Howard Phillips Lovecraft is probably the most important and influential author of supernatural fiction in the twentieth century. A life-long resident of Providence, Rhode Island, many of his tales are set in the fear-haunted towns of an imaginary area of Massachusetts, or in the cosmic vistas that exist beyond space and time. Since his untimely death, Lovecraft has become acknowledged as a master of fantasy fiction and a mainstream American writer second only to Edgar Allan Poe, while his relatively small body of work has influenced countless imitators and formed the basis of a world-wide industry of books, games and movies based on his concepts.

H.P. Lovecraft's tales of the tentacled Elder God Cthulhu and his pantheon of alien deities were initially written for the pulp magazines of the 1920s and '30s. These astonishing tales blend elements of horror and science fiction and are as powerful today as they were when they initially appeared. This companion volume to the best-selling *Necronomicon: The Best Weird Tales of H.P. Lovecraft* brings together in chronological order all of Lovecraft's remaining major stories, his 'Fungi from Yuggoth' cycle and other important weird poetry, a number of obscure revisions and some notable nonfiction, including the seminal critical essay 'Supernatural Horror in Literature'.

'Lovecraft opened the way for me, as he had done for others before me'
Stephen King

'H.P. Lovecraft built the stage on which most of the last century's horror fiction was performed. As doomed as any of his protagonists, he put a worldview into words that has spread to infect the world. You need to read him – he's where the darkness starts'
Neil Gaiman

'As a writer he stands among the best in the field'
August Derleth

'H.P. Lovecraft is not only the essential link between Edgar Allan Poe and the present day, he has become an almost unimaginably influential force throughout the whole of our popular culture'   Peter Straub

'H.P. Lovecraft is the most important single writer of the weird … his achievement lies not so much in his influence as in the enduring qualities of his finest work'   Ramsey Campbell

'In his case the highest literary genius was allied to the most brilliant and most endearing personal qualities'
                                                        Clark Ashton Smith

'It's hard to name a single modern writer of weird fiction who hasn't to some extent, often profoundly, felt the influence of Howard Phillips Lovecraft … It's possible that I personally would never have written anything if I hadn't first read H.P. Lovecraft. And I fancy I'm but one of many …'
                                                            Brian Lumley

'The thing that particularly drew me to Lovecraft as a young and innocent child was the way his stories and the concepts in them would – in a genuinely eerie way – activate the creative machinery in my head'   Gahan Wilson

'One of the twentieth century's most original writers'
                                                        Arthur C. Clarke

'He's an American original, whose influence on subsequent writers in the field is all-pervasive'   Joyce Carol Oates

'In a genre blessed with many great stylists, H. P. Lovecraft's baroque imagination and outrageous use of language still manages to stand head and shoulders above the rest. A timeless master of the macabre, and the true connoisseur of dread'
                                                    Michael Marshall Smith

'There will never be another like him'   Edmond Hamilton

ELDRITCH TALES

A Miscellany of the
Macabre by H.P. Lovecraft

SPECIAL COLLECTOR'S EDITION

Edited with an Afterword by
STEPHEN JONES

Illustrated by
LES EDWARDS

GOLLANCZ
LONDON

First published in Great Britain in 2011 by Gollancz
An imprint of the Orion Publishing Group
Orion House, 5 Upper St Martin's Lane, London WC2H 9EA
An Hachette UK Company

A CIP catalogue record for this book is available
from the British Library

ISBN 978 0 575 09935 7 (Cased)
ISBN 978 0 575 09963 0 (Export Trade Paperback)

3 5 7 9 10 8 6 4 2

Typeset by Input Data Services Ltd, Bridgwater, Somerset

Printed in the UK by CPI William Clowes Beccles NR34 7TL

The Orion Publishing Group's policy is to use papers that
are natural, renewable and recyclable products and made
from wood grown in sustainable forests. The logging and
manufacturing processes are expected to conform to the
environmental regulations of the country of origin.

www.orionbooks.co.uk

ACKNOWLEDGEMENTS

Grateful acknowledgement is made to the following individuals, whose work was consulted (and in some cases quoted from) in the compilation of this volume: August Derleth, Victor Gollancz, Otis Kline Associates, Laurence Pollinger, Mr J.J. Jeffery, John Bush, E.D. Nisbet, Mr R. Denton, Giles Gordon, Forrest D. Hartmann, Les Edwards and Gahan Wilson.

Special thanks also go, as always, to my editor Jo Fletcher, Malcolm Edwards, Lail Finlay Hernandez, Val and Les Edwards, Charlie Panayiotou and Marcus Gipps for all their help and support.

'History of the *Necronomicon*', originally published in *A History of the Necronomicon* (1938).

'The Alchemist', originally published in *The United Amateur* Vo.16, No.4, November 1916.

'A Reminiscence of Dr Samuel Johnson', originally published (as by Humphry Littlewit, Esq.) in *The United Amateur* Vol.17, No.2, September 1917.

'The Beast in the Cave', originally published in *The Vagrant* No.7, June 1918.

'The Poe-et's Nightmare', originally published in *The Vagrant* No.8, July 1918.

'Memory', originally published in *The United Co-operative* Vol.1, No.2, June 1919.

'Despair', originally published in *Pine Cones* Vol.1, No.4, June 1919.

'The Picture in the House', originally published in *The National Amateur* Vol.41, No.6, July 1919 (1921).

'Beyond the Wall of Sleep', originally published in *Pine Cones* Vol.1, No.6, October 1919.

'Psychopompos: A Tale in Rhyme', originally published in *The Vagrant*, October 1919.

'The White Ship', originally published in *The United Amateur* Vol.19, No.2, November 1919.

'The House', originally published in *National Enquirer* Vol.9, No.11, December 11, 1919.

'The Nightmare Lake', originally published in *The Vagrant* No.12, December 1919.

'Poetry and the Gods' originally published (as by Anna Helen Crofts and Henry Paget-Lowe) in *The United Amateur* Vol.20, No.1, September 1920.

'Nyarlathotep', originally published in *The United Amateur* Vol.20, No.2, November 1920.

'Polaris', originally published in *The Philosopher* Vol.1, No.1, December 1920.

'The Street', originally published in *The Wolverine* No.8, December 1920.

'Ex Oblivione', originally published (as by Ward Phillips) in *The United Amateur* Vol.20, No.4, March 1921.

'Facts Concerning the Late Arthur Jermyn and His Family', originally published in *The Wolverine* No.9, March 1921.

'The Crawling Chaos' originally published (as by Elizabeth Neville Berkeley and Lewis Theobald, Jr) in *The United Co-operative* Vol.1, No.3, April 1921.

'The Terrible Old Man', originally published in *The Tryout* Vol.7, No.4, July 1921.

'The Tree', originally published in *The Tryout* Vol.7, No.7, October 1921.

'The Tomb', originally published in *The Vagrant* No.14, March 1922.

'Celephaïs', originally published in *The Rainbow* No.2, May 1922.

'Hypnos', originally published in *The National Amateur* Vol.45, No.5, May 1923.

'What the Moon Brings', originally published in *The National Amateur* Vol.45 No.5, May 1923.

'The Horror at Martin's Beach' originally published under the title 'The Invisible Monster' in *Weird Tales*, November 1923.

'The Festival', originally published in *Weird Tales*, January 1925.

'The Temple', originally published in *Weird Tales*, September 1925.

'Hallowe'en in a Suburb', originally published (as 'In a Suburb') in *The National Amateur* Vol.48, No.4, March 1926.

'The Moon-Bog', originally published in *Weird Tales*, June 1926.

'He', originally published in *Weird Tales*, September 1926.

'Festival', originally published (as 'Yule Horror') in *Weird Tales*, December 1926.

'The Green Meadow' originally published (as Translated by Elizabeth Neville Berkeley and Lewis Theobald, Jr) in *The Vagrant*, Spring 1927.

'Nathicana', originally published in *The Vagrant*, Spring 1927.

'Two Black Bottles' originally published in *Weird Tales*, August 1927.

'The Last Test' originally published in *Weird Tales*, November 1928. (A revision of 'A Sacrifice to Science', originally published in *In the Confessional and the Following*, 1893.)

'The Wood', originally published (as by Lewis Theobold, Jr) in *The Tryout*, Vol.11, No.2, January 1929.

'The Ancient Track', originally published in *Weird Tales*, March 1930.

'The Electric Executioner' originally published in *Weird Tales*, August 1930. (A revision of 'The Automatic Executioner', originally published in *The Wave*, November 14, 1891.)

'Fungi from Yuggoth'

   '1: The Book', originally published in *The Fantasy Fan* Vol.2, No.2, October 1934.

   '2: Pursuit', originally published in *The Fantasy Fan* Vol.2, No.2, October 1934.

   '3: The Key', originally published in *The Fantasy Fan* Vol.2, No.5, January 1935.

   '4: Recognition', originally published in *Driftwind* Vol.11, No.5, December 1936.

   '5: Homecoming', originally published in *The Fantasy Fan* Vol.2, No.6, January 1935.

   '6: The Lamp', originally published in *Driftwind* Vol.5, No.5, March 1931.

   '7: Zaman's Hill', originally published in *Driftwind* Vol.9, No.4, October 1934.

   '8: The Port', originally published in *Driftwind* Vol.5, No.3, November 1930.

   '9: The Courtyard', originally published in *Weird Tales*, September 1930.

   '10: The Pigeon-Flyers', originally published in *Beyond the Wall of Sleep* (1943).

'11: The Well', originally published in *The Providence Journal* Vol.102, No.116, May 14, 1930.

'12: The Howler' originally published in *Driftwind* Vol.7, No.3, November 1932.

'13: Hesperia', originally published in *Weird Tales*, October 1930.

'14: Star-Winds', originally published in *Weird Tales*, September 1930.

'15: Antarktos', originally published in *Weird Tales*, November 1930.

'16: The Window', originally published in *Driftwind*, April 1931.

'17: A Memory', originally published (as 'Memory' by Lewis Theobold) in *The United Co-operative*, April 1921.

'18: The Gardens of Yin', originally published in *Driftwind*, March 1932.

'19: The Bells', originally published in *Weird Tales*, December 1930.

'20: Night-Gaunts' originally published in *The Providence Journal*, March 26, 1930.

'21: Nyarlathotep', originally published in *The United Amateur*, November 1920.

'22: Azathoth', originally published in *Weird Tales*, January 1931.

'23: Mirage', originally published in *Weird Tales*, February–March 1931.

'24: The Canal', originally published in *Driftwind*, March 1932.

'25: St Toads', originally published in *Beyond the Wall of Sleep* (1943).

'26: The Familiars', originally published in *Driftwind*, July 1930.

'27: The Elder Pharos', originally published in *Weird Tales*, February–March 1931.

'28: Expectancy', originally published in *Beyond the Wall of Sleep* (1943).

'29: Nostalgia', originally published in *The Providence Journal*, March 12, 1930.

'30: Background', originally published in *The Providence Journal*, April 16, 1930.

'31: The Dweller', originally published in *The Providence Journal*, May 7, 1930.

'32: Alienation', originally published in *Weird Tales*, April–May 1931.

ACKNOWLEDGEMENTS

'33: Harbour Whistles', originally published in *The Silver Fern*, May 1930.

'34: Recapture', originally published in *Weird Tales*, May 1930.

'35: Evening Star', originally published in *Beyond the Wall of Sleep* (1943).

'36: Continuity', originally published in *Causerie*, February 1936.

'The Trap' originally published in *Strange Tales of Mystery and Terror*, Vol.2, No.1, March 1932.

'The Other Gods', originally published in *The Fantasy Fan* Vol.1, No.3, November 1933.

'The Quest of Iranon', originally published in *The Galleon* Vol.1, No.5, July–August 1935.

'The Challenge from Beyond', originally published in *Fantasy Magazine* Vol.5, No.4, September 1935. 'Fragment from the Eltdown Shards' was originally written for 'The Sealed Casket' by Richard F. Searight (*Weird Tales*, March 1935), but omitted from the published version.

'In a Sequester'd Providence Churchyard Where Once Poe Walk'd', originally published in *Four Acrostic Sonnets on Edgar Allan Poe* (1936).

'Ibid', originally published in *O-Wash-Ta-Nong* Vol.3, No.1, January 1938.

'Azathoth', originally published in *Leaves* No.2, 1938.

'The Descendant', originally published in *Leaves* No.2, 1938.

'The Book', originally published in *Leaves* No.2, 1938.

'The Messenger', originally published in *Weird Tales*, July 1938.

'The Evil Clergyman', originally published (as 'The Wicked Clergyman') in *Weird Tales*, April 1939.

'The Very Old Folk', originally published in *Scienti-Snaps* Vol.3, No.3, Summer 1940.

'The Thing in the Moonlight', originally published in *Bizarre* Vol.4, No.1, January 1941.

'The Transition of Juan Romero', originally published in *Marginalia* (1944).

'Supernatural Horror in Literature', originally published in *The Recluse* (1927) and *The Fantasy Fan*, October 1933–February 1935.

'Afterword: Lovecraft in Britain' copyright © Stephen Jones 2007, 2011. Originally published in slightly different form in *H.P.*

Every effort has been made to trace the owners of any copyright material in this book. In the case of any question arising as to the use of such material, the publisher, while expressing regret for any errors, will be pleased to make the necessary corrections in future editions of the book.

CONTENTS

CONTENTS

For
S.T. JOSHI
and
ROBERT M. PRICE
for also keeping the
Nightmares alive.

History of the Necronomicon

Original title Al Azif — azif being the word used by the Arabs to designate that nocturnal sound (made by insects) suppos'd to be the howling of daemons.

Composed by Abdul Alhazred, a mad poet of Sanaá, in Yemen, who is said to have flourished during the period of the Ommiade caliphs, circa 700 A.D. He visited the ruins of Babylon & the subterranean secrets of Memphis & spent ten years alone in the great southern desert of Arabia — the Roba el Khaliyeh or "Empty Space" of the ancients — & "Dahna" or "Crimson" desert of the modern Arabs, which is held to be inhabited by protective evil spirits & monsters of death. Of this desert many strange & unbelievable marvels are told by those who pretend to have penetrated it. In his last years Alhazred dwelt in Damascus, where the Necronomicon (Al Azif) was written, & of his final death or disappearance (738 A.D.) many terrible & conflicting things are told. He is said by Ebn Khallikan (12th cent. biographer) to have been seized by an invisible monster in broad daylight & devoured horribly before a large number of fright-frozen witnesses. Of his madness many things are told. He claimed to have seen the fabulous Irem, or city of Pillars, & to have found beneath the ruins of a certain nameless desert town the shocking annals & secrets of a race older than mankind. He was only an indifferent Moslem, worshipping unknown Entities whom he called Yog-Sothoth & Cthulhu.

In A.D. 950 the Azif, which had gained a considerable tho' surreptitious circulation amongst the philosophers of the age, was secretly translated into Greek by Theodorus Philetas of Constantinople under the title Necronomicon. For a century it impelled certain experimenters to terrible attempts, when it was suppressed & burnt by the patriarch Michael. After this it is only heard of furtively, but (1228) Olaus Wormius made a Latin translation later in the Middle Ages, & the Latin text was printed twice — once in the 15th century (evidently in Germany) & once in the 17th — (prob. Spanish) both in black-letter (over)

HISTORY OF THE *NECRONOMICON*

ORIGINAL TITLE *Al Azif* – *azif* being the word used by Arabs to designate that nocturnal sound (made by insects) suppos'd to be the howling of daemons.

Composed by Abdul Alhazred, a mad poet of Sanaá, in Yemen, who is said to have flourished during the period of the Ommiade caliphs, circa AD 700. He visited the ruins of Babylon and the subterranean secrets of Memphis and spent ten years alone in the great southern desert of Arabia – the Roba el Khaliyeh or 'Empty Space' of the ancients – and 'Dahna' or 'Crimson' desert of the modern Arabs, which is held to be inhabited by protective evil spirits and monsters of death. Of this desert many strange and unbelievable marvels are told by those who pretend to have penetrated it. In his last years Alhazred dwelt in Damascus, where the *Necronomicon* (*Al Azif*) was written, and of his final death or disappearance (AD 738) many terrible and conflicting things are told. He is said by Ebn Khallikan (12th cent. biographer) to have been seized by an invisible monster in broad daylight and devoured horribly before a large number of fright-frozen witnesses. Of his madness many things are told. He claimed to have seen fabulous Irem, or City of Pillars, and to have found beneath the ruins of a certain nameless desert town the shocking annals and secrets of a race older than mankind. He was only an indifferent Moslem, worshipping unknown entities whom he called Yog-Sothoth and Cthulhu.

In AD 950 the *Azif*, which had gained a considerable tho' surreptitious circulation amongst the philosophers of the age, was secretly translated into Greek by Theodorus Philetas of Constantinople under the title *Necronomicon*. For a century it impelled certain experimenters to terrible attempts, when it was suppressed and burnt by the patriarch Michael. After this it is only heard of furtively, but (1228) Olaus Wormius made a Latin translation later in the Middle Ages, and the Latin text was printed twice – once in the fifteenth century in black-letter (evidently in Germany) and once in the seventeenth (prob. Spanish) – both editions being without identifying marks, and located as to time and place by internal typographical evidence only. The work both Latin and Greek was banned by Pope Gregory IX in 1232, shortly after its Latin translation, which called attention to it. The Arabic original was lost as early as Wormius' time, as indicated by his prefatory note; and no sight of the Greek copy – which was printed in Italy between 1500 and 1550 – has been reported since the burning of a certain Salem man's library in 1692. An English translation made by Dr Dee was never printed, and exists only in fragments recovered from the original manuscript. Of the Latin texts now existing one (15th cent.) is known to be in the British Museum under lock and key, while another (17th cent.) is in the Bibliothèque Nationale at Paris. A seventeenth-century edition is in the Widener Library at Harvard, and in the library of Miskatonic University at Arkham. Also in the library of the University of Buenos Aires. Numerous other copies probably exist in secret, and a fifteenth-century one is persistently rumoured to form part of the collection of a celebrated American millionaire. A still vaguer rumour credits the preservation of a sixteenth-century Greek text in the Salem family of Pickman; but if it was so preserved, it vanished with the artist R.U. Pickman, who disappeared early in 1926. The book is rigidly suppressed by the authorities of most countries, and by all branches of organised ecclesiasticism. Reading leads to terrible consequences. It was from rumours of this book (of which relatively few of the general public know) that Robert W. Chambers is said to have derived the idea of his early novel *The King in Yellow*

Chronology

Al Azif written circa AD 730 at Damascus by Abdul Alhazred
Tr to Greek AD 950 as *Necronomicon* by Theodorus Philetas
Burnt by Patriarch Michael 1050 (i.e., Greek text). Arabic now lost.
Olaus translates Gr. To Latin 1228
1232 Latin ed. (and Gr.) suppr. by Pope Gregory IX
14 ... Black-letter printed edition (Germany)
15 ... Gr. Text printed in Italy
16 ... Spanish reprint of Latin text

Editions being without identifying marks, & located as to time & place by internal typographical evidence only. The Arabic original was lost as early as Wormius' time, as indicated by his prefatory note; & no sight of the Greek copy — which was printed in Italy 1500 + 1550 — has been reported since the burning of a certain Salem man's library in 1692. Of the Latin texts now existing one (15th cent.) is known to be locked up in the British Museum under lock & key, while another (17th cent.) is in the Bibliotheque Nationale at Paris. A 17th cent. edition is in the Widener Library at Harvard, & in the library of Miskatonic University at Arkham. Also in the library of the Univ. of Buenos Ayres. Numerous other copies probably exist in secret, & a 15th cent. one is persistently rumoured to form part of the collection of a celebrated American millionaire. A still vaguer rumour credits the preservation of a 16th cent. Greek text in the Salem family of Pickman; but if it was so preserved, it vanished with the artist R. U. Pickman, who disappeared early in 1926. The book is rigidly suppressed by the authorities of most countries, & by all branches of organised ecclesiasticism. Reading leads to terrible consequences. It was from rumours of this book (of which relatively few of the general public know) that R. W. Chambers is said to have derived the idea of his early novel "The King in Yellow."

— H. P. Lovecraft

The work was banned by Pope Gregory IX shortly after its Latin translation, which called attention to it.

CHRONOLOGY

Al Azif written circa 730 A.D. at Damascus by Abdul Alhazred
Tr. to Greek 950 A.D. as Necronomicon by Theodorus Philetas
Burnt by Patriarch Michael 1050 (i.e. Greek text).
Arabic text now lost
Trans. translated gr. to Latin 1228
1232 Latin ed. (& Gr.) suppressed by Pope Gregory IX
14... black-letter edition (Germany)
15... Gr. text printed in Italy
16... Spanish reprint of Latin text

My Dear Mr. Lovecraft:

I have inclosed your questionnaire with the letter to Dr. Fisher of Brown University with a request that he fill it out and return it to me. As soon as I got it, I will send it on to you. Dr. Fisher no doubt has all the informa-tion you wish as he told me he has been visit-ing most of the localities and knows far more about them than I do as yet. I have only lived here two years and have not had a chance to see many of the outcrops.

Yours very truly,

William L. Bryant
Director of the Museum.

PARK MUSEUM
ROGER WILLIAMS PARK
PROVIDENCE, R.I.

CITY OF PROVIDENCE

PARK COMMISSIONERS
EDWARD A. McHUGH, Chairman
JOSEPH E. C. FARNHAM
FREDERIC C. GORHAM

WILLIAM L. BRYANT
Director

10 Barn Street
Providence, Rhode Island
Mr. H. P. Lovecraft
April 27, 1927

THE ALCHEMIST

HIGH UP, crowning the grassy summit of a swelling mount whose sides are wooded near the base with the gnarled trees of the primeval forest stands the old chateau of my ancestors. For centuries its lofty battlements have frowned down upon the wild and rugged countryside about, serving as a home and stronghold for the proud house whose honoured line is older even than the moss-grown castle walls. These ancient turrets, stained by the storms of generations and crumbling under the slow yet mighty pressure of time, formed in the ages of feudalism one of the most dreaded and formidable fortresses in all France. From its machico-lated parapets and mounted battlements Barons, Counts, and even Kings had been defied, yet never had its spacious halls resounded to the footsteps of the invader.

But since those glorious years, all is changed. A poverty but little above the level of dire want, together with a pride of name that forbids its alleviation by the pursuits of commercial life, have prevented the scions of our line from maintaining their estates in pristine splendour; and the falling stones of the walls, the overgrown vegetation in the parks, the dry and dusty moat, the ill-paved courtyards, and toppling towers without, as well as the sagging floors, the worm-eaten wainscots, and the faded tapestries within, all tell a gloomy tale of fallen grandeur. As the ages passed, first one, then another of the four great turrets were left to ruin, until at last but a single tower housed the sadly reduced descendants of the once mighty lords of the estate.

It was in one of the vast and gloomy chambers of this remaining tower that I, Antoine, last of the unhappy and accursed Counts de C—, first saw the light of day, ninety long years ago. Within these walls and amongst the dark and shadowy forests, the wild ravines and grottoes of the hillside below, were spent the first years of my troubled life. My parents I never knew. My father had been killed at the age of thirty-two, a month before I was born, by the fall of a stone somehow dislodged from one of the deserted parapets of the castle. And my mother having died at my birth, my care and education devolved solely upon one remaining servitor, an old and trusted man of considerable intelligence, whose name I remember as Pierre. I was an only child and the lack of companionship which this fact entailed upon me was augmented by the strange care exercised by my aged guardian, in excluding me from the society of the peasant children whose abodes were scattered here and there upon the plains that surround the base of the hill. At that time, Pierre said that this restriction was imposed upon me because my noble birth placed me above association with such plebeian company. Now I know that its real object was to keep from my ears the idle tales of the dread curse upon our line that were nightly told and magnified by the simple tenantry as they conversed in hushed accents in the glow of their cottage hearths.

Thus isolated, and thrown upon my own resources, I spent the hours of my childhood in poring over the ancient tomes that filled the shadow-haunted library of the chateau, and in roaming without aim or purpose through the perpetual dust of the spectral wood that clothes the side of the hill near its foot. It was perhaps an effect of such surroundings that my mind early acquired a shade of melancholy. Those studies and pursuits which partake of the dark and occult in nature most strongly claimed my attention.

Of my own race I was permitted to learn singularly little, yet what small knowledge of it I was able to gain seemed to depress me much. Perhaps it was at first only the manifest reluctance of my old preceptor to discuss with me my paternal ancestry that gave rise to the terror which I ever felt at the mention of my great house, yet as I grew out of childhood, I was able to piece together disconnected fragments of discourse, let slip from the unwilling tongue which had begun to falter in approaching senility, that had a sort of relation to a certain circumstance which I had always deemed strange, but which now became dimly terrible. The circumstance to which I allude is the early age at which all the Counts of my line had met their end. Whilst I had hitherto considered this but a natural attribute of a family of short-lived men, I afterward pondered long upon these premature deaths, and began to connect them with the wanderings of the old man, who often spoke of a curse which for centuries had prevented the lives of the holders of my title from much exceeding the span of thirty-two years. Upon my twenty-first birthday, the aged Pierre gave to me a family document which he said had for many generations been handed down from father to son, and continued by each possessor. Its contents were of the most startling nature, and its perusal confirmed the gravest of my apprehensions. At this time, my belief in the supernatural was firm and deep-seated, else I should have dismissed with scorn the incredible narrative unfolded before my eyes.

The paper carried me back to the days of the thirteenth century, when the old castle in which I sat had been a feared and impregnable fortress. It told of a certain ancient man who had once dwelled on our estates, a person of no small accomplishments, though little above the rank of peasant, by name, Michel, usually designated by the surname of Mauvais, the Evil, on account of his sinister reputation. He had studied beyond the custom of his kind, seeking such things as the Philosopher's Stone or the Elixir of Eternal Life, and was reputed wise in the terrible secrets of Black Magic and Alchemy. Michel Mauvais had one son, named Charles, a youth as proficient as himself in the hidden arts, who had therefore been called Le Sorcier, or the Wizard. This pair, shunned by all honest folk, were suspected of the most hideous practices. Old Michel was said to have burnt his wife alive as a sacrifice to the Devil, and the unaccountable disappearance of many small peasant children was laid at the dreaded door of these two. Yet through the dark natures of the father and son ran one redeeming ray of humanity; the evil old man loved his offspring with fierce intensity, whilst the youth had for his parent a more than filial affection.

One night the castle on the hill was thrown into the wildest confusion by the vanishment of young Godfrey, son to Henri, the Count. A searching party, headed by the frantic father, invaded the cottage of the sorcerers and there came upon old Michel Mauvais, busy over a huge and violently boiling cauldron. Without certain cause, in the ungoverned madness of fury and despair, the Count laid hands on the aged wizard, and ere he released his murderous hold, his victim was no more. Meanwhile, joyful servants were proclaiming the finding of young Godfrey in a distant and unused chamber of the great edifice, telling too late that poor Michel had been killed in vain. As the Count and his associates turned away from the lowly abode of the alchemist, the form of Charles Le Sorcier appeared through the trees. The excited chatter of the menials standing about told him what had occurred, yet he seemed at first unmoved at his father's fate. Then, slowly advancing to meet the Count, he pronounced in dull yet terrible accents the curse that ever afterward haunted the house of C—.

'May ne'er a noble of thy murd'rous line
Survive to reach a greater age than thine!'
spake he, when, suddenly leaping backwards into the black woods, he drew from his tunic a phial of colourless liquid which he threw into the face of his father's slayer as he disappeared behind the inky curtain of the night. The Count died without utterance, and was buried the next day, but little more than two and thirty years from the hour of his birth. No trace of the assassin could be found, though relentless bands of peasants scoured the neighbouring woods and the meadowland around the hill.

Thus time and the want of a reminder dulled the memory of the curse in the minds of the late Count's family, so that when Godfrey, innocent cause of the whole tragedy and now bearing the title, was killed by an arrow whilst hunting at the age of thirty-two, there were no thoughts save those of grief at his demise. But when, years afterward, the next young Count, Robert by name, was found dead in a nearby field of no apparent cause, the peasants told in whispers that their seigneur had but lately passed his thirty-second birthday when surprised by early death. Louis, son to Robert, was found drowned in the moat at the same fateful age, and thus down through

8

the centuries ran the ominous chronicle: Henris, Roberts, Antoines, and Armands snatched from happy and virtuous lives when little below the age of their unfortunate ancestor at his murder.

That I had left at most but eleven years of further existence was made certain to me by the words which I had read. My life, previously held at small value, now became dearer to me each day, as I delved deeper and deeper into the mysteries of the hidden world of black magic. Isolated as I was, modern science had produced no impression upon me, and I laboured as in the Middle Ages, as wrapt as had been old Michel and young Charles themselves in the acquisition of demonological and alchemical learning. Yet read as I might, in no manner could I account for the strange curse upon my line. In unusually rational moments I would even go so far as to seek a natural explanation, attributing the early deaths of my ancestors to the sinister Charles Le Sorcier and his heirs; yet, having found upon careful inquiry that there were no known descendants of the alchemist, I would fall back to occult studies, and once more endeavour to find a spell, that would release my house from its terrible burden. Upon one thing I was absolutely resolved. I should never wed, for, since no other branch of my family was in existence, I might thus end the curse with myself.

As I drew near the age of thirty, old Pierre was called to the land beyond. Alone I buried him beneath the stones of the courtyard about which he had loved to wander in life. Thus was I left to ponder on myself as the only human creature within the great fortress, and in my utter solitude my mind began to cease its vain protest against the impending doom, to become almost reconciled to the fate which so many of my ancestors had met. Much of my time was now occupied in the exploration of the ruined and abandoned halls and towers of the old chateau, which in youth fear had caused me to shun, and some of which old Pierre had once told me had not been trodden by human foot for over four centuries. Strange and awesome were many of the objects I encountered. Furniture, covered by the dust of ages and crumbling with the rot of long dampness, met my eyes. Cobwebs in a profusion never before seen by me were spun everywhere, and huge bats flapped their bony and uncanny wings on all sides of the otherwise untenanted gloom.

Of my exact age, even down to days and hours, I kept a most

careful record, for each movement of the pendulum of the massive clock in the library told off so much of my doomed existence. At length I approached that time which I had so long viewed with apprehension. Since most of my ancestors had been seized some little while before they reached the exact age of Count Henri at his end, I was every moment on the watch for the coming of the unknown death. In what strange form the curse should overtake me, I knew not; but I was resolved at least that it should not find me a cowardly or a passive victim. With new vigour I applied myself to my examination of the old chateau and its contents.

It was upon one of the longest of all my excursions of discovery in the deserted portion of the castle, less than a week before that fatal hour which I felt must mark the utmost limit of my stay on earth, beyond which I could have not even the slightest hope of continuing to draw breath that I came upon the culminating event of my whole life. I had spent the better part of the morning in climbing up and down half ruined staircases in one of the most dilapidated of the ancient turrets. As the afternoon progressed, I sought the lower levels, descending into what appeared to be either a mediaeval place of confinement, or a more recently excavated storehouse for gunpowder. As I slowly traversed the nitre-encrusted passageway at the foot of the last staircase, the paving became very damp, and soon I saw by the light of my flickering torch that a blank, water-stained wall impeded my journey. Turning to retrace my steps, my eye fell upon a small trapdoor with a ring, which lay directly beneath my foot. Pausing, I succeeded with difficulty in raising it, whereupon there was revealed a black aperture, exhaling noxious fumes which caused my torch to sputter, and disclosing in the unsteady glare the top of a flight of stone steps.

As soon as the torch which I lowered into the repellent depths burned freely and steadily, I commenced my descent. The steps were many, and led to a narrow stone-flagged passage which I knew must be far underground. This passage proved of great length, and terminated in a massive oaken door, dripping with the moisture of the place, and stoutly resisting all my attempts to open it. Ceasing after a time my efforts in this direction, I had proceeded back some distance toward the steps when there suddenly fell to my experience one of the most profound and maddening shocks capable of reception by the human mind. Without warning, I heard the heavy door behind me creak slowly open upon its rusted hinges. My immediate sensations were incapable of analysis. To be confronted in a place as thoroughly deserted as I had deemed the old castle with evidence of the presence of man or spirit produced in my brain a horror of the most acute description. When at last I turned and faced the seat of the sound, my eyes must have started from their orbits at the sight that they beheld.

There in the ancient Gothic doorway stood a human figure. It was that of a man clad in a skull-cap and long mediaeval tunic of dark colour. His long hair and flowing beard were of a terrible and intense black hue, and of incredible profusion. His forehead, high beyond the usual dimensions; his cheeks, deep-sunken and heavily lined with wrinkles; and his hands, long, claw-like, and gnarled, were of such a deadly marble-like whiteness as I have never else-where seen in man. His figure, lean to the proportions of a skeleton, was strangely bent and almost lost within the voluminous folds of his peculiar garment. But strangest of all were his eyes, twin caves of abysmal blackness, profound in expression of understanding, yet inhuman in degree of wickedness. These were now fixed upon me, piercing my soul with their hatred, and rooting me to the spot whereon I stood.

At last the figure spoke in a rumbling voice that chilled me through with its dull hollowness and latent malevolence. The language in which the discourse was clothed was that debased form of Latin in use amongst the more learned men of the Middle Ages, and made familiar to me by my prolonged researches into the works of the old alchemists and demonologists. The apparition spoke of the curse which had hovered over my house, told me of my coming end, dwelt on the wrong perpetrated by my ancestor against old Michel Mauvais, and gloated over the revenge of Charles Le Sorcier. He told how young Charles has escaped into the night, returning in after years to kill Godfrey the heir with an arrow just as he approached the age which had been his father's at his assassination; how he had secretly returned to the estate and estab-lished himself, unknown, in the even then deserted subterranean chamber whose doorway now framed the hideous narrator, how he had seized Robert, son of Godfrey, in a field, forced poison down his throat, and left him to die at the age of thirty-two, thus main-taining the foul provisions of his vengeful curse. At this point I was left to imagine the solution of the greatest mystery of all, how the curse had been fulfilled since that time when Charles Le Sorcier must in the course of nature have died, for the man digressed into an account of the deep alchemical studies of the two wizards, father and son, speaking most particularly of the researches of Charles Le Sorcier concerning the elixir which should grant to him who partook of it eternal life and youth.

His enthusiasm had seemed for the moment to remove from his terrible eyes the black malevolence that had first so haunted me, but suddenly the fiendish glare returned and, with a shocking sound like the hissing of a serpent, the stranger raised a glass phial with the evident intent of ending my life as had Charles Le Sorcier, six hundred years before, ended that of my ancestor. Prompted by some preserving instinct of self-defence, I broke through the spell that had hitherto held me immovable, and flung my now dying torch at the creature who menaced my existence. I heard the phial break harmlessly against the stones of the passage as the tunic of the strange man caught fire and lit the horrid scene with a ghastly radiance. The shriek of fright and impotent malice emitted by the would-be assassin proved too much for my already shaken nerves, and I fell prone upon the slimy floor in a total faint.

When at last my senses returned, all was frightfully dark, and my mind, remembering what had occurred, shrank from the idea of beholding any more; yet curiosity over-mastered all. Who, I asked myself, was this man of evil, and how came he within the castle walls? Why should he seek to avenge the death of Michel Mauvais, and how had the curse been carried on through all the long centuries since the time of Charles Le Sorcier? The dread of years was lifted from my shoulder, for I knew that he whom I had felled was the source of all my danger from the curse; and now that I was free, I burned with the desire to learn more of the sinister thing which had haunted my line for centuries, and made of my own youth one long-continued nightmare. Determined upon further exploration, I felt in my pockets for flint and steel, and lit the unused torch which I had with me.

First of all, new light revealed the distorted and blackened form of the mysterious stranger. The hideous eyes were now closed. Disliking the sight, I turned away and entered the chamber beyond the Gothic door. Here I found what seemed much like an alchemist's laboratory. In one corner was an immense pile of shining yellow metal that sparkled gorgeously in the light of the torch. It may have been gold, but I did not pause to examine it, for I was strangely affected by that which I had undergone. At the farther end of the apartment was an opening leading out into one of the many wild ravines of the dark hillside forest. Filled with wonder, yet now realising how the man had obtained access to the chateau, I proceeded to return. I had intended to pass by the remains of the stranger with averted face but, as I approached the body, I seemed to hear emanating from it a faint sound, as though life were not yet wholly extinct. Aghast, I turned to examine the charred and shrivelled figure on the floor.

Then all at once the horrible eyes, blacker even than the seared face in which they were set, opened wide with an expression which I was unable to interpret. The cracked lips tried to frame words which I could not well understand. Once I caught the name of Charles Le Sorcier, and again I fancied that the words 'years' and 'curse' issued from the twisted mouth. Still I was at a loss to gather the purport of his disconnected speech. At my evident ignorance of his meaning, the pitchy eyes once more flashed malevolently at me, until, helpless as I saw my opponent to be, I trembled as I watched him.

Suddenly the wretch, animated with his last burst of strength, raised his piteous head from the damp and sunken pavement. Then, as I remained, paralysed with fear, he found his voice and in his dying breath screamed forth those words which have ever afterward haunted my days and nights. 'Fool!' he shrieked, 'Can you not guess my secret? Have you no brain whereby you may recognise the will which has through six long centuries fulfilled the dreadful curse upon the house? Have I not told you of the great elixir of eternal life? Know you not how the secret of Alchemy was solved? I tell you, it is I! I! I! that have lived for six hundred years to maintain my revenge, for I am Charles Le Sorcier!'

A REMINISCENCE OF
DR SAMUEL JOHNSON

T HE PRIVILEGE OF REMINISCENCE, however rambling or tire-
some, is one generally allow'd to the very aged; indeed, 'tis
frequently by means of such Recollections that the obscure occur-
rences of History, and the lesser Anecdotes of the Great, are transmitted to Posterity.

Tho' many of my readers have at times observ'd and remark'd a
Sort of antique Flow in my Stile of Writing, it hath pleased me to
pass amongst the Members of this Generation as a young Man,
giving out the Fiction that I was born in 1890, in *America*. I am now,
however, resolv'd to unburthen myself of a Secret which I have
hitherto kept thro' Dread of Incredulity; and to impart to the
Publick a true knowledge of my long years, in order to gratifie their
taste for authentick Information of an Age with whose famous
Personages I was on familiar Terms. Be it then known that I was
born on the family Estate in *Devonshire*, of the 10th day of August,
1690 (or in the new *Gregorian* Stile of Reckoning, the 20th of August),
being therefore now in my 228th year. Coming early to *London*,
I saw as a Child many of the celebrated Men of King *William's*

Reign, including the lamented Mr *Dryden*, who sat much at the Tables of *Will's* Coffee-House. With Mr *Addison* and Dr *Swift* I later became very well acquainted, and was an even more familiar Friend to Mr *Pope*, whom I knew and respected till the Day of his Death. But since it is of my more recent Associate, the late Dr *Johnson*, that I am at this time desir'd to write; I will pass over my Youth for the present.

I had first Knowledge of the Doctor in May of the year 1738, tho' I did not at that Time meet him. Mr *Pope* had just compleated his Epilogue to his Satires (the Piece beginning: 'Not twice a Twelvemonth you appear in Print.'), and had arrang'd for its Publication. On the very Day it appear'd, there was also publish'd a Satire in Imitation of *Juvenal*, intitul'd '*London*', by the then unknown *Johnson*; and this so struck the Town, that many Gentlemen of Taste declared, it was the Work of a greater Poet than Mr *Pope*. Notwithstanding what some Detractors have said of Mr *Pope's* petty jealousy, he gave the Verses of his new Rival no small Praise; and having learnt thro' Mr *Richardson* who the Poet was, told me, 'that Mr *Johnson* wou'd soon be *deterré*'.

I had no personal Acquaintance with the Doctor till 1763, when I was presented to him at the *Mitre* Tavern by Mr *James Boswell*, a young *Scotchman* of excellent Family and great Learning, but small Wit, whose metrical Effusions I had sometimes revis'd.

Dr *Johnson*, as I beheld him, was a full, pursy Man, very ill drest, and of slovenly Aspect. I recall him to have worn a bushy Bob-Wig, untyed and without Powder, and much too small for his Head. His cloaths were of rusty brown, much wrinkled, and with more than one Button missing. His Face, too full to be handsom, was likewise marred by the Effects of some scrofulous Disorder; and his Head was continually rolling about in a sort of convulsive way. Of this Infirmity, indeed, I had known before; having heard of it from Mr *Pope*, who took the Trouble to make particular Inquiries.

Being nearly seventy-three, full nineteen Years older than Dr *Johnson* (I say Doctor, tho' his Degree came not till two Years afterward), I naturally expected him to have some Regard for my Age; and was therefore not in that Fear of him, which others confess'd. On my asking him what he thought of my favourable Notice of his Dictionary in *The Londoner*, my periodical Paper, he said: 'Sir,

I possess no Recollection of having perus'd your Paper, and have not a great Interest in the Opinions of the less thoughtful Part of Mankind.' Being more than a little piqued at the Incivility of one whose Celebrity made me solicitous of his Approbation, I ventur'd to retaliate in kind, and told him, I was surpris'd that a Man of Sense shou'd judge the Thoughtfulness of one whose Productions he admitted never having read. 'Why, Sir,' reply'd *Johnson*, 'I do not require to become familiar with a Man's Writings in order to estimate the Superficiality of his Attainments, when he plainly shews it by his Eagerness to mention his own Productions in the first Question he puts to me.' Having thus become Friends, we convers'd on many Matters. When, to agree with him, I said I was distrustful of the Authenticity of *Ossian's* Poems, Mr *Johnson* said: 'That, Sir, does not do your Understanding particular Credit; for what all the Town is sensible of, is no great Discovery for a *Grub-Street* Critick to make. You might as well say, you have a strong Suspicion that *Milton* wrote *Paradise Lost.*'

I thereafter saw *Johnson* very frequently, most often at Meetings of THE LITERARY CLUB, which was founded the next Year by the Doctor, together with Mr *Burke*, the parliamentary Orator, Mr *Beauclerk*, a Gentleman of Fashion, Mr *Langton*, a pious Man and Captain of Militia, Sir J. *Reynolds*, the widely known Painter, Dr *Goldsmith*, the prose and poetick Writer, Dr *Nugent*, father-in-law to Mr *Burke*, Sir *John Hawkins*, Mr *Anthony Charmier*, and my self. We assembled generally at seven o'clock of an Evening, once a Week, at the *Turk's-Head*, in *Gerrard-Street*, *Soho*, till that Tavern was sold and made into a private Dwelling; after which Event we mov'd our Gatherings successively to *Prince's* in *Sackville-Street*, *Le Tellier's* in *Dover-Street*, and *Parsloe's* and *The Thatched House* in *St. James's-Street*. In these Meetings we preserv'd a remarkable Degree of Amity and Tranquillity, which contrasts very favourably with some of the Dissensions and Disruptions I observe in the literary and amateur Press Associations of today. This Tranquillity was the more remarkable, because we had amongst us Gentlemen of very opposed Opinions. Dr *Johnson* and I, as well as many others, were high Tories; whilst Mr *Burke* was a *Whig*, and against the *American War*, many of his Speeches on that Subject having been widely publish'd. The least congenial Member was one of the Founders, Sir *John Hawkins*, who hath since written many misrepresentations of our Society. Sir *John*, an eccentrick Fellow, once declin'd to pay his part of the Reckoning for Supper, because 'twas his Custom at Home to eat no Supper. Later he insulted Mr *Burke* in so intolerable a Manner, that we all took Pains to shew our Disapproval; after which Incident he came no more to our Meetings. However, he never openly fell out with the Doctor, and was the Executor of his Will; tho' Mr *Boswell* and others have Reason to question the genuineness of his Attachment. Other and later Members of the CLUB were Mr *David Garrick*, the Actor and early Friend of Dr *Johnson*, Messieurs *Tho* and *Jos Warton*, Dr *Adam Smith*, Dr *Percy*, Author of the *Reliques*, Mr *Edw. Gibbon*, the Historian, Dr *Burney*, the Musician, Mr *Malone*, the Critick, and Mr *Boswell*. Mr Garrick obtain'd Admittance only with Difficulty; for the Doctor, not-withstanding his great Friendship, was for ever affecting to decry the Stage and all Things connected with it. *Johnson*, indeed, had a most singular Habit of speaking for *Davy* when others were against him, and of arguing against him, when others were for him. I have no Doubt that he sincerely lov'd Mr *Garrick*, for he never alluded to him as he did to *Foote*, who was a very coarse Fellow despite his comick Genius. Mr *Gibbon* was none too well lik'd, for he had an odious sneering Way which offended even those of us who most admir'd his historical Productions. Mr *Goldsmith*, a little Man very vain of his Dress and very deficient in Brilliancy of Conversation, was my particular Favourite; since I was equally unable to shine in the Discourse. He was vastly jealous of Dr *Johnson*, tho' none the less liking and respecting him. I remember that once a Foreigner, a *German*, I think, was in our Company; and that whilst *Goldsmith* was speaking, he observ'd the Doctor preparing to utter something. Unconsciously looking upon *Goldsmith* as a meer Encumbrance when compar'd to the greater Man, the Foreigner bluntly inter-rupted him and incurr'd his lasting Hostility by crying, 'Hush, Toctor *Shonson* iss going to speak!'

In this luminous Company I was tolerated more because of my Years than for my Wit or Learning; being no Match at all for the rest. My Friendship for the celebrated Monsieur *Voltaire* was ever a Cause of Annoyance to the Doctor; who was deeply orthodox, and who us'd to say of the *French* Philosopher: 'Vir est acerrimi Ingenii et paucarum Literarum.'

Mr *Boswell*, a little teazing Fellow whom I had known for some

Time previously, us'd to make Sport of my aukward Manners and old-fashion'd Wig and Cloaths. Once coming in a little the worse for Wine (to which he was addicted) he endeavour'd to lampoon me by means of an Impromptu in verse, writ on the Surface of the Table; but lacking the Aid he usually had in his Composition, he made a bad grammatical Blunder. I told him, he shou'd not try to pasquinade the Source of his Poesy. At another Time *Bozzy* (as we us'd to call him) complain'd of my Harshness toward new Writers in the Articles I prepar'd for *The Monthly Review*. He said, I push'd every Aspirant off the Slopes of Parnassus. 'Sir,' I reply'd, 'you are mistaken. They who lose their Hold do so from their own Want of Strength; but desiring to conceal their Weakness, they attribute the Absence of Success to the first Critick that mentions them.' I am glad to recall that Dr *Johnson* upheld me in this Matter.

Dr Johnson was second to no Man in the Pains he took to revise the bad Verses of others; indeed, 'tis said that in the book of poor blind old Mrs Williams, there are scarce two lines which are not the Doctor's. At one Time *Johnson* recited to me some lines by a Servant to the Duke of *Leeds*, which had so amus'd him, that he had got them by Heart. They are on the Duke's Wedding, and so much resemble in Quality the Work of other and more recent poetick Dunces, that I cannot forbear copying them:

> '*When the Duke of Leeds shall marry'd be*
> *To a fine young Lady of high Quality*
> *How happy will that Gentlewoman be*
> *In his Grace of Leeds' good Company.*'

I ask'd the Doctor, if he had ever try'd making Sense of this Piece; and upon his saying he had not, I amus'd myself with the following Amendment of it:

> *When Gallant LEEDS auspiciously shall wed*
> *The virtuous Fair, of antient Lineage bred,*
> *How must the Maid rejoice with conscious*
>   *Pride*
> *To win so great an Husband to her Side!*

On shewing this to Dr Johnson, he said, 'Sir, you have straightened out the Feet, but you have put neither Wit nor Poetry into the Lines.'

It wou'd afford me Gratification to tell more of my Experiences with Dr Johnson and his circle of Wits; but I am an old Man, and easily fatigued. I seem to ramble along without much Logick or Continuity when I endeavour to recall the Past; and fear I light upon but few Incidents which others have not before discuss'd. Shou'd my present Recollections meet with Favour, I might later set down some further Anecdotes of old Times of which I am the only Survivor. I recall many things of *Sam Johnson* and his Club, having kept up my Membership in the Latter long after the Doctor's Death, at which I sincerely mourn'd. I remember how *John Burgoyne*, Esq, the General, whose Dramatick and Poetical Works were printed after his Death, was blackballed by three Votes; probably because of his unfortunate Defeat in the *American* War, at *Saratoga*. Poor *John!* His Son fared better, I think, and was made a Baronet. But I am very tired. I am old, very old, and it is Time for my Afternoon Nap.

THE BEAST IN THE CAVE

THE HORRIBLE CONCLUSION which had been gradually intruding itself upon my confused and reluctant mind was now an awful certainty. I was lost, completely, hopelessly lost in the vast and labyrinthine recess of the Mammoth Cave. Turn as I might, in no direction could my straining vision seize on any object capable of serving as a guidepost to set me on the outward path. That nevermore should I behold the blessed light of day, or scan the pleasant hills and dales of the beautiful world outside, my reason could no longer entertain the slightest unbelief. Hope had departed. Yet, indoctrinated as I was by a life of philosophical study, I derived no small measure of satisfaction from my unimpassioned demeanour; for although I had frequently read of the wild frenzies into which were thrown the victims of similar situations, I experienced none of these, but stood quiet as soon as I clearly realised the loss of my bearings.

Nor did the thought that I had probably wandered beyond the utmost limits of an ordinary search cause me to abandon my composure even for a moment. If I must die, I reflected, then was this terrible yet majestic cavern as welcome a sepulchre as that which any churchyard might afford, a conception which carried with it more of tranquillity than of despair.

Starving would prove my ultimate fate; of this I was certain. Some, I knew, had gone mad under circumstances such as these, but I felt that this end would not be mine. My disaster was the result of no fault save my own, since unknown to the guide I had separated myself from the regular party of sightseers; and, wandering for over an hour in forbidden avenues of the cave, had found myself unable to retrace the devious windings which I had pursued since forsaking my companions.

Already my torch had begun to expire; soon I would be enveloped by the total and almost palpable blackness of the bowels of the earth. As I stood in the waning, unsteady light, I idly wondered over the exact circumstances of my coming end. I remembered the accounts which I had heard of the colony of consumptives, who, taking their residence in this gigantic grotto to find health from the apparently salubrious air of the underground world, with its steady, uniform temperature, pure air, and peaceful quiet, had found, instead, death in strange and ghastly form. I had seen the sad remains of their ill-made cottages as I passed them by with the party, and had wondered what unnatural influence a long sojourn in this immense and silent cavern would exert upon one as healthy and vigorous as I. Now, I grimly told myself, my opportunity for settling this point had arrived, provided that want of food should not bring me too speedy a departure from this life.

As the last fitful rays of my torch faded into obscurity, I resolved to leave no stone unturned, no possible means of escape neglected; so, summoning all the powers possessed by my lungs, I set up a series of loud shoutings, in the vain hope of attracting the attention of the guide by my clamour. Yet, as I called, I believed in my heart that my cries were to no purpose, and that my voice, magnified and reflected by the numberless ramparts of the black maze about me, fell upon no ears save my own.

All at once, however, my attention was fixed with a start as I fancied that I heard the sound of soft approaching steps on the rocky floor of the cavern.

Was my deliverance about to be accomplished so soon? Had, then, all my horrible apprehensions been for naught, and was the guide, having marked my unwarranted absence from the party, following my course and seeking me out in this limestone labyrinth? Whilst these joyful queries arose in my brain, I was on the point of renewing my cries, in order that my discovery might come the sooner, when in an instant my delight was turned to horror as I listened; for my ever acute ear, now sharpened in even greater degree by the complete silence of the cave, bore to my benumbed understanding the unexpected and dreadful knowledge that these footfalls *were not like those of any mortal man.* In the unearthly stillness of this subterranean region, the tread of the booted guide would have sounded like a series of sharp and incisive blows. These impacts were soft, and stealthy, as of the paws of some feline. Besides, when I listened carefully, I seemed to trace the falls of *four* instead of *two* feet.

I was now convinced that I had by my own cries aroused and attracted some wild beast, perhaps a mountain lion which had accidentally strayed within the cave. Perhaps, I considered, the Almighty had chosen for me a swifter and more merciful death than that of hunger; yet the instinct of self-preservation, never wholly dormant, was stirred in my breast, and though escape from the on-coming peril might but spare me for a sterner and more lingering end, I determined nevertheless to part with my life at as high a price as I could command. Strange as it may seem, my mind conceived of no intent on the part of the visitor save that of hostility. Accordingly, I became very quiet, in the hope that the unknown beast would, in the absence of a guiding sound, lose its direction as had I, and thus pass me by. But this hope was not destined for realisation, for the strange footfalls steadily advanced, the animal evidently having obtained my scent, which in an atmosphere so absolutely free from all distracting influences as is that of the cave, could doubtless be followed at great distance.

Seeing therefore that I must be armed for defence against an uncanny and unseen attack in the dark, I groped about me the largest of the fragments of rock which were strewn upon all parts of the floor of the cavern in the vicinity, and grasping one in each hand for immediate use, awaited with resignation the inevitable result. Meanwhile the hideous pattering of the paws drew near. Certainly, the conduct of the creature was exceedingly strange. Most of the time, the tread seemed to be that of a quadruped, walking with a singular *lack of unison* betwixt hind and fore feet, yet at brief and infrequent intervals I fancied that but two feet were engaged in the process of locomotion. I wondered what species of animal was to confront me; it must, I thought, be some unfortunate beast who had paid for its curiosity to investigate one of the entrances of the fearful grotto with a life-long confinement in its interminable recesses. It doubtless obtained as food the eyeless fish, bats and rats of the cave, as well as some of the ordinary fish that are wafted in at every freshet of Green River, which communicates in some occult manner with the waters of the cave. I occupied my terrible vigil with grotesque conjectures of what alteration cave life might have wrought in the physical structure of the beast, remembering the awful appearances ascribed by local tradition to the consumptives who had died after long residence in the cave. Then I remembered with a start that, even should I succeed in felling my antagonist, I should *never behold its form*, as my torch had long since been extinct, and I was entirely unprovided with matches. The tension on my brain now became frightful. My disordered fancy conjured up hideous and fearsome shapes from the sinister darkness that surrounded me, and that actually seemed to *press* upon my body. Nearer, nearer, the dreadful footfalls approached. It seemed that I must give vent to a piercing scream, yet had I been sufficiently irresolute to attempt such a thing, my voice could scarce have responded. I was petrified, rooted to the spot. I doubted if my right arm would allow me to hurl its missile at the oncoming thing when the crucial moment should arrive. Now the steady *pat, pat,* of the steps was close at hand; now *very* close. I could hear the laboured breathing of the animal, and terror-struck as I was, I realised that it must have come from a considerable distance, and was correspondingly fatigued. Suddenly the spell broke. My right hand, guided by my ever trustworthy sense of hearing, threw with full force the sharp-angled bit of limestone which it contained, toward that point in the darkness from which emanated the breathing and pattering, and, wonderful to relate, it nearly reached its goal, for I heard the thing jump, landing at a distance away, where it seemed to pause.

Having readjusted my aim, I discharged my second missile, this time most effectively, for with a flood of joy I listened as the creature fell in what sounded like a complete collapse and evidently remained prone and unmoving. Almost overpowered by the great relief which rushed over me, I reeled back against the wall. The breathing continued, in heavy, gasping inhalations and expirations, whence I realised that I had no more than wounded the creature. And now all desire to examine the *thing* ceased. At last something allied to groundless, superstitious fear had entered my brain, and I did not approach the body, nor did I continue to cast stones at it in order to complete the extinction of its life. Instead, I ran at full speed in what was, as nearly as I could estimate in my frenzied condition, the direction from which I had come. Suddenly I heard a sound or rather, a regular succession of sounds. In another instant they had resolved themselves into a series of sharp, metallic clicks. This time there was no doubt. *It was the guide.* And then I shouted, yelled, screamed, even shrieked with joy as I beheld in the vaulted arches above the faint and glimmering effulgence which I knew to be the reflected light of an approaching torch. I ran to meet the flare, and before I could completely understand what had occurred, was lying upon the ground at the feet of the guide, embracing his boots and gibbering, despite my boasted reserve, in a most meaningless and idiotic manner, pouring out my terrible story, and at the same time overwhelming my auditor with protestations of gratitude. At length, I awoke to something like my normal consciousness. The guide had noted my absence upon the arrival of the party at the entrance of the cave, and had, from his own intuitive sense of direction, proceeded to make a thorough canvass of by-passages just ahead of where he had last spoken to me, locating my whereabouts after a quest of about four hours.

By the time he had related this to me, I, emboldened by his torch and his company, began to reflect upon the strange beast which I had wounded but a short distance back in the darkness, and suggested that we ascertain, by the flashlight's aid, what manner of creature was my victim. Accordingly I retraced my steps, this time with a courage born of companionship, to the scene of my terrible experience. Soon we descried a white object upon the floor, an object whiter even than the gleaming limestone itself. Cautiously advancing, we gave vent to a simultaneous ejaculation of wonderment, for of all the unnatural monsters either of us had in our lifetimes beheld, this was in surpassing degree the strangest. It appeared to be an anthropoid ape of large proportions, escaped, perhaps, from some itinerant menagerie. Its hair was snow-white, a thing due no doubt to the bleaching action of a long existence within the inky confines of the cave, but it was also surprisingly thin, being indeed largely absent save on the head, where it was of such length and abundance that it fell over the shoulders in considerable profusion. The face was turned away from us, as the creature lay almost directly upon it. The inclination of the limbs was very singular, explaining, however, the alternation in their use which I had before noted, whereby the beast used sometimes all four, and on other occasions but two for its progress. From the tips of the fingers or toes, long rat-like claws extended. The hands or feet were not prehensile, a fact that I ascribed to that long residence in the cave which, as I before mentioned, seemed evident from the all-pervading and almost unearthly whiteness so characteristic of the whole anatomy. No tail seemed to be present.

The respiration had now grown very feeble, and the guide had drawn his pistol with the evident intent of despatching the creature, when a sudden *sound* emitted by the latter caused the weapon to fall unused. The sound was of a nature difficult to describe. It was not like the normal note of any known species of simian, and I wonder if this unnatural quality were not the result of a long continued and complete silence, broken by the sensations produced by the advent of the light, a thing which the beast could not have seen since its first entrance into the cave. The sound, which I might feebly attempt to classify as a kind of deep-tone chattering, was faintly continued.

All at once a fleeting spasm of energy seemed to pass through the frame of the beast. The paws went through a convulsive motion, and the limbs contracted. With a jerk, the white body rolled over so that its face was turned in our direction. For a moment I was so struck with horror at the eyes thus revealed that I noted nothing else. They were black, those eyes, deep jetty black, in hideous contrast to the snow-white hair and flesh. Like those of other cave denizens, they were deeply sunken in their orbits, and were entirely destitute of iris. As I looked more closely, I saw that they were set in a face less prognathous than that of the average ape, and infinitely less hairy. The nose was quite distinct. As we gazed upon the uncanny sight presented to our vision, the thick lips opened, and several *sounds* issued from them, after which the *thing* relaxed in death.

The guide clutched my coat sleeve and trembled so violently that the light shook fitfully, casting weird moving shadows on the walls.

I made no motion, but stood rigidly still, my horrified eyes fixed upon the floor ahead.

The fear left, and wonder, awe, compassion, and reverence succeeded in its place, for the *sounds* uttered by the stricken figure that lay stretched out on the limestone had told us the awesome truth. The creature I had killed, the strange beast of the unfathomed cave, was, or had at one time been a *MAN!!!*

THE POE-ET'S NIGHTMARE

A Fable

Luxus tumultus semper causa est.

LUCULLUS LANGUISH, student of the skies,
And connoisseur of rarebits and mince pies,
A bard by choice, a grocer's clerk by trade,
(Grown pessimist thro' honours long delay'd),
A secret yearning bore, that he might shine
In breathing numbers, and in song divine.
Each day his fountain pen was wont to drop
An ode or dirge or two about the shop,
Yet naught could strike the chord within his heart
That throbb'd for poesy, and cry'd for art.
Each eve he sought his bashful Muse to wake
With overdoses of ice-cream and cake;
But thou' th' ambitious youth a dreamer grew,
Th' Aonian Nymph declin'd to come to view.
Sometimes at dusk he scour'd the heav'ns afar,

Searching for raptures in the evening star;
One night he strove to catch a tale untold
In crystal deeps – but only caught a cold.
So pin'd Lucullus with his lofty woe,
Till one drear day he bought a set of Poe:
Charm'd with the cheerful horrors there display'd,
He vow'd with gloom to woo the Heav'nly Maid.
Of Auber's tarn and Yaanek's slope he dreams,
And weaves an hundred Ravens in his schemes.
Not far from our young hero's peaceful home
Lies the fair grove wherein he loves to roam.
Tho' but a stunted copse in vacant lot,
He dubs it Tempe, and adores the spot;
When shallow puddles dot the wooded plain,
And brim o'er muddy banks with muddy rain,
He calls them limpid lakes or poison pools
(Depending on which bard his fancy rules).
'Tis here he comes with Heliconian fire
On Sundays when he smites the Attic lyre;
And here one afternoon he brought his gloom,
Resolv'd to chant a poet's lay of doom.
Roget's Thesaurus, and a book of rhymes,
Provide the rungs whereon his spirit climbs:
With this grave retinue he trod the grove
And pray'd the Fauns he might a Poe-et prove.
But sad to tell, ere Pegasus flew high,
The not unrelish'd supper hour drew nigh;
Our tuneful swain th' imperious call attends,
And soon above the groaning table bends.
Tho' it were too prosaic to relate
Th' exact particulars of what he ate
(Such long-drawn lists the hasty reader skips,
Like Homer's well-known catalogue of ships),
This much we swear: that as adjournment near'd,
A monstrous lot of cake had disappear'd!
Soon to his chamber the young bard repairs,
And courts soft Somnus with sweet Lydian airs;
Thro' open casement scans the star-strown deep,
And 'neath Orion's beams sinks off to sleep.

Now start from airy dell the elfin train
That dance each midnight o'er the sleeping plain,
To bless the just, or cast a warning spell
On those who dine not wisely, but too well.
First Deacon Smith they plague, whose nasal glow
Comes from what Holmes hath call'd 'Elixir Pro';
Group'd round the couch his visage they deride,
Whilst thro' his dreams unnumber'd serpents glide.
Next troop the little folk into the room
Where snores our young Endymion, swath'd in gloom:
A smile lights up his boyish face, whilst he
Dreams of the moon – or what he ate at tea.
The chieftain elf th' unconscious youth surveys,
And on his form a strange enchantment lays:
Those lips, that lately thrill'd with frosted cake,
Uneasy sounds in slumbrous fashion make;
At length their owner's fancies they rehearse,
And lisp this awesome Poe-em in blank verse:

Aletheia Phrikodes

Omnia risus et omnia pulvis et omnia nihil.

Demoniac clouds, up-pil'd in chasmy reach
Of soundless heav'n, smother'd the brooding night;
Nor came the wonted whisp'rings of the swamp,
Nor voice of autumn wind along the moor,
Nor mutter'd noises of th' insomnious grove
Whose black recesses never saw the sun.
Within that grove a hideous hollow lies,
Half bare of trees; a pool in centre lurks
That none dares sound; a tarn of murky face
(Tho' naught can prove its hue, since light of day,
Affrighted, shuns the forest-shadow'd banks).
Hard by, a yawning hillside grotto breathes,
From deeps unvisited, a dull, dank air
That sears the leaves on certain stunted trees
Which stand about, clawing the spectral gloom
With evil boughs. To this accursed dell

Come woodland creatures, seldom to depart:
Once I behold, upon a crumbling stone
Set altar-like before the cave, a thing
I saw not clearly, yet from glimpsing, fled.
In this half-dusk I meditate alone
At many a weary noontide, when without
A world forgets me in its sun-blest mirth.
Here howl by night the werewolves, and the souls
Of those that knew me well in other days.
Yet on this night the grove spake not to me;
Nor spake the swamp, nor wind along the moor,
Nor moan'd the wind about the lonely eaves
Of the bleak, haunted pile wherein I lay.
I was afraid to sleep, or quench the spark
Of the low-burning taper by my couch.
I was afraid when thro' the vaulted space
Of the old tow'r, the clock-ticks died away
Into a silence so profound and chill
That my teeth chatter'd – giving yet no sound.
Then flicker'd low the light, and all dissolv'd,
Leaving me floating in the hellish grasp
Of body'd blackness, from whose beating wings
Came ghoulish blasts of charnel-scented mist.
Things vague, unseen, unfashion'd, and unnam'd
Jostled each other in the seething void
That gap'd, chaotic, downward to a sea
Of speechless horror, foul with writhing thoughts.
All this I felt, and felt the mocking eyes
Of the curs'd universe upon my soul;
Yet naught I saw nor heard, till flash'd a beam
Of lurid lustre thro' the rotting heav'ns,
Playing on scenes I labour'd not to see.
Methought the nameless tarn, alight at last,
Reflected shapes, and more reveal'd within
Those shocking depths than ne'er were seen before;
Methought from out the cave a demon train,
Grinning and smirking, reel'd in fiendish rout;
Bearing within their reeking paws a load
Of carrion viands for an impious feast.

Methought the stunted trees with hungry arms
Grop'd greedily for things I dare not name;
The while a stifling, wraith-like noisomeness
Fill'd all the dale, and spoke a larger life
Of uncorporeal hideousness awake
In the half-sentient wholeness of the spot.
Now glow'd the ground, and tarn, and cave, and trees,
And moving forms, and things not spoken of,
With such a phosphorescence as men glimpse
In the putrescent thickets of the swamp
Where logs decaying lie, and rankness reigns.
Methought a fire-mist drap'd with lucent fold
The well-remember'd features of the grove,
Whilst whirling ether bore in eddying streams
The hot, unfinish'd stuff of nascent worlds
Hither and thither thro' infinities
Of light and darkness, strangely intermix'd;
Wherein all entity had consciousness,
Without th' accustom'd outward shape of life.
Of these swift-circling currents was my soul,
Free from the flesh, a true constituent part;
Nor felt I less myself, for want of form.
Then clear'd the mist, and o'er a star-strown scene,
Divine and measureless, I gaz'd in awe.
Alone in space, I view'd a feeble fleck
Of silvern light, marking the narrow ken
Which mortals call the boundless universe.
On ev'ry side, each as a tiny star,
Shone more creations, vaster than our own,
And teeming with unnumber'd forms of life;
Tho' we as life would recognise it not,
Being bound to earthy thoughts of human mould.
As on a moonless night the Milky Way
In solid sheen displays its countless orbs
To weak terrestrial eyes, each orb a sun;
So beam'd the prospect on my wond'ring soul:
A spangled curtain, rich with twinkling gems,
Yet each a mighty universe of suns.
But as I gaz'd, I sens'd a spirit voice

In speech didactic, tho' no voice it was,
Save as it carried thought. It bade me mark
That all the universes in my view
Form'd but an atom in infinity;
Whose reaches pass the ether-laden realms
Of heat and light, extending to far fields
Where flourish worlds invisible and vague,
Fill'd with strange wisdom and uncanny life,
And yet beyond; to myriad spheres of light,
To spheres of darkness, to abysmal voids
That know the pulses of disorder'd force.
Big with these musings, I survey'd the surge
Of boundless being, yet I us'd not eyes,
For spirit leans not on the props of sense.
The docent presence swell'd my strength of soul;
All things I knew, but knew with mind alone.
Time's endless vista spread before my thought
With its vast pageant of unceasing change
And sempiternal strife of force and will;
I saw the ages flow in stately stream
Past rise and fall of universe and life;
I saw the birth of suns and worlds, their death,
Their transmutation into limpid flame,
Their second birth and second death, their course
Perpetual thro' the aeons' termless flight,
Never the same, yet born again to serve
The varying purpose of omnipotence.
And whilst I watch'd, I knew each second's space
Was greater than the lifetime of our world.
Then turn'd my musings to that speck of dust
Whereon my form corporeal took its rise;
That speck, born but a second, which must die
In one brief second more; that fragile earth;
That crude experiment; that cosmic sport
Which holds our proud, aspiring race of mites
And moral vermin; those presuming mites
Whom ignorance with empty pomp adorns,
And misinstructs in specious dignity;
Those mites who, reas'ning outward, vaunt themselves

As the chief work of Nature, and enjoy
In fatuous fancy the particular care
Of all her mystic, super-regnant pow'r.
And as I strove to vision the sad sphere
Which lurk'd, lost in ethereal vortices,
Methought my soul, tun'd to the infinite,
Refus'd to glimpse that poor atomic blight;
That misbegotten accident of space;
That globe of insignificance, whereon
(My guide celestial told me) dwells no part
Of empyrean virtue, but where breed
The coarse corruptions of divine disease;
The fest'ring ailments of infinity;
The morbid matter by itself call'd man:
Such matter (said my guide) as oft breaks forth
On broad Creation's fabric, to annoy
For a brief instant, ere assuaging death
Heal up the malady its birth provok'd.
Sicken'd, I turn'd my heavy thoughts away.
Then spake th' ethereal guide with mocking mien,
Upbraiding me for searching after Truth;
Visiting on my mind the searing scorn
Of mind superior; laughing at the woe
Which rent the vital essence of my soul.
Methought he brought remembrance of the time
When from my fellows to the grove I stray'd,
In solitude and dusk to meditate
On things forbidden, and to pierce the veil
Of seeming good and seeming beauteousness
That covers o'er the tragedy of Truth,
Helping mankind forget his sorry lot,
And raising Hope where Truth would crush it down.
He spake, and as he ceas'd, methought the flames
Of fuming Heav'n resolv'd in torments dire;
Whirling in maelstroms of rebellious might,
Yet ever bound by laws I fathom'd not.
Cycles and epicycles, of such girth
That each a cosmos seem'd, dazzled my gaze
Till all a wild phantasmal glow became.

Now burst athwart the fulgent formlessness
A rift of purer sheen, a sight supernal,
Broader than all the void conceiv'd by man,
Yet narrow here. A glimpse of heav'ns beyond;
Of weird creations so remote and great
That ev'n my guide assum'd a tone of awe.
Borne on the wings of stark immensity,
A touch of rhythm celestial reach'd my soul;
Thrilling me more with horror than with joy.
Again the spirit mock'd my human pangs,
And deep revil'd me for presumptuous thoughts:
Yet changing now his mien, he bade me scan
The wid'ning rift that clave the walls of space;
He bade me search it for the ultimate;
He bade me find the Truth I sought so long;
He bade me brave th' unutterable Thing,
The final Truth of moving entity.
All this he bade and offer'd – but my soul,
Clinging to life, fled without aim or knowledge,
Shrieking in silence thro' the gibbering deeps.

Thus shriek'd the young Lucullus, as he fled
Thro' gibbering deeps – and tumbled out of bed;
Within the room the morning sunshine gleams,
Whilst the poor youth recalls his troubled dreams.
He feels his aching limbs, whose woeful pain
Informs his soul his body lives again,
And thanks his stars – or cosmoses – or such
That he survives the noxious nightmare's clutch.
Thrill'd with the music of th' eternal spheres
(Or is it the alarm-clock that he hears?),
He vows to all the Pantheon, high and low,
No more to feed on cake, or pie, or Poe.
And now his gloomy spirits seem to rise,
As he the world beholds with clearer eyes;
The cup he thought too full of dregs to quaff
Affords him wine enough to raise a laugh.
(All this is metaphor – you must not think
Our late Endymion prone to stronger drink!)

With brighter visage and with lighter heart,
He turns his fancies to the grocer's mart;
And strange to say, at last he seems to find
His daily duties worthy of his mind.
Since Truth prov'd such a high and dang'rous goal,
Our bard seeks one less trying to his soul;
With deep-drawn breath he flouts his dreary woes,
And a good clerk from a bad poet grows!
Now close attend my lay, ye scribbling crew
That bay the moon in numbers strange and new;
That madly for the spark celestial bawl
In metres short or long, or none at all:
Curb your rash force, in numbers or at tea,
Nor overzealous for high fancies be;
Reflect, ere ye the draught Pierian take,
What worthy clerks or plumbers ye might make;
Wax not too frenzied in the leaping line
That neither sense nor measure can confine,
Lest ye, like young Lucullus Languish, groan
Beneath Poe-etic nightmares of your own!

MEMORY

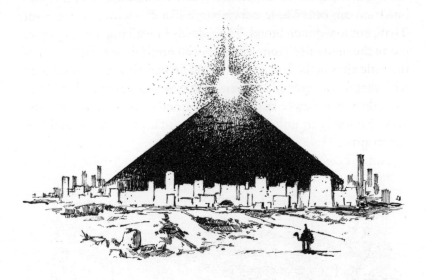

I N THE VALLEY OF NIS the accursed waning moon shines thinly,
tearing a path for its light with feeble horns through the lethal
foliage of a great uperas-tree. And within the depths of the valley,
where the light reaches not, move forms not meant to be beheld.
Rank is the herbage on each slope, where evil vines and creeping
plants crawl amidst the stones of ruined palaces, twining tightly
about broken columns and strange monoliths, and heaving up
marble pavements laid by forgotten hands. And in trees that grow
gigantic in crumbling courtyards leap little apes, while in and out
of deep treasure-vaults writhe poison serpents and scaly things
without a name.

Vast are the stones which sleep beneath coverlets of dank moss,
and mighty were the walls from which they fell. For all time did
their builders erect them, and in sooth they yet serve nobly, for
beneath them the grey toad makes his habitation.

At the very bottom of the valley lies the river Than, whose waters
are slimy and filled with weeds. From hidden springs it rises, and
to subterranean grottoes it flows, so that the Daemon of the Valley

knows not why its waters are red, nor whither they are bound.

The Genie that haunts the moonbeams spake to the Daemon of the Valley, saying, 'I am old, and forget much. Tell me the deeds and aspect and name of them who built these things of Stone.' And the Daemon replied, 'I am Memory, and am wise in lore of the past, but I too am old. These beings were like the waters of the river Than, not to be understood. Their deeds I recall not, for they were but of the moment. Their aspect I recall dimly, it was like to that of the little apes in the trees. Their name I recall clearly, for it rhymed with that of the river. These beings of yesterday were called Man.'

So the Genie flew back to the thin horned moon, and the Daemon looked intently at a little ape in a tree that grew in a crumbling courtyard.

DESPAIR

O 'ER THE MIDNIGHT moorlands crying,
   Thro' the cypress forests sighing,
In the night-wind madly flying,
   Hellish forms with streaming hair;
In the barren branches creaking,
By the stagnant swamp-pools speaking,
Past the shore-cliffs ever shrieking;
   Damn'd daemons of despair.

Once, I think I half remember,
Ere the grey skies of November
Quench'd my youth's aspiring ember,
   Liv'd there such a thing as bliss;
Skies that now are dark were beaming,
Gold and azure, splendid seeming
Till I learn'd it all was dreaming—
   Deadly drowsiness of Dis.

But the stream of Time, swift flowing,
Brings the torment of half-knowing—
Dimly rushing, blindly going
    Past the never-trodden lea;
And the voyager, repining,
Sees the wicked death-fires shining,
Hears the wicked petrel's whining
    As he helpless drifts to sea.

Evil wings in ether beating;
Vultures at the spirit eating;
Things unseen forever fleeting
    Black against the leering sky.
Ghastly shades of bygone gladness,
Clawing fiends of future sadness,
Mingle in a cloud of madness
    Ever on the soul to lie.

Thus the living, lone and sobbing,
In the throes of anguish throbbing,
With the loathsome Furies robbing
    Night and noon of peace and rest.
But beyond the groans and grating
Of abhorrent Life, is waiting
Sweet Oblivion, culminating
    All the years of fruitless quest.

THE PICTURE IN THE HOUSE

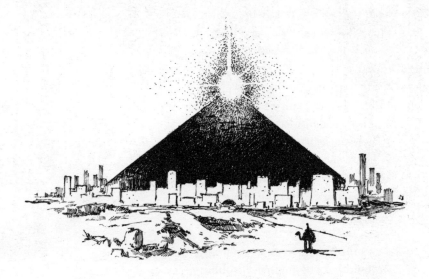

SEARCHERS AFTER HORROR haunt strange, far places. For them are the catacombs of Ptolemais, and the carven mausolea of the nightmare countries. They climb to the moonlit towers of ruined Rhine castles, and falter down black cobwebbed steps beneath the scattered stones of forgotten cities in Asia. The haunted wood and the desolate mountain are their shrines, and they linger around the sinister monoliths on uninhabited islands. But the true epicure in the terrible, to whom a new thrill of unutterable ghastliness is the chief end and justification of existence, esteems most of all the ancient, lonely farmhouses of backwoods New England; for there the dark elements of strength, solitude, grotesqueness, and ignorance combine to form the perfection of the hideous.

Most horrible of all sights are the little unpainted wooden houses remote from travelled ways, usually squatted upon some damp, grassy slope or leaning against some gigantic outcropping of rock. Two hundred years and more they have leaned or squatted there, while the vines have crawled and the trees have swelled and spread. They are almost hidden now in lawless luxuriances of green and

guardian shrouds of shadow; but the small-paned windows still stare shockingly, as if blinking through a lethal stupor which wards off madness by dulling the memory of unutterable things.

In such houses have dwelt generations of strange people, whose like the world has never seen. Seized with a gloomy and fanatical belief which exiled them from their kind, their ancestors sought the wilderness for freedom. There the scions of a conquering race indeed flourished free from the restrictions of their fellows, but cowered in an appalling slavery to the dismal phantasms of their own minds. Divorced from the enlightenment of civilisation, the strength of these Puritans turned into singular channels; and in their isolation, morbid self-repression, and struggle for life with relentless Nature, there came to them dark furtive traits from the prehistoric depths of their cold Northern heritage. By necessity practical and by philosophy stern, these folk were not beautiful in their sins. Erring as all mortals must, they were forced by their rigid code to seek concealment above all else; so that they came to use less and less taste in what they concealed. Only the silent, sleepy, staring houses in the backwoods can tell all that has lain hidden since the early days; and they are not communicative, being loath to shake off the drowsiness which helps them forget. Sometimes one feels that it would be merciful to tear down these houses, for they must often dream.

It was to a time-battered edifice of this description that I was driven one afternoon in November, 1896, by a rain of such chilling copiousness that any shelter was preferable to exposure. I had been travelling for some time amongst the people of the Miskatonic Valley in quest of certain genealogical data; and from the remote, devious, and problematical nature of my course, had deemed it convenient to employ a bicycle despite the lateness of the season. Now I found myself upon an apparently abandoned road which I had chosen as the shortest cut to Arkham; overtaken by the storm at a point far from any town, and confronted with no refuge save the antique and repellent wooden building which blinked with bleared windows from between two huge leafless elms near the foot of a rocky hill. Distant though it was from the remnant of a road, the house none the less impressed me unfavourably the very moment I espied it. Honest, wholesome structures do not stare at travellers so slyly and hauntingly, and in my genealogical researches I had encountered legends of a century before which biased me against places of this kind. Yet the force of the elements was such as to overcome my scruples, and I did not hesitate to wheel my machine up the weedy rise to the closed door which seemed at once so suggestive and secretive.

I had somehow taken it for granted that the house was abandoned, yet as I approached it I was not so sure; for though the walks were indeed overgrown with weeds, they seemed to retain their nature a little too well to argue complete desertion. Therefore instead of trying the door I knocked, feeling as I did so a trepidation I could scarcely explain. As I waited on the rough, mossy rock which served as a doorstep, I glanced at the neighbouring windows and the panes of the transom above me, and noticed that although old, rattling, and almost opaque with dirt, they were not broken. The building, then, must still be inhabited, despite its isolation and general neglect. However, my rapping evoked no response, so after repeating the summons I tried the rusty latch and found the door unfastened. Inside was a little vestibule with walls from which the plaster was falling, and through the doorway came a faint but peculiarly hateful odour. I entered, carrying my bicycle, and closed the door behind me. Ahead rose a narrow staircase, flanked by a small door probably leading to the cellar, while to the left and right were closed doors leading to rooms on the ground floor.

Leaning my cycle against the wall I opened the door at the left, and crossed into a small low-ceiled chamber but dimly lighted by its two dusty windows and furnished in the barest and most primitive possible way. It appeared to be a kind of sitting-room, for it had a table and several chairs, and an immense fireplace above which ticked an antique clock on a mantel. Books and papers were very few, and in the prevailing gloom I could not readily discern the titles. What interested me was the uniform air of archaism as displayed in every visible detail. Most of the houses in this region I had found rich in relics of the past, but here the antiquity was curiously complete; for in all the room I could not discover a single article of definitely post-revolutionary date. Had the furnishings been less humble, the place would have been a collector's paradise.

As I surveyed this quaint apartment, I felt an increase in that aversion first excited by the bleak exterior of the house. Just what it was that I feared or loathed, I could by no means define; but something in the whole atmosphere seemed redolent of unhallowed age, of unpleasant crudeness, and of secrets which should be forgotten. I felt disinclined to sit down, and wandered about examining the various articles which I had noticed. The first object of my curiosity was a book of medium size lying upon the table and presenting such an antediluvian aspect that I marvelled at beholding it outside a museum or library. It was bound in leather with metal fittings, and was in an excellent state of preservation; being altogether an unusual sort of volume to encounter in an abode so lowly. When I opened it to the title page my wonder grew even greater, for it proved to be nothing less rare than Pigafetta's account of the Congo region, written in Latin from the notes of the sailor Lopez and printed at Frankfort in 1598. I had often heard of this work, with its curious illustrations by the brothers De Bry, hence for a moment forgot my uneasiness in my desire to turn the pages before me. The engravings were indeed interesting, drawn wholly from imagination and careless descriptions, and represented Negroes with white skins and Caucasian features; nor would I soon have closed the book had not an exceedingly trivial circumstance upset my tired nerves and revived my sensation of disquiet. What annoyed me was merely the persistent way in which the volume tended to fall open of itself at Plate XII, which represented in gruesome detail a butcher's shop of the cannibal Anziques. I experienced some shame at my susceptibility to so slight a thing, but the drawing nevertheless disturbed me, especially in connection with some adjacent passages descriptive of Anzique gastronomy.

I had turned to a neighbouring shelf and was examining its meagre literary contents – an eighteenth-century Bible, a *Pilgrim's Progress* of like period, illustrated with grotesque woodcuts and printed by the almanack-maker Isaiah Thomas, the rotting bulk of Cotton Mather's *Magnalia Christi Americana*, and a few other books of evidently equal age – when my attention was aroused by the unmistakable sound of walking in the room overhead. At first astonished and startled, considering the lack of response to my recent knocking at the door, I immediately afterward concluded that the walker had just awakened from a sound sleep; and listened with less surprise as the footsteps sounded on the creaking stairs. The tread was heavy, yet seemed to contain a curious quality of cautiousness; a quality which I disliked the more because the tread was heavy.

When I had entered the room I had shut the door behind me. Now, after a moment of silence during which the walker may have been inspecting my bicycle in the hall, I heard a fumbling at the latch and saw the panelled portal swing open again.

In the doorway stood a person of such singular appearance that I should have exclaimed aloud but for the restraints of good breeding. Old, white-bearded, and ragged, my host possessed a countenance and physique which inspired equal wonder and respect. His height could not have been less than six feet, and despite a general air of age and poverty he was stout and powerful in proportion. His face, almost hidden by a long beard which grew high on the cheeks, seemed abnormally ruddy and less wrinkled than one might expect; while over a high forehead fell a shock of white hair little thinned by the years. His blue eyes, though a trifle bloodshot, seemed inexplicably keen and burning. But for his horrible unkemptness the man would have been as distinguished-looking as he was impressive. This unkemptness, however, made him offensive despite his face and figure. Of what his clothing consisted I could hardly tell, for it seemed to me no more than a mass of tatters surmounting a pair of high, heavy boots; and his lack of cleanliness surpassed description.

The appearance of this man, and the instinctive fear he inspired, prepared me for something like enmity; so that I almost shuddered through surprise and a sense of uncanny incongruity when he motioned me to a chair and addressed me in a thin, weak voice full of fawning respect and ingratiating hospitality. His speech was very curious, an extreme form of Yankee dialect I had thought long extinct; and I studied it closely as he sat down opposite me for conversation.

'Ketched in the rain, be ye?' he greeted. 'Glad ye was nigh the haouse en' hed the sense ta come right in. I calc'late I was asleep, else I'd a heerd ye – I ain't as young as I uster be, an' I need a paowerful sight o' naps naowadays. Trav'lin' fur? I hain't seed many folks 'long this rud sence they tuk off the Arkham stage.'

I replied that I was going to Arkham, and apologised for my rude entry into his domicile, whereupon he continued.

'Glad ta see ye, young Sir – new faces is scurce arount here, an' I hain't got much ta cheer me up these days. Guess yew hail from Bosting, don't ye? I never ben thar, but I kin tell a taown man when

I see 'im – we hed one fer deestrick schoolmaster in 'eighty-four, but he quit suddent an' no one never heerd on 'im sence—' Here the old man lapsed into a kind of chuckle, and made no explanation when I questioned him. He seemed to be in an aboundingly good humour, yet to possess those eccentricities which one might guess from his grooming. For some time he rambled on with an almost feverish geniality, when it struck me to ask him how he came by so rare a book as Pigafetta's *Regnum Congo*. The effect of this volume had not left me, and I felt a certain hesitancy in speaking of it; but curiosity overmastered all the vague fears which had steadily accumulated since my first glimpse of the house. To my relief, the question did not seem an awkward one; for the old man answered freely and volubly.

'Oh, thet Afriky book? Cap'n Ebenezer Holt traded me thet in 'sixty-eight – him as was kilt in the war.' Something about the name of Ebenezer Holt caused me to look up sharply. I had encountered it in my genealogical work, but not in any record since the Revolution. I wondered if my host could help me in the task at which I was labouring, and resolved to ask him about it later on. He continued.

'Ebenezer was on a Salem merchantman for years, an' picked up a sight o' queer stuff in every port. He got this in London, I guess – he uster like ter buy things at the shops. I was up ta his haouse onct, on the hill, tradin' hosses, when I see this book. I relished the picters, so he give it in on a swap. 'Tis a queer book – here, leave me git on my spectacles—' The old man fumbled among his rags, producing a pair of dirty and amazingly antique glasses with small octagonal lenses and steel bows. Donning these, he reached for the volume on the table and turned the pages lovingly.

'Ebenezer cud read a leetle o' this – 'tis Latin – but I can't. I hed two er three schoolmasters read me a bit, and Passon Clark, him they say got draownded in the pond – kin yew make anything outen it?' I told him that I could, and translated for his benefit a paragraph near the beginning. If I erred, he was not scholar enough to correct me; for he seemed childishly pleased at my English version. His proximity was becoming rather obnoxious, yet I saw no way to escape without offending him. I was amused at the childish fondness of this ignorant old man for the pictures in a book he could not read, and wondered how much better he could read the few books in English which adorned the room. This revelation of simplicity

46

removed much of the ill-defined apprehension I had felt, and I smiled as my host rambled on:

'Queer haow picters kin set a body thinkin'. Take this un here near the front. Hev yew ever seed trees like thet, with big leaves a-floppin' over an' daown? And them men – them can't be niggers – they dew beat all. Kinder like Injuns, I guess, even ef they be in Afriky. Some o' these here critters looks like monkeys, or half monkeys an' half men, but I never heerd o' nothing like this un.' Here he pointed to a fabulous creature of the artist, which one might describe as a sort of dragon with the head of an alligator.

'But naow I'll shew ye the best un – over here nigh the middle—' The old man's speech grew a trifle thicker and his eyes assumed a brighter glow; but his fumbling hands, though seemingly clumsier than before, were entirely adequate to their mission. The book fell open, almost of its own accord and as if from frequent consultation at this place, to the repellent twelfth plate shewing a butcher's shop amongst the Anzique cannibals. My sense of restlessness returned, though I did not exhibit it. The especially bizarre thing was that the artist had made his Africans look like white men – the limbs and quarters hanging about the walls of the shop were ghastly, while the butcher with his axe was hideously incongruous. But my host seemed to relish the view as much as I disliked it.

'What d'ye think o' this – ain't never see the like hereabouts, eh? When I see this I telled Eb Holt, "That's suthin' ta stir ye up an' make yer blood tickle!" When I read in Scripter about slayin' – like them Midianites was slew – I kinder think things, but I ain't got no picter of it. Here a body kin see all they is to it – I s'pose 'tis sinful, but ain't we all born an' livin' in sin? – Thet feller bein' chopped up gives me a tickle every time I look at 'im – I hev ta keep lookin' at 'im – see whar the butcher cut off his feet? Thar's his head on thet bench, with one arm side of it, an' t'other arm's on the graound side o' the meat block.'

As the man mumbled on in his shocking ecstasy the expression on his hairy, spectacled face became indescribable, but his voice sank rather than mounted. My own sensations can scarcely be recorded. All the terror I had dimly felt before rushed upon me actively and vividly, and I knew that I loathed the ancient and abhorrent creature so near me with an infinite intensity. His madness, or at least his partial perversion, seemed beyond dispute.

47

He was almost whispering now, with a huskiness more terrible than a scream, and I trembled as I listened.

'As I says, 'tis queer haow picters sets ye thinkin'. D'ye know, young Sir, I'm right sot on this un here. Arter I got the book off Eb I uster look at it a lot, especial when I'd heerd Passon Clark rant o' Sundays in his big wig. Onct I tried suthin' funny – here, young Sir, don't git skeert – all I done was ter look at the picter afore I kilt the sheep for market – killin' sheep was kinder more fun arter lookin' at it—' The tone of the old man now sank very low, sometimes becoming so faint that his words were hardly audible. I listened to the rain, and to the rattling of the bleared, small-paned windows, and marked a rumbling of approaching thunder quite unusual for the season. Once a terrific flash and peal shook the frail house to its foundations, but the whisperer seemed not to notice it.

'Killin' sheep was kinder more fun – but d'ye know, 'twan't quite *satisfyin'*. Queer haow a *cravin'* gits a holt on ye– As ye love the Almighty, young man, don't tell nobody, but I swar ter Gawd thet picter begun ta make me *hungry fer victuals I couldn't raise nor buy* – here, set still, what's ailin' ye? – I didn't do nothin', only I wondered haow 'twud be ef I *did*– They say meat makes blood an' flesh, an' gives ye new life, so I wondered ef 'twudn't make a man live longer an' longer ef 'twas *more the same*–' But the whisperer never continued. The interruption was not produced by my fright, nor by the rapidly increasing storm amidst whose fury I was presently to open my eyes on a smoky solitude of blackened ruins. It was produced by a very simple though somewhat unusual happening.

The open book lay flat between us, with the picture staring repulsively upward. As the old man whispered the words '*more the same*' a tiny spattering impact was heard, and something shewed on the yellowed paper of the upturned volume. I thought of the rain and of a leaky roof, but rain is not red. On the butcher's shop of the Anzique cannibals a small red spattering glistened picturesquely, lending vividness to the horror of the engraving. The old man saw it, and stopped whispering even before my expression of horror made it necessary; saw it and glanced quickly toward the floor of the room he had left an hour before. I followed his glance, and beheld just above us on the loose plaster of the ancient ceiling a large irregular spot of wet crimson which seemed to spread even as I viewed it. I did not shriek or move, but merely shut my eyes. A moment later came the titanic thunderbolt of thunderbolts; blasting that accursed house of unutterable secrets and bringing the oblivion which alone saved my mind.

BEYOND THE WALL OF SLEEP

'I have an exposition of sleep come upon me.'
—*Shakespeare*

I HAVE FREQUENTLY WONDERED if the majority of mankind ever pause to reflect upon the occasionally titanic significance of dreams, and of the obscure world to which they belong. Whilst the greater number of our nocturnal visions are perhaps no more than faint and fantastic reflections of our waking experiences – Freud to the contrary with his puerile symbolism – there are still a certain remainder whose immundane and ethereal character permits of no ordinary interpretation, and whose vaguely exciting and disquieting effect suggests possible minute glimpses into a sphere of mental existence no less important than physical life, yet separated from that life by an all but impassable barrier. From my experience I cannot doubt but that man, when lost to terrestrial consciousness, is indeed sojourning in another and uncorporeal life of far different nature from the life we know; and of which only the slightest and most indistinct memories linger after waking. From

purpose (whatever it may have been originally) became that of a sheriff's posse after one of the seldom popular state troopers had by accident observed, then questioned, and finally joined the seekers.

On the third day Slater was found unconscious in the hollow of a tree, and taken to the nearest gaol; where alienists from Albany examined him as soon as his senses returned. To them he told a simple story. He had, he said, gone to sleep one afternoon about sundown after drinking much liquor. He had awaked to find himself standing bloody-handed in the snow before his cabin, the mangled corpse of his neighbour Peter Slader at his feet. Horrified, he had taken to the woods in a vague effort to escape from the scene of what must have been his crime. Beyond these things he seemed to know nothing, nor could the expert questioning of his interrogators bring out a single additional fact. That night Slater slept quietly, and the next morning he wakened with no singular feature save a certain alteration of expression. Dr Barnard, who had been watching the patient, thought he noticed in the pale blue eyes a certain gleam of peculiar quality; and in the flaccid lips an all but imperceptible tightening, as if of intelligent determination. But when questioned, Slater relapsed into the habitual vacancy of the mountaineer, and only reiterated what he had said on the preceding day.

On the third morning occurred the first of the man's mental attacks. After some show of uneasiness in sleep, he burst forth into a frenzy so powerful that the combined efforts of four men were needed to bind him in a strait-jacket. The alienists listened with keen attention to his words, since their curiosity had been aroused to a high pitch by the suggestive yet mostly conflicting and incoherent stories of his family and neighbours. Slater raved for upward of fifteen minutes, babbling in his backwoods dialect of great edifices of light, oceans of space, strange music, and shadowy mountains and valleys. But most of all did he dwell upon some mysterious blazing entity that shook and laughed and mocked at him. This vast, vague personality seemed to have done him a terrible wrong, and to kill it in triumphant revenge was his paramount desire. In order to reach it, he said, he would soar through abysses of emptiness, *burning* every obstacle that stood in his way. Thus ran his discourse, until with the greatest suddenness he ceased. The fire of madness died from his eyes, and in dull wonder he looked at his questioners and asked why he was bound. Dr Barnard unbuckled the leathern harness and did not restore it till night, when he succeeded in persuading Slater to don it of his own volition, for his own good. The man had now admitted that he sometimes talked queerly, though he knew not why.

Within a week two more attacks appeared, but from them the doctors learned little. On the *source* of Slater's visions they speculated at length, for since he could neither read nor write, and had apparently never heard a legend or fairy tale, his gorgeous imagery was quite inexplicable. That it could not come from any known myth or romance was made especially clear by the fact that the unfortunate lunatic expressed himself only in his own simple manner. He raved of things he did not understand and could not interpret; things which he claimed to have experienced, but which he could not have learned through any normal or connected narration. The alienists soon agreed that abnormal dreams were the foundation of the trouble; dreams whose vividness could for a time completely dominate the waking mind of this basically inferior man. With due formality Slater was tried for murder, acquitted on the ground of insanity, and committed to the institution wherein I held so humble a post.

I have said that I am a constant speculator concerning dream life, and from this you may judge of the eagerness with which I applied myself to the study of the new patient as soon as I had fully ascertained the facts of his case. He seemed to sense a certain friendliness in me; born no doubt of the interest I could not conceal, and the gentle manner in which I questioned him. Not that he ever recognised me during his attacks, when I hung breathlessly upon his chaotic but cosmic word-pictures; but he knew me in his quiet hours, when he would sit by his barred window weaving baskets of straw and willow, and perhaps pining for the mountain freedom he could never enjoy again. His family never called to see him; probably it had found another temporary head, after the manner of decadent mountain folk.

By degrees I commenced to feel an overwhelming wonder at the mad and fantastic conceptions of Joe Slater. The man himself was pitiably inferior in mentality and language alike; but his glowing, titanic visions, though described in a barbarous and disjointed jargon, were assuredly things which only a superior or even exceptional brain could conceive. How, I often asked myself, could the stolid imagination of a Catskill degenerate conjure up sights whose very possession argued a lurking spark of genius? How could any backwoods dullard have gained so much as an idea of those glittering realms of supernal radiance and space about which Slater ranted in his furious delirium? More and more I inclined to the belief that in the pitiful personality who cringed before me lay the disordered nucleus of something beyond my comprehension; something infinitely beyond the comprehension of my more experienced but less imaginative medical and scientific colleagues.

And yet I could extract nothing definite from the man. The sum of all my investigation was, that in a kind of semi-uncorporeal dream life Slater wandered or floated through resplendent and prodigious valleys, meadows, gardens, cities, and palaces of light; in a region unbounded and unknown to man. That there he was no peasant or degenerate, but a creature of importance and vivid life; moving proudly and dominantly, and checked only by a certain deadly enemy, who seemed to be a being of visible yet ethereal structure, and who did not appear to be of human shape, since Slater never referred to it as a *man*, or as aught save a *thing*. This *thing* had done Slater some hideous but unnamed wrong, which the maniac (if maniac he were) yearned to avenge. From the manner in which Slater alluded to their dealings, I judged that he and the luminous *thing* had met on equal terms; that in his dream existence the man was himself a luminous *thing* of the same race as his enemy. This impression was sustained by his frequent references to *flying through space* and *burning* all that impeded his progress. Yet these conceptions were formulated in rustic words wholly inadequate to convey them, a circumstance which drove me to the conclusion that if a true dream-world indeed existed, oral language was not its medium for the transmission of thought. Could it be that the dream-soul inhabiting this inferior body was desperately struggling to speak things which the simple and halting tongue of dullness could not utter? Could it be that I was face to face with intellectual emanations which would explain the mystery if I could but learn to discover and read them? I did not tell the older physicians of these things, for middle age is sceptical, cynical, and disinclined to accept new ideas. Besides, the head of the institution had but lately warned me in his paternal way that I was overworking; that my mind needed a rest.

It had long been my belief that human thought consists basically of atomic or molecular motion, convertible into ether waves of radiant energy like heat, light, and electricity. This belief had early led me to contemplate the possibility of telepathy or mental communication by means of suitable apparatus, and I had in my college days prepared a set of transmitting and receiving instruments somewhat similar to the cumbrous devices employed in wireless telegraphy at that crude, pre-radio period. These I had tested with a fellow-student; but achieving no result, had soon packed them away with other scientific odds and ends for possible future use. Now, in my intense desire to probe into the dream life of Joe Slater, I sought these instruments again; and spent several days in repairing them for action. When they were complete once more I missed no opportunity for their trial. At each outburst of Slater's violence, I would fit the transmitter to his forehead and the receiver to my own; constantly making delicate adjustments for various hypothetical wave-lengths of intellectual energy. I had but little notion of how the thought-impressions would, if successfully conveyed, arouse an intelligent response in my brain; but I felt certain that I could detect and interpret them. Accordingly I continued my experiments, though informing no one of their nature.

It was on the twenty-first of February, 1901, that the thing finally occurred. As I look back across the years I realise how unreal it seems; and sometimes half wonder if old Dr Fenton was not right when he charged it all to my excited imagination. I recall that he listened with great kindness and patience when I told him, but afterward gave me a nerve-powder and arranged for the half-year's vacation on which I departed the next week. That fateful night I was wildly agitated and perturbed, for despite the excellent care he had received, Joe Slater was unmistakably dying. Perhaps it was his mountain freedom that he missed, or perhaps the turmoil in his brain had grown too acute for his rather sluggish physique; but at all events the flame of vitality flickered low in the decadent body. He was drowsy near the end, and as darkness fell he dropped off into a troubled sleep. I did not strap on the strait-jacket as was customary when he slept, since I saw that he was too feeble to be dangerous, even if he woke in mental disorder once more before passing away. But I did place upon his head and mine the two ends of my cosmic 'radio'; hoping against hope for a first and last message from the dream-world in the brief time remaining. In the cell with us was one nurse, a mediocre fellow who did not understand the purpose of the apparatus, or think to inquire into my course. As the hours wore on I saw his head droop awkwardly in sleep, but I did not disturb him. I myself, lulled by the rhythmical breathing of the healthy and the dying man, must have nodded a little later.

The sound of weird lyric melody was what aroused me. Chords, vibrations, and harmonic ecstasies echoed passionately on every hand; while on my ravished sight burst the stupendous spectacle of ultimate beauty. Walls, columns, and architraves of living fire blazed effulgently around the spot where I seemed to float in air; extending upward to an infinitely high vaulted dome of indescribable splendour. Blending with this display of palatial magnificence, or rather, supplanting it at times in kaleidoscopic rotation, were glimpses of wide plains and graceful valleys, high mountains and inviting grottoes; covered with every lovely attribute of scenery which my delighted eye could conceive of, yet formed wholly of some glowing, ethereal, plastic entity, which in consistency partook as much of spirit as of matter. As I gazed, I perceived that my own brain held the key to these enchanting metamorphoses; for each vista which appeared to me, was the one my changing mind most wished to behold. Amidst this elysian realm I dwelt not as a stranger, for each sight and sound was familiar to me; just as it had been for uncounted aeons of eternity before, and would be for like eternities to come.

Then the resplendent aura of my brother of light drew near and held colloquy with me, soul to soul, with silent and perfect interchange of thought. The hour was one of approaching triumph, for was not my fellow-being escaping at last from a degrading periodic bondage; escaping forever, and preparing to follow the accursed oppressor even unto the uttermost fields of ether, that upon it might be wrought a flaming cosmic vengeance which would shake the spheres? We floated thus for a little time, when I perceived a slight blurring and fading of the objects around us, as though some force were recalling me to earth – where I least wished to go. The form near me seemed to feel a change also, for it gradually brought its discourse toward a conclusion, and itself prepared to quit the scene; fading from my sight at a rate somewhat less rapid than that of the other objects. A few more thoughts were exchanged, and I knew that the luminous one and I were being recalled to bondage, though for my brother of light it would be the last time. The sorry planet-shell being well-nigh spent, in less than an hour my fellow would be free to pursue the oppressor along the Milky Way and past the hither stars to the very confines of infinity.

A well-defined shock separates my final impression of the fading scene of light from my sudden and somewhat shamefaced awakening and straightening up in my chair as I saw the dying figure on the couch move hesitantly. Joe Slater was indeed awaking, though probably for the last time. As I looked more closely, I saw that in the sallow cheeks shone spots of colour which had never before been present. The lips, too, seemed unusual; being tightly compressed, as if by the force of a stronger character than had been Slater's. The whole face finally began to grow tense, and the head turned restlessly with closed eyes. I did not arouse the sleeping nurse, but readjusted the slightly disarranged head-bands of my telepathic 'radio', intent to catch any parting message the dreamer might have to deliver. All at once the head turned sharply in my direction and the eyes fell open, causing me to stare in blank amazement at what I beheld. The man who had been Joe Slater, the Catskill decadent, was now gazing at me with a pair of luminous, expanded eyes whose blue seemed subtly to have deepened. Neither mania nor degeneracy was visible in that gaze, and I felt beyond a doubt that I was viewing a face behind which lay an active mind of high order.

At this juncture my brain became aware of a steady external influence operating upon it. I closed my eyes to concentrate my thoughts more profoundly, and was rewarded by the positive knowledge that *my long-sought mental message had come at last.* Each transmitted idea formed rapidly in my mind, and though no actual language was employed, my habitual association of conception and expression was so great that I seemed to be receiving the message in ordinary English.

'*Joe Slater is dead,*' came the soul-petrifying voice or agency from beyond the wall of sleep. My opened eyes sought the couch of pain in curious horror, but the blue eyes were still calmly gazing, and the countenance was still intelligently animated. 'He is better dead, for he was unfit to bear the active intellect of cosmic entity. His gross body could not undergo the needed adjustments between ethereal life and planet life. He was too much of an animal, too little a man; yet it is through his deficiency that you have come to discover me, for the cosmic and planet souls rightly should never meet. He has been my torment and diurnal prison for forty-two of your terrestrial years. I am an entity like that which you yourself become in the freedom of dreamless sleep. I am your brother of light, and have floated with you in the effulgent valleys. It is not permitted me to tell your waking earth-self of your real self, but we are all roamers of vast spaces and travellers in many ages. Next year I may be dwelling in the dark Egypt which you call ancient, or in the cruel empire of Tsan-Chan which is to come three thousand years hence. You and I have drifted to the worlds that reel about the red Arcturus, and dwelt in the bodies of the insect-philosophers that crawl proudly over the fourth moon of Jupiter. How little does the earth-self know of life and its extent! How little, indeed, ought it to know for its own tranquillity! Of the oppressor I cannot speak. You on earth have unwittingly felt its distant presence – you who without knowing idly gave to its blinking beacon the name of *Algol, the Daemon-Star.* It is to meet and conquer the oppressor that I have vainly striven for aeons, held back by bodily encumbrances. Tonight I go as a Nemesis bearing just and blazingly cataclysmic vengeance. *Watch me in the sky close by the Daemon-Star.* I cannot speak longer, for the body of Joe Slater grows cold and rigid, and the coarse brains are ceasing to vibrate as I wish. You have been my friend in the cosmos; you have been my only friend on this planet – the only soul to sense and seek for me within the repellent form which lies on this couch. We shall meet again – perhaps in the shining mists of Orion's Sword, perhaps on a bleak plateau in prehistoric Asia. Perhaps in unremembered dreams tonight; perhaps in some other form an aeon hence, when the solar system shall have been swept away.'

At this point the thought-waves abruptly ceased, and the pale eyes of the dreamer – or can I say dead man? – commenced to glaze fishily. In a half-stupor I crossed over to the couch and felt of his wrist, but found it cold, stiff, and pulseless. The sallow cheeks paled again, and the thick lips fell open, disclosing the repulsively rotten fangs of the degenerate Joe Slater. I shivered, pulled a blanket over the hideous face, and awakened the nurse. Then I left the cell and went silently to my room. I had an insistent and unaccountable craving for a sleep whose dreams I should not remember.

The climax? What plain tale of science can boast of such a rhetorical effect? I have merely set down certain things appealing to me as facts, allowing you to construe them as you will. As I have already admitted, my superior, old Dr Fenton, denies the reality of everything I have related. He vows that I was broken down with nervous strain, and badly in need of the long vacation on full pay which he so generously gave me. He assures me on his professional honour that Joe Slater was but a low-grade paranoiac, whose fantastic notions must have come from the crude hereditary folk-tales which circulate in even the most decadent of communities. All this he tells me – yet I cannot forget what I saw in the sky on the night after Slater died. Lest you think me a biased witness, another's pen must add this final testimony, which may perhaps supply the climax you expect. I will quote the following account of the star *Nova Persei* verbatim from the pages of that eminent astronomical authority, Prof. Garrett P. Serviss:

'On February 22, 1901, a marvellous new star was discovered by Dr Anderson, of Edinburgh, *not very far from Algol.* No star had been visible at that point before. Within twenty-four hours the stranger had become so bright that it outshone Capella. In a week or two it had visibly faded, and in the course of a few months it was hardly discernible with the naked eye.'

PSYCHOPOMPOS

I am He who howls in the night;
   I am He who moans in the snow;
I am He who hath never seen light;
   I am He who mounts from below.

My car is the car of Death;
   My wings are the wings of dread;
My breath is the north wind's breath;
   My prey are the cold and the dead.

IN OLD AUVERGNE, when schools were poor and few,
And peasants fancy'd what they scarcely knew,
When lords and gentry shunn'd their monarch's throne
For solitary castles of their own,
There dwelt a man of rank, whose fortress stood
In the hush'd twilight of a hoary wood.
De Blois his name; his lineage high and vast,
A proud memorial of an honour'd past;

But curious swains would whisper now and then
That Sieur De Blois was not as other men.
In person dark and lean, with glossy hair,
And gleaming teeth that he would often bare,
With piercing eye, and stealthy roving glance,
And tongue that clipt the soft, sweet speech of France;
The Sieur was little lov'd and seldom seen,
So close he kept within his own demesne.
The castle servants, few, discreet, and old,
Full many a tale of strangeness might have told;
But bow'd with years, they rarely left the door
Wherein their sires and grandsires serv'd before.
Thus gossip rose, as gossip rises best,
When mystery imparts a keener zest;
Seclusion oft the poison tongue attracts,
And scandal prospers on a dearth of facts.
'Twas said, the Sieur had more than once been spy'd
Alone at midnight by the river's side,
With aspect so uncouth, and gaze so strange,
That rustics cross'd themselves to see the change;
Yet none, when press'd, could clearly say or know
Just what it was, or why they trembled so.
De Blois, as rumour whisper'd, fear'd to pray,
Nor us'd his chapel on the Sabbath day;
Howe'er this may have been, 'twas known at least
His household had no chaplain, monk, or priest.
But if the Master liv'd in dubious fame,
Twice fear'd and hated was his noble Dame;
As dark as he, in features wild and proud,
And with a weird supernal grace endow'd,
The haughty mistress scorn'd the rural train
Who sought to learn her source, but sought in vain.
Old women call'd her eyes too bright by half,
And nervous children shiver'd at her laugh;
Richard, the dwarf (whose word had little weight),
Vow'd she was like a serpent in her gait,
Whilst ancient Pierre (the aged often err)
Laid all her husband's mystery to her.
Still more absurd were those odd mutter'd things

62

That calumny to curious list'ners brings;
Those subtle slanders, told with downcast face,
And muffled voice ... those tales no man may trace;
Tales that the faith of old wives can command,
Tho' always heard at sixth or seventh hand.
Thus village legend darkly would imply
That Dame De Blois possess'd an evil eye;
Or going further, furtively suggest
A lurking spark of sorcery in her breast;
Old Mère Allard (herself half witch) once said
The lady's glance work'd strangely on the dead.
So liv'd the pair, like many another two
That shun the crowd, and shrink from public view.
They scorn'd the doubts by ev'ry peasant shown,
And ask'd but one thing ... to be let alone!

'Twas Candlemas, the dreariest time of year,
With fall long gone, and spring too far to cheer,
When little Jean, the bailiff's son and heir,
Fell sick and threw the doctors in despair.
A child so stout and strong that few would think
An hour might carry him to death's dark brink,
Yet pale he lay, though hidden was the cause,
And Galens search'd in vain through Nature's laws.
But stricken sadness could not quite suppress
The roving thought, or wrinkled grandam's guess:
Though spoke by stealth, 'twas known to half a score
That Dame De Blois rode by the day before;
She had (they said) with glances weird and wild
Paus'd by the gate to view the prattling child,
Nor did they like the smile which seem'd to trace
New lines of evil on her proud, dark face.
These things they whisper'd, when the mother's cry
Told of the end ... the gentle soul gone by;
In genuine grief the kindly watcher wept,
Whilst the lov'd babe with saints and angels slept.
The village priest his simple rites went through,
And good Michel nail'd up the box of yew;
Around the corpse the holy candles burn'd,

The mourners sighed, the parents dumbly yearn'd.
Then one by one each sought his humble bed,
And left the lonely mother with her dead.
Late in the night it was, when o'er the vale
The storm-king swept with pandemoniac gale;
Deep pil'd the cruel snow, yet strange to tell,
The lightning sputter'd while the white flakes fell;
A hideous presence seem'd abroad to steal,
And terror sounded in the thunder's peal.
Within the house of grief the tapers glow'd
Whilst the poor mother bow'd beneath her load;
Her salty eyes too tired now to weep,
Too pain'd to see, too sad to close in sleep.
The clock struck three, above the tempest heard,
When something near the lifeless infant stirr'd;
Some slipp'ry thing, that flopp'd in awkward way,
And climb'd the table where the coffin lay.
With scaly convolutions strove to find
The cold, still clay that death had left behind.
The nodding mother hears ... starts broad awake ...
Empower'd to reason, yet too stunn'd to shake;
The pois'nous thing she sees, and nimbly foils
The ghoulish purpose of the quiv'ring coils:
With ready ax the serpent's head she cleaves,
And thrills with savage triumph whilst she grieves.
The injur'd reptile hissing glides from sight,
And hides its cloven carcass in the night.

The weeks slipp'd by, and gossip's tongue began
To call the Sieur De Blois an alter'd man;
With curious mien he oft would pace along
The village street, and eye the gaping throng.
Yet whilst he showed himself as ne'er before,
His wild-eyed lady was observ'd no more.
In course of time, 'twas scarce thought odd or ill
That he his ears with village lore should fill;
Nor was the town with special rumour rife
When he sought out the bailiff and his wife:
Their tale of sorrow, with its ghastly end,

Was told, indeed, by ev'ry wond'ring friend.
The Sieur heard all, and low'ring rode away,
Nor was he seen again for many a day.

When vernal sunshine shed its cheering glow,
And genial zephyrs blew away the snow,
To frighten'd swains a horror was reveal'd
In the damp herbage of a melting field.
There (half preserved by winter's frigid bed)
Lay the dark Dame De Blois, untimely dead;
By some assassin's stroke most foully slain,
Her shapely brow and temples cleft in twain.
Reluctant hands the dismal burden bore
To the stone arches of the husband's door,
Where silent serfs the ghastly thing receiv'd,
Trembling with fright, but less amaz'd than griev'd;
The Sieur his dame beheld with blazing eyes,
And shook with anger, more than with surprise.
(At least 'tis thus the stupid peasants told
Their wide-mouth'd wives when they the tale unroll'd.)
The village wonder'd why De Blois had kept
His spouse's loss unmention'd and unwept,
Nor were there lacking sland'rous tongues to claim
That the dark master was himself to blame.
But village talk could scarcely hope to solve
A crime so deep, and thus the months revolve:
The rural train repeat the gruesome tale,
And gape and marvel more than they bewail.

Swift flew the sun, and winter once again
With icy talons gripp'd the frigid plain.
December brought its store of Christmas cheer,
And grateful peasants hail'd the op'ning year;
But by the hearth as Candlemas drew nigh,
The whisp'ring ancients spoke of things gone by.
Few had forgot the dark demoniac lore
Of things that came the Candlemas before,
And many a crone intently ey'd the house
Where dwelt the sadden'd bailiff and his spouse.

At last the day arriv'd, the sky o'erspread
With dark'ning messengers and clouds of lead;
Each neighb'ring grove Æolian warnings sigh'd,
And thick'ning terrors broadcast seem'd to bide.
The good folk, though they knew not why, would run
Swift past the bailiff's door, the scene to shun;
Within the house the grieving couple wept,
And mourn'd the child who now for ever slept.
On rush'd the dusk in doubly hideous form,
Borne on the pinions of the gath'ring storm;
Unusual murmurs fill'd the rainless wind,
And hast'ning travellers fear'd to glance behind.
Mad o'er the hills the demon tempest tore;
The rising river lash'd the troubled shore;
Black through the night the awful storm-god prowl'd,
And froze the list'ners' life-blood as he howled;
Gigantic trees like supple rushes sway'd,
Whilst for his home the trembling cotter pray'd.
Now falls a sudden lull amidst the gale;
With less'ning force the circling currents wail;
Far down the stream that laves the neighb'ring mead
Burst a new ululation, wildly key'd;
The peasant train a frantic mien assume,
And huddle closer in the spectral gloom:
To each strain'd ear the truth too well is known,
For that dread sound can come from wolves alone!
The rustics close attend, when ere they think,
A lupine army swarms the river's brink;
From out the waters leap a howling train
That rend the air, and scatter o'er the plain:
With flaming orbs the frothing creatures fly,
And chant with hellish voice their hungry cry.
First of the pack a mighty monster leaps
With fearless tread, and martial order keeps;
Th' attendant wolves his yelping tones obey,
And form in columns for the coming fray:
No frighten'd swain they harm, but silent bound
With a fix'd purpose o'er the frozen ground.
Straight course the monsters through the village street,

66

Unholy vigour in their flying feet;
Through half-shut blinds the shelter'd peasants peer,
And wax in wonder as they lose in fear.
Th' excited pack at last their goal perceive,
And the vex'd air with deaf'ning clamour cleave;
The churls, astonish'd, watch th' unnatural herd
Flock round a cottage at the leader's word:
Quick spreads the fearsome fact, by rumour blown,
That the doom'd cottage is the bailiff's own!
Round and around the howling daemons glide,
Whilst the fierce leader scales the vine-clad side;
The frantic wind its horrid wail renews,
And mutters madly through the lifeless yews.
In the frail house the bailiff calmly waits
The rav'ning horde, and trusts th' impartial Fates,
But the wan wife revives with curious mien
Another monster and an older scene;
Amidst th' increasing wind that rocks the walls,
The dame to him the serpent's deed recalls:
Then as a nameless thought fills both their minds,
The bare-fang'd leader crashes through the blinds.
Across the room, with murd'rous fury rife,
Leaps the mad wolf, and seizes on the wife;
With strange intent he drags his shrieking prey
Close to the spot where once the coffin lay.
Wilder and wilder roars the mounting gale
That sweeps the hills and hurtles through the vale;
The ill-made cottage shakes, the pack without
Dance with new fury in demoniac rout.
Quick as his thought, the valiant bailiff stands
Above the wolf, a weapon in his hands;
The ready ax that served a year before,
Now serves as well to slay one monster more.
The creature drops inert, with shatter'd head,
Full on the floor, and silent as the dead;
The rescu'd wife recalls the dire alarms,
And faints from terror in her husband's arms.
But as he holds her, all the cottage quakes,
And with full force the titan tempest breaks:

Down crash the walls, and o'er their shrinking forms
Burst the mad revels of the storm of storms.
Th' encircling wolves advance with ghastly pace,
Hunger and murder in each gleaming face,
But as they close, from out the hideous night
Flashes a bolt of unexpected light:
The vivid scene to ev'ry eye appears,
And peasants shiver with returning fears.
Above the wreck the scatheless chimney stays,
Its outline glimm'ring in the fitful rays,
Whilst o'er the hearth still hangs the household shrine,
The Saviour's image and the Cross divine!
Round the blest spot a lambent radiance glows,
And shields the cotters from their stealthy foes:
Each monstrous creature marks the wondrous glare,
Drops, fades, and vanishes in empty air!
The village train with startled eyes adore,
And count their beads in rev'rence o'er and o'er.
Now fades the light, and dies the raging blast,
The hour of dread and reign of horror past.
Pallid and bruis'd, from out his toppled walls
The panting bailiff with his good wife crawls:
Kind hands attend them, whilst o'er all the town
A strange sweet peace of spirit settles down.
Wonder and fear are still'd in soothing sleep,
As through the breaking clouds the moon rays peep.

Here paus'd the prattling grandam in her speech,
Confus'd with age, the tale half out of reach;
The list'ning guest, impatient for a clue,
Fears 'tis not one tale, but a blend of two;
He fain would know how far'd the widow'd lord
Whose eerie ways th' initial theme afford,
And marvels that the crone so quick should slight
His fate, to babble of the wolf-rack'd night.
The old wife, press'd, for greater clearness strives,
Nods wisely, and her scatter'd wits revives;

Yet strangely lingers on her latter tale

Of wolf and bailiff, miracle and gale.
When (quoth the crone) the dawn's bright radiance bath'd
Th' eventful scene, so late in terror swath'd,
The chatt'ring churls that sought the ruin'd cot
Found a new marvel in the gruesome spot.
From fallen walls a trail of gory red,
As of the stricken wolf, erratic led;
O'er road and mead the new-dript crimson wound,
Till lost amidst the neighb'ring swampy ground:
With wonder unappeas'd the peasants burn'd,
For what the quicksand takes is ne'er return'd.

Once more the grandam, with a knowing eye,
Stops in her tale, to watch a hawk soar by;
The weary list'ner, baffled, seeks anew
For some plain statement, or enlight'ning clue.
Th' indulgent crone attends the puzzled plea,
Yet strangely mutters o'er the mystery.
The Sieur? Ah, yes ... that morning all in vain
His shaking servants scour'd the frozen plain;
No man had seen him since he rode away
In silence on the dark preceding day.
His horse, wild-eyed with some unusual fright,
Came wand'ring from the river bank that night.
His hunting-hound, that mourn'd with piteous woe,
Howl'd by the quicksand swamp, his grief to show.
The village folk thought much, but utter'd less;
The servants' search wore out in emptiness:
For Sieur De Blois (the old wife's tale is o'er)
Was lost to mortal sight forevermore.

THE WHITE SHIP

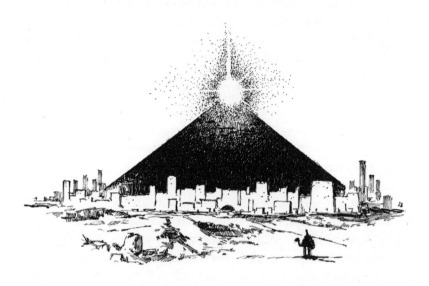

I AM BASIL ELTON, keeper of the North Point light that my father and grandfather kept before me. Far from the shore stands the grey lighthouse, above sunken slimy rocks that are seen when the tide is low, but unseen when the tide is high. Past that beacon for a century have swept the majestic barques of the seven seas. In the days of my grandfather there were many; in the days of my father not so many; and now there are so few that I sometimes feel strangely alone, as though I were the last man on our planet.

From far shores came those white-sailed argosies of old; from far Eastern shores where warm suns shine and sweet odours linger about strange gardens and gay temples. The old captains of the sea came often to my grandfather and told him of these things, which in turn he told to my father, and my father told to me in the long autumn evenings when the wind howled eerily from the East. And I have read more of these things, and of many things besides, in the books men gave me when I was young and filled with wonder.

But more wonderful than the lore of old men and the lore of books is the secret lore of ocean. Blue, green, grey, white, or black;

smooth, ruffled, or mountainous; that ocean is not silent. All my days have I watched it and listened to it, and I know it well. At first it told to me only the plain little tales of calm beaches and near ports, but with the years it grew more friendly and spoke of other things; of things more strange and more distant in space and in time. Sometimes at twilight the grey vapours of the horizon have parted to grant me glimpses of the ways beyond; and sometimes at night the deep waters of the sea have grown clear and phosphorescent, to grant me glimpses of the ways beneath. And these glimpses have been as often of the ways that were and the ways that might be, as of the ways that are; for ocean is more ancient than the mountains, and freighted with the memories and the dreams of Time.

Out of the South it was that the White Ship used to come when the moon was full and high in the heavens. Out of the South it would glide very smoothly and silently over the sea. And whether the sea was rough or calm, and whether the wind was friendly or adverse, it would always glide smoothly and silently, its sails distant and its long strange tiers of oars moving rhythmically. One night I espied upon the deck a man, bearded and robed, and he seemed to beckon me to embark for fair unknown shores. Many times afterward I saw him under the full moon, and ever did he beckon me.

Very brightly did the moon shine on the night I answered the call, and I walked out over the waters to the White Ship on a bridge of moonbeams. The man who had beckoned now spoke a welcome to me in a soft language I seemed to know well, and the hours were filled with soft songs of the oarsmen as we glided away into a mysterious South, golden with the glow of that full, mellow moon.

And when the day dawned, rosy and effulgent, I beheld the green shore of far lands, bright and beautiful, and to me unknown. Up from the sea rose lordly terraces of verdure, tree-studded, and shewing here and there the gleaming white roofs and colonnades of strange temples. As we drew nearer the green shore the bearded man told me of that land, the Land of Zar, where dwell all the dreams and thoughts of beauty that come to men once and then are forgotten. And when I looked upon the terraces again I saw that what he said was true, for among the sights before me were many things I had once seen through the mists beyond the horizon and in the phosphorescent depths of ocean. There too were forms and fantasies more splendid than any I had ever known; the visions of young poets who died in want before the world could learn of what they had seen and dreamed. But we did not set foot upon the sloping meadows of Zar, for it is told that he who treads them may nevermore return to his native shore.

As the White Ship sailed silently away from the templed terraces of Zar, we beheld on the distant horizon ahead the spires of a mighty city; and the bearded man said to me: 'This is Thalarion, the City of a Thousand Wonders, wherein reside all those mysteries that man has striven in vain to fathom.' And I looked again, at closer range, and saw that the city was greater than any city I had known or dreamed of before. Into the sky the spires of its temples reached, so that no man might behold their peaks; and far back beyond the horizon stretched the grim, grey walls, over which one might spy only a few roofs, weird and ominous, yet adorned with rich friezes and alluring sculptures. I yearned mightily to enter this fascinating yet repellent city, and besought the bearded man to land me at the stone pier by the huge carven gate Akariel; but he gently denied my wish, saying: 'Into Thalarion, the City of a Thousand Wonders, many have passed but none returned. Therein walk only daemons and mad things that are no longer men, and the streets are white with the unburied bones of those who have looked upon the eidolon Lathi, that reigns over the city.' So the White Ship sailed on past the walls of Thalarion, and followed for many days a southward-flying bird, whose glossy plumage matched the sky out of which it had appeared.

Then came we to a pleasant coast gay with blossoms of every hue, where as far inland as we could see basked lovely groves and radiant arbours beneath a meridian sun. From bowers beyond our view came bursts of song and snatches of lyric harmony, interspersed with faint laughter so delicious that I urged the rowers onward in my eagerness to reach the scene. And the bearded man spoke no word, but watched me as we approached the lily-lined shore. Suddenly a wind blowing from over the flowery meadows and leafy woods brought a scent at which I trembled. The wind grew stronger, and the air was filled with the lethal, charnel odour of plague-stricken towns and uncovered cemeteries. And as we sailed madly away from that damnable coast the bearded man spoke at last, saying: 'This is Xura, the Land of Pleasures Unattained.'

So once more the White Ship followed the bird of heaven, over warm blessed seas fanned by caressing, aromatic breezes. Day after day and night after night did we sail, and when the moon was full we would listen to soft songs of the oarsmen, sweet as on that distant night when we sailed away from my far native land. And it was by moonlight that we anchored at last in the harbour of Sona-Nyl, which is guarded by twin headlands of crystal that rise from the sea and meet in a resplendent arch. This is the Land of Fancy, and we walked to the verdant shore upon a golden bridge of moonbeams.

In the Land of Sona-Nyl there is neither time nor space, neither suffering nor death; and there I dwelt for many aeons. Green are the groves and pastures, bright and fragrant the flowers, blue and musical the streams, clear and cool the fountains, and stately and gorgeous the temples, castles, and cities of Sona-Nyl. Of that land there is no bound, for beyond each vista of beauty rises another more beautiful. Over the countryside and amidst the splendour of cities rove at will the happy folk, of whom all are gifted with unmarred grace and unalloyed happiness. For the aeons that I dwelt there I wandered blissfully through gardens where quaint pagodas peep from pleasing clumps of bushes, and where the white walks are bordered with delicate blossoms. I climbed gentle hills from whose summits I could see entrancing panoramas of loveliness, with steepled towns nestling in verdant valleys, and with the golden domes of gigantic cities glittering on the infinitely distant horizon. And I viewed by moonlight the sparkling sea, the crystal headlands, and the placid harbour wherein lay anchored the White Ship.

It was against the full moon one night in the immemorial year of Tharp that I saw outlined the beckoning form of the celestial bird, and felt the first stirrings of unrest. Then I spoke with the bearded man, and told him of my new yearnings to depart for remote Cathuria, which no man hath seen, but which all believe to lie beyond the basalt pillars of the West. It is the Land of Hope, and in it shine the perfect ideals of all that we know elsewhere; or at least so men relate. But the bearded man said to me: 'Beware of those perilous seas wherein men say Cathuria lies. In Sona-Nyl there is no pain nor death, but who can tell what lies beyond the basalt pillars of the West?' Natheless at the next full moon I boarded the

White Ship, and with the reluctant bearded man left the happy harbour for untravelled seas.

And the bird of heaven flew before, and led us toward the basalt pillars of the West, but this time the oarsmen sang no soft songs under the full moon. In my mind I would often picture the unknown Land of Cathuria with its splendid groves and palaces, and would wonder what new delights there awaited me. 'Cathuria,' I would say to myself, 'is the abode of gods and the land of unnumbered cities of gold. Its forests are of aloe and sandalwood, even as the fragrant groves of Camorin, and among the trees flutter gay birds sweet with song. On the green and flowery mountains of Cathuria stand temples of pink marble, rich with carven and painted glories, and having in their courtyards cool fountains of silver, where purl with ravishing music the scented waters that come from the grotto-born river Narg. And the cities of Cathuria are cinctured with golden walls, and their pavements also are of gold. In the gardens of these cities are strange orchids, and perfumed lakes whose beds are of coral and amber. At night the streets and the gardens are lit with gay lanthorns fashioned from the three-coloured shell of the tortoise, and here resound the soft notes of the singer and the lutanist. And the houses of the cities of Cathuria are all palaces, each built over a fragrant canal bearing the waters of the sacred Narg. Of marble and porphyry are the houses, and roofed with glittering gold that reflects the rays of the sun and enhances the splendour of the cities as blissful gods view them from the distant peaks. Fairest of all is the palace of the great monarch Dorieb, whom some say to be a demigod and others a god. High is the palace of Dorieb, and many are the turrets of marble upon its walls. In its wide halls many multitudes assemble, and here hang the trophies of the ages. And the roof is of pure gold, set upon tall pillars of ruby and azure, and having such carven figures of gods and heroes that he who looks up to those heights seems to gaze upon the living Olympus. And the floor of the palace is of glass, under which flow the cunningly lighted waters of the Narg, gay with gaudy fish not known beyond the bounds of lovely Cathuria.'

Thus would I speak to myself of Cathuria, but ever would the bearded man warn me to turn back to the happy shores of Sona-Nyl; for Sona-Nyl is known of men, while none hath ever beheld Cathuria.

And on the thirty-first day that we followed the bird, we beheld the basalt pillars of the West. Shrouded in mist they were, so that no man might peer beyond them or see their summits – which indeed some say reach even to the heavens. And the bearded man again implored me to turn back, but I heeded him not; for from the mists beyond the basalt pillars I fancied there came the notes of singer and lutanist; sweeter than the sweetest songs of Sona-Nyl, and sounding mine own praises; the praises of me, who had voyaged far under the full moon and dwelt in the Land of Fancy.

So to the sound of melody the White Ship sailed into the mist betwixt the basalt pillars of the West. And when the music ceased and the mist lifted, we beheld not the Land of Cathuria, but a swift-rushing resistless sea, over which our helpless barque was borne toward some unknown goal. Soon to our ears came the distant thunder of falling waters, and to our eyes appeared on the far horizon ahead the titanic spray of a monstrous cataract, wherein the oceans of the world drop down to abysmal noth-ingness. Then did the bearded man say to me with tears on his cheek: 'We have rejected the beautiful Land of Sona-Nyl, which we may never behold again. The gods are greater than men, and they have conquered.' And I closed my eyes before the crash that I knew would come, shutting out the sight of the celestial bird which flapped its mocking blue wings over the brink of the torrent.

Out of that crash came darkness, and I heard the shrieking of men and of things which were not men. From the East tempestuous winds arose, and chilled me as I crouched on the slab of damp stone which had risen beneath my feet. Then as I heard another crash I opened my eyes and beheld myself upon the platform of that lighthouse from whence I had sailed so many aeons ago. In the darkness below there loomed the vast blurred outlines of a vessel breaking up on the cruel rocks, and as I glanced out over the waste I saw that the light had failed for the first time since my grandfather had assumed its care.

And in the later watches of the night, when I went within the tower, I saw on the wall a calendar which still remained as when I had left it at the hour I sailed away. With the dawn I descended the tower and looked for wreckage upon the rocks, but what I found was only this: a strange dead bird whose hue was as of the azure

sky, and a single shattered spar, of a whiteness greater than that of
the wave-tips or of the mountain snow.

And thereafter the ocean told me its secrets no more; and though
many times since has the moon shone full and high in the heavens,
the White Ship from the South came never again.

THE HOUSE

'TIS A GROVE-CIRCLED dwelling
   Set close to a hill,
Where the branches are telling
Strange legends of ill;
Over timbers so old
That they breathe of the dead,
Crawl the vines, green and cold,
By strange nourishment fed;
And no man knows the juices they suck
   from the depths of their dank slimy bed.

In the gardens are growing
Tall blossoms and fair,
Each pallid bloom throwing
Perfume on the air;
But the afternoon sun
With its shining red rays
Makes the picture loom dun

On the curious gaze,
And above the sweet scent of the blossoms
   rise odours of numberless days.

The rank grasses are waving
On terrace and lawn,
Dim memories sav'ring
Of things that have gone;
The stones of the walks
Are encrusted and wet,
And a strange spirit stalks
When the red sun has set,
And the soul of the watcher is fill'd
   with faint pictures he fain would forget.

It was in the hot June-time
I stood by that scene,
When the gold rays of noon-time
Beat bright on the green.
But I shiver'd with cold,
Groping feebly for light,
As a picture unroll'd—
And my age-spanning sight
Saw the time I had been there before
   flash like fulgury out of the night.

THE NIGHTMARE LAKE

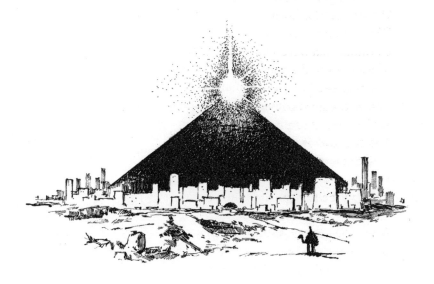

THERE IS A LAKE in distant Zan,
   Beyond the wonted haunts of man,
Where broods alone in a hideous state
A spirit dead and desolate;
A spirit ancient and unholy,
Heavy with fearsome melancholy,
Which from the waters dull and dense
Draws vapours cursed with pestilence.
Around the banks, a mire of clay,
Sprawl things offensive in decay,
And curious birds that reach that shore
Are seen by mortals nevermore.
Here shines by day the searing sun
On glassy wastes beheld by none,
And here by night pale moonbeams flow
Into the deeps that yawn below.
In nightmares only is it told
What scenes beneath those beams unfold;

What scenes, too old for human sight,
Lie sunken there in endless night;
For in those depths there only pace
The shadows of a voiceless race.
One midnight, redolent of ill,
I saw that lake, asleep and still;
While in the lurid sky there rode
A gibbous moon that glow'd and glow'd.
I saw the stretching marshy shore,
And the foul things those marshes bore:
Lizards and snakes convuls'd and dying;
Ravens and vampires putrefying;
All these, and hov'ring o'er the dead,
Narcophagi that on them fed.
And as the dreadful moon climb'd high,
Fright'ning the stars from out the sky,
I saw the lake's dull water glow
Till sunken things appear'd below.
There shone unnumber'd fathoms down,
The tow'rs of a forgotten town;
The tarnish'd domes and mossy walls;
Weed-tangled spires and empty halls;
Deserted fanes and vaults of dread,
And streets of gold uncoveted.
These I beheld, and saw beside
A horde of shapeless shadows glide;
A noxious horde which to my glance
Seem'd moving in a hideous dance
Round slimy sepulchres that lay
Beside a never-travell'd way.
Straight from those tombs a heaving rose
That vex'd the waters' dull repose,
While lethal shades of upper space
Howl'd at the moon's sardonic face.
Then sank the lake within its bed,
Suck'd down to caverns of the dead,
Till from the reeking, new-stript earth
Curl'd foetid fumes of noisome birth.
About the city, nigh uncover'd,

The monstrous dancing shadows hover'd,
When lo! there oped with sudden stir
The portal of each sepulchre!
No ear may learn, no tongue may tell
What nameless horror then befell.
I see that lake – that moon agrin–
That city and the *things* within–
Waking, I pray that on that shore
The nightmare lake may sink *no more*!

POETRY AND THE GODS

(with Anna Helen Crofts)

A DAMP, GLOOMY EVENING in April it was, just after the close of the Great War, when Marcia found herself alone with strange thoughts and wishes; unheard-of yearnings which floated out of the spacious twentieth-century drawing-room, up the misty deeps of the air, and eastward to far olive-groves in Arcady which she had seen only in her dreams. She had entered the room in abstraction, turned off the glaring chandeliers, and now reclined on a soft divan by a solitary lamp which shed over the reading table a green glow as soothing and delicious as moonlight through the foliage about an antique shrine.

Attired simply, in a low-cut evening dress of black, she appeared outwardly a typical product of modern civilisation; but tonight she felt the immeasurable gulf that separated her soul from all her prosaic surroundings. Was it because of the strange home in which she lived; that abode of coldness where relations were always strained and the inmates scarcely more than strangers? Was it that, or was it some greater and less explicable misplacement in Time and Space, whereby she had been born too late, too early, or too far away from the haunts of her spirit ever to harmonise with the unbeautiful things of contemporary reality? To dispel the mood which was engulfing her more deeply each moment, she took a magazine from the table and searched for some healing bit of poetry. Poetry had always relieved her troubled mind better than anything else, though many things in the poetry she had seen detracted from the influence. Over parts of even the sublimest verses hung a chill vapour of sterile ugliness and restraint, like dust on a window-pane through which one views a magnificent sunset.

Listlessly turning the magazine's pages, as if searching for an elusive treasure, she suddenly came upon something which dispelled her languor. An observer could have read her thoughts and told that she had discovered some image or dream which brought her nearer to her unattained goal than any image or dream she had seen before. It was only a bit of *vers libre*, that pitiful compromise of the poet who overleaps prose yet falls short of the divine melody of numbers; but it had in it all the unstudied music of a bard who lives and feels, and who gropes ecstatically for unveiled beauty. Devoid of regularity, it yet had the wild harmony of winged, spontaneous words; a harmony missing from the formal, convention-bound verse she had known. As she read on, her surroundings gradually faded, and soon there lay about her only the mists of dream; the purple, star-strewn mists beyond Time, where only gods and dreamers walk.

> *Moon over Japan,*
> *White butterfly moon!*
> *Where the heavy-lidded Buddhas dream*
> *To the sound of the cuckoo's call ...*
> *The white wings of moon-butterflies*
> *Flicker down the streets of the city,*
> *Blushing into silence the useless wicks of round*
> *   lanterns in the hands of girls.*

> *Moon over the tropics,*
> *A white-curved bud*
> *Opening its petals slowly in the warmth of heaven ...*
> *The air is full of odours*
> *And languorous warm sounds ...*

A flute drones its insect music to the night
Below the curving moon-petal of the heavens.

Moon over China,
Weary moon on the river of the sky,
The stir of light in the willows is like the flashing of
   a thousand silver minnows
Through dark shoals;
The tiles on graves and rotting temples flash like
   ripples,
The sky is flecked with clouds like the scales of a
   dragon.

Amid the mists of dream the reader cried to the rhythmical stars, of her delight at the coming of a new age of song, a rebirth of Pan. Half closing her eyes, she repeated words whose melody lay hid like crystals at the bottom of a stream before the dawn; hidden but to gleam effulgently at the birth of day.

Moon over Japan,
White butterfly moon!

Moon over the tropics,
A white-curved bud
Opening its petals slowly in the warmth of heaven.
The air is full of odours
And languorous warm sounds ... languorous
   warm sounds.

Moon over China,
Weary moon on the river of the sky ... weary moon!

Out of the mists gleamed godlike the form of a youth in winged helmet and sandals, caduceus-bearing, and of a beauty like to nothing on earth. Before the face of the sleeper he thrice waved the rod which Apollo had given him in trade for the nine-corded shell of melody, and upon her brow he placed a wreath of myrtle and roses. Then, adoring, Hermes spoke:

'O Nymph more fair than the golden-haired sisters of Cyane or the sky-inhabiting Atlantides, beloved of Aphrodite and blessed of Pallas, thou hast indeed discovered the secret of the Gods, which lieth in beauty and song. O Prophetess more lovely than the Sybil of Cumae when Apollo first knew her, thou hast truly spoken of the new age, for even now on Maenalus, Pan sighs and stretches in his sleep, wishful to awake and behold about him the little rose-crowned Fauns and the antique Satyrs. In thy yearning hast thou divined what no mortal else, saving only a few whom the world rejects, remembereth; *that the Gods were never dead*, but only sleeping the sleep and dreaming the dreams of Gods in lotos-filled Hesperian gardens beyond the golden sunset. And now draweth nigh the time of their awaking, when coldness and ugliness shall perish, and Zeus sit once more on Olympus. Already the sea about Paphos trembleth into a foam which only ancient skies have looked on before, and at night on Helicon the shepherds hear strange murmurings and half-remembered notes. Woods and fields are tremulous at twilight with the shimmering of white saltant forms, and immemorial Ocean yields up curious sights beneath thin moons. The Gods are patient, and have slept long, but neither man nor giant shall defy the Gods forever. In Tartarus the Titans writhe, and beneath the fiery Aetna groan the children of Uranus and Gaea. The day now dawns when man must answer for centuries of denial, but in sleeping the Gods have grown kind, and will not hurl him to the gulf made for deniers of Gods. Instead will their vengeance smite the darkness, fallacy, and ugliness which have turned the mind of man; and under the sway of bearded Saturnus shall mortals, once more sacrificing unto him, dwell in beauty and delight. This night shalt thou know the favour of the Gods, and behold on Parnassus those dreams which the Gods have through ages sent to earth to shew that they are not dead. For poets are the dreams of the Gods, and in each age someone hath sung unknowing the message and the promise from the lotos-gardens beyond the sunset.'

Then in his arms Hermes bore the dreaming maiden through the skies. Gentle breezes from the tower of Aiolos wafted them high above warm, scented seas, till suddenly they came upon Zeus holding court on the double-headed Parnassus; his golden throne flanked by Apollo and the Muses on the right hand, and by ivy-wreathed Dionysus and pleasure-flushed Bacchae on the left hand. So much of splendour Marcia had never seen before, either awake or in dreams, but its radiance did her no injury, as would have the radiance of lofty Olympus; for in this lesser court the Father of Gods had tempered his glories for the sight of mortals. Before the laurel-draped mouth of the Corycian cave sat in a row six noble forms with the aspect of mortals, but the countenances of Gods. These the dreamer recognised from images of them which she had beheld, and she knew that they were none else than the divine Maeonides, the Avernian Dante, the more than mortal Shakespeare, the chaos-exploring Milton, the cosmic Goethe, and the Musaean Keats. These were those messengers whom the Gods had sent to tell men that Pan had passed not away, but only slept; for it is in poetry that Gods speak to men. Then spake the Thunderer:

'O Daughter – for, being one of my endless line, thou art indeed my daughter – behold upon ivory thrones of honour the august messengers that Gods have sent down, that in the words and writings of men there may be still some trace of divine beauty. Other bards have men justly crowned with enduring laurels, but these hath Apollo crowned, and these have I set in places apart, as mortals who have spoken the language of the Gods. Long have we dreamed in lotos-gardens beyond the West, and spoken only through our dreams; but the time approaches when our voices shall not be silent. It is a time of awaking and of change. Once more hath Phaeton ridden low, searing the fields and drying the streams. In Gaul lone nymphs with disordered hair weep beside fountains that are no more, and pine over rivers turned red with the blood of mortals. Ares and his train have gone forth with the madness of Gods, and have returned, Deimos and Phobos glutted with unnatural delight. Tellus moans with grief, and the faces of men are as the faces of the Erinyes, even as when Astraea fled to the skies, and the waves of our bidding encompassed all the land saving this high peak alone. Amidst this chaos, prepared to herald his coming yet to conceal his arrival, even now toileth our latest-born messenger, in whose dreams are all the images which other messengers have dreamed before him. He it is that we have chosen to blend into one glorious whole all the beauty that the world hath known before, and to write words wherein shall echo all the wisdom and the loveliness of the past. He it is who shall proclaim our return, and sing of the days to come when Fauns and Dryads shall haunt their accustomed groves in beauty. Guided was our choice by those who now sit before the

Corycian grotto on thrones of ivory, and in whose songs thou shalt hear notes of sublimity by which years hence thou shalt know the greater messenger when he cometh. Attend their voices as one by one they sing to thee here. Each note shalt thou hear again in the poetry which is to come; the poetry which shall bring peace and pleasure to thy soul, though search for it through bleak years thou must. Attend with diligence, for each chord that vibrates away into hiding shall appear again to thee after thou hast returned to earth, as Alpheus, sinking his waters into the soul of Hellas, appears as the crystal Arethusa in remote Sicilia.'

Then arose Homeros, the ancient among bards, who took his lyre and chaunted his hymn to Aphrodite. No word of Greek did Marcia know, yet did the message not fall vainly upon her ears; for in the cryptic rhythm was that which spake to all mortals and Gods, and needed no interpreter.

So too the songs of Dante and Goethe, whose unknown words clave the ether with melodies easy to read and to adore. But at last remembered accents resounded before the listener. It was the Swan of Avon, once a God among men, and still a God among Gods:

> Write, write, that from the bloody course of war,
> My dearest master, your dear son, may hie;
> Bless him at home in peace, whilst I from far,
> His name with zealous fervour sanctify.

Accents still more familiar arose as Milton, blind no more, declaimed immortal harmony:

> Or let thy lamp at midnight hour
> Be seen in some high lonely tower,
> Where I might oft outwatch the Bear
> With thrice-great Hermes, or unsphere
> The spirit of Plato, to unfold
> What worlds or what vast regions hold
> Th' immortal mind, that hath forsook
> Her mansion in this fleshly nook.
>
> Sometime let gorgeous Tragedy
> In sceptred pall come sweeping by,

Presenting Thebes, or Pelops' line,
Or the tale of Troy divine.

Last of all came the young voice of Keats, closest of all the messengers to the beauteous faun-folk:

Heard melodies are sweet, but those unheard
Are sweeter; therefore, ye soft pipes, play on …

When old age shall this generation waste,
Thou shalt remain, in midst of other woe
Than ours, a friend to man, to whom thou say'st,
'Beauty is truth – truth beauty' – that is all
Ye know on earth, and all ye need to know.

As the singer ceased, there came a sound in the wind blowing from far Egypt, where at night Aurora mourns by the Nile for her slain son Memnon. To the feet of the Thunderer flew the rosy-fingered Goddess, and kneeling, cried, 'Master, it is time I unlocked the gates of the East.' And Phoebus, handing his lyre to Calliope, his bride among the Muses, prepared to depart for the jewelled and column-raised Palace of the Sun, where fretted the steeds already harnessed to the golden car of day. So Zeus descended from his carven throne and placed his hand upon the head of Marcia, saying:
'Daughter, the dawn is nigh, and it is well that thou shouldst return before the awaking of mortals to thy home. Weep not at the bleakness of thy life, for the shadow of false faiths will soon be gone, and the Gods shall once more walk among men. Search thou unceasingly for our messenger, for in him wilt thou find peace and comfort. By his word shall thy steps be guided to happiness, and in his dreams of beauty shall thy spirit find all that it craveth.' As Zeus ceased, the young Hermes gently seized the maiden and bore her up toward the fading stars; up, and westward over unseen seas.

Many years have passed since Marcia dreamt of the Gods and of their Parnassian conclave. Tonight she sits in the same spacious drawing-room, but she is not alone. Gone is the old spirit of unrest, for beside her is one whose name is luminous with celebrity; the young poet of poets at whose feet sits all the world. He is reading from a manuscript words which none has ever heard before, but which when heard will bring to men the dreams and fancies they lost so many centuries ago, when Pan lay down to doze in Arcady, and the greater Gods withdrew to sleep in lotos-gardens beyond the lands of the Hesperides. In the subtle cadences and hidden melodies of the bard the spirit of the maiden has found rest at last, for there echo the divinest notes of Thracian Orpheus; notes that moved the very rocks and trees by Hebrus' banks. The singer ceases, and with eagerness asks a verdict, yet what can Marcia say but that the strain is 'fit for the Gods'?

And as she speaks there comes again a vision of Parnassus and the far-off sound of a mighty voice saying, 'By his word shall thy steps be guided to happiness, and in his dreams of beauty shall thy spirit find all that it craveth.'

NYARLATHOTEP

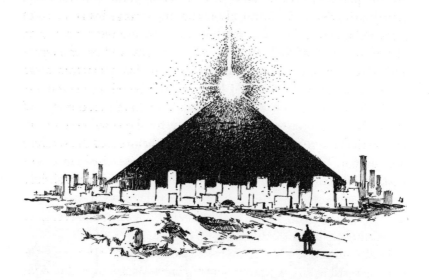

NYARLATHOTEP ... the crawling chaos ... I am the last ...
I will tell the audient void ...

I do not recall distinctly when it began, but it was months ago.
The general tension was horrible. To a season of political and
social upheaval was added a strange and brooding apprehension of
hideous physical danger; a danger widespread and all-embracing,
such a danger as may be imagined only in the most terrible phantasms of the night. I recall that the people went about with pale
and worried faces, and whispered warnings and prophecies which
no one dared consciously repeat or acknowledge to himself that he
had heard. A sense of monstrous guilt was upon the land, and out
of the abysses between the stars swept chill currents that made men
shiver in dark and lonely places. There was a demoniac alteration
in the sequence of the seasons, the autumn heat lingered fearsomely,
and everyone felt that the world and perhaps the universe had
passed from the control of known gods or forces to that of gods or
forces which were unknown.

And it was then that Nyarlathotep came out of Egypt. Who he

was, none could tell, but he was of the old native blood and looked
like a Pharaoh. The fellahin knelt when they saw him, yet could
not say why. He said he had risen up out of the blackness of twenty-
seven centuries, and that he had heard messages from places not
on this planet. Into the lands of civilisation came Nyarlathotep,
swarthy, slender, and sinister, always buying strange instruments of
glass and metal and combining them into instruments yet stranger.
He spoke much of the sciences – of electricity and psychology –
and gave exhibitions of power which sent his spectators away
speechless, yet which swelled his fame to exceeding magnitude.
Men advised one another to see Nyarlathotep, and shuddered. And
where Nyarlathotep went, rest vanished, for the small hours were
rent with the screams of nightmare. Never before had the screams
of nightmare been such a public problem; now the wise men almost
wished they could forbid sleep in the small hours, that the shrieks
of cities might less horribly disturb the pale, pitying moon as it
glimmered on green waters gliding under bridges, and old steeples
crumbling against a sickly sky.

I remember when Nyarlathotep came to my city – the great, the
old, the terrible city of unnumbered crimes. My friend had told me
of him, and of the impelling fascination and allurement of his
revelations, and I burned with eagerness to explore his uttermost
mysteries. My friend said they were horrible and impressive beyond
my most fevered imaginings; and what was thrown on a screen in
the darkened room prophesied things none but Nyarlathotep dared
prophesy, and in the sputter of his sparks there was taken from men
that which had never been taken before yet which showed only
in the eyes. And I heard it hinted abroad that those who knew
Nyarlathotep looked on sights which others saw not.

It was in the hot autumn that I went through the night with the
restless crowds to see Nyarlathotep; through the stifling night and
up the endless stairs into the choking room. And shadowed on a
screen, I saw hooded forms amidst ruins, and yellow evil faces
peering from behind fallen monuments. And I saw the world
battling against blackness; against the waves of destruction from
ultimate space; whirling, churning, struggling around the dimming,
cooling sun. Then the sparks played amazingly around the heads
of the spectators, and hair stood up on end whilst shadows more
grotesque than I can tell came out and squatted on the heads. And

when I, who was colder and more scientific than the rest, mumbled a trembling protest about 'imposture' and 'static electricity', Nyar-lathotep drove us all out, down the dizzy stairs into the damp, hot, deserted midnight streets. I screamed aloud that I was *not* afraid; that I never could be afraid; and others screamed with me for solace. We swore to one another that the city *was* exactly the same, and still alive; and when the electric lights began to fade we cursed the company over and over again, and laughed at the queer faces we made.

I believe we felt something coming down from the greenish moon, for when we began to depend on its light we drifted into curious involuntary marching formations and seemed to know our destinations though we dared not think of them. Once we looked at the pavement and found the blocks loose and displaced by grass, with scarce a line of rusted metal to show where the tramways had run. And again we saw a tram-car, lone, windowless, dilapidated, and almost on its side. When we gazed around the horizon, we could not find the third tower by the river, and noticed that the silhouette of the second tower was ragged at the top. Then we split up into narrow columns, each of which seemed drawn in a different direction. One disappeared in a narrow alley to the left, leaving only the echo of a shocking moan. Another filed down a weed-choked subway entrance, howling with a laughter that was mad. My own column was sucked toward the open country, and presently I felt a chill which was not of the hot autumn; for as we stalked out on the dark moor, we beheld around us the hellish moon-glitter of evil snows. Trackless, inexplicable snows, swept asunder in one direction only, where lay a gulf all the blacker for its glittering walls. The column seemed very thin indeed as it plodded dreamily into the gulf. I lingered behind, for the black rift in the green-litten snow was frightful, and I thought I had heard the reverberations of a disquieting wail as my companions vanished; but my power to linger was slight. As if beckoned by those who had gone before, I half-floated between the titanic snowdrifts, quivering and afraid, into the sightless vortex of the unimaginable.

Screamingly sentient, dumbly delirious, only the gods that were can tell. A sickened, sensitive shadow writhing in hands that are not hands, and whirled blindly past ghastly midnights of rotting creation, corpses of dead worlds with sores that were cities, charnel winds that brush the pallid stars and make them flicker low. Beyond the worlds vague ghosts of monstrous things; half-seen columns of unsanctified temples that rest on nameless rocks beneath space and reach up to dizzy vacua above the spheres of light and darkness. And through this revolting graveyard of the universe the muffled, maddening beating of drums, and thin, monotonous whine of blasphemous flutes from inconceivable, unlighted chambers beyond Time; the detestable pounding and piping whereunto dance slowly, awkwardly, and absurdly the gigantic, tenebrous ultimate gods – the blind, voiceless, mindless gargoyles whose soul is Nyarlathotep.

POLARIS

INTO THE NORTH WINDOW of my chamber glows the Pole
Star with uncanny light. All through the long hellish hours
of blackness it shines there. And in the autumn of the year,
when the winds from the north curse and whine, and the red-
leaved trees of the swamp mutter things to one another in the
small hours of the morning under the horned waning moon,
I sit by the casement and watch that star. Down from the
heights reels the glittering Cassiopeia as the hours wear on,
while Charles' Wain lumbers up from behind the vapour-soaked
swamp trees that sway in the night-wind. Just before dawn Arcturus
winks ruddily from above the cemetery on the low hillock, and
Coma Berenices shimmers weirdly afar off in the mysterious east;
but still the Pole Star leers down from the same place in the black
vault, winking hideously like an insane watching eye which strives
to convey some strange message, yet recalls nothing save that it
once had a message to convey. Sometimes, when it is cloudy, I can
sleep.

Well do I remember the night of the great Aurora, when over

the swamp played the shocking coruscations of the daemon-light. After the beams came clouds, and then I slept.

And it was under a horned waning moon that I saw the city for the first time. Still and somnolent did it lie, on a strange plateau in a hollow betwixt strange peaks. Of ghastly marble were its walls and its towers, its columns, domes, and pavements. In the marble streets were marble pillars, the upper parts of which were carven into the images of grave bearded men. The air was warm and stirred not. And overhead, scarce ten degrees from the zenith, glowed that watching Pole Star. Long did I gaze on the city, but the day came not. When the red Aldebaran, which blinked low in the sky but never set, had crawled a quarter of the way around the horizon, I saw light and motion in the houses and the streets. Forms strangely robed, but at once noble and familiar, walked abroad, and under the horned waning moon men talked wisdom in a tongue which I understood, though it was unlike any language I had ever known. And when the red Aldebaran had crawled more than half way around the horizon, there were again darkness and silence.

When I awaked, I was not as I had been. Upon my memory was graven the vision of the city, and within my soul had arisen another and vaguer recollection, of whose nature I was not then certain. Thereafter, on the cloudy nights when I could sleep, I saw the city often; sometimes under that horned waning moon, and sometimes under the hot yellow rays of a sun which did not set, but which wheeled low around the horizon. And on the clear nights the Pole Star leered as never before.

Gradually I came to wonder what might be my place in that city on the strange plateau betwixt strange peaks. At first content to view the scene as an all-observant uncorporeal presence, I now desired to define my relation to it, and to speak my mind amongst the grave men who conversed each day in the public squares. I said to myself, 'This is no dream, for by what means can I prove the greater reality of that other life in the house of stone and brick south of the sinister swamp and the cemetery on the low hillock, where the Pole Star peers into my north window each night?'

One night as I listened to the discourse in the large square containing many statues, I felt a change; and perceived that I had at last a bodily form. Nor was I a stranger in the streets of Olathoë, which lies on the plateau of Sarkis, betwixt the peaks Noton and

Kadiphonek. It was my friend Alos who spoke, and his speech was one that pleased my soul, for it was the speech of a true man and patriot. That night had the news come of Daikos' fall, and of the advance of the Inutos; squat, hellish, yellow fiends who five years ago had appeared out of the unknown west to ravage the confines of our kingdom, and finally to besiege our towns. Having taken the fortified places at the foot of the mountains, their way now lay open to the plateau, unless every citizen could resist with the strength of ten men. For the squat creatures were mighty in the arts of war, and knew not the scruples of honour which held back our tall, grey-eyed men of Lomar from ruthless conquest.

Alos, my friend, was commander of all the forces on the plateau, and in him lay the last hope of our country. On this occasion he spoke of the perils to be faced, and exhorted the men of Olathoë, bravest of the Lomarians, to sustain the traditions of their ancestors, who when forced to move southward from Zobna before the advance of the great ice-sheet (even as our descendants must some day flee from the land of Lomar), valiantly and victoriously swept aside the hairy, long-armed, cannibal Gnophkehs that stood in their way. To me Alos denied a warrior's part, for I was feeble and given to strange faintings when subjected to stress and hardships. But my eyes were the keenest in the city, despite the long hours I gave each day to the study of the Pnakotic manuscripts and the wisdom of the Zobnarian Fathers; so my friend, desiring not to doom me to inaction, rewarded me with that duty which was second to nothing in importance. To the watch-tower of Thapnen he sent me, there to serve as the eyes of our army. Should the Inutos attempt to gain the citadel by the narrow pass behind the peak Noton, and thereby surprise the garrison, I was to give the signal of fire which would warn the waiting soldiers and save the town from immediate disaster.

Alone I mounted the tower, for every man of stout body was needed in the passes below. My brain was sore dazed with excitement and fatigue, for I had not slept in many days; yet was my purpose firm, for I loved my native land of Lomar, and the marble city of Olathoë that lies betwixt the peaks of Noton and Kadiphonek.

But as I stood in the tower's topmost chamber, I beheld the horned waning moon, red and sinister, quivering through the vapours that hovered over the distant valley of Banof. And through an opening in the roof glittered the pale Pole Star, fluttering as if alive, and leering like a fiend and tempter. Methought its spirit whispered evil counsel, soothing me to traitorous somnolence with a damnable rhythmical promise which it repeated over and over:

> 'Slumber, watcher, till the spheres
> Six and twenty thousand years
> Have revolv'd, and I return
> To the spot where now I burn.
> Other stars anon shall rise
> To the axis of the skies;
> Stars that soothe and stars that bless
> With a sweet forgetfulness:
> Only when my round is o'er
> Shall the past disturb thy door.'

Vainly did I struggle with my drowsiness, seeking to connect these strange words with some lore of the skies which I had learnt from the Pnakotic manuscripts. My head, heavy and reeling, drooped to my breast, and when next I looked up it was in a dream; with the Pole Star grinning at me through a window from over the horrible swaying trees of a dream-swamp. And I am still dreaming.

In my shame and despair I sometimes scream frantically, begging the dream-creatures around me to waken me ere the Inutos steal up the pass behind the peak Noton and take the citadel by surprise; but these creatures are daemons, for they laugh at me and tell me I am not dreaming. They mock me whilst I sleep, and whilst the squat yellow foe may be creeping silently upon us. I have failed in my duty and betrayed the marble city of Olathoë; I have proven false to Alos, my friend and commander. But still these shadows of my dream deride me. They say there is no land of Lomar, save in my nocturnal imaginings; that in those realms where the Pole Star shines high and red Aldebaran crawls low around the horizon, there has been naught save ice and snow for thousands of years, and never a man save squat yellow creatures, blighted by the cold, whom they call 'Esquimaux'.

And as I writhe in my guilty agony, frantic to save the city whose peril every moment grows, and vainly striving to shake off this unnatural dream of a house of stone and brick south of a sinister swamp and a cemetery on a low hillock; the Pole Star, evil and monstrous, leers down from the black vault, winking hideously like an insane watching eye which strives to convey some strange message, yet recalls nothing save that it once had a message to convey.

THE STREET

T HERE BE THOSE WHO SAY that things and places have souls, and there be those who say they have not; I dare not say, myself, but I will tell of the Street.

Men of strength and honour fashioned that Street: good valiant men of our blood who had come from the Blessed Isles across the sea. At first it was but a path trodden by bearers of water from the woodland spring to the cluster of houses by the beach. Then, as more men came to the growing cluster of houses and looked about for places to dwell, they built cabins along the north side, cabins of stout oaken logs with masonry on the side toward the forest, for many Indians lurked there with fire-arrows. And in a few years more, men built cabins on the south side of the Street.

Up and down the Street walked grave men in conical hats, who most of the time carried muskets or fowling pieces. And there were also their bonneted wives and sober children. In the evening these men with their wives and children would sit about gigantic hearths and read and speak. Very simple were the things of which they read and spoke, yet things which gave them courage and goodness and helped them by day to subdue the forest and till the fields. And the children would listen and learn of the laws and deeds of old, and of that dear England which they had never seen or could not remember.

There was war, and thereafter no more Indians troubled the Street. The men, busy with labour, waxed prosperous and as happy as they knew how to be. And the children grew up comfortable, and more families came from the Mother Land to dwell on the Street. And the children's children, and the newcomers' children, grew up. The town was now a city, and one by one the cabins gave place to houses – simple, beautiful houses of brick and wood, with stone steps and iron railings and fanlights over the doors. No flimsy creations were these houses, for they were made to serve many a generation. Within there were carven mantels and graceful stairs, and sensible, pleasing furniture, china, and silver, brought from the Mother Land.

So the Street drank in the dreams of a young people and rejoiced as its dwellers became more graceful and happy. Where once had been only strength and honour, taste and learning now abode as well. Books and paintings and music came to the houses, and the young men went to the university which rose above the plain to the north. In the place of conical hats and small-swords, of lace and snowy periwigs, there were cobblestones over which clattered many a blooded horse and rumbled many a gilded coach; and brick sidewalks with horse blocks and hitching-posts.

There were in that Street many trees: elms and oaks and maples of dignity; so that in the summer, the scene was all soft verdure and twittering bird-song. And behind the houses were walled rose-gardens with hedged paths and sundials, where at evening the moon and stars would shine bewitchingly while fragrant blossoms glistened with dew.

So the Street dreamed on, past wars, calamities, and change. Once, most of the young men went away, and some never came back. That was when they furled the old flag and put up a new banner of stripes and stars. But though men talked of great changes, the Street felt them not, for its folk were still the same, speaking of the old familiar things in the old familiar accounts. And the trees still sheltered singing birds, and at evening the moon and stars looked down upon dewy blossoms in the walled rose-gardens.

In time there were no more swords, three-cornered hats, or periwigs in the Street. How strange seemed the inhabitants with their walking-sticks, tall beavers, and cropped heads! New sounds came from the distance – first strange puffings and shrieks from the river a mile away, and then, many years later, strange puffings and shrieks and rumblings from other directions. The air was not quite so pure as before, but the spirit of the place had not changed. The blood and soul of their ancestors had fashioned the Street. Nor did the spirit change when they tore open the earth to lay down strange pipes, or when they set up tall posts bearing weird wires. There was so much ancient lore in that Street, that the past could not easily be forgotten.

Then came days of evil, when many who had known the Street of old knew it no more, and many knew it who had not known it before, and went away, for their accents were coarse and strident, and their mien and faces unpleasing. Their thoughts, too, fought with the wise, just spirit of the Street, so that the Street pined silently as its houses fell into decay, and its trees died one by one, and its rose-gardens grew rank with weeds and waste. But it felt a stir of pride one day when again marched forth young men, some of whom never came back. These young men were clad in blue.

With the years, worse fortune came to the Street. Its trees were all gone now, and its rose-gardens were displaced by the backs of cheap, ugly new buildings on parallel streets. Yet the houses remained, despite the ravages of the years and the storms and worms, for they had been made to serve many a generation. New kinds of faces appeared in the Street, swarthy, sinister faces with furtive eyes and odd features, whose owners spoke unfamiliar words and placed signs in known and unknown characters upon most of the musty houses. Push-carts crowded the gutters. A sordid, undefinable stench settled over the place, and the ancient spirit slept.

Great excitement once came to the Street. War and revolution were raging across the seas; a dynasty had collapsed, and its degenerate subjects were flocking with dubious intent to the Western Land. Many of these took lodgings in the battered houses that had once known the songs of birds and the scent of roses. Then the Western Land itself awoke and joined the Mother Land in her titanic struggle for civilisation. Over the cities once more floated the old flag, companioned by the new flag, and by a plainer, yet glorious tricolour. But not many flags floated over the Street, for therein brooded only fear and hatred and ignorance. Again young men went forth, but not quite as did the young men of those other days. Something was lacking. And the sons of those young men of other days, who did indeed go forth in olive-drab with the true spirit of their ancestors, went from distant places and knew not the Street and its ancient spirit.

Over the seas there was a great victory, and in triumph most of the young men returned. Those who had lacked something lacked it no longer, yet did fear and hatred and ignorance still brood over the Street; for many had stayed behind, and many strangers had come from distant places to the ancient houses. And the young men who had returned dwelt there no longer. Swarthy and sinister were most of the strangers, yet among them one might find a few faces like those who fashioned the Street and moulded its spirit. Like and yet unlike, for there was in the eyes of all a weird, unhealthy glitter as of greed, ambition, vindictiveness, or misguided zeal. Unrest and treason were abroad amongst an evil few who plotted to strike the Western Land its death blow, that they might mount to power over its ruins, even as assassins had mounted in that unhappy, frozen land from whence most of them had come. And the heart of that plotting was in the Street, whose crumbling houses teemed with alien makers of discord and echoed with the plans and speeches of those who yearned for the appointed day of blood, flame and crime.

Of the various odd assemblages in the Street, the Law said much but could prove little. With great diligence did men of hidden badges linger and listen about such places as Petrovitch's Bakery, the squalid Rifkin School of Modern Economics, the Circle Social Club, and the Liberty Cafe. There congregated sinister men in great numbers, yet always was their speech guarded or in a foreign tongue. And still the old houses stood, with their forgotten lore of nobler, departed centuries; of sturdy Colonial tenants and dewy rose-gardens in the moonlight. Sometimes a lone poet or traveller would come to view them, and would try to picture them in their vanished glory; yet of such travellers and poets there were not many.

The rumour now spread widely that these houses contained the leaders of a vast band of terrorists, who on a designated day were to launch an orgy of slaughter for the extermination of America and of all the fine old traditions which the Street had loved. Hand-bills and papers fluttered about filthy gutters; handbills and papers printed in many tongues and in many characters, yet all bearing messages of crime and rebellion. In these writings the people were urged to tear down the laws and virtues that our fathers had exalted, to stamp out the soul of the old America – the soul that was bequeathed through a thousand and a half years of Anglo-Saxon freedom, justice, and moderation. It was said that the swart men who dwelt in the Street and congregated in its rotting edifices were the brains of a hideous revolution, that at their word of command many millions of brainless, besotted beasts would stretch forth their noisome talons from the slums of a thousand cities, burning, slaying, and destroying till the land of our fathers should be no more. All this was said and repeated, and many looked forward in dread to the fourth day of July, about which the strange writings hinted much; yet could nothing be found to place the guilt. None could tell just whose arrest might cut off the damnable plotting at its source. Many times came bands of blue-coated police to search the shaky houses, though at last they ceased to come; for they too had grown tired of law and order, and had abandoned all the city to its fate. Then men in olive-drab came, bearing muskets, till it seemed as if in its sad sleep the Street must have some haunting dreams of those other days, when musket-bearing men in conical hats walked along it from the woodland spring to the cluster of houses by the beach. Yet could no act be performed to check the impending cataclysm, for the swart, sinister men were old in cunning.

So the Street slept uneasily on, till one night there gathered in Petrovitch's Bakery, and the Rifkin School of Modern Economics, and the Circle Social Club, and Liberty Café, and in other places as well, vast hordes of men whose eyes were big with horrible triumph and expectation. Over hidden wires strange messages trav-elled, and much was said of still stranger messages yet to travel; but most of this was not guessed till afterward, when the Western Land was safe from the peril. The men in olive-drab could not tell what was happening, or what they ought to do; for the swart, sinister men were skilled in subtlety and concealment.

And yet the men in olive-drab will always remember that night, and will speak of the Street as they tell of it to their grandchildren; for many of them were sent there toward morning on a mission unlike that which they had expected. It was known that this nest of anarchy was old, and that the houses were tottering from the ravages of the years and the storms and worms; yet was the happening of that summer night a surprise because of its very queer uniformity. It was, indeed, an exceedingly singular happening, though after all, a simple one. For without warning, in one of the small hours beyond midnight, all the ravages of the years and the storms and the worms came to a tremendous climax; and after the crash there was nothing left standing in the Street save two ancient chimneys and part of a stout brick wall. Nor did anything that had been alive come alive from the ruins. A poet and a traveller, who came with the mighty crowd that sought the scene, tell odd stories. The poet says that all through the hours before dawn he beheld sordid ruins indistinctly in the glare of the arc-lights; that there loomed above the wreckage another picture wherein he could describe moonlight and fair houses and elms and oaks and maples of dignity. And the traveller declares that instead of the place's wonted stench there lingered a delicate fragrance as of roses in full bloom. But are not the dreams of poets and the tales of travellers notoriously false?

There be those who say that things and places have souls, and there be those who say they have not; I dare not say, myself, but I have told you of the Street.

EX OBLIVIONE

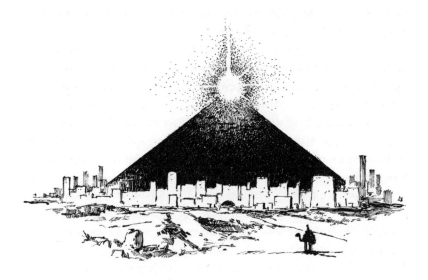

WHEN THE LAST DAYS WERE UPON ME, and the ugly trifles of existence began to drive me to madness like the small drops of water that torturers let fall ceaselessly upon one spot of their victim's body, I loved the irradiate refuge of sleep. In my dreams I found a little of the beauty I had vainly sought in life, and wandered through old gardens and enchanted woods.

Once when the wind was soft and scented I heard the south calling, and sailed endlessly and languorously under strange stars.

Once when the gentle rain fell I glided in a barge down a sunless stream under the earth till I reached another world of purple twilight, iridescent arbours, and undying roses.

And once I walked through a golden valley that led to shadowy groves and ruins, and ended in a mighty wall green with antique vines, and pierced by a little gate of bronze.

Many times I walked through that valley, and longer and longer would I pause in the spectral half-light where the giant trees squirmed and twisted grotesquely, and the grey ground stretched damply from trunk to trunk, sometimes disclosing the mould-stained stones of buried temples. And always the goal of my fancies was the mighty vine-grown wall with the little gate of bronze therein.

After awhile, as the days of waking became less and less bearable from their greyness and sameness, I would often drift in opiate peace through the valley and the shadowy groves, and wonder how I might seize them for my eternal dwelling-place, so that I need no more crawl back to a dull world stript of interest and new colours. And as I looked upon the little gate in the mighty wall, I felt that beyond it lay a dream-country from which, once it was entered, there would be no return.

So each night in sleep I strove to find the hidden latch of the gate in the ivied antique wall, though it was exceedingly well hidden. And I would tell myself that the realm beyond the wall was not more lasting merely, but more lovely and radiant as well.

Then one night in the dream-city of Zakarion I found a yellowed papyrus filled with the thoughts of dream-sages who dwelt of old in that city, and who were too wise ever to be born in the waking world. Therein were written many things concerning the world of dream, and among them was lore of a golden valley and a sacred grove with temples, and a high wall pierced by a little bronze gate. When I saw this lore, I knew that it touched on the scenes I had haunted, and I therefore read long in the yellowed papyrus.

Some of the dream-sages wrote gorgeously of the wonders beyond the irrepassable gate, but others told of horror and disappointment. I knew not which to believe, yet longed more and more to cross forever into the unknown land; for doubt and secrecy are the lure of lures, and no new horror can be more terrible than the daily torture of the commonplace. So when I learned of the drug which would unlock the gate and drive me through, I resolved to take it when next I awaked.

Last night I swallowed the drug and floated dreamily into the golden valley and the shadowy groves; and when I came this time to the antique wall, I saw that the small gate of bronze was ajar. From beyond came a glow that weirdly lit the giant twisted trees and the tops of the buried temples, and I drifted on songfully, expectant of the glories of the land from whence I should never return.

But as the gate swung wider and the sorcery of the drug and the dream pushed me through, I knew that all sights and glories were at an end; for in that new realm was neither land nor sea, but only the white void of unpeopled and illimitable space. So, happier than I had ever dared hope to be, I dissolved again into that native infinity of crystal oblivion from which the daemon Life had called me for one brief and desolate hour.

FACTS CONCERNING THE LATE ARTHUR JERMYN AND HIS FAMILY

LIFE IS A HIDEOUS THING, and from the background behind what we know of it peer daemoniacal hints of truth which make it sometimes a thousandfold more hideous. Science, already oppressive with its shocking revelations, will perhaps be the ultimate exterminator of our human species – if separate species we be – for its reserve of unguessed horrors could never be borne by mortal brains if loosed upon the world. If we knew what we are, we should do as Sir Arthur Jermyn did; and Arthur Jermyn soaked himself in oil and set fire to his clothing one night. No one placed the charred fragments in an urn or set a memorial to him who had been; for certain papers and a certain boxed *object* were found, which made men wish to forget. Some who knew him do not admit that he ever existed.

Arthur Jermyn went out on the moor and burned himself after seeing the boxed *object* which had come from Africa. It was this *object*, and not his peculiar personal appearance, which made him end his life. Many would have disliked to live if possessed of the peculiar features of Arthur Jermyn, but he had been a poet and

scholar and had not minded. Learning was in his blood, for his great-grandfather, Sir Robert Jermyn, Bt., had been an anthropologist of note, whilst his great-great-great-grandfather, Sir Wade Jermyn, was one of the earliest explorers of the Congo region, and had written eruditely of its tribes, animals, and supposed antiquities. Indeed, old Sir Wade had possessed an intellectual zeal amounting almost to a mania; his bizarre conjectures on a prehistoric white Congolese civilisation earning him much ridicule when his book, *Observations on the Several Parts of Africa*, was published. In 1765 this fearless explorer had been placed in a madhouse at Huntingdon.

Madness was in all the Jermyns, and people were glad there were not many of them. The line put forth no branches, and Arthur was the last of it. If he had not been, one cannot say what he would have done when the *object* came. The Jermyns never seemed to look quite right – something was amiss, though Arthur was the worst, and the old family portraits in Jermyn House shewed fine faces enough before Sir Wade's time. Certainly, the madness began with Sir Wade, whose wild stories of Africa were at once the delight and terror of his few friends. It shewed in his collection of trophies and specimens, which were not such as a normal man would accumulate and preserve, and appeared strikingly in the Oriental seclusion in which he kept his wife. The latter, he had said, was the daughter of a Portuguese trader whom he had met in Africa; and did not like English ways. She, with an infant son born in Africa, had accompanied him back for the second and longest of his trips, and had gone with him on the third and last, never returning. No one had ever seen her closely, not even the servants; for her disposition had been violent and singular. During her brief stay at Jermyn House she occupied a remote wing, and was waited on by her husband alone. Sir Wade was, indeed, most peculiar in his solicitude for his family; for when he returned to Africa he would permit no one to care for his young son save a loathsome black woman from Guinea. Upon coming back, after the death of Lady Jermyn, he himself assumed complete care of the boy.

But it was the talk of Sir Wade, especially when in his cups, which chiefly led his friends to deem him mad. In a rational age like the eighteenth century it was unwise for a man of learning to talk about wild sights and strange scenes under a Congo moon; of the gigantic walls and pillars of a forgotten city, crumbling and vine-grown, and of damp, silent, stone steps leading interminably down into the darkness of abysmal treasure-vaults and inconceivable catacombs. Especially was it unwise to rave of the living things that might haunt such a place; of creatures half of the jungle and half of the impiously aged city – fabulous creatures which even a Pliny might describe with scepticism; things that might have sprung up after the great apes had overrun the dying city with the walls and the pillars, the vaults and the weird carvings. Yet after he came home for the last time Sir Wade would speak of such matters with a shudderingly uncanny zest, mostly after his third glass at the Knight's Head; boasting of what he had found in the jungle and of how he had dwelt among terrible ruins known only to him. And finally he had spoken of the living things in such a manner that he was taken to the madhouse. He had shewn little regret when shut into the barred room at Huntingdon, for his mind moved curiously. Ever since his son had commenced to grow out of infancy he had liked his home less and less, till at last he had seemed to dread it. The Knight's Head had been his headquarters, and when he was confined he expressed some vague gratitude as if for protection. Three years later he died.

Wade Jermyn's son Philip was a highly peculiar person. Despite a strong physical resemblance to his father, his appearance and conduct were in many particulars so coarse that he was universally shunned. Though he did not inherit the madness which was feared by some, he was densely stupid and given to brief periods of uncontrollable violence. In frame he was small, but intensely powerful, and was of incredible agility. Twelve years after succeeding to his title he married the daughter of his gamekeeper, a person said to be of gypsy extraction, but before his son was born joined the navy as a common sailor, completing the general disgust which his habits and misalliance had begun. After the close of the American war he was heard of as a sailor on a merchantman in the African trade, having a kind of reputation for feats of strength and climbing, but finally disappearing one night as his ship lay off the Congo coast.

In the son of Sir Philip Jermyn the now accepted family peculiarity took a strange and fatal turn. Tall and fairly handsome, with a sort of weird Eastern grace despite certain slight oddities of proportion, Robert Jermyn began life as a scholar and investigator. It was he who first studied scientifically the vast collection of relics which his mad grandfather had brought from Africa, and who made the family name as celebrated in ethnology as in exploration. In 1815 Sir Robert married a daughter of the seventh Viscount Brightholme and was subsequently blessed with three children, the eldest and youngest of whom were never publicly seen on account of deformities in mind and body. Saddened by these family misfortunes, the scientist sought relief in work, and made two long expeditions in the interior of Africa. In 1849 his second son, Nevil, a singularly repellent person who seemed to combine the surliness of Philip Jermyn with the hauteur of the Brightholmes, ran away with a vulgar dancer, but was pardoned upon his return in the following year. He came back to Jermyn House a widower with an infant son, Alfred, who was one day to be the father of Arthur Jermyn.

Friends said that it was this series of griefs which unhinged the mind of Sir Robert Jermyn, yet it was probably merely a bit of African folklore which caused the disaster. The elderly scholar had been collecting legends of the Onga tribes near the field of his grandfather's and his own explorations, hoping in some way to account for Sir Wade's wild tales of a lost city peopled by strange hybrid creatures. A certain consistency in the strange papers of his ancestor suggested that the madman's imagination might have been stimulated by native myths. On October 19, 1852, the explorer Samuel Seaton called at Jermyn House with a manuscript of notes collected among the Ongas, believing that certain legends of a grey city of white apes ruled by a white god might prove valuable to the ethnologist. In his conversation he probably supplied many additional details; the nature of which will never be known, since a hideous series of tragedies suddenly burst into being. When Sir Robert Jermyn emerged from his library he left behind the strangled corpse of the explorer, and before he could be restrained, had put an end to all three of his children; the two who were never seen, and the son who had run away. Nevil Jermyn died in the successful defence of his own two-year-old son, who had apparently been included in the old man's madly murderous scheme. Sir Robert himself, after repeated attempts at suicide and a stubborn refusal to utter any articulate sound, died of apoplexy in the second year of his confinement.

Sir Alfred Jermyn was a baronet before his fourth birthday, but his tastes never matched his title. At twenty he had joined a band of music-hall performers, and at thirty-six had deserted his wife and child to travel with an itinerant American circus. His end was very revolting. Among the animals in the exhibition with which he travelled was a huge bull gorilla of lighter colour than the average; a surprisingly tractable beast of much popularity with the performers. With this gorilla Alfred Jermyn was singularly fascinated, and on many occasions the two would eye each other for long periods through the intervening bars. Eventually Jermyn asked and obtained permission to train the animal, astonishing audiences and fellow-performers alike with his success. One morning in Chicago, as the gorilla and Alfred Jermyn were rehearsing an exceedingly clever boxing match, the former delivered a blow of more than usual force, hurting both the body and dignity of the amateur trainer. Of what followed, members of 'The Greatest Show on Earth' do not like to speak. They did not expect to hear Sir Alfred Jermyn emit a shrill, inhuman scream, or to see him seize his clumsy antagonist with both hands, dash it to the floor of the cage, and bite fiendishly at its hairy throat. The gorilla was off its guard, but not for long, and before anything could be done by the regular trainer the body which had belonged to a baronet was past recognition.

2

Arthur Jermyn was the son of Sir Alfred Jermyn and a music-hall singer of unknown origin. When the husband and father deserted his family, the mother took the child to Jermyn House; where there was none left to object to her presence. She was not without notions of what a nobleman's dignity should be, and saw to it that her son received the best education which limited money could provide. The family resources were now sadly slender, and Jermyn House had fallen into woeful disrepair, but young Arthur loved the old edifice and all its contents. He was not like any other Jermyn who had ever lived, for he was a poet and a dreamer. Some of the neighbouring families who had heard tales of old Sir Wade Jermyn's unseen Portuguese wife declared that her Latin blood must be shewing itself; but most persons merely sneered at his sensitiveness to beauty, attributing it to his music-hall mother, who was socially unrecognised. The poetic delicacy of Arthur Jermyn was the more remarkable because of his uncouth personal appearance. Most of the Jermyns had possessed a subtly odd and repellent cast, but Arthur's case was very striking. It is hard to say just what he resembled, but his expression, his facial angle, and the length of his arms gave a thrill of repulsion to those who met him for the first time.

It was the mind and character of Arthur Jermyn which atoned for his aspect. Gifted and learned, he took highest honours at Oxford and seemed likely to redeem the intellectual fame of his family. Though of poetic rather than scientific temperament, he planned to continue the work of his forefathers in African ethnology and antiquities, utilising the truly wonderful though strange collection of Sir Wade. With his fanciful mind he thought often of the prehistoric civilisation in which the mad explorer had so implicitly believed, and would weave tale after tale about the silent jungle city mentioned in the latter's wilder notes and paragraphs. For the nebulous utterances concerning a nameless, unsuspected race of jungle hybrids he had a peculiar feeling of mingled terror and attraction; speculating on the possible basis of such a fancy, and seeking to obtain light among the more recent data gleaned by his great-grandfather and Samuel Seaton amongst the Ongas.

In 1911, after the death of his mother, Sir Arthur Jermyn determined to pursue his investigations to the utmost extent. Selling a portion of his estate to obtain the requisite money, he outfitted an expedition and sailed for the Congo. Arranging with the Belgian authorities for a party of guides, he spent a year in the Onga and Kaliri country, finding data beyond the highest of his expectations. Among the Kaliris was an aged chief called Mwanu, who possessed not only a highly retentive memory, but a singular degree of intelligence and interest in old legends. This ancient confirmed every tale which Jermyn had heard, adding his own account of the stone city and the white apes as it had been told to him.

According to Mwanu, the grey city and the hybrid creatures were no more, having been annihilated by the warlike N'bangus many years ago. This tribe, after destroying most of the edifices and killing the live beings, had carried off the stuffed goddess which had been the object of their quest; the white ape-goddess which the strange beings worshipped, and which was held by Congo tradition to be the form of one who had reigned as a princess among those beings. Just what the white ape-like creatures could have been, Mwanu had no idea, but he thought they were the builders of the ruined city. Jermyn could form no conjecture, but by close questioning obtained a very picturesque legend of the stuffed goddess.

The ape-princess, it was said, became the consort of a great white god who had come out of the West. For a long time they had reigned over the city together, but when they had a son all three went away. Later the god and the princess had returned, and upon the death of the princess her divine husband had mummified the body and enshrined it in a vast house of stone, where it was worshipped. Then he had departed alone. The legend here seemed to present three variants. According to one story nothing further happened save that the stuffed goddess became a symbol of supremacy for whatever tribe might possess it. It was for this reason that the N'bangus carried it off. A second story told of the god's return and death at the feet of his enshrined wife. A third told of the return of the son, grown to manhood – or apehood or godhood, as the case might be – yet unconscious of his identity. Surely the imaginative blacks had made the most of whatever events might lie behind the extravagant legendry.

Of the reality of the jungle city described by old Sir Wade, Arthur Jermyn had no further doubt; and was hardly astonished when early in 1912 he came upon what was left of it. Its size must have been exaggerated, yet the stones lying about proved that it was no mere Negro village. Unfortunately no carvings could be found, and the small size of the expedition prevented operations toward clearing the one visible passageway that seemed to lead down into the system of vaults which Sir Wade had mentioned. The white apes and the stuffed goddess were discussed with all the native chiefs of the region, but it remained for a European to improve on the data offered by old Mwanu. M. Verhaeren, Belgian agent at a trading-post on the Congo, believed that he could not only locate but obtain the stuffed goddess, of which he had vaguely heard; since the once mighty N'bangus were now the submissive servants of King Albert's government, and with but little persuasion could be induced to part with the gruesome deity they had carried off. When Jermyn sailed for England, therefore, it was with the exultant probability that he would within a few months receive a priceless ethnological relic confirming the wildest of his great-great-great-grandfather's narratives – that is, the wildest which he had ever heard. Countrymen near Jermyn House had perhaps heard wilder tales handed down from ancestors who had listened to Sir Wade around the tables of the Knight's Head.

Arthur Jermyn waited very patiently for the expected box from M. Verhaeren, meanwhile studying with increased diligence the manuscripts left by his mad ancestor. He began to feel closely akin to Sir Wade, and to seek relics of the latter's personal life in England as well as of his African exploits. Oral accounts of the mysterious and secluded wife had been numerous, but no tangible relic of her stay at Jermyn House remained. Jermyn wondered what circumstance had prompted or permitted such an effacement, and decided that the husband's insanity was the prime cause. His great-great-great-grandmother, he recalled, was said to have been the daughter of a Portuguese trader in Africa. No doubt her practical heritage and superficial knowledge of the Dark Continent had caused her to flout Sir Wade's talk of the interior, a thing which such a man would not be likely to forgive. She had died in Africa, perhaps dragged thither by a husband determined to prove what he had told. But as Jermyn indulged in these reflections he could not but smile at their futility, a century and a half after the death of both of his strange progenitors.

In June, 1913, a letter arrived from M. Verhaeren, telling of the finding of the stuffed goddess. It was, the Belgian averred, a most extraordinary object; an object quite beyond the power of a layman to classify. Whether it was human or simian only a scientist could determine, and the process of determination would be greatly hampered by its imperfect condition. Time and the Congo climate are not kind to mummies; especially when their preparation is as amateurish as seemed to be the case here. Around the creature's neck had been found a golden chain bearing an empty locket on which were armorial designs; no doubt some hapless traveller's keepsake, taken by the N'bangus and hung upon the goddess as a charm. In commenting on the contour of the mummy's face, M. Verhaeren suggested a whimsical comparison; or rather, expressed a humorous wonder just how it would strike his correspondent, but was too much interested scientifically to waste many words in levity.

The stuffed goddess, he wrote, would arrive duly packed about a month after receipt of the letter.

The boxed object was delivered at Jermyn House on the afternoon of August 3, 1913, being conveyed immediately to the large chamber which housed the collection of African specimens as arranged by Sir Robert and Arthur. What ensued can best be gathered from the tales of servants and from things and papers later examined. Of the various tales that of aged Soames, the family butler, is most ample and coherent.

According to this trustworthy man, Sir Arthur Jermyn dismissed everyone from the room before opening the box, though the instant sound of hammer and chisel shewed that he did not delay the operation. Nothing was heard for some time; just how long Soames cannot exactly estimate; but it was certainly less than a quarter of an hour later that the horrible scream, undoubtedly in Jermyn's voice, was heard. Immediately afterward Jermyn emerged from the room, rushing frantically toward the front of the house as if pursued by some hideous enemy. The expression on his face, a face ghastly enough in repose, was beyond description. When near the front door he seemed to think of something, and turned back in his flight, finally disappearing down the stairs to the cellar. The servants were utterly dumbfounded, and watched at the head of the stairs, but their master did not return. A smell of oil was all that came up from the regions below. After dark a rattling was heard at the door leading from the cellar into the courtyard; and a stable-boy saw Arthur Jermyn, glistening from head to foot with oil and redolent of that fluid, steal furtively out and vanish on the black moor surrounding the house. Then, in an exaltation of supreme horror, everyone saw the end. A spark appeared on the moor, a flame arose, and a pillar of human fire reached to the heavens. The house of Jermyn no longer existed.

The reason why Arthur Jermyn's charred fragments were not collected and buried lies in what was found afterward, principally the thing in the box. The stuffed goddess was a nauseous sight, withered and eaten away, but it was clearly a mummified white ape of some unknown species, less hairy than any recorded variety, and infinitely nearer mankind – quite shockingly so. Detailed description would be rather unpleasant, but two salient particulars must be told, for they fit in revoltingly with certain notes of Sir Wade

Jermyn's African expeditions and with the Congolese legends of the white god and the ape-princess. The two particulars in question are these: the arms on the golden locket about the creature's neck were the Jermyn arms, and the jocose suggestion of M. Verhaeren about a certain resemblance as connected with the shrivelled face applied with vivid, ghastly, and unnatural horror to none other than the sensitive Arthur Jermyn, great-great-great-grandson of Sir Wade Jermyn and an unknown wife. Members of the Royal Anthropological Institute burned the thing and threw the locket into a well, and some of them do not admit that Arthur Jermyn ever existed.

THE CRAWLING CHAOS

(with Winifred Virginia Jackson)

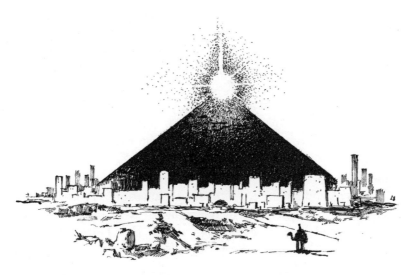

OF THE PLEASURES and pains of opium much has been written. The ecstasies and horrors of De Quincey and the *paradis artificiels* of Baudelaire are preserved and interpreted with an art which makes them immortal, and the world knows well the beauty, the terror and the mystery of those obscure realms into which the inspired dreamer is transported. But much as has been told, no man has yet dared intimate the *nature* of the phantasms thus unfolded to the mind, or hint at the *direction* of the unheard-of roads along whose ornate and exotic course the partaker of the drug is so irresistibly borne. De Quincey was drawn back into Asia, that teeming land of nebulous shadows whose hideous antiquity is so impressive that 'the vast age of the race and name overpowers the sense of youth in the individual,' but farther than that he dared not go. Those who *have* gone farther seldom returned, and even when they have, they have been either silent or quite mad. I took opium but once – in the year of the plague, when doctors sought to deaden the agonies they could not cure. There was an overdose – my physician was worn out with horror and exertion – and I travelled very far indeed. In the end I returned and lived, but my nights are filled with strange memories, nor have I ever permitted a doctor to give me opium again.

The pain and pounding in my head had been quite unendurable when the drug was administered. Of the future I had no heed; to escape, whether by cure, unconsciousness, or death, was all that concerned me. I was partly delirious, so that it is hard to place the exact moment of transition, but I think the effect must have begun shortly before the pounding ceased to be painful. As I have said, there was an overdose; so my reactions were probably far from normal. The sensation of falling, curiously dissociated from the idea of gravity or direction, was paramount; though there was subsidiary impression of unseen throngs in incalculable profusion, throngs of infinitely diverse nature, but all more or less related to me. Sometimes it seemed less as though I were falling, than as though the universe or the ages were falling past me. Suddenly my pain ceased, and I began to associate the pounding with an external rather than internal force. The falling had ceased also, giving place to a sensation of uneasy, temporary rest; and when I listened closely, I fancied the pounding was that of the vast, inscrutable sea as its sinister, colossal breakers lacerated some desolate shore after a storm of titanic magnitude. Then I opened my eyes.

For a moment my surroundings seemed confused, like a pro-jected image hopelessly out of focus, but gradually I realised my solitary presence in a strange and beautiful room lighted by many windows. Of the exact nature of the apartment I could form no idea, for my thoughts were still far from settled, but I noticed vari-coloured rugs and draperies, elaborately fashioned tables, chairs, ottomans, and divans, and delicate vases and ornaments which conveyed a suggestion of the exotic without being actually alien. These things I noticed, yet they were not long uppermost in my mind. Slowly but inexorably crawling upon my consciousness and rising above every other impression, came a dizzying fear of the unknown; a fear all the greater because I could not analyse it, and seeming to concern a stealthily approaching menace; not death, but some nameless, unheard-of thing inexpressibly more ghastly and abhorrent.

Presently I realised that the direct symbol and excitant of my fear was the hideous pounding whose incessant reverberations throbbed maddeningly against my exhausted brain. It seemed to come from a point outside and below the edifice in which I stood, and to associate itself with the most terrifying mental images. I felt that some horrible scene or object lurked beyond the silk-hung walls, and shrank from glancing through the arched, latticed windows that opened so bewilderingly on every hand. Perceiving shutters attached to these windows, I closed them all, averting my eyes from the exterior as I did so. Then, employing a flint and steel which I found on one of the small tables, I lit the many candles reposing about the walls in arabesque sconces. The added sense of security brought by closed shutters and artificial light calmed my nerves to some degree, but I could not shut out the monotonous pounding. Now that I was calmer, the sound became as fascinating as it was fearful, and I felt a contradictory desire to seek out its source despite my still powerful shrinking. Opening a portiere at the side of the room nearest the pounding, I beheld a small and richly draped corridor ending in a cavern door and large oriel window. To this window I was irresistibly drawn, though my ill-defined apprehensions seemed almost equally bent on holding me back. As I approached it I could see a chaotic whirl of waters in the distance. Then, as I attained it and glanced out on all sides, the stupendous picture of my surroundings burst upon me with full and devastating force.

I beheld such a sight as I had never beheld before, and which no living person can have seen save in the delirium of fever or the inferno of opium. The building stood on a narrow point of land – or what was now a narrow point of land – fully three hundred feet above what must lately have been a seething vortex of mad waters. On either side of the house there fell a newly washed-out precipice of red earth, whilst ahead of me the hideous waves were still rolling in frightfully, eating away the land with ghastly monotony and deliberation. Out a mile or more there rose and fell menacing breakers at least fifty feet in height, and on the far horizon ghoulish black clouds of grotesque contour were resting and brooding like unwholesome vultures. The waves were dark and purplish, almost black, and clutched at the yielding red mud of the bank as if with uncouth, greedy hands. I could not but feel that some noxious marine mind had declared a war of extermination upon all the solid ground, perhaps abetted by the angry sky.

Recovering at length from the stupor into which this unnatural spectacle had thrown me, I realised that my actual physical danger was acute. Even whilst I gazed, the bank had lost many feet, and it could not be long before the house would fall undermined into the awful pit of lashing waves. Accordingly I hastened to the opposite side of the edifice, and finding a door, emerged at once, locking it after me with a curious key which had hung inside. I now beheld more of the strange region about me, and marked a singular division which seemed to exist in the hostile ocean and firmament. On each side of the jutting promontory different conditions held sway. At my left as I faced inland was a gently heaving sea with great green waves rolling peacefully in under a brightly shining sun. Something about that sun's nature and position made me shudder, but I could not then tell, and cannot tell now, what it was. At my right also was the sea, but it was blue, calm, and only gently undulating, while the sky above it was darker and the washed-out bank more nearly white than reddish.

I now turned my attention to the land, and found occasion for fresh surprise; for the vegetation resembled nothing I had ever seen or read about. It was apparently tropical or at least sub-tropical – a conclusion borne out by the intense heat of the air. Sometimes I thought I could trace strange analogies with the flora of my native land, fancying that the well-known plants and shrubs might assume such forms under a radical change of climate; but the gigantic and omnipresent palm trees were plainly foreign. The house I had just left was very small – hardly more than a cottage – but its material was evidently marble, and its architecture was weird and composite, involving a quaint fusion of Western and Eastern forms. At the corners were Corinthian columns, but the red tile roof was like that of a Chinese pagoda. From the door inland there stretched a path of singularly white sand, about four feet wide, and lined on either side with stately palms and unidentifiable flowering shrubs and plants. It lay toward the side of the promontory where the sea was blue and the bank rather whitish. Down this path I felt impelled to flee, as if pursued by some malignant spirit from the pounding ocean. At first it was slightly uphill, then I reached a gentle crest. Behind me I saw the scene I had left; the entire point with the cottage and the black water, with the green sea on one side and the blue sea on the other, and a curse unnamed and unnameable lowering over all. I never saw it again, and often wonder ... After this last look I strode ahead and surveyed the inland panorama before me.

The path, as I have intimated, ran along the right-hand shore as one went inland. Ahead and to the left I now viewed a magnificent valley comprising thousands of acres, and covered with a swaying growth of tropical grass higher than my head. Almost at the limit of vision was a colossal palm tree which seemed to fascinate and beckon me. By this time wonder and escape from the imperilled peninsula had largely dissipated my fear, but as I paused and sank fatigued to the path, idly digging with my hands into the warm, whitish-golden sand, a new and acute sense of danger seized me. Some terror in the swishing tall grass seemed added to that of the diabolically pounding sea, and I started up crying aloud and disjointedly, 'Tiger? Tiger? Is it Tiger? Beast? Beast? Is it a Beast that I am afraid of?' My mind wandered back to an ancient and classical story of tigers which I had read; I strove to recall the author, but had difficulty. Then in the midst of my fear I remembered that the tale was by Rudyard Kipling; nor did the grotesqueness of deeming him an ancient author occur to me; I wished for the volume containing this story, and had almost started back toward the doomed cottage to procure it when my better sense and the lure of the palm prevented me.

Whether or not I could have resisted the backward beckoning without the counter-fascination of the vast palm tree, I do not know. This attraction was now dominant, and I left the path and crawled on hands and knees down the valley's slope despite my fear of the grass and of the serpents it might contain. I resolved to fight for life and reason as long as possible against all menaces of sea or land, though I sometimes feared defeat as the maddening swish of the uncanny grasses joined the still audible and irritating pounding of the distant breakers. I would frequently pause and put my hands to my ears for relief, but could never quite shut out the detestable sound. It was, as it seemed to me, only after ages that I finally dragged myself to the beckoning palm tree and lay quiet beneath its protecting shade.

There now ensued a series of incidents which transported me to the opposite extremes of ecstasy and horror; incidents which I tremble to recall and dare not seek to interpret. No sooner had

I crawled beneath the overhanging foliage of the palm, than there dropped from its branches a young child of such beauty as I never beheld before. Though ragged and dusty, this being bore the features of a faun or demigod, and seemed almost to diffuse a radiance in the dense shadow of the tree. It smiled and extended its hand, but before I could arise and speak I heard in the upper air the exquisite melody of singing; notes high and low blent with a sublime and ethereal harmoniousness. The sun had by this time sunk below the horizon, and in the twilight I saw an aureole of lambent light encircled the child's head. Then in a tone of silver it addressed me: 'It is the end. They have come down through the gloaming from the stars. Now all is over, and beyond the Arinurian streams we shall dwell blissfully in Teloe.' As the child spoke, I beheld a soft radiance through the leaves of the palm tree, and rising, greeted a pair whom I knew to be the chief singers among those I had heard. A god and goddess they must have been, for such beauty is not mortal; and they took my hands, saying, 'Come, child, you have heard the voices, and all is well. In Teloe beyond the Milky Way and the Arinurian streams are cities all of amber and chalcedony. And upon their domes of many facets glisten the images of strange and beautiful stars. Under the ivory bridges of Teloe flow rivers of liquid gold bearing pleasure-barges bound for blossomy Cytharion of the Seven Suns. And in Teloe and Cytharion abide only youth, beauty, and pleasure, nor are any sounds heard, save of laughter, song, and the lute. Only the gods dwell in Teloe of the golden rivers, but among them shalt thou dwell.'

As I listened, enchanted, I suddenly became aware of a change in my surroundings. The palm tree, so lately overshadowing my exhausted form, was now some distance to my left and considerably below me. I was obviously floating in the atmosphere; companioned not only by the strange child and the radiant pair, but by a constantly increasing throng of half-luminous, vine-crowned youths and maidens with wind-blown hair and joyful countenance. We slowly ascended together, as if borne on a fragrant breeze which blew not from the earth but from the golden nebulae, and the child whispered in my ear that I must look always upward to the pathways of light, and never backward to the sphere I had just left. The youths and maidens now chanted mellifluous choriambics to the accompaniment of lutes, and I felt enveloped in a peace and happiness more profound than any I had in life imagined, when the intrusion of a single sound altered my destiny and shattered my soul. Through the ravishing strains of the singers and the lutanists, as if in mocking, daemoniac concord, throbbed from gulfs below the damnable, the detestable pounding of that hideous ocean. As those black breakers beat their message into my ears I forgot the words of the child and looked back, down upon the doomed scene from which I thought I had escaped.

Down through the aether I saw the accursed earth slowly turning, ever turning, with angry and tempestuous seas gnawing at wild desolate shores and dashing foam against the tottering towers of deserted cities. And under a ghastly moon there gleamed sights I can never describe, sights I can never forget; deserts of corpselike clay and jungles of ruin and decadence where once stretched the populous plains and villages of my native land, and maelstroms of frothing ocean where once rose the mighty temples of my fore-fathers. Around the northern pole steamed a morass of noisome growths and miasmal vapours, hissing before the onslaught of the ever-mounting waves that curled and fretted from the shuddering deep. Then a rending report clave the night, and athwart the desert of deserts appeared a smoking rift. Still the black ocean foamed and gnawed, eating away the desert on either side as the rift in the centre widened and widened.

There was now no land left but the desert, and still the fuming ocean ate and ate. All at once I thought even the pounding sea seemed afraid of something, afraid of dark gods of the inner earth that are greater than the evil god of waters, but even if it was it could not turn back; and the desert had suffered too much from those nightmare waves to help them now. So the ocean ate the last of the land and poured into the smoking gulf, thereby giving up all it had ever conquered. From the new-flooded lands it flowed again, uncovering death and decay; and from its ancient and immemorial bed it trickled loathsomely, uncovering nighted secrets of the years when Time was young and the gods unborn. Above the waves rose weedy remembered spires. The moon laid pale lilies of light on dead London, and Paris stood up from its damp grave to be sanc-tified with star-dust. Then rose spires and monoliths that were weedy but not remembered; terrible spires and monoliths of lands that men never knew were lands.

There was not any pounding now, but only the unearthly roaring and hissing of waters tumbling into the rift. The smoke of that rift had changed to steam, and almost hid the world as it grew denser and denser. It seared my face and hands, and when I looked to see how it affected my companions I found they had all disappeared. Then very suddenly it ended, and I knew no more till I awaked upon a bed of convalescence. As the cloud of steam from the Plutonic gulf finally concealed the entire surface from my sight, all the firmament shrieked at a sudden agony of mad reverberations which shook the trembling aether. In one delirious flash and burst it happened; one blinding, deafening holocaust of fire, smoke, and thunder that dissolved the wan moon as it sped outward to the void.

And when the smoke cleared away, and I sought to look upon the earth, I beheld against the background of cold, humorous stars only the dying sun and the pale mournful planets searching for their sister.

THE TERRIBLE OLD MAN

I T WAS THE DESIGN of Angelo Ricci and Joe Czanek and Manuel Silva to call on the Terrible Old Man. This old man dwells all alone in a very ancient house on Water Street near the sea, and is reputed to be both exceedingly rich and exceedingly feeble; which forms a situation very attractive to men of the profession of Messrs Ricci, Czanek, and Silva, for that profession was nothing less dignified than robbery.

The inhabitants of Kingsport say and think many things about the Terrible Old Man which generally keep him safe from the attention of gentlemen like Mr Ricci and his colleagues, despite the almost certain fact that he hides a fortune of indefinite magnitude somewhere about his musty and venerable abode. He is, in truth, a very strange person, believed to have been a captain of East India clipper ships in his day; so old that no one can remember when he was young, and so taciturn that few know his real name. Among the gnarled trees in the front yard of his aged and neglected place he maintains a strange collection of large stones, oddly grouped and painted so that they resemble the idols in some obscure Eastern temple. This collection frightens away most of the small boys who love to taunt the Terrible Old Man about his long white hair and beard, or to break the small-paned windows of his dwelling with wicked missiles; but there are other things which frighten the older and more curious folk who sometimes steal up to the house to peer in through the dusty panes. These folk say that on a table in a bare room on the ground floor are many peculiar bottles, in each a small piece of lead suspended pendulum-wise from a string. And they say that the Terrible Old Man talks to these bottles, addressing them by such names as Jack, Scar-Face, Long Tom, Spanish Joe, Peters, and Mate Ellis, and that whenever he speaks to a bottle the little lead pendulum within makes certain definite vibrations as if in answer. Those who have watched the tall, lean, Terrible Old Man in these peculiar conversations, do not watch him again. But Angelo Ricci and Joe Czanek and Manuel Silva were not of Kingsport blood; they were of that new and heterogeneous alien stock which lies outside the charmed circle of New England life and traditions, and they saw in the Terrible Old Man merely a tottering, almost helpless greybeard, who could not walk without the aid of his knotted cane, and whose thin, weak hands shook pitifully. They were really quite sorry in their way for the lonely, unpopular old fellow, whom everybody shunned, and at whom all the dogs barked singularly. But business is business, and to a robber whose soul is in his profession, there is a lure and a challenge about a very old and very feeble man who has no account at the bank, and who pays for his few necessities at the village store with Spanish gold and silver minted two centuries ago.

Messrs Ricci, Czanek, and Silva selected the night of April 11th for their call. Mr Ricci and Mr Silva were to interview the poor old gentleman, whilst Mr Czanek waited for them and their presumable metallic burden with a covered motor-car in Ship Street, by the gate in the tall rear wall of their host's grounds. Desire to avoid needless explanations in case of unexpected police intrusions prompted these plans for a quiet and unostentatious departure.

As prearranged, the three adventurers started out separately in order to prevent any evil-minded suspicions afterward. Messrs Ricci and Silva met in Water Street by the old man's front gate, and although they did not like the way the moon shone down upon the painted stones through the budding branches of the gnarled trees, they had more important things to think about than mere idle superstition. They feared it might be unpleasant work making the Terrible Old Man loquacious concerning his hoarded gold and silver, for aged sea-captains are notably stubborn and perverse. Still, he was very old and very feeble, and there were two visitors. Messrs Ricci and Silva were experienced in the art of making unwilling persons voluble, and the screams of a weak and exceptionally venerable man can be easily muffled. So they moved up to the one lighted window and heard the Terrible Old Man talking childishly to his bottles with pendulums. Then they donned masks and knocked politely at the weather-stained oaken door.

Waiting seemed very long to Mr Czanek as he fidgeted restlessly in the covered motor-car by the Terrible Old Man's back gate in Ship Street. He was more than ordinarily tender-hearted, and he did not like the hideous screams he had heard in the ancient house just after the hour appointed for the deed. Had he not told his colleagues to be as gentle as possible with the pathetic old sea-captain? Very nervously he watched that narrow oaken gate in the high and ivy-clad stone wall. Frequently he consulted his watch, and wondered at the delay. Had the old man died before revealing where his treasure was hidden, and had a thorough search become necessary? Mr Czanek did not like to wait so long in the dark in such a place. Then he sensed a soft tread or tapping on the walk inside the gate, heard a gentle fumbling at the rusty latch, and saw the narrow, heavy door swing inward. And in the pallid glow of the single dim street-lamp he strained his eyes to see what his colleagues had brought out of that sinister house which loomed so close behind. But when he looked, he did not see what he had expected; for his colleagues were not there at all, but only the Terrible Old Man leaning quietly on his knotted cane and smiling hideously. Mr Czanek had never before noticed the colour of that man's eyes; now he saw that they were yellow.

Little things make considerable excitement in little towns, which is the reason that Kingsport people talked all that spring and summer about the three unidentifiable bodies, horribly slashed as with many cutlasses, and horribly mangled as by the tread of many cruel boot-heels, which the tide washed in. And some people even spoke of things as trivial as the deserted motor-car found in Ship Street, or certain especially inhuman cries, probably of a stray animal or migratory bird, heard in the night by wakeful citizens. But in this idle village gossip the Terrible Old Man took no interest at all. He was by nature reserved, and when one is aged and feeble one's reserve is doubly strong. Besides, so ancient a sea-captain must have witnessed scores of things much more stirring in the far-off days of his unremembered youth.

THE TREE

'Fata viam invenient.'

ON A VERDANT SLOPE of Mount Maenalus, in Arcadia, there stands an olive grove about the ruins of a villa. Close by is a tomb, once beautiful with the sublimest sculptures, but now fallen into as great decay as the house. At one end of that tomb, its curious roots displacing the time-stained blocks of Pentelic marble, grows an unnaturally large olive tree of oddly repellent shape; so like to some grotesque man, or death-distorted body of a man, that the country folk fear to pass it at night when the moon shines faintly through the crooked boughs. Mount Maenalus is a chosen haunt of dreaded Pan, whose queer companions are many, and simple swains believe that the tree must have some hideous kinship to these weird Panisci; but an old bee-keeper who lives in the neighbouring cottage told me a different story.

Many years ago, when the hillside villa was new and resplendent, there dwelt within it the two sculptors Kalos and Musides. From Lydia to Neapolis the beauty of their work was praised, and none

131

dared say that the one excelled the other in skill. The Hermes of Kalos stood in a marble shrine in Corinth, and the Pallas of Musides surmounted a pillar in Athens, near the Parthenon. All men paid homage to Kalos and Musides, and marvelled that no shadow of artistic jealousy cooled the warmth of their brotherly friendship.

But though Kalos and Musides dwelt in unbroken harmony, their natures were not alike. Whilst Musides revelled by night amidst the urban gaieties of Tegea, Kalos would remain at home; stealing away from the sight of his slaves into the cool recesses of the olive grove. There he would meditate upon the visions that filled his mind, and there devise the forms of beauty which later became immortal in breathing marble. Idle folk, indeed, said that Kalos conversed with the spirits of the grove, and that his statues were but images of the fauns and dryads he met there – for he patterned his work after no living model.

So famous were Kalos and Musides, that none wondered when the Tyrant of Syracuse sent to them deputies to speak of the costly statue of Tyché which he had planned for his city. Of great size and cunning workmanship must the statue be, for it was to form a wonder of nations and a goal of travellers. Exalted beyond thought would be he whose work should gain acceptance, and for this honour Kalos and Musides were invited to compete. Their brotherly love was well known, and the crafty Tyrant surmised that each, instead of concealing his work from the other, would offer aid and advice; this charity producing two images of unheard-of beauty, the lovelier of which would eclipse even the dreams of poets.

With joy the sculptors hailed the Tyrant's offer, so that in the days that followed their slaves heard the ceaseless blows of chisels. Not from each other did Kalos and Musides conceal their work, but the sight was for them alone. Saving theirs, no eyes beheld the two divine figures released by skilful blows from the rough blocks that had imprisoned them since the world began.

At night, as of yore, Musides sought the banquet halls of Tegea whilst Kalos wandered alone in the olive grove. But as time passed, men observed a want of gaiety in the once sparkling Musides. It was strange, they said amongst themselves, that depression should thus seize one with so great a chance to win art's loftiest reward. Many months passed, yet in the sour face of Musides came nothing of the sharp expectancy which the situation should arouse.

Then one day Musides spoke of the illness of Kalos, after which none marvelled again at his sadness, since the sculptors' attachment was known to be deep and sacred. Subsequently many went to visit Kalos, and indeed noticed the pallor of his face; but there was about him a happy serenity which made his glance more magical than the glance of Musides – who was clearly distracted with anxiety, and who pushed aside all the slaves in his eagerness to feed and wait upon his friend with his own hands. Hidden behind heavy curtains stood the two unfinished figures of Tyché, little touched of late by the sick man and his faithful attendant.

As Kalos grew inexplicably weaker and weaker despite the ministrations of puzzled physicians and of his assiduous friend, he desired to be carried often to the grove which he so loved. There he would ask to be left alone, as if wishing to speak with unseen things. Musides ever granted his requests, though his eyes filled with visible tears at the thought that Kalos should care more for the fauns and the dryads than for him. At last the end drew near, and Kalos discoursed of things beyond this life. Musides, weeping, promised him a sepulchre more lovely than the tomb of Mausolus; but Kalos bade him speak no more of marble glories. Only one wish now haunted the mind of the dying man; that twigs from certain olive trees in the grove be buried by his resting-place – close to his head. And one night, sitting alone in the darkness of the olive grove, Kalos died.

Beautiful beyond words was the marble sepulchre which stricken Musides carved for his beloved friend. None but Kalos himself could have fashioned such bas-reliefs, wherein were displayed all the splendours of Elysium. Nor did Musides fail to bury close to Kalos' head the olive twigs from the grove.

As the first violence of Musides' grief gave place to resignation, he laboured with diligence upon his figure of Tyché. All honour was now his, since the Tyrant of Syracuse would have the work of none save him or Kalos. His task proved a vent for his emotion, and he toiled more steadily each day, shunning the gaieties he once had relished. Meanwhile his evenings were spent beside the tomb of his friend, where a young olive tree had sprung up near the sleeper's head. So swift was the growth of this tree, and so strange was its form, that all who beheld it exclaimed in surprise; and Musides seemed at once fascinated and repelled.

Three years after the death of Kalos, Musides despatched a messenger to the Tyrant, and it was whispered in the agora at Tegea that the mighty statue was finished. By this time the tree by the tomb had attained amazing proportions, exceeding all other trees of its kind, and sending out a singularly heavy branch above the apartment in which Musides laboured. As many visitors came to view the prodigious tree, as to admire the art of the sculptor, so that Musides was seldom alone. But he did not mind his multitude of guests; indeed, he seemed to dread being alone now that his absorbing work was done. The bleak mountain wind, sighing through the olive grove and the tomb-tree, had an uncanny way of forming vaguely articulate sounds.

The sky was dark on the evening that the Tyrant's emissaries came to Tegea. It was definitely known that they had come to bear away the great image of Tyché and bring eternal honour to Musides, so their reception by the proxenoi was of great warmth. As the night wore on, a violent storm of wind broke over the crest of Maenalus, and the men from far Syracuse were glad that they rested snugly in the town. They talked of their illustrious Tyrant, and of the splendour of his capital; and exulted in the glory of the statue which Musides had wrought for him. And then the men of Tegea spoke of the goodness of Musides, and of his heavy grief for his friend; and how not even the coming laurels of art could console him in the absence of Kalos, who might have worn those laurels instead. Of the tree which grew by the tomb, near the head of Kalos, they also spoke. The wind shrieked more horribly, and both the Syracusans and the Arcadians prayed to Aiolos.

In the sunshine of the morning the proxenoi led the Tyrant's messengers up the slope to the abode of the sculptor, but the night-wind had done strange things. Slaves' cries ascended from a scene of desolation, and no more amidst the olive grove rose the gleaming colonnades of that vast hall wherein Musides had dreamed and toiled. Lone and shaken mourned the humble courts and the lower walls, for upon the sumptuous greater peristyle had fallen squarely the heavy overhanging bough of the strange new tree, reducing the stately poem in marble with odd completeness to a mound of unsightly ruins. Strangers and Tegeans stood aghast, looking from the wreckage to the great, sinister tree whose aspect was so weirdly human and whose roots reached so queerly into the sculptured sepulchre of Kalos. And their fear and dismay increased when they searched the fallen apartment; for of the gentle Musides, and of the marvellously fashioned image of Tyché, no trace could be discovered. Amidst such stupendous ruin only chaos dwelt, and the representatives of two cities left disappointed; Syracusans that they had no statue to bear home, Tegeans that they had no artist to crown. However, the Syracusans obtained after a while a very splendid statue in Athens, and the Tegeans consoled themselves by erecting in the agora a marble temple commemorating the gifts, virtues, and brotherly piety of Musides.

But the olive grove still stands, as does the tree growing out of the tomb of Kalos, and the old bee-keeper told me that sometimes the boughs whisper to one another in the night-wind, saying over and over again, '*Οιδα! Οιδα! – I know! I know!*'

THE TOMB

'Sedibus ut saltem placidis in morte quiescam.'
—*Virgil*

I N RELATING the circumstances which have led to my confinement within this refuge for the demented, I am aware that
my present position will create a natural doubt of the authenticity
of my narrative. It is an unfortunate fact that the bulk of humanity
is too limited in its mental vision to weigh with patience and
intelligence those isolated phenomena, seen and felt only by a
psychologically sensitive few, which lie outside its common experience. Men of broader intellect know that there is no sharp distinction betwixt the real and the unreal; that all things appear as
they do only by virtue of the delicate individual physical and
mental media through which we are made conscious of them; but
the prosaic materialism of the majority condemns as madness the
flashes of super-sight which penetrate the common veil of obvious
empiricism.

My name is Jervas Dudley, and from earliest childhood I have

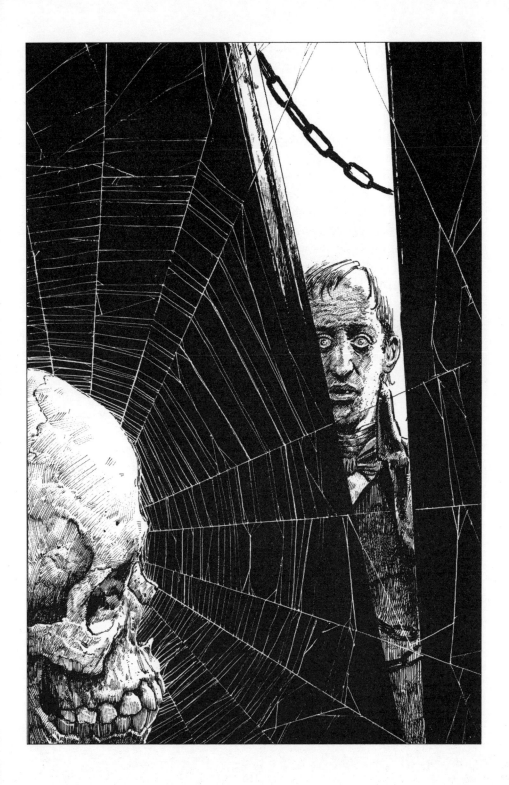

been a dreamer and a visionary. Wealthy beyond the necessity of a commercial life, and temperamentally unfitted for the formal studies and social recreations of my acquaintances, I have dwelt ever in realms apart from the visible world; spending my youth and adolescence in ancient and little-known books, and in roaming the fields and groves of the region near my ancestral home. I do not think that what I read in these books or saw in these fields and groves was exactly what other boys read and saw there; but of this I must say little, since detailed speech would but confirm those cruel slanders upon my intellect which I sometimes overhear from the whispers of the stealthy attendants around me. It is sufficient for me to relate events without analysing causes.

I have said that I dwelt apart from the visible world, but I have not said that I dwelt alone. This no human creature may do; for lacking the fellowship of the living, he inevitably draws upon the companionship of things that are not, or are no longer, living. Close by my home there lies a singular wooded hollow, in whose twilight deeps I spent most of my time; reading, thinking, and dreaming. Down its moss-covered slopes my first steps of infancy were taken, and around its grotesquely gnarled oak trees my first fancies of boyhood were woven. Well did I come to know the presiding dryads of those trees, and often have I watched their wild dances in the struggling beams of a waning moon – but of these things I must not now speak. I will tell only of the lone tomb in the darkest of the hillside thickets; the deserted tomb of the Hydes, an old and exalted family whose last direct descendant had been laid within its black recesses many decades before my birth.

The vault to which I refer is of ancient granite, weathered and discoloured by the mists and dampness of generations. Excavated back into the hillside, the structure is visible only at the entrance. The door, a ponderous and forbidding slab of stone, hangs upon rusted iron hinges, and is fastened *ajar* in a queerly sinister way by means of heavy iron chains and padlocks, according to a gruesome fashion of half a century ago. The abode of the race whose scions are here inurned had once crowned the declivity which holds the tomb, but had long since fallen victim to the flames which sprang up from a disastrous stroke of lightning. Of the midnight storm which destroyed this gloomy mansion, the older inhabitants of the region sometimes speak in hushed and uneasy voices; alluding to what they call 'divine wrath' in a manner that in later years vaguely increased the always strong fascination which I felt for the forest-darkened sepulchre. One man only had perished in the fire. When the last of the Hydes was buried in this place of shade and stillness, the sad urnful of ashes had come from a distant land; to which the family had repaired when the mansion burned down. No one remains to lay flowers before the granite portal, and few care to brave the depressing shadows which seem to linger strangely about the water-worn stones.

I shall never forget the afternoon when first I stumbled upon the half-hidden house of death. It was in mid-summer, when the alchemy of Nature transmutes the sylvan landscape to one vivid and almost homogeneous mass of green; when the senses are well-nigh intoxicated with the surging seas of moist verdure and the subtly indefinable odours of the soil and the vegetation. In such surroundings the mind loses its perspective; time and space become trivial and unreal, and echoes of a forgotten prehistoric past beat insistently upon the enthralled consciousness. All day I had been wandering through the mystic groves of the hollow; thinking thoughts I need not discuss, and conversing with things I need not name. In years a child of ten, I had seen and heard many wonders unknown to the throng; and was oddly aged in certain respects. When, upon forcing my way between two savage clumps of briers, I suddenly encountered the entrance of the vault, I had no knowledge of what I had discovered. The dark blocks of granite, the door so curiously ajar, and the funereal carvings above the arch, aroused in me no associations of mournful or terrible character. Of graves and tombs I knew and imagined much, but had on account of my peculiar temperament been kept from all personal contact with churchyards and cemeteries. The strange stone house on the woodland slope was to me only a source of interest and speculation; and its cold, damp interior, into which I vainly peered through the aperture so tantalisingly left, contained for me no hint of death or decay. But in that instant of curiosity was born the madly unreasoning desire which has brought me to this hell of confinement. Spurred on by a voice which must have come from the hideous soul of the forest, I resolved to enter the beckoning gloom in spite of the ponderous chains which barred my passage. In the waning light of day I alternately rattled the rusty impediments with a view to throwing wide the stone door, and essayed to squeeze my slight form through the space already provided; but neither plan met with success. At first curious, I was now frantic; and when in the thickening twilight I returned to my home, I had sworn to the hundred gods of the grove that *at any cost* I would some day force an entrance to the black, chilly depths that seemed calling out to me. The physician with the iron-grey beard who comes each day to my room once told a visitor that this decision marked the beginning of a pitiful monomania; but I will leave final judgement to my readers when they shall have learnt all.

The months following my discovery were spent in futile attempts to force the complicated padlock of the slightly open vault, and in carefully guarded inquiries regarding the nature and history of the structure. With the traditionally receptive ears of the small boy, I learned much; though an habitual secretiveness caused me to tell no one of my information or my resolve. It is perhaps worth mentioning that I was not at all surprised or terrified on learning of the nature of the vault. My rather original ideas regarding life and death had caused me to associate the cold clay with the breathing body in a vague fashion; and I felt that the great and sinister family of the burned-down mansion was in some way represented within the stone space I sought to explore. Mumbled tales of the weird rites and godless revels of bygone years in the ancient hall gave to me a new and potent interest in the tomb, before whose door I would sit for hours at a time each day. Once I thrust a candle within the nearly closed entrance, but could see nothing save a flight of damp stone steps leading downward. The odour of the place repelled yet bewitched me. I felt I had known it before, in a past remote beyond all recollection; beyond even my tenancy of the body I now possess.

The year after I first beheld the tomb, I stumbled upon a worm-eaten translation of Plutarch's *Lives* in the book-filled attic of my home. Reading the life of Theseus, I was much impressed by that passage telling of the great stone beneath which the boyish hero was to find his tokens of destiny whenever he should become old enough to lift its enormous weight. This legend had the effect of dispelling my keenest impatience to enter the vault, for it made me feel that the time was not yet ripe. Later, I told myself, I should grow to a strength and ingenuity which might enable me to unfasten the heavily chained door with ease; but until then I would do better by conforming to what seemed the will of Fate.

Accordingly my watches by the dank portal became less persistent, and much of my time was spent in other though equally strange pursuits. I would sometimes rise very quietly in the night, stealing out to walk in those churchyards and places of burial from which I had been kept by my parents. What I did there I may not say, for I am not now sure of the reality of certain things; but I know that on the day after such a nocturnal ramble I would often astonish those about me with my knowledge of topics almost forgotten for many generations. It was after a night like this that I shocked the community with a queer conceit about the burial of the rich and celebrated Squire Brewster, a maker of local history who was interred in 1711, and whose slate headstone, bearing a graven skull and crossbones, was slowly crumbling to powder. In a moment of childish imagination I vowed not only that the undertaker, Goodman Simpson, had stolen the silver-buckled shoes, silken hose, and satin small-clothes of the deceased before burial; but that the Squire himself, not fully inanimate, had turned twice in his mound-covered coffin on the day after interment.

But the idea of entering the tomb never left my thoughts; being indeed stimulated by the unexpected genealogical discovery that my own maternal ancestry possessed at least a slight link with the supposedly extinct family of the Hydes. Last of my paternal race, I was likewise the last of this older and more mysterious line. I began to feel that the tomb was *mine*, and to look forward with hot eagerness to the time when I might pass within that stone door and down those slimy stone steps in the dark. I now formed the habit of *listening* very intently at the slightly open portal, choosing my favourite hours of midnight stillness for the odd vigil. By the time I came of age, I had made a small clearing in the thicket before the mould-stained façade of the hillside, allowing the surrounding vegetation to encircle and overhang the space like the walls and roof of a sylvan bower. This bower was my temple, the fastened door my shrine, and here I would lie outstretched on the mossy ground, thinking strange thoughts and dreaming strange dreams.

The night of the first revelation was a sultry one. I must have fallen asleep from fatigue, for it was with a distinct sense of awakening that I heard the *voices*. Of those tones and accents I hesitate

ELDRITCH TALES

to speak; of their *quality* I will not speak; but I may say that they presented certain uncanny differences in vocabulary, pronunciation, and mode of utterance. Every shade of New England dialect, from the uncouth syllables of the Puritan colonists to the precise rhetoric of fifty years ago, seemed represented in that shadowy colloquy, though it was only later that I noticed the fact. At the time, indeed, my attention was distracted from this matter by another phenomenon; a phenomenon so fleeting that I could not take oath upon its reality. I barely fancied that as I awoke, a *light* had been hurriedly extinguished within the sunken sepulchre. I do not think I was either astounded or panic-stricken, but I know that I was greatly and permanently *changed* that night. Upon returning home I went with much directness to a rotting chest in the attic, wherein I found the key which next day unlocked with ease the barrier I had so long stormed in vain.

It was in the soft glow of late afternoon that I first entered the vault on the abandoned slope. A spell was upon me, and my heart leaped with an exultation I can but ill describe. As I closed the door behind me and descended the dripping steps by the light of my lone candle, I seemed to know the way; and though the candle sputtered with the stifling reek of the place, I felt singularly at home in the musty, charnel-house air. Looking about me, I beheld many marble slabs bearing coffins, or the remains of coffins. Some of these were sealed and intact, but others had nearly vanished, leaving the silver handles and plates isolated amidst certain curious heaps of whitish dust. Upon one plate I read the name of Sir Geoffrey Hyde, who had come from Sussex in 1640 and died here a few years later. In a conspicuous alcove was one fairly well-preserved and untenanted casket, adorned with a single name which brought to me both a smile and a shudder. An odd impulse caused me to climb upon the broad slab, extinguish my candle, and lie down within the vacant box.

In the grey light of dawn I staggered from the vault and locked the chain of the door behind me. I was no longer a young man, though but twenty-one winters had chilled my bodily frame. Early-rising villagers who observed my homeward progress looked at me strangely, and marvelled at the signs of ribald revelry which they saw in one whose life was known to be sober and solitary. I did not appear before my parents till after a long and refreshing sleep.

Henceforward I haunted the tomb each night; seeing, hearing, and doing things I must never reveal. My speech, always susceptible to environmental influences, was the first thing to succumb to the change; and my suddenly acquired archaism of diction was soon remarked upon. Later a queer boldness and recklessness came into my demeanour, till I unconsciously grew to possess the bearing of a man of the world despite my lifelong seclusion. My formerly silent tongue waxed voluble with the easy grace of a Chesterfield or the godless cynicism of a Rochester. I displayed a peculiar erudition utterly unlike the fantastic, monkish lore over which I had pored in youth; and covered the flyleaves of my books with facile impromptu epigrams which brought up suggestions of Gay, Prior, and the sprightliest of the Augustan wits and rimesters. One morning at breakfast I came close to disaster by declaiming in palpably liquor-ish accents an effusion of eighteenth-century Bacchanalian mirth; a bit of Georgian playfulness never recorded in a book, which ran something like this:

> Come hither, my lads, with your tankards of ale,
> And drink to the present before it shall fail;
> Pile each on your platter a mountain of beef,
> For 'tis eating and drinking that bring us relief:
>> So fill up your glass,
>> For life will soon pass;
> When you're dead ye'll ne'er drink to your king or your lass!

> Anacreon had a red nose, so they say;
> But what's a red nose if ye're happy and gay?
> Gad split me! I'd rather be red whilst I'm here,
> Than white as a lily – and dead half a year!
>> So Betty, my miss,
>> Come give me a kiss;
> In hell there's no innkeeper's daughter like this!

> Young Harry, propp'd up just as straight as he's able,
> Will soon lose his wig and slip under the table;
> But fill up your goblets and pass 'em around—
> Better under the table than under the ground!
>> So revel and chaff

As ye thirstily quaff:
Under six feet of dirt 'tis less easy to laugh!

The fiend strike me blue! I'm scarce able to walk,
And damn me if I can stand upright or talk!
Here, landlord, bid Betty to summon a chair;
I'll try home for a while, for my wife is not there!
  So lend me a hand;
  I'm not able to stand,
But I'm gay whilst I linger on top of the land!

About this time I conceived my present fear of fire and thunder-storms. Previously indifferent to such things, I had now an unspeak-able horror of them; and would retire to the innermost recesses of the house whenever the heavens threatened an electrical display. A favourite haunt of mine during the day was the ruined cellar of the mansion that had burned down, and in fancy I would picture the structure as it had been in its prime. On one occasion I startled a villager by leading him confidently to a shallow sub-cellar, of whose existence I seemed to know in spite of the fact that it had been unseen and forgotten for many generations.

At last came that which I had long feared. My parents, alarmed at the altered manner and appearance of their only son, commenced to exert over my movements a kindly espionage which threatened to result in disaster. I had told no one of my visits to the tomb, having guarded my secret purpose with religious zeal since childhood; but now I was forced to exercise care in threading the mazes of the wooded hollow, that I might throw off a possible pursuer. My key to the vault I kept suspended from a cord about my neck, its presence known only to me. I never carried out of the sepulchre any of the things I came upon whilst within its walls.

One morning as I emerged from the damp tomb and fastened the chain of the portal with none too steady hand, I beheld in an adjacent thicket the dreaded face of a watcher. Surely the end was near; for my bower was discovered, and the objective of my nocturnal journeys revealed. The man did not accost me, so I hastened home in an effort to overhear what he might report to my careworn father. Were my sojourns beyond the chained door about to be proclaimed to the world? Imagine my delighted astonishment on hearing the spy inform my parent in a cautious whisper *that I had spent the night in the bower outside the tomb;* my sleep-filmed eyes fixed upon the crevice where the padlocked portal stood ajar! By what miracle had the watcher been thus deluded? I was now convinced that a supernatural agency protected me. Made bold by this heaven-sent circumstance, I began to resume perfect openness in going to the vault; confident that no one could witness my entrance. For a week I tasted to the full the joys of that charnel conviviality which I must not describe, when the *thing* happened, and I was borne away to this accursed abode of sorrow and monotony.

I should not have ventured out that night; for the taint of thunder was in the clouds, and a hellish phosphorescence rose from the rank swamp at the bottom of the hollow. The call of the dead, too, was different. Instead of the hillside tomb, it was the charred cellar on the crest of the slope whose presiding daemon beckoned to me with unseen fingers. As I emerged from an intervening grove upon the plain before the ruin, I beheld in the misty moonlight a thing I had always vaguely expected. The mansion, gone for a century, once more reared its stately height to the raptured vision; every window ablaze with the splendour of many candles. Up the long drive rolled the coaches of the Boston gentry, whilst on foot came a numerous assemblage of powdered exquisites from the neighbouring mansions. With this throng I mingled, though I knew I belonged with the hosts rather than with the guests. Inside the hall were music, laughter, and wine on every hand. Several faces I recognised; though I should have known them better had they been shrivelled or eaten away by death and decomposition. Amidst a wild and reckless throng I was the wildest and most abandoned. Gay blasphemy poured in torrents from my lips, and in my shocking sallies I heeded no law of God, Man, or Nature. Suddenly a peal of thunder, resonant even above the din of the swinish revelry, clave the very roof and laid a hush of fear upon the boisterous company. Red tongues of flame and searing gusts of heat engulfed the house; and the roysterers, struck with terror at the descent of a calamity which seemed to transcend the bounds of unguided Nature, fled shrieking into the night. I alone remained, riveted to my seat by a grovelling fear which I had never felt before. And then a second horror took possession of my soul. Burnt alive to ashes, my body dispersed by the four winds, *I might never lie in the tomb of the Hydes!* Was not my coffin prepared for me? Had I not a right to rest till eternity amongst the descendants of Sir Geoffrey Hyde? Aye! I would claim my heritage of death, even though my soul go seeking through the ages for another corporeal tenement to represent it on that vacant slab in the alcove of the vault. *Jervas Hyde* should never share the sad fate of Palinurus!

As the phantom of the burning house faded, I found myself screaming and struggling madly in the arms of two men, one of whom was the spy who had followed me to the tomb. Rain was pouring down in torrents, and upon the southern horizon were flashes of the lightning that had so lately passed over our heads. My father, his face lined with sorrow, stood by as I shouted my demands to be laid within the tomb; frequently admonishing my captors to treat me as gently as they could. A blackened circle on the floor of the ruined cellar told of a violent stroke from the heavens; and from this spot a group of curious villagers with lanterns were prying a small box of antique workmanship which the thunderbolt had brought to light. Ceasing my futile and now objectless writhing, I watched the spectators as they viewed the treasure-trove, and was permitted to share in their discoveries. The box, whose fastenings were broken by the stroke which had unearthed it, contained many papers and objects of value; but I had eyes for one thing alone. It was the porcelain miniature of a young man in a smartly curled bag-wig, and bore the initials 'J. H.' The face was such that as I gazed, I might well have been studying my mirror.

On the following day I was brought to this room with the barred windows, but I have been kept informed of certain things through an aged and simple-minded servitor, for whom I bore a fondness in infancy, and who like me loves the churchyard. What I have dared relate of my experiences within the vault has brought me only pitying smiles. My father, who visits me frequently, declares that at no time did I pass the chained portal, and swears that the rusted padlock had not been touched for fifty years when he examined it. He even says that all the village knew of my journeys to the tomb, and that I was often watched as I slept in the bower outside the grim façade, my half-open eyes fixed on the crevice that leads to the interior. Against these assertions I have no tangible proof to offer, since my key to the padlock was lost in the struggle on that night of horrors. The strange things of the past which I learnt during those nocturnal meetings with the dead he dismisses as the fruits of my lifelong and omnivorous browsing amongst the ancient volumes of the family library. Had it not been for my old servant Hiram, I should have by this time become quite convinced of my madness.

But Hiram, loyal to the last, has held faith in me, and has done that which impels me to make public at least a part of my story. A week ago he burst open the lock which chains the door of the tomb perpetually ajar, and descended with a lantern into the murky depths. On a slab in an alcove he found an old but empty coffin whose tarnished plate bears the single word '*Jervas*'. In that coffin and in that vault they have promised me I shall be buried.

CELEPHAÏS

IN A DREAM Kuranes saw the city in the valley, and the sea-coast beyond, and the snowy peak overlooking the sea, and the gaily painted galleys that sail out of the harbour toward the distant regions where the sea meets the sky. In a dream it was also that he came by his name of Kuranes, for when awake he was called by another name. Perhaps it was natural for him to dream a new name; for he was the last of his family, and alone among the indifferent millions of London, so there were not many to speak to him and remind him who he had been. His money and lands were gone, and he did not care for the ways of people about him, but preferred to dream and write of his dreams. What he wrote was laughed at by those to whom he shewed it, so that after a time he kept his writings to himself, and finally ceased to write. The more he withdrew from the world about him, the more wonderful became his dreams; and it would have been quite futile to try to describe them on paper. Kuranes was not modern, and did not think like others who wrote. Whilst they strove to strip from life its embroidered robes of myth, and to shew in naked ugliness the foul thing that is reality, Kuranes sought for beauty alone. When truth and experience failed to reveal it, he sought it in fancy and illusion, and found it on his very doorstep, amid the nebulous memories of childhood tales and dreams.

There are not many persons who know what wonders are opened to them in the stories and visions of their youth; for when as children we listen and dream, we think but half-formed thoughts, and when as men we try to remember, we are dulled and prosaic with the poison of life. But some of us awake in the night with strange phantasms of enchanted hills and gardens, of fountains that sing in the sun, of golden cliffs overhanging murmuring seas, of plains that stretch down to sleeping cities of bronze and stone, and of shadowy companies of heroes that ride caparisoned white horses along the edges of thick forests; and then we know that we have looked back through the ivory gates into that world of wonder which was ours before we were wise and unhappy.

Kuranes came very suddenly upon his old world of childhood. He had been dreaming of the house where he was born; the great stone house covered with ivy, where thirteen generations of his ancestors had lived, and where he had hoped to die. It was moonlight, and he had stolen out into the fragrant summer night, through the gardens, down the terraces, past the great oaks of the park, and along the long white road to the village. The village seemed very old, eaten away at the edge like the moon which had commenced to wane, and Kuranes wondered whether the peaked roofs of the small houses hid sleep or death. In the streets were spears of long grass, and the window-panes on either side were either broken or filmily staring. Kuranes had not lingered, but had plodded on as though summoned toward some goal. He dared not disobey the summons for fear it might prove an illusion like the urges and aspirations of waking life, which do not lead to any goal. Then he had been drawn down a lane that led off from the village street toward the channel cliffs, and had come to the end of things – to the precipice and the abyss where all the village and all the world fell abruptly into the unechoing emptiness of infinity, and where even the sky ahead was empty and unlit by the crumbling moon and the peering stars. Faith had urged him on, over the precipice and into the gulf, where he had floated down, down, down; past dark, shapeless, undreamed dreams, faintly glowing spheres that may have been partly dreamed dreams, and laughing winged things that seemed to mock the dreamers of all the worlds. Then a rift seemed to open in the darkness before him, and he saw the city of the valley, glistening radiantly far, far below, with a background of sea and sky, and a snow-capped mountain near the shore.

Kuranes had awaked the very moment he beheld the city, yet he knew from his brief glance that it was none other than Celephaïs, in the Valley of Ooth-Nargai beyond the Tanarian Hills, where his spirit had dwelt all the eternity of an hour one summer afternoon very long ago, when he had slipt away from his nurse and let the warm sea-breeze lull him to sleep as he watched the clouds from the cliff near the village. He had protested then, when they had found him, waked him, and carried him home, for just as he was aroused he had been about to sail in a golden galley for those alluring regions where the sea meets the sky. And now he was equally resentful of awaking, for he had found his fabulous city after forty weary years.

But three nights afterward Kuranes came again to Celephaïs. As before, he dreamed first of the village that was asleep or dead, and of the abyss down which one must float silently; then the rift appeared again, and he beheld the glittering minarets of the city, and saw the graceful galleys riding at anchor in the blue harbour, and watched the gingko trees of Mount Aran swaying in the sea-breeze. But this time he was not snatched away, and like a winged being settled gradually over a grassy hillside till finally his feet rested gently on the turf. He had indeed come back to the Valley of Ooth-Nargai and the splendid city of Celephaïs.

Down the hill amid scented grasses and brilliant flowers walked Kuranes, over the bubbling Naraxa on the small wooden bridge where he had carved his name so many years ago, and through the whispering grove to the great stone bridge by the city gate. All was as of old, nor were the marble walls discoloured, nor the polished bronze statues upon them tarnished. And Kuranes saw that he need not tremble lest the things he knew be vanished; for even the sentries on the ramparts were the same, and still as young as he remembered them. When he entered the city, past the bronze gates and over the onyx pavements, the merchants and camel-drivers greeted him as if he had never been away; and it was the same at the turquoise temple of Nath-Horthath, where the orchid-wreathed priests told him that there is no time in Ooth-Nargai, but only perpetual youth. Then Kuranes walked through the Street of Pillars to the seaward wall, where gathered the traders and sailors, and strange men from the regions where the sea meets the sky. There he stayed long, gazing out over the bright harbour where the ripples sparkled beneath an unknown sun, and where rode lightly the galleys from far places over the water. And he gazed also upon Mount Aran rising regally from the shore, its lower slopes green with swaying trees and its white summit touching the sky.

More than ever Kuranes wished to sail in a galley to the far places of which he had heard so many strange tales, and he sought again the captain who had agreed to carry him so long ago. He found the man, Athib, sitting on the same chest of spices he had sat upon before, and Athib seemed not to realise that any time had passed. Then the two rowed to a galley in the harbour, and giving orders to the oarsmen, commenced to sail out into the billowy Cerenerian Sea that leads to the sky. For several days they glided undulatingly over the water, till finally they came to the horizon, where the sea meets the sky. Here the galley paused not at all, but floated easily in the blue of the sky among fleecy clouds tinted with rose. And far beneath the keel Kuranes could see strange lands and rivers and cities of surpassing beauty, spread indolently in the sunshine which seemed never to lessen or disappear. At length Athib told him that their journey was near its end, and that they would soon enter the harbour of Serannian, the pink marble city of the clouds, which is built on that ethereal coast where the west wind flows into the sky; but as the highest of the city's carven towers came into sight there was a sound somewhere in space, and Kuranes awaked in his London garret.

For many months after that Kuranes sought the marvellous city of Celephaïs and its sky-bound galleys in vain; and though his dreams carried him to many gorgeous and unheard-of places, no one whom he met could tell him how to find Ooth-Nargai, beyond the Tanarian Hills. One night he went flying over dark mountains where there were faint, lone campfires at great distances apart, and strange, shaggy herds with tinkling bells on the leaders; and in the wildest part of this hilly country, so remote that few men could ever have seen it, he found a hideously ancient wall or causeway of stone zigzagging along the ridges and valleys; too gigantic ever to have risen by human hands, and of such a length that neither end of it could be seen. Beyond that wall in the grey dawn he came to a land of quaint gardens and cherry trees, and when the sun rose he beheld such beauty of red and white flowers, green foliage and lawns, white paths, diamond brooks, blue lakelets, carven bridges, and red-roofed pagodas, that he for a moment forgot Celephaïs in sheer delight. But he remembered it again when he walked down a white path toward a red-roofed pagoda, and would have questioned the people of that land about it, had he not found that there were no people there, but only birds and bees and butterflies. On another night Kuranes walked up a damp stone spiral stairway endlessly, and came to a tower window overlooking a mighty plain and river lit by the full moon; and in the silent city that spread away from the river-bank he thought he beheld some feature or arrangement which he had known before. He would have descended and asked the way to Ooth-Nargai had not a fearsome aurora sputtered up from some remote place beyond the horizon, shewing the ruin and antiquity of the city, and the stagnation of the reedy river, and the death lying upon that land, as it had lain since King Kynaratholis came home from his conquests to find the vengeance of the gods.

So Kuranes sought fruitlessly for the marvellous city of Cele-phaïs and its galleys that sail to Serannian in the sky, meanwhile seeing many wonders and once barely escaping from the high-priest not to be described, which wears a yellow silken mask over its face and dwells all alone in a prehistoric stone monastery on the cold desert plateau of Leng. In time he grew so impatient of the bleak intervals of day that he began buying drugs in order to increase his periods of sleep. Hasheesh helped a great deal, and once sent him to a part of space where form does not exist, but where glowing gases study the secrets of existence. And a violet-coloured gas told him that this part of space was outside what he had called infinity. The gas had not heard of planets and organisms before, but identified Kuranes merely as one from the infinity where matter, energy, and gravitation exist. Kuranes was now very anxious to return to minaret-studded Celephaïs, and increased his doses of drugs; but eventually he had no more money left, and could buy no drugs. Then one summer day he was turned out of his garret, and wandered aimlessly through the streets, drifting over a bridge to a place where the houses grew thinner and thinner. And it was there that fulfilment came, and he met the cortege of knights come from Celephaïs to bear him thither forever.

Handsome knights they were, astride roan horses and clad in shining armour with tabards of cloth-of-gold curiously emblazoned. So numerous were they, that Kuranes almost mistook them for an army, but their leader told him they were sent in his honour; since it was he who had created Ooth-Nargai in his dreams, on which account he was now to be appointed its chief god for evermore. Then they gave Kuranes a horse and placed him at the head of the cavalcade, and all rode majestically through the downs of Surrey and onward toward the region where Kuranes and his ancestors were born. It was very strange, but as the riders went on they seemed to gallop back through Time; for whenever they passed through a village in the twilight they saw only such houses and villages as Chaucer or men before him might have seen, and sometimes they saw knights on horseback with small companies of retainers. When it grew dark they travelled more swiftly, till soon they were flying uncannily as if in the air. In the dim dawn they came upon the village which Kuranes had seen alive in his childhood, and asleep or dead in his dreams. It was alive now, and early villagers curtsied as the horsemen clattered down the street and turned off into the lane that ends in the abyss of dream. Kuranes had previously entered that abyss only at night, and wondered what it would look like by day; so he watched anxiously as the column approached its brink. Just as they galloped up the rising ground to the precipice a golden glare came somewhere out of the east and hid all the landscape in its effulgent draperies. The abyss was now a seething chaos of roseate and cerulean splendour, and invisible voices sang exultantly as the knightly entourage plunged over the edge and floated gracefully down past glittering clouds and silvery coruscations. Endlessly down the horsemen floated, their chargers pawing the aether as if galloping over golden sands; and then the luminous vapours spread apart to reveal a greater brightness, the brightness of the city Celephaïs, and the sea-coast beyond, and the snowy peak overlooking the sea, and the gaily painted galleys that sail out of the harbour toward distant regions where the sea meets the sky.

And Kuranes reigned thereafter over Ooth-Nargai and all the neighbouring regions of dream, and held his court alternately in

Celephaïs and in the cloud-fashioned Serannian. He reigns there still, and will reign happily forever, though below the cliffs at Innsmouth the channel tides played mockingly with the body of a tramp who had stumbled through the half-deserted village at dawn; played mockingly, and cast it upon the rocks by ivy-covered Trevor Towers, where a notably fat and especially offensive millionaire brewer enjoys the purchased atmosphere of extinct nobility.

HYPNOS

To S.L.

'Apropos of sleep, that sinister adventure of all our nights, we may say that men go to bed daily with an audacity that would be incomprehensible if we did not know that it is the result of ignorance of the danger.'

—*Baudelaire*

MAY THE MERCIFUL GODS, if indeed there be such, guard those hours when no power of the will, or drug that the cunning of man devises, can keep me from the chasm of sleep. Death is merciful, for there is no return therefrom, but with him who has come back out of the nethermost chambers of night, haggard and knowing, peace rests nevermore. Fool that I was to plunge with such unsanctioned phrensy into mysteries no man was meant to penetrate; fool or god that he was – my only friend, who led me and went before me, and who in the end passed into terrors which may yet be mine.

We met, I recall, in a railway station, where he was the centre of a crowd of the vulgarly curious. He was unconscious, having fallen in a kind of convulsion which imparted to his slight black-clad body a strange rigidity. I think he was then approaching forty years of age, for there were deep lines in the face, wan and hollow-cheeked, but oval and actually beautiful; and touches of grey in the thick, waving hair and small full beard which had once been of the deepest raven black. His brow was white as the marble of Pentelicus, and of a height and breadth almost godlike. I said to myself, with all the ardour of a sculptor, that this man was a faun's statue out of antique Hellas, dug from a temple's ruins and brought somehow to life in our stifling age only to feel the chill and pressure of dev-astating years. And when he opened his immense, sunken, and wildly luminous black eyes I knew he would be thenceforth my only friend – the only friend of one who had never possessed a friend before – for I saw that such eyes must have looked fully upon the grandeur and the terror of realms beyond normal consciousness and reality; realms which I had cherished in fancy, but vainly sought. So as I drove the crowd away I told him he must come home with me and be my teacher and leader in unfathomed mysteries, and he assented without speaking a word. Afterward I found that his voice was music – the music of deep viols and of crystalline spheres. We talked often in the night, and in the day, when I chiselled busts of him and carved miniature heads in ivory to immortalise his differ-ent expressions.

Of our studies it is impossible to speak, since they held so slight a connection with anything of the world as living men conceive it. They were of that vaster and more appalling universe of dim entity and consciousness which lies deeper than matter, time, and space, and whose existence we suspect only in certain forms of sleep – those rare dreams beyond dreams which come never to common men, and but once or twice in the lifetime of imaginative men. The cosmos of our waking knowledge, born from such an universe as a bubble is born from the pipe of a jester, touches it only as such a bubble may touch its sardonic source when sucked back by the jester's whim. Men of learning suspect it little, and ignore it mostly. Wise men have interpreted dreams, and the gods have laughed. One man with Oriental eyes has said that all time and space are relative, and men have laughed. But even that man with Oriental eyes has done no more than suspect. I had wished and tried to do more than suspect, and my friend had tried and partly succeeded.

Then we both tried together, and with exotic drugs courted terrible and forbidden dreams in the tower studio chamber of the old manor-house in hoary Kent.

Among the agonies of these after days is that chief of torments – inarticulateness. What I learned and saw in those hours of impious exploration can never be told – for want of symbols or suggestions in any language. I say this because from first to last our discoveries partook only of the nature of sensations; sensations correlated with no impression which the nervous system of normal humanity is capable of receiving. They were sensations, yet within them lay unbelievable elements of time and space – things which at bottom possess no distinct and definite existence. Human utterance can best convey the general character of our experiences by calling them plungings or soarings; for in every period of revelation some part of our minds broke boldly away from all that is real and present, rushing aërially along shocking, unlighted, and fear-haunted abysses, and occasionally tearing through certain well-marked and typical obstacles describable only as viscous, uncouth clouds or vapours. In these black and bodiless flights we were sometimes alone and sometimes together. When we were together, my friend was always far ahead; I could comprehend his presence despite the absence of form by a species of pictorial memory whereby his face appeared to me, golden from a strange light and frightful with its weird beauty, its anomalously youthful cheeks, its burning eyes, its Olympian brow, and its shadowing hair and growth of beard.

Of the progress of time we kept no record, for time had become to us the merest illusion. I know only that there must have been something very singular involved, since we came at length to marvel why we did not grow old. Our discourse was unholy, and always hideously ambitious – no god or daemon could have aspired to discoveries and conquests like those which we planned in whispers. I shiver as I speak of them, and dare not be explicit; though I will say that my friend once wrote on paper a wish which he dared not utter with his tongue, and which made me burn the paper and look affrightedly out of the window at the spangled night sky. I will hint – only hint – that he had designs which involved the rulership of the visible universe and more; designs whereby the earth and the stars would move at his command, and the destinies of all living things be his. I affirm – I swear – that I had no share in these extreme aspirations. Anything my friend may have said or written to the contrary must be erroneous, for I am no man of strength to risk the unmentionable warfare in unmentionable spheres by which alone one might achieve success.

There was a night when winds from unknown spaces whirled us irresistibly into limitless vacua beyond all thought and entity. Perceptions of the most maddeningly untransmissible sort thronged upon us; perceptions of infinity which at the time convulsed us with joy, yet which are now partly lost to my memory and partly incapable of presentation to others. Viscous obstacles were clawed through in rapid succession, and at length I felt that we had been borne to realms of greater remoteness than any we had previously known. My friend was vastly in advance as we plunged into this awesome ocean of virgin aether, and I could see the sinister exultation on his floating, luminous, too youthful memory-face. Suddenly that face became dim and quickly disappeared, and in a brief space I found myself projected against an obstacle which I could not penetrate. It was like the others, yet incalculably denser; a sticky, clammy mass, if such terms can be applied to analogous qualities in a non-material sphere.

I had, I felt, been halted by a barrier which my friend and leader had successfully passed. Struggling anew, I came to the end of the drug-dream and opened my physical eyes to the tower studio in whose opposite corner reclined the pallid and still unconscious form of my fellow-dreamer, weirdly haggard and wildly beautiful as the moon shed gold-green light on his marble features. Then, after a short interval, the form in the corner stirred; and may pitying heaven keep from my sight and sound another thing like that which took place before me. I cannot tell you how he shrieked, or what vistas of unvisitable hells gleamed for a second in black eyes crazed with fright. I can only say that I fainted, and did not stir till he himself recovered and shook me in his phrensy for someone to keep away the horror and desolation.

That was the end of our voluntary searchings in the caverns of dream. Awed, shaken, and portentous, my friend who had been beyond the barrier warned me that we must never venture within those realms again. What he had seen, he dared not tell me; but he said from his wisdom that we must sleep as little as possible, even if drugs were necessary to keep us awake. That he was right, I soon learned from the unutterable fear which engulfed me whenever consciousness lapsed. After each short and inevitable sleep I seemed older, whilst my friend aged with a rapidity almost shocking. It is hideous to see wrinkles form and hair whiten almost before one's eyes. Our mode of life was now totally altered. Heretofore a recluse so far as I know – his true name and origin never having passed his lips – my friend now became frantic in his fear of solitude. At night he would not be alone, nor would the company of a few persons calm him. His sole relief was obtained in revelry of the most general and boisterous sort; so that few assemblies of the young and the gay were unknown to us. Our appearance and age seemed to excite in most cases a ridicule which I keenly resented, but which my friend considered a lesser evil than solitude. Especially was he afraid to be out of doors alone when the stars were shining, and if forced to this condition he would often glance furtively at the sky as if hunted by some monstrous thing therein. He did not always glance at the same place in the sky – it seemed to be a different place at different times. On spring evenings it would be low in the northeast. In the summer it would be nearly overhead. In the autumn it would be in the northwest. In winter it would be in the east, but mostly if in the small hours of morning. Midwinter evenings seemed least dreadful to him. Only after two years did I connect this fear with anything in particular; but then I began to see that he must be looking at a special spot on the celestial vault whose position at different times corresponded to the direction of his glance – a spot roughly marked by the constellation Corona Borealis.

We now had a studio in London, never separating, but never discussing the days when we had sought to plumb the mysteries of the unreal world. We were aged and weak from our drugs, dissipations, and nervous overstrain, and the thinning hair and beard of my friend had become snow-white. Our freedom from long sleep was surprising, for seldom did we succumb more than an hour or two at a time to the shadow which had now grown so frightful a menace. Then came one January of fog and rain, when money ran low and drugs were hard to buy. My statues and ivory heads were all sold, and I had no means to purchase new materials, or energy to fashion them even had I possessed them. We suffered terribly, and on a certain night my friend sank into a deep-breathing sleep from which I could not awaken him. I can recall the scene now – the desolate, pitch-black garret studio under the eaves with the rain beating down; the ticking of the lone clock; the fancied ticking of our watches as they rested on the dressing-table; the creaking of some swaying shutter in a remote part of the house; certain distant city noises muffled by fog and space; and worst of all the deep, steady, sinister breathing of my friend on the couch – a rhythmical breathing which seemed to measure moments of supernal fear and agony for his spirit as it wandered in spheres forbidden, unimagined, and hideously remote.

The tension of my vigil became oppressive, and a wild train of trivial impressions and associations thronged through my almost unhinged mind. I heard a clock strike somewhere – not ours, for that was not a striking clock – and my morbid fancy found in this a new starting-point for idle wanderings. Clocks – time – space – infinity – and then my fancy reverted to the local as I reflected that even now, beyond the roof and the fog and the rain and the atmosphere, Corona Borealis was rising in the northeast. Corona Borealis, which my friend had appeared to dread, and whose scintillant semicircle of stars must even now be glowing unseen through the measureless abysses of aether. All at once my feverishly sensitive ears seemed to detect a new and wholly distinct component in the soft medley of drug-magnified sounds – a low and damnably insistent whine from very far away; droning, clamouring, mocking, calling, from the northeast.

But it was not that distant whine which robbed me of my faculties and set upon my soul such a seal of fright as may never in life be removed; not that which drew the shrieks and excited the convulsions which caused lodgers and police to break down the door. It was not what I heard, but what I saw; for in that dark, locked, shuttered, and curtained room there appeared from the black northeast corner a shaft of horrible red-gold light – a shaft which bore with it no glow to disperse the darkness, but which streamed only upon the recumbent head of the troubled sleeper, bringing out in hideous duplication the luminous and strangely youthful memory-face as I had known it in dreams of abysmal space and unshackled time, when my friend had pushed behind the barrier to those secret, innermost, and forbidden caverns of nightmare.

And as I looked, I beheld the head rise, the black, liquid, and deep-sunken eyes open in terror, and the thin, shadowed lips part as if for a scream too frightful to be uttered. There dwelt in that ghastly and flexible face, as it shone bodiless, luminous, and rejuvenated in the blackness, more of stark, teeming, brain-shattering fear than all the rest of heaven and earth has ever revealed to me. No word was spoken amidst the distant sound that grew nearer and nearer, but as I followed the memory-face's mad stare along that cursed shaft of light to its source, the source whence also the whining came, I too saw for an instant what it saw, and fell with ringing ears in that fit of shrieking and epilepsy which brought the lodgers and the police. Never could I tell, try as I might, what it actually was that I saw; nor could the still face tell, for although it must have seen more than I did, it will never speak again. But always I shall guard against the mocking and insatiate Hypnos, lord of sleep, against the night sky, and against the mad ambitions of knowledge and philosophy.

Just what happened is unknown, for not only was my own mind unseated by the strange and hideous thing, but others were tainted with a forgetfulness which can mean nothing if not madness. They have said, I know not for what reason, that I never had a friend, but that art, philosophy, and insanity had filled all my tragic life. The lodgers and police on that night soothed me, and the doctor administered something to quiet me, nor did anyone see what a nightmare event had taken place. My stricken friend moved them to no pity, but what they found on the couch in the studio made them give me a praise which sickened me, and now a fame which I spurn in despair as I sit for hours, bald, grey-bearded, shrivelled, palsied, drug-crazed, and broken, adoring and praying to the object they found.

For they deny that I sold the last of my statuary, and point with ecstasy at the thing which the shining shaft of light left cold, petrified, and unvocal. It is all that remains of my friend; the friend who led me on to madness and wreckage; a godlike head of such marble as only old Hellas could yield, young with the youth that is outside time, and with beauteous bearded face, curved, smiling lips, Olympian brow, and dense locks waving and poppy-crowned. They say that that haunting memory-face is modelled from my own, as it was at twenty-five, but upon the marble base is carven a single name in the letters of Attica –'ΥΠΝΟΣ.

WHAT THE MOON BRINGS

I HATE THE MOON – I am afraid of it – for when it shines on certain scenes familiar and loved it sometimes makes them unfamiliar and hideous.

It was in the spectral summer when the moon shone down on the old garden where I wandered; the spectral summer of narcotic flowers and humid seas of foliage that bring wild and many-coloured dreams. And as I walked by the shallow crystal stream I saw unwonted ripples tipped with yellow light, as if those placid waters were drawn on in resistless currents to strange oceans that are not in the world. Silent and sparkling, bright and baleful, those moon-cursed waters hurried I knew not whither; whilst from the embowered banks white lotos-blossoms fluttered one by one in the opiate night-wind and dropped despairingly into the stream, swirling away horribly under the arched, carven bridge, and staring back with the sinister resignation of calm, dead faces.

And as I ran along the shore, crushing sleeping flowers with heedless feet and maddened ever by the fear of unknown things and the lure of the dead faces, I saw that the garden had no end under that moon; for where by day the walls were, there stretched now only new vistas of trees and paths, flowers and shrubs, stone idols and pagodas, and bendings of the yellow-litten stream past grassy banks and under grotesque bridges of marble. And the lips of the dead lotos-faces whispered sadly, and bade me follow, nor did I cease my steps till the stream became a river, and joined amidst marshes of swaying reeds and beaches of gleaming sand the shore of a vast and nameless sea.

Upon that sea the hateful moon shone, and over its unvocal waves weird perfumes breeded. And as I saw therein the lotos-faces vanish, I longed for nets that I might capture them and learn from them the secrets which the moon had brought upon the night. But when that moon went over to the west and the still tide ebbed from the sullen shore, I saw in that light old spires that the waves almost uncovered, and white columns gay with festoons of green seaweed. And knowing that to this sunken place all the dead had come, I trembled and did not wish again to speak with the lotos-faces.

Yet when I saw afar out in the sea a black condor descend from the sky to seek rest on a vast reef, I would fain have questioned him, and asked him of those whom I had known when they were alive. This I would have asked him had he not been so far away, but he was very far, and could not be seen at all when he drew nigh that gigantic reef.

So I watched the tide go out under that sinking moon, and saw gleaming the spires, the towers, and the roofs of that dead, dripping city. And as I watched, my nostrils tried to close against the perfume-conquering stench of the world's dead; for truly, in this unplaced and forgotten spot had all the flesh of the churchyards gathered for puffy sea-worms to gnaw and glut upon.

Over these horrors the evil moon now hung very low, but the puffy worms of the sea need no moon to feed by. And as I watched the ripples that told of the writhing of worms beneath, I felt a new chill from afar out whither the condor had flown, as if my flesh had caught a horror before my eyes had seen it.

Nor had my flesh trembled without cause, for when I raised my eyes I saw that the waters had ebbed very low, shewing much of the vast reef whose rim I had seen before. And when I saw that the reef was but the black basalt crown of a shocking eikon whose monstrous forehead now shewed in the dim moonlight and whose vile hooves must paw the hellish ooze miles below, I shrieked and shrieked lest the hidden face rise above the waters, and lest the hidden eyes look at me after the slinking away of that leering and treacherous yellow moon.

And to escape this relentless thing I plunged gladly and unhesitantly into the stinking shallows where amidst weedy walls and sunken streets fat sea-worms feast upon the world's dead.

THE HORROR AT MARTIN'S BEACH

(with Sonia H. Greene)

I HAVE NEVER HEARD an even approximately adequate explanation of the horror at Martin's Beach. Despite the large number of witnesses, no two accounts agree; and the testimony taken by local authorities contains the most amazing discrepancies.

Perhaps this haziness is natural in view of the unheard-of character of the horror itself, the almost paralytic terror of all who saw it, and the efforts made by the fashionable Wavecrest Inn to hush it up after the publicity created by Prof. Alton's article 'Are Hypnotic Powers Confined to Recognised Humanity?'

Against all these obstacles I am striving to present a coherent version; for I beheld the hideous occurrence, and believe it should be known in view of the appalling possibilities it suggests. Martin's Beach is once more popular as a watering-place, but I shudder when I think of it. Indeed, I cannot look at the ocean at all now without shuddering.

Fate is not always without a sense of drama and climax, hence the terrible happening of August 8, 1922, swiftly followed a period of minor and agreeably wonder-fraught excitement at Martin's

Beach. On May 17 the crew of the fishing smack *Alma* of Gloucester, under Capt. James P. Orne, killed, after a battle of nearly forty hours, a marine monster whose size and aspect produced the greatest possible stir in scientific circles and caused certain Boston naturalists to take every precaution for its taxidermic preservation.

The object was some fifty feet in length, of roughly cylindrical shape, and about ten feet in diameter. It was unmistakably a gilled fish in its major affiliations; but with certain curious modifications, such as rudimentary forelegs and six-toed feet in place of pectoral fins, which prompted the widest speculation. Its extraordinary mouth, its thick and scaly hide, and its single, deep-set eye were wonders scarcely less remarkable than its colossal dimensions; and when the naturalists pronounced it an infant organism, which could not have been hatched more than a few days, public interest mounted to extraordinary heights.

Capt. Orne, with typical Yankee shrewdness, obtained a vessel large enough to hold the object in its hull, and arranged for the exhibition of his prize. With judicious carpentry he prepared what amounted to an excellent marine museum, and, sailing south to the wealthy resort district of Martin's Beach, anchored at the hotel wharf and reaped a harvest of admission fees.

The intrinsic marvellousness of the object, and the importance which it clearly bore in the minds of many scientific visitors from near and far, combined to make it the season's sensation. That it was absolutely unique – unique to a scientifically revolutionary degree – was well understood. The naturalists had shown plainly that it radically differed from the similarly immense fish caught off the Florida coast; that, while it was obviously an inhabitant of almost incredible depths, perhaps thousands of feet, its brain and principal organs indicated a development startlingly vast, and out of all proportion to anything hitherto associated with the fish tribe.

On the morning of July 20 the sensation was increased by the loss of the vessel and its strange treasure. In the storm of the preceding night it had broken from its moorings and vanished forever from the sight of man, carrying with it the guard who had slept aboard despite the threatening weather. Capt. Orne, backed by extensive scientific interests and aided by large numbers of fishing boats from Gloucester, made a thorough and exhaustive searching cruise, but with no result other than the prompting of interest and conversation. By August 7 hope was abandoned, and Capt. Orne had returned to the Wavecrest Inn to wind up his business affairs at Martin's Beach and confer with certain of the scientific men who remained there. The horror came on August 8.

It was in the twilight, when grey sea-birds hovered low near the shore and a rising moon began to make a glittering path across the waters. The scene is important to remember, for every impression counts. On the beach were several strollers and a few late bathers; stragglers from the distant cottage colony that rose modestly on a green hill to the north, or from the adjacent cliff-perched Inn whose imposing towers proclaimed its allegiance to wealth and grandeur.

Well within viewing distance was another set of spectators, the loungers on the Inn's high-ceiled and lantern-lighted veranda, who appeared to be enjoying the dance music from the sumptuous ballroom inside. These spectators, who included Capt. Orne and his group of scientific confreres, joined the beach group before the horror progressed far; as did many more from the Inn. Certainly there was no lack of witnesses, confused though their stories be with fear and doubt of what they saw.

There is no exact record of the time the thing began, although a majority say that the fairly round moon was 'about a foot' above the low-lying vapours of the horizon. They mention the moon because what they saw seemed subtly connected with it – a sort of stealthy, deliberate, menacing ripple which rolled in from the far skyline along the shimmering lane of reflected moonbeams, yet which seemed to subside before it reached the shore.

Many did not notice this ripple until reminded by later events; but it seems to have been very marked, differing in height and motion from the normal waves around it. Some called it *cunning* and *calculating*. And as it died away craftily by the black reefs afar out, there suddenly came belching up out of the glitter-streaked brine a cry of death; a scream of anguish and despair that moved pity even while it mocked it.

First to respond to the cry were the two life guards then on duty; sturdy fellows in white bathing attire, with their calling proclaimed in large red letters across their chests. Accustomed as they were to rescue work, and to the screams of the drowning, they could find nothing familiar in the unearthly ululation; yet with a trained sense of duty they ignored the strangeness and proceeded to follow their usual course.

Hastily seizing an air-cushion, which with its attached coil of rope lay always at hand, one of them ran swiftly along the shore to the scene of the gathering crowd; whence, after whirling it about to gain momentum, he flung the hollow disc far out in the direction from which the sound had come. As the cushion disappeared in the waves, the crowd curiously awaited a sight of the hapless being whose distress had been so great; eager to see the rescue made by the massive rope.

But that rescue was soon acknowledged to be no swift and easy matter; for, pull as they might on the rope, the two muscular guards could not move the object at the other end. Instead, they found that object pulling with equal or even greater force in the very opposite direction, till in a few seconds they were dragged off their feet and into the water by the strange power which had seized on the proffered life-preserver.

One of them, recovering himself, called immediately for help from the crowd on the shore, to whom he flung the remaining coil of rope; and in a moment the guards were seconded by all the hardier men, among whom Capt. Orne was foremost. More than a dozen strong hands were now tugging desperately at the stout line, yet wholly without avail.

Hard as they tugged, the strange force at the other end tugged harder; and since neither side relaxed for an instant, the rope became rigid as steel with the enormous strain. The struggling participants, as well as the spectators, were by this time consumed with curiosity as to the nature of the force in the sea. The idea of a drowning man had long been dismissed; and hints of whales, submarines, monsters, and demons now passed freely around. Where humanity had first led the rescuers, wonder kept them at their task; and they hauled with a grim determination to uncover the mystery.

It being decided at last that a whale must have swallowed the air-cushion, Capt. Orne, as a natural leader, shouted to those on that a boat must be obtained in order to approach, harpoon, and land the unseen leviathan. Several men at once prepared to scatter in quest of a suitable craft, while others came to supplant the captain at the straining rope, since his place was logically with whatever boat party might be formed. His own idea of the situation was very broad, and by no means limited to whales, since he had to do with a monster so much stranger. He wondered what might be the acts and manifestations of an adult of the species of which the fifty-foot creature had been the merest infant.

And now there developed with appalling suddenness the crucial fact which changed the entire scene from one of wonder to one of horror, and dazed with fright the assembled band of toilers and onlookers. Capt. Orne, turning to leave his post at the rope, found his hands held in their place with unaccountable strength; and in a moment he realised that he was unable to let go of the rope. His plight was instantly divined, and as each companion tested his own situation the same condition was encountered. The fact could not be denied – every struggler was irresistibly held in some mysterious bondage to the hempen line which was slowly, hideously, and relentlessly pulling them out to sea.

Speechless horror ensued; a horror in which the spectators were petrified to utter inaction and mental chaos. Their complete demor- alisation is reflected in the conflicting accounts they give, and the sheepish excuses they offer for their seemingly callous inertia. I was one of them, and know.

Even the strugglers, after a few frantic screams and futile groans, succumbed to the paralysing influence and kept silent and fatalistic in the face of unknown powers. There they stood in the pallid moonlight, blindly pulling against a spectral doom and swaying monotonously backward and forward as the water rose first to their knees, then to their hips. The moon went partly under a cloud, and in the half-light the line of swaying men resembled some sinister and gigantic centipede, writhing in the clutch of a terrible creeping death.

Harder and harder grew the rope, as the tug in both directions increased, and the strands swelled with the undisturbed soaking of the rising waves. Slowly the tide advanced, till the sands so lately peopled by laughing children and whispering lovers were now swallowed by the inexorable flow. The herd of panic-stricken watch- ers surged blindly backward as the water crept above their feet, while the frightful line of strugglers swayed hideously on, half submerged, and now at a substantial distance from their audience. Silence was complete.

The crowd, having gained a huddling-place beyond reach of the tide, stared in mute fascination; without offering a word of advice or encouragement, or attempting any kind of assistance. There was in the air a nightmare fear of impending evils such as the world had never before known.

Minutes seemed lengthened into hours, and still that human snake of swaying torsos was seen above the fast rising tide. Rhythmically it undulated; slowly, horribly, with the seal of doom upon it. Thicker clouds now passed over the ascending moon, and the glittering path on the waters faded nearly out.

Very dimly writhed the serpentine line of nodding heads, with now and then the livid face of a backward-glancing victim gleaming pale in the darkness. Faster and faster gathered the clouds, till at length their angry rifts shot down sharp tongues of febrile flame. Thunders rolled, softly at first, yet soon increasing to a deafening, maddening intensity. Then came a culminating crash – a shock whose reverberations seemed to shake land and sea alike – and on its heels a cloudburst whose drenching violence overpowered the darkened world as if the heavens themselves had opened to pour forth a vindictive torrent.

The spectators, instinctively acting despite the absence of conscious and coherent thought, now retreated up the cliff steps to the hotel veranda. Rumours had reached the guests inside, so that the refugees found a state of terror nearly equal to their own. I think a few frightened words were uttered, but cannot be sure.

Some, who were staying at the Inn, retired in terror to their rooms; while others remained to watch the fast sinking victims as the line of bobbing heads showed above the mounting waves in the fitful lightning flashes. I recall thinking of those heads, and the bulging eyes they must contain; eyes that might well reflect all the fright, panic, and delirium of a malignant universe – all the sorrow, sin, and misery, blasted hopes and unfulfilled desires, fear, loathing and anguish of the ages since time's beginning; eyes alight with all the soul-racking pain of eternally blazing infernos.

And as I gazed out beyond the heads, my fancy conjured up still another eye; a single eye, equally alight, yet with a purpose so revolting to my brain that the vision soon passed. Held in the clutches of an unknown vice, the line of the damned dragged on; their silent screams and unuttered prayers known only to the demons of the black waves and the night-wind.

There now burst from the infuriate sky such a mad cataclysm of satanic sound that even the former crash seemed dwarfed. Amidst a blinding glare of descending fire the voice of heaven resounded with the blasphemies of hell, and the mingled agony of all the lost reverberated in one apocalyptic, planet-rending peal of Cyclopean din. It was the end of the storm, for with uncanny suddenness the rain ceased and the moon once more cast her pallid beams on a strangely quieted sea.

There was no line of bobbing heads now. The waters were calm and deserted, and broken only by the fading ripples of what seemed to be a whirlpool far out in the path of the moonlight whence the strange cry had first come. But as I looked along that treacherous lane of silvery sheen, with fancy fevered and senses overwrought, there trickled upon my ears from some abysmal sunken waste the faint and sinister echoes of a laugh.

THE FESTIVAL

'Efficiunt Daemones, ut quae non sunt, sic tamen
quasi sint, conspicienda hominibus exhibeant.'
—Lactantius

I WAS FAR FROM HOME, and the spell of the eastern sea was upon
me. In the twilight I heard it pounding on the rocks, and I knew
it lay just over the hill where the twisting willows writhed against
the clearing sky and the first stars of evening. And because my
fathers had called me to the old town beyond, I pushed on through
the shallow, new-fallen snow along the road that soared lonely up
to where Aldebaran twinkled among the trees; on toward the very
ancient town I had never seen but often dreamed of.

It was the Yuletide, that men call Christmas though they know
in their hearts it is older than Bethlehem and Babylon, older than
Memphis and mankind. It was the Yuletide, and I had come at last
to the ancient sea town where my people had dwelt and kept festival
in the elder time when festival was forbidden; where also they had
commanded their sons to keep festival once every century, that the

memory of primal secrets might not be forgotten. Mine were an old people, and were old even when this land was settled three hundred years before. And they were strange, because they had come as dark furtive folk from opiate southern gardens of orchids, and spoken another tongue before they learnt the tongue of the blue-eyed fishers. And now they were scattered, and shared only the rituals of mysteries that none living could understand. I was the only one who came back that night to the old fishing town as legend bade, for only the poor and the lonely remember.

Then beyond the hill's crest I saw Kingsport outspread frostily in the gloaming; snowy Kingsport with its ancient vanes and steeples, ridgepoles and chimney-pots, wharves and small bridges, willow-trees and graveyards; endless labyrinths of steep, narrow, crooked streets, and dizzy church-crowned central peak that time durst not touch; ceaseless mazes of colonial houses piled and scattered at all angles and levels like a child's disordered blocks; antiquity hovering on grey wings over winter-whitened gables and gambrel roofs; fanlights and small-paned windows one by one gleaming out in the cold dusk to join Orion and the archaic stars. And against the rotting wharves the sea pounded; the secretive, immemorial sea out of which the people had come in the elder time.

Beside the road at its crest a still higher summit rose, bleak and windswept, and I saw that it was a burying-ground where black gravestones stuck ghoulishly through the snow like the decayed fingernails of a gigantic corpse. The printless road was very lonely, and sometimes I thought I heard a distant horrible creaking as of a gibbet in the wind. They had hanged four kinsmen of mine for witchcraft in 1692, but I did not know just where.

As the road wound down the seaward slope I listened for the merry sounds of a village at evening, but did not hear them. Then I thought of the season, and felt that these old Puritan folk might well have Christmas customs strange to me, and full of silent hearth-side prayer. So after that I did not listen for merriment or look for wayfarers, but kept on down past the hushed lighted farmhouses and shadowy stone walls to where the signs of ancient shops and sea-taverns creaked in the salt breeze, and the grotesque knockers of pillared doorways glistened along deserted, unpaved lanes in the light of little, curtained windows.

I had seen maps of the town, and knew where to find the home of my people. It was told that I should be known and welcomed, for village legend lives long; so I hastened through Back Street to Circle Court, and across the fresh snow on the one full flagstone pavement in the town, to where Green Lane leads off behind the Market house. The old maps still held good, and I had no trouble; though at Arkham they must have lied when they said the trolleys ran to this place, since I saw not a wire overhead. Snow would have hid the rails in any case. I was glad I had chosen to walk, for the white village had seemed very beautiful from the hill; and now I was eager to knock at the door of my people, the seventh house on the left in Green Lane, with an ancient peaked roof and jutting second story, all built before 1650.

There were lights inside the house when I came upon it, and I saw from the diamond window-panes that it must have been kept very close to its antique state. The upper part overhung the narrow grass-grown street and nearly met the overhanging part of the house opposite, so that I was almost in a tunnel, with the low stone doorstep wholly free from snow. There was no sidewalk, but many houses had high doors reached by double flights of steps with iron railings. It was an odd scene, and because I was strange to New England I had never known its like before. Though it pleased me, I would have relished it better if there had been footprints in the snow, and people in the streets, and a few windows without drawn curtains.

When I sounded the archaic iron knocker I was half afraid. Some fear had been gathering in me, perhaps because of the strangeness of my heritage, and the bleakness of the evening, and the queerness of the silence in that aged town of curious customs. And when my knock was answered I was fully afraid, because I had not heard any footsteps before the door creaked open. But I was not afraid long, for the gowned, slippered old man in the doorway had a bland face that reassured me; and though he made signs that he was dumb, he wrote a quaint and ancient welcome with the stylus and wax tablet he carried.

He beckoned me into a low, candle-lit room with massive exposed rafters and dark, stiff, sparse furniture of the seventeenth century. The past was vivid there, for not an attribute was missing. There was a cavernous fireplace and a spinning-wheel at which a bent old woman in loose wrapper and deep poke-bonnet sat back toward me, silently spinning despite the festive season. An indefinite dampness seemed upon the place, and I marvelled that no fire should be blazing. The high-backed settle faced the row of curtained windows at the left, and seemed to be occupied, though I was not sure. I did not like everything about what I saw, and felt again the fear I had had. This fear grew stronger from what had before lessened it, for the more I looked at the old man's bland face the more its very blandness terrified me. The eyes never moved, and the skin was too like wax. Finally I was sure it was not a face at all, but a fiendishly cunning mask. But the flabby hands, curiously gloved, wrote genially on the tablet and told me I must wait a while before I could be led to the place of festival.

Pointing to a chair, table, and pile of books, the old man now left the room; and when I sat down to read I saw that the books were hoary and mouldy, and that they included old Morryster's wild *Marvells of Science*, the terrible *Saducismus Triumphatus* of Joseph Glanvill, published in 1681, the shocking *Daemonolatreia* of Remigius, printed in 1595 at Lyons, and worst of all, the unmentionable *Necronomicon* of the mad Arab Abdul Alhazred, in Olaus Wormius' forbidden Latin translation; a book which I had never seen, but of which I had heard monstrous things whispered. No one spoke to me, but I could hear the creaking of signs in the wind outside, and the whir of the wheel as the bonneted old woman continued her silent spinning, spinning. I thought the room and the books and the people very morbid and disquieting, but because an old tradition of my fathers had summoned me to strange feastings, I resolved to expect queer things. So I tried to read, and soon became tremblingly absorbed by something I found in that accursed *Necronomicon*, a thought and a legend too hideous for sanity or consciousness. But I disliked it when I fancied I heard the closing of one of the windows that the settle faced, as if it had been stealthily opened. It had seemed to follow a whirring that was not of the old woman's spinning-wheel. This was not much, though, for the old woman was spinning very hard, and the aged clock had been striking. After that I lost the feeling that there were persons on the settle, and was reading intently and shudderingly when the old man came back booted and dressed in a loose antique costume, and sat down on that very bench, so that I could not see him. It was certainly nervous waiting, and the blasphemous book in my hands made it doubly so.

When eleven struck, however, the old man stood up, glided to a massive carved chest in a corner, and got two hooded cloaks; one of which he donned, and the other of which he draped round the old woman, who was ceasing her monotonous spinning. Then they both started for the outer door; the woman lamely creeping, and the old man, after picking up the very book I had been reading, beckoning me as he drew his hood over that unmoving face or mask.

We went out into the moonless and tortuous network of that incredibly ancient town; went out as the lights in the curtained windows disappeared one by one, and the Dog Star leered at the throng of cowled, cloaked figures that poured silently from every doorway and formed monstrous processions up this street and that, past the creaking signs and antediluvian gables, the thatched roofs and diamond-paned windows; threading precipitous lanes where decaying houses overlapped and crumbled together, gliding across open courts and churchyards where the bobbing lanthorns made eldritch drunken constellations.

Amid these hushed throngs I followed my voiceless guides; jostled by elbows that seemed preternaturally soft, and pressed by chests and stomachs that seemed abnormally pulpy; but seeing never a face and hearing never a word. Up, up, up the eerie columns slithered, and I saw that all the travellers were converging as they flowed near a sort of focus of crazy alleys at the top of a high hill in the centre of the town, where perched a great white church. I had seen it from the road's crest when I looked at Kingsport in the new dusk, and it had made me shiver because Aldebaran had seemed to balance itself a moment on the ghostly spire.

There was an open space around the church; partly a churchyard with spectral shafts, and partly a half-paved square swept nearly bare of snow by the wind, and lined with unwholesomely archaic houses having peaked roofs and overhanging gables. Death-fires danced over the tombs, revealing gruesome vistas, though queerly failing to cast any shadows. Past the churchyard, where there were no houses, I could see over the hill's summit and watch the glimmer of stars on the harbour, though the town was invisible in the dark. Only once in a while a lanthorn bobbed horribly through serpentine alleys on its way to overtake the throng that was now slipping speechlessly into the church. I waited till the crowd had oozed into the black doorway, and till all the stragglers had followed. The old man was pulling at my sleeve, but I was determined to be the last. Then I finally went, the sinister man and the old spinning woman before me. Crossing the threshold into that swarming temple of unknown darkness, I turned once to look at the outside world as the churchyard phosphorescence cast a sickly glow on the hill-top pavement. And as I did so I shuddered. For though the wind had not left much snow, a few patches did remain on the path near the door; and in that fleeting backward look it seemed to my troubled eyes that they bore no mark of passing feet, not even mine.

The church was scarce lighted by all the lanthorns that had entered it, for most of the throng had already vanished. They had streamed up the aisle between the high white pews to the trap-door of the vaults which yawned loathsomely open just before the pulpit, and were now squirming noiselessly in. I followed dumbly down the footworn steps and into the dank, suffocating crypt. The tail of that sinuous line of night-marchers seemed very horrible, and as I saw them wriggling into a venerable tomb they seemed more horrible still. Then I noticed that the tomb's floor had an aperture down which the throng was sliding, and in a moment we were all descending an ominous staircase of rough-hewn stone; a narrow spiral staircase damp and peculiarly odorous, that wound endlessly down into the bowels of the hill past monotonous walls of dripping stone blocks and crumbling mortar. It was a silent, shocking descent, and I observed after a horrible interval that the walls and steps were changing in nature, as if chiselled out of the solid rock. What mainly troubled me was that the myriad footfalls made no sound and set up no echoes. After more aeons of descent I saw some side passages or burrows leading from unknown recesses of blackness to this shaft of nighted mystery. Soon they became excessively numerous, like impious catacombs of nameless menace; and their pungent odour of decay grew quite unbearable. I knew we must have passed down through the mountain and beneath the earth of Kingsport itself, and I shivered that a town should be so aged and maggoty with subterraneous evil.

Then I saw the lurid shimmering of pale light, and heard the insidious lapping of sunless waters. Again I shivered, for I did not like the things that the night had brought, and wished bitterly that no forefather had summoned me to this primal rite. As the steps and the passage grew broader, I heard another sound, the thin, whining mockery of a feeble flute; and suddenly there spread out before me the boundless vista of an inner world – a vast fungous shore litten by a belching column of sick greenish flame and washed by a wide oily river that flowed from abysses frightful and unsuspected to join the blackest gulfs of immemorial ocean.

Fainting and gasping, I looked at that unhallowed Erebus of titan toadstools, leprous fire, and slimy water, and saw the cloaked throngs forming a semicircle around the blazing pillar. It was the Yule-rite, older than man and fated to survive him; the primal rite of the solstice and of spring's promise beyond the snows; the rite of fire and evergreen, light and music. And in the Stygian grotto I saw them do the rite, and adore the sick pillar of flame, and throw into the water handfuls gouged out of the viscous vegetation which glittered green in the chlorotic glare. I saw this, and I saw something amorphously squatted far away from the light, piping noisomely on a flute; and as the thing piped I thought I heard noxious muffled flutterings in the foetid darkness where I could not see. But what frightened me most was that flaming column; spouting volcanically from depths profound and inconceivable, casting no shadows as healthy flame should, and coating the nitrous stone above with a nasty, venomous verdigris. For in all that seething combustion no warmth lay, but only the clamminess of death and corruption.

The man who had brought me now squirmed to a point directly beside the hideous flame, and made stiff ceremonial motions to the semicircle he faced. At certain stages of the ritual they did grovelling obeisance, especially when he held above his head that abhorrent *Necronomicon* he had taken with him; and I shared all the obeisances because I had been summoned to this festival by the writings of my forefathers. Then the old man made a signal to the half-seen flute-player in the darkness, which player thereupon changed its feeble drone to a scarce louder drone in another key; precipitating as it did so a horror unthinkable and unexpected. At this horror I sank nearly to the lichened earth, transfixed with a dread not of this nor any world, but only of the mad spaces between the stars.

Out of the unimaginable blackness beyond the gangrenous glare of that cold flame, out of the Tartarean leagues through which that oily river rolled uncanny, unheard, and unsuspected, there flopped rhythmically a horde of tame, trained, hybrid winged things that no sound eye could ever wholly grasp, or sound brain ever wholly remember. They were not altogether crows, nor moles, nor buzzards, nor ants, nor vampire bats, nor decomposed human beings; but something I cannot and must not recall. They flopped limply along, half with their webbed feet and half with their membraneous wings; and as they reached the throng of celebrants the cowled figures seized and mounted them, and rode off one by one along the reaches of that unlighted river, into pits and galleries of panic where poison springs feed frightful and undiscoverable cataracts.

The old spinning woman had gone with the throng, and the old man remained only because I had refused when he motioned me to seize an animal and ride like the rest. I saw when I staggered to my feet that the amorphous flute-player had rolled out of sight, but that two of the beasts were patiently standing by. As I hung back, the old man produced his stylus and tablet and wrote that he was the true deputy of my fathers who had founded the Yule worship in this ancient place; that it had been decreed I should come back, and that the most secret mysteries were yet to be performed. He wrote this in a very ancient hand, and when I still hesitated he pulled from his loose robe a seal ring and a watch, both with my family arms, to prove that he was what he said. But it was a hideous proof, because I knew from old papers that that watch had been buried with my great-great-great-great-grandfather in 1698.

Presently the old man drew back his hood and pointed to the family resemblance in his face, but I only shuddered, because I was sure that the face was merely a devilish waxen mask. The flopping animals were now scratching restlessly at the lichens, and I saw that the old man was nearly as restless himself. When one of the things began to waddle and edge away, he turned quickly to stop it; so that the suddenness of his motion dislodged the waxen mask from what should have been his head. And then, because that nightmare's position barred me from the stone staircase down which we had come, I flung myself into the oily underground river that bubbled somewhere to the caves of the sea; flung myself into that putrescent juice of earth's inner horrors before the madness of my screams could bring down upon me all the charnel legions these pest-gulfs might conceal.

At the hospital they told me I had been found half frozen in

Kingsport Harbour at dawn, clinging to the drifting spar that accident sent to save me. They told me I had taken the wrong fork of the hill road the night before, and fallen over the cliffs at Orange Point; a thing they deduced from prints found in the snow. There was nothing I could say, because everything was wrong. Everything was wrong, with the broad window shewing a sea of roofs in which only about one in five was ancient, and the sound of trolleys and motors in the streets below. They insisted that this was Kingsport, and I could not deny it. When I went delirious at hearing that the hospital stood near the old churchyard on Central Hill, they sent me to St. Mary's Hospital in Arkham, where I could have better care. I liked it there, for the doctors were broad-minded, and even lent me their influence in obtaining the carefully sheltered copy of Alhazred's objectionable *Necronomicon* from the library of Miskatonic University. They said something about a 'psychosis', and agreed I had better get any harassing obsessions off my mind.

So I read again that hideous chapter, and shuddered doubly because it was indeed not new to me. I had seen it before, let footprints tell what they might; and where it was I had seen it were best forgotten. There was no one – in waking hours – who could remind me of it; but my dreams are filled with terror, because of phrases I dare not quote. I dare quote only one paragraph, put into such English as I can make from the awkward Low Latin.

'The nethermost caverns,' wrote the mad Arab, 'are not for the fathoming of eyes that see; for their marvels are strange and terrific. Cursed the ground where dead thoughts live new and oddly bodied, and evil the mind that is held by no head. Wisely did Ibn Schacabao say, that happy is the tomb where no wizard hath lain, and happy the town at night whose wizards are all ashes. For it is of old rumour that the soul of the devil-bought hastes not from his charnel clay, but fats and instructs *the very worm that gnaws;* till out of corruption horrid life springs, and the dull scavengers of earth wax crafty to vex it and swell monstrous to plague it. Great holes secretly are digged where earth's pores ought to suffice, and things have learnt to walk that ought to crawl.'

THE TEMPLE

(Manuscript found on the coast of Yucatan.)

ON AUGUST 20, 1917, I, Karl Heinrich, Graf von Altberg-Ehrenstein, Lieutenant-Commander in the Imperial German Navy and in charge of the submarine U-29, deposit this bottle and record in the Atlantic Ocean at a point to me unknown but probably about N. Latitude 20°, W. Longitude 35°, where my ship lies disabled on the ocean floor. I do so because of my desire to set certain unusual facts before the public; a thing I shall not in all probability survive to accomplish in person, since the circumstances surrounding me are as menacing as they are extraordinary, and involve not only the hopeless crippling of the U-29, but the impairment of my iron German will in a manner most disastrous.

On the afternoon of June 18, as reported by wireless to the U-61, bound for Kiel, we torpedoed the British freighter Victory, New York to Liverpool, in N. Latitude 45° 16', W. Longitude 28° 34'; permitting the crew to leave in boats in order to obtain a good cinema view for the admiralty records. The ship sank quite picturesquely, bow first, the stern rising high out of the water whilst the hull shot down perpendicularly to the bottom of the sea. Our camera missed nothing, and I regret that so fine a reel of film should never reach Berlin. After that we sank the lifeboats with our guns and submerged.

When we rose to the surface about sunset a seaman's body was found on the deck, hands gripping the railing in curious fashion. The poor fellow was young, rather dark, and very handsome; probably an Italian or Greek, and undoubtedly of the Victory's crew. He had evidently sought refuge on the very ship which had been forced to destroy his own – one more victim of the unjust war of aggression which the English pig-dogs are waging upon the Fatherland. Our men searched him for souvenirs, and found in his coat pocket a very odd bit of ivory carved to represent a youth's head crowned with laurel. My fellow-officer, Lieut. Klenze, believed that the thing was of great age and artistic value, so took it from the men for himself. How it had ever come into the possession of a common sailor, neither he nor I could imagine.

As the dead man was thrown overboard there occurred two incidents which created much disturbance amongst the crew. The fellow's eyes had been closed; but in the dragging of his body to the rail they were jarred open, and many seemed to entertain a queer delusion that they gazed steadily and mockingly at Schmidt and Zimmer, who were bent over the corpse. The Boatswain Müller, an elderly man who would have known better had he not been a superstitious Alsatian swine, became so excited by this impression that he watched the body in the water; and swore that after it sank a little it drew its limbs into a swimming position and sped away to the south under the waves. Klenze and I did not like these displays of peasant ignorance, and severely reprimanded the men, particularly Müller.

The next day a very troublesome situation was created by the indisposition of some of the crew. They were evidently suffering from the nervous strain of our long voyage, and had had bad dreams. Several seemed quite dazed and stupid; and after satisfying myself that they were not feigning their weakness, I excused them from their duties. The sea was rather rough, so we descended to a depth where the waves were less troublesome. Here we were comparatively calm, despite a somewhat puzzling southward current which we could not identify from our oceanographic charts. The

moans of the sick men were decidedly annoying; but since they did not appear to demoralise the rest of the crew, we did not resort to extreme measures. It was our plan to remain where we were and intercept the liner Dacia, mentioned in information from agents in New York.

In the early evening we rose to the surface, and found the sea less heavy. The smoke of a battleship was on the northern horizon, but our distance and ability to submerge made us safe. What worried us more was the talk of Boatswain Müller, which grew wilder as night came on. He was in a detestably childish state, and babbled of some illusion of dead bodies drifting past the undersea portholes; bodies which looked at him intensely, and which he recognised in spite of bloating, having seen them dying during some of our victorious German exploits. And he said that the young man we had found and tossed overboard was their leader. This was very gruesome and abnormal, so we confined Müller in irons and had him soundly whipped. The men were not pleased at his punishment, but discipline was necessary. We also denied the request of a delegation headed by Seaman Zimmer, that the curious carved ivory head be cast into the sea.

On June 20, Seamen Bohm and Schmidt, who had been ill the day before, became violently insane. I regretted that no physician was included in our complement of officers, since German lives are precious; but the constant ravings of the two concerning a terrible curse were most subversive of discipline, so drastic steps were taken. The crew accepted the event in a sullen fashion, but it seemed to quiet Müller; who thereafter gave us no trouble. In the evening we released him, and he went about his duties silently.

In the week that followed we were all very nervous, watching for the Dacia. The tension was aggravated by the disappearance of Müller and Zimmer, who undoubtedly committed suicide as a result of the fears which had seemed to harass them, though they were not observed in the act of jumping overboard. I was rather glad to be rid of Müller, for even his silence had unfavourably affected the crew. Everyone seemed inclined to be silent now, as though holding a secret fear. Many were ill, but none made a disturbance. Lieut. Klenze chafed under the strain, and was annoyed by the merest trifles – such as the school of dolphins which gathered about the U-29 in increasing numbers, and the growing intensity of that southward current which was not on our chart.

It at length became apparent that we had missed the Dacia altogether. Such failures are not uncommon, and we were more pleased than disappointed; since our return to Wilhelmshaven was now in order. At noon June 28 we turned northeastward, and despite some rather comical entanglements with the unusual masses of dolphins were soon under way.

The explosion in the engine room at 2 p.m. was wholly a surprise. No defect in the machinery or carelessness in the men had been noticed, yet without warning the ship was racked from end to end with a colossal shock. Lieut. Klenze hurried to the engine room, finding the fuel-tank and most of the mechanism shattered, and Engineers Raabe and Schneider instantly killed. Our situation had suddenly become grave indeed; for though the chemical air regenerators were intact, and though we could use the devices for raising and submerging the ship and opening the hatches as long as compressed air and storage batteries might hold out, we were powerless to propel or guide the submarine. To seek rescue in the lifeboats would be to deliver ourselves into the hands of enemies unreasonably embittered against our great German nation, and our wireless had failed ever since the Victory affair to put us in touch with a fellow U-boat of the Imperial Navy.

From the hour of the accident till July 2 we drifted constantly to the south, almost without plans and encountering no vessel. Dolphins still encircled the U-29, a somewhat remarkable circumstance considering the distance we had covered. On the morning of July 2 we sighted a warship flying American colours, and the men became very restless in their desire to surrender. Finally Lieut. Klenze had to shoot a seaman named Traube, who urged this un-German act with especial violence. This quieted the crew for the time, and we submerged unseen.

The next afternoon a dense flock of sea-birds appeared from the south, and the ocean began to heave ominously. Closing our hatches, we awaited developments until we realised that we must either submerge or be swamped in the mounting waves. Our air pressure and electricity were diminishing, and we wished to avoid all unnecessary use of our slender mechanical resources; but in this case there was no choice. We did not descend far, and when after several hours the sea was calmer, we decided to return to the surface. Here, however, a new trouble developed; for the ship failed to respond to our direction in spite of all that the mechanics could do. As the men grew more frightened at this undersea imprisonment, some of them began to mutter again about Lieut. Klenze's ivory image, but the sight of an automatic pistol calmed them. We kept the poor devils as busy as we could, tinkering at the machinery even when we knew it was useless.

Klenze and I usually slept at different times; and it was during my sleep, about 5 a.m., July 4, that the general mutiny broke loose. The six remaining pigs of seamen, suspecting that we were lost, had suddenly burst into a mad fury at our refusal to surrender to the Yankee battleship two days before; and were in a delirium of cursing and destruction. They roared like the animals they were, and broke instruments and furniture indiscriminately; screaming about such nonsense as the curse of the ivory image and the dark dead youth who looked at them and swam away. Lieut. Klenze seemed paralysed and inefficient, as one might expect of a soft, womanish Rhinelander. I shot all six men, for it was necessary, and made sure that none remained alive.

We expelled the bodies through the double hatches and were alone in the U-29. Klenze seemed very nervous, and drank heavily. It was decided that we remain alive as long as possible, using the large stock of provisions and chemical supply of oxygen, none of which had suffered from the crazy antics of those swine-hound seamen. Our compasses, depth gauges, and other delicate instruments were ruined; so that henceforth our only reckoning would be guesswork, based on our watches, the calendar, and our apparent drift as judged by any objects we might spy through the portholes or from the conning tower. Fortunately we had storage batteries still capable of long use, both for interior lighting and for the searchlight. We often cast a beam around the ship, but saw only dolphins, swimming parallel to our own drifting course. I was scientifically interested in those dolphins; for though the ordinary Delphinus delphis is a cetacean mammal, unable to subsist without air, I watched one of the swimmers closely for two hours, and did not see him alter his submerged condition.

With the passage of time Klenze and I decided that we were still drifting south, meanwhile sinking deeper and deeper. We noted the marine fauna and flora, and read much on the subject in the books

I had carried with me for spare moments. I could not help observing, however, the inferior scientific knowledge of my companion. His mind was not Prussian, but given to imaginings and speculations which have no value. The fact of our coming death affected him curiously, and he would frequently pray in remorse over the men, women, and children we had sent to the bottom; forgetting that all things are noble which serve the German state. After a time he became noticeably unbalanced, gazing for hours at his ivory image and weaving fanciful stories of the lost and forgotten things under the sea. Sometimes, as a psychological experiment, I would lead him on in these wanderings, and listen to his endless poetical quotations and tales of sunken ships. I was very sorry for him, for I dislike to see a German suffer; but he was not a good man to die with. For myself I was proud, knowing how the Fatherland would revere my memory and how my sons would be taught to be men like me.

On August 9, we espied the ocean floor, and sent a powerful beam from the searchlight over it. It was a vast undulating plain, mostly covered with seaweed, and strown with the shells of small molluscs. Here and there were slimy objects of puzzling contour, draped with weeds and encrusted with barnacles, which Klenze declared must be ancient ships lying in their graves. He was puzzled by one thing, a peak of solid matter, protruding above the ocean bed nearly four feet at its apex; about two feet thick, with flat sides and smooth upper surfaces which met at a very obtuse angle. I called the peak a bit of outcropping rock, but Klenze thought he saw carvings on it. After a while he began to shudder, and turned away from the scene as if frightened; yet could give no explanation save that he was overcome with the vastness, darkness, remoteness, antiquity, and mystery of the oceanic abysses. His mind was tired, but I am always a German, and was quick to notice two things; that the U-29 was standing the deep-sea pressure splendidly, and that the peculiar dolphins were still about us, even at a depth where the existence of high organisms is considered impossible by most naturalists. That I had previously overestimated our depth, I was sure; but none the less we must still be deep enough to make these phenomena remarkable. Our southward speed, as gauged by the ocean floor, was about as I had estimated from the organisms passed at higher levels.

It was at 3:15 p.m., August 12, that poor Klenze went wholly mad. He had been in the conning tower using the searchlight when I saw him bound into the library compartment where I sat reading, and his face at once betrayed him. I will repeat here what he said, underlining the words he emphasised: 'He is <u>calling</u>! He is <u>calling</u>! I <u>hear</u> him! We must <u>go</u>!' As he spoke he took his ivory image from the table, pocketed it, and seized my arm in an effort to drag me up the companionway to the deck. In a moment I understood that he meant to open the hatch and plunge with me into the water outside, a vagary of suicidal and homicidal mania for which I was scarcely prepared. As I hung back and attempted to soothe him he grew more violent, saying: 'Come now – do not wait until later; it is better to repent and be forgiven than to defy and be condemned.' Then I tried the opposite of the soothing plan, and told him he was mad – pitifully demented. But he was unmoved, and cried: 'If I am mad, it is mercy! May the gods pity the man who in his callousness can remain sane to the hideous end! Come and be mad whilst he still calls with mercy!'

This outburst seemed to relieve a pressure in his brain; for as he finished he grew much milder, asking me to let him depart alone if I would not accompany him. My course at once became clear. He was a German, but only a Rhinelander and a commoner; and he was now a potentially dangerous madman. By complying with his suicidal request I could immediately free myself from one who was no longer a companion but a menace. I asked him to give me the ivory image before he went, but this request brought from him such uncanny laughter that I did not repeat it. Then I asked him if he wished to leave any keepsake or lock of hair for his family in Germany in case I should be rescued, but again he gave me that strange laugh. So as he climbed the ladder I went to the levers, and allowing proper time-intervals operated the machinery which sent him to his death. After I saw that he was no longer in the boat I threw the searchlight around the water in an effort to obtain a last glimpse of him; since I wished to ascertain whether the water-pressure would flatten him as it theoretically should, or whether the body would be unaffected, like those extraordinary dolphins. I did not, however, succeed in finding my late companion, for the dolphins were massed thickly and obscuringly about the conning tower.

That evening I regretted that I had not taken the ivory image surreptitiously from poor Klenze's pocket as he left, for the memory of it fascinated me. I could not forget the youthful, beautiful head with its leafy crown, though I am not by nature an artist. I was also sorry that I had no one with whom to converse. Klenze, though not my mental equal, was much better than no one. I did not sleep well that night, and wondered exactly when the end would come. Surely, I had little enough chance of rescue.

The next day I ascended to the conning tower and commenced the customary searchlight explorations. Northward the view was much the same as it had been all the four days since we had sighted the bottom, but I perceived that the drifting of the U-29 was less rapid. As I swung the beam around to the south, I noticed that the ocean floor ahead fell away in a marked declivity, and bore curiously regular blocks of stone in certain places, disposed as if in accordance with definite patterns. The boat did not at once descend to match the greater ocean depth, so I was soon forced to adjust the searchlight to cast a sharply downward beam. Owing to the abruptness of the change a wire was disconnected, which necessitated a delay of many minutes for repairs; but at length the light streamed on again, flooding the marine valley below me.

I am not given to emotion of any kind, but my amazement was very great when I saw what lay revealed in that electrical glow. And yet as one reared in the best Kultur of Prussia I should not have been amazed, for geology and tradition alike tell us of great transpositions in oceanic and continental areas. What I saw was an extended and elaborate array of ruined edifices; all of magnificent though unclassified architecture, and in various stages of preservation. Most appeared to be of marble, gleaming whitely in the rays of the searchlight, and the general plan was of a large city at the bottom of a narrow valley, with numerous isolated temples and villas on the steep slopes above. Roofs were fallen and columns were broken, but there still remained an air of immemorially ancient splendour which nothing could efface.

Confronted at last with the Atlantis I had formerly deemed largely a myth, I was the most eager of explorers. At the bottom of that valley a river once had flowed; for as I examined the scene more closely I beheld the remains of stone and marble bridges and sea-walls, and terraces and embankments once verdant and beautiful. In my enthusiasm I became nearly as idiotic and sentimental as poor Klenze, and was very tardy in noticing that the southward current had ceased at last, allowing the U-29 to settle slowly down upon the sunken city as an aëroplane settles upon a town of the upper earth. I was slow, too, in realising that the school of unusual dolphins had vanished.

In about two hours the boat rested in a paved plaza close to the rocky wall of the valley. On one side I could view the entire city as it sloped from the plaza down to the old river-bank; on the other side, in startling proximity, I was confronted by the richly ornate and perfectly preserved façade of a great building, evidently a temple, hollowed from the solid rock. Of the original workmanship of this titanic thing I can only make conjectures. The façade, of immense magnitude, apparently covers a continuous hollow recess; for its windows are many and widely distributed. In the centre yawns a great open door, reached by an impressive flight of steps, and surrounded by exquisite carvings like the figures of Bacchanals in relief. Foremost of all are the great columns and frieze, both decorated with sculptures of inexpressible beauty; obviously portraying idealised pastoral scenes and processions of priests and priestesses bearing strange ceremonial devices in adoration of a radiant god. The art is of the most phenomenal perfection, largely Hellenic in idea, yet strangely individual. It imparts an impression of terrible antiquity, as though it were the remotest rather than the immediate ancestor of Greek art. Nor can I doubt that every detail of this massive product was fashioned from the virgin hillside rock of our planet. It is palpably a part of the valley wall, though how the vast interior was ever excavated I cannot imagine. Perhaps a cavern or series of caverns furnished the nucleus. Neither age nor submersion has corroded the pristine grandeur of this awful fane – for fane indeed it must be – and today after thousands of years it rests untarnished and inviolate in the endless night and silence of an ocean chasm.

I cannot reckon the number of hours I spent in gazing at the sunken city with its buildings, arches, statues, and bridges, and the colossal temple with its beauty and mystery. Though I knew that death was near, my curiosity was consuming; and I threw the searchlight's beam about in eager quest. The shaft of light permitted me to learn many details, but refused to shew anything within the gaping door of the rock-hewn temple; and after a time I turned off the current, conscious of the need of conserving power. The rays were now perceptibly dimmer than they had been during the weeks of drifting. And as if sharpened by the coming deprivation of light, my desire to explore the watery secrets grew. I, a German, should be the first to tread those aeon-forgotten ways!

I produced and examined a deep-sea diving suit of joined metal, and experimented with the portable light and air regenerator. Though I should have trouble in managing the double hatches alone, I believed I could overcome all obstacles with my scientific skill and actually walk about the dead city in person.

On August 16 I effected an exit from the U-29, and laboriously made my way through the ruined and mud-choked streets to the ancient river. I found no skeletons or other human remains, but gleaned a wealth of archaeological lore from sculptures and coins. Of this I cannot now speak save to utter my awe at a culture in the full noon of glory when cave-dwellers roamed Europe and the Nile flowed unwatched to the sea. Others, guided by this manuscript if it shall ever be found, must unfold the mysteries at which I can only hint. I returned to the boat as my electric batteries grew feeble, resolved to explore the rock temple on the following day.

On the 17th, as my impulse to search out the mystery of the temple waxed still more insistent, a great disappointment befell me; for I found that the materials needed to replenish the portable light had perished in the mutiny of those pigs in July. My rage was unbounded, yet my German sense forbade me to venture unprepared into an utterly black interior which might prove the lair of some indescribable marine monster or a labyrinth of passages from whose windings I could never extricate myself. All I could do was to turn on the waning searchlight of the U-29, and with its aid walk up the temple steps and study the exterior carvings. The shaft of light entered the door at an upward angle, and I peered in to see if I could glimpse anything, but all in vain. Not even the roof was visible; and though I took a step or two inside after testing the floor with a staff, I dared not go farther. Moreover, for the first time in my life I experienced the emotion of dread. I began to realise how some of poor Klenze's moods had arisen, for as the temple drew me more and more, I feared its aqueous abysses with a blind and mounting terror. Returning to the submarine, I turned off the lights and sat thinking in the dark. Electricity must now be saved for emergencies.

Saturday the 18th I spent in total darkness, tormented by thoughts and memories that threatened to overcome my German will. Klenze had gone mad and perished before reaching this sinister remnant of a past unwholesomely remote, and had advised me to go with him. Was, indeed, Fate preserving my reason only to draw me irresistibly to an end more horrible and unthinkable than any man has dreamed of? Clearly, my nerves were sorely taxed, and I must cast off these impressions of weaker men.

I could not sleep Saturday night, and turned on the lights regardless of the future. It was annoying that the electricity should not last out the air and provisions. I revived my thoughts of euthanasia, and examined my automatic pistol. Toward morning I must have dropped asleep with the lights on, for I awoke in darkness yesterday afternoon to find the batteries dead. I struck several matches in succession, and desperately regretted the improvidence which had caused us long ago to use up the few candles we carried.

After the fading of the last match I dared to waste, I sat very quietly without a light. As I considered the inevitable end my mind ran over preceding events, and developed a hitherto dormant impression which would have caused a weaker and more superstitious man to shudder. The head of the radiant god in the sculptures on the rock temple is the same as that carven bit of ivory which the dead sailor brought from the sea and which poor Klenze carried back into the sea.

I was a little dazed by this coincidence, but did not become terrified. It is only the inferior thinker who hastens to explain the singular and the complex by the primitive short cut of supernaturalism. The coincidence was strange, but I was too sound a reasoner to connect circumstances which admit of no logical connection, or to associate in any uncanny fashion the disastrous events which had led from the Victory affair to my present plight. Feeling the need of more rest, I took a sedative and secured some more sleep. My nervous condition was reflected in my dreams, for I seemed to hear the cries of drowning persons, and to see dead faces pressing against the portholes of the boat. And among the dead faces was the living, mocking face of the youth with the ivory image.

I must be careful how I record my awaking today, for I am unstrung, and much hallucination is necessarily mixed with fact. Psychologically my case is most interesting, and I regret that it cannot be observed scientifically by a competent German authority. Upon opening my eyes my first sensation was an overmastering desire to visit the rock temple; a desire which grew every instant, yet which I automatically sought to resist through some emotion of fear which operated in the reverse direction. Next there came to me the impression of light amidst the darkness of dead batteries, and I seemed to see a sort of phosphorescent glow in the water through the porthole which opened toward the temple. This aroused my curiosity, for I knew of no deep-sea organism capable of emitting such luminosity. But before I could investigate there came a third impression which because of its irrationality caused me to doubt the objectivity of anything my senses might record. It was an aural delusion; a sensation of rhythmic, melodic sound as of some wild yet beautiful chant or choral hymn, coming from the outside through the absolutely sound-proof hull of the U-29. Convinced of my psychological and nervous abnormality, I lighted some matches and poured a stiff dose of sodium bromide solution, which seemed to calm me to the extent of dispelling the illusion of sound. But the phosphorescence remained, and I had difficulty in repressing a childish impulse to go to the porthole and seek its source. It was horribly realistic, and I could soon distinguish by its aid the familiar objects around me, as well as the empty sodium bromide glass of which I had had no former visual impression in its present location. The last circumstance made me ponder, and I crossed the room and touched the glass. It was indeed in the place where I had seemed to see it. Now I knew that the light was either real or part of an hallucination so fixed and consistent that I could not hope to dispel it, so abandoning all resistance I ascended to the conning tower to look for the luminous agency. Might it not actually be another U-boat, offering possibilities of rescue?

It is well that the reader accept nothing which follows as objective truth, for since the events transcend natural law, they are necessarily the subjective and unreal creations of my overtaxed mind. When I attained the conning tower I found the sea in general far less luminous than I had expected. There was no animal or vegetable phosphorescence about, and the city that sloped down to the river was invisible in blackness. What I did see was not spectacular, not grotesque or terrifying, yet it removed my last vestige of trust in my consciousness. For the door and windows of the undersea temple hewn from the rocky hill were vividly aglow with a flickering radiance, as from a mighty altar-flame far within.

Later incidents are chaotic. As I stared at the uncannily lighted door and windows, I became subject to the most extravagant visions – visions so extravagant that I cannot even relate them. I fancied that I discerned objects in the temple – objects both stationary and moving – and seemed to hear again the unreal chant that had floated to me when first I awaked. And over all rose thoughts and fears which centred in the youth from the sea and the ivory image whose carving was duplicated on the frieze and columns of the temple before me. I thought of poor Klenze, and wondered where his body rested with the image he had carried back into the sea. He had warned me of something, and I had not heeded – but he was a soft-headed Rhinelander who went mad at troubles a Prussian could bear with ease.

The rest is very simple. My impulse to visit and enter the temple has now become an inexplicable and imperious command which ultimately cannot be denied. My own German will no longer controls my acts, and volition is henceforward possible only in minor matters. Such madness it was which drove Klenze to his death, bareheaded and unprotected in the ocean; but I am a Prussian and a man of sense, and will use to the last what little will I have. When first I saw that I must go, I prepared my diving suit, helmet, and air regenerator for instant donning; and immediately commenced to write this hurried chronicle in the hope that it may some day reach the world. I shall seal the manuscript in a bottle and entrust it to the sea as I leave the U-29 forever.

I have no fear, not even from the prophecies of the madman Klenze. What I have seen cannot be true, and I know that this madness of my own will at most lead only to suffocation when my air is gone. The light in the temple is a sheer delusion, and I shall die calmly, like a German, in the black and forgotten depths. This daemoniac laughter which I hear as I write comes only from my own weakening brain. So I will carefully don my diving suit and walk boldly up the steps into that primal shrine; that silent secret of unfathomed waters and uncounted years.

HALLOWE'EN IN A SUBURB

T HE STEEPLES are white in the wild moonlight,
  And the trees have a silver glare;
Past the chimneys high see the vampires fly,
  And the harpies of upper air,
  That flutter and laugh and stare.

For the village dead to the moon outspread
  Never shone in the sunset's gleam,
But grew out of the deep that the dead years keep
  Where the rivers of madness stream
  Down the gulfs to a pit of dream.

A chill wind weaves thro' the rows of sheaves
  In the meadows that shimmer pale,
And comes to twine where the headstones shine
  And the ghouls of the churchyard wail
  For harvests that fly and fail.

Not a breath of the strange grey gods of change
    That tore from the past its own
Can quicken this hour, when a spectral pow'r
    Spreads sleep o'er the cosmic throne
    And looses the vast unknown.

So here again stretch the vale and plain
    That moons long-forgotten saw,
And the dead leap gay in the pallid ray,
    Sprung out of the tomb's black maw
    To shake all the world with awe.

And all that the morn shall greet forlorn,
    The ugliness and the pest
Of rows where thick rise the stones and brick,
    Shall some day be with the rest,
    And brood with the shades unblest.

Then wild in the dark let the lemurs bark,
    And the leprous spires ascend;
For new and old alike in the fold
    Of horror and death are penn'd,
    For the hounds of Time to rend.

THE MOON-BOG

SOMEWHERE, to what remote and fearsome region I know not, Denys Barry has gone. I was with him the last night he lived among men, and heard his screams when the thing came to him; but all the peasants and police in County Meath could never find him, or the others, though they searched long and far. And now I shudder when I hear the frogs piping in swamps, or see the moon in lonely places.

I had known Denys Barry well in America, where he had grown rich, and had congratulated him when he bought back the old castle by the bog at sleepy Kilderry. It was from Kilderry that his father had come, and it was there that he wished to enjoy his wealth among ancestral scenes. Men of his blood had once ruled over Kilderry and built and dwelt in the castle, but those days were very remote, so that for generations the castle had been empty and decaying. After he went to Ireland Barry wrote me often, and told me how under his care the grey castle was rising tower by tower to its ancient splendour; how the ivy was climbing slowly over the restored walls as it had climbed so many centuries ago, and how

197

the peasants blessed him for bringing back the old days with his gold from over the sea. But in time there came troubles, and the peasants ceased to bless him, and fled away instead as from a doom. And then he sent a letter and asked me to visit him, for he was lonely in the castle with no one to speak to save the new servants and labourers he had brought from the north.

The bog was the cause of all these troubles, as Barry told me the night I came to the castle. I had reached Kilderry in the summer sunset, as the gold of the sky lighted the green of the hills and groves and the blue of the bog, where on a far islet a strange olden ruin glistened spectrally. That sunset was very beautiful, but the peasants at Ballylough had warned me against it and said that Kilderry had become accursed, so that I almost shuddered to see the high turrets of the castle gilded with fire. Barry's motor had met me at the Ballylough station, for Kilderry is off the railway. The villagers had shunned the car and the driver from the north, but had whispered to me with pale faces when they saw I was going to Kilderry. And that night, after our reunion, Barry told me why.

The peasants had gone from Kilderry because Denys Barry was to drain the great bog. For all his love of Ireland, America had not left him untouched, and he hated the beautiful wasted space where peat might be cut and land opened up. The legends and super-stitions of Kilderry did not move him, and he laughed when the peasants first refused to help, and then cursed him and went away to Ballylough with their few belongings as they saw his deter-mination. In their place he sent for labourers from the north, and when the servants left he replaced them likewise. But it was lonely among strangers, so Barry had asked me to come.

When I heard the fears which had driven the people from Kil-derry I laughed as loudly as my friend had laughed, for these fears were of the vaguest, wildest, and most absurd character. They had to do with some preposterous legend of the bog, and of a grim guardian spirit that dwelt in the strange olden ruin on the far islet I had seen in the sunset. There were tales of dancing lights in the dark of the moon, and of chill winds when the night was warm; of wraiths in white hovering over the waters, and of an imagined city of stone deep down below the swampy surface. But foremost among the weird fancies, and alone in its absolute unanimity, was that of the curse awaiting him who should dare to touch or drain the vast reddish morass. There were secrets, said the peasants, which must not be uncovered; secrets that had lain hidden since the plague came to the children of Partholan in the fabulous years beyond history. In the *Book of Invaders* it is told that these sons of the Greeks were all buried at Tallaght, but old men in Kilderry said that one city was overlooked save by its patron moon-goddess; so that only the wooded hills buried it when the men of Nemed swept down from Scythia in their thirty ships.

Such were the idle tales which had made the villagers leave Kilderry, and when I heard them I did not wonder that Denys Barry had refused to listen. He had, however, a great interest in antiquities; and proposed to explore the bog thoroughly when it was drained. The white ruins on the islet he had often visited, but though their age was plainly great, and their contour very little like that of most ruins in Ireland, they were too dilapidated to tell the days of their glory. Now the work of drainage was ready to begin, and the labourers from the north were soon to strip the forbidden bog of its green moss and red heather, and kill the tiny shell-paved streamlets and quiet blue pools fringed with rushes.

After Barry had told me these things I was very drowsy, for the travels of the day had been wearying and my host had talked late into the night. A manservant shewed me to my room, which was in a remote tower overlooking the village, and the plain at the edge of the bog, and the bog itself; so that I could see from my windows in the moonlight the silent roofs from which the peasants had fled and which now sheltered the labourers from the north, and too, the parish church with its antique spire, and far out across the brooding bog the remote olden ruin on the islet gleaming white and spectral. Just as I dropped to sleep I fancied I heard faint sounds from the distance; sounds that were wild and half musical, and stirred me with a weird excitement which coloured my dreams. But when I awaked next morning I felt it had all been a dream, for the visions I had seen were more wonderful than any sound of wild pipes in the night. Influenced by the legends that Barry had related, my mind had in slumber hovered around a stately city in a green valley, where marble streets and statues, villas and temples, carvings and inscriptions, all spoke in certain tones the glory that was Greece. When I told this dream to Barry we both laughed; but I laughed the louder, because he was perplexed about his labourers from the north. For the sixth time they had all overslept, waking very slowly and dazedly, and acting as if they had not rested, although they were known to have gone early to bed the night before.

That morning and afternoon I wandered alone through the sun-gilded village and talked now and then with idle labourers, for Barry was busy with the final plans for beginning his work of drainage. The labourers were not as happy as they might have been, for most of them seemed uneasy over some dream which they had had, yet which they tried in vain to remember. I told them of my dream, but they were not interested till I spoke of the weird sounds I thought I had heard. Then they looked oddly at me, and said that they seemed to remember weird sounds, too.

In the evening Barry dined with me and announced that he would begin the drainage in two days. I was glad, for although I disliked to see the moss and the heather and the little streams and lakes depart, I had a growing wish to discern the ancient secrets the deep-matted peat might hide. And that night my dreams of piping flutes and marble peristyles came to a sudden and dis-quieting end; for upon the city in the valley I saw a pestilence descend, and then a frightful avalanche of wooded slopes that covered the dead bodies in the streets and left unburied only the temple of Artemis on the high peak, where the aged moon-priestess Cleis lay cold and silent with a crown of ivory on her silver head.

I have said that I awaked suddenly and in alarm. For some time I could not tell whether I was waking or sleeping, for the sound of flutes still rang shrilly in my ears; but when I saw on the floor the icy moonbeams and the outlines of a latticed Gothic window I decided I must be awake and in the castle at Kilderry. Then I heard a clock from some remote landing below strike the hour of two, and I knew I was awake. Yet still there came that monotonous piping from afar; wild, weird airs that made me think of some dance of fauns on distant Maenalus. It would not let me sleep, and in impa-tience I sprang up and paced the floor. Only by chance did I go to the north window and look out upon the silent village and the plain at the edge of the bog. I had no wish to gaze abroad, for I wanted to sleep; but the flutes tormented me, and I had to do or see something. How could I have suspected the thing I was to behold?

There in the moonlight that flooded the spacious plain was a spectacle which no mortal, having seen it, could ever forget. To the sound of reedy pipes that echoed over the bog there glided silently and eerily a mixed throng of swaying figures, reeling through such a revel as the Sicilians may have danced to Demeter in the old days under the harvest moon beside the Cyane. The wide plain, the golden moonlight, the shadowy moving forms, and above all the shrill monotonous piping, produced an effect which almost paralysed me; yet I noted amidst my fear that half of these tireless, mechanical dancers were the labourers whom I had thought asleep, whilst the other half were strange airy beings in white, half indeterminate in nature, but suggesting pale wistful naiads from the haunted fountains of the bog. I do not know how long I gazed at this sight from the lonely turret window before I dropped suddenly in a dreamless swoon, out of which the high sun of morning aroused me.

My first impulse on awaking was to communicate all my fears and observations to Denys Barry, but as I saw the sunlight glowing through the latticed east window I became sure that there was no reality in what I thought I had seen. I am given to strange phantasms, yet am never weak enough to believe in them; so on this occasion contented myself with questioning the labourers, who slept very late and recalled nothing of the previous night save misty dreams of shrill sounds. This matter of the spectral piping harassed me greatly, and I wondered if the crickets of autumn had come before their time to vex the night and haunt the visions of men. Later in the day I watched Barry in the library poring over his plans for the great work which was to begin on the morrow, and for the first time felt a touch of the same kind of fear that had driven the peasants away. For some unknown reason I dreaded the thought of disturbing the ancient bog and its sunless secrets, and pictured terrible sights lying black under the unmeasured depth of age-old peat. That these secrets should be brought to light seemed injudicious, and I began to wish for an excuse to leave the castle and the village. I went so far as to talk casually to Barry on the subject, but did not dare continue after he gave his resounding laugh. So I was silent when the sun set fulgently over the far hills, and Kilderry blazed all red and gold in a flame that seemed a portent.

Whether the events of that night were of reality or illusion I shall never ascertain. Certainly they transcend anything we dream of in Nature and the universe; yet in no normal fashion can I explain those disappearances which were known to all men after it was over. I retired early and full of dread, and for a long time could not sleep in the uncanny silence of the tower. It was very dark, for although the sky was clear the moon was now well in the wane, and would not rise till the small hours. I thought as I lay there of Denys Barry, and of what would befall that bog when the day came, and found myself almost frantic with an impulse to rush out into the night, take Barry's car, and drive madly to Ballylough out of the menaced lands. But before my fears could crystallise into action I had fallen asleep, and gazed in dreams upon the city in the valley, cold and dead under a shroud of hideous shadow.

Probably it was the shrill piping that awaked me, yet that piping was not what I noticed first when I opened my eyes. I was lying with my back to the east window overlooking the bog, where the waning moon would rise, and therefore expected to see light cast on the opposite wall before me; but I had not looked for such a sight as now appeared. Light indeed glowed on the panels ahead, but it was not any light that the moon gives. Terrible and piercing was the shaft of ruddy refulgence that streamed through the Gothic window, and the whole chamber was brilliant with a splendour intense and unearthly. My immediate actions were peculiar for such a situation, but it is only in tales that a man does the dramatic and foreseen thing. Instead of looking out across the bog toward the source of the new light, I kept my eyes from the window in panic fear, and clumsily drew on my clothing with some dazed idea of escape. I remember seizing my revolver and hat, but before it was over I had lost them both without firing the one or donning the other. After a time the fascination of the red radiance overcame my fright, and I crept to the east window and looked out whilst the maddening, incessant piping whined and reverberated through the castle and over all the village.

Over the bog was a deluge of flaring light, scarlet and sinister, and pouring from the strange olden ruin on the far islet. The aspect of that ruin I cannot describe – I must have been mad, for it seemed to rise majestic and undecayed, splendid and column-cinctured, the flame-reflecting marble of its entablature piercing the sky like the apex of a temple on a mountain-top. Flutes shrieked and drums began to beat, and as I watched in awe and terror I thought I saw dark saltant forms silhouetted grotesquely against the vision of marble and effulgence. The effect was titanic – altogether unthinkable – and I might have stared indefinitely had not the sound of the piping seemed to grow stronger at my left. Trembling with a terror oddly mixed with ecstasy I crossed the circular room to the north window from which I could see the village and the plain at the edge of the bog. There my eyes dilated again with a wild wonder as great as if I had not just turned from a scene beyond the pale of Nature, for on the ghastly red-litten plain was moving a procession of beings in such a manner as none ever saw before save in nightmares.

Half gliding, half floating in the air, the white-clad bog-wraiths were slowly retreating toward the still waters and the island ruin in fantastic formations suggesting some ancient and solemn ceremonial dance. Their waving translucent arms, guided by the detestable piping of those unseen flutes, beckoned in uncanny rhythm to a throng of lurching labourers who followed dog-like with blind, brainless, floundering steps as if dragged by a clumsy but resistless daemon-will. As the naiads neared the bog, without altering their course, a new line of stumbling stragglers zigzagged drunkenly out of the castle from some door far below my window, groped sightlessly across the courtyard and through the intervening bit of village, and joined the floundering column of labourers on the plain. Despite their distance below me I at once knew they were the servants brought from the north, for I recognised the ugly and unwieldy form of the cook, whose very absurdness had now become unutterably tragic. The flutes piped horribly, and again I heard the beating of the drums from the direction of the island ruin. Then silently and gracefully the naiads reached the water and melted one by one into the ancient bog; while the line of followers, never checking their speed, splashed awkwardly after them and vanished amidst a tiny vortex of unwholesome bubbles which I could barely see in the scarlet light. And as the last pathetic straggler, the fat cook, sank heavily out of sight in that sullen pool, the flutes and the drums grew silent, and the blinding red rays from the ruins snapped instantaneously out, leaving the village of doom lone and desolate in the wan beams of a new-risen moon.

My condition was now one of indescribable chaos. Not knowing whether I was mad or sane, sleeping or waking, I was saved only by a merciful numbness. I believe I did ridiculous things such as offering prayers to Artemis, Latona, Demeter, Persephone, and Plouton. All that I recalled of a classic youth came to my lips as the horrors of the situation roused my deepest superstitions. I felt that I had witnessed the death of a whole village, and knew I was alone in the castle with Denys Barry, whose boldness had brought down a doom. As I thought of him new terrors convulsed me, and I fell to the floor; not fainting, but physically helpless. Then I felt the icy blast from the east window where the moon had risen, and began to hear the shrieks in the castle far below me. Soon those shrieks had attained a magnitude and quality which cannot be written of, and which make me faint as I think of them. All I can say is that they came from something I had known as a friend.

At some time during this shocking period the cold wind and the screaming must have roused me, for my next impression is of racing madly through inky rooms and corridors and out across the courtyard into the hideous night. They found me at dawn wandering mindless near Ballylough, but what unhinged me utterly was not any of the horrors I had seen or heard before. What I muttered about as I came slowly out of the shadows was a pair of fantastic incidents which occurred in my flight; incidents of no significance, yet which haunt me unceasingly when I am alone in certain marshy places or in the moonlight.

As I fled from that accursed castle along the bog's edge I heard a new sound; common, yet unlike any I had heard before at Kilderry. The stagnant waters, lately quite devoid of animal life, now teemed with a horde of slimy enormous frogs which piped shrilly and incessantly in tones strangely out of keeping with their size. They glistened bloated and green in the moonbeams, and seemed to gaze up at the fount of light. I followed the gaze of one very fat and ugly frog, and saw the second of the things which drove my senses away.

Stretching directly from the strange olden ruin on the far islet to the waning moon, my eyes seemed to trace a beam of faint quivering radiance having no reflection in the waters of the bog. And upward along that pallid path my fevered fancy pictured a thin shadow slowly writhing; a vague contorted shadow struggling as if drawn by unseen daemons. Crazed as I was, I saw in that awful shadow a monstrous resemblance – a nauseous, unbelievable caricature – a blasphemous effigy of him who had been Denys Barry.

HE

I SAW HIM on a sleepless night when I was walking desperately to save my soul and my vision. My coming to New York had been a mistake; for whereas I had looked for poignant wonder and inspiration in the teeming labyrinths of ancient streets that twist endlessly from forgotten courts and squares and waterfronts to courts and squares and waterfronts equally forgotten, and in the Cyclopean modern towers and pinnacles that rise blackly Babylonian under waning moons, I had found instead only a sense of horror and oppression which threatened to master, paralyse, and annihilate me.

The disillusion had been gradual. Coming for the first time upon the town, I had seen it in the sunset from a bridge, majestic above its waters, its incredible peaks and pyramids rising flower-like and delicate from pools of violet mist to play with the flaming golden clouds and the first stars of evening. Then it had lighted up window by window above the shimmering tides where lanterns nodded and glided and deep horns bayed weird harmonies, and itself become a starry firmament of dream, redolent of faery music, and one with the marvels of Carcassonne and Samarcand and El Dorado and all glorious and half-fabulous cities. Shortly afterward I was taken through those antique ways so dear to my fancy – narrow, curving alleys and passages where rows of red Georgian brick blinked with small-paned dormers above pillared doorways that had looked on gilded sedans and panelled coaches – and in the first flush of realisation of these long-wished things I thought I had indeed achieved such treasures as would make me in time a poet.

But success and happiness were not to be. Garish daylight shewed only squalor and alienage and the noxious elephantiasis of climbing, spreading stone where the moon had hinted of loveliness and elder magic; and the throngs of people that seethed through the flume-like streets were squat, swarthy strangers with hardened faces and narrow eyes, shrewd strangers without dreams and without kinship to the scenes about them, who could never mean aught to a blue-eyed man of the old folk, with the love of fair green lanes and white New England village steeples in his heart.

So instead of the poems I had hoped for, there came only a shuddering blankness and ineffable loneliness; and I saw at last a fearful truth which no one had ever dared to breathe before – the unwhisperable secret of secrets – the fact that this city of stone and stridor is not a sentient perpetuation of Old New York as London is of Old London and Paris of Old Paris, but that it is in fact quite dead, its sprawling body imperfectly embalmed and infested with queer animate things which have nothing to do with it as it was in life. Upon making this discovery I ceased to sleep comfortably; though something of resigned tranquillity came back as I gradually formed the habit of keeping off the streets by day and venturing abroad only at night, when darkness calls forth what little of the past still hovers wraith-like about, and old white doorways remember the stalwart forms that once passed through them. With this mode of relief I even wrote a few poems, and still refrained from going home to my people lest I seem to crawl back ignobly in defeat.

Then, on a sleepless night's walk, I met the man. It was in a grotesque hidden courtyard of the Greenwich section, for there in my ignorance I had settled, having heard of the place as the natural home of poets and artists. The archaic lanes and houses and unex-pected bits of square and court had indeed delighted me, and when

I found the poets and artists to be loud-voiced pretenders whose quaintness is tinsel and whose lives are a denial of all that pure beauty which is poetry and art, I stayed on for love of these venerable things. I fancied them as they were in their prime, when Greenwich was a placid village not yet engulfed by the town; and in the hours before dawn, when all the revellers had slunk away, I used to wander alone among their cryptical windings and brood upon the curious arcana which generations must have deposited there. This kept my soul alive, and gave me a few of those dreams and visions for which the poet far within me cried out.

The man came upon me at about two one cloudy August morning, as I was threading a series of detached courtyards; now accessible only through the unlighted hallways of intervening buildings, but once forming parts of a continuous network of picturesque alleys. I had heard of them by vague rumour, and realised that they could not be upon any map of today; but the fact that they were forgotten only endeared them to me, so that I had sought them with twice my usual eagerness. Now that I had found them, my eagerness was again redoubled; for something in their arrangement dimly hinted that they might be only a few of many such, with dark, dumb counterparts wedged obscurely betwixt high blank walls and deserted rear tenements, or lurking lamplessly behind archways, unbetrayed by hordes of the foreign-speaking or guarded by furtive and uncommunicative artists whose practices do not invite publicity or the light of day.

He spoke to me without invitation, noting my mood and glances as I studied certain knockered doorways above iron-railed steps, the pallid glow of traceried transoms feebly lighting my face. His own face was in shadow, and he wore a wide-brimmed hat which somehow blended perfectly with the out-of-date cloak he affected; but I was subtly disquieted even before he addressed me. His form was very slight, thin almost to cadaverousness; and his voice proved phenomenally soft and hollow, though not particularly deep. He had, he said, noticed me several times at my wanderings; and inferred that I resembled him in loving the vestiges of former years. Would I not like the guidance of one long practised in these explorations, and possessed of local information profoundly deeper than any which an obvious newcomer could possibly have gained?

As he spoke, I caught a glimpse of his face in the yellow beam from a solitary attic window. It was a noble, even a handsome, elderly countenance; and bore the marks of a lineage and refinement unusual for the age and place. Yet some quality about it disturbed me almost as much as its features pleased me – perhaps it was too white, or too expressionless, or too much out of keeping with the locality, to make me feel easy or comfortable. Nevertheless I followed him; for in those dreary days my quest for antique beauty and mystery was all that I had to keep my soul alive, and I reckoned it a rare favour of Fate to fall in with one whose kindred seekings seemed to have penetrated so much farther than mine.

Something in the night constrained the cloaked man to silence, and for a long hour he led me forward without needless words; making only the briefest of comments concerning ancient names and dates and changes, and directing my progress very largely by gestures as we squeezed through interstices, tiptoed through corridors, clambered over brick walls, and once crawled on hands and knees through a low, arched passage of stone whose immense length and tortuous twistings effaced at last every hint of geographical location I had managed to preserve. The things we saw were very old and marvellous, or at least they seemed so in the few straggling rays of light by which I viewed them, and I shall never forget the tottering Ionic columns and fluted pilasters and urn-headed iron fence-posts and flaring-lintelled windows and decorative fanlights that appeared to grow quainter and stranger the deeper we advanced into this inexhaustible maze of unknown antiquity.

We met no person, and as time passed the lighted windows became fewer and fewer. The street-lights we first encountered had been of oil, and of the ancient lozenge pattern. Later I noticed some with candles; and at last, after traversing a horrible unlighted court where my guide had to lead with his gloved hand through total blackness to a narrow wooden gate in a high wall, we came upon a fragment of alley lit only by lanterns in front of every seventh house – unbelievably colonial tin lanterns with conical tops and holes punched in the sides. This alley led steeply uphill – more steeply than I thought possible in this part of New York – and the upper end was blocked squarely by the ivy-clad wall of a private estate, beyond which I could see a pale cupola, and the tops of trees waving against a vague lightness in the sky. In this wall was a small, low-arched gate of nail-studded black oak, which the man proceeded to unlock with a ponderous key. Leading me within, he steered a course in utter blackness over what seemed to be a gravel path, and finally up a flight of stone steps to the door of the house, which he unlocked and opened for me.

We entered, and as we did so I grew faint from a reek of infinite mustiness which welled out to meet us, and which must have been the fruit of unwholesome centuries of decay. My host appeared not to notice this, and in courtesy I kept silent as he piloted me up a curving stairway, across a hall, and into a room whose door I heard him lock behind us. Then I saw him pull the curtains of the three small-paned windows that barely shewed themselves against the lightening sky; after which he crossed to the mantel, struck flint and steel, lighted two candles of a candelabrum of twelve sconces, and made a gesture enjoining soft-toned speech.

In this feeble radiance I saw that we were in a spacious, well-furnished, and panelled library dating from the first quarter of the eighteenth century, with splendid doorway pediments, a delightful Doric cornice, and a magnificently carved overmantel with scroll-and-urn top. Above the crowded bookshelves at intervals along the walls were well-wrought family portraits; all tarnished to an enigmatical dimness, and bearing an unmistakable likeness to the man who now motioned me to a chair beside the graceful Chippendale table. Before seating himself across the table from me, my host paused for a moment as if in embarrassment; then, tardily removing his gloves, wide-brimmed hat, and cloak, stood theatrically revealed in full mid-Georgian costume from queued hair and neck ruffles to knee-breeches, silk hose, and the buckled shoes I had not previously noticed. Now slowly sinking into a lyre-back chair, he commenced to eye me intently.

Without his hat he took on an aspect of extreme age which was scarcely visible before, and I wondered if this unperceived mark of singular longevity were not one of the sources of my original disquiet. When he spoke at length, his soft, hollow, and carefully muffled voice not infrequently quavered; and now and then I had great difficulty in following him as I listened with a thrill of amazement and half-disavowed alarm which grew each instant.

'You behold, Sir,' my host began, 'a man of very eccentrical habits, for whose costume no apology need be offered to one with your wit and inclinations. Reflecting upon better times, I have not scrupled to ascertain their ways and adopt their dress and manners; an indulgence which offends none if practised without ostentation. It hath been my good fortune to retain the rural seat of my ancestors, swallowed though it was by two towns, first Greenwich, which built up hither after 1800, then New-York, which joined on near 1830. There were many reasons for the close keeping of this place in my family, and I have not been remiss in discharging such obligations. The squire who succeeded to it in 1768 studied sartain arts and made sartain discoveries, all connected with influences residing in this particular plot of ground, and eminently desarving of the strongest guarding. Some curious effects of these arts and dis-coveries I now purpose to shew you, under the strictest secrecy; and I believe I may rely on my judgement of men enough to have no distrust of either your interest or your fidelity.'

He paused, but I could only nod my head. I have said that I was alarmed, yet to my soul nothing was more deadly than the material daylight world of New York, and whether this man were a harmless eccentric or a wielder of dangerous arts I had no choice save to follow him and slake my sense of wonder on whatever he might have to offer. So I listened.

'To – my ancestor—' he softly continued, 'there appeared to reside some very remarkable qualities in the will of mankind; qualities having a little-suspected dominance not only over the acts of one's self and of others, but over every variety of force and substance in Nature, and over many elements and dimensions deemed more univarsal than Nature herself. May I say that he flouted the sanctity of things as great as space and time, and that he put to strange uses the rites of sartain half-breed red Indians once encamped upon this hill? These Indians shewed choler when the place was built, and were plaguey pestilent in asking to visit the grounds at the full of the moon. For years they stole over the wall each month when they could, and by stealth performed sartain acts. Then, in '68, the new squire catched them at their doings, and stood still at what he saw. Thereafter he bargained with them and exchanged the free access of his grounds for the exact inwardness of what they did; larning that their grandfathers got part of their custom from red ancestors and part from an old Dutchman in the time of the States-General. And pox on him, I'm afeared the squire must have sarved them monstrous bad rum – whether or not by intent – for a week after he larnt the secret he was the only man living that knew it. You, Sir, are the first outsider to be told there is a secret, and split me if I'd have risked tampering that much with – the powers – had ye not been so hot after bygone things.'

I shuddered as the man grew colloquial – and with familiar speech of another day. He went on.

'But you must know, Sir, that what – the squire – got from those mongrel savages was but a small part of the larning he came to have. He had not been at Oxford for nothing, nor talked to no account with an ancient chymist and astrologer in Paris. He was, in fine, made sensible that all the world is but the smoke of our intellects; past the bidding of the vulgar, but by the wise to be puffed out and drawn in like any cloud of prime Virginia tobacco. What we want, we may make about us; and what we don't want, we may sweep away. I won't say that all this is wholly true in body, but 'tis sufficient true to furnish a very pretty spectacle now and then. You, I conceive, would be tickled by a better sight of sartain other years than your fancy affords you; so be pleased to hold back any fright at what I design to shew. Come to the window and be quiet.'

My host now took my hand to draw me to one of the two windows on the long side of the malodorous room, and at the first touch of his ungloved fingers I turned cold. His flesh, though dry and firm, was of the quality of ice; and I almost shrank away from his pulling. But again I thought of the emptiness and horror of reality, and boldly prepared to follow whithersoever I might be led. Once at the window, the man drew apart the yellow silk curtains and di-rected my stare into the blackness outside. For a moment I saw nothing save a myriad of tiny dancing lights, far, far before me. Then, as if in response to an insidious motion of my host's hand, a flash of heat-lightning played over the scene, and I looked out upon a sea of luxuriant foliage – foliage unpolluted, and not the sea of roofs to be expected by any normal mind. On my right the Hudson glittered wickedly, and in the distance ahead I saw the unhealthy shimmer of a vast salt marsh constellated with nervous fireflies. The flash died, and an evil smile illumined the waxy face of the aged necromancer.

'That was before my time – before the new squire's time. Pray let us try again.'

I was faint, even fainter than the hateful modernity of that accursed city had made me.

'Good God!' I whispered, 'can you do that for *any time?*' And as he nodded, and bared the black stumps of what had once been yellow fangs, I clutched at the curtains to prevent myself from falling. But he steadied me with that terrible, ice-cold claw, and once more made his insidious gesture.

Again the lightning flashed – but this time upon a scene not wholly strange. It was Greenwich, the Greenwich that used to be, with here and there a roof or row of houses as we see it now, yet with lovely green lanes and fields and bits of grassy common. The marsh still glittered beyond, but in the farther distance I saw the steeples of what was then all of New York; Trinity and St Paul's and the Brick Church dominating their sisters, and a faint haze of wood smoke hovering over the whole. I breathed hard, but not so much from the sight itself as from the possibilities my imagination terrifiedly conjured up.

'Can you – dare you – go *far?*' I spoke with awe, and I think he shared it for a second, but the evil grin returned.

'*Far?* What I have seen would blast ye to a mad statue of stone! Back, back – forward, *forward* – look, ye puling lack-wit!'

And as he snarled the phrase under his breath he gestured anew; bringing to the sky a flash more blinding than either which had come before. For full three seconds I could glimpse that pandaemoniac sight, and in those seconds I saw a vista which will ever afterward torment me in dreams. I saw the heavens verminous with strange flying things, and beneath them a hellish black city of giant stone terraces with impious pyramids flung savagely to the moon, and devil-lights burning from unnumbered windows. And swarming loathsomely on aërial galleries I saw the yellow, squint-eyed people of that city, robed horribly in orange and red, and dancing insanely to the pounding of fevered kettle-drums, the clatter of obscene crotala, and the maniacal moaning of muted horns whose ceaseless dirges rose and fell undulantly like the waves of an unhallowed ocean of bitumen.

I saw this vista, I say, and heard as with the mind's ear the blasphemous domdaniel of cacophony which companioned it. It was the shrieking fulfilment of all the horror which that corpse-city had ever stirred in my soul, and forgetting every injunction to silence I screamed and screamed and screamed as my nerves gave way and the walls quivered about me.

Then, as the flash subsided, I saw that my host was trembling too; a look of shocking fear half blotting from his face the serpent distortion of rage which my screams had excited. He tottered, clutched at the curtains as I had done before, and wriggled his head wildly, like a hunted animal. God knows he had cause, for as the echoes of my screaming died away there came another sound so hellishly suggestive that only numbed emotion kept me sane and conscious. It was the steady, stealthy creaking of the stairs beyond the locked door, as with the ascent of a barefoot or skin-shod horde; and at last the cautious, purposeful rattling of the brass latch that glowed in the feeble candlelight. The old man clawed and spat at me through the mouldy air, and barked things in his throat as he swayed with the yellow curtain he clutched.

'The full moon – damn ye – ye ... ye yelping dog – ye called 'em, and they've come for me! Moccasined feet – dead men – Gad sink ye, ye red devils, but I poisoned no rum o' yours – han't I kept your pox-rotted magic safe? – ye swilled yourselves sick, curse ye, and ye must needs blame the squire – let go, you! Unhand that latch – I've naught for ye here—'

At this point three slow and very deliberate raps shook the panels of the door, and a white foam gathered at the mouth of the frantic magician. His fright, turning to steely despair, left room for a resurgence of his rage against me; and he staggered a step toward the table on whose edge I was steadying myself. The curtains, still clutched in his right hand as his left clawed out at me, grew taut and finally crashed down from their lofty fastenings; admitting to the room a flood of that full moonlight which the brightening of the sky had presaged. In those greenish beams the candles paled, and a new semblance of decay spread over the musk-reeking room with its wormy panelling, sagging floor, battered mantel, rickety furniture, and ragged draperies. It spread over the old man, too, whether from the same source or because of his fear and vehemence, and I saw him shrivel and blacken as he lurched near and strove to rend me with vulturine talons. Only his eyes stayed whole, and they glared with a propulsive, dilated incandescence which grew as the face around them charred and dwindled.

The rapping was now repeated with greater insistence, and this time bore a hint of metal. The black thing facing me had become only a head with eyes, impotently trying to wriggle across the sinking floor in my direction, and occasionally emitting feeble little spits of immortal malice. Now swift and splintering blows assailed the sickly panels, and I saw the gleam of a tomahawk as it cleft the rending wood. I did not move, for I could not; but watched dazedly as the door fell in pieces to admit a colossal, shapeless influx of inky substance starred with shining, malevolent eyes. It poured thickly, like a flood of oil bursting a rotten bulkhead, overturned a chair as it spread, and finally flowed under the table and across the room to where the blackened head with the eyes still glared at me. Around that head it closed, totally swallowing it up, and in another moment it had begun to recede; bearing away its invisible burden without touching me, and flowing again out of that black doorway and down the unseen stairs, which creaked as before, though in reverse order.

Then the floor gave way at last, and I slid gaspingly down into the nighted chamber below, choking with cobwebs and half-swooning with terror. The green moon, shining through broken windows, shewed me the hall door half open; and as I rose from the plaster-strown floor and twisted myself free from the sagged ceilings, I saw sweep past it an awful torrent of blackness, with scores of baleful eyes glowing in it. It was seeking the door to the cellar, and when it found it, it vanished therein. I now felt the floor of this lower room giving as that of the upper chamber had done, and once a crashing above had been followed by the fall past the west window of something which must have been the cupola. Now liberated for the instant from the wreckage, I rushed through the hall to the front door; and finding myself unable to open it, seized a chair and broke a window, climbing frenziedly out upon the unkempt lawn where moonlight danced over yard-high grass and weeds. The wall was high, and all the gates were locked; but moving a pile of boxes in a corner I managed to gain the top and cling to the great stone urn set there.

About me in my exhaustion I could see only strange walls and windows and old gambrel roofs. The steep street of my approach was nowhere visible, and the little I did see succumbed rapidly to a mist that rolled in from the river despite the glaring moonlight. Suddenly the urn to which I clung began to tremble, as if sharing my own lethal dizziness; and in another instant my body was plunging downward to I knew not what fate.

The man who found me said that I must have crawled a long way despite my broken bones, for a trail of blood stretched off as far as he dared look. The gathering rain soon effaced this link with the scene of my ordeal, and reports could state no more than that I had appeared from a place unknown, at the entrance of a little black court off Perry Street.

I never sought to return to those tenebrous labyrinths, nor would I direct any sane man thither if I could. Of who or what that ancient creature was, I have no idea; but I repeat that the city is dead and full of unsuspected horrors. Whither *he* has gone, I do not know; but I have gone home to the pure New England lanes up which fragrant sea-winds sweep at evening.

FESTIVAL

T HERE IS SNOW on the ground,
　And the valleys are cold,
And a midnight profound
　Blackly squats o'er the wold;
But a light on the hilltops half-seen hints of
　　feastings unhallow'd and old.

There is death in the clouds,
　There is fear in the night,
For the dead in their shrouds
　Hail the sun's turning flight,
And chant wild in the woods as they dance round
　　a Yule-altar fungous and white.

To no gale of earth's kind
　Sways the forest of oak,
Where the sick boughs entwin'd
　By mad mistletoes choke,

For these pow'rs are the pow'rs of the dark,
    from the graves of the lost Druid-folk.

And mayst thou to such deeds
    Be an abbot and priest,
Singing cannibal greeds
    At each devil-wrought feast,
And to all the incredulous world shewing
    dimly the sign of the beast.

THE GREEN MEADOW

(with Winifred Virginia Jackson)

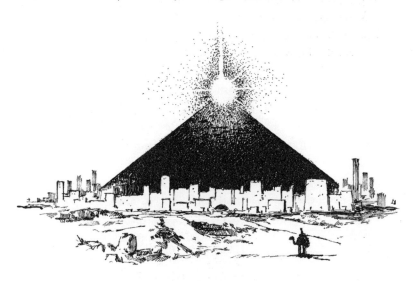

Translated by Elizabeth Neville Berkeley and
Lewis Theobald, Jun.

I NTRODUCTORY NOTE: The following very singular narrative
or record of impressions was discovered under circumstances so
extraordinary that they deserve careful description. On the evening
of Wednesday, August 27, 1913, at about 8:30 o'clock, the population
of the small seaside village of Potowonket, Maine, USA, was aroused
by a thunderous report accompanied by a blinding flash; and
persons near the shore beheld a mammoth ball of fire dart from
the heavens into the sea but a short distance out, sending up a
prodigious column of water. The following Sunday a fishing party
composed of John Richmond, Peter B. Carr, and Simon Canfield
caught in their trawl and dragged ashore a mass of metallic rock,
weighing 360 pounds, and looking (as Mr Canfield said) like a piece
of slag. Most of the inhabitants agreed that this heavy body was
none other than the fireball which had fallen from the sky four days
before; and Dr Richmond M. Jones, the local scientific authority,

allowed that it must be an aerolite or meteoric stone. In chipping off specimens to send to an expert Boston analyst, Dr Jones discovered imbedded in the semi-metallic mass the strange book containing the ensuing tale, which is still in his possession.

In form the discovery resembles an ordinary notebook, about 5 × 3 inches in size, and containing thirty leaves. In material, however, it presents marked peculiarities. The covers are apparently of some dark stony substance unknown to geologists, and unbreakable by any mechanical means. No chemical reagent seems to act upon them. The leaves are much the same, save that they are lighter in colour, and so infinitely thin as to be quite flexible. The whole is bound by some process not very clear to those who have observed it; a process involving the adhesion of the leaf substance to the cover substance. These substances cannot now be separated, nor can the leaves be torn by any amount of force. The writing is *Greek of the purest classical quality*, and several students of palaeography declare that the characters are in a cursive hand used about the second century BC. There is little in the text to determine the date. The mechanical mode of writing cannot be deduced beyond the fact that it must have resembled that of the modern slate and slate-pencil. During the course of analytical efforts made by the late Prof. Chambers of Harvard, several pages, mostly at the conclusion of the narrative, were blurred to the point of utter effacement before being read; a circumstance forming a well-nigh irreparable loss. What remains of the contents was done into modern Greek letters by the palaeographer Rutherford and in this form submitted to the translators.

Prof. Mayfield of the Massachusetts Institute of Technology, who examined samples of the strange stone, declares it a true meteorite; an opinion in which Dr. von Winterfeldt of Heidelberg (interned in 1918 as a dangerous enemy alien) does not concur. Prof. Bradley of Columbia College adopts a less dogmatic ground; pointing out that certain utterly unknown ingredients are present in large quantities, and warning that no classification is as yet possible.

The presence, nature, and message of the strange book form so momentous a problem, that no explanation can even be attempted. The text, as far as preserved, is here rendered as literally as our language permits, in the hope that some reader may eventually hit upon an interpretation and solve one of the greatest scientific mysteries of recent years.

—E.N.B.–L.T., Jun.

(The Story)

I T WAS A NARROW PLACE, and I was alone. On one side, beyond a margin of vivid waving green, was the sea; blue, bright, and billowy, and sending up vaporous exhalations which intoxicated me. So profuse, indeed, were these exhalations, that they gave me an odd impression of a coalescence of sea and sky; for the heavens were likewise bright and blue. On the other side was the forest, ancient almost as the sea itself, and stretching infinitely inland. It was very dark, for the trees were grotesquely huge and luxuriant, and incredibly numerous. Their giant trunks were of a horrible green which blended weirdly with the narrow green tract whereon I stood. At some distance away, on either side of me, the strange forest extended down to the water's edge; obliterating the shore line and completely hemming in the narrow tract. Some of the trees, I observed, stood in the water itself; as though impatient of any barrier to their progress.

I saw no living thing, nor sign that any living thing save myself had ever existed. The sea and the sky and the wood encircled me, and reached off into regions beyond my imagination. Nor was there any sound save of the wind-tossed wood and of the sea.

As I stood in this silent place, I suddenly commenced to tremble; for though I knew not how I came there, and could scarce remember what my name and rank had been, I felt that I should go mad if I could understand what lurked about me. I recalled things I had learned, things I had dreamed, things I had imagined and yearned for in some other distant life. I thought of long nights when I had gazed up at the stars of heaven and cursed the gods that my free soul could not traverse the vast abysses which were inaccessible to my body. I conjured up ancient blasphemies, and terrible delvings into the papyri of Democritus; but as memories appeared, I shuddered in deeper fear, for I knew that I was alone – horribly alone. Alone, yet close to sentient impulses of vast, vague kind; which

I prayed never to comprehend nor encounter. In the voice of the swaying green branches I fancied I could detect a kind of malignant hatred and daemoniac triumph. Sometimes they struck me as being in horrible colloquy with ghastly and unthinkable things which the scaly green bodies of the trees half hid; hid from sight but not from consciousness. The most oppressive of my sensations was a sinister feeling of alienage. Though I saw about me objects which I could name – trees, grass, sea, and sky; I felt that their relation to me was not the same as that of the trees, grass, sea, and sky I knew in another and dimly remembered life. The nature of the difference I could not tell, yet I shook in stark fright as it impressed itself upon me.

And then, in a spot where I had before discerned nothing but the misty sea, I beheld the Green Meadow; separated from me by a vast expanse of blue rippling water with sun-tipped wavelets, yet strangely near. Often I would peep fearfully over my right shoulder at the trees, but I preferred to look at the Green Meadow, which affected me oddly.

It was while my eyes were fixed upon this singular tract, that I first felt the ground in motion beneath me. Beginning with a kind of throbbing agitation which held a fiendish suggestion of conscious action, the bit of bank on which I stood detached itself from the grassy shore and commenced to float away; borne slowly onward as if by some current of resistless force. I did not move, astonished and startled as I was by the unprecedented phenomenon; but stood rigidly still until a wide lane of water yawned betwixt me and the land of trees. Then I sat down in a sort of daze, and again looked at the sun-tipped water and the Green Meadow.

Behind me the trees and the things they may have been hiding seemed to radiate infinite menace. This I knew without turning to view them, for as I grew more used to the scene I became less and less dependent upon the five senses that once had been my sole reliance. I knew the green scaly forest hated me, yet now I was safe from it, for my bit of bank had drifted far from the shore.

But though one peril was past, another loomed up before me. Pieces of earth were constantly crumbling from the floating isle which held me, so that death could not be far distant in any event. Yet even then I seemed to sense that death would be death to me no more, for I turned again to watch the Green Meadow, imbued with a curious feeling of security in strange contrast to my general horror.

Then it was that I heard, at a distance immeasurable, the sound of falling water. Not that of any trivial cascade such as I had known, but that which might be heard in the far Scythian lands if all the Mediterranean were poured down an unfathomable abyss. It was toward this sound that my shrinking island was drifting, yet I was content.

Far in the rear were happening weird and terrible things; things which I turned to view, yet shivered to behold. For in the sky dark vaporous forms hovered fantastically, brooding over trees and seeming to answer the challenge of the waving green branches. Then a thick mist arose from the sea to join the sky-forms, and the shore was erased from my sight. Though the sun – what sun I knew not – shone brightly on the water around me, the land I had left seemed involved in a daemoniac tempest where clashed the will of the hellish trees and what they hid, with that of the sky and the sea. And when the mist vanished, I saw only the blue sky and the blue sea, for the land and the trees were no more.

It was at this point that my attention was arrested by the *singing* in the Green Meadow. Hitherto, as I have said, I had encountered no sign of human life; but now there arose to my ears a dull chant whose origin and nature were apparently unmistakable. While the words were utterly undistinguishable, the chant awaked in me a peculiar train of associations; and I was reminded of some vaguely disquieting lines I had once translated out of an Egyptian book, which in turn were taken from a papyrus of ancient Meroë. Through my brain ran lines that I fear to repeat; lines telling of very antique things and forms of life in the days when our earth was exceeding young. Of things which thought and moved and were alive, yet which gods and men would not consider alive. It was a strange book.

As I listened, I became gradually conscious of a circumstance which had before puzzled me only subconsciously. At no time had my sight distinguished any definite objects in the Green Meadow, an impression of vivid homogeneous verdure being the sum total of my perception. Now, however, I saw that the current would cause my island to pass the shore at but a little distance; so that I might learn more of the land and of the singing thereon. My curiosity to behold the singers had mounted high, though it was mingled with apprehension.

Bits of sod continued to break away from the tiny tract which carried me, but I heeded not their loss; for I felt that I was not to die with the body (or appearance of a body) which I seemed to possess. That everything about me, even life and death, was illusory; that I had overleaped the bounds of mortality and corporeal entity, becoming a free, detached thing; impressed me as almost certain. Of my location I knew nothing, save that I felt I could not be on the earth-planet once so familiar to me. My sensations, apart from a kind of haunting terror, were those of a traveller just embarked upon an unending voyage of discovery. For a moment I thought of the lands and persons I had left behind; and of strange ways whereby I might some day tell them of my adventurings, even though I might never return.

I had now floated very near the Green Meadow, so that the voices were clear and distinct; but though I knew many languages I could not quite interpret the words of the chanting. Familiar they indeed were, as I had subtly felt when at a greater distance, but beyond a sensation of vague and awesome remembrance I could make nothing of them. A most extraordinary *quality* in the voices – a quality which I cannot describe – at once frightened and fascinated me. My eyes could now discern several things amidst the omnipresent verdure – rocks, covered with bright green moss, shrubs of considerable height, and less definable shapes of great magnitude which seemed to move or vibrate amidst the shrubbery in a peculiar way. The chanting, whose authors I was so anxious to glimpse, seemed loudest at points where these shapes were most numerous and most vigorously in motion.

And then, as my island drifted closer and the sound of the distant waterfall grew louder, I saw clearly the *source* of the chanting, and in one horrible instant remembered everything. Of such things I cannot, dare not tell, for therein was revealed the hideous solution of all which had puzzled me; and that solution would drive you mad, even as it almost drove me ... I knew now the change through which I had passed, and through which certain others who once were men had passed! and I knew the endless cycle of the future which none like me may escape ... I shall live forever, be conscious forever, though my soul cries out to the gods for the boon of death and oblivion ... All is before me: beyond the deafening torrent lies the land of Stethelos, where young men are infinitely old ... The Green Meadow ... I will send a message across the horrible immeasurable abyss ...

[At this point the text becomes illegible.]

NATHICANA

I T WAS IN THE PALE garden of Zaïs;
The mist-shrouded gardens of Zaïs,
Where blossoms the white nephalotë,
The redolent herald of midnight.
There slumber the still lakes of crystal,
And streamlets that flow without murm'ring;
Smooth streamlets from caverns of Kathos
Where brood the calm spirits of twilight.
And over the lakes and the streamlets
Are bridges of pure alabaster,
White bridges all cunningly carven
With figures of fairies and daemons.
Here glimmer strange suns and strange planets,
And strange is the crescent Banapis
That sets 'yond the ivy-grown ramparts
Where thickens the dust of the evening.
Here fall the white vapours of Yabon;
And here in the swirl of vapours

226

I saw the divine Nathicana;
The garlanded, white Nathicana;
The slender, black-hair'd Nathicana;
The sloe-ey'd, red-lipp'd Nathicana;
The silver-voic'd, sweet Nathicana;
The pale-rob'd, belov'd Nathicana.
And ever was she my belovèd,
From ages when Time was unfashion'd;
From days when the stars were not fashion'd
Nor any thing fashion'd but Yabon.
And here dwelt we ever and ever,
The innocent children of Zaïs,
At peace in the paths and the arbours,
White-crown'd with the blest nephalotë.
How oft would we float in the twilight
O'er flow'r-cover'd pastures and hillsides
All white with the lowly astalthon;
The lowly yet lovely astalthon,
And dream in a world made of dreaming
The dreams that are fairer than Aidenn;
Bright dreams that are truer than reason!
So dream'd and so lov'd we thro' ages,
Till came the curs'd season of Dzannin;
The daemon-damn'd season of Dzannin;
When red shone the suns and the planets,
And red gleamed the crescent Banapis,
And red fell the vapours of Yabon.
Then redden'd the blossoms and streamlets
And lakes that lay under the bridges,
And even the calm alabaster
Glow'd pink with uncanny reflections
Till all the carv'd fairies and daemons
Leer'd redly from the backgrounds of shadow.
Now redden'd my vision, and madly
I strove to peer thro' the dense curtain
And glimpse the divine Nathicana;
The pure, ever-pale Nathicana;
The lov'd, the unchang'd Nathicana.
But vortex on vortex of madness

Beclouded my labouring vision;
My damnable, reddening vision
That built a new world for my seeing;
A new world of redness and darkness,
A horrible coma call'd living.
So now in this coma call'd living
I view the bright phantoms of beauty;
The false, hollow phantoms of beauty
That cloak all the evils of Dzannin.
I view them with infinite longing,
So like do they seem to my lov'd one;
So shapely and fair like my lov'd one;
Yet foul from their eyes shines their evil;
Their cruel and pitiless evil,
More evil than Thaphron and Latgoz,
Twice ill for its gorgeous concealment.
And only in slumbers of midnight
Appears the lost maid Nathicana,
The pallid, the pure Nathicana,
Who fades at the glance of the dreamer.
Again and again do I seek her;
I woo with deep draughts of Plathotis,
Deep draughts brew'd in wine of Astarte
And strengthen'd with tears of long weeping.
I yearn for the gardens of Zaïs;
The lovely lost garden of Zaïs
Where blossoms the white nephalotë,
The redolent herald of midnight.
The last potent draught I am brewing;
A draught that the daemons delight in;
A draught that will banish the redness;
The horrible coma call'd living.
Soon, soon, if I fail not in brewing,
The redness and madness will vanish,
And deep in the worm-peopled darkness
Will rot the base chains that have bound me.
Once more shall the gardens of Zaïs
Dawn white on my long-tortur'd vision,
And there midst the vapours of Yabon

Will stand the divine Nathicana;
The deathless, restor'd Nathicana
Whose like is not met with in living.

TWO BLACK BOTTLES

(with Wilfred Blanch Talman)

N OT ALL OF THE FEW remaining inhabitants of Daalbergen, that dismal little village in the Ramapo Mountains, believe that my uncle, old Dominie Vanderhoof, is really dead. Some of them believe he is suspended somewhere between heaven and hell because of the old sexton's curse. If it had not been for that old magician, he might still be preaching in the little damp church across the moor.

After what has happened to me in Daalbergen, I can almost share the opinion of the villagers. I am not sure that my uncle is dead, but I am very sure that he is not alive upon this earth. There is no doubt that the old sexton buried him once, but he is not in that grave now. I can almost feel him behind me as I write, impelling me to tell the truth about those strange happenings in Daalbergen so many years ago.

It was the fourth day of October when I arrived at Daalbergen in answer to a summons. The letter was from a former member of my uncle's congregation, who wrote that the old man had passed away and that there should be some small estate which I, as his only living relative, might inherit. Having reached the secluded little hamlet by a wearying series of changes on branch railways, I found my way to the grocery store of Mark Haines, writer of the letter, and he, leading me into a stuffy back room, told me a peculiar tale concerning Dominie Vanderhoof's death.

'Y' should be careful, Hoffman,' Haines told me, 'when y' meet that old sexton, Abel Foster. He's in league with the devil, sure's you're alive. 'Twa'n't two weeks ago Sam Pryor, when he passed the old graveyard, heared him mumblin 't' the dead there. 'Twa'n't right he should talk that way – an' Sam does vow that there was a voice answered him – a kind o' half-voice, hollow and muffled-like, as though it come out o' th' ground. There's others, too, as could tell y' about seein' him standin' afore old Dominie Slott's grave – that one right agin' the church wall – a-wringin' his hands an' a-talkin' t' th' moss on th' tombstone as though it was the old Dominie himself.'

Old Foster, Haines said, had come to Daalbergen about ten years before, and had been immediately engaged by Vanderhoof to take care of the damp stone church at which most of the villagers worshipped. No one but Vanderhoof seemed to like him, for his presence brought a suggestion almost of the uncanny. He would sometimes stand by the door when the people came to church, and the men would coldly return his servile bow while the women brushed past in haste, holding their skirts aside to avoid touching him. He could be seen on week days cutting the grass in the cemetery and tending the flowers around the graves, now and then crooning and muttering to himself. And few failed to notice the particular attention he paid to the grave of the Reverend Guilliam Slott, first pastor of the church in 1701.

It was not long after Foster's establishment as a village fixture that disaster began to lower. First came the failure of the mountain mine where most of the men worked. The vein of iron had given out, and many of the people moved away to better localities, while those who had large holdings of land in the vicinity took to farming and managed to wrest a meagre living from the rocky hillsides. Then came the disturbances in the church. It was whispered about that the Reverend Johannes Vanderhoof had made a compact with the devil, and was preaching his word in the house of God. His sermons had become weird and grotesque – redolent with sinister things which the ignorant people of Daalbergen did not understand. He transported them back over ages of fear and superstition to regions of hideous, unseen spirits, and peopled their fancy with night-haunting ghouls. One by one the congregation dwindled, while the elders and deacons vainly pleaded with Vanderhoof to change the subject of his sermons. Though the old man continually promised to comply, he seemed to be enthralled by some higher power which forced him to do its will.

A giant in stature, Johannes Vanderhoof was known to be weak and timid at heart, yet even when threatened with expulsion he continued his eerie sermons, until scarcely a handful of people remained to listen to him on Sunday morning. Because of weak finances, it was found impossible to call a new pastor, and before long not one of the villagers dared venture near the church or the parsonage which adjoined it. Everywhere there was fear of those spectral wraiths with whom Vanderhoof was apparently in league.

My uncle, Mark Haines told me, had continued to live in the parsonage because there was no one with sufficient courage to tell him to move out of it. No one ever saw him again, but lights were visible in the parsonage at night, and were even glimpsed in the church from time to time. It was whispered about the town that Vanderhoof preached regularly in the church every Sunday morning, unaware that his congregation was no longer there to listen. He had only the old sexton, who lived in the basement of the church, to take care of him, and Foster made a weekly visit to what remained of the business section of the village to buy provisions. He no longer bowed servilely to everyone he met, but instead seemed to harbour a demoniac and ill-concealed hatred. He spoke to no one except as was necessary to make his purchases, and glanced from left to right out of evil-filled eyes as he walked the street with his cane tapping the uneven pavements. Bent and shrivelled with extreme age, his presence could actually be felt by anyone near him, so powerful was that personality which, said the townspeople, had made Vanderhoof accept the devil as his master. No person in Daalbergen doubted that Abel Foster was at the bottom of all the town's ill luck, but not a one dared lift a finger against him, or could even approach him without a tremor of fear. His name, as well as Vanderhoof's, was never mentioned aloud.

Whenever the matter of the church across the moor was discussed, it was in whispers; and if the conversation chanced to be nocturnal, the whisperers would keep glancing over their shoulders to make sure that nothing shapeless or sinister crept out of the darkness to bear witness to their words.

The churchyard continued to be kept just as green and beautiful as when the church was in use, and the flowers near the graves in the cemetery were tended just as carefully as in times gone by. The old sexton could occasionally be seen working there, as if still being paid for his services, and those who dared venture near said that he maintained a continual conversation with the devil and with those spirits which lurked within the graveyard walls.

One morning, Haines went on to say, Foster was seen digging a grave where the steeple of the church throws its shadow in the afternoon, before the sun goes down behind the mountain and puts the entire village in semi-twilight. Later, the church bell, silent for months, tolled solemnly for a half-hour. And at sundown those who were watching from a distance saw Foster bring a coffin from the parsonage on a wheelbarrow, dump it into the grave with slender ceremony, and replace the earth in the hole.

The sexton came to the village the next morning, ahead of his usual weekly schedule, and in much better spirits than was customary. He seemed willing to talk, remarking that Vanderhoof had died the day before, and that he had buried his body beside that of Dominie Slott near the church wall. He smiled from time to time, and rubbed his hands in an untimely and unaccountable glee. It was apparent that he took a perverse and diabolic delight in Vanderhoof's death. The villagers were conscious of an added uncanniness in his presence, and avoided him as much as they could. With Vanderhoof gone they felt more insecure than ever, for the old sexton was now free to cast his worst spells over the town from the church across the moor. Muttering something in a tongue which no one understood, Foster made his way back along the road over the swamp.

It was then, it seems, that Mark Haines remembered having heard Dominie Vanderhoof speak of me as his nephew. Haines accordingly sent for me, in the hope that I might know something which would clear up the mystery of my uncle's last years. I assured my summoner, however, that I knew nothing about my uncle or his past, except that my mother had mentioned him as a man of gigantic physique but with little courage or power of will.

Having heard all that Haines had to tell me, I lowered the front legs of my chair to the floor and looked at my watch. It was late afternoon.

'How far is it out to the church?' I inquired. 'Think I can make it before sunset?'

'Sure, lad, y' ain't goin' out there t'night! Not t' that place!' The old man trembled noticeably in every limb and half rose from his chair, stretching out a lean, detaining hand. 'Why, it's plumb foolishness!' he exclaimed.

I laughed aside his fears and informed him that, come what may, I was determined to see the old sexton that evening and get the whole matter over as soon as possible. I did not intend to accept the superstitions of ignorant country folk as truth, for I was convinced that all I had just heard was merely a chain of events which the over-imaginative people of Daalbergen had happened to link with their ill-luck. I felt no sense of fear or horror whatever.

Seeing that I was determined to reach my uncle's house before nightfall, Haines ushered me out of his office and reluctantly gave me the few required directions, pleading from time to time that I change my mind. He shook my hand when I left, as though he never expected to see me again.

'Take keer that old devil, Foster, don't git ye!' he warned, again and again. 'I wouldn't go near him after dark fer love n'r money. No siree!' He re-entered his store, solemnly shaking his head, while I set out along a road leading to the outskirts of the town.

I had walked barely two minutes before I sighted the moor of which Haines had spoken. The road, flanked by a whitewashed fence, passed over the great swamp, which was overgrown with clumps of underbrush dipping down into the dank, slimy ooze. An odour of deadness and decay filled the air, and even in the sunlit afternoon little wisps of vapour could be seen rising from the unhealthful spot.

On the opposite side of the moor I turned sharply to the left, as I had been directed, branching from the main road. There were several houses in the vicinity, I noticed; houses which were scarcely more than huts, reflecting the extreme poverty of their owners. The road here passed under the drooping branches of enormous willows which almost completely shut out the rays of the sun. The miasmal odour of the swamp was still in my nostrils, and the air was damp and chilly. I hurried my pace to get out of that dismal tunnel as soon as possible.

Presently I found myself in the light again. The sun, now hanging like a red ball upon the crest of the mountain, was beginning to dip low, and there, some distance ahead of me, bathed in its bloody iridescence, stood the lonely church. I began to sense that uncanniness which Haines had mentioned; that feeling of dread which made all Daalbergen shun the place. The squat, stone hulk of the church itself, with its blunt steeple, seemed like an idol to which the tombstones that surrounded it bowed down and worshipped, each with an arched top like the shoulders of a kneeling person, while over the whole assemblage the dingy, grey parsonage hovered like a wraith.

I had slowed my pace a trifle as I took in the scene. The sun was disappearing behind the mountain very rapidly now, and the damp air chilled me. Turning my coat collar up about my neck, I plodded on. Something caught my eye as I glanced up again. In the shadow of the church wall was something white – a thing which seemed to have no definite shape. Straining my eyes as I came nearer, I saw that it was a cross of new timber, surmounting a mound of freshly turned earth. The discovery sent a new chill through me. I realised that this must be my uncle's grave, but something told me that it was not like the other graves near it. It did not seem like a *dead* grave. In some intangible way it appeared to be *living*, if a grave can be said to live. Very close to it, I saw as I came nearer, was another grave; an old mound with a crumbling stone about it. Dominie Slott's tomb, I thought, remembering Haines's story.

There was no sign of life anywhere about the place. In the semi-twilight I climbed the low knoll upon which the parsonage stood, and hammered upon the door. There was no answer. I skirted the house and peered into the windows. The whole place seemed deserted.

The lowering mountains had made night fall with disarming suddenness the minute the sun was fully hidden. I realised that I could see scarcely more than a few feet ahead of me. Feeling my way carefully, I rounded a corner of the house and paused, wondering what to do next.

Everything was quiet. There was not a breath of wind, nor were there even the usual noises made by animals in their nocturnal ramblings. All dread had been forgotten for a time, but in the presence of that sepulchral calm my apprehensions returned. I imagined the air peopled with ghastly spirits that pressed around me, making the air almost unbreathable. I wondered, for the hundredth time, where the old sexton might be.

As I stood there, half expecting some sinister demon to creep from the shadows, I noticed two lighted windows glaring from the belfry of the church. I then remembered what Haines had told me about Foster's living in the basement of the building. Advancing cautiously through the blackness, I found a side door of the church ajar.

The interior had a musty and mildewed odour. Everything I touched was covered with a cold, clammy moisture. I struck a match and began to explore, to discover, if I could, how to get into the belfry. Suddenly I stopped in my tracks.

A snatch of song, loud and obscene, sung in a voice that was guttural and thick with drink, came from above me. The match burned my fingers, and I dropped it. Two pin-points of light pierced the darkness of the farther wall of the church, and below them, to one side, I could see a door outlined where light filtered through its cracks. The song stopped as abruptly as it had commenced, and there was absolute silence again. My heart was thumping and blood racing through my temples. Had I not been petrified with fear, I should have fled immediately.

Not caring to light another match, I felt my way among the pews until I stood in front of the door. So deep was the feeling of depression which had come over me that I felt as though I were acting in a dream. My actions were almost involuntary.

The door was locked, as I found when I turned the knob. I hammered upon it for some time, but there was no answer. The silence was as complete as before. Feeling around the edge of the door, I found the hinges, removed the pins from them, and allowed the door to fall toward me. Dim light flooded down a steep flight of steps. There was a sickening odour of whisky. I could now hear someone stirring in the belfry room above. Venturing a low halloo, I thought I heard a groan in reply, and cautiously climbed the stairs.

My first glance into that unhallowed place was indeed startling.

Strewn about the little room were old and dusty books and manu-scripts – strange things that bespoke almost unbelievable age. On rows of shelves which reached to the ceiling were horrible things in glass jars and bottles – snakes and lizards and bats. Dust and mould and cobwebs encrusted everything. In the centre, behind a table upon which was a lighted candle, a nearly empty bottle of whisky, and a glass, was a motionless figure with a thin, scrawny, wrinkled face and wild eyes that stared blankly through me. I recog-nised Abel Foster, the old sexton, in an instant. He did not move or speak as I came slowly and fearfully toward him.

'Mr Foster?' I asked, trembling with unaccountable fear when I heard my voice echo within the close confines of the room. There was no reply, and no movement from the figure behind the table. I wondered if he had not drunk himself to insensibility, and went behind the table to shake him.

At the mere touch of my arm upon his shoulder, the strange old man started from his chair as though terrified. His eyes, still having in them that same blank stare, were fixed upon me. Swinging his arms like flails, he backed away.

'Don't!' he screamed. 'Don't touch me! Go back – go back!'

I saw that he was both drunk and struck with some kind of a nameless terror. Using a soothing tone, I told him who I was and why I had come. He seemed to understand vaguely and sank back into his chair, sitting limp and motionless.

'I thought ye was him,' he mumbled. 'I thought ye was him come back fer it. He's been a-tryin' t' get out – a-tryin' t' get out sence I put him in there.' His voice again rose to a scream and he clutched his chair. 'Maybe he's got out now! Maybe he's out!'

I looked about, half expecting to see some spectral shape coming up the stairs.

'Maybe who's out?' I inquired.

'Vanderhoof!' he shrieked. 'Th' cross over his grave keeps fallin' down in th' night! Every morning the earth is loose, and gets harder t' pat down. He'll come out an' I won't be able t' do nothin'.'

Forcing him back into the chair, I seated myself on a box near him. He was trembling in mortal terror, with the saliva dripping from the corners of his mouth. From time to time I felt that sense of horror which Haines had described when he told me of the old sexton. Truly, there was something uncanny about the man. His head had now sunk forward upon his breast, and he seemed calmer, mumbling to himself.

I quietly arose and opened a window to let out the fumes of whisky and the musty odour of dead things. Light from a dim moon, just risen, made objects below barely visible. I could just see Dominie Vanderhoof's grave from my position in the belfry, and blinked my eyes as I gazed at it. That cross *was* tilted! I remembered that it had been vertical an hour ago. Fear took possession of me again. I turned quickly. Foster sat in his chair watching me. His glance was saner than before.

'So ye're Vanderhoof's nephew,' he mumbled in a nasal tone. 'Waal, ye might's well know it all. He'll be back arter me afore long, he will – jus' as soon as he can get out o' that there grave. Ye might's well know all about it now.'

His terror appeared to have left him. He seemed resigned to some horrible fate which he expected any minute. His head dropped down upon his chest again, and he went on muttering in that nasal monotone.

'Ye see all them there books and papers? Waal, they was once Dominie Slott's – Dominie Slott, who was here years ago. All them things is got t' do with magic – black magic that th' old Dominie knew afore he come t' this country. They used t' burn 'em an' boil 'em in oil fer knowin' that over there, they did. But old Slott knew, and he didn't go fer t' tell nobody. No sir, old Slott used to preach here generations ago, an' he used to come up here an' study them books, an' use all them dead things in jars, an' pronounce magic curses an' things, but he didn't let nobody know it. No, nobody knowed it but Dominie Slott an' me.'

'You?' I ejaculated, leaning across the table toward him.

'That is, me after I learned it.' His face showed lines of trickery as he answered me. 'I found all this stuff here when I come t' be church sexton, an' I used t' read it when I wa'n't at work. An' I soon got t' know all about it.'

The old man droned on, while I listened, spellbound. He told about learning the difficult formulae of demonology, so that, by means of incantations, he could cast spells over human beings. He had performed horrible occult rites of his hellish creed, calling down anathema upon the town and its inhabitants. Crazed by his desires, he tried to bring the church under his spell, but the power of God was too strong. Finding Johannes Vanderhoof very weak-willed, he bewitched him so that he preached strange and mystic sermons which struck fear into the simple hearts of the country folk. From his position in the belfry room, he said, behind a painting of the temptation of Christ which adorned the rear wall of the church, he would glare at Vanderhoof while he was preaching, through holes which were the eyes of the Devil in the picture. Terrified by the uncanny things which were happening in their midst, the congregation left one by one, and Foster was able to do what he pleased with the church and with Vanderhoof.

'But what did you do with him?' I asked in a hollow voice as the old sexton paused in his confession. He burst into a cackle of laughter, throwing back his head in drunken glee.

'I took his soul!' he howled in a tone that set me trembling. 'I took his soul and put it in a bottle – in a little black bottle! And I buried him! But he ain't got his soul, an' he cain't go neither t' heaven n'r hell! But he's a-comin' back after it. He's a-tryin' t' get out o' his grave now. I can hear him pushin' his way up through the ground, he's that strong!"

As the old man had proceeded with his story, I had become more and more convinced that he must be telling me the truth, and not merely gibbering in drunkenness. Every detail fitted what Haines had told me. Fear was growing upon me by degrees. With the old wizard now shouting with demoniac laughter, I was tempted to bolt down the narrow stairway and leave that accursed neighbourhood. To calm myself, I rose and again looked out of the window. My eyes nearly started from their sockets when I saw that the cross above Vanderhoof's grave had fallen per-ceptibly since I had last looked at it. It was now tilted to an angle of forty-five degrees!

'Can't we dig up Vanderhoof and restore his soul?' I asked almost breathlessly, feeling that something must be done in a hurry. The old man rose from his chair in terror.

'No, no, no!' he screamed. 'He'd kill me! I've fergot th' formula, an' if he gets out he'll be alive, without a soul. He'd kill us both!'

'Where is the bottle that contains his soul?' I asked, advancing threateningly toward him. I felt that some ghastly thing was about to happen, which I must do all in my power to prevent.

'I won't tell ye, ye young whelp!' he snarled. I felt, rather than saw, a queer light in his eyes as he backed into a corner. 'An' don't ye touch me, either, or ye'll wish ye hadn't!'

I moved a step forward, noticing that on a low stool behind him there were two black bottles. Foster muttered some peculiar words in a low singsong voice. Everything began to turn grey before my eyes, and something within me seemed to be dragged upward, trying to get out at my throat. I felt my knees become weak.

Lurching forward, I caught the old sexton by the throat, and with my free arm reached for the bottles on the stool. But the old man fell backward, striking the stool with his foot, and one bottle fell to the floor as I snatched the other. There was a flash of blue flame, and a sulfurous smell filled the room. From the little heap of broken glass a white vapour rose and followed the draft out the window.

'Curse ye, ye rascal!' sounded a voice that seemed faint and far away. Foster, whom I had released when the bottle broke, was crouching against the wall, looking smaller and more shrivelled than before. His face was slowly turning greenish-black.

'Curse ye!' said the voice again, hardly sounding as though it came from his lips. 'I'm done fer! That one in there was mine! *Dominie Slott took it out two hundred years ago!*'

He slid slowly toward the floor, gazing at me with hatred in eyes that were rapidly dimming. His flesh changed from white to black, and then to yellow. I saw with horror that his body seemed to be crumbling away and his clothing falling into limp folds.

The bottle in my hand was growing warm. I glanced at it, fearfully. It glowed with a faint phosphorescence. Stiff with fright, I set it upon the table, but could not keep my eyes from it. There was an ominous moment of silence as its glow became brighter, and then there came distinctly to my ears the sound of sliding earth. Gasping for breath, I looked out of the window. The moon was now well up in the sky, and by its light I could see that the fresh cross above Vanderhoof's grave had completely fallen. Once again there came the sound of trickling gravel, and no longer able to control myself, I stumbled down the stairs and found my way out of doors. Falling now and then as I raced over the uneven ground, I ran on in abject terror. When I had reached the foot of the knoll, at the entrance to that gloomy tunnel beneath the willows, I heard a horrible roar behind me. Turning, I glanced back toward the church. Its wall reflected the light of the moon, and silhouetted against it was a gigantic, loathsome, black shadow climbing from my uncle's grave and floundering gruesomely toward the church.

I told my story to a group of villagers in Haines's store the next morning. They looked from one to the other with little smiles during my tale, I noticed, but when I suggested that they accompany me to the spot, gave various excuses for not caring to go. Though there seemed to be a limit to their credulity, they cared to run no risks. I informed them that I would go alone, though I must confess that the project did not appeal to me.

As I left the store, one old man with a long, white beard hurried after me and caught my arm.

'I'll go wi' ye, lad,' he said. 'It do seem that I once heared my gran'pap tell o' su'thin' o' the sort concernin' old Dominie Slott. A queer old man I've heared he were, but Vanderhoof's been worse.'

Dominie Vanderhoof's grave was open and deserted when we arrived. Of course it could have been grave-robbers, the two of us agreed, and yet ... In the belfry the bottle which I had left upon the table was gone, though the fragments of the broken one were found on the floor. And upon the heap of yellow dust and crumpled clothing that had once been Abel Foster were certain immense footprints.

After glancing at some of the books and papers strewn about the belfry room, we carried them down the stairs and burned them, as something unclean and unholy. With a spade which we found in the church basement we filled in the grave of Johannes Vanderhoof, and, as an afterthought, flung the fallen cross upon the flames.

Old wives say that now, when the moon is full, there walks about the churchyard a gigantic and bewildered figure clutching a bottle and seeking some unremembered goal.

THE LAST TEST

(with Adolphe de Castro)

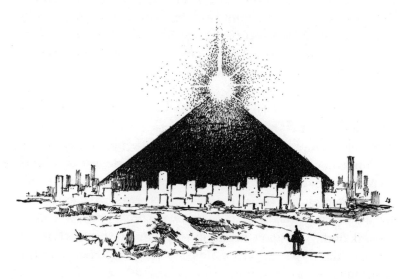

1

F EW PERSONS KNOW the inside of the Clarendon story, or even that there is an inside not reached by the newspapers. It was a San Francisco sensation in the days before the fire, both because of the panic and menace that kept it company, and because of its close linkage with the governor of the state. Governor Dalton, it will be recalled, was Clarendon's best friend, and later married his sister. Neither Dalton nor Mrs Dalton would ever discuss the painful affair, but somehow the facts have leaked out to a limited circle. But for that and for the years which have given a sort of vagueness and impersonality to the actors, one would still pause before probing into secrets so strictly guarded at the time.

The appointment of Dr Alfred Clarendon as medical director of San Quentin Penitentiary in 189– was greeted with the keenest enthusiasm throughout California. San Francisco had at last the honour of harbouring one of the greatest biologists and physicians of the period, and solid pathological leaders from all over the world might be expected to flock thither to study his methods, profit by his advice and researches, and learn how to cope with their own local problems. California, almost over night, would become a centre of medical scholarship with earthwide influence and reputation.

Governor Dalton, anxious to spread the news in its fullest significance, saw to it that the press carried ample and dignified accounts of his new appointee. Pictures of Dr Clarendon and his new home near old Goat Hill, sketches of his career and manifold honours, and popular accounts of his salient scientific discoveries were all presented in the principal California dailies, till the public soon felt a sort of reflected pride in the man whose studies of pyemia in India, of the pest in China, and of every sort of kindred disorder elsewhere would soon enrich the world of medicine with an antitoxin of revolutionary importance – a basic antitoxin combating the whole febrile principle at its very source, and ensuring the ultimate conquest and extirpation of fever in all its diverse forms.

Back of the appointment stretched an extended and not wholly unromantic history of early friendship, long separation, and dramatically renewed acquaintance. James Dalton and the Clarendon family had been friends in New York ten years before – friends and more than friends, since the doctor's only sister, Georgina, was the sweetheart of Dalton's youth, while the doctor himself had been his closest associate and almost his protégé in the days of school and college. The father of Alfred and Georgina, a Wall Street pirate of the ruthless elder breed, had known Dalton's father well; so well, indeed, that he had finally stripped him of all he possessed in a memorable afternoon's fight on the stock exchange. Dalton Senior, hopeless of recuperation and wishing to give his one adored child the benefit of his insurance, had promptly blown out his brains; but James had not sought to retaliate. It was, as he viewed it, all in the game; and he wished no harm to the father of the girl he meant to marry and of the budding young scientist whose admirer and protector he had been throughout their years of fellowship and study. Instead, he turned to the law, established himself in a small way, and in due course of time asked 'Old Clarendon' for Georgina's hand.

Old Clarendon had refused very firmly and loudly, vowing that no pauper and upstart lawyer was fit to be his son-in-law; and a scene of considerable violence had occurred. James, telling the wrinkled freebooter at last what he ought to have been told long before, had left the house and the city in a high temper; and was embarked within a month upon the California life which was to lead him to the governorship through many a fight with ring and politician. His farewells to Alfred and Georgina had been brief, and he had never known the aftermath of that scene in the Clarendon library. Only by a day did he miss the news of Old Clarendon's death from apoplexy, and by so missing it, changed the course of his whole career. He had not written Georgina in the decade that followed; knowing her loyalty to her father, and waiting till his own fortune and position might remove all obstacles to the match. Nor had he sent any word to Alfred, whose calm indifference in the face of affection and hero-worship had always savoured of conscious destiny and the self-sufficiency of genius. Secure in the ties of a constancy rare even then, he had worked and risen with thoughts only of the future; still a bachelor, and with a perfect intuitive faith that Georgina also was waiting.

In this faith Dalton was not deceived. Wondering perhaps why no message ever came, Georgina found no romance save in her dreams and expectations; and in the course of time became busy with the new responsibilities brought by her brother's rise to greatness. Alfred's growth had not belied the promise of his youth, and the slim boy had darted quietly up the steps of science with a speed and permanence almost dizzying to contemplate. Lean and ascetic, with steel-rimmed pince-nez and pointed brown beard, Dr Alfred Clarendon was an authority at twenty-five and an international figure at thirty. Careless of worldly affairs with the negligence of genius, he depended vastly on the care and management of his sister, and was secretly thankful that her memories of James had kept her from other and more tangible alliances.

Georgina conducted the business and household of the great bacteriologist, and was proud of his strides toward the conquest of fever. She bore patiently with his eccentricities, calmed his occasional bursts of fanaticism, and healed those breaches with his friends which now and then resulted from his unconcealed scorn of anything less than a single-minded devotion to pure truth and its progress. Clarendon was undeniably irritating at times to ordinary folk; for he never tired of depreciating the service of the individual as contrasted with the service of mankind as a whole, and in censuring men of learning who mingled domestic life or outside interests with their pursuit of abstract science. His enemies called him a bore; but his admirers, pausing before the white heat of ecstasy into which he would work himself, became almost ashamed of ever having any standards or aspirations outside the one divine sphere of unalloyed knowledge.

The doctor's travels were extensive and Georgina generally accompanied him on the shorter ones. Three times, however, he had taken long, lone jaunts to strange and distant places in his studies of exotic fevers and half-fabulous plagues; for he knew that it is out of the unknown lands of cryptic and immemorial Asia that most of the earth's diseases spring. On each of these occasions he had brought back curious mementoes which added to the eccentricity of his home, not least among which was the needlessly large staff of eight Tibetan servants picked up somewhere in U-tsang during an epidemic of which the world never heard, but amidst which Clarendon had discovered and isolated the germ of black fever. These men, taller than most Tibetans and clearly belonging to a stock but little investigated in the outside world, were of a skeletonic leanness which made one wonder whether the doctor had sought to symbolise in them the anatomical models of his college years. Their aspect, in the loose black silk robes of Bonpa priests which he chose to give them, was grotesque in the highest degree; and there was an unsmiling silence and stiffness in their motions which enhanced their air of fantasy and gave Georgina a queer, awed feeling of having stumbled into the pages of Vathek or the Arabian Nights.

But queerest of all was the general factotum or clinic-man, whom Clarendon addressed as Surama, and whom he had brought back with him after a long stay in Northern Africa, during which he had studied certain odd intermittent fevers among the mysterious Saharan Tuaregs, whose descent from the primal race of lost Atlantis is an old archaeological rumour. Surama, a man of great intelligence and seemingly inexhaustible erudition, was as morbidly lean as the Tibetan servants; with swarthy, parchment-like skin drawn so tightly over his bald pate and hairless face that every line of the skull stood out in ghastly prominence – this death's-head effect being heightened by lustrelessly burning black eyes set with a depth which left to common visibility only a pair of dark, vacant sockets. Unlike the ideal subordinate, he seemed despite his impassive features to spend no effort in concealing such emotions as he possessed. Instead, he carried about an insidious atmosphere of irony or amusement, accompanied at certain moments by a deep, guttural chuckle like that of a giant turtle which has just torn to pieces some furry animal and is ambling away toward the sea. His race appeared to be Caucasian, but could not be classified more closely than that. Some of Clarendon's friends thought he looked like a high-caste Hindoo notwithstanding his accentless speech, while many agreed with Georgina – who disliked him – when she gave her opinion that a Pharaoh's mummy, if miraculously brought to life, would form a very apt twin for this sardonic skeleton.

Dalton, absorbed in his uphill political battles and isolated from Eastern interests through the peculiar self-sufficiency of the old West, had not followed the meteoric rise of his former comrade; Clarendon had actually heard nothing of one so far outside his chosen world of science as the governor. Being of independent and even of abundant means, the Clarendons had for many years stuck to their old Manhattan mansion in East Nineteenth Street, whose ghosts must have looked sorely askance at the bizarrerie of Surama and the Tibetans. Then, through the doctor's wish to transfer his base of medical observation, the great change had suddenly come, and they had crossed the continent to take up a secluded life in San Francisco; buying the gloomy old Bannister place near Goat Hill, overlooking the bay, and establishing their strange household in a rambling, French-roofed relic of mid-Victorian design and gold-rush parvenu display, set amidst high-walled grounds in a region still half suburban.

Dr Clarendon, though better satisfied than in New York, still felt cramped for lack of opportunities to apply and test his pathological theories. Unworldly as he was, he had never thought of using his reputation as an influence to gain public appointment; though more and more he realised that only the medical directorship of a government or a charitable institution – a prison, almshouse, or hospital – would give him a field of sufficient width to complete his researches and make his discoveries of the greatest use to humanity and science at large.

Then he had run into James Dalton by sheer accident one afternoon in Market Street as the governor was swinging out of the Royal Hotel. Georgina had been with him, and an almost instant recognition had heightened the drama of the reunion. Mutual ignorance of one another's progress had bred long explanation and histories, and Clarendon was pleased to find that he had so important an official for a friend. Dalton and Georgina, exchanging many a glance, felt more than a trace of their youthful tenderness; and a friendship was then and there revived which led to frequent calls and a fuller and fuller exchange of confidences.

James Dalton learned of his old protégé's need for political appointment, and sought, true to his protective role of school and college days, to devise some means of giving 'Little Alf' the needed position and scope. He had, it is true, wide appointive powers; but the legislature's constant attacks and encroachments forced him to exercise these with the utmost discretion. At length, however, scarcely three months after the sudden reunion, the foremost institutional medical office in the state fell vacant. Weighing all the elements with care, and conscious that his friend's achievements and reputation would justify the most substantial rewards, the governor felt at last able to act. Formalities were few, and on the eighth of November, 189—, Dr Alfred Schuyler Clarendon became medical director of the California State Penitentiary at San Quentin.

2

In scarcely more than a month the hopes of Dr Clarendon's admirers were amply fulfilled. Sweeping changes in methods brought to the prison's medical routine an efficiency never before dreamed of; and though the subordinates were naturally not without jealousy, they were obliged to admit the magical results of a really great man's superintendence. Then came a time where mere appreciation might well have grown to devout thankfulness at a providential conjunction of time, place, and man; for one morning Dr Jones came to his new chief with a grave face to announce his discovery of a case which he could not but identify as that selfsame black fever whose germ Clarendon had found and classified.

Dr Clarendon shewed no surprise, but kept on at the writing before him.

'I know,' he said evenly; 'I came across that case yesterday. I'm glad you recognised it. Put the man in a separate ward, though I don't believe this fever is contagious.'

Dr Jones, with his own opinion of the malady's contagiousness, was glad of this deference to caution; and hastened to execute the order. Upon his return Clarendon rose to leave, declaring that he would himself take charge of the case alone. Disappointed in his wish to study the great man's methods and technique, the junior physician watched his chief stride away toward the lone ward where he had placed the patient, more critical of the new regime than at any time since admiration had displaced his first jealous pangs.

Reaching the ward, Clarendon entered hastily, glancing at the bed and stepping back to see how far Dr Jones's obvious curiosity might have led him. Then, finding the corridor still vacant, he shut the door and turned to examine the sufferer. The man was a convict of a peculiarly repulsive type, and seemed to be racked by the keenest throes of agony. His features were frightfully contracted, and his knees drawn sharply up in the mute desperation of the stricken. Clarendon studied him closely, raising his tightly shut eyelids, took his pulse and temperature, and finally dissolving a tablet in water, forced the solution between the sufferer's lips. Before long the height of the attack abated, as shewn by the relaxing body and returning normality of expression, and the patient began to breathe more easily. Then, by a soft rubbing of the ears, the doctor caused the man to open his eyes. There was life in them, for they moved from side to side, though they lacked the fine fire which we are wont to deem the image of the soul. Clarendon smiled as he surveyed the peace his help had brought, feeling behind him the power of an all-capable science. He had long known of this case, and had snatched the victim from death with the work of a moment. Another hour and this man would have gone – yet Jones had seen the symptoms for days before discovering them, and having discovered them, did not know what to do.

Man's conquest of disease, however, cannot be perfect. Clarendon, assuring the dubious trusty-nurses that the fever was not contagious, had had the patient bathed, sponged in alcohol, and put to bed; but was told the next morning that the case was lost. The man had died after midnight in the most intense agony, and with such cries and distortions of face that the nurses were driven almost to panic. The doctor took this news with his usual calm, whatever his scientific feelings may have been, and ordered the burial of the patient in quicklime. Then, with a philosophic shrug of the shoulders, he made the usual rounds of the penitentiary.

Two days later the prison was hit again. Three men came down at once this time, and there was no concealing the fact that a black fever epidemic was under way. Clarendon, having adhered so firmly to his theory of non-contagiousness, suffered a distinct loss of prestige, and was handicapped by the refusal of the trusty-nurses to attend the patients. Theirs was not the soul-free devotion of those who sacrifice themselves to science and humanity. They were convicts, serving only because of the privileges they could not otherwise buy, and when the price became too great they preferred to resign the privileges.

But the doctor was still master of the situation. Consulting with the warden and sending urgent messages to his friend the governor, he saw to it that special rewards in cash and in reduced terms were offered to the convicts for the dangerous nursing service; and by this method succeeded in getting a very fair quota of volunteers. He was steeled for action now, and nothing could shake his poise and determination. Additional cases brought only a curt nod, and he seemed a stranger to fatigue as he hastened from bedside to bedside all over the vast stone home of sadness and evil. More than forty cases developed within another week, and nurses had to be brought from the city. Clarendon went home very seldom at this stage, often sleeping on a cot in the warden's quarters, and always giving himself up with typical abandon to the service of medicine and of mankind.

Then came the first mutterings of that storm which was soon to convulse San Francisco. News will out, and the menace of black fever spread over the town like a fog from the bay. Reporters trained in the doctrine of 'sensation first' used their imagination without restraint, and gloried when at last they were able to produce a case in the Mexican quarter which a local physician – fonder perhaps of money than of truth or civic welfare – pronounced black fever.

That was the last straw. Frantic at the thought of the crawling death so close upon them, the people of San Francisco went mad en masse, and embarked upon that historic exodus of which all the country was soon to hear over busy wires. Ferries and rowboats, excursion steamers and launches, railways and cable cars, bicycles and carriages, moving-vans and work carts, all were pressed into instant and frenzied service. Sausalito and Tamalpais, as lying in the direction of San Quentin, shared in the flight; while housing space in Oakland, Berkeley, and Alameda rose to fabulous prices. Tent colonies sprang up, and improvised villages lined the crowded southward highways from Millbrae to San Jose. Many sought refuge with friends in Sacramento, while the fright-shaken residue forced by various causes to stay behind could do little more than maintain the basic necessities of a nearly dead city.

Business, save for quack doctors with 'sure cures' and 'preventives' for use against the fever, fell rapidly to the vanishing-point. At first the saloons offered 'medicated drinks', but soon found that the populace preferred to be duped by charlatans of more professional aspect. In strangely noiseless streets persons peered into one another's faces to glimpse possible plague symptoms, and shopkeepers began more and more to refuse admission to their clientele, each customer seeming to them a fresh fever menace. Legal and judicial machinery began to disintegrate as attorneys and county clerks succumbed one by one to the urge for flight. Even the doctors deserted in large numbers, many of them pleading the need of vacations among the mountains and the lakes in the northern part of the state. Schools and colleges, theatres and cafés, restaurants and saloons, all gradually closed their doors; and in a single week San Francisco lay prostrate and inert with only its light, power, and water service even half normal, with newspapers in skeletonic form, and with a crippled parody on transportation maintained by the horse and cable cars.

This was the lowest ebb. It could not last long, for courage and observation are not altogether dead in mankind; and sooner or later the non-existence of any widespread black fever epidemic outside San Quentin became too obvious a fact to deny, notwithstanding several actual cases and the undeniable spread of typhoid in the unsanitary suburban tent colonies. The leaders and editors of the community conferred and took action, enlisting in their service the very reporters whose energies had done so much to bring on the trouble, but now turning their 'sensation first' avidity into more constructive channels. Editorials and fictitious interviews appeared, telling of Dr Clarendon's complete control of the disease, and of the absolute impossibility of its diffusion beyond the prison walls. Reiteration and circulation slowly did their work, and gradually a slim backward trickle of urbanites swelled into a vigorous refluent stream. One of the first healthy symptoms was the start of a newspaper controversy of the approved acrimonious kind, attempting to fix blame for the panic wherever the various participants thought it belonged. The returning doctors, jealously strengthened by their timely vacations, began striking at Clarendon, assuring the public that they as well as he would keep the fever in leash, and censuring him for not doing even more to check its spread within San Quentin.

Clarendon had, they averred, permitted far more deaths than were necessary. The veriest tyro in medicine knew how to check fever contagion; and if this renowned savant did not do it, it was clearly because he chose for scientific reasons to study the final effects of the disease, rather than to prescribe properly and save the victims. This policy, they insinuated, might be proper enough among convicted murderers in a penal institution, but it would not do in San Francisco, where life was still a precious and sacred thing. Thus they went on, and the papers were glad to publish all they wrote, since the sharpness of the campaign, in which Dr Clarendon would doubtless join, would help to obliterate confusion and restore confidence among the people.

But Clarendon did not reply. He only smiled, while his singular clinic-man Surama indulged in many a deep, testudinous chuckle. He was at home more nowadays, so that reporters began besieging the gate of the great wall the doctor had built around his house, instead of pestering the warden's office at San Quentin. Results, though, were equally meagre; for Surama formed an impassable barrier between the doctor and the outer world – even after the reporters had got into the grounds. The newspaper men getting access to the front hall had glimpses of Clarendon's singular entourage and made the best they could in a 'write-up' of Surama and the queer skeletonic Tibetans. Exaggeration, of course, occurred in every fresh article, and the net effect of the publicity was distinctly adverse to the great physician. Most persons hate the unusual, and hundreds who could have excused heartlessness or incompetence stood ready to condemn the grotesque taste manifested in the chuckling attendant and the eight black-robed Orientals.

Early in January an especially persistent young man from the *Observer* climbed the moated eight-foot brick wall in the rear of the Clarendon grounds and began a survey of the varied outdoor appearances which trees concealed from the front walk. With quick, alert brain he took in everything – the rose-arbour, the aviaries, the animal cages where all sorts of mammalia from monkeys to guinea-pigs might be seen and heard, the stout wooden clinic building with barred windows in the northwest corner of the yard – and bent searching glances throughout the thousand square feet of intramural privacy. A great article was brewing, and he would have escaped unscathed but for the barking of Dick, Georgina Clarendon's gigantic and beloved St Bernard. Surama, instant in his response, had the youth by the collar before a protest could be uttered, and was presently shaking him as a terrier shakes a rat, and dragging him through the trees to the front yard and the gate.

Breathless explanations and quavering demands to see Dr Clarendon were useless. Surama only chuckled and dragged his victim on. Suddenly a positive fright crept over the dapper scribe, and he began to wish desperately that this unearthly creature would speak if only to prove that he really was a being of honest flesh and blood belonging to this planet. He became deathly sick, and strove not to glimpse the eyes which he knew must lie at the base of those gaping black sockets. Soon he heard the gate open and felt himself propelled violently through; in another moment waking rudely to the things of earth as he landed wetly and muddily in the ditch which Clarendon had had dug around the entire length of the wall. Fright gave a place to rage as he heard the massive gate slam shut, and he rose dripping to shake his fist at the forbidding portal. Then, as he turned to go, a soft sound grated behind him, and through a small wicket in the gate he felt the sunken eyes of Surama and heard the echoes of a deep-voiced, blood-freezing chuckle.

This young man, feeling perhaps justly that his handling had been rougher than he deserved, resolved to revenge himself upon the household responsible for his treatment. Accordingly he pre-pared a fictitious interview with Dr Clarendon, supposed to be held in the clinic building, during which he was careful to describe the agonies of a dozen black fever patients whom his imagination ranged on orderly rows of couches. His master-stroke was the picture of one especially pathetic sufferer gasping for water, while the doctor held a glass of the sparkling fluid just out of his reach, in a scientific attempt to determine the effect of a tantalising emotion on the course of the disease. This invention was followed by paragraphs of insinuating comment so outwardly respectful that it bore a double venom. Dr Clarendon was, the article ran, undoubtedly the greatest and most single-minded scientist in the world; but science is no friend to individual welfare, and one would not like to have one's gravest ills drawn out and aggravated merely to satisfy an investigator on some point of abstract truth. Life is too short for that.

Altogether, the article was diabolically skilful, and succeeded in horrifying nine readers out of ten against Dr Clarendon and his supposed methods. Other papers were quick to copy and enlarge upon its substance, taking the cue it offered, and commencing a series of 'faked' interviews which fairly ran the gamut of derogatory fantasy. In no case, however, did the doctor condescend to offer a contradiction. He had no time to waste on fools and liars, and cared little for the esteem of a thoughtless rabble he despised. When James Dalton telegraphed his regrets and offered aid, Clarendon replied with an almost boorish curtness. He did not heed the barking of dogs, and could not bother to muzzle them. Nor would he thank anyone for messing with a matter wholly beneath notice. Silent and contemptuous, he continued his duties with tranquil evenness.

But the young reporter's spark had done its work. San Francisco was insane again, and this time as much with rage as with fear. Sober judgement became a lost art; and though no second exodus occurred, there ensued a reign of vice and recklessness born of desperation, and suggesting parallel phenomena in mediaeval times of pestilence. Hatred ran riot against the man who had found the disease and was struggling to restrain it, and a light-headed public forgot his great services to knowledge in their efforts to fan the flames of resentment. They seemed, in their blindness, to hate him in person, rather than the plague which had come to their breeze-cleaned and usually healthy city.

Then the young reporter, playing in the Neronic fire he had

kindled, added a crowning personal touch of his own. Remembering the indignities he had suffered at the hands of the cadaverous clinic-man, he prepared a masterly article on the home and environment of Dr Clarendon, giving especial prominence to Surama, whose very aspect he declared sufficient to scare the healthiest person into any sort of fever. He tried to make the gaunt chuckler appear equally ridiculous and terrible, succeeding best, perhaps, in the latter half of his intention, since a tide of horror always welled up whenever he thought of his brief proximity to the creature. He collected all the rumours current about the man, elaborated on the unholy depth of his reputed scholarship, and hinted darkly that it could have been no godly realm of secret and aeon-weighted Africa wherein Dr Clarendon had found him.

Georgina, who followed the papers closely, felt crushed and hurt by these attacks upon her brother, but James Dalton, who called often at the house, did his best to comfort her. In this he was warm and sincere; for he wished not only to console the woman he loved, but to utter some measure of the reverence he had always felt for the starward-bound genius who had been his youth's closest comrade. He told Georgina how greatness can never be exempted from the shafts of envy, and cited the long, sad list of splendid brains crushed beneath vulgar heels. The attacks, he pointed out, formed the truest of all proofs of Alfred's solid eminence.

'But they hurt just the same,' she rejoined, 'and all the more because I know that Al really suffers from them, no matter how indifferent he tries to be.'

Dalton kissed her hand in a manner not then obsolete among well-born persons.

'And it hurts me a thousand times more, knowing that it hurts you and Alf. But never mind, Georgie, we'll stand together and pull through it!'

Thus it came about that Georgina came more and more to rely on the strength of the steel-firm, square-jawed governor who had been her youthful swain, and more and more to confide in him the things she feared. The press attacks and the epidemic were not quite all. There were aspects of the household which she did not like. Surama, cruel in equal measure to man and beast, filled her with the most unnameable repulsion; and she could not but feel that he meant some vague, indefinable harm to Alfred. She did not like the Tibetans, either, and thought it very peculiar that Surama was able to talk with them. Alfred would not tell her who or what Surama was, but had once explained rather haltingly that he was a much older man than would be commonly thought credible, and that he had mastered secrets and been through experiences calculated to make him a colleague of phenomenal value for any scientist seeking Nature's hidden mysteries.

Urged by her uneasiness, Dalton became a still more frequent visitor at the Clarendon home, though he saw that his presence was deeply resented by Surama. The bony clinic-man formed the habit of glaring peculiarly from those spectral sockets when admitting him, and would often, after closing the gate when he left, chuckle monotonously in a manner that made his flesh creep. Meanwhile Dr Clarendon seemed oblivious of everything save his work at San Quentin, whither he went each day in his launch – alone save for Surama, who managed the wheel while the doctor read or collated his notes. Dalton welcomed these regular absences, for they gave him constant opportunities to renew his suit for Georgina's hand. When he would overstay and meet Alfred, however, the latter's greeting was always friendly despite his habitual reserve. In time the engagement of James and Georgina grew to be a definite thing, and the two awaited only a favourable chance to speak to Alfred.

The governor, whole-soulled in everything and firm in his protective loyalty, spared no pains in spreading propaganda on his old friend's behalf. Press and officialdom both felt his influence, and he even succeeded in interesting scientists in the East, many of whom came to California to study the plague and investigate the anti-fever bacillus which Clarendon was so rapidly isolating and perfecting. These doctors and biologists, however, did not obtain the information they wished; so that several of them left with a very unfortunate impression. Not a few prepared articles hostile to Clarendon, accusing him of an unscientific and fame-seeking attitude, and intimating that he concealed his methods through a highly unprofessional desire for ultimate personal profit.

Others, fortunately, were more liberal in their judgements, and wrote enthusiastically of Clarendon and his work. They had seen the patients, and could appreciate how marvellously he held the dread disease in leash. His secrecy regarding the antitoxin they deemed quite justifiable, since its public diffusion in unperfected form could not but do more harm than good. Clarendon himself, whom many of their number had met before, impressed them more profoundly than ever, and they did not hesitate to compare him with Jenner, Lister, Koch, Pasteur, Metchnikoff, and the rest of those whose whole lives have served pathology and humanity. Dalton was careful to save for Alfred all the magazines that spoke well of him, bringing them in person as an excuse to see Georgina. They did not, however, produce much effect save a contemptuous smile; and Clarendon would generally throw them to Surama, whose deep, disturbing chuckle upon reading them formed a close parallel to the doctor's own ironic amusement.

One Monday evening early in February Dalton called with the definite intention of asking Clarendon for his sister's hand. Georgina herself admitted him to the grounds, and as they walked toward the house he stopped to pat the great dog which rushed up and laid friendly fore paws on his breast. It was Dick, Georgina's cherished St Bernard, and Dalton was glad to feel that he had the affection of a creature which meant so much to her.

Dick was excited and glad, and turned the governor nearly half about with his vigorous pressure as he gave a soft quick bark and sprang off through the trees toward the clinic. He did not vanish, though, but presently stopped and looked back, softly barking again as if he wished Dalton to follow. Georgina, fond of obeying her huge pet's playful whims, motioned to James to see what he wanted; and they both walked slowly after him as he trotted relievedly to the rear of the yard where the top of the clinic building stood silhouetted against the stars above the great brick wall.

The outline of lights within shewed around the edges of the dark window-curtains so they knew that Alfred and Surama were at work. Suddenly from the interior came a thin, subdued sound like a cry of a child – a plaintive call of 'Mamma! Mamma!' at which Dick barked, while James and Georgina started perceptibly. Then Georgina smiled, remembering the parrots that Clarendon always kept for experimental uses, and patted Dick on the head either to forgive him for having fooled her and Dalton, or to console him for having been fooled himself.

As they turned slowly toward the house Dalton mentioned his resolve to speak to Alfred that evening about their engagement, and Georgina supplied no objection. She knew that her brother would not relish the loss of a faithful manager and companion, but believed his affection would place no barrier in the way of her happiness.

Later that evening Clarendon came into the house with a springy step and aspect less grim than usual. Dalton, seeing a good omen in this easy buoyancy, took heart as the doctor wrung his hand with a jovial 'Ah, Jimmy, how's politics this year?' He glanced at Georgina, and she quietly excused herself, while the two men settled down to a chat on general subjects. Little by little, amidst many reminders of their old youthful days, Dalton worked toward his point; till at last he came out plainly with the crucial query.

'Alf, I want to marry Georgina. Have we your blessing?'

Keenly watching his old friend, Dalton saw a shadow steal over his face. The dark eyes flashed for a moment, then veiled themselves as wonted placidity returned. So science or selfishness was at work after all!

'You're asking an impossibility, James. Georgina isn't the aimless butterfly she was years ago. She has a place in the service of truth and mankind now, and that place is here. She's decided to devote her life to my work – to the household that makes my work possible – and there's no room for desertion or personal caprice.'

Dalton waited to see if he had finished. The same old fanaticism – humanity versus the individual – and the doctor was going to let it spoil his sister's life! Then he tried to answer.

'But look here, Alf, do you mean to say that Georgina, in particular, is so necessary to your work that you must make a slave and martyr of her? Use your sense of proportion, man! If it were a question of Surama or somebody in the utter thick of your experiments it might be different; but after all, Georgina is only a housekeeper to you in the last analysis. She has promised to be my wife and says that she loves me. Have you the right to cut her off from the life that belongs to her? Have you the right—'

'That'll do, James!' Clarendon's face was set and white. 'Whether or not I have the right to govern my own family is no business of an outsider.'

'Outsider – you can say that to a man who—' Dalton almost choked as the steely voice of the doctor interrupted him again.

'An outsider to my family, and from now on an outsider to my home. Dalton, your presumption goes just a little too far! Good evening, Governor!'

And Clarendon strode from the room without extending his hand.

Dalton hesitated for a moment, almost at a loss what to do, when presently Georgina entered. Her face shewed that she had spoken with her brother, and Dalton took both her hands impetuously.

'Well, Georgie, what do you say? I'm afraid it's a choice between Alf and me. You know how I feel – you know how I felt before, when it was your father I was up against. What's your answer this time?'

He paused as she responded slowly.

'James, dear, do you believe that I love you?'

He nodded and pressed her hands expectantly.

'Then, if you love me, you'll wait a while. Don't think of Al's rudeness. He's to be pitied. I can't tell you the whole thing now, but you know how worried I am – what with the strain of his work, the criticisms, and the staring and cackling of that horrible creature Surama! I'm afraid he'll break down – he shews the strain more than anyone outside the family could tell. I can see it, for I've watched him all my life. He's changing – slowly bending under his burdens – and he puts on his extra brusqueness to hide it. You can see what I mean, can't you, dear?"

She paused, and Dalton nodded again, pressing one of her hands to his breast. Then she concluded.

'So promise me, dear, to be patient. I must stand by him; I must! I must!'

Dalton did not speak for a while, but his head inclined in what was almost a bow of reverence. There was more of Christ in this devoted woman than he had thought any human being possessed; and in the face of such love and loyalty he could do no urging.

Words of sadness and parting were brief; and James, whose blue eyes were misty, scarcely saw the gaunt clinic-man as the gate to the street was at last opened to him. But when it slammed to behind him he heard that blood-curdling chuckle he had come to recognise so well, and knew that Surama was there – Surama, whom Georgina had called her brother's evil genius. Walking away with a firm step, Dalton resolved to be watchful, and to act at the first sign of trouble.

3

Meanwhile San Francisco, the epidemic still on the lips of all, seethed with anti-Clarendon feeling. Actually the cases outside the penitentiary were very few, and confined almost wholly to the lower Mexican element whose lack of sanitation was a standing invitation to disease of every kind; but politicians and the people needed no more than this to confirm the attacks made by the doctor's enemies. Seeing that Dalton was immovable in his championship of Clarendon, the malcontents, medical dogmatists, and ward-heelers turned their attention to the state legislature; lining up the anti-Clarendonists and the governor's old enemies with great shrewdness, and preparing to launch a law – with a veto-proof majority – transferring the authority for minor institutional appointments from the chief executive to the various boards or commissions concerned.

In the furtherance of this measure no lobbyist was more active than Clarendon's chief assistant, Dr Jones. Jealous of his superior from the first, he now saw an opportunity for turning matters to his liking; and he thanked fate for the circumstance – responsible indeed for his present position – of his relationship to the chairman of the prison board. The new law, if passed, would certainly mean the removal of Clarendon and the appointment of himself in his stead; so, mindful of his own interest, he worked hard for it. Jones was all that Clarendon was not – a natural politician and sycophantic opportunist who served his own advancement first and science only incidentally. He was poor, and avid for salaried position, quite in contrast to the wealthy and independent savant he sought to displace. So with a rat-like cunning and persistence he laboured to undermine the great biologist above him, and was one day rewarded by the news that the new law was passed. Thenceforward the governor was powerless to make appointments to the state institutions, and the medical directorship of San Quentin lay at the disposal of the prison board.

Of all this legislative turmoil Clarendon was singularly oblivious. Wrapped wholly in matters of administration and research, he was blind to the treason of 'that ass Jones' who worked by his side, and deaf to all the gossip of the warden's office. He had never in his life read the newspapers, and the banishment of Dalton from his house cut off his last real link with the world of outside events. With the naiveté of a recluse, he at no time thought of his position as insecure. In view of Dalton's loyalty, and of his forgiveness of even the greatest wrongs, as shewn in his dealings with the elder Clarendon who had crushed his father to death on the stock exchange, the possibility of a gubernatorial dismissal was, of course, out of the question; nor could the doctor's political ignorance envisage a sudden shift of power which might place the matter of retention or dismissal in very different hands. Thereupon he merely smiled with satisfaction when Dalton left for Sacramento; convinced that his place in San Quentin and his sister's place in his household were alike secure from disturbance. He was accustomed to having what he wanted, and fancied his luck was still holding out.

The first week in March, a day or so after the enactment of the new law, the chairman of the prison board called at San Quentin. Clarendon was out, but Dr Jones was glad to shew the august visitor – his own uncle, incidentally – through the great infirmary, including the fever ward made so famous by press and panic. By this time converted against his will to Clarendon's belief in the fever's non-contagiousness, Jones smilingly assured his uncle that nothing was to be feared, and encouraged him to inspect the patients in detail – especially a ghastly skeleton, once a very giant of bulk and vigour, who was, he insinuated, slowly and painfully dying because Clarendon would not administer the proper medicine.

'Do you mean to say,' cried the chairman, 'that Dr Clarendon refuses to let the man have what he needs, knowing his life could be saved?'

'Just that,' snapped Dr Jones, pausing as the door opened to admit none other than Clarendon himself. Clarendon nodded coldly to Jones and surveyed the visitor, whom he did not know, with disapproval.

'Dr Jones, I thought you knew this case was not to be disturbed at all. And haven't I said that visitors aren't to be admitted except by special permission?' But the chairman interrupted before his nephew could introduce him.

'Pardon me, Dr Clarendon, but am I to understand that you refuse to give this man the medicine that would save him?'

Clarendon glared coldly, and rejoined with steel in his voice. 'That's an impertinent question, sir. I am in authority here, and visitors are not allowed. Please leave the room at once.'

The chairman, his sense of drama secretly tickled, answered with greater pomp and hauteur than were necessary.

'You mistake me, sir! I, not you, am master here. You are address-ing the chairman of the prison board. I must say, moreover, that I deem your activity a menace to the welfare of the prisoners, and must request your resignation. Henceforth Dr Jones will be in charge, and if you wish to remain until your formal dismissal you will take your orders from him.'

It was Wilfred Jones's great moment. Life never gave him another such climax, and we need not grudge him this one. After all, he was a small rather than a bad man, and he had only obeyed a small man's code of looking to himself at all costs. Clarendon stood still, gazing at the speaker as if he thought him mad, till in another second the look of triumph on Dr Jones's face convinced him that something important was indeed afoot. He was icily courteous as he replied.

'No doubt you are what you claim to be, sir. But fortunately my appointment came from the governor of the state, and can therefore be revoked only by him.'

The chairman and his nephew both stared perplexedly, for they had not realised to what lengths unworldly ignorance can go. Then the older man, grasping the situation, explained at some length.

'Had I found that the current reports did you an injustice,' he concluded, 'I would have deferred action; but the case of this poor man and your own arrogant manner left me no choice. As it is—'

But Dr Clarendon interrupted with a new razor-sharpness in his voice. 'As it is, I am the director in charge at present, and I ask you to leave this room at once.'

The chairman reddened and exploded. 'Look here, sir, who do you think you're talking to? I'll have you chucked out of here – damn your impertinence!'

But he had time only to finish the sentence. Transformed by the insult to a sudden dynamo of hate, the slender scientist launched out with both fists in a burst of preternatural strength of which no one would have thought him capable. And if his strength was preternatural, his accuracy of aim was no less so; for not even a champion of the ring could have wrought a neater result. Both men – the chairman and Dr Jones – were squarely hit; the one full in the face and the other on the point of the chin. Going down like felled trees, they lay motionless and unconscious on the floor; while Clarendon, now clear and completely master of himself, took his hat and cane and went out to join Surama in the launch. Only when seated in the moving boat did he at last give audible vent to the frightful rage that consumed him. Then, with face convulsed, he called down imprecations from the stars and the gulfs beyond the stars; so that even Surama shuddered, made an elder sign that no book of history records, and forgot to chuckle.

4

Georgina soothed her brother's hurt as best she could. He had come home mentally and physically exhausted and thrown himself on the library lounge; and in that gloomy room, little by little, the faithful sister had taken in the almost incredible news. Her consolations were instantaneous and tender, and she made him realise how vast, though unconscious, a tribute to his greatness the attacks, persecution, and dismissal all were. He had tried to cultivate the indifference she preached, and could have done so had personal dignity alone been involved. But the loss of scientific opportunity was more than he could calmly bear, and he sighed again and again as he repeated how three months more of study in the prison might have given him at last the long-sought bacillus which would make all fever a thing of the past.

Then Georgina tried another mode of cheering, and told him that surely the prison board would send for him again if the fever did not abate, or if it broke out with increased force. But even this was ineffective, and Clarendon answered only in a string of bitter, ironic, and half-meaningless little sentences whose tone shewed all too clearly how deeply despair and resentment had bitten.

'Abate? Break out again? Oh, it'll abate all right! At least, they'll think it has abated. They'd think anything, no matter what happens! Ignorant eyes see nothing, and bunglers are never discoverers. Science never shews her face to that sort. And they call themselves doctors! Best of all, fancy that ass Jones in charge!'

Ceasing with a quick sneer, he laughed so daemoniacally that Georgina shivered.

The days that followed were dismal ones indeed at the Clarendon mansion. Depression, stark and unrelieved, had taken hold of the doctor's usually tireless mind; and he would even have refused food had not Georgina forced it upon him. His great notebook of observations lay unopened on the library table, and his little gold syringe of anti-fever serum – a clever device of his own, with a self-contained reservoir, attached to a broad gold finger ring, and single-pressure action peculiar to itself – rested idly in a small leather case beside it. Vigour, ambition, and the desire for study and observation seemed to have died within him; and he made no inquiries about his clinic, where hundreds of germ cultures stood in their orderly phials awaiting his attention.

The countless animals held for experiments played, lively and well fed, in the early spring sunshine; and as Georgina strolled out through the rose-arbour to the cages she felt a strangely incongruous sense of happiness about her. She knew, though, how tragically transient that happiness must be; since the start of new work would soon make all these small creatures unwilling martyrs to science. Knowing this, she glimpsed a sort of compensating element in her brother's inaction, and encouraged him to keep on in a rest he needed so badly. The eight Tibetan servants moved noiselessly about, each as impeccably effective as usual; and Georgina saw to it that the order of the household did not suffer because of the master's relaxation.

Study and starward ambition laid aside in slippered and dressing-gowned indifference, Clarendon was content to let Georgina treat him as an infant. He met her maternal fussiness with a slow, sad smile, and always obeyed her multitude of orders and precepts. A kind of faint, wistful felicity came over the languid household, amidst which the only dissenting note was supplied by Surama. He indeed was miserable, and looked often with sullen and resentful eyes at the sunny serenity in Georgina's face. His only joy had been the turmoil of experiment, and he missed the routine of seizing the fated animals, bearing them to the clinic in clutching talons, and watching them with hot brooding gaze and evil chuckles as they gradually fell into the final coma with wide-opened, red-rimmed eyes, and swollen tongue lolling from froth-covered mouth.

Now he was seemingly driven to desperation by the sight of the carefree creatures in their cages, and frequently came to ask Clarendon if there were any orders. Finding the doctor apathetic and unwilling to begin work, he would go away muttering under his breath and glaring curses upon everything; stealing with cat-like tread to his own quarters in the basement, where his voice would sometimes ascend in deep, muffled rhythms of blasphemous strangeness and uncomfortably ritualistic suggestion.

All this wore on Georgina's nerves, but not by any means so gravely as her brother's continued lassitude itself. The duration of the state alarmed her, and little by little she lost the air of cheerfulness which had so provoked the clinic-man. Herself skilled in medicine, she found the doctor's condition highly unsatisfactory from an alienist's point of view; and she now feared as much from his absence of interest and activity as she had formerly feared from his fanatical zeal and overstudy. Was lingering melancholy about to turn the once brilliant man of intellect into an innocuous imbecile?

Then, toward the end of May, came the sudden change. Georgina always recalled the smallest details connected with it; details as trivial as the box delivered to Surama the day before, postmarked Algiers, and emitting a most unpleasant odour; and the sharp, sudden thunderstorm, rare in the extreme for California, which sprang up that night as Surama chanted his rituals behind his locked basement door in a droning chest-voice louder and more intense than usual.

It was a sunny day, and she had been in the garden gathering flowers for the dining-room. Re-entering the house, she glimpsed her brother in the library, fully dressed and seated at the table, alternately consulting the notes in his thick observation book, and making fresh entries with brisk assured strokes of the pen. He was alert and vital, and there was a satisfying resilience about his movements as he now and then turned a page, or reached for a book from the rear of the great table. Delighted and relieved, Georgina hastened to deposit her flowers in the dining-room and return; but when she reached the library again she found that her brother was gone.

She knew, of course, that he must be in the clinic at work, and rejoiced to think that his old mind and purpose had snapped back into place. Realising it would be of no use to delay the luncheon for him, she ate alone and set aside a bite to be kept warm in case of his return at an odd moment. But he did not come. He was making up for lost time, and was still in the great stout-planked clinic when she went for a stroll through the rose-arbour.

As she walked among the fragrant blossoms she saw Surama fetching animals for the test. She wished she could notice him less, for he always made her shudder; but her very dread had sharpened her eyes and ears where he was concerned. He always went hatless around the yard, and the total hairlessness of his head enhanced his skeleton-like aspect horribly. Now she heard a faint chuckle as he took a small monkey from its cage against the wall and carried it to the clinic, his long, bony fingers pressing so cruelly into its furry sides that it cried out in frightened anguish. The sight sickened her, and brought her walk to an end. Her inmost soul rebelled at the ascendancy this creature had gained over her brother, and she reflected bitterly that the two had almost changed places as master and servant.

Night came without Clarendon's return to the house, and Georgina concluded that he was absorbed in one of his very longest sessions, which meant total disregard of time. She hated to retire without a talk with him about his sudden recovery; but finally, feeling it would be futile to wait up, she wrote a cheerful note and propped it before his chair on the library table; then started resolutely for bed.

She was not quite asleep when she heard the outer door open and shut. So it had not been an all-night session after all! Determined to see that her brother had a meal before retiring she rose, slipped on a robe, and descended to the library, halting only when she heard voices from behind the half-opened door. Clarendon and Surama were talking, and she waited till the clinic-man might go.

Surama, however, shewed no inclination to depart; and indeed, the whole heated tenor of the discourse seemed to bespeak absorption and promise length. Georgina, though she had not meant to listen, could not help catching a phrase now and then, and presently became aware of a sinister undercurrent which frightened her very much without being wholly clear to her. Her brother's voice, nervous, incisive, held her notice with disquieting persistence.

'But anyway,' he was saying, 'we haven't enough animals for

another day, and you know how hard it is to get a decent supply at short notice. It seems silly to waste so much effort on comparative trash when human specimens could be had with just a little extra care.'

Georgina sickened at the possible implication, and caught at the hall rack to steady herself. Surama was replying in that deep, hollow tone which seemed to echo with the evil of a thousand ages and a thousand planets.

'Steady, steady – what a child you are with your haste and impatience! You crowd things so! When you've lived as I have, so that a whole life will seem only an hour, you won't be so fretful about a day or week or month! You work too fast. You've plenty of specimens in the cages for a full week if you'll only go at a sensible rate. You might even begin on the older material if you'd be sure not to overdo it.'

'Never mind my haste!' the reply was snapped out sharply; 'I have my own methods. I don't want to use our material if I can help it, for I prefer them as they are. And you'd better be careful of them anyway – you know the knives those sly dogs carry.'

Surama's deep chuckle came.

'Don't worry about that. The brutes eat, don't they? Well, I can get you one any time you need it. But go slow – with the boy gone, there are only eight, and now that you've lost San Quentin it'll be hard to get new ones by the wholesale. I'd advise you to start in on Tsanpo – he's the least use to you as he is, and—'

But that was all Georgina heard. Transfixed by a hideous dread from the thoughts this talk excited, she nearly sank to the floor where she stood, and was scarcely able to drag herself up the stairs and into her room. What was the evil monster Surama planning? Into what was he guiding her brother? What monstrous circumstances lay behind these cryptic sentences? A thousand phantoms of darkness and menace danced before her eyes, and she flung herself upon the bed without hope of sleep. One thought above the rest stood out with fiendish prominence, and she almost screamed aloud as it beat itself into her brain with renewed force. Then Nature, kinder than she expected, intervened at last. Closing her eyes in a dead faint, she did not awake till morning, nor did any fresh nightmare come to join the lasting one which the overheard words had brought.

266

With the morning sunshine came a lessening of the tension. What happens in the night when one is tired often reaches the consciousness in distorted forms, and Georgina could see that her brain must have given strange colour to scraps of common medical conversation. To suppose her brother – only son of the gentle Frances Schuyler Clarendon – guilty of savage sacrifices in the name of science would be to do an injustice to their blood, and she decided to omit all mention of her trip downstairs, lest Alfred ridicule her fantastic notions.

When she reached the breakfast table she found that Clarendon was already gone, and regretted that not even this second morning had given her a chance to congratulate him on his revived activity. Quietly taking the breakfast served by stone-deaf old Margarita, the Mexican cook, she read the morning paper and seated herself with some needlework by the sitting-room window overlooking the great yard. All was silent out there, and she could see that the last of the animal cages had been emptied. Science was served, and the lime-pit held all that was left of the once pretty and lively little creatures. This slaughter had always grieved her, but she had never complained, since she knew it was all for humanity. Being a scientist's sister, she used to say to herself, was like being the sister of a soldier who kills to save his countrymen from their foes.

After luncheon Georgina resumed her post by the window, and had been busily sewing for some time when the sound of a pistol shot from the yard caused her to look out in alarm. There, not far from the clinic, she saw the ghastly form of Surama, a revolver in his hand, and his skull-face twisted into a strange expression as he chuckled at a cowering figure robed in black silk and carrying a long Tibetan knife. It was the servant Tsanpo, and as she recognised the shrivelled face Georgina remembered horribly what she had overheard the night before. The sun flashed on the polished blade, and suddenly Surama's revolver spat once more. This time the knife flew from the Mongol's hand, and Surama glanced greedily at his shaking and bewildered prey.

Then Tsanpo, glancing quickly at his unhurt hand and at the fallen knife, sprang nimbly away from the stealthily approaching clinic-man and made a dash for the house. Surama, however, was too swift for him, and caught him in a single leap, seizing his shoulder and almost crushing him. For a moment the Tibetan tried to struggle, but Surama lifted him like an animal by the scruff of the neck and bore him off toward the clinic. Georgina heard him chuckling and taunting the man in his own tongue, and saw the yellow face of the victim twist and quiver with fright. Suddenly realising against her own will what was taking place, a great horror mastered her and she fainted for the second time within twenty-four hours.

When consciousness returned, the golden light of late afternoon was flooding the room. Georgina, picking up her fallen work-basket and scattered materials, was lost in a daze of doubt; but finally felt convinced that the scene which had overcome her must have been all too tragically real. Her worst fears, then, were horrible truths. What to do about it, nothing in her experience could tell her; and she was vaguely thankful that her brother did not appear. She must talk to him, but not now. She could not talk to anybody now. And, thinking shudderingly of the monstrous happening behind those barred clinic windows, she crept into bed for a long night of anguished sleeplessness.

Rising haggardly on the following day, Georgina saw the doctor for the first time since his recovery. He was bustling about pre-occupiedly, circulating between the house and the clinic, and paying little attention to anything besides his work. There was no chance for the dreaded interview, and Clarendon did not even notice his sister's worn-out aspect and hesitant manner.

In the evening she heard him in the library, talking to himself in a fashion most unusual for him, and she felt that he was under a great strain which might culminate in the return of his apathy. Entering the room, she tried to calm him without referring to any trying subject, and forced a steadying cup of bouillon upon him. Finally she asked gently what was distressing him, and waited anxiously for his reply, hoping to hear that Surama's treatment of the poor Tibetan had horrified and outraged him.

There was a note of fretfulness in his voice as he responded.

'What's distressing me? Good God, Georgina, what *isn't*? Look at the cages and see if you have to ask again! Cleaned out – milked dry – not a cursed specimen left; and a line of the most important bacterial cultures incubating in their tubes without a chance to do an ounce of good! Days' work wasted – whole programme set back –

it's enough to drive a man mad! How shall I ever get anywhere if I can't scrape up some decent subjects?'

Georgina stroked his forehead.

'I think you ought to rest a while, Al dear.'

He moved away.

'Rest? That's good! That's damn good! What else have I been doing but resting and vegetating and staring blankly into space for the last fifty or a hundred or a thousand years? Just as I manage to shake off the clouds, I have to run short of material – and then I'm told to lapse back again into drooling stupefaction! God! And all the while some sneaking thief is probably working with my data and getting ready to come out ahead of me with the credit for my own work. I'll lose by a neck – some fool with the proper specimens will get the prize, when one week more with even half-adequate facilities would see me through with flying colours!'

His voice rose querulously, and there was an overtone of mental strain which Georgina did not like. She answered softly, yet not so softly as to hint at the soothing of a psychopathic case.

'But you're killing yourself with this worry and tension, and if you're dead, how can you do your work?'

He gave a smile that was almost a sneer.

'I guess a week or a month – all the time I need – wouldn't quite finish me, and it doesn't much matter what becomes of me or any other individual in the end. Science is what must be served – science – the austere cause of human knowledge. I'm like the monkeys and birds and guinea-pigs I use – just a cog in the machine, to be used to the advantage of the whole. They had to be killed – I may have to be killed – what of it? Isn't the cause we serve worth that and more?'

Georgina sighed. For a moment she wondered whether, after all, this ceaseless round of slaughter really was worth while.

'But are you absolutely sure your discovery will be enough of a boon to humanity to warrant these sacrifices?'

Clarendon's eyes flashed dangerously.

'Humanity! What the deuce is humanity? Science! Dolts! Just individuals over and over again! Humanity is made for preachers to whom it means the blindly credulous. Humanity is made for the predatory rich to whom it speaks in terms of dollars and cents. Humanity is made for the politician to whom it signifies collective power to be used to his advantage. What is humanity? Nothing! Thank God that crude illusion doesn't last! What a grown man worships is truth – knowledge – science – light – the rending of the veil and the pushing back of the shadow. Knowledge, the juggernaut! There is death in our own ritual. We must kill – dissect – destroy – and all for the sake of discovery – the worship of the ineffable light. The goddess Science demands it. We test a doubtful poison by killing. How else? No thought for self – just knowledge – the effect must be known.'

His voice trailed off in a kind of temporary exhaustion, and Georgina shuddered slightly.

'But this is horrible, Al! You shouldn't think of it that way!'

Clarendon cackled sardonically, in a manner which stirred odd and repugnant associations in his sister's mind.

'Horrible? You think what *I* say is horrible? You ought to hear Surama! I tell you, things were known to the priests of Atlantis that would have you drop dead of fright if you heard a hint of them. Knowledge was knowledge a hundred thousand years ago, when our especial forbears were shambling about Asia as speechless semi-apes! They know something of it in the Hoggar region – there are rumours in the farther uplands of Tibet – and once I heard an old man in China calling on Yog-Sothoth—'

He turned pale, and made a curious sign in the air with his extended forefinger. Georgina felt genuinely alarmed, but became somewhat calmer as his speech took a less fantastic form.

'Yes, it may be horrible, but it's glorious too. The pursuit of knowledge, I mean. Certainly, there's no slovenly sentiment con-nected with it. Doesn't Nature kill – constantly and remorselessly – and are any but fools horrified at the struggle? Killings are neces-sary. They are the glory of science. We learn something from them, and we can't sacrifice learning to sentiment. Hear the sen-timentalists howl against vaccination! They fear it will kill the child. Well, what if it does? How else can we discover the laws of disease concerned? As a scientist's sister you ought to know better than to prate sentiment. You ought to help my work instead of hindering it!'

'But, Al,' protested Georgina, 'I haven't the slightest intention of hindering your work. Haven't I always tried to help as much as I could? I am ignorant, I suppose, and can't help very actively; but at least I'm proud of you – proud for my own sake and for the family's sake – and I've always tried to smooth the way. You've given me credit for that many a time.'

Clarendon looked at her keenly.

'Yes,' he said jerkily as he rose and strode from the room, 'you're right. You've always tried to help as best you knew. You may yet have a chance to help still more.'

Georgina, seeing him disappear through the front door, followed him into the yard. Some distance away a lantern was shining through the trees, and as they approached it they saw Surama bending over a large object stretched on the ground. Clarendon, advancing, gave a short grunt; but when Georgina saw what it was she rushed up with a shriek. It was Dick, the great St Bernard, and he was lying still with reddened eyes and protruding tongue.

'He's sick, Al!' she cried. 'Do something for him, quick!'

The doctor looked at Surama, who had uttered something in a tongue unknown to Georgina.

'Take him to the clinic,' he ordered; 'I'm afraid Dick's caught the fever.'

Surama took up the dog as he had taken poor Tsanpo the day before, and carried him silently to the building near the mall. He did not chuckle this time, but glanced at Clarendon with what appeared to be real anxiety. It almost seemed to Georgina that Surama was asking the doctor to save her pet.

Clarendon, however, made no move to follow, but stood still for a moment and then sauntered slowly toward the house. Georgina, astonished at such callousness, kept up a running fire of entreaties on Dick's behalf, but it was of no use. Without paying the slightest attention to her pleas he made directly for the library and began to read in a large old book which had lain face down on the table. She put her hand on his shoulder as he sat there, but he did not speak or turn his head. He only kept on reading, and Georgina, glancing curiously over his shoulder, wondered in what strange alphabet this brass-bound tome was written.

In the cavernous parlour across the hall, sitting alone in the dark a quarter of an hour later, Georgina came to her decision. Something was gravely wrong – just what, and to what extent, she scarcely dared formulate to herself – and it was time that she called in some stronger force to help her. Of course it must be James. He was powerful and capable, and his sympathy and affection would shew him the right thing to do. He had known Al always, and would understand.

It was by this time rather late, but Georgina had resolved on action. Across the hall the light still shone from the library, and she looked wistfully at the doorway as she quietly donned a hat and left the house. Outside the gloomy mansion and forbidding grounds, it was only a short walk to Jackson Street, where by good luck she found a carriage to take her to the Western Union telegraph office. There she carefully wrote out a message to James Dalton in Sacramento, asking him to come at once to San Francisco on a matter of the greatest importance to them all.

5

Dalton was frankly perplexed by Georgina's sudden message. He had had no word from the Clarendons since that stormy February evening when Alfred had declared him an outsider to his home; and he in turn had studiously refrained from communicating, even when he had longed to express sympathy after the doctor's summary ousting from office. He had fought hard to frustrate the politicians and keep the appointive power, and was bitterly sorry to watch the unseating of a man who, despite recent estrangements, still represented to him the ultimate ideal of scientific competence.

Now, with this clearly frightened summons before him, he could not imagine what had happened. He knew, though, that Georgina was not one to lose her head or send forth a needless alarm; hence he wasted no time, but took the Overland which left Sacramento within the hour, going at once to his club and sending word to Georgina by a messenger that he was in town and wholly at her service.

Meanwhile things had been quiescent at the Clarendon home, notwithstanding the doctor's continued taciturnity and his absolute refusal to report on the dog's condition. Shadows of evil seemed omnipresent and thickening, but for the moment there was a lull. Georgina was relieved to get Dalton's message and learn that he was close at hand, and sent back word that she would call him when necessity arose. Amidst all the gathering tension some faint compensating element seemed manifest, and Georgina finally decided that it was the absence of the lean Tibetans, whose stealthy, sinuous ways and disturbing exotic aspect had always annoyed her. They had vanished all at once; and old Margarita, the sole visible servant left in the house, told her they were helping their master and Surama at the clinic.

The following morning – the twenty-eighth of May – long to be remembered – was dark and lowering, and Georgina felt the precarious calm wearing thin. She did not see her brother at all, but knew he was in the clinic hard at work at something despite the lack of specimens he had bewailed. She wondered how poor Tsanpo was getting along, and whether he had really been subjected to any serious inoculation, but it must be confessed that she wondered more about Dick. She longed to know whether Surama had done anything for the faithful dog amidst his master's oddly callous indifference. Surama's apparent solicitude on the night of Dick's seizure had impressed her greatly, giving her perhaps the kindliest feeling she had ever had for the detested clinic-man. Now, as the day advanced, she found herself thinking more and more of Dick; till at last her harassed nerves, finding in this one detail a sort of symbolic summation of the whole horror that lay upon the household, could stand the suspense no longer.

Up to that time she had always respected Alfred's imperious wish that he be never approached or disturbed at the clinic; but as this fateful afternoon advanced, her resolution to break through the barrier grew stronger and stronger. Finally she set out with determined face, crossing the yard and entering the unlocked vestibule of the forbidden structure with the fixed intention of discovering how the dog was or of knowing the reason for her brother's secrecy.

The inner door, as usual, was locked; and behind it she heard voices in heated conversation. When her knocking brought no response she rattled the knob as loudly as possible, but still the voices argued on unheeding. They belonged, of course, to Surama and her brother; and as she stood there trying to attract attention she could not help catch something of their drift. Fate had made her for the second time an eavesdropper, and once more the matter she overheard seemed likely to tax her mental poise and nervous endurance to their ultimate bounds. Alfred and Surama were plainly quarrelling with increasing violence, and the purport of their speech was enough to arouse the wildest fears and confirm the gravest apprehensions. Georgina shivered as her brother's voice mounted shrilly to dangerous heights of fanatical tension.

'You, damn you – you're a fine one to talk defeat and moderation to me! Who started all this, anyway? Did *I* have any idea of your cursed devil-gods and elder world? Did *I* ever in my life think of your damned spaces beyond the stars and your crawling chaos Nyarlathotep? I was a normal scientific man, confound you, till I was fool enough to drag you out of the vaults with your devilish Atlantean secrets. You egged me on, and now you want to cut me off! You loaf around doing nothing and telling me to go slow when you might just as well as not be going out and getting material. You know damn well that I don't know how to go about such things, whereas you must have been an old hand at it before the earth was made. It's like you, you damned walking corpse, to start something you won't or can't finish!'

Surama's evil chuckle came.

'You're insane, Clarendon. That's the only reason I let you rave on when I could send you to hell in three minutes. Enough is enough, and you've certainly had enough material for any novice at your stage. You've had all I'm going to get you, anyhow! You're only a maniac on the subject now – what a cheap, crazy thing to sacrifice even your poor sister's pet dog, when you could have spared him as well as not! You can't look at any living thing now without wanting to jab that gold syringe into it. No – Dick had to go where the Mexican boy went – where Tsanpo and the other seven went – where all the animals went! What a pupil! You're no fun any more – you've lost your nerve. You set out to control things, and they're controlling you. I'm about done with you, Clarendon. I thought you had the stuff in you, but you haven't. It's about time I tried somebody else. I'm afraid you'll have to go!'

In the doctor's shouted reply there was both fear and frenzy.

'Be careful, you—! There are powers against your powers – I didn't go to China for nothing, and there are things in Alhazred's *Azif* which weren't known in Atlantis! We've both meddled in dangerous things, but you needn't think you know all my resources. How about the Nemesis of Flame? I talked in Yemen with an old man who had come back alive from the Crimson Desert – he had seen Irem, the City of Pillars, and had worshipped at the underground shrines of Nug and Yeb – Iä! Shub-Niggurath!'

Through Clarendon's shrieking falsetto cut the deep chuckle of the clinic-man.

'Shut up, you fool! Do you suppose your grotesque nonsense has any weight with me? Words and formulae – words and formulae – what do they all mean to one who has the substance behind them? We're in a material sphere now, and subject to material laws. You have your fever; I have my revolver. You'll get no specimens, and I'll get no fever so long as I have you in front of me with this gun between!'

That was all Georgina could hear. She felt her senses reeling, and staggered out of the vestibule for a saving breath of the lowering outside air. She saw that the crisis had come at last, and that help must now arrive quickly if her brother was to be saved from the unknown gulfs of madness and mystery. Summoning up all her reserve energy, she managed to reach the house and get to the library, where she scrawled a hasty note for Margarita to take to James Dalton.

When the old woman had gone, Georgina had just strength enough to cross to the lounge and sink weakly down into a sort of semi-stupor. There she lay for what seemed like years, conscious only of the fantastic creeping up of the twilight from the lower corners of the great, dismal room, and plagued by a thousand shadowy shapes of terror which filed with phantasmal, half-limned pageantry through her tortured and stifled brain. Dusk deepened into darkness, and still the spell held. Then a firm tread sounded in the hall, and she heard someone enter the room and fumble at the match-safe. Her heart almost stopped beating as the gas-jets of the chandelier flared up one by one, but then she saw that the arrival was her brother. Relieved to the bottom of her heart that he was still alive, she gave vent to an involuntary sigh, profound, long-drawn, and tremulous, and lapsed at last into kindly oblivion.

At the sound of that sigh Clarendon turned in alarm toward the lounge, and was inexpressibly shocked to see the pale and unconscious form of his sister there. Her face had a death-like quality that frightened his inmost spirit, and he flung himself on his knees by her side, awake to a realisation of what her passing away would mean to him. Long unused to private practice amidst his ceaseless quest for truth, he had lost the physician's instinct of first aid, and could only call out her name and chafe her wrists mechanically as fear and grief possessed him. Then he thought of water, and ran to the dining-room for a carafe. Stumbling about in a darkness which seemed to harbour vague terrors, he was some time in finding what he sought; but at last he clutched it in shaking hand and hastened back to dash the cold fluid in Georgina's face. The method was crude but effective. She stirred, sighed a second time, and finally opened her eyes.

'You are alive!' he cried, and put his cheek to hers as she stroked his head maternally. She was almost glad she fainted, for the circumstance seemed to have dispelled the strange Alfred and brought her own brother back to her. She sat up slowly and tried to reassure him.

'I'm all right, Al. Just give me a glass of water. It's a sin to waste it this way – to say nothing of spoiling my waist! Is that the way to behave every time your sister drops off for a nap? You needn't think I'm going to be sick, for I haven't time for such nonsense!'

Alfred's eyes shewed that her cool, common-sense speech had had its effect. His brotherly panic dissolved in an instant, and instead there came into his face a vague, calculating expression, as if some marvellous possibility had just dawned upon him. As she watched the subtle waves of cunning and appraisal pass fleetingly over his countenance she became less and less certain that her mode of reassurance had been a wise one, and before he spoke she found herself shivering at something she could not define. A keen medical instinct almost told her that his moment of sanity had passed, and that he was now once more the unrestrained fanatic for scientific research. There was something morbid in the quick narrowing of his eyes at her casual mention of good health. What was he thinking? To what unnatural extreme was his passion for experiment about to be pushed? Wherein lay the special significance of her pure blood and absolutely flawless organic state? None of these misgivings, however, troubled Georgina for more than a second, and she was quite natural and unsuspicious as she felt her brother's steady fingers at her pulse.

'You're a bit feverish, Georgie,' he said in a precise, elaborately restrained voice as he looked professionally into her eyes.

'Why, nonsense, I'm all right,' she replied. 'One would think you were on the watch for fever patients just for the sake of shewing off your discovery! It *would* be poetic, though, if you could make your final proof and demonstration by curing your own sister!'

Clarendon started violently and guiltily. Had she suspected his wish? Had he muttered anything aloud? He looked at her closely, and saw that she had no inkling of the truth. She smiled up sweetly into his face and patted his hand as he stood by the side of the lounge. Then he took a small oblong leather case from his vest pocket, and taking out a little gold syringe, he began fingering it thoughtfully, pushing the piston speculatively in and out of the empty cylinder.

'I wonder,' he began with suave sententiousness, 'whether you would really be willing to help science in – something like that way – if the need arose? Whether you would have the devotion to offer yourself to the cause of medicine as a sort of Jephthah's daughter if you knew it meant the absolute perfection and completion of my work?'

Georgina, catching the odd and unmistakable glitter in her brother's eyes, knew at last that her worst fears were true. There was nothing to do now but keep him quiet at all hazards and to pray that Margarita had found James Dalton at his club.

'You look tired, Al dear,' she said gently. 'Why not take a little morphia and get some of the sleep you need so badly?'

He replied with a kind of crafty deliberation.

'Yes, you're right. I'm worn out, and so are you. Each of us needs a good sleep. Morphine is just the thing – wait till I go and fill the syringe and we'll both take a proper dose.'

Still fingering the empty syringe, he walked softly out of the room. Georgina looked about her with the aimlessness of desperation, ears alert for any sign of possible help. She thought she heard Margarita again in the basement kitchen, and rose to ring the bell, in an effort to learn of the fate of her message. The old servant answered her summons at once, and declared she had given the message at the club hours ago. Governor Dalton had been out, but the clerk had promised to deliver the note at the very moment of his arrival.

Margarita waddled below stairs again, but still Clarendon did not reappear. What was he doing? What was he planning? She had heard the outer door slam, so knew he must be at the clinic. Had he forgotten his original intention with the vacillating mind of madness? The suspense grew almost unbearable, and Georgina had to keep her teeth clenched tightly to avoid screaming.

It was the gate bell, which rang simultaneously in house and clinic, that broke the tension at last. She heard the cat-like tread of Surama on the walk as he left the clinic to answer it; and then, with an almost hysterical sigh of relief, she caught the firm, familiar accents of Dalton in conversation with the sinister attendant. Rising, she almost tottered to meet him as he loomed up in the library doorway; and for a moment no word was spoken while he kissed her hand in his courtly, old-school fashion. Then Georgina burst forth into a torrent of hurried explanation, telling all that had happened, all she had glimpsed and overheard, and all she feared and suspected.

Dalton listened gravely and comprehendingly, his first bewilderment gradually giving place to astonishment, sympathy, and resolution. The message, held by a careless clerk, had been slightly delayed, and had found him appropriately enough in the midst of a warm lounging-room discussion about Clarendon. A fellow-member, Dr MacNeil, had brought in a medical journal with an article well calculated to disturb the devoted scientist, and Dalton had just asked to keep the paper for future reference when the message was handed him at last. Abandoning his half-formed plan to take Dr MacNeil into his confidence regarding Alfred, he called at once for his hat and stick, and lost not a moment in getting a cab for the Clarendon home.

Surama, he thought, appeared alarmed at recognising him; though he had chuckled as usual when striding off again toward the clinic. Dalton always recalled Surama's stride and chuckle on this ominous night, for he was never to see the unearthly creature again. As the chuckler entered the clinic vestibule his deep, guttural gurgles seemed to blend with some low mutterings of thunder which troubled the far horizon.

When Dalton had heard all Georgina had to say, and learned that Alfred was expected back at any moment with a hypodermic dose of morphine, he decided he had better talk with the doctor alone. Advising Georgina to retire to her room and await developments, he walked about the gloomy library, scanning the shelves and listening for Clarendon's nervous footstep on the clinic path outside. The vast room's corners were dismal despite the chandelier, and the closer Dalton looked at his friend's choice of books the less he liked them. It was not the balanced collection of a normal physician, biologist, or man of general culture. There were too many volumes on doubtful borderland themes; dark speculations and forbidden rituals of the Middle Ages, and strange exotic mysteries in alien alphabets both known and unknown.

The great notebook of observations on the table was unwholesome, too. The handwriting had a neurotic cast, and the spirit of the entries was far from reassuring. Long passages were inscribed in crabbed Greek characters, and as Dalton marshalled his linguistic memory for their translation he gave a sudden start, and wished his college struggles with Xenophon and Homer had been more conscientious. There was something wrong – something hideously wrong – here, and the governor sank limply into the chair by the table as he pored more and more closely over the doctor's barbarous Greek. Then a sound came, startlingly near, and he jumped nervously at a hand laid sharply on his shoulder.

'What, may I ask, is the cause of this intrusion? You might have stated your business to Surama.'

Clarendon was standing icily by the chair, the little gold syringe in one hand. He seemed very calm and rational, and Dalton fancied for a moment that Georgina must have exaggerated his condition. How, too, could a rusty scholar be absolutely sure about these Greek entries? The governor decided to be very cautious in his interview, and thanked the lucky chance which had placed a specious pretext in his coat pocket. He was very cool and assured as he rose to reply.

'I didn't think you'd care to have things dragged before a subordinate, but I thought you ought to see this article at once.'

He drew forth the magazine given him by Dr MacNeil and handed it to Clarendon.

'On page 542 – you see the heading, "Black Fever Conquered by New Serum". It's by Dr Miller of Philadelphia – and he thinks he's got ahead of you with your cure. They were discussing it at the club, and MacNeil thought the exposition very convincing. I, as a layman, couldn't pretend to judge; but at all events I thought you oughtn't to miss a chance to digest the thing while it's fresh. If you're busy, of course, I won't disturb you—'

Clarendon cut in sharply.

'I'm going to give my sister an hypodermic – she's not quite well – but I'll look at what that quack has to say when I get back. I know Miller – a damn sneak and incompetent – and I don't believe he has the brains to steal my methods from the little he's seen of them.'

Dalton suddenly felt a wave of intuition warning him that Georgina must not receive that intended dose. There was something sinister about it. From what she had said, Alfred must have been inordinately long preparing it, far longer than was needed for the dissolving of a morphine tablet. He decided to hold his host as long as possible, meanwhile testing his attitude in a more or less subtle way.

'I'm sorry Georgina isn't well. Are you sure that the injection will do her good? That it won't do her any harm?'

Clarendon's spasmodic start shewed that something had been struck home.

'Do her harm?' he cried. 'Don't be absurd! You know Georgina must be in the best of health – the very best, I say – in order to serve science as a Clarendon should serve it. She, at least, appreciates the fact that she is my sister. She deems no sacrifice too great in my service. She is a priestess of truth and discovery, as I am a priest.'

He paused in his shrill tirade, wild-eyed, and somewhat out of breath. Dalton could see that his attention had been momentarily shifted.

'But let me see what this cursed quack has to say,' he continued. 'If he thinks his pseudo-medical rhetoric can take a real doctor in, he is even simpler than I thought!'

Clarendon nervously found the right page and began reading as he stood there clutching his syringe. Dalton wondered what the real facts were. MacNeil had assured him that the author was a pathologist of the highest standing, and that whatever errors the article might have, the mind behind it was powerful, erudite, and absolutely honourable and sincere.

Watching the doctor as he read, Dalton saw the thin, bearded face grow pale. The great eyes blazed, and the pages crackled in the tenser grip of the long, lean fingers. A perspiration broke out on the high, ivory-white forehead where the hair was already thinning, and the reader sank gaspingly into the chair his visitor had vacated as he kept on with his devouring of the text. Then came a wild scream as from a haunted beast, and Clarendon lurched forward on the table, his outflung arms sweeping books and paper before them as consciousness went dark like a wind-quenched candle-flame.

Dalton, springing to help his stricken friend, raised the slim form and tilted it back in the chair. Seeing the carafe on the floor near the lounge, he dashed some water into the twisted face, and was rewarded by seeing the large eyes slowly open. They were sane eyes now – deep and sad and unmistakably sane – and Dalton felt awed in the presence of a tragedy whose ultimate depth he could never hope or dare to plumb.

The golden hypodermic was still clutched in the lean left hand, and as Clarendon drew a deep, shuddering breath he unclosed his fingers and studied the glittering thing that rolled about on his palm. Then he spoke – slowly, and with the ineffable sadness of utter, absolute despair.

'Thanks, Jimmy, I'm quite all right. But there's much to be done. You asked me a while back if this shot of morphia would do Georgie any harm. I'm in a position now to tell you that it won't.'

He turned a small screw in the syringe and laid a finger on the piston, at the same time pulling with his left hand at the skin of his own neck. Dalton cried out in alarm as a lightning motion of his right hand injected the contents of the cylinder into the ridge of distended flesh.

'Good Lord, Al, what have you done?'

Clarendon smiled gently – a smile almost of peace and resignation, different indeed from the sardonic sneer of the past few weeks.

'You ought to know, Jimmy, if you've still the judgement that made you a governor. You must have pieced together enough from my notes to realise that there's nothing else to do. With your marks in Greek back at Columbia I guess you couldn't have missed much. All I can say is that it's true.

'James, I don't like to pass blame along, but it's only right to tell you that Surama got me into this. I can't tell you who or what he is, for I don't fully know myself, and what I do know is stuff that no sane person ought to know; but I will say that I don't consider him a human being in the fullest sense, and that I'm not sure whether or not he's alive as we know life.

'You think I'm talking nonsense. I wish I were, but the whole hideous mess is damnably real. I started out in life with a clean mind and purpose. I wanted to rid the world of fever. I tried and failed – and I wish to God I had been honest enough to say that I'd failed. Don't let my old talk of science deceive you, James – *I found no antitoxin and was never even half on the track of one!*

'Don't look so shaken up, old fellow! A veteran politician-fighter like you must have seen plenty of unmaskings before. I tell you, I never had even the start of a fever cure. But my studies had taken me into some queer places, and it was just my damned luck to listen to the stories of some still queerer people. James, if you ever wish any man well, tell him to keep clear of the ancient, hidden places of the earth. Old backwaters are dangerous – things are handed down there that don't do healthy people any good. I talked too much with old priests and mystics, and got to hoping I might achieve things in dark ways that I couldn't achieve in lawful ways.

'I shan't tell you just what I mean, for if I did I'd be as bad as the old priests that were the ruin of me. All I need say is that after what I've learned I shudder at the thought of the world and what it's been through. The world is cursed old, James, and there have been whole chapters lived and closed before the dawn of our organic life and the geologic eras connected with it. It's an awful thought – whole forgotten cycles of evolution with beings and races and wisdom and diseases – all lived through and gone before the first amoeba ever stirred in the tropic seas geology tells us about.

'I said gone, but I didn't quite mean that. It would have been better that way, but it wasn't quite so. In places traditions have kept on – I can't tell you how – and certain archaic life-forms have managed to struggle thinly down the aeons in hidden spots. There were cults, you know – bands of evil priests in lands now buried under the sea. Atlantis was the hotbed. That was a terrible place. If heaven is merciful, no one will ever drag up that horror from the deep.

'It had a colony, though, that didn't sink; and when you get too confidential with one of the Tuareg priests in Africa, he's likely to tell you wild tales about it – tales that connect up with whispers you'll hear among the mad lamas and flighty yak-drivers on the secret table-lands of Asia. I'd heard all the common tales and whispers when I came on the big one. What that was, you'll never know – but it pertained to somebody or something that had come down from a blasphemously long time ago, and could be made to live again – or seem alive again – through certain processes that weren't very clear to the man who told me.

'Now, James, in spite of my confession about the fever, you know I'm not bad as a doctor. I plugged hard at medicine, and soaked up about as much as the next man – maybe a little more, because down there in the Hoggar country I did something no priest had ever been able to do. They led me blindfolded to a place that had been sealed up for generations – and I came back with Surama.

'Easy, James! I know what you want to say. How does he know all he knows? – why does he speak English – or any other language, for that matter – without an accent? – why did he come away with me? – and all that. I can't tell you altogether, but I can say that he takes in ideas and images and impressions with something besides his brain and senses. He had a use for me and my science. He told me things, and opened up vistas. He taught me to worship ancient, primordial, and unholy gods, and mapped out a road to a terrible goal which I can't even hint to you. Don't press me, James – it's for the sake of your sanity and the world's sanity!

'The creature is beyond all bounds. He's in league with the stars and all the forces of Nature. Don't think I'm still crazy, James – I swear to you I'm not! I've had too many glimpses to doubt. He gave me new pleasures that were forms of his palaeogean worship, and the greatest of those was the black fever.

'God, James! Haven't you seen through the business by this time? Do you still believe the black fever came out of Tibet, and that I learned about it there? Use your brains, man! Look at Miller's article here! He's found a basic antitoxin that will end all fever within half a century, when other men learn how to modify it for the different forms. He's cut the ground of my youth from under me – done what I'd have given my life to do – taken the wind out of all the honest sails I ever flung to the breeze of science! Do you wonder his article gave me a turn? Do you wonder it shocks me out of my madness back to the old dreams of my youth? Too late! Too late! But not too late to save others!

'I guess I'm rambling a bit now, old man. You know – the

hypodermic. I asked you why you didn't tumble to the facts about black fever. How could you, though? Doesn't Miller say he's cured seven cases with his serum? A matter of diagnosis, James. He only thinks it is black fever. I can read between his lines. Here, old chap, on page 551, is the key to the whole thing. Read it again.

'You see, don't you? The fever cases *from the Pacific Coast* didn't respond to his serum. They puzzled him. They didn't even seem like any true fever he knew. Well, those were *my* cases! Those were the *real* black fever cases! And there can't ever be an antitoxin on earth that'll cure black fever!

'How do I know? *Because black fever isn't of this earth!* It's from *somewhere else*, James – and Surama alone knows where, because he brought it here. He *brought it and I spread it!* That's the secret, James! That's all I wanted the appointment for – that's all I ever did – *just spread the fever that I carried in this gold syringe and in the deadlier finger-ring-pump-syringe you see on my index finger!* Science? A blind! I wanted to kill, and kill, and kill! A single pressure on my finger, and the black fever was inoculated. I wanted to see living things writhe and squirm, scream and froth at the mouth. A single pressure of the pump-syringe and I could watch them as they died, and I couldn't live or think unless I had plenty to watch. That's why I jabbed everything in sight with the accursed hollow needle. Animals, criminals, children, servants – and the next would have been—'

Clarendon's voice broke, and he crumpled up perceptibly in his chair.

'That – that, James – was – my life. Surama made it so – he taught me, and kept me at it till I couldn't stop. Then – then it got too much *even for him*. He tried to check me. Fancy – *he* trying to check anybody in that line! But now I've got my last specimen. That is my last test. Good subject, James – I'm healthy – devilish healthy. Deuced ironic, though – the madness has gone now, so there won't be any fun watching the agony! Can't be – can't—'

A violent shiver of fever racked the doctor, and Dalton mourned amidst his horror-stupefaction that he could give no grief. How much of Alfred's story was sheer nonsense, and how much night-mare truth he could not say; but in any case he felt that the man was a victim rather than a criminal, and above all, he was a boyhood comrade and Georgina's brother. Thoughts of the old days came back kaleidoscopically. 'Little Alf' – the yard at Phillips Exeter –

the quadrangle at Columbia – the fight with Tom Cortland when he saved Alf from a pommelling ...

He helped Clarendon to the lounge and asked gently what he could do. There was nothing. Alfred could only whisper now, but he asked forgiveness for all his offences, and commended his sister to the care of his friend.

'You – you'll – make her happy,' he gasped. 'She deserves it. Martyr – to – a myth! Make it up to her, James. Don't – let – her – know – more – than she has to!'

His voice trailed off in a mumble, and he fell into a stupor. Dalton rang the bell, but Margarita had gone to bed, so he called up the stairs for Georgina. She was firm of step, but very pale. Alfred's scream had tried her sorely, but she had trusted James. She trusted him still as he shewed her the unconscious form on the lounge and asked her to go back to her room and rest, no matter what sounds she might hear. He did not wish her to witness the awful spectacle of delirium certain to come, but bade her kiss her brother a final farewell as he lay there calm and still, very like the delicate boy he had once been. So she left him – the strange, moonstruck, star-reading genius she had mothered so long – and the picture she carried away was a very merciful one.

Dalton must bear to his grave a sterner picture. His fears of delirium were not vain, and all through the black midnight hours his giant strength restrained the frenzied contortions of the mad sufferer. What he heard from those swollen, blackening lips he will never repeat. He has never been quite the same man since, and he knows that no one who hears such things can ever be wholly as he was before. So, for the world's good, he dares not speak, and he thanks God that his layman's ignorance of certain subjects makes many of the revelations cryptic and meaningless to him.

Toward morning Clarendon suddenly woke to a sane con-sciousness and began to speak in a firm voice.

'James, I didn't tell you what must be done – about everything. Blot out these entries in Greek and send my notebook to Dr Miller. All my other notes, too, that you'll find in the files. He's the big authority today – his article proves it. Your friend at the club was right.

'But everything in the clinic must go. *Everything without exception, dead or alive or – otherwise.* All the plagues of hell are in those bottles on the shelves. Burn them – burn it all – if one thing escapes, Surama will spread black death throughout the world. *And above all burn Surama!* That – that *thing* – must not breathe the wholesome air of heaven. You know now – what I told you – you know why such an entity can't be allowed on earth. It won't be murder – Surama isn't human – if you're as pious as you used to be, James, I shan't have to urge you. Remember the old text – "Thou shalt not suffer a witch to live" – or something of the sort.

'*Burn him, James!* Don't let him chuckle again over the torture of mortal flesh! I say, *burn him* – the Nemesis of Flame – that's all that can reach him, James, unless you can catch him asleep and drive a stake through his heart … *Kill him – extirpate him – cleanse the decent universe of its primal taint – the taint I recalled from its age-long sleep …*'

The doctor had risen on his elbow, and his voice was a piercing shriek toward the last. The effort was too much, however, and he lapsed very suddenly into a deep, tranquil coma. Dalton, himself fearless of fever, since he knew the dread germ to be non-contagious, composed Alfred's arms and legs on the lounge and threw a light afghan over the fragile form. After all, mightn't much of this horror be exaggeration and delirium? Mightn't old Doc MacNeil pull him through on a long chance? The governor strove to keep awake, and walked briskly up and down the room, but his energies had been taxed too deeply for such measures. A second's rest in the chair by the table took matters out of his hands, and he was presently sleeping soundly despite his best intentions.

Dalton started up as a fierce light shone in his eyes, and for a moment he thought the dawn had come. But it was not the dawn, and as he rubbed his heavy lids he saw that it was the glare of the burning clinic in the yard, whose stout planks flamed and roared and crackled heavenward in the most stupendous holocaust he had ever seen. It was indeed the 'Nemesis of Flame' that Clarendon had wished, and Dalton felt that some strange com-bustibles must be involved in a blaze so much wilder than anything normal pine or redwood could afford. He glanced alarmedly at the lounge, but Alfred was not there. Starting up, he went to call Georgina, but met her in the hall, roused as he was by the mountain of living fire.

'The clinic's burning down!' she cried. 'How is Al now?'

'He's disappeared – disappeared while I dropped asleep!' replied

Dalton, reaching out a steadying arm to the form which faintness had begun to sway.

Gently leading her upstairs toward her room, he promised to search at once for Alfred, but Georgina slowly shook her head as the flames from outside cast a weird glow through the window on the landing.

'He must be dead, James – he could never live, sane and knowing what he did. I heard him quarrelling with Surama, and know that awful things were going on. He is my brother, but – it is best as it is.'

Her voice had sunk to a whisper.

Suddenly through the open window came the sound of a deep, hideous chuckle, and the flames of the burning clinic took fresh contours till they half resembled some nameless, Cyclopean creatures of nightmare. James and Georgina paused hesitant, and peered out breathlessly through the landing window. Then from the sky came a thunderous peal, as a forked bolt of lightning shot down with terrible directness into the very midst of the blazing ruin. The deep chuckle ceased, and in its place came a frantic, ululant yelp as of a thousand ghouls and werewolves in torment. It died away with long, reverberant echoes, and slowly the flames resumed their normal shape.

The watchers did not move, but waited till the pillar of fire had shrunk to a smouldering glow. They were glad of a half-rusticity which had kept the firemen from trooping out, and of the wall that excluded the curious. What had happened was not for vulgar eyes – it involved too much of the universe's inner secrets for that.

In the pale dawn, James spoke softly to Georgina, who could do no more than put her head on his breast and sob.

'Sweetheart, I think he has atoned. He must have set the fire, you know, while I was asleep. He told me it ought to be burned – the clinic, and everything in it, Surama, too. It was the only way to save the world from the unknown horrors he had loosed upon it. He knew, and he did what was best.

'He was a great man, Georgie. Let's never forget that. We must always be proud of him, for he started out to help mankind, and was titanic even in his sins. I'll tell you more sometime. What he did, be it good or evil, was what no man ever did before. He was the first and last to break through certain veils, and even Apollonius of Tyana takes second place beside him. But we mustn't talk about that. We must remember him only as the Little Alf we knew – as the boy who wanted to master medicine and conquer fever.'

In the afternoon the leisurely firemen overhauled the ruins and found two skeletons with bits of blackened flesh adhering – only two, thanks to the undisturbed lime-pits. One was of a man; the other is still a subject of debate among the biologists of the coast. It was not exactly an ape's or a saurian's skeleton, but it had disturbing suggestions of lines of evolution of which palaeontology has revealed no trace. The charred skull, oddly enough, was very human, and reminded people of Surama; but the rest of the bones were beyond conjecture. Only well-cut clothing could have made such a body look like a man.

But the human bones were Clarendon's. No one disputed this, and the world at large still mourns the untimely death of the greatest doctor of his age; the bacteriologist whose universal fever serum would have far eclipsed Dr Miller's kindred antitoxin had he lived to bring it to perfection. Much of Miller's late success, indeed, is credited to the notes bequeathed him by the hapless victim of the flames. Of the old rivalry and hatred almost none survived, and even Dr Wilfred Jones has been known to boast of his association with the vanished leader.

James Dalton and his wife Georgina have always preserved a reticence which modesty and family grief might well account for. They published certain notes as a tribute to the great man's memory, but have never confirmed or contradicted either the popular esti-mate or the rare hints of marvels that a very few keen thinkers have been known to whisper. It was very subtly and slowly that the facts filtered out. Dalton probably gave Dr MacNeil an inkling of the truth, and that good soul had not many secrets from his son.

The Daltons have led, on the whole, a very happy life; for their cloud of terror lies far in the background, and a strong mutual love has kept the world fresh for them. But there are things which disturb them oddly – little things, of which one would scarcely ever think of complaining. They cannot bear persons who are lean or deep-voiced beyond certain limits, and Georgina turns pale at the sound of any guttural chuckling. Senator Dalton has a mixed horror of occultism, travel, hypodermics, and strange alphabets which most find hard to unify, and there are still those who blame him for the vast proportion of the doctor's library that he destroyed with such painstaking completeness.

MacNeil, though, seemed to realise. He was a simple man, and he said a prayer as the last of Alfred Clarendon's strange books crumbled to ashes. Nor would anyone who had peered under-standingly within those books wish a word of that prayer unsaid.

THE WOOD

T HEY CUT IT DOWN, and where the pitch-black aisles
   Of forest night had hid eternal things,
They scal'd the sky with tow'rs and marble piles
   To make a city for their revellings.

White and amazing to the lands around
   That wondrous wealth of domes and turrets rose;
Crystal and ivory, sublimely crown'd
   With pinnacles that bore unmelting snows.

And through its halls the pipe and sistrum rang,
   While wine and riot brought their scarlet stains;
Never a voice of elder marvels sang,
   Nor any eye call'd up the hills and plains.

Thus down the years, till on one purple night
   A drunken minstrel in his careless verse
Spoke the vile words that should not see the light,
   And stirr'd the shadows of an ancient curse.

Forests may fall, but not the dusk they shield;
   So on the spot where that proud city stood,
The shuddering dawn no single stone reveal'd,
   But fled the blackness of a primal wood.

THE ANCIENT TRACK

T HERE WAS NO HAND to hold me back
  That night I found the ancient track
Over the hill, and strained to see
The fields that teased my memory.
This tree, that wall – I knew them well,
And all the roofs and orchards fell
Familiarly upon my mind
As from a past not far behind.
I knew what shadows would be cast
When the late moon came up at last
From back of Zaman's Hill, and how
The vale would shine three hours from now.
And when the path grew steep and high,
And seemed to end against the sky,
I had no fear of what might rest
Beyond that silhouetted crest.
Straight on I walked, while all the night
Grew pale with phosphorescent light,

And wall and farmhouse gable glowed
Unearthly by the climbing road.
There was the milestone that I knew—
'Two miles to Dunwich' – now the view
Of distant spire and roofs would dawn
With ten more upward paces gone . . .

There was no hand to hold me back
That night I found the ancient track,
And reached the crest to see outspread
A valley of the lost and dead:
And over Zaman's Hill the horn
Of a malignant moon was born,
To light the weeds and vines that grew
On ruined walls I never knew.
The fox-fire glowed in field and bog,
And unknown waters spewed a fog
Whose curling talons mocked the thought
That I had ever known this spot.
Too well I saw from the mad scene
That my loved past had never been—
Nor was I now upon the trail
Descending to that long-dead vale.
Around was fog – ahead, the spray
Of star-streams in the Milky Way . . .
There was no hand to hold me back
That night I found the ancient track.

THE ELECTRIC EXECUTIONER

(with Adolphe de Castro)

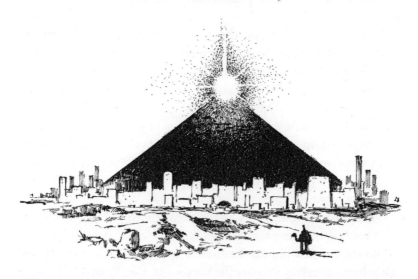

FOR ONE WHO HAS NEVER faced the danger of legal execution, I have a rather queer horror of the electric chair as a subject. Indeed, I think the topic gives me more of a shudder than it gives many a man who has been on trial for his life. The reason is that I associate the thing with an incident of forty years ago – a very strange incident which brought me close to the edge of the unknown's black abyss.

In 1889 I was an auditor and investigator connected with the Tlaxcala Mining Company of San Francisco, which operated several small silver and copper properties in the San Mateo Mountains in Mexico. There had been some trouble at Mine No. 3, which had a surly, furtive assistant superintendent named Arthur Feldon; and on August 6th the firm received a telegram saying that Feldon had decamped, taking with him all the stock records, securities, and private papers, and leaving the whole clerical and financial situation in dire confusion.

This development was a severe blow to the company, and late in the afternoon President McComb called me into his office to give orders for the recovery of the papers at any cost. There were, he knew, grave drawbacks. I had never seen Feldon, and there were only very indifferent photographs to go by. Moreover, my own wedding was set for Thursday of the following week – only nine days ahead – so that I was naturally not eager to be hurried off to Mexico on a man-hunt of indefinite length. The need, however, was so great that McComb felt justified in asking me to go at once; and I for my part decided that the effect on my status with the company would make ready acquiescence eminently worth while.

I was to start that night, using the president's private car as far as Mexico City, after which I would have to take a narrow-gauge railway to the mines. Jackson, the superintendent of No. 3, would give me all details and any possible clues upon my arrival; and then the search would begin in earnest – through the mountains, down to the coast, or among the byways of Mexico City, as the case might be. I set out with a grim determination to get the matter done – and successfully done – as swiftly as possible; and tempered my discontent with pictures of an early return with papers and culprit, and of a wedding which would be almost a triumphal ceremony.

Having notified my family, fiancée, and principal friends, and made hasty preparations for the trip, I met President McComb at eight p.m. at the Southern Pacific depot, received from him some written instructions and a check-book, and left in his car attached to the 8:15 eastbound transcontinental train. The journey that followed seemed destined for uneventfulness, and after a good night's sleep I revelled in the ease of the private car so thoughtfully assigned me; reading my instructions with care, and formulating plans for the capture of Feldon and the recovery of the documents. I knew the Tlaxcala country quite well – probably much better than the missing man – hence had a certain amount of advantage in my search unless he had already used the railway.

According to the instructions, Feldon had been a subject of worry to Superintendent Jackson for some time; acting secretively, and working unaccountably in the company's laboratory at odd hours. That he was implicated with a Mexican boss and several peons in some thefts of ore was strongly suspected; but though the natives had been discharged, there was not enough evidence to warrant any positive step regarding the subtle official. Indeed, despite his furtiveness, there seemed to be more of defiance than of guilt in the man's bearing. He wore a chip on his shoulder, and talked as if the company were cheating him instead of his cheating the company. The obvious surveillance of his colleagues, Jackson wrote, appeared to irritate him increasingly; and now he had gone with everything of importance in the office. Of his possible whereabouts no guess could be made; though Jackson's final telegram suggested the wild slopes of the Sierra de Malinche, that tall, myth-surrounded peak with the corpse-shaped silhouette, from whose neighbourhood the thieving natives were said to have come.

At El Paso, which we reached at two a.m. of the night following our start, my private car was detached from the transcontinental train and joined to an engine specially ordered by telegraph to take it southward to Mexico City. I continued to drowse till dawn, and all the next day grew bored on the flat, desert Chihuahua landscape. The crew had told me we were due in Mexico City at noon Friday, but I soon saw that countless delays were wasting precious hours. There were waits on sidings all along the single-tracked route, and now and then a hot-box or other difficulty would further complicate the schedule.

At Torreón we were six hours late, and it was almost eight o'clock on Friday evening – fully twelve hours behind schedule – when the conductor consented to do some speeding in an effort to make up time. My nerves were on edge, and I could do nothing but pace the car in desperation. In the end I found that the speeding had been purchased at a high cost indeed, for within a half-hour the symptoms of a hot-box had developed in my car itself; so that after a maddening wait the crew decided that all the bearings would have to be overhauled after a quarter-speed limp ahead to the next station with shops – the factory town of Querétaro. This was the last straw, and I almost stamped like a child. Actually I sometimes caught myself pushing at my chair-arm as if trying to urge the train forward at a less snail-like pace.

It was almost ten in the evening when we drew into Querétaro, and I spent a fretful hour on the station platform while my car was sidetracked and tinkered at by a dozen native mechanics. At last they told me the job was too much for them, since the forward truck needed new parts which could not be obtained nearer than Mexico City. Everything indeed seemed against me, and I gritted my teeth when I thought of Feldon getting farther and farther away – perhaps to the easy cover of Vera Cruz with its shipping or Mexico City with its varied rail facilities – while fresh delays kept me tied and helpless. Of course Jackson had notified the police in all the cities around, but I knew with sorrow what their efficiency amounted to.

The best I could do, I soon found out, was to take the regular night express for Mexico City, which ran from Aguas Calientes and made a five-minute stop at Querétaro. It would be along at one a.m. if on time, and was due in Mexico City at five o'clock Saturday morning. When I purchased my ticket I found that the train would be made up of European compartment carriages instead of long American cars with rows of two-seat chairs. These had been much used in the early days of Mexican railroading, owing to the European construction interests back of the first lines; and in 1889 the Mexican Central was still running a fair number of them on its shorter trips. Ordinarily I prefer the American coaches, since I hate to have people facing me; but for this once I was glad of the foreign carriage. At such a time of night I stood a good chance of having a whole compartment to myself, and in my tired, nervously hyper-sensitive state I welcomed the solitude – as well as the comfortably upholstered seat with soft arm-rests and head-cushion, running the whole width of the vehicle. I bought a first-class ticket, obtained my valise from the sidetracked private car, telegraphed both President McComb and Jackson of what had happened, and settled down in the station to wait for the night express as patiently as my strained nerves would let me.

For a wonder, the train was only half an hour late; though even so, the solitary station vigil had about finished my endurance. The conductor, shewing me into a compartment, told me he expected to make up the delay and reach the capital on time; and I stretched myself comfortably on the forward-facing seat in the expectation of a quiet three-and-a-half hour run. The light from the overhead oil lamp was soothingly dim, and I wondered whether I could snatch some much-needed sleep in spite of my anxiety and nerve-tension. It seemed, as the train jolted into motion, that I was alone; and I was heartily glad of it. My thoughts leaped ahead to my quest, and I nodded with the accelerating rhythm of the speeding string of carriages.

Then suddenly I perceived that I was not alone after all. In the corner diagonally opposite me, slumped down so that his face was invisible, sat a roughly clad man of unusual size, whom the feeble light had failed to reveal before. Beside him on the seat was a huge valise, battered and bulging, and tightly gripped even in his sleep by one of his incongruously slender hands. As the engine whistled sharply at some curve or crossing, the sleeper started nervously into a kind of watchful half-awakening; raising his head and disclosing a handsome face, bearded and clearly Anglo-Saxon, with dark, lustrous eyes. At sight of me his wakefulness became complete, and I wondered at the rather hostile wildness of his glance. No doubt, I thought, he resented my presence when he had hoped to have the compartment alone all the way; just as I was myself disappointed to find strange company in the half-lighted carriage. The best we could do, however, was to accept the situation gracefully; so I began apologising to the man for my intrusion. He seemed to be a fellow-American, and we could both feel more at ease after a few civilities. Then we could leave each other in peace for the balance of the journey.

To my surprise, the stranger did not respond to my courtesies with so much as a word. Instead, he kept staring at me fiercely and almost appraisingly, and brushed aside my embarrassed proffer of a cigar with a nervous lateral movement of his disengaged hand. His other hand still tensely clutched the great, worn valise, and his whole person seemed to radiate some obscure malignity. After a time he abruptly turned his face toward the window, though there was nothing to see in the dense blackness outside. Oddly, he appeared to be looking at something as intently as if there really were something to look at. I decided to leave him to his own curious devices and meditations without further annoyance; so settled back in my seat, drew the brim of my soft hat over my face, and closed my eyes in an effort to snatch the sleep I had half counted on.

I could not have dozed very long or very fully when my eyes fell open as if in response to some external force. Closing them again with some determination, I renewed my quest of a nap, yet wholly without avail. An intangible influence seemed bent on keeping me awake; so raising my head, I looked about the dimly lighted compartment to see if anything were amiss. All appeared normal, but I noticed that the stranger in the opposite corner was looking at me very intently – intently, though without any of the geniality or friendliness which would have implied a change from his former surly attitude. I did not attempt conversation this time, but leaned back in my previous sleepy posture; half closing my eyes as if I had dozed off once more, yet continuing to watch him curiously from beneath my down-turned hat brim.

As the train rattled onward through the night I saw a subtle and gradual metamorphosis come over the expression of the staring man. Evidently satisfied that I was asleep, he allowed his face to reflect a curious jumble of emotions, the nature of which seemed anything but reassuring. Hatred, fear, triumph, and fanaticism flickered compositely over the lines of his lips and the angles of his eyes, while his gaze became a glare of really alarming greed and ferocity. Suddenly it dawned upon me that this man was mad, and dangerously so.

I will not pretend that I was anything but deeply and thoroughly frightened when I saw how things stood. Perspiration started out all over me, and I had hard work to maintain my attitude of relaxation and slumber. Life had many attractions for me just then, and the thought of dealing with a homicidal maniac – possibly armed and certainly powerful to a marvellous degree – was a dismaying and terrifying one. My disadvantage in any sort of struggle was enormous; for the man was a virtual giant, evidently in the best of athletic trim, while I have always been rather frail, and was then almost worn out with anxiety, sleeplessness, and nervous tension. It was undeniably a bad moment for me, and I felt pretty close to a horrible death as I recognised the fury of madness in the stranger's eyes. Events from the past came up into my consciousness as if for a farewell – just as a drowning man's whole life is said to resurrect itself before him at the last moment.

Of course I had my revolver in my coat pocket, but any motion of mine to reach and draw it would be instantly obvious. Moreover, if I did secure it, there was no telling what effect it would have on the maniac. Even if I shot him once or twice he might have enough remaining strength to get the gun from me and deal with me in his own way; or if he were armed himself he might shoot or stab without trying to disarm me. One can cow a sane man by covering him with a pistol, but an insane man's complete indifference to consequences gives him a strength and menace quite superhuman for the time being. Even in those pre-Freudian days I had a common-sense realisation of the dangerous power of a person without normal inhibitions. That the stranger in the corner was indeed about to start some murderous action, his burning eyes and twitching facial muscles did not permit me to doubt for a moment.

Suddenly I heard his breath begin to come in excited gasps, and saw his chest heaving with mounting excitement. The time for a showdown was close, and I tried desperately to think of the best thing to do. Without interrupting my pretence of sleep, I began to slide my right hand gradually and inconspicuously toward the pocket containing my pistol; watching the madman closely as I did so, to see if he would detect any move. Unfortunately he did – almost before he had time to register the fact in his expression. With a bound so agile and abrupt as to be almost incredible in a man of his size, he was upon me before I knew what had happened; looming up and swaying forward like a giant ogre of legend, and pinioning me with one powerful hand while with the other he forestalled me in reaching the revolver. Taking it from my pocket and placing it in his own, he released me contemptuously, well knowing how fully his physique placed me at his mercy. Then he stood up at his full height – his head almost touching the roof of the carriage – and stared down at me with eyes whose fury had quickly turned to a look of pitying scorn and ghoulish calculation.

I did not move, and after a moment the man resumed his seat opposite me; smiling a ghastly smile as he opened his great bulging valise and extracted an article of peculiar appearance – a rather large cage of semi-flexible wire, woven somewhat like a baseball catcher's mask, but shaped more like the helmet of a diving-suit. Its top was connected with a cord whose other end remained in the valise. This device he fondled with obvious affection, cradling it in his lap as he looked at me afresh and licked his bearded lips with an almost feline motion of the tongue. Then, for the first time, he spoke – in a deep, mellow voice of softness and cultivation start-lingly at variance with his rough corduroy clothes and unkempt aspect.

'You are fortunate, sir. I shall use you first of all. You shall go into history as the first fruits of a remarkable invention. Vast sociological consequences – I shall let my light shine, as it were. I'm radiating all the time, but nobody knows it. Now you shall know. Intelligent guinea-pig. Cats and burros – it worked even with a burro ...'

He paused, while his bearded features underwent a convulsive motion closely synchronised with a vigorous gyratory shaking of the whole head. It was as though he were shaking clear of some nebulous obstructing medium, for the gesture was followed by a clarification or subtilisation of expression which hid the more obvious madness in a look of suave composure through which the craftiness gleamed only dimly. I glimpsed the difference at once, and put in a word to see if I could lead his mind into harmless channels.

'You seem to have a marvellously fine instrument, if I'm any judge. Won't you tell me how you came to invent it?'

He nodded.

'Mere logical reflection, dear sir. I consulted the needs of the age and acted upon them. Others might have done the same had their minds been as powerful – that is, as capable of sustained concentration – as mine. I had the sense of conviction – the available will power – that is all. I realised, as no one else has yet realised, how imperative it is to remove everybody from the earth before Quetzalcoatl comes back, and realised also that it must be done elegantly. I hate butchery of any kind, and hanging is barbarously crude. You know last year the New York legislature voted to adopt electric execution for condemned men – but all the apparatus they have in mind is as primitive as Stephenson's "Rocket" or Davenport's first electric engine. I knew of a better way, and told them so, but they paid no attention to me. God, the fools! As if I didn't know all there is to know about men and death and electricity – student, man, and boy – technologist and engineer – soldier of fortune ...'

He leaned back and narrowed his eyes.

'I was in Maximilian's army twenty years and more ago. They were going to make me a nobleman. Then those damned greasers killed him and I had to go home. But I came back – back and forth, back and forth. I live in Rochester, N.Y. ...'

His eyes grew deeply crafty, and he leaned forward, touching me on the knee with the fingers of a paradoxically delicate hand.

'I came back, I say, and I went deeper than any of them. I hate greasers, but I like Mexicans! A puzzle? Listen to me, young fellow – you don't think Mexico is really Spanish, do you? God, if you knew the tribes I know! In the mountains – in the mountains – Anahuac – Tenochtitlan – the old ones ...'

His voice changed to a chanting and not unmelodious howl.

'Iä! Huitzilopotchli! ... Nahuatlacatl! Seven, seven, seven ... Xochimilca, Chalca, Tepaneca, Acolhua, Tlahuica, Tlascalteca, Azteca! ... Iä! Iä! I have been to the Seven Caves of Chicomoztoc, but no one shall ever know! I tell you *because you will never repeat it.*'

He subsided, and resumed a conversational tone.

'It would surprise you to know what things are told in the mountains. Huitzilopotchli is coming back ... of that there can be no doubt. Any peon south of Mexico City can tell you that. But I meant to do nothing about it. I went home, as I tell you, again and again, and was going to benefit society with my electric executioner when that cursed Albany legislature adopted the other way. A joke, sir, a joke! Grandfather's chair – sit by the fireside – Hawthorne—'

The man was chuckling with a morbid parody of good nature.

'Why, sir, I'd like to be the first man to sit in their damned chair and feel their little two-bit battery current! It wouldn't make a frog's legs dance! And they expect to kill murderers with it – reward of merit – everything! But then, young man, I saw the uselessness – the pointless illogicality, as it were – of killing just a few. Everybody is a murderer – they murder ideas – steal inventions – stole mine by watching, and watching, and watching—'

The man choked and paused, and I spoke soothingly.

'I'm sure your invention was much the better, and probably they'll come to use it in the end.'

Evidently my tact was not great enough, for his response shewed fresh irritation.

'"Sure," are you? Nice, mild, conservative assurance! Cursed lot you care – *but you'll soon know!* Why, damn you, all the good there ever will be in that electric chair will have been stolen from me. The ghost of Nezahualpilli told me that on the sacred mountain. They watched, and watched, and watched—'

He choked again, then gave another of those gestures in which he seemed to shake both his head and his facial expression. That seemed temporarily to steady him.

'What my invention needs is testing. That is it – here. The wire hood or head-net is flexible, and slips on easily. Neckpiece binds but doesn't choke. Electrodes touch forehead and base of cerebellum – all that's necessary. Stop the head, and what else can go? The fools up at Albany, with their carved oak easy-chair, think they've got to make it a head-to-foot affair. Idiots! – don't they know that you don't need to shoot a man through the body after you've plugged him through the brain? I've seen men die in battle – I know better. And then their silly high-power circuit – dynamos – all that. Why didn't they see what I've done with the storage-battery? Not a hearing – nobody knows – I alone have the secret – that's why I and Quetzalcoatl and Huitzilopotchli will rule the world alone – I and they, if I choose to let them ... But I must have experimental subjects – subjects – *do you know whom I've chosen for the first?*'

I tried jocoseness, quickly merging into friendly seriousness, as a sedative. Quick thought and apt words might save me yet.

'Well, there are lots of fine subjects among the politicians of San Francisco, where I come from! They need your treatment, and I'd like to help you introduce it! But really, I think I can help you in all truth. I have some influence in Sacramento, and if you'll go back to the States with me after I'm through with my business in Mexico, I'll see that you get a hearing.'

He answered soberly and civilly.

'No – I can't go back. I swore not to when those criminals at Albany turned down my invention and set spies to watch me and steal from me. But I must have American subjects. Those greasers are under a curse, and would be too easy; and the full-blood Indians – the real children of the feathered serpent – are sacred and inviolate except for proper sacrificial victims ... and even those must be slain according to ceremony. I must have Americans without going back – and the first man I choose will be signally honoured. Do you know who he is?'

I temporised desperately.

'Oh, if that's all the trouble, I'll find you a dozen first-rate Yankee specimens as soon as we get to Mexico City! I know where there are lots of small mining men who wouldn't be missed for days—'

But he cut me short with a new and sudden air of authority which had a touch of real dignity in it.

'That'll do – we've trifled long enough. Get up and stand erect like a man. You're the subject I've chosen, and you'll thank me for the honour in the other world, just as the sacrificial victim thanks the priest for transferring him to eternal glory. A new principle – no other man alive has dreamed of such a battery, and it might never again be hit on if the world experimented a thousand years.

Do you know that atoms aren't what they seem? Fools! A century after this some dolt would be guessing if I were to let the world live!'

As I arose at his command, he drew additional feet of cord from the valise and stood erect beside me; the wire helmet outstretched toward me in both hands, and a look of real exaltation on his tanned and bearded face. For an instant he seemed like a radiant Hellenic mystagogue or hierophant.

'Here, O Youth – a libation! Wine of the cosmos – nectar of the starry spaces – Linos – Iacchus – Ialmenos – Zagreus – Dionysos – Atys – Hylas – sprung from Apollo and slain by the hounds of Argos – seed of Psamathe – child of the sun – Evoë! Evoë!'

He was chanting again, and this time his mind seemed far back amongst the classic memories of his college days. In my erect posture I noticed the nearness of the signal cord overhead, and wondered whether I could reach it through some gesture of ostensible response to his ceremonial mood. It was worth trying, so with an antiphonal cry of 'Evoë!' I put my arms forward and upward toward him in a ritualistic fashion, hoping to give the cord a tug before he could notice the act. But it was useless. He saw my purpose, and moved one hand toward the right-hand coat pocket where my revolver lay. No words were needed, and we stood for a moment like carven figures. Then he quietly said, 'Make haste!'

Again my mind rushed frantically about seeking avenues of escape. The doors, I knew, were not locked on Mexican trains; but my companion could easily forestall me if I tried to unlatch one and jump out. Besides, our speed was so great that success in that direction would probably be as fatal as failure. The only thing to do was to play for time. Of the three-and-a-half hour trip a good slice was already worn away, and once we got to Mexico City the guards and police in the station would provide instant safety.

There would, I thought, be two distinct times for diplomatic stalling. If I could get him to postpone the slipping on of the hood, that much time would be gained. Of course I had no belief that the thing was really deadly; but I knew enough of madmen to understand what would happen when it failed to work. To his disappointment would be added a mad sense of my responsibility for the failure, and the result would be a red chaos of murderous rage. Therefore the experiment must be postponed as long as possible. Yet the second opportunity did exist, for if I planned cleverly I might devise explanations for the failure which would hold his attention and lead him into more or less extended searches for corrective influences. I wondered just how far his credulity went, and whether I could prepare in advance a prophecy of failure which would make the failure itself stamp me as a seer or initiate, or perhaps a god. I had enough of a smattering of Mexican mythology to make it worth trying; though I would try other delaying influences first and let the prophecy come as a sudden revelation. Would he spare me in the end if I could make him think me a prophet or divinity? Could I 'get by' as Quetzalcoatl or Huitzilopotchli? Anything to drag matters out till five o'clock, when we were due in Mexico City.

But my opening 'stall' was the veteran will-making ruse. As the maniac repeated his command for haste, I told him of my family and intended marriage, and asked for the privilege of leaving a message and disposing of my money and effects. If, I said, he would lend me some paper and agree to mail what I should write, I could die more peacefully and willingly. After some cogitation he gave a favourable verdict and fished in his valise for a pad, which he handed me solemnly as I resumed my seat. I produced a pencil, artfully breaking the point at the outset and causing some delay while he searched for one of his own. When he gave me his, he took my broken pencil and proceeded to sharpen it with a large, horn-handled knife which had been in his belt under his coat. Evidently a second pencil-breaking would not profit me greatly.

What I wrote, I can hardly recall at this date. It was largely gibberish, and composed of random scraps of memorised literature when I could think of nothing else to set down. I made my handwriting as illegible as I could without destroying its nature as writing; for I knew he would be likely to look at the result before commencing his experiment, and realised how he would react to the sight of obvious nonsense. The ordeal was a terrible one, and I chafed each second at the slowness of the train. In the past I had often whistled a brisk gallop to the sprightly 'tac' of wheels on rails, but now the tempo seemed slowed down to that of a funeral march – my funeral march, I grimly reflected.

My ruse worked till I had covered over four pages, six by nine; when at last the madman drew out his watch and told me I could have but five minutes more. What should I do next? I was hastily going through the form of concluding the will when a new idea struck me. Ending with a flourish and handing him the finished sheets, which he thrust carelessly into his left-hand coat pocket, I reminded him of my influential Sacramento friends who would be so much interested in his invention.

'Oughtn't I to give you a letter of introduction to them?' I said. 'Oughtn't I to make a signed sketch and description of your executioner so that they'll grant you a cordial hearing? They can make you famous, you know – and there's no question at all but that they'll adopt your method for the state of California if they hear of it through someone like me, whom they know and trust.'

I was taking this tack on the chance that his thoughts as a disappointed inventor would let him forget the Aztec-religious side of his mania for a while. When he veered to the latter again, I reflected, I would spring the 'revelation' and 'prophecy'. The scheme worked, for his eyes glowed an eager assent, though he brusquely told me to be quick. He further emptied the valise, lifting out a queer-looking congeries of glass cells and coils to which the wire from the helmet was attached, and delivering a fire of running comment too technical for me to follow yet apparently quite plausible and straightforward. I pretended to note down all he said, wondering as I did so whether the queer apparatus was really a battery after all. Would I get a slight shock when he applied the device? The man surely talked as if he were a genuine electrician. Description of his own invention was clearly a congenial task for him, and I saw he was not as impatient as before. The hopeful grey of dawn glimmered red through the windows before he wound up, and I felt at last that my chance of escape had really become tangible.

But he, too, saw the dawn, and began glaring wildly again. He knew the train was due in Mexico City at five, and would certainly force quick action unless I could override all his judgement with engrossing ideas. As he rose with a determined air, setting the battery on the seat beside the open valise, I reminded him that I had not made the needed sketch; and asked him to hold the headpiece so that I could draw it near the battery. He complied and resumed his seat, with many admonitions to me to hurry. After another moment I paused for some information, asking him how the victim was placed for execution, and how his presumable struggles were overcome.

'Why,' he replied, 'the criminal is securely strapped to a post. It does not matter how much he tosses his head, for the helmet fits tightly and draws even closer when the current comes on. We turn the switch gradually – you see it here, a carefully arranged affair with a rheostat.'

A new idea for delay occurred to me as the tilled fields and increasingly frequent houses in the dawnlight outside told of our approach to the capital at last.

'But,' I said, 'I must draw the helmet in place on a human head as well as beside the battery. Can't you slip it on yourself a moment so that I can sketch you with it? The papers as well as the officials will want all this, and they are strong on completeness.'

I had, by chance, made a better shot than I had planned; for at my mention of the press the madman's eyes lit up afresh.

'The papers? Yes – damn them, you can make even the papers give me a hearing! They all laughed at me and wouldn't print a word. Here, you, hurry up! We've not a second to lose!'

He had slipped the headpiece on and was watching my flying pencil avidly. The wire mesh gave him a grotesque, comic look as he sat there with nervously twitching hands.

'Now, curse 'em, they'll print pictures! I'll revise your sketch if you make any blunders – must be accurate at any cost. Police will find you afterward – they'll tell how it works. Associated Press item – back up your letter – immortal fame … Hurry, I say – hurry, confound you!'

The train was lurching over the poorer roadbed near the city and we swayed disconcertingly now and then. With this excuse I managed to break the pencil again, but of course the maniac at once handed me my own which he had sharpened. My first batch of ruses was about used up, and I felt that I should have to submit to the headpiece in a moment. We were still a good quarter-hour from the terminal, and it was about time for me to divert my companion to his religious side and spring the divine prophecy.

Mustering up my scraps of Nahuan-Aztec mythology, I suddenly threw down pencil and paper and commenced to chant.

'Iä! Iä! Tloquenahuaque, Thou Who Art All In Thyself! Thou

too, Ipalnemoan, By Whom We Live! I hear, I hear! I see, I see! Serpent-bearing Eagle, hail! A message! A message! Huitzilopotchli, in my soul echoes thy thunder!'

At my intonations the maniac stared incredulously through his odd mask, his handsome face shewn in a surprise and perplexity which quickly changed to alarm. His mind seemed to go blank a moment, and then to recrystallise in another pattern. Raising his hands aloft, he chanted as if in a dream.

'Mictlanteuctli, Great Lord, a sign! A sign from within thy black cave! Iä! Tonatiuh-Metztli! Cthulhutl! Command, and I serve!'

Now in all this responsive gibberish there was one word which struck an odd chord in my memory. Odd, because it never occurs in any printed account of Mexican mythology, yet had been overheard by me more than once as an awe-struck whisper amongst the peons in my own firm's Tlaxcala mines. It seemed to be part of an exceedingly secret and ancient ritual; for there were characteristic whispered responses which I had caught now and then, and which were as unknown as itself to academic scholarship. This maniac must have spent considerable time with the hill peons and Indians, just as he had said; for surely such unrecorded lore could have come from no mere book-learning. Realising the importance he must attach to this doubly esoteric jargon, I determined to strike at his most vulnerable spot and give him the gibberish responses the natives used.

'Ya-R'lyeh! Ya-R'lyeh!' I shouted. 'Cthulhutl fhtaghn! Niguratl-Yig! Yog-Sototl—'

But I never had a chance to finish. Galvanised into a religious epilepsy by the exact response which his subconscious mind had probably not really expected, the madman scrambled down to a kneeling posture on the floor, bowing his wire-helmeted head again and again, and turning it to the right and left as he did so. With each turn his obeisances became more profound, and I could hear his foaming lips repeating the syllable 'kill, kill, kill,' in a rapidly swelling monotone. It occurred to me that I had overreached myself, and that my response had unloosed a mounting mania which would rouse him to the slaying-point before the train reached the station.

As the arc of the madman's turnings gradually increased, the slack in the cord from his headpiece to the battery had naturally been taken up more and more. Now, in an all-forgetting delirium of ecstasy, he began to magnify his turns to complete circles, so that the cord wound round his neck and began to tug at its moorings to the battery on the seat. I wondered what he would do when the inevitable would happen, and the battery would be dragged to presumable destruction on the floor.

Then came the sudden cataclysm. The battery, yanked over the seat's edge by the maniac's last gesture of orgiastic frenzy, did indeed fall; but it did not seem to have wholly broken. Instead, as my eye caught the spectacle in one too-fleeting instant, the actual impact was borne by the rheostat, so that the switch was jerked over instantly to full current. And the marvellous thing is that there *was* a current. The invention was no mere dream of insanity.

I saw a blinding blue auroral coruscation, heard an ululating shriek more hideous than any of the previous cries of that mad, horrible journey, and smelled the nauseous odour of burning flesh. That was all my overwrought consciousness could bear, and I sank instantly into oblivion.

When the train guard at Mexico City revived me, I found a crowd on the station platform around my compartment door. At my involuntary cry the pressing faces became curious and dubious, and I was glad when the guard shut out all but the trim doctor who had pushed his way through to me. My cry was a very natural thing, but it had been prompted by something more than the shocking sight on the carriage floor which I had expected to see. Or should say, by something *less*, because in truth there was not anything on the floor at all.

Nor, said the guard, had there been when he opened the door and found me unconscious within. My ticket was the only one sold for that compartment, and I was the only person found within it. Just myself and my valise, nothing more. I had been alone all the way from Querétaro. Guard, doctor, and spectators alike tapped their foreheads significantly at my frantic and insistent questions.

Had it all been a dream, or was I indeed mad? I recalled my anxiety and overwrought nerves, and shuddered. Thanking the guard and doctor, and shaking free of the curious crowd, I staggered into a cab and was taken to the Fonda Nacional, where, after telegraphing Jackson at the mine, I slept till afternoon in an effort to get a fresh grip on myself. I had myself called at one o'clock, in time to catch the narrow-gauge for the mining country, but when I got up I found a telegram under the door. It was from Jackson, and said that Feldon had been found dead in the mountains that morning, the news reaching the mine about ten o'clock. The papers were all safe, and the San Francisco office had been duly notified. So the whole trip, with its nervous haste and harrowing mental ordeal, had been for nothing!

Knowing that McComb would expect a personal report despite the course of events, I sent another wire ahead and took the narrow-gauge after all. Four hours later I was rattled and jolted into the station of Mine No. 3, where Jackson was waiting to give a cordial greeting. He was so full of the affair at the mine that he did not notice my still shaken and seedy appearance.

The superintendent's story was brief, and he told me it as he led me toward the shack up the hillside above the *arrastre*, where Feldon's body lay. Feldon, he said, had always been a queer, sullen character, ever since he was hired the year before; working at some secret mechanical device and complaining of constant espionage, and being disgustingly familiar with the native workmen. But he certainly knew the work, the country, and the people. He used to make long trips into the hills where the peons lived, and even to take part in some of their ancient, heathenish ceremonies. He hinted at odd secrets and strange powers as often as he boasted of his mechanical skill. Of late he had disintegrated rapidly; growing morbidly suspicious of his colleagues, and undoubtedly joining his native friends in ore-thieving after his cash got low. He needed unholy amounts of money for something or other – was always having boxes come from laboratories and machine shops in Mexico City or the States.

As for the final absconding with all the papers – it was only a crazy gesture of revenge for what he called 'spying'. He was certainly stark mad, for he had gone across country to a hidden cave on the wild slope of the haunted Sierra de Malinche, where no white men live, and had done some amazingly queer things. The cave, which would never have been found but for the final tragedy, was full of hideous old Aztec idols and altars; the latter covered with the charred bones of recent burnt-offerings of doubtful nature. The natives would tell nothing – indeed, they swore they knew nothing – but it was easy to see that the cave was an old rendezvous of theirs, and that Feldon had shared their practices to the fullest extent.

The searchers had found the place only because of the chanting and the final cry. It had been close to five that morning, and after an all-night encampment the party had begun to pack up for its empty-handed return to the mines. Then somebody had heard faint rhythms in the distance, and knew that one of the noxious old native rituals was being howled from some lonely spot up the slope of the corpse-shaped mountain. They heard the same old names – Mictlanteuctli, Tonatiuh-Metzli, Cthulhutl, Ya-R'lyeh, and all the rest – but the queer thing was that some English words were mixed with them. Real white man's English, and no greaser patter. Guided by the sound, they had hastened up the weed-entangled mountainside toward it, when after a spell of quiet the shriek had burst upon them. It was a terrible thing – a worse thing than any of them had ever heard before. There seemed to be some smoke, too, and a morbid acrid smell.

Then they stumbled on the cave, its entrance screened by scrub mesquites, but now emitting clouds of foetid smoke. It was lighted within, the horrible altars and grotesque images revealed flickeringly by candles which must have been changed less than a half-hour before; and on the gravelly floor lay the horror that made all the crowd reel backward. It was Feldon, head burned to a crisp by some odd device he had slipped over it – a kind of wire cage connected with a rather shaken-up battery which had evidently fallen to the floor from a nearby altar-pot. When the men saw it they exchanged glances, thinking of the 'electric executioner' Feldon had always boasted of inventing – the thing which everyone had rejected, but had tried to steal and copy. The papers were safe in Feldon's open portmanteau which stood close by, and an hour later the column of searchers started back for No. 3 with a grisly burden on an improvised stretcher.

That was all, but it was enough to make me turn pale and falter as Jackson led me up past the *arrastre* to the shed where he said the body lay. For I was not without imagination, and knew only too well into what hellish nightmare this tragedy somehow supernaturally dovetailed. I knew what I should see inside that gaping door around which the curious miners clustered, and did not flinch when my eyes took in the giant form, the rough corduroy clothes, the oddly

311

delicate hands, the wisps of burnt beard, and the hellish machine itself – battery slightly broken, and headpiece blackened by the charring of what was inside. The great, bulging portmanteau did not surprise me, and I quailed only at two things – the folded sheets of paper sticking out of the left-hand pocket, and the queer sagging of the corresponding right-hand pocket. In a moment when no one was looking I reached out and seized the too familiar sheets, crushing them in my hand without daring to look at their penmanship. I ought to be sorry now that a kind of panic fear made me burn them that night with averted eyes. They would have been a positive proof or disproof of something – but for that matter I could still have had proof by asking about the revolver the coroner afterward took from that sagging right-hand coat pocket. I never had the courage to ask about that – because my own revolver was missing after the night on the train. My pocket pencil, too, shewed signs of a crude and hasty sharpening unlike the precise pointing I had given it Friday afternoon on the machine in President McComb's private car.

So in the end I went home still puzzled – mercifully puzzled, perhaps. The private car was repaired when I got back to Querétaro, but my greatest relief was crossing the Rio Grande into El Paso and the States. By the next Friday I was in San Francisco again, and the postponed wedding came off the following week.

As to what really happened that night – as I've said, I simply don't dare to speculate. That chap Feldon was insane to start with, and on top of his insanity he had piled a lot of prehistoric Aztec witch-lore that nobody has any right to know. He was really an inventive genius, and that battery must have been the genuine stuff. I heard later how he had been brushed aside in former years by press, public, and potentates alike. Too much disappointment isn't good for men of a certain kind. Anyhow, some unholy combination of influences was at work. He had really, by the way, been a soldier of Maximilian's.

When I tell my story most people call me a plain liar. Others lay it to abnormal psychology – and heaven knows I *was* overwrought – while still others talk of 'astral projection' of some sort. My zeal to catch Feldon certainly sent my thoughts ahead toward him, and with all his Indian magic he'd be about the first one to recognise and meet them. Was he in the railway carriage or was I in the cave on the corpse-shaped haunted mountain? What would have happened to me, had I not delayed him as I did? I'll confess I don't know, and I'm not sure that I want to know. I've never been in Mexico since – and as I said at the start, I don't enjoy hearing about electric executions.

Homecoming

The daemon said that he would take me home
To the pale, shadowy land I half-recalled
As a high place of stair and terrace, walled
With marble balustrades that sky-winds comb,
While miles below a maze of dome on dome
And tower on tower beside a sea lies sprawled.
Once more, he told me, I would stand enthralled
On those old heights, and hear the far-off foam.

All this he promised, and through sunset's gate
He swept me, past the lapping lakes of flame,
And red-gold thrones of gods without a name
Who shriek in fear at some impending fate.
Then a black gulf with sea-sounds in the night:
"Here was your home", he mocked, "when you had sight!"

—— H. P. LOVECRAFT

H

FUNGI FROM YUGGOTH

1. The Book

THE PLACE WAS DARK and dusty and half-lost
  In tangles of old alleys near the quays,
Reeking of strange things brought in from the seas,
And with queer curls of fog that west winds tossed.
Small lozenge panes, obscured by smoke and frost,
Just shewed the books, in piles like twisted trees,
Rotting from floor to roof – congeries
Of crumbling elder lore at little cost.

I entered, charmed, and from a cobwebbed heap
Took up the nearest tome and thumbed it through,
Trembling at curious words that seemed to keep
Some secret, monstrous if one only knew.
Then, looking for some seller old in craft,
I could find nothing but a voice that laughed.

2. Pursuit

I held the book beneath my coat, at pains
To hide the thing from sight in such a place;
Hurrying through the ancient harbour lanes
With often-turning head and nervous pace.
Dull, furtive windows in old tottering brick
Peered at me oddly as I hastened by,
And thinking what they sheltered, I grew sick
For a redeeming glimpse of clean blue sky.

No one had seen me take the thing – but still
A blank laugh echoed in my whirling head,
And I could guess what nighted worlds of ill
Lurked in that volume I had coveted.
The way grew strange – the walls alike and madding–
And far behind me, unseen feet were padding.

3. The Key

I do not know what windings in the waste
Of those strange sea-lanes brought me home once more,
But on my porch I trembled, white with haste
To get inside and bolt the heavy door.
I had the book that told the hidden way
Across the void and through the space-hung screens
That hold the undimensioned worlds at bay,
And keep lost aeons to their own demesnes.

At last the key was mine to those vague visions
Of sunset spires and twilight woods that brood
Dim in the gulfs beyond this earth's precisions,
Lurking as memories of infinitude.
The key was mine, but as I sat there mumbling,
The attic window shook with a faint fumbling.

4. Recognition

The day had come again, when as a child
I saw – just once – that hollow of old oaks,
Grey with a ground-mist that enfolds and chokes
The slinking shapes which madness has defiled.
It was the same – an herbage rank and wild
Clings round an altar whose carved sign invokes
That Nameless One to whom a thousand smokes
Rose, aeons gone, from unclean towers up-piled.

I saw the body spread on that dank stone,
And knew those things which feasted were not men;
I knew this strange, grey world was not my own,
But Yuggoth, past the starry voids – and then
The body shrieked at me with a dead cry,
And all too late I knew that it was I!

5. Homecoming

The daemon said that he would take me home
To the pale, shadowy land I half recalled
As a high place of stair and terrace, walled
With marble balustrades that sky-winds comb,
While miles below a maze of dome on dome
And tower on tower beside a sea lies sprawled.
Once more, he told me, I would stand enthralled
On those old heights, and hear the far-off foam.

All this he promised, and through sunset's gate
He swept me, past the lapping lakes of flame,
And red-gold thrones of gods without a name
Who shriek in fear at some impending fate.
Then a black gulf with sea-sounds in the night:
'Here was your home,' he mocked, 'when you had sight!'

6. The Lamp

We found the lamp inside those hollow cliffs
Whose chiselled sign no priest in Thebes could read,
And from whose caverns frightened hieroglyphs
Warned every creature of earth's breed.
No more was there – just that one brazen bowl
With traces of a curious oil within;
Fretted with some obscurely patterned scroll,
And symbols hinting vaguely of strange sin.

Little the fears of forty centuries meant
To us as we bore off our slender spoil,
And when we scanned it in our darkened tent
We struck a match to test the ancient oil.
It blazed – great God! ... But the vast shapes we saw
In that mad flash have seared our lives with awe.

7. Zaman's Hill

The great hill hung close over the old town,
A precipice against the main street's end;
Green, tall, and wooded, looking darkly down
Upon the steeple at the highway bend.
Two hundred years the whispers had been heard
About what happened on the man-shunned slope—
Tales of an oddly mangled deer or bird,
Or of lost boys whose kin had ceased to hope.

One day the mail-man found no village there,
Nor were its folk or houses seen again;
People came out from Aylesbury to stare—
Yet they all told the mail-man it was plain
That he was mad for saying he had spied
The great hill's gluttonous eyes, and jaws stretched wide.

8. The Port

Ten miles from Arkham I had struck the trail
That rides the cliff-edge over Boynton Beach,
And hoped that just at sunset I could reach
The crest that looks on Innsmouth in the vale.
Far out at sea was a retreating sail,
White as hard years of ancient winds could bleach,
But evil with some portent beyond speech,
So that I did not wave my hand or hail.

Sails out of lnnsmouth! echoing old renown
Of long-dead times. But now a too-swift night
Is closing in, and I have reached the height
Whence I so often scan the distant town.
The spires and roofs are there – but look! The gloom
Sinks on dark lanes, as lightless as the tomb!

9. The Courtyard

It was the city I had known before;
The ancient, leprous town where mongrel throngs
Chant to strange gods, and beat unhallowed gongs
In crypts beneath foul alleys near the shore.
The rotting, fish-eyed houses leered at me
From where they leaned, drunk and half-animate,
As edging through the filth I passed the gate
To the black courtyard where the man would be.

The dark walls closed me in, and loud I cursed
That ever I had come to such a den,
When suddenly a score of windows burst
Into wild light, and swarmed with dancing men:
Mad, soundless revels of the dragging dead—
And not a corpse had either hands or head!

10. The Pigeon-Flyers

They took me slumming, where gaunt walls of brick
Bulge outward with a viscous stored-up evil,
And twisted faces, thronging foul and thick,
Wink messages to alien god and devil.
A million fires were blazing in the streets,
And from flat roofs a furtive few would fly
Bedraggled birds into the yawning sky
While hidden drums droned on with measured beats.

I knew those fires were brewing monstrous things,
And that those birds of space had been *Outside*—
I guessed to what dark planet's crypts they plied,
And what they brought from Thog beneath their wings.
The others laughed – till struck too mute to speak
By what they glimpsed in one bird's evil beak.

11. The Well

Farmer Seth Atwood was past eighty when
He tried to sink that deep well by his door,
With only Eb to help him bore and bore.
We laughed, and hoped he'd soon be sane again.
And yet, instead, young Eb went crazy, too,
So that they shipped him to the county farm.
Seth bricked the well-mouth up as tight as glue—
Then hacked an artery in his gnarled left arm.

After the funeral we felt bound to get
Out to that well and rip the bricks away,
But all we saw were iron hand-holds set
Down a black hole deeper than we could say.
And yet we put the bricks back – for we found
The hole too deep for any line to sound.

12. The Howler

They told me not to take the Briggs' Hill path
That used to be the highroad through to Zoar,
For Goody Watkins, hanged in seventeen-four,
Had left a certain monstrous aftermath.
Yet when I disobeyed, and had in view
The vine-hung cottage by the great rock slope,
I could not think of elms or hempen rope,
But wondered why the house still seemed so new.

Stopping a while to watch the fading day,
I heard faint howls, as from a room upstairs,
When through the ivied panes one sunset ray
Struck in, and caught the howler unawares.
I glimpsed – and ran in frenzy from the place,
And from a four-pawed thing with human face.

13. Hesperia

The winter sunset, flaming beyond spires
And chimneys half-detached from this dull sphere,
Opens great gates to some forgotten year
Of elder splendours and divine desires.
Expectant wonders burn in those rich fires,
Adventure-fraught, and not untinged with fear;
A row of sphinxes where the way leads clear
Toward walls and turrets quivering to far lyres.

It is the land where beauty's meaning flowers;
Where every unplaced memory has a source;
Where the great river Time begins its course
Down the vast void in starlit streams of hours.
Dreams bring us close – but ancient lore repeats
That human tread has never soiled these streets.

14. Star-Winds

It is a certain hour of twilight glooms,
Mostly in autumn, when the star-wind pours
Down hilltop streets, deserted out-of-doors,
But shewing early lamplight from snug rooms.
The dead leaves rush in strange, fantastic twists,
And chimney-smoke whirls round with alien grace,
Heeding geometries of outer space,
While Fomalhaut peers in through southward mists.

This is the hour when moonstruck poets know
What fungi sprout in Yuggoth, and what scents
And tints of flowers fill Nithon's continents,
Such as in no poor earthly garden blow.
Yet for each dream these winds to us convey,
A dozen more of ours they sweep away!

15. Antarktos

Deep in my dream the great bird whispered queerly
Of the black cone amid the polar waste;
Pushing above the ice-sheet lone and drearly,
By storm-crazed aeons battered and defaced.
Hither no living earth-shapes take their courses,
And only pale auroras and faint suns
Glow on that pitted rock, whose primal sources
Are guessed at dimly by the Elder Ones.

If men should glimpse it, they would merely wonder
What tricky mound of Nature's build they spied;
But the bird told of vaster parts, that under
The mile-deep ice-shroud crouch and brood and bide.
God help the dreamer whose mad visions shew
Those dead eyes set in crystal gulfs below!

16. The Window

The house was old, with tangled wings outthrown,
Of which no one could ever half keep track,
And in a small room somewhat near the back
Was an odd window sealed with ancient stone.
There, in a dream-plagued childhood, quite alone
I used to go, where night reigned vague and black;
Parting the cobwebs with a curious lack
Of fear, and with a wonder each time grown.

One later day I brought the masons there
To find what view my dim forbears had shunned,
But as they pierced the stone, a rush of air
Burst from the alien voids that yawned beyond.
They fled – but I peered through and found unrolled
All the wild worlds of which my dreams had told.

17. A Memory

There were great steppes, and rocky table-lands
Stretching half-limitless in starlit night,
With alien campfires shedding feeble light
On beasts with tinkling bells, in shaggy bands.
Far to the south the plain sloped low and wide
To a dark zigzag line of wall that lay
Like a huge python of some primal day
Which endless time had chilled and petrified.

I shivered oddly in the cold, thin air,
And wondered where I was and how I came,
When a cloaked form against a campfire's glare
Rose and approached, and called me by my name.
Staring at that dead face beneath the hood,
I ceased to hope – because I understood.

18. The Gardens of Yin

Beyond that wall, whose ancient masonry
Reached almost to the sky in moss-thick towers,
There would be terraced gardens, rich with flowers,
And flutter of bird and butterfly and bee.
There would be walks, and bridges arching over
Warm lotus-pools reflecting temple eaves,
And cherry-trees with delicate boughs and leaves
Against a pink sky where the herons hover.

All would be there, for had not old dreams flung
Open the gate to that stone-lanterned maze
Where drowsy streams spin out their winding ways,
Trailed by green vines from bending branches hung?
I hurried – but when the wall rose, grim and great,
I found there was no longer any gate.

19. The Bells

Year after year I heard that faint, far ringing
Of deep-toned bells on the black midnight wind;
Peals from no steeple I could ever find,
But strange, as if across some great void winging.
I searched my dreams and memories for a clue,
And thought of all the chimes my visions carried;
Of quiet Innsmouth, where the white gulls tarried
Around an ancient spire that once I knew.

Always perplexed I heard those far notes falling,
Till one March night the bleak rain splashing cold
Beckoned me back through gateways of recalling
To elder towers where the mad clappers tolled.
They tolled – but from the sunless tides that pour
Through sunken valleys on the sea's dead floor.

20. Night-Gaunts

Out of what crypt they crawl, I cannot tell,
But every night I see the rubbery things,
Black, horned, and slender, with membraneous wings,
And tails that bear the bifid barb of hell.
They come in legions on the north wind's swell,
With obscene clutch that titillates and stings,
Snatching me off on monstrous voyagings
To grey worlds hidden deep in nightmare's well.

Over the jagged peaks of Thok they sweep,
Heedless of all the cries I try to make,
And down the nether pits to that foul lake
Where the puffed shoggoths splash in doubtful sleep.
But oh! If only they would make some sound,
Or wear a face where faces should be found!

21. Nyarlathotep

And at the last from inner Egypt came
The strange dark One to whom the fellahs bowed;
Silent and lean and cryptically proud,
And wrapped in fabrics red as sunset flame.
Throngs pressed around, frantic for his commands,
But leaving, could not tell what they had heard;
While through the nations spread the awestruck word
That wild beasts followed him and licked his hands.

Soon from the sea a noxious birth began;
Forgotten lands with weedy spires of gold;
The ground was cleft, and mad auroras rolled
Down on the quaking citadels of man.
Then, crushing what he chanced to mould in play,
The idiot Chaos blew Earth's dust away.

22. Azathoth

Out in the mindless void the daemon bore me,
Past the bright clusters of dimensioned space,
Till neither time nor matter stretched before me,
But only Chaos, without form or place.
Here the vast Lord of All in darkness muttered
Things he had dreamed but could not understand,
While near him shapeless bat-things flopped and fluttered
In idiot vortices that ray-streams fanned.

They danced insanely to the high, thin whining
Of a cracked flute clutched in a monstrous paw,
Whence flow the aimless waves whose chance combining
Gives each frail cosmos its eternal law.
'I am His Messenger,' the daemon said,
As in contempt he struck his Master's head.

23. Mirage

I do not know if ever it existed—
That lost world floating dimly on Time's stream—
And yet I see it often, violet-misted,
And shimmering at the back of some vague dream.
There were strange towers and curious lapping rivers,
Labyrinths of wonder, and low vaults of light,
And bough-crossed skies of flame, like that which quivers
Wistfully just before a winter's night.

Great moors led off to sedgy shores unpeopled,
Where vast birds wheeled, while on a windswept hill
There was a village, ancient and white-steepled,
With evening chimes for which I listen still.
I do not know what land it is – or dare
Ask when or why I was, or will be, there.

24. The Canal

Somewhere in dream there is an evil place
Where tall, deserted buildings crowd along
A deep, black, narrow channel, reeking strong
Of frightful things whence oily currents race.
Lanes with old walls half meeting overhead
Wind off to streets one may or may not know,
And feeble moonlight sheds a spectral glow
Over long rows of windows, dark and dead.

There are no footfalls, and the one soft sound
Is of the oily water as it glides
Under stone bridges, and along the sides
Of its deep flume, to some vague ocean bound.
None lives to tell when that stream washed away
Its dream-lost region from the world of clay.

25. St Toad's

'Beware St Toad's cracked chimes!' I heard him scream
As I plunged into those mad lanes that wind
In labyrinths obscure and undefined
South of the river where old centuries dream.
He was a furtive figure, bent and ragged,
And in a flash had staggered out of sight,
So still I burrowed onward in the night
Toward where more roof-lines rose, malign and jagged.

No guide-book told of what was lurking here—
But now I heard another old man shriek:
'Beware St Toad's cracked chimes!' And growing weak,
I paused, when a third greybeard croaked in fear:
'Beware St Toad's cracked chimes!' Aghast, I fled—
Till suddenly that black spire loomed ahead.

26. The Familiars

John Whateley lived about a mile from town,
Up where the hills began to huddle thick;
We never thought his wits were very quick,
Seeing the way he let his farm run down.
He used to waste his time on some queer books
He'd found around the attic of his place,
Till funny lines got creased into his face,
And folks all said they didn't like his looks.

When he began those night-howls we declared
He'd better be locked up away from harm,
So three men from the Aylesbury town farm
Went for him – but came back alone and scared.
They'd found him talking to two crouching things
That at their step flew off on great black wings.

27. The Elder Pharos

From Leng, where rocky peaks climb bleak and bare
Under cold stars obscure to human sight,
There shoots at dusk a single beam of light
Whose far blue rays make shepherds whine in prayer.
They say (though none has been there) that it comes
Out of a pharos in a tower of stone,
Where the last Elder One lives on alone,
Talking to Chaos with the beat of drums.

The Thing, they whisper, wears a silken mask
Of yellow, whose queer folds appear to hide
A face not of this earth, though none dares ask
Just what those features are, which bulge inside.
Many, in man's first youth, sought out that glow,
But what they found, no one will ever know.

329

28. Expectancy

I cannot tell why some things hold for me
A sense of unplumbed marvels to befall,
Or of a rift in the horizon's wall
Opening to worlds where only gods can be.
There is a breathless, vague expectancy,
As of vast ancient pomps I half recall,
Or wild adventures, uncorporeal,
Ecstasy-fraught, and as a day-dream free.

It is in sunsets and strange city spires,
Old villages and woods and misty downs,
South winds, the sea, low hills, and lighted towns,
Old gardens, half-heard songs, and the moon's fires.
But though its lure alone makes life worth living,
None gains or guesses what it hints at giving.

29. Nostalgia

Once every year, in autumn's wistful glow,
The birds fly out over an ocean waste,
Calling and chattering in a joyous haste
To reach some land their inner memories know.
Great terraced gardens where bright blossoms blow,
And lines of mangoes luscious to the taste,
And temple-groves with branches interlaced
Over cool paths – all these their vague dreams shew.

They search the sea for marks of their old shore—
For the tall city, white and turreted—
But only empty waters stretch ahead,
So that at last they turn away once more.
Yet sunken deep where alien polyps throng,
The old towers miss their lost, remembered song.

30. Background

I never can be tied to raw, new things,
For I first saw the light in an old town,
Where from my window huddled roofs sloped down
To a quaint harbour rich with visionings.
Streets with carved doorways where the sunset beams
Flooded old fanlights and small window-panes,
And Georgian steeples topped with gilded vanes—
These were the sights that shaped my childhood dreams.

Such treasures, left from times of cautious leaven,
Cannot but loose the hold of flimsier wraiths
That flit with shifting ways and muddled faiths
Across the changeless walls of earth and heaven.
They cut the moment's thongs and leave me free
To stand alone before eternity.

31. The Dweller

It had been old when Babylon was new;
None knows how long it slept beneath that mound,
Where in the end our questing shovels found
Its granite blocks and brought it back to view.
There were vast pavements and foundation-walls,
And crumbling slabs and statues, carved to shew
Fantastic beings of some long ago
Past anything the world of man recalls.

And then we saw those stone steps leading down
Through a choked gate of graven dolomite
To some black haven of eternal night
Where elder signs and primal secrets frown.
We cleared a path – but raced in mad retreat
When from below we heard those clumping feet.

32. Alienation

His solid flesh had never been away,
For each dawn found him in his usual place,
But every night his spirit loved to race
Through gulfs and worlds remote from common day.
He had seen Yaddith, yet retained his mind,
And come back safely from the Ghooric zone,
When one still night across curved space was thrown
That beckoning piping from the voids behind.

He waked that morning as an older man,
And nothing since has looked the same to him.
Objects around float nebulous and dim—
False, phantom trifles of some vaster plan.
His folk and friends are now an alien throng
To which he struggles vainly to belong.

33. Harbour Whistles

Over old roofs and past decaying spires
The harbour whistles chant all through the night;
Throats from strange ports, and beaches far and white,
And fabulous oceans, ranged in motley choirs.
Each to the other alien and unknown,
Yet all, by some obscurely focussed force
From brooding gulfs beyond the Zodiac's course,
Fused into one mysterious cosmic drone.

Through shadowy dreams they send a marching line
Of still more shadowy shapes and hints and views;
Echoes from outer voids, and subtle clues
To things which they themselves cannot define.
And always in that chorus, faintly blent,
We catch some notes no earth-ship ever sent.

34. Recapture

The way led down a dark, half-wooded heath
Where moss-grey boulders humped above the mould,
And curious drops, disquieting and cold,
Sprayed up from unseen streams in gulfs beneath.
There was no wind, nor any trace of sound
In puzzling shrub, or alien-featured tree,
Nor any view before – till suddenly,
Straight in my path, I saw a monstrous mound.

Half to the sky those steep sides loomed upspread,
Rank-grassed, and cluttered by a crumbling flight
Of lava stairs that scaled the fear-topped height
In steps too vast for any human tread.
I shrieked – and *knew* what primal star and year
Had sucked me back from man's dream-transient sphere!

35. Evening Star

I saw it from that hidden, silent place
Where the old wood half shuts the meadow in.
It shone through all the sunset's glories – thin
At first, but with a slowly brightening face.
Night came, and that lone beacon, amber-hued,
Beat on my sight as never it did of old;
The evening star – but grown a thousandfold
More haunting in this hush and solitude.

It traced strange pictures on the quivering air—
Half-memories that had always filled my eyes—
Vast towers and gardens; curious seas and skies
Of some dim life – I never could tell where.
But now I knew that through the cosmic dome
Those rays were calling from my far, lost home.

36. Continuity

There is in certain ancient things a trace
Of some dim essence – more than form or weight;
A tenuous aether, indeterminate,
Yet linked with all the laws of time and space.
A faint, veiled sign of continuities
That outward eyes can never quite descry;
Of locked dimensions harbouring years gone by,
And out of reach except for hidden keys.

It moves me most when slanting sunbeams glow
On old farm buildings set against a hill,
And paint with life the shapes which linger still
From centuries less a dream than this we know.
In that strange light I feel I am not far
From the fixt mass whose sides the ages are.

Dec. 27, 1929–Jan. 4, 1930.

THE TRAP

(with Henry S. Whitehead)

I T WAS ON A CERTAIN Thursday morning in December that the whole thing began with that unaccountable motion I thought I saw in my antique Copenhagen mirror. Something, it seemed to me, stirred – something reflected in the glass, though I was alone in my quarters. I paused and looked intently, then, deciding that the effect must be a pure illusion, resumed the interrupted brushing of my hair.

I had discovered the old mirror, covered with dust and cobwebs, in an outbuilding of an abandoned estate-house in Santa Cruz's sparsely settled Northside territory, and had brought it to the United States from the Virgin Islands. The venerable glass was dim from more than two hundred years' exposure to a tropical climate, and the graceful ornamentation along the top of the gilt frame had been badly smashed. I had had the detached pieces set back into the frame before placing it in storage with my other belongings.

Now, several years later, I was staying half as a guest and half as a tutor at the private school of my old friend Browne on a windy

Connecticut hillside – occupying an unused wing in one of the dormitories, where I had two rooms and a hallway to myself. The old mirror, stowed securely in mattresses, was the first of my possessions to be unpacked on my arrival; and I had set it up majestically in the living-room, on top of an old rosewood console which had belonged to my great-grandmother.

The door of my bedroom was just opposite that of the living-room, with a hallway between; and I had noticed that by looking into my chiffonier glass I could see the larger mirror through the two doorways – which was exactly like glancing down an endless, though diminishing, corridor. On this Thursday morning I thought I saw a curious suggestion of motion down that normally empty corridor – but, as I have said, soon dismissed the notion.

When I reached the dining-room I found everyone complaining of the cold, and learned that the school's heating-plant was temporarily out of order. Being especially sensitive to low temperatures, I was myself an acute sufferer; and at once decided not to brave any freezing schoolroom that day. Accordingly I invited my class to come over to my living-room for an informal session around my grate-fire – a suggestion which the boys received enthusiastically.

After the session one of the boys, Robert Grandison, asked if he might remain; since he had no appointment for the second morning period. I told him to stay, and welcome. He sat down to study in front of the fireplace in a comfortable chair.

It was not long, however, before Robert moved to another chair somewhat farther away from the freshly replenished blaze, this change bringing him directly opposite the old mirror. From my own chair in another part of the room I noticed how fixedly he began to look at the dim, cloudy glass, and, wondering what so greatly interested him, was reminded of my own experience earlier that morning. As time passed he continued to gaze, a slight frown knitting his brows.

At last I quietly asked him what had attracted his attention. Slowly, and still wearing the puzzled frown, he looked over and replied rather cautiously:

'It's the corrugations in the glass – or whatever they are, Mr Canevin. I was noticing how they all seem to run from a certain point. Look – I'll show you what I mean.'

The boy jumped up, went over to the mirror, and placed his finger on a point near its lower left-hand corner.

'It's right here, sir,' he explained, turning to look toward me and keeping his finger on the chosen spot.

His muscular action in turning may have pressed his finger against the glass. Suddenly he withdrew his hand as though with some slight effort, and with a faintly muttered 'Ouch.' Then he looked at the glass in obvious mystification.

'What happened?' I asked, rising and approaching.

'Why – it—' He seemed embarrassed. 'It – I – felt – well, as though it were pulling my finger into it. Seems – er – perfectly foolish, sir, but – well – it was a most peculiar sensation.' Robert had an unusual vocabulary for his fifteen years.

I came over and had him show me the exact spot he meant.

'You'll think I'm rather a fool, sir,' he said shamefacedly, 'but – well, from right here I can't be absolutely sure. From the chair it seemed to be clear enough.'

Now thoroughly interested, I sat down in the chair Robert had occupied and looked at the spot he selected on the mirror. Instantly the thing 'jumped out at me'. Unmistakably, from that particular angle, all the many whorls in the ancient glass appeared to converge like a large number of spread strings held in one hand and radiating out in streams.

Getting up and crossing to the mirror, I could no longer see the curious spot. Only from certain angles, apparently, was it visible. Directly viewed, that portion of the mirror did not even give back a normal reflection – for I could not see my face in it. Manifestly I had a minor puzzle on my hands.

Presently the school gong sounded, and the fascinated Robert Grandison departed hurriedly, leaving me alone with my odd little problem in optics. I raised several window-shades, crossed the hallway, and sought for the spot in the chiffonier mirror's reflection. Finding it readily, I looked very intently and thought I again detected something of the 'motion'. I craned my neck, and at last, at a certain angle of vision, the thing again 'jumped out at me'.

The vague 'motion' was now positive and definite – an appearance of torsional movement, or of whirling; much like a minute yet intense whirlwind or waterspout, or a huddle of autumn leaves dancing circularly in an eddy of wind along a level lawn. It was, like the earth's, a double motion – around and around, and at the same time *inward*, as if the whorls poured themselves endlessly toward some point inside the glass. Fascinated, yet realising that the thing must be an illusion, I grasped an impression of quite distinct *suction*, and thought of Robert's embarrassed explanation: '*I felt as though it were pulling my finger into it.*'

A kind of slight chill ran suddenly up and down my backbone. There was something here distinctly worth looking into. And as the idea of investigation came to me, I recalled the rather wistful expression of Robert Grandison when the gong called him to class. I remembered how he had looked back over his shoulder as he walked obediently out into the hallway, and resolved that he should be included in whatever analysis I might make of this little mystery.

Exciting events connected with that same Robert, however, were soon to chase all thoughts of the mirror from my consciousness for a time. I was away all that afternoon, and did not return to the school until the five-fifteen 'Call-Over' – a general assembly at which the boys' attendance was compulsory. Dropping in at this function with the idea of picking Robert up for a session with the mirror, I was astonished and pained to find him absent – a very unusual and unaccountable thing in his case. That evening Browne told me that the boy had actually disappeared, a search in his room, in the gymnasium, and in all other accustomed places being unavailing, though all his belongings – including his outdoor clothing – were in their proper places.

He had not been encountered on the ice or with any of the hiking groups that afternoon, and telephone calls to all the school-catering merchants of the neighbourhood were in vain. There was, in short, no record of his having been seen since the end of the lesson periods at two-fifteen; when he had turned up the stairs toward his room in Dormitory Number Three.

When the disappearance was fully realised, the resulting sensation was tremendous throughout the school. Browne, as head-master, had to bear the brunt of it; and such an unprecedented occurrence in his well-regulated, highly organised institution left him quite bewildered. It was learned that Robert had not run away to his home in western Pennsylvania, nor did any of the searching-parties of boys and masters find any trace of him in the snowy

ELDRITCH TALES

countryside around the school. So far as could be seen, he had simply vanished.

Robert's parents arrived on the afternoon of the second day after his disappearance. They took their trouble quietly, though, of course, they were staggered by this unexpected disaster. Browne looked ten years older for it, but there was absolutely nothing that could be done. By the fourth day the case had settled down in the opinion of the school as an insoluble mystery. Mr and Mrs Grandison went reluctantly back to their home, and on the following morning the ten days' Christmas vacation began.

Boys and masters departed in anything but the usual holiday spirit; and Browne and his wife were left, along with the servants, as my only fellow-occupants of the big place. Without the masters and boys it seemed a very hollow shell indeed.

That afternoon I sat in front of my grate-fire thinking about Robert's disappearance and evolving all sorts of fantastic theories to account for it. By evening I had acquired a bad headache, and ate a light supper accordingly. Then, after a brisk walk around the massed buildings, I returned to my living-room and took up the burden of thought once more.

A little after ten o'clock I awakened in my armchair, stiff and chilled, from a doze during which I had let the fire go out. I was physically uncomfortable, yet mentally aroused by a peculiar sensation of expectancy and possible hope. Of course it had to do with the problem that was harassing me. For I had started from that inadvertent nap with a curious, persistent idea – the odd idea that a tenuous, hardly recognisable Robert Grandison had been trying desperately to communicate with me. I finally went to bed with one conviction unreasoningly strong in my mind. Somehow I was sure that young Robert Grandison was still alive.

That I should be receptive of such a notion will not seem strange to those who know my long residence in the West Indies and my close contact with unexplained happenings there. It will not seem strange, either, that I fell asleep with an urgent desire to establish some sort of mental communication with the missing boy. Even the most prosaic scientists affirm, with Freud, Jung, and Adler, that the subconscious mind is most open to external impressions in sleep; though such impressions are seldom carried over intact into the waking state.

Going a step further and granting the existence of telepathic forces, it follows that such forces must act most strongly on a sleeper; so that if I were ever to get a definite message from Robert, it would be during a period of profoundest slumber. Of course, I might lose the message in waking; but my aptitude for retaining such things has been sharpened by types of mental discipline picked up in various obscure corners of the globe.

I must have dropped asleep instantaneously, and from the vividness of my dreams and the absence of wakeful intervals I judge that my sleep was a very deep one. It was six-forty-five when I awakened, and there still lingered with me certain impressions which I knew were carried over from the world of somnolent cerebration. Filling my mind was the vision of Robert Grandison strangely transformed to a boy of a dull greenish dark-blue colour; Robert desperately endeavouring to communicate with me by means of speech, yet finding some almost insuperable difficulty in so doing. A wall of curious spatial separation seemed to stand between him and me – a mysterious, invisible wall which completely baffled us both.

I had seen Robert as though at some distance, yet queerly enough he seemed at the same time to be just beside me. He was both larger and smaller than in real life, his apparent size varying *directly*, instead of *inversely*, with the distance as he advanced and retreated in the course of conversation. That is, he grew larger instead of smaller to my eye when he stepped away or backwards, and vice versa; as if the laws of perspective in his case had been wholly reversed. His aspect was misty and uncertain – as if he lacked sharp or permanent outlines; and the anomalies of his colouring and clothing baffled me utterly at first.

At some point in my dream Robert's vocal efforts had finally crystallised into audible speech – albeit speech of an abnormal thickness and dullness. I could not for a time understand anything he said, and even in the dream racked my brain for a clue to where he was, what he wanted to tell, and why his utterance was so clumsy and unintelligible. Then little by little I began to distinguish words and phrases, the very first of which sufficed to throw my dreaming self into the wildest excitement and to establish a certain mental connection which had previously refused to take conscious form because of the utter incredibility of what it implied.

341

I do not know how long I listened to those halting words amidst my deep slumber, but hours must have passed while the strangely remote speaker struggled on with his tale. There was revealed to me such a circumstance as I cannot hope to make others believe without the strongest corroborative evidence, yet which I was quite ready to accept as truth – both in the dream and after waking – because of my former contacts with uncanny things. The boy was obviously watching my face – mobile in receptive sleep – as he choked along; for about the time I began to comprehend him, his own expression brightened and gave signs of gratitude and hope.

Any attempt to hint at Robert's message, as it lingered in my ears after a sudden awakening in the cold, brings this narrative to a point where I must choose my words with the greatest care. Everything involved is so difficult to record that one tends to flounder help-lessly. I have said that the revelation established in my mind a certain connection which reason had not allowed me to formulate consciously before. This connection, I need no longer hesitate to hint, had to do with the old Copenhagen mirror whose suggestions of motion had so impressed me on the morning of the dis-appearance, and whose whorl-like contours and apparent illusions of suction had later exerted such a disquieting fascination on both Robert and me.

Resolutely, though my outer consciousness had previously rejected what my intuition would have liked to imply, it could reject that stupendous conception no longer. What was fantasy in the tale of 'Alice' now came to me as a grave and immediate reality. That looking-glass had indeed possessed a malign, abnormal suction; and the struggling speaker in my dream made clear the extent to which it violated all the known precedents of human experience and all the age-old laws of our three sane dimensions. It was more than a mirror – it was a gate; a trap; a link with spatial recesses not meant for the denizens of our visible universe, and realisable only in terms of the most intricate non-Euclidean mathematics. *And in some outrageous fashion Robert Grandison had passed out of our ken into the glass and was there immured, waiting for release.*

It is significant that upon awakening I harboured no genuine doubt of the reality of the revelation. That I had actually held conversation with a trans-dimensional Robert, rather than evoked the whole episode from my broodings about his disappearance and about the old illusions of the mirror, was as certain to my utmost instincts as any of the instinctive certainties commonly recognised as valid.

The tale thus unfolded to me was of the most incredibly bizarre character. As had been clear on the morning of his disappearance, Robert was intensely fascinated by the ancient mirror. All through the hours of school, he had it in mind to come back to my living-room and examine it further. When he did arrive, after the close of the school day, it was somewhat later than two-twenty, and I was absent in town. Finding me out and knowing that I would not mind, he had come into my living-room and gone straight to the mirror; standing before it and studying the place where, as we had noted, the whorls appeared to converge.

Then, quite suddenly, there had come to him an overpowering urge to place his hand upon this whorl-centre. Almost reluctantly, against his better judgement, he had done so; and upon making the contact had felt at once the strange, almost painful suction which had perplexed him that morning. Immediately thereafter – quite without warning, but with a wrench which seemed to twist and tear every bone and muscle in his body and to bulge and press and cut at every nerve – he had been abruptly *drawn through* and found himself *inside*.

Once through, the excruciatingly painful stress upon his entire system was suddenly released. He felt, he said, as though he had just been born – a feeling that made itself evident every time he tried to do anything; walk, stoop, turn his head, or utter speech. Everything about his body seemed a misfit.

These sensations wore off after a long while, Robert's body becoming an organised whole rather than a number of protesting parts. Of all the forms of expression, speech remained the most difficult; doubtless because it is complicated, bringing into play a number of different organs, muscles, and tendons. Robert's feet, on the other hand, were the first members to adjust themselves to the new conditions within the glass.

During the morning hours I rehearsed the whole reason-defying problem; correlating everything I had seen and heard, dismissing the natural scepticism of a man of sense, and scheming to devise possible plans for Robert's release from his incredible prison. As

I did so a number of originally perplexing points became clear — or at least, clearer — to me.

There was, for example, the matter of Robert's colouring. His face and hands, as I have indicated, were a kind of dull greenish dark-blue; and I may add that his familiar blue Norfolk jacket had turned to a pale lemon-yellow while his trousers remained a neutral grey as before. Reflecting on this after waking, I found the circumstance closely allied to the reversal of perspective which made Robert seem to grow larger when receding and smaller when approaching. Here, too, was a physical *reversal* — for every detail of his colouring in the unknown dimension was the exact reverse or complement of the corresponding colour detail in normal life. In physics the typical complementary colours are blue and yellow, and red and green. These pairs are opposites, and when mixed yield grey. Robert's natural colour was a pinkish-buff, the opposite of which is the greenish-blue I saw. His blue coat had become yellow, while the grey trousers remained grey. This latter point baffled me until I remembered that grey is itself a mixture of opposites. There is no opposite for grey — or rather, it is its own opposite.

Another clarified point was that pertaining to Robert's curiously dulled and thickened speech — as well as to the general awkwardness and sense of misfit bodily parts of which he complained. This, at the outset, was a puzzle indeed; though after long thought the clue occurred to me. Here again was the same *reversal* which affected perspective and coloration. Anyone in the fourth dimension must necessarily be reversed in just this way — hands and feet, as well as colours and perspectives, being changed about. It would be the same with all the other dual organs, such as nostrils, ears, and eyes. Thus Robert had been talking with a reversed tongue, teeth, vocal cords, and kindred speech-apparatus; so that his difficulties in utterance were little to be wondered at.

As the morning wore on, my sense of the stark reality and maddening urgency of the dream-disclosed situation increased rather than decreased. More and more I felt that something must be done, yet realised that I could not seek advice or aid. Such a story as mine — a conviction based upon mere dreaming — could not conceivably bring me anything but ridicule or suspicions as to my mental state. And what, indeed, could I do, aided or unaided,

with as little working data as my nocturnal impressions had provided? I must, I finally recognised, have more information before
I could even think of a possible plan for releasing Robert. This
could come only through the receptive conditions of sleep, and it
heartened me to reflect that according to every probability my
telepathic contact would be resumed the moment I fell into deep
slumber again.

I accomplished sleeping that afternoon, after a midday dinner at
which, through rigid self-control, I succeeded in concealing from
Browne and his wife the tumultuous thoughts that crashed through
my mind. Hardly had my eyes closed when a dim telepathic image
began to appear; and I soon realised to my infinite excitement that
it was identical with what I had seen before. If anything, it was more
distinct; and when it began to speak I seemed able to grasp a greater
proportion of the words.

During this sleep I found most of the morning's deductions
confirmed, though the interview was mysteriously cut off long prior
to my awakening. Robert had seemed apprehensive just before
communication ceased, but had already told me that in his strange
fourth-dimensional prison colours and spatial relationships were
indeed reversed – black being white, distance increasing apparent
size, and so on.

He had also intimated that, notwithstanding his possession of
full physical form and sensations, most human vital properties
seemed curiously suspended. Nutriment, for example, was quite
unnecessary – a phenomenon really more singular than the omnipresent reversal of objects and attributes, since the latter was a
reasonable and mathematically indicated state of things. Another
significant piece of information was that the only exit from the glass
to the world was the entrance-way, and that this was permanently
barred and impenetrably sealed, so far as egress was concerned.

That night I had another visitation from Robert; nor did such
impressions, received at odd intervals while I slept receptively
minded, cease during the entire period of his incarceration. His
efforts to communicate were desperate and often pitiful; for at
times the telepathic bond would weaken, while at other times
fatigue, excitement, or fear of interruption would hamper and
thicken his speech.

I may as well narrate as a continuous whole all that Robert told me throughout the whole series of transient mental contacts – perhaps supplementing it at certain points with facts directly related after his release. The telepathic information was fragmentary and often nearly inarticulate, but I studied it over and over during the waking intervals of three intense days; classifying and cogitating with feverish diligence, since it was all that I had to go upon if the boy were to be brought back into our world.

The fourth-dimensional region in which Robert found himself was not, as in scientific romance, an unknown and infinite realm of strange sights and fantastic denizens; but was rather a projection of certain limited parts of our own terrestrial sphere within an alien and normally inaccessible aspect or direction of space. It was a curiously fragmentary, intangible, and heterogeneous world – a series of apparently dissociated scenes merging indistinctly one into the other; their constituent details having an obviously different status from that of an object drawn into the ancient mirror as Robert had been drawn. These scenes were like dream-vistas or magic-lantern images – elusive visual impressions of which the boy was not really a part, but which formed a sort of panoramic background or ethereal environment against which or amidst which he moved.

He could not touch any of the parts of these scenes – walls, trees, furniture, and the like – but whether this was because they were truly non-material, or because they always receded at his approach, he was singularly unable to determine. Everything seemed fluid, mutable, and unreal. When he walked, it appeared to be on whatever lower surface the visible scene might have – floor, path, greensward, or such; but upon analysis he always found that the contact was an illusion. There was never any difference in the resisting force met by his feet – and by his hands when he would stoop experimentally – no matter what changes of apparent surface might be involved. He could not describe this foundation or limiting plane on which he walked as anything more definite than a virtually abstract pressure balancing his gravity. Of definite tactile distinctiveness it had none, and supplementing it there seemed to be a kind of restricted levitational force which accomplished transfers of altitude. He could never actually climb stairs, yet would gradually walk up from a lower level to a higher.

Passage from one definite scene to another involved a sort of

346

gliding through a region of shadow or blurred focus where the details of each scene mingled curiously. All the vistas were distinguished by the absence of transient objects, and the indefinite or ambiguous appearance of such semi-transient objects as furniture or details of vegetation. The lighting of every scene was diffuse and perplexing, and of course the scheme of reversed colours – bright red grass, yellow sky with confused black and grey cloud-forms, white tree-trunks, and green brick walls – gave to everything an air of unbelievable grotesquerie. There was an alteration of day and night, which turned out to be a reversal of the normal hours of light and darkness at whatever point on the earth the mirror might be hanging.

This seemingly irrelevant diversity of the scenes puzzled Robert until he realised that they comprised merely such places as had been reflected for long continuous periods in the ancient glass. This also explained the odd absence of transient objects, the generally arbitrary boundaries of vision, and the fact that all exteriors were framed by the outlines of doorways or windows. The glass, it appeared, had power to store up these intangible scenes through long exposure; though it could never absorb anything corporeally, as Robert had been absorbed, except by a very different and particular process.

But – to me at least – the most incredible aspect of the mad phenomenon was the monstrous subversion of our known laws of space involved in the relation of various illusory scenes to the actual terrestrial regions represented. I have spoken of the glass as storing up the images of these regions, but this is really an inexact definition. In truth, each of the mirror scenes formed a true and quasi-permanent fourth-dimensional projection of the corresponding mundane region; so that whenever Robert moved to a certain part of a certain scene, as he moved into the image of my room when sending his telepathic messages, *he was actually in that place itself, on earth* – though under spatial conditions which cut off all sensory communication, in either direction, between him and the present tri-dimensional aspect of the place.

Theoretically speaking, a prisoner in the glass could in a few moments go anywhere on our planet – into any place, that is, which had ever been reflected in the mirror's surface. This probably applied even to places where the mirror had not hung long enough to produce a clear illusory scene; the terrestrial region being then represented by a zone of more or less formless shadow. Outside the definite scenes was a seemingly limitless waste of neutral grey shadow about which Robert could never be certain, and into which he never dared stray far lest he become hopelessly lost to the real and mirror worlds alike.

Among the earliest particulars which Robert gave, was the fact that he was not alone in his confinement. Various others, all in antique garb, were in there with him – a corpulent middle-aged gentleman with tied queue and velvet knee-breeches who spoke English fluently though with a marked Scandinavian accent; a rather beautiful small girl with very blonde hair which appeared a glossy dark blue; two apparently mute Negroes whose features contrasted grotesquely with the pallor of their reversed-coloured skins; three young men; one young woman; a very small child, almost an infant; and a lean, elderly Dane of extremely distinctive aspect and a kind of half-malign intellectuality of countenance.

This last-named individual – Axel Holm, who wore the satin small-clothes, flared-skirted coat, and voluminous full-bottomed periwig of an age more than two centuries in the past – was notable among the little band as being the one responsible for the presence of them all. He it was who, skilled equally in the arts of magic and glass working, had long ago fashioned this strange dimensional prison in which himself, his slaves, and those whom he chose to invite or allure thither were immured unchangingly for as long as the mirror might endure.

Holm was born early in the seventeenth century, and had followed with tremendous competence and success the trade of a glass-blower and moulder in Copenhagen. His glass, especially in the form of large drawing-room mirrors, was always at a premium. But the same bold mind which had made him the first glazier of Europe also served to carry his interests and ambitions far beyond the sphere of mere material craftsmanship. He had studied the world around him, and chafed at the limitations of human knowledge and capability. Eventually he sought for dark ways to overcome those limitations, and gained more success than is good for any mortal.

He had aspired to enjoy something like eternity, the mirror being his provision to secure this end. Serious study of the fourth dimension was far from beginning with Einstein in our own era; and Holm, more than erudite in all the methods of his day, knew that a bodily entrance into that hidden phase of space would prevent him from dying in the ordinary physical sense. Research showed him that the principle of reflection undoubtedly forms the chief gate to all dimensions beyond our familiar three; and chance placed in his hands a small and very ancient glass whose cryptic properties he believed he could turn to advantage. Once 'inside' this mirror according to the method he had envisaged, he felt that 'life' in the sense of form and consciousness would go on virtually forever, provided the mirror could be preserved indefinitely from breakage or deterioration.

Holm made a magnificent mirror, such as would be prized and carefully preserved; and in it deftly fused the strange whorl-con-figured relic he had acquired. Having thus prepared his refuge and his trap, he began to plan his mode of entrance and conditions of tenancy. He would have with him both servitors and companions; and as an experimental beginning he sent before him into the glass two dependable Negro slaves brought from the West Indies. What his sensations must have been upon beholding this first concrete demonstration of his theories, only imagination can conceive.

Undoubtedly a man of his knowledge realised that absence from the outside world, if deferred beyond the natural span of life of those within, must mean instant dissolution at the first attempt to return to that world. But, barring that misfortune or accidental breakage, those within would remain forever as they were at the time of entrance. They would never grow old, and would need neither food nor drink.

To make his prison tolerable he sent ahead of him certain books and writing materials, a chair and table of stoutest workmanship, and a few other accessories. He knew that the images which the glass would reflect or absorb would not be tangible, but would merely extend around him like a background of dream. His own transition in 1687 was a momentous experience; and must have been attended by mixed sensations of triumph and terror. Had anything gone wrong, there were frightful possibilities of being lost in dark and inconceivable multiple dimensions.

For over fifty years he had been unable to secure any additions to the little company of himself and slaves, but later on he had perfected his telepathic method of visualising small sections of the outside world close to the glass, and attracting certain individuals in those areas through the mirror's strange entrance. Thus Robert, influenced into a desire to press upon the 'door', had been lured within. Such visualisations depended wholly on telepathy, since no one inside the mirror could see out into the world of men.

It was, in truth, a strange life that Holm and his company had lived inside the glass. Since the mirror had stood for fully a century with its face to the dusty stone wall of the shed where I found it, Robert was the first being to enter this limbo after all that interval. His arrival was a gala event, for he brought news of the outside world which must have been of the most startling impressiveness to the more thoughtful of those within. He, in his turn – young though he was – felt overwhelmingly the weirdness of meeting and talking with persons who had been alive in the seventeenth and eighteenth centuries.

The deadly monotony of life for the prisoners can only be vaguely conjectured. As mentioned, its extensive spatial variety was limited to localities which had been reflected in the mirror for long periods; and many of these had become dim and strange as tropical climates had made inroads on the surface. Certain localities were bright and beautiful, and in these the company usually gathered. But no scene could be fully satisfying; since the visible objects were all unreal and intangible, and often of perplexingly indefinite outline. When the tedious periods of darkness came, the general custom was to indulge in memories, reflections, or conversations. Each one of that strange, pathetic group had retained his or her personality unchanged and unchangeable, since becoming immune to the time effects of outside space.

The number of inanimate objects within the glass, aside from the clothing of the prisoners, was very small; being largely limited to the accessories Holm had provided for himself. The rest did without even furniture, since sleep and fatigue had vanished along with most other vital attributes. Such inorganic things as were present, seemed as exempt from decay as the living beings. The lower forms of animal life were wholly absent.

Robert derived most of his information from Herr Thiele, the gentleman who spoke English with a Scandinavian accent. This portly Dane had taken a fancy to him, and talked at considerable length. The others, too, had received him with courtesy and good-will; Holm himself, seeming well-disposed, had told him about various matters including the door of the trap.

The boy, as he told me later, was sensible enough never to attempt communication with me when Holm was nearby. Twice, while thus engaged, he had seen Holm appear; and had accordingly ceased at once. At no time could I see the world behind the mirror's surface. Robert's visual image, which included his bodily form and the clothing connected with it, was – like the aural image of his halting voice and like his own visualisation of myself – a case of purely telepathic transmission; and did not involve true interdimensional sight. However, had Robert been as trained a telepathist as Holm, he might have transmitted a few strong images apart from his immediate person.

Throughout this period of revelation I had, of course, been desperately trying to devise a method for Robert's release. On the fourth day – the ninth after the disappearance – I hit on a solution. Everything considered, my laboriously formulated process was not a very complicated one; though I could not tell beforehand how it would work, while the possibility of ruinous consequences in case of a slip was appalling. This process depended, basically, on the fact that there was no possible exit from inside the glass. If Holm and his prisoners were permanently sealed in, then release must come wholly from outside. Other considerations included the disposal of the other prisoners, if any survived, and especially of Axel Holm. What Robert had told me of him was anything but reassuring; and I certainly did not wish him loose in my apartment, free once more to work his evil will upon the world. The telepathic messages had not made fully clear the effect of liberation on those who had entered the glass so long ago.

There was, too, a final though minor problem in case of success – that of getting Robert back into the routine of school life without having to explain the incredible. In case of failure, it was highly inadvisable to have witnesses present at the release operations – and lacking these, I simply could not attempt to relate the actual facts if I should succeed. Even to me the reality seemed a mad one whenever I let my mind turn from the data so compellingly presented in that tense series of dreams.

When I had thought these problems through as far as possible,

I procured a large magnifying-glass from the school laboratory and studied minutely every square millimetre of that whorl-centre which presumably marked the extent of the original ancient mirror used by Holm. Even with this aid I could not quite trace the exact boundary between the old area and the surface added by the Danish wizard: but after a long study decided on a conjectural oval boundary which I outlined very precisely with a soft blue pencil. I then made a trip to Stamford, where I procured a heavy glass-cutting tool; for my primary idea was to remove the ancient and magically potent mirror from its later setting.

My next step was to figure out the best time of day to make the crucial experiment. I finally settled on two-thirty a.m. – both because it was a good season for uninterrupted work, and because it was the 'opposite' of two-thirty p.m., the probable moment at which Robert had entered the mirror. This form of 'oppositeness' may or may not have been relevant, but I knew at least that the chosen hour was as good as any – and perhaps better than most.

I finally set to work in the early morning of the eleventh day after the disappearance, having drawn all the shades of my living-room and closed and locked the door into the hallway. Following with breathless care the elliptical line I had traced, I worked around the whorl-section with my steel-wheeled cutting tool. The ancient glass, half an inch thick, crackled crisply under the firm, uniform pressure; and upon completing the circuit I cut around it a second time, crunching the roller more deeply into the glass.

Then, very carefully indeed, I lifted the heavy mirror down from its console and leaned it face-inward against the wall; prying off two of the thin, narrow boards nailed to the back. With equal caution I smartly tapped the cut-around space with the heavy wooden handle of the glass-cutter.

At the very first tap the whorl-containing section of glass dropped out on the Bokhara rug beneath. I did not know what might happen, but was keyed up for anything, and took a deep involuntary breath. I was on my knees for convenience at the moment, with my face quite near the newly made aperture; and as I breathed there poured into my nostrils a powerful *dusty* odour – a smell not comparable to any other I have ever encountered. Then everything within my range of vision suddenly turned to a dull grey before my failing eyesight as I felt myself overpowered by an invisible force which robbed my muscles of their power to function.

I remember grasping weakly and futilely at the edge of the nearest window drapery and feeling it rip loose from its fastening. Then I sank slowly to the floor as the darkness of oblivion passed over me.

When I regained consciousness I was lying on the Bokhara rug with my legs held unaccountably up in the air. The room was full of that hideous and inexplicable dusty smell – and as my eyes began to take in definite images I saw that Robert Grandison stood in front of me. It was he – fully in the flesh and with his colouring normal – who was holding my legs aloft to bring the blood back to my head as the school's first-aid course had taught him to do with persons who had fainted. For a moment I was struck mute by the stifling odour and by a bewilderment which quickly merged into a sense of triumph. Then I found myself able to move and speak collectedly.

I raised a tentative hand and waved feebly at Robert.

'All right, old man,' I murmured, 'you can let my legs down now. Many thanks. I'm all right again, I think. It was the smell – I imagine – that got me. Open that farthest window, please – wide – from the bottom. That's it – thanks. No – leave the shade down the way it was.'

I struggled to my feet, my disturbed circulation adjusting itself in waves, and stood upright hanging on to the back of a big chair. I was still 'groggy', but a blast of fresh, bitterly cold air from the window revived me rapidly. I sat down in the big chair and looked at Robert, now walking toward me.

'First,' I said hurriedly, 'tell me, Robert – those others – Holm? What happened to *them*, when I – opened the exit?'

Robert paused half-way across the room and looked at me very gravely.

'I saw them fade away – into nothingness – Mr Canevin,' he said with solemnity; 'and with them – everything. There isn't any more "inside", sir – thank God, and you, sir!'

And young Robert, at last yielding to the sustained strain which he had borne through all those terrible eleven days, suddenly broke down like a little child and began to weep hysterically in great, stifling, dry sobs.

I picked him up and placed him gently on my davenport, threw a rug over him, sat down by his side, and put a calming hand on his forehead.

'Take it easy, old fellow,' I said soothingly.

The boy's sudden and very natural hysteria passed as quickly as it had come on as I talked to him reassuringly about my plans for his quiet restoration to the school. The interest of the situation and the need of concealing the incredible truth beneath a rational explanation took hold of his imagination as I had expected; and at last he sat up eagerly, telling the details of his release and listening to the instructions I had thought out. He had, it seems, been in the 'projected area' of my bedroom when I opened the way back, and had emerged in that actual room – hardly realising that he was 'out'. Upon hearing a fall in the living-room he had hastened thither, finding me on the rug in my fainting spell.

I need mention only briefly my method of restoring Robert in a seemingly normal way – how I smuggled him out of the window in an old hat and sweater of mine, took him down the road in my quietly started car, coached him carefully in a tale I had devised, and returned to arouse Browne with the news of his discovery. He had, I explained, been walking alone on the afternoon of his disappearance; and had been offered a motor ride by two young men who, as a joke and over his protests that he could go no farther than Stamford and back, had begun to carry him past that town. Jumping from the car during a traffic stop with the intention of hitch-hiking back before Call-Over, he had been hit by another car just as the traffic was released – awakening ten days later in the Greenwich home of the people who had hit him. On learning the date, I added, he had immediately telephoned the school; and I, being the only one awake, had answered the call and hurried after him in my car without stopping to notify anyone.

Browne, who at once telephoned to Robert's parents, accepted my story without question; and forbore to interrogate the boy because of the latter's manifest exhaustion. It was arranged that he should remain at the school for a rest, under the expert care of Mrs Browne, a former trained nurse. I naturally saw a good deal of him during the remainder of the Christmas vacation, and was thus enabled to fill in certain gaps in his fragmentary dream-story.

Now and then we would almost doubt the actuality of what had occurred; wondering whether we had not both shared some monstrous delusion born of the mirror's glittering hypnotism, and whether the tale of the ride and accident were not after all the real truth. But whenever we did so we would be brought back to belief by some monstrous and haunting memory; with me, of Robert's dream-figure and its thick voice and inverted colours; with him, of the whole fantastic pageantry of ancient people and dead scenes that he had witnessed. And then there was that joint recollection of that damnable dusty odour ... We knew what it meant: the instant dissolution of those who had entered an alien dimension a century and more ago.

There are, in addition, at least two lines of rather more positive evidence; one of which comes through my researches in Danish annals concerning the sorcerer, Axel Holm. Such a person, indeed, left many traces in folklore and written records; and diligent library sessions, plus conferences with various learned Danes, have shed much more light on his evil fame. At present I need say only that the Copenhagen glass-blower – born in 1612 – was a notorious Luciferian whose pursuits and final vanishing formed a matter of awed debate over two centuries ago. He had burned with a desire to know all things and to conquer every limitation of mankind – to which end he had delved deeply into occult and forbidden fields ever since he was a child.

He was commonly held to have joined a coven of the dreaded witch-cult, and the vast lore of ancient Scandinavian myth – with its Loki the Sly One and the accursed Fenris-Wolf – was soon an open book to him. He had strange interests and objectives, few of which were definitely known, but some of which were recognised as intolerably evil. It is recorded that his two Negro helpers, originally slaves from the Danish West Indies, had become mute soon after their acquisition by him; and that they had disappeared not long before his own disappearance from the ken of mankind.

Near the close of an already long life the idea of a glass of immortality appears to have entered his mind. That he had acquired an enchanted mirror of inconceivable antiquity was a matter of common whispering; it being alleged that he had purloined it from a fellow-sorcerer who had entrusted it to him for polishing.

This mirror – according to popular tales a trophy as potent in its way as the better-known Aegis of Minerva or Hammer of Thor – was a small oval object called 'Loki's Glass', made of some polished fusible mineral and having magical properties which included the divination of the immediate future and the power to show the possessor his enemies. That it had deeper potential properties, realisable in the hands of an erudite magician, none of the common people doubted; and even educated persons attached much fearful importance to Holm's rumoured attempts to incorporate it in a larger glass of immortality. Then had come the wizard's disappearance in 1687, and the final sale and dispersal of his goods amidst a growing cloud of fantastic legendry. It was, altogether, just such a story as one would laugh at if possessed of no particular key; yet to me, remembering those dream messages and having Robert Grandison's corroboration before me, it formed a positive confirmation of all the bewildering marvels that had been unfolded.

But as I have said, there is still another line of rather positive evidence – of a very different character – at my disposal. Two days after his release, as Robert, greatly improved in strength and appearance, was placing a log on my living-room fire, I noticed a certain awkwardness in his motions and was struck by a persistent idea. Summoning him to my desk I suddenly asked him to pick up an ink-stand – and was scarcely surprised to note that, despite lifelong right-handedness, he obeyed unconsciously with his left hand. Without alarming him, I then asked that he unbutton his coat and let me listen to his cardiac action. What I found upon placing my ear to his chest – and what I did not tell him for some time afterward – was that *his heart was beating on his right side.*

He had gone into the glass right-handed and with all organs in their normal positions. Now he was left-handed and with organs reversed, and would doubtless continue so for the rest of his life. Clearly, the dimensional transition had been no illusion – for this physical change was tangible and unmistakable. Had there been a natural exit from the glass, Robert would probably have undergone a thorough re-reversal and emerged in perfect normality – as indeed the colour-scheme of his body and clothing did emerge. The forcible nature of his release, however, undoubtedly set something awry; so that dimensions no longer had a chance to right themselves as chromatic wave-frequencies still did.

I had not merely *opened* Holm's trap; I had *destroyed* it; and at the particular stage of destruction marked by Robert's escape some of the reversing properties had perished. It is significant that in escaping Robert had felt no pain comparable to that experienced in entering. Had the destruction been still more sudden, I shiver to think of the monstrosities of colour the boy would always have been forced to bear. I may add that after discovering Robert's reversal I examined the rumpled and discarded clothing he had worn in the glass, and found, as I had expected, a complete reversal of pockets, buttons, and all other corresponding details.

At this moment Loki's Glass, just as it fell on my Bokhara rug from the now patched and harmless mirror, weighs down a sheaf of papers on my writing-table here in St Thomas, venerable capital of the Danish West Indies – now the American Virgin Islands. Various collectors of old Sandwich glass have mistaken it for an odd bit of that early American product – but I privately realise that my paper-weight is an antique of far subtler and more palaeogean craftsmanship. Still, I do not disillusion such enthusiasts.

THE OTHER GODS

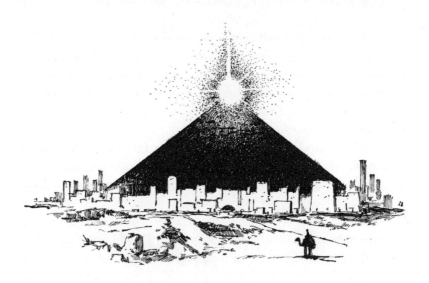

ATOP THE TALLEST of earth's peaks dwell the gods of earth, and suffer not man to tell that he hath looked upon them. Lesser peaks they once inhabited; but ever the men from the plains would scale the slopes of rock and snow, driving the gods to higher and higher mountains till now only the last remains. When they left their old peaks they took with them all signs of themselves, save once, it is said, when they left a carven image on the face of the mountain which they called Ngranek.

But now they have betaken themselves to unknown Kadath in the cold waste where no man treads, and are grown stern, having no higher peak whereto to flee at the coming of men. They are grown stern, and where once they suffered men to displace them, they now forbid men to come; or coming, to depart. It is well for men that they know not of Kadath in the cold waste; else they would seek injudiciously to scale it.

Sometimes when earth's gods are homesick they visit in the still of the night the peaks where once they dwelt, and weep softly as they try to play in the olden way on remembered slopes. Men have felt the tears of the gods on white-capped Thurai, though they have thought it rain; and have heard the sighs of the gods in the plaintive dawn-winds of Lerion. In cloud-ships the gods are wont to travel, and wise cotters have legends that keep them from certain high peaks at night when it is cloudy, for the gods are not lenient as of old.

In Ulthar, which lies beyond the river Skai, once dwelt an old man avid to behold the gods of earth; a man deeply learned in the seven cryptical books of Hsan, and familiar with the *Pnakotic Manuscripts* of distant and frozen Lomar. His name was Barzai the Wise, and the villagers tell of how he went up a mountain on the night of the strange eclipse.

Barzai knew so much of the gods that he could tell of their comings and goings, and guessed so many of their secrets that he was deemed half a god himself. It was he who wisely advised the burgesses of Ulthar when they passed their remarkable law against the slaying of cats, and who first told the young priest Atal where it is that black cats go at midnight on St John's Eve. Barzai was learned in the lore of the earth's gods, and had gained a desire to look upon their faces. He believed that his great secret knowledge of gods could shield him from their wrath, so resolved to go up to the summit of high and rocky Hatheg-Kla on a night when he knew the gods would be there.

Hatheg-Kla is far in the stony desert beyond Hatheg, for which it is named, and rises like a rock statue in a silent temple. Around its peak the mists play always mournfully, for mists are the memories of the gods, and the gods loved Hatheg-Kla when they dwelt upon it in the old days. Often the gods of earth visit Hatheg-Kla in their ships of clouds, casting pale vapours over the slopes as they dance reminiscently on the summit under a clear moon. The villagers of Hatheg say it is ill to climb the Hatheg-Kla at any time, and deadly to climb it by night when pale vapours hide the summit and the moon; but Barzai heeded them not when he came from neighbouring Ulthar with the young priest Atal, who was his disciple. Atal was only the son of an innkeeper, and was sometimes afraid; but Barzai's father had been a landgrave who dwelt in an ancient castle, so he had no common superstition in his blood, and only laughed at the fearful cotters.

Barzai and Atal went out of Hatheg into the stony desert despite the prayers of peasants, and talked of earth's gods by their campfires at night. Many days they travelled, and from afar saw lofty Hatheg-Kla with his aureole of mournful mist. On the thirteenth day they reached the mountain's lonely base, and Atal spoke of his fears. But Barzai was old and learned and had no fears, so led the way up the slope that no man had scaled since the time of Sansu, who is written of with fright in the mouldy *Pnakotic Manuscripts.*

The way was rocky, and made perilous by chasms, cliffs, and falling stones. Later it grew cold and snowy; and Barzai and Atal often slipped and fell as they hewed and plodded upward with staves and axes. Finally the air grew thin, and the sky changed colour, and the climbers found it hard to breathe; but still they toiled up and up, marvelling at the strangeness of the scene and thrilling at the thought of what would happen on the summit when the moon was out and the pale vapours spread around. For three days they climbed higher and higher toward the roof of the world; then they camped to wait for the clouding of the moon.

For four nights no clouds came, and the moon shone down cold through the thin mournful mist around the silent pinnacle. Then on the fifth night, which was the night of the full moon, Barzai saw some dense clouds far to the north, and stayed up with Atal to watch them draw near. Thick and majestic they sailed, slowly and deliberately onward; ranging themselves round the peak high above the watchers, and hiding the moon and the summit from view. For a long hour the watchers gazed, whilst the vapours swirled and the screen of clouds grew thicker and more restless. Barzai was wise in the lore of earth's gods, and listened hard for certain sounds, but Atal felt the chill of the vapours and the awe of the night, and feared much. And when Barzai began to climb higher and beckon eagerly, it was long before Atal would follow.

So thick were the vapours that the way was hard, and though Atal followed at last, he could scarce see the grey shape of Barzai on the dim slope above in the clouded moonlight. Barzai forged very far ahead, and seemed despite his age to climb more easily than Atal; fearing not the steepness that began to grow too great for any save a strong and dauntless man, nor pausing at wide black chasms that Atal could scarce leap. And so they went up wildly over rocks and gulfs, slipping and stumbling, and sometimes awed at the vastness and horrible silence of bleak ice pinnacles and mute granite steeps.

Very suddenly Barzai went out of Atal's sight, scaling a hideous cliff that seemed to bulge outward and block the path for any climber not inspired of earth's gods. Atal was far below, and planning what he should do when he reached the place, when curiously he noticed that the light had grown strong, as if the cloudless peak and moonlit meeting-place of the gods were very near. And as he scrambled on toward the bulging cliff and litten sky he felt fears more shocking than any he had known before. Then through the high mists he heard the voice of Barzai shouting wildly in delight:

'I have heard the gods. I have heard earth's gods singing in revelry on Hatheg-Kla! The voices of earth's gods are known to Barzai the Prophet! The mists are thin and the moon is bright, and I shall see the gods dancing wildly on Hatheg-Kla that they loved in youth. The wisdom of Barzai hath made him greater than earth's gods, and against his will their spells and barriers are as naught; Barzai will behold the gods, the proud gods, the secret gods, the gods of earth who spurn the sight of man!'

Atal could not hear the voices Barzai heard, but he was now close to the bulging cliff and scanning it for footholds. Then he heard Barzai's voice grow shriller and louder:

'The mist is very thin, and the moon casts shadows on the slope; the voices of earth's gods are high and wild, and they fear the coming of Barzai the Wise, who is greater than they ... The moon's light flickers, as earth's gods dance against it; I shall see the dancing forms of the gods that leap and howl in the moonlight ... The light is dimmer and the gods are afraid ...'

Whilst Barzai was shouting these things Atal felt a spectral change in all the air, as if the laws of earth were bowing to greater laws; for though the way was steeper than ever, the upward path was now grown fearsomely easy, and the bulging cliff proved scarce an obstacle when he reached it and slid perilously up its convex face. The light of the moon had strangely failed, and as Atal plunged upward through the mists he heard Barzai the Wise shrieking in the shadows:

'The moon is dark, and the gods dance in the night; there is terror in the sky, for upon the moon hath sunk an eclipse foretold in no books of men or of earth's gods … There is unknown magic on Hatheg-Kla, for the screams of the frightened gods have turned to laughter, and the slopes of ice shoot up endlessly into the black heavens whither I am plunging … Hei! Hei! At last! In the dim light I behold the gods of earth!'

And now Atal, slipping dizzily up over inconceivable steeps, heard in the dark a loathsome laughing, mixed with such a cry as no man else ever heard save in the Phlegethon of unrelatable nightmares; a cry wherein reverberated the horror and anguish of a haunted lifetime packed into one atrocious moment:

'The other gods! The other gods! The gods of the outer hells that guard the feeble gods of earth! … Look away … Go back … Do not see! Do not see! The vengeance of the infinite abysses … That cursed, that damnable pit … Merciful gods of earth, I am falling into the sky!'

And as Atal shut his eyes and stopped his ears and tried to hump downward against the frightful pull from unknown heights, there resounded on Hatheg-Kla that terrible peal of thunder which awaked the good cotters of the plains and the honest burgesses of Hatheg, Nir and Ulthar, and caused them to behold through the clouds that strange eclipse of the moon that no book ever predicted. And when the moon came out at last Atal was safe on the lower snows of the mountain without sight of earth's gods, or of the other gods.

Now it is told in the mouldy *Pnakotic Manuscripts* that Sansu found naught but wordless ice and rock when he did climb Hatheg-Kla in the youth of the world. Yet when the men of Ulthar and Nir and Hatheg crushed their fears and scaled that haunted steep by day in search of Barzai the Wise, they found graven in the naked stone of the summit a curious and cyclopean symbol fifty cubits wide, as if the rock had been riven by some titanic chisel. And the symbol was like to one that learned men have discerned in those frightful parts of the *Pnakotic Manuscripts* which were too ancient to be read. This they found.

Barzai the Wise they never found, nor could the holy priest Atal ever be persuaded to pray for his soul's repose. Moreover, to this day the people of Ulthar and Nir and Hatheg fear eclipses, and pray by night when pale vapours hide the mountain-top and the moon. And above the mists on Hatheg-Kla, earth's gods sometimes dance reminiscently; for they know they are safe, and love to come from unknown Kadath in ships of clouds and play in the olden way, as they did when earth was new and men not given to the climbing of inaccessible places.

THE QUEST OF IRANON

INTO THE GRANITE CITY of Teloth wandered the youth, vine-crowned, his yellow hair glistening with myrrh and his purple robe torn with briers of the mountain Sidrak that lies across the antique bridge of stone. The men of Teloth are dark and stern, and dwell in square houses, and with frowns they asked the stranger whence he had come and what were his name and fortune. So the youth answered:

'I am Iranon, and come from Aira, a far city that I recall only dimly but seek to find again. I am a singer of songs that I learned in the far city, and my calling is to make beauty with the things remembered of childhood. My wealth is in little memories and dreams, and in hopes that I sing in gardens when the moon is tender and the west wind stirs the lotos-buds.'

When the men of Teloth heard these things they whispered to one another; for though in the granite city there is no laughter or song, the stern men sometimes look to the Karthian hills in the spring and think of the lutes of distant Oonai whereof travellers have told. And thinking thus, they bade the stranger stay and sing in the square before the Tower of Mlin, though they liked not the colour of his tattered robe, nor the myrrh in his hair, nor his chaplet of vine-leaves, nor the youth in his golden voice. At evening Iranon sang, and while he sang an old man prayed and a blind man said he saw a nimbus over the singer's head. But most of the men of Teloth yawned, and some laughed and some went away to sleep; for Iranon told nothing useful, singing only his memories, his dreams, and his hopes.

'I remember the twilight, the moon, and soft songs, and the window where I was rocked to sleep. And through the window was the street where the golden lights came, and where the shadows danced on houses of marble. I remember the square of moonlight on the floor, that was not like any other light, and the visions that danced in the moonbeams when my mother sang to me. And too, I remember the sun of morning bright above the many-coloured hills in summer, and the sweetness of flowers borne on the south wind that made the trees sing.

'O Aira, city of marble and beryl, how many are thy beauties! How loved I the warm and fragrant groves across the hyaline Nithra, and the falls of the tiny Kra that flowed through the verdant valley! In those groves and in that vale the children wove wreaths for one another, and at dusk I dreamed strange dreams under the yath-trees on the mountain as I saw below me the lights of the city, and the curving Nithra reflecting a ribbon of stars.

'And in the city were palaces of veined and tinted marble, with golden domes and painted walls, and green gardens with cerulean pools and crystal fountains. Often I played in the gardens and waded in the pools, and lay and dreamed among the pale flowers under the trees. And sometimes at sunset I would climb the long hilly street to the citadel and the open place, and look down upon Aira, the magic city of marble and beryl, splendid in a robe of golden flame.

'Long have I missed thee, Aira, for I was but young when we went into exile; but my father was thy King and I shall come again to thee, for it is so decreed of Fate. All through seven lands have I sought thee, and some day shall I reign over thy groves and gardens, thy streets and palaces, and sing to men who shall know whereof I sing, and laugh not nor turn away. For I am Iranon, who was a Prince in Aira.'

That night the men of Teloth lodged the stranger in a stable, and in the morning an archon came to him and told him to go to the shop of Athok the cobbler, and be apprenticed to him.

'But I am Iranon, a singer of songs,' he said, 'and have no heart for the cobbler's trade.'

'All in Teloth must toil,' replied the archon, 'for that is the law.' Then said Iranon,

'Wherefore do ye toil; is it not that ye may live and be happy? And if ye toil only that ye may toil more, when shall happiness find you? Ye toil to live, but is not life made of beauty and song? And if ye suffer no singers among you, where shall be the fruits of your toil? Toil without song is like a weary journey without an end. Were not death more pleasing?' But the archon was sullen and did not understand, and rebuked the stranger.

'Thou art a strange youth, and I like not thy face nor thy voice. The words thou speakest are blasphemy, for the gods of Teloth have said that toil is good. Our gods have promised us a haven of light beyond death, where there shall be rest without end, and crystal coldness amidst which none shall vex his mind with thought or his eyes with beauty. Go thou then to Athok the cobbler or be gone out of the city by sunset. All here must serve, and song is folly.'

So Iranon went out of the stable and walked over the narrow stone streets between the gloomy square houses of granite, seeking something green in the air of spring. But in Teloth was nothing green, for all was of stone. On the faces of men were frowns, but by the stone embankment along the sluggish river Zuro sat a young boy with sad eyes gazing into the waters to spy green budding branches washed down from the hills by the freshets. And the boy said to him:

'Art thou not indeed he of whom the archons tell, who seekest a far city in a fair land? I am Romnod, and born of the blood of Teloth, but am not old in the ways of the granite city, and yearn daily for the warm groves and the distant lands of beauty and song. Beyond the Karthian hills lieth Oonai, the city of lutes and dancing, which men whisper of and say is both lovely and terrible. Thither would I go were I old enough to find the way, and thither shouldst thou go and thou wouldst sing and have men listen to thee. Let us leave the city Teloth and fare together among the hills of spring.

Thou shalt shew me the ways of travel and I will attend thy songs at evening when the stars one by one bring dreams to the minds of dreamers. And peradventure it may be that Oonai the city of lutes and dancing is even the fair Aira thou seekest, for it is told that thou hast not known Aira since old days, and a name often changeth. Let us go to Oonai, O Iranon of the golden head, where men shall know our longings and welcome us as brothers, nor ever laugh or frown at what we say.' And Iranon answered:

'Be it so, small one; if any in this stone place yearn for beauty he must seek the mountains and beyond, and I would not leave thee to pine by the sluggish Zuro. But think not that delight and understanding dwell just across the Karthian hills, or in any spot thou canst find in a day's, or a year's, or a lustrum's journey. Behold, when I was small like thee I dwelt in the valley of Narthos by the frigid Xari, where none would listen to my dreams; and I told myself that when older I would go to Sinara on the southern slope, and sing to smiling dromedary-men in the market-place. But when I went to Sinara I found the dromedary-men all drunken and ribald, and saw that their songs were not as mine, so I travelled in a barge down the Xari to onyx-walled Jaren. And the soldiers at Jaren laughed at me and drave me out, so that I wandered to many other cities. I have seen Stethelos that is below the great cataract, and have gazed on the marsh where Sarnath once stood. I have been to Thraa, Ilarnek, and Kadatheron on the winding river Ai, and have dwelt long in Olathoë in the land of Lomar. But though I have had listeners sometimes, they have ever been few, and I know that welcome shall await me only in Aira, the city of marble and beryl where my father once ruled as King. So for Aira shall we seek, though it were well to visit distant and lute-blessed Oonai across the Karthian hills, which may indeed be Aira, though I think not. Aira's beauty is past imagining, and none can tell of it without rapture, whilst of Oonai the camel-drivers whisper leeringly.'

At the sunset Iranon and small Romnod went forth from Teloth, and for long wandered amidst the green hills and cool forests. The way was rough and obscure, and never did they seem nearer to Oonai the city of lutes and dancing; but in the dusk as the stars came out Iranon would sing of Aira and its beauties and Romnod would listen, so that they were both happy after a fashion. They ate plentifully of fruit and red berries, and marked not the passing of time, but many years must have slipped away. Small Romnod was now not so small, and spoke deeply instead of shrilly, though Iranon was always the same, and decked his golden hair with vines and fragrant resins found in the woods. So it came to pass one day that Romnod seemed older than Iranon, though he had been very small when Iranon had found him watching for green budding branches in Teloth beside the sluggish stone-banked Zuro.

Then one night when the moon was full the travellers came to a mountain crest and looked down upon the myriad lights of Oonai. Peasants had told them they were near, and Iranon knew that this was not his native city of Aira. The lights of Oonai were not like those of Aira; for they were harsh and glaring, while the lights of Aira shine as softly and magically as shone the moonlight on the floor by the window where Iranon's mother once rocked him to sleep with song. But Oonai was a city of lutes and dancing, so Iranon and Romnod went down the steep slope that they might find men to whom songs and dreams would bring pleasure. And when they were come into the town they found rose-wreathed revellers bound from house to house and leaning from windows and balconies, who listened to the songs of Iranon and tossed him flowers and applauded when he was done. Then for a moment did Iranon believe he had found those who thought and felt even as he, though the town was not an hundredth as fair as Aira.

When dawn came Iranon looked about with dismay, for the domes of Oonai were not golden in the sun, but grey and dismal. And the men of Oonai were pale with revelling and dull with wine, and unlike the radiant men of Aira. But because the people had thrown him blossoms and acclaimed his songs Iranon stayed on, and with him Romnod, who liked the revelry of the town and wore in his dark hair roses and myrtle. Often at night Iranon sang to the revellers, but he was always as before, crowned only with the vine of the mountains and remembering the marble streets of Aira and the hyaline Nithra. In the frescoed halls of the Monarch did he sing, upon a crystal dais raised over a floor that was a mirror, and as he sang he brought pictures to his hearers till the floor seemed to reflect old, beautiful, and half-remembered things instead of the wine-reddened feasters who pelted him with roses. And the King bade him put away his tattered purple, and clothed him in satin and cloth-of-gold, with rings of green jade and bracelets of tinted ivory, and lodged him in a gilded and tapestried chamber on a bed of sweet carven wood with canopies and coverlets of flower-embroidered silk. Thus dwelt Iranon in Oonai, the city of lutes and dancing.

It is not known how long Iranon tarried in Oonai, but one day the King brought to the palace some wild whirling dancers from the Liranian desert, and dusky flute-players from Drinen in the East, and after that the revellers threw their roses not so much at Iranon as at the dancers and the flute-players. And day by day that Romnod who had been a small boy in granite Teloth grew coarser and redder with wine, till he dreamed less and less, and listened with less delight to the songs of Iranon. But though Iranon was sad he ceased not to sing, and at evening told again his dreams of Aira, the city of marble and beryl. Then one night the red and fattened Romnod snorted heavily amidst the poppied silks of his banquet-couch and died writhing, whilst Iranon, pale and slender, sang to himself in a far corner. And when Iranon had wept over the grave of Romnod and strown it with green budding branches, such as Romnod used to love, he put aside his silks and gauds and went forgotten out of Oonai the city of lutes and dancing clad only in the ragged purple in which he had come, and garlanded with fresh vines from the mountains.

Into the sunset wandered Iranon, seeking still for his native land and for men who would understand and cherish his songs and dreams. In all the cities of Cydathria and in the lands beyond the Bnazic desert gay-faced children laughed at his olden songs and tattered robe of purple; but Iranon stayed ever young, and wore wreaths upon his golden head whilst he sang of Aira, delight of the past and hope of the future.

So came he one night to the squalid cot of an antique shepherd, bent and dirty, who kept lean flocks on a stony slope above a quicksand marsh. To this man Iranon spoke, as to so many others:

'Canst thou tell me where I may find Aira, the city of marble and beryl, where flows the hyaline Nithra and where the falls of the tiny Kra sing to verdant valleys and hills forested with yath trees?' And the shepherd, hearing, looked long and strangely at Iranon, as if recalling something very far away in time, and noted each line of the stranger's face, and his golden hair, and his crown of vine-leaves. But he was old, and shook his head as he replied:

'O stranger, I have indeed heard the name of Aira, and the other names thou hast spoken, but they come to me from afar down the waste of long years. I heard them in my youth from the lips of a playmate, a beggar's boy given to strange dreams, who would weave long tales about the moon and the flowers and the west wind. We used to laugh at him, for we knew him from his birth though he thought himself a King's son. He was comely, even as thou, but full of folly and strangeness; and he ran away when small to find those who would listen gladly to his songs and dreams. How often hath he sung to me of lands that never were, and things that never can be! Of Aira did he speak much; of Aira and the river Nithra, and the falls of the tiny Kra. There would he ever say he once dwelt as a Prince, though here we knew him from his birth. Nor was there ever a marble city of Aira, nor those who could delight in strange songs, save in the dreams of mine old playmate Iranon who is gone.'

And in the twilight, as the stars came out one by one and the moon cast on the marsh a radiance like that which a child sees quivering on the floor as he is rocked to sleep at evening, there walked into the lethal quicksands a very old man in tattered purple, crowned with withered vine-leaves and gazing ahead as if upon the golden domes of a fair city where dreams are understood. That night something of youth and beauty died in the elder world.

THE CHALLENGE FROM BEYOND

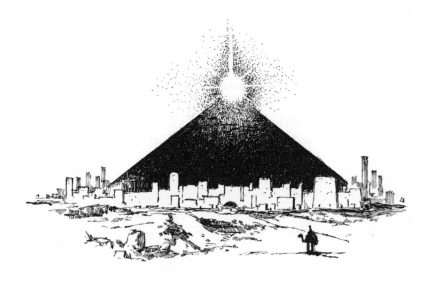

... And it is recorded that in the Elder Times, Om Oris, mightiest of the wizards, laid crafty snare for the demon Avaloth, and pitted dark magic against him; for Avaloth plagued the earth with a strange growth of ice and snow that crept as if alive, ever southward, and swallowed up the forests and the mountains. And the outcome of the contest with the demon is not known; but wizards of that day maintained that Avaloth, who was not easily discernible, could not be destroyed save by a great heat, the means whereof was not then known, although certain of the wizards foresaw that one day it should be. Yet, at this time the ice fields began to shrink and dwindle and finally vanished; and the earth bloomed forth afresh.

—Fragment from the Eltdown Shards

A S THE MIST-BLURRED LIGHT of the sapphire suns grew more and more intense, the outlines of the globe ahead wavered and dissolved to a churning chaos. Its pallor and its motion and its music all blended themselves with the engulfing mist – bleaching it to a pale steel-colour and setting it undulantly in motion. And the sapphire suns, too, melted imperceptibly into the greying infinity of shapeless pulsation.

Meanwhile the sense of forward, outward motion grew intolerably, incredibly, cosmically swift. Every standard of speed known to earth seemed dwarfed, and Campbell knew that any such flight in physical reality would mean instant death to a human being. Even as it was – in this strange, hellish hypnosis or nightmare – the quasi-visual impression of meteor-like hurtling almost unhinged his mind. Though there were no real points of reference in the grey, pulsing void, he felt that he was approaching and passing the speed of light itself. Finally his consciousness did go under – and merciful blackness swallowed everything.

It was very suddenly, and amidst the most impenetrable darkness, that thoughts and ideas again came to George Campbell. Of how many moments – or years – or eternities – had elapsed since his flight through the grey void, he could form no estimate. He knew only that he seemed to be at rest and without pain. Indeed, the absence of all physical sensation was the salient quality of his condition. It made even the blackness seem less solidly black – suggesting as it did that he was rather a disembodied intelligence in a state beyond physical senses, than a corporeal being with senses deprived of their accustomed objects of perception. He could think sharply and quickly – almost preternaturally so – yet could form no idea whatsoever of his situation.

Half by instinct, he realised that he was not in his own tent. True, he might have awaked there from a nightmare to a world equally black; yet he knew this was not so. There was no camp cot beneath him – he had no hands to feel the blankets and canvas surface and flashlight that ought to be around him – there was no sensation of cold in the air – no flap through which he could glimpse the pale night outside ... something was wrong, dreadfully wrong.

He cast his mind backward and thought of the fluorescent cube which had hypnotised him – of that, and all which had followed. He had known that his mind was going, yet had been unable to draw back. At the last moment there had been a shocking, panic fear – a subconscious fear beyond even that caused by the sensation of daemoniac flight. It had come from some vague flash or remote recollection – just what, he could not at once tell. Some cell-group in the back of his head had seemed to find a cloudily familiar quality in the cube – and that familiarity was fraught with dim terror. Now he tried to remember what the familiarity and the terror were.

Little by little it came to him. Once – long ago, in connection with his geological life-work – he had read of something like that cube. It had to do with those debatable and disquieting clay fragments called the Eltdown Shards, dug up from pre-carboniferous strata in southern England thirty years before. Their shape and markings were so queer that a few scholars hinted at artificiality, and made wild conjectures about them and their origin. They came, clearly, from a time when no human beings could exist on the globe – but their contours and figurings were damnably puzzling. That was how they got their name.

It was not, however, in the writings of any sober scientist that Campbell had seen that reference to a crystal, disc-holding globe. The source was far less reputable, and infinitely more vivid. About 1912 a deeply learned Sussex clergyman of occultist leanings – the Reverend Arthur Brooke Winters-Hall – had professed to identify the markings on the Eltdown Shards with some of the so-called 'pre-human hieroglyphs' persistently cherished and esoterically handed down in certain mystical circles, and had published at his own expense what purported to be a 'translation' of the primal and baffling 'inscriptions' – a 'translation' still quoted frequently and seriously by occult writers. In this 'translation' – a surprisingly long brochure in view of the limited number of 'shards' existing – had occurred the narrative, supposedly of pre-human authorship, containing the now frightening reference.

As the story went, there dwelt on a world – and eventually on countless other worlds – of outer space a mighty order of worm-like beings whose attainments and whose control of nature surpassed anything within the range of terrestrial imagination. They had mastered the art of interstellar travel early in their career, and had peopled every habitable planet in their own galaxy – killing off the races they found.

Beyond the limits of their own galaxy – which was not ours – they could not navigate in person; but in their quest for knowledge of all space and time they discovered a means of spanning certain trans-galactic gulfs with their minds. They devised peculiar objects – strangely energised cubes of a curious crystal containing hypnotic talismans and enclosed in space-resisting spherical envelopes of an unknown substance – which could be forcibly expelled beyond the limits of their universe, and which would respond to the attraction of cool solid matter only. These, of which a few would necessarily land on various inhabited worlds in outside universes, formed the ether-bridges needed for mental communication. Atmospheric friction burned away the protecting envelope, leaving the cube exposed and subject to discovery by the intelligent minds of the world where it fell. By its very nature, the cube would attract and rivet attention. This, when coupled with the action of light, was sufficient to set its special properties working. The mind that noticed the cube would be drawn into it by the power of the disc, and would be sent on a thread of obscure energy to the place whence the disc had come – the remote world of the worm-like space-explorers across stupendous galactic abysses. Received in one of the machines to which each cube was attuned, the captured mind would remain suspended without body or senses until examined by one of the dominant race. Then it would, by an obscure process of interchange, be pumped of all its contents. The investigator's mind would now occupy the strange machine while the captive mind occupied the interrogator's worm-like body. Then, in another interchange, the interrogator's mind would leap across boundless space to the captive's vacant and unconscious body on the trans-galactic world – animating the alien tenement as best it might, and exploring the alien world in the guise of one of its denizens.

When done with exploration, the adventurer would use the cube and its disc in accomplishing his return – and sometimes the captured mind would be restored safely to its own remote world. Not always, however, was the dominant race so kind. Sometimes, when a potentially important race capable of space travel was found, the worm-like folk would employ the cube to capture and annihilate minds by the thousands, and would extirpate the race for diplomatic reasons – using the exploring minds as agents of destruction.

In other cases sections of the worm-folk would permanently occupy a trans-galactic planet – destroying the captured minds and wiping out the remaining inhabitants preparatory to settling down in unfamiliar bodies. Never, however, could the parent civilisation be quite duplicated in such a case; since the new planet would not contain all the materials necessary for the worm-race's arts. The cubes, for example, could be made only on the home planet.

Only a few of the numberless cubes sent forth ever found a landing and response on an inhabited world – since there was no such thing as *aiming* them at goals beyond sight or knowledge. Only three, ran the story, had ever landed on peopled worlds in our own particular universe. One of these had struck a planet near the galactic rim two thousand billion years ago, while another had lodged three billion years ago on a world near the centre of the galaxy. The third – and the only one ever known to have invaded the solar system – had reached our own earth a hundred and fifty million years ago.

It was with this latter that Dr Winters-Hall's 'translation' chiefly dealt. When the cube struck the earth, he wrote, the ruling terrestrial species was a huge, cone-shaped race surpassing all others before or since in mentality and achievements. This race was so advanced that it had actually sent minds abroad in both space *and time* to explore the cosmos, hence recognised something of what had happened when the cube fell from the sky and certain individuals had suffered mental change after gazing at it.

Realising that the changed individuals represented invading minds, the race's leaders had them destroyed – even at the cost of leaving the displaced minds exiled in alien space. They had had experience with even stranger transitions. When, through a mental exploration of space and time, they formed a rough idea of what the cube was, they carefully hid the thing from light and sight, and guarded it as a menace. They did not wish to destroy a thing so rich in later experimental possibilities. Now and then some rash, unscrupulous adventurer would furtively gain access to it and sample its perilous powers despite the consequences – but all such cases were discovered, and safely and drastically dealt with.

Of this evil meddling the only bad result was that the worm-like outside race learned from the new exiles what had happened to their explorers on earth, and conceived a violent hatred of the planet and all its life-forms. They would have depopulated it if they could, and indeed sent additional cubes into space in the wild hope of striking it by accident in unguarded places – but that accident never came to pass.

The cone-shaped terrestrial beings kept the one existing cube in a special shrine as a relique and basis for experiments, till after aeons it was lost amidst the chaos of war and the destruction of the great polar city where it was guarded. When, fifty million years ago, the beings sent their minds ahead into the infinite future to avoid a nameless peril of inner earth, the whereabouts of the sinister cube from space were unknown.

This much, according to the learned occultist, the Eltdown Shards had said. What now made the account so obscurely frightful to Campbell was the minute accuracy with which the alien cube had been described. Every detail tallied – dimensions, consistency, hieroglyphed central disc, hypnotic effects. As he thought the matter over and over amidst the darkness of his strange situation, he began to wonder whether his whole experience with the crystal cube – indeed, its very existence – were not a nightmare brought on by some freakish subconscious memory of this old bit of extravagant, charlatanic reading. If so, though, the nightmare must still be in force; since his present apparently bodiless state had nothing of normality in it.

Of the time consumed by this puzzled memory and reflection, Campbell could form no estimate. Everything about his state was so unreal that ordinary dimensions and measurements became meaningless. It seemed an eternity, but perhaps it was not really long before the sudden interruption came. What happened was as strange and inexplicable as the blackness it succeeded. There was a sensation – of the mind rather than of the body – and all at once Campbell felt his thoughts swept or sucked beyond his control in tumultuous and chaotic fashion. Memories arose irresponsibly and irrelevantly. All that he knew – all his personal background, traditions, experiences, scholarship, dreams, ideas, and inspirations – welled up abruptly and simultaneously, with a dizzying speed and abundance which soon made him unable to keep track of any separate concept. The parade of all his mental contents became an avalanche, a cascade, a vortex. It was as horrible and vertiginous as his hypnotic flight through space when the crystal cube pulled him. Finally it sapped his consciousness and brought on fresh oblivion.

Another measureless blank – and then a slow trickle of sensations.

This time it was physical, not mental. Sapphire light, and a low rumble of distant sound. There were tactile impressions – he could realise that he was lying at full length on something, though there was a baffling strangeness about the feel of his posture. He could not reconcile the pressure of the supporting surface with his own outlines – or with the outlines of the human form at all. He tried to move his arms, but found no definite response to the attempt. Instead, there were little, ineffectual nervous twitches all over the area which seemed to mark his body.

He tried to open his eyes more widely, but found himself unable to control their mechanism. The sapphire light came in a diffused, nebulous manner, and could nowhere be voluntarily focussed into definiteness. Gradually, though, visual images began to trickle in curiously and indecisively. The limits and qualities of vision were not those which he was used to, but he could roughly correlate the sensation with what he had known as sight. As this sensation gained some degree of stability, Campbell realised that he must still be in the throes of nightmare.

He seemed to be in a room of considerable extent – of medium height, but with a large proportionate area. On every side – and he could apparently see all four sides at once – were high, narrowish slits which seemed to serve as combined doors and windows. There were singular low tables or pedestals, but no furniture of normal nature and proportions. Through the slits streamed floods of sapphire light, and beyond them could be mistily seen the sides and roofs of fantastic buildings like clustered cubes. On the walls – in the vertical panels between the slits – were strange markings of an oddly disquieting character. It was some time before Campbell understood why they disturbed him so – then he saw that they were, in repeated instances, precisely like some of the hieroglyphs on the disc within the crystal cube.

The actual nightmare element, though, was something more than this. It began with the living thing which presently entered through one of the slits, advancing deliberately toward him and bearing a metal box of bizarre proportions and glassy, mirror-like surfaces. For this thing was nothing human – nothing of earth – nothing even of man's myths and dreams. It was a gigantic, pale-grey worm or centipede, as large around as a man and twice as long, with a disc-like, apparently eyeless, cilia-fringed head bearing a purple central orifice. It glided on its rear pairs of legs, with its fore part raised vertically – the legs, or at least two pairs of them, serving as arms. Along its spinal ridge was a curious purple comb, and a fan-shaped tail of some grey membrane ended its grotesque bulk. There was a ring of flexible red spikes around its neck, and from the twistings of these came clicking, twanging sounds in measured, deliberate rhythms.

Here, indeed, was outré nightmare at its height – capricious fantasy at its apex. But even this vision of delirium was not what caused George Campbell to lapse a third time into unconsciousness. It took one more thing – one final, unbearable touch – to do that. As the nameless worm advanced with its glistening box, the reclining man caught in the mirror-like surface a glimpse of what should have been his own body. Yet – horribly verifying his disordered and unfamiliar sensations – it was not his own body at all that he saw reflected in the burnished metal. It was, instead, the loathsome, pale-grey bulk of one of the great centipedes.

IN A SEQUESTER'D PROVIDENCE CHURCHYARD WHERE ONCE POE WALK'D

ETERNAL BROOD the shadows on this ground,
Dreaming of centuries that have gone before;
Great elms rise solemnly by slab and mound,
Arch'd high above a hidden world of yore.
Round all the scene a light of memory plays,
And dead leaves whisper of departed days,
Longing for sights and sounds that are no more.

Lonely and sad, a spectre glides along
Aisles where of old his living footsteps fell;
No common glance discerns him, tho' his song
Peals down thro' time with a mysterious spell:
Only the few who sorcery's secret know
Espy amidst these tombs the shade of Poe.

IBID

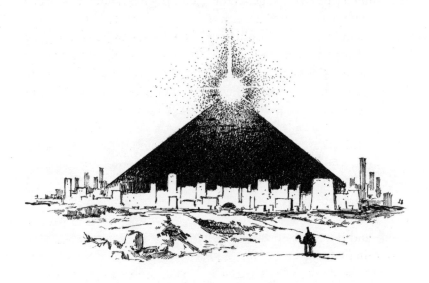

('… as Ibid says in his famous *Lives of the Poets.*'
—*From a student theme.*)

T HE ERRONEOUS IDEA that Ibid is the author of the *Lives* is so
frequently met with, even among those pretending to a degree
of culture, that it is worth correcting. It should be a matter of
general knowledge that Cf. is responsible for this work. Ibid's
masterpiece, on the other hand, was the famous *Op. Cit.* wherein all
the significant undercurrents of Graeco-Roman expression were
crystallised once for all – and with admirable acuteness, notwithstanding the surprisingly late date at which Ibid wrote. There
is a false report – very commonly reproduced in modern books
prior to Von Schweinkopf's monumental *Geschichte der Ostrogothen
in Italien* – that Ibid was a Romanised Visigoth of Ataulf's horde
who settled in Placentia about AD 410. The contrary cannot be too
strongly emphasised; for Von Schweinkopf, and since his time
Littlewit[1] and Bêtenoir,[2] have shewn with irrefutable force that this
strikingly isolated figure was a genuine Roman – or at least as

genuine a Roman as that degenerate and mongrelised age could produce – of whom one might well say what Gibbon said of Boethius, 'that he was the last whom Cato or Tully could have acknowledged for their countryman.' He was, like Boethius and nearly all the eminent men of his age, of the great Anician family, and traced his genealogy with much exactitude and self-satisfaction to all the heroes of the republic. His full name – long and pompous according to the custom of an age which had lost the trinomial simplicity of classic Roman nomenclature – is stated by Von Schweinkopf[3] to have been Caius Anicius Magnus Furius Camillus Aemilianus Cornelius Valerius Pompeius Julius Ibidus; though Littlewit[4] rejects *Aemilianus* and adds *Claudius Decius Junianus*, whilst Bêtenoir[5] differs radically, giving the full name as Magnus Furius Camillus Aurelius Antoninus Flavius Anicius Petronius Valentinianus Aegidus Ibidus.

The eminent critic and biographer was born in the year 486, shortly after the extinction of the Roman rule in Gaul by Clovis. Rome and Ravenna are rivals for the honour of his birth, though it is certain that he received his rhetorical and philosophical training in the schools of Athens – the extent of whose suppression by Theodosius a century before is grossly exaggerated by the superficial. In 512, under the benign rule of the Ostrogoth Theodoric, we behold him as a teacher of rhetoric at Rome, and in 516 he held the consulship together with Pompilius Numantius Bombastes Marcellinus Deodamnatus. Upon the death of Theodoric in 526, Ibidus retired from public life to compose his celebrated work (whose pure Ciceronian style is as remarkable a case of classic atavism as is the verse of Claudius Claudianus, who flourished a century before Ibidus); but he was later recalled to scenes of pomp to act as court rhetorician for Theodatus, nephew of Theodoric.

Upon the usurpation of Vitiges, Ibidus fell into disgrace and was for a time imprisoned; but the coming of the Byzantine-Roman army under Belisarius soon restored him to liberty and honours. Throughout the siege of Rome he served bravely in the army of the defenders, and afterward followed the eagles of Belisarius to Alba, Porto, and Centumcellae. After the Frankish siege of Milan, Ibidus was chosen to accompany the learned Bishop Datius to Greece, and resided with him at Corinth in the year 539. About 541 he removed to Constantinopolis, where he received every mark of imperial favour both from Justinianus and Justinus the Second. The Emperors Tiberius and Maurice did kindly honour to his old age, and contributed much to his immortality – especially Maurice, whose delight it was to trace his ancestry to old Rome notwithstanding his birth at Arabiscus, in Cappadocia. It was Maurice who, in the poet's 101st year, secured the adoption of his work as a textbook in the schools of the empire, an honour which proved a fatal tax on the aged rhetorician's emotions, since he passed away peacefully at his home near the church of St Sophia on the sixth day before the Kalends of September, AD 587, in the 102nd year of his age.

His remains, notwithstanding the troubled state of Italy, were taken to Ravenna for interment; but being interred in the suburb of Classe, were exhumed and ridiculed by the Lombard Duke of Spoleto, who took his skull to King Autharis for use as a wassail-bowl. Ibid's skull was proudly handed down from king to king of the Lombard line. Upon the capture of Pavia by Charlemagne in 774, the skull was seized from the tottering Desiderius and carried in the train of the Frankish conqueror. It was from this vessel, indeed, that Pope Leo administered the royal unction which made of the hero-nomad a Holy Roman Emperor. Charlemagne took Ibid's skull to his capital at Aix, soon afterward presenting it to his Saxon teacher Alcuin, upon whose death in 804 it was sent to Alcuin's kinsfolk in England.

William the Conqueror, finding it in an abbey niche where the pious family of Alcuin had placed it (believing it to be the skull of a saint[6] who had miraculously annihilated the Lombards by his prayers), did reverence to its osseous antiquity; and even the rough soldiers of Cromwell, upon destroying Ballylough Abbey in Ireland in 1650 (it having been secretly transported thither by a devout Papist in 1539, upon Henry VIII's dissolution of the English monasteries), declined to offer violence to a relic so venerable.

It was captured by the private soldier Read-'em-and-Weep Hopkins, who not long after traded it to Rest-in-Jehovah Stubbs for a quid of new Virginia weed. Stubbs, upon sending forth his son Zerubbabel to seek his fortune in New England in 1661 (for he thought ill of the Restoration atmosphere for a pious young yeoman), gave him St Ibid's – or rather Brother Ibid's, for he abhorred all that was Popish – skull as a talisman. Upon landing in

Salem Zerubbabel set it up in his cupboard beside the chimney, he having built a modest house near the town pump. However, he had not been wholly unaffected by the Restoration influence; and having become addicted to gaming, lost the skull to one Epenetus Dexter, a visiting freeman of Providence.

It was in the house of Dexter, in the northern part of the town near the present intersection of North Main and Olney Streets, on the occasion of Canonchet's raid of March 30, 1676, during King Philip's War; and the astute sachem, recognising it at once as a thing of singular venerableness and dignity, sent it as a symbol of alliance to a faction of the Pequots in Connecticut with whom he was negotiating. On April 4 he was captured by the colonists and soon after executed, but the austere head of Ibid continued on its wanderings.

The Pequots, enfeebled by a previous war, could give the now stricken Narragansetts no assistance; and in 1680 a Dutch fur-trader of Albany, Petrus van Schaack, secured the distinguished cranium for the modest sum of two guilders, he having recognised its value from the half-effaced inscription carved in Lombardic minuscules (palaeography, it might be explained, was one of the leading accomplishments of New-Netherland fur-traders of the seventeenth century).

Ibidus rhetor romanus

From van Schaack, sad to say, the relic was stolen in 1683 by a French trader, Jean Grenier, whose Popish zeal recognised the features of one whom he had been taught at his mother's knee to revere as St Ibide. Grenier, fired with virtuous rage at the possession of this holy symbol by a Protestant, crushed van Schaack's head one night with an axe and escaped to the north with his booty; soon, however, being robbed and slain by the half-breed voyageur Michel Savard, who took the skull – despite the illiteracy which prevented his recognising it – to add to a collection of similar but more recent material.

Upon his death in 1701 his half-breed son Pierre traded it among other things to some emissaries of the Sacs and Foxes, and it was found outside the chief's tepee a generation later by Charles de

Langlade, founder of the trading post at Green Bay, Wisconsin. De Langlade regarded this sacred object with proper veneration and ransomed it at the expense of many glass beads; yet after his time it found itself in many other hands, being traded to settlements at the head of Lake Winnebago, to tribes around Lake Mendota, and finally, early in the nineteenth century, to one Solomon Juneau, a Frenchman, at the new trading post of Milwaukee on the Menominee River and the shore of Lake Michigan.

Later traded to Jacques Caboche, another settler, it was in 1850 lost in a game of chess or poker to a newcomer named Hans Zimmerman; being used by him as a beer-stein until one day, under the spell of its contents, he suffered it to roll from his front stoop to the prairie path before his home – where, falling into the burrow of a prairie-dog, it passed beyond his power of discovery or recovery upon his awaking.

So for generations did the sainted skull of Caius Anicius Magnus Furius Camillus Aemilianus Cornelius Valerius Pompeius Julius Ibidus, consul of Rome, favourite of emperors, and saint of the Romish church, lie hidden beneath the soil of a growing town. At first worshipped with dark rites by the prairie-dogs, who saw in it a deity sent from the upper world, it afterward fell into dire neglect as the race of simple, artless burrowers succumbed before the onslaught of the conquering Aryan. Sewers came, but they passed by it. Houses went up – 2303 of them, and more – and at last one fateful night a titan thing occurred. Subtle Nature, convulsed with a spiritual ecstasy, like the froth of that region's quondam beverage, laid low the lofty and heaved high the humble – and behold! In the roseal dawn the burghers of Milwaukee rose to find a former prairie turned to a highland! Vast and far-reaching was the great upheaval. Subterrene arcana, hidden for years, came at last to the light. For there, full in the rifted roadway, lay bleached and tranquil in bland, saintly, and consular pomp the dome-like skull of Ibid!

NOTES

1. *Rome and Byzantium: A Study in Survival* (Waukesha, 1869), Vol.XX, p.598.
2. *Influences Romains dans le Moyen Age* (Fond du Lac, 1877), Vol.XV, p.720.
3. Following Procopius, *Goth.* x.y.z.

[4] Following Jornandes, Codex Murat. Xxj. 4144
[5] After Pagi, 50–50
[6] Not till the appearance of Schweinkopf's work in 1797 were St Ibid and the rhetorician properly re-identified.

AZATHOTH

WHEN AGE FELL upon the world, and wonder went out of the minds of men; when grey cities reared to smoky skies tall towers grim and ugly, in whose shadow none might dream of the sun or of Spring's flowering meads; when learning stripped the Earth of her mantle of beauty and poets sang no more save of twisted phantoms seen with bleared and inward-looking eyes; when these things had come to pass, and childish hopes had gone forever, there was a man who travelled out of life on a quest into spaces whither the world's dreams had fled.

Of the name and abode of this man little is written, for they were of the waking world only; yet it is said that both were obscure. It is enough to say that he dwelt in a city of high walls where sterile twilight reigned, that he toiled all day among shadow and turmoil, coming home at evening to a room whose one window opened not to open fields and groves but on to a dim court where other windows stared in dull despair. From that casement one might see only walls and windows, except sometimes when one leaned so far out and peered at the small stars that passed. And because mere walls and windows must soon drive a man to madness who dreams and reads much, the dweller in that room used night after night to lean out and peer aloft to glimpse some fragment of things beyond the waking world and the tall cities. After years he began to call the slow sailing stars by name, and to follow them in fancy when they glided regretfully out of sight; till at length his vision opened to many secret vistas whose existence no common eye suspected. And one night a mighty gulf was bridged, and the dream-haunted skies swelled down to the lonely watcher's window to merge with the close air of his room and to make him a part of their fabulous wonder.

There came to that room wild streams of violet midnight glittering with dust of gold, vortices of dust and fire, swirling out of the ultimate spaces and heavy perfumes from beyond the worlds. Opiate oceans poured there, litten by suns that the eye may never behold and having in their whirlpools strange dolphins and sea-nymphs of unrememberable depths. Noiseless infinity eddied around the dreamer and wafted him away without touching the body that leaned stiffly from the lonely window; and for days not counted in men's calendars the tides of far spheres that bore him gently to join the course of other cycles that tenderly left him sleeping on a green sunrise shore, a green shore fragrant with lotus blossoms and starred by red camalates ...

THE DESCENDANT

WRITING ON WHAT my doctor tells me is my deathbed, my most hideous fear is that the man is wrong. I suppose I shall seem to be buried next week, but ... *(foregoing deleted)*.

In London there is a man who screams when the church bells ring. He lives all alone with his streaked cat in Gray's Inn, and people call him harmlessly mad. His room is filled with books of the tamest and most puerile kind, and hour after hour he tries to lose himself in their feeble pages. All he seeks from life is not to think. For some reason thought is very horrible to him, and anything which stirs the imagination he flees as a plague. He is very thin and grey and wrinkled, but there are those who declare he is not nearly so old as he looks. Fear has its grisly claws upon him, and a sound will make him start with staring eyes and sweat-beaded forehead. Friends and companions he shuns, for he wishes to answer no questions. Those who once knew him as scholar and aesthete say it is very pitiful to see him now. He dropped them all years ago, and no one feels sure whether he left the country or merely sank from sight in some hidden byway.

It is a decade now since he moved into Gray's Inn, and of where he had been he would say nothing till the night young Williams bought the *Necronomicon*.

Williams was a dreamer, and only twenty-three, and when he moved into the ancient house he felt a strangeness and a breath of cosmic wind about the grey wizened man in the next room. He forced his friendship where old friends dared not force theirs, and marvelled at the fright that sat upon this gaunt, haggard watcher and listener. For that the man always watched and listened no one could doubt. He watched and listened with his mind more than with his eyes and ears, and strove every moment to drown something in his ceaseless poring over gay, insipid novels. And when the church bells rang he would stop his ears and scream, and the grey cat that dwelt with him would howl in unison till the last peal died reverberantly away.

But try as Williams would, he could not make his neighbour speak of anything profound or hidden. The old man would not live up to his aspect and manner, but would feign a smile and a light tone and prattle feverishly and frantically of cheerful trifles; his voice every moment rising and thickening till at last it would split in a piping and incoherent falsetto. That his learning was deep and thorough, his most trivial remarks made abundantly clear; and Williams was not surprised to hear that he had been to Harrow and Oxford. Later it developed that he was none other than Lord Northam, of whose ancient hereditary castle on the Yorkshire coast so many odd things were told; but when Williams tried to talk of the castle, and of its reputed Roman origin, he refused to admit that there was anything unusual about it. He even tittered shrilly when the subject of the supposed under crypts, hewn out of the solid crag that frowns on the North Sea, was brought up.

So matters went till that night when Williams brought home the infamous *Necronomicon* of the mad Arab Abdul Alhazred. He had known of the dreaded volume since his sixteenth year, when his dawning love of the bizarre had led him to ask queer questions of a bent old bookseller in Chandos Street; and he had always wondered why men paled when they spoke of it. The old bookseller had told him that only five copies were known to have survived the shocked edicts of the priests and lawgivers against it and that all of these were locked up with frightened care by custodians who had ventured to begin a reading of the hateful black-letter. But now, at last, he had not only found an accessible copy but had made it his own at a ludicrously low figure. It was at a Jew's shop in the squalid precincts of Clare Market, where he had often bought strange things before, and he almost fancied the gnarled old Levite smiled amidst tangles of beard as the great discovery was made. The bulky leather cover with the brass clasp had been so prominently visible, and the price was so absurdly slight.

The one glimpse he had had of the title was enough to send him into transports, and some of the diagrams set in the vague Latin text excited the tensest and most disquieting recollections in his brain. He felt it was highly necessary to get the ponderous thing home and begin deciphering it, and bore it out of the shop with such precipitate haste that the old Jew chuckled disturbingly behind him. But when at last it was safe in his room he found the combination of black-letter and debased idiom too much for his powers as a linguist, and reluctantly called on his strange, frightened friend for help with the twisted, mediaeval Latin. Lord Northam was simpering inanities to his streaked cat, and started violently when the young man entered. Then he saw the volume and shuddered wildly, and fainted altogether when Williams uttered the title. It was when he regained his senses that he told his story; told his fantastic figment of madness in frantic whispers, lest his friend be not quick to burn the accursed book and give wide scattering to its ashes.

There must, Lord Northam whispered, have been something wrong at the start; but it would never have come to a head if he had not explored too far. He was the nineteenth Baron of a line whose beginnings went uncomfortably far back into the past – unbeliev-ably far, if vague tradition could be heeded, for there were family tales of a descent from pre-Saxon times, when a certain Lunaeus Gabinius Capito, military tribune in the Third Augustan Legion then stationed at Lindum in Roman Britain, had been summarily expelled from his command for participation in certain rites uncon-nected with any known religion. Gabinius had, the rumour ran, come upon a cliffside cavern where strange folk met together and made the Elder Sign in the dark; strange folk whom the Britons knew not save in fear, and who were the last to survive from a great land in the west that had sunk, leaving only the islands with the roths and circles and shrines of which Stonehenge was the greatest. There was no certainty, of course, in the legend that Gabinius had built an impregnable fortress over the forbidden cave and founded a line which Pict and Saxon, Dane and Norman were powerless to obliterate; or in the tacit assumption that from this line sprang the bold companion and lieutenant of the Black Prince whom Edward the Third created Baron of Northam. These things were not certain, yet they were often told; and in truth the stonework of Northam Keep did look alarmingly like the masonry of Hadrian's Wall. As a child Lord Northam had had peculiar dreams when sleeping in the older parts of the castle, and had acquired a constant habit of looking back through his memory for half-amorphous scenes and patterns and impressions which formed no part of his waking experience. He became a dreamer who found life tame and unsatisfying; a searcher for strange realms and relationships once familiar, yet lying nowhere in the visible regions of Earth.

Filled with a feeling that our tangible world is only an atom in a fabric vast and ominous, and that unknown demesnes press on and permeate the sphere of the known at every point, Northam in youth and young manhood drained in turn the founts of formal religion and occult mystery. Nowhere, however, could he find ease and content; and as he grew older the staleness and limitations of life became more and more maddening to him. During the 'nineties he dabbled in Satanism, and at all times he devoured avidly any doctrine or theory which seemed to promise escape from the close vistas of science and the dully unvarying laws of Nature. Books like Ignatius Donnelly's commercial account of Atlantis he absorbed with zest, and a dozen obscure precursors of Charles Fort enthralled him with their vagaries. He would travel leagues to follow up a furtive village tale of abnormal wonder, and once went into the desert of Araby to seek a Nameless City of faint report, which no man has ever beheld. There rose within him the tantalising faith that somewhere an easy gate existed, which if found would admit him freely to those outer deeps whose echoes rattled so dimly at the back of his memory. It might be in the visible world, yet it might be only in his mind and soul. Perhaps he held within his own half-explored brain that cryptic link which would awaken him to elder and future lives in forgotten dimensions; which would bind him to the stars, and to the infinities and eternities beyond them.

THE BOOK

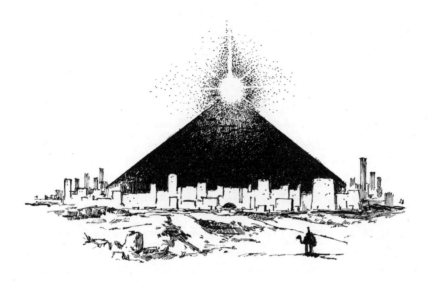

M Y MEMORIES ARE VERY CONFUSED. There is even much
doubt as to where they begin; for at times I feel appalling
vistas of years stretching behind me, while at other times it seems
as if the present moment were an isolated point in a grey, formless
infinity. I am not even certain how I am communicating this
message. While I know I am speaking, I have a vague impression
that some strange and perhaps terrible mediation will be needed
to bear what I say to the points where I wish to be heard. My
identity, too, is bewilderingly cloudy. I seem to have suffered a
great shock – perhaps from some utterly monstrous outgrowth of
my cycles of unique, incredible experience.

These cycles of experience, of course, all stem from that worm-
riddled book. I remember when I found it – in a dimly lighted place
near the black, oily river where the mists always swirl. That place
was very old, and the ceiling-high shelves full of rotting volumes
reached back endlessly through windowless inner rooms and
alcoves. There were, besides, great formless heaps of books on the
floor and in crude bins; and it was in one of these heaps that I found

the thing. I never learned its title, for the early pages were missing; but it fell open toward the end and gave me a glimpse of something which sent my senses reeling.

There was a formula – a sort of list of things to say and do – which I recognised as something black and forbidden; something which I had read of before in furtive paragraphs of mixed abhorrence and fascination penned by those strange ancient delvers into the universe's guarded secrets whose decaying texts I loved to absorb. It was a key – a guide – to certain gateways and transitions of which mystics have dreamed and whispered since the race was young, and which lead to freedoms and discoveries beyond the three dimensions and realms of life and matter that we know. Not for centuries had any man recalled its vital substance or known where to find it, but this book was very old indeed. No printing-press, but the hand of some half-crazed monk, had traced these ominous Latin phrases in uncials of awesome antiquity.

I remember how the old man leered and tittered, and made a curious sign with his hand when I bore it away. He had refused to take pay for it, and only long afterwards did I guess why. As I hurried home through those narrow, winding, mist-cloaked waterfront streets I had a frightful impression of being stealthily followed by softly padding feet. The centuried, tottering houses on both sides seemed alive with a fresh and morbid malignity – as if some hitherto closed channel of evil understanding had abruptly been opened. I felt that those walls and over-hanging gables of mildewed brick and fungoid plaster and timber – with eyelike, diamond-paned windows that leered – could hardly desist from advancing and crushing me … yet I had read only the least fragment of that blasphemous rune before closing the book and bringing it away.

I remember how I read the book at last – white-faced, and locked in the attic room that I had long devoted to strange searchings. The great house was very still, for I had not gone up till after midnight. I think I had a family then – though the details are very uncertain – and I know there were many servants. Just what the year was I cannot say; for since then I have known many ages and dimensions, and have had all my notions of time dissolved and refashioned. It was by the light of candles that I read – I recall the relentless dripping of the wax – and there were chimes that came every now and then from distant belfries. I seemed to keep track of those chimes with a peculiar intentness, as if I feared to hear some very remote, intruding note among them.

Then came the first scratching and fumbling at the dormer window that looked out high above the other roofs of the city. It came as I droned aloud the ninth verse of that primal lay, and I knew amidst my shudders what it meant. For he who passes the gateways always wins a shadow, and never again can he be alone. I had evoked – and the book was indeed all I had suspected. That night I passed the gateway to a vortex of twisted time and vision, and when morning found me in the attic room I saw in the walls and shelves and fittings that which I had never seen before.

Nor could I ever after see the world as I had known it. Mixed with the present scene was always a little of the past and a little of the future, and every once-familiar object loomed alien in the new perspective brought by my widened sight. From then on I walked in a fantastic dream of unknown and half-known shapes; and with each new gateway crossed, the less plainly could I recognise the things of the narrow sphere to which I had so long been bound. What I saw about me, none else saw; and I grew doubly silent and aloof lest I be thought mad. Dogs had a fear of me, for they felt the outside shadow which never left my side. But still I read more – in hidden, forgotten books and scrolls to which my new vision led me – and pushed through fresh gateways of space and being and life-patterns toward the core of the unknown cosmos.

I remember the night I made the five concentric circles of fire on the floor, and stood in the innermost one chanting that monstrous litany the messenger from Tartary had brought. The walls melted away, and I was swept by a black wind through gulfs of fathomless grey with the needle-like pinnacles of unknown mountains miles below me. After a while there was utter blackness, and then the light of myriad stars forming strange, alien constellations. Finally I saw a green-litten plain far below me, and discerned on it the twisted towers of a city built in no fashion I had ever known or read or dreamed of. As I floated closer to that city I saw a great square building of stone in an open space, and felt a hideous fear clutching at me. I screamed and struggled, and after a blankness was again in my attic room sprawled flat over the five phosphorescent circles on the floor. In that night's wandering there was no more of strangeness than in many a former night's wandering;

but there was more of terror because I knew I was closer to those outside gulfs and worlds than I had ever been before. Thereafter I was more cautious with my incantations, for I had no wish to be cut off from my body and from the earth in unknown abysses whence I could never return ...

THE MESSENGER

To Bertrand K. Hart, Esq.

THE THING, he said, would come that night at three
From the old churchyard on the hill below;
But crouching by an oak fire's wholesome glow,
I tried to tell myself it could not be.
Surely, I mused, it was a pleasantry
Devised by one who did not truly know
The Elder Sign, bequeathed from long ago,
That sets the fumbling forms of darkness free.

He had not meant it – no – but still I lit
Another lamp as starry Leo climbed
Out of the Seekonk, and a steeple chimed
Three – and the firelight faded, bit by bit.
Then at the door that cautious rattling came—
And the mad truth devoured me like a flame!

THE EVIL CLERGYMAN

I WAS SHEWN into the attic chamber by a grave, intelligent-looking man with quiet clothes and an iron-grey beard, who spoke to me in this fashion:

'Yes, *he* lived here – but I don't advise your doing anything. Your curiosity makes you irresponsible. *We* never come here at night, and it's only because of *his* will that we keep it this way. You know what *he* did. That abominable society took charge at last, and we don't know where *he* is buried. There was no way the law or anything else could reach the society.

'I hope you won't stay till after dark. And I beg of you to let that thing on the table – the thing that looks like a match box – alone. We don't know what it is, but we suspect it has something to do with what *he* did. We even avoid looking at it very steadily.'

After a time the man left me alone in the attic room. It was very dingy and dusty, and only primitively furnished, but it had a neatness which shewed it was not a slum-denizen's quarters. There were shelves full of theological and classical books, and another bookcase containing treatises on magic – Paracelsus, Albertus

Magnus, Trithemius, Hermes Trismegistus, Borellus, and others in strange alphabets whose titles I could not decipher. The furniture was very plain. There was a door, but it led only into a closet. The only egress was the aperture in the floor up to which the crude, steep staircase led. The windows were of bull's-eye pattern, and the black oak beams bespoke unbelievable antiquity. Plainly, this house was of the old world. I seemed to know where I was, but cannot recall what I then knew. Certainly the town was *not* London. My impression is of a small seaport.

The small object on the table fascinated me intensely. I seemed to know what to do with it, for I drew a pocket electric light – or what looked like one – out of my pocket and nervously tested its flashes. The light was not white but violet, and seemed less like true light than like some radio-active bombardment. I recall that I did not regard it as a common flashlight – indeed, I *had* a common flashlight in another pocket.

It was getting dark, and the ancient roofs and chimney-pots outside looked very queer through the bull's-eye window-panes. Finally I summoned up courage and propped the small object up on the table against a book – then turned the rays of the peculiar violet light upon it. The light seemed now to be more like a rain or hail of small violet particles than like a continuous beam. As the particles struck the glassy surface at the centre of the strange device, they seemed to produce a crackling noise like the sputtering of a vacuum tube through which sparks are passed. The dark glassy surface displayed a pinkish glow, and a vague white shape seemed to be taking form at its centre. Then I noticed that I was not alone in the room – and put the ray-projector back in my pocket.

But the newcomer did not speak – nor did I hear any sound whatever during all the immediately following moments. Everything was shadowy pantomime, as if seen at a vast distance through some intervening haze – although on the other hand the newcomer and all subsequent comers loomed large and close, as if both near and distant, according to some abnormal geometry.

The newcomer was a thin, dark man of medium height attired in the clerical garb of the Anglican church. He was apparently about thirty years old, with a sallow, olive complexion and fairly good features, but an abnormally high forehead. His black hair was well cut and neatly brushed, and he was clean-shaven though blue-chinned with a heavy growth of beard. He wore rimless spectacles with steel bows. His build and lower facial features were like other clergymen I had seen, but he had a vastly higher forehead, and was darker and more intelligent-looking – also more subtly and concealedly *evil*-looking. At the present moment – having just lighted a faint oil lamp – he looked nervous, and before I knew it he was casting all his magical books into a fireplace on the window side of the room (where the wall slanted sharply) which I had not noticed before. The flames devoured the volumes greedily – leaping up in strange colours and emitting indescribably hideous odours as the strangely hieroglyphed leaves and wormy bindings succumbed to the devastating element. All at once I saw there were others in the room – grave-looking men in clerical costume, one of whom wore the bands and knee-breeches of a bishop. Though I could hear nothing, I could see that they were bringing a decision of vast import to the first-comer. They seemed to hate and fear him at the same time, and he seemed to return these sentiments. His face set itself into a grim expression, but I could see his right hand shaking as he tried to grip the back of a chair. The bishop pointed to the empty case and to the fireplace (where the flames had died down amidst a charred, non-committal mass), and seemed filled with a peculiar loathing. The first-comer then gave a wry smile and reached out with his left hand toward the small object on the table. Everyone then seemed frightened. The procession of clerics began filing down the steep stairs through the trap-door in the floor, turning and making menacing gestures as they left. The bishop was last to go.

The first-comer now went to a cupboard on the inner side of the room and extracted a coil of rope. Mounting a chair, he attached one end of the rope to a hook in the great exposed central beam of black oak, and began making a noose with the other end. Realising he was about to hang himself, I started forward to dissuade or save him. He saw me and ceased his preparations, looking at me with a kind of *triumph* which puzzled and disturbed me. He slowly stepped down from the chair and began gliding toward me with a positively wolfish grin on his dark, thin-lipped face.

I felt somehow in deadly peril, and drew out the peculiar ray-projector as a weapon of defence. Why I thought it could help me, I do not know. I turned it on – full in his face, and saw the sallow features glow first with violet and then with pinkish light. His expression of wolfish exultation began to be crowded aside by a look of profound fear – which did not, however, wholly displace the exultation. He stopped in his tracks – then, flailing his arms wildly in the air, began to stagger backward. I saw he was edging toward the open stair-well in the floor, and tried to shout a warning, but he did not hear me. In another instant he had lurched backward through the opening and was lost to view.

I found difficulty in moving toward the stair-well, but when I did get there I found no crushed body on the floor below. Instead there was a clatter of people coming up with lanterns, for the spell of phantasmal silence had broken, and I once more heard sounds and saw figures as normally tri-dimensional. Something had evidently drawn a crowd to this place. Had there been a noise I had not heard? Presently the two people (simply villagers, apparently) farthest in the lead saw me – and stood paralysed. One of them shrieked loudly and reverberantly:

'Ahrrh! ... It be'ee, zur? Again?'

Then they all turned and fled frantically. All, that is, but one. When the crowd was gone I saw the grave-bearded man who had brought me to this place – standing alone with a lantern. He was gazing at me gaspingly and fascinatedly, but did not seem afraid. Then he began to ascend the stairs, and joined me in the attic. He spoke:

'So you *didn't* let it alone! I'm sorry. I know what has happened. It happened once before, but the man got frightened and shot himself. You ought not to have made *him* come back. You know what *he* wants. But you mustn't get frightened like the other man he got. Something very strange and terrible has happened to you, but it didn't get far enough to hurt your mind and personality. If you'll keep cool, and accept the need for making certain radical readjustments in your life, you can keep right on enjoying the world, and the fruits of your scholarship. But you can't live here – and I don't think you'll wish to go back to London. I'd advise America.

'You mustn't try anything more with that – thing. Nothing can be put back now. It would only make matters worse to do – or summon – anything. You are not as badly off as you might be – but you must get out of here at once and stay away. You'd better thank heaven it didn't go further ...

'I'm going to prepare you as bluntly as I can. There's been a certain change – in your personal appearance. *He* always causes that. But in a new country you can get used to it. There's a mirror up at the other end of the room, and I'm going to take you to it. You'll get a shock – though you will see nothing repulsive.'

I was now shaking with a deadly fear, and the bearded man almost had to hold me up as he walked me across the room to the mirror, the faint lamp (i.e., that formerly on the table, not the still fainter lantern he had brought) in his free hand. This is what I saw in the glass:

A thin, dark man of medium stature attired in the clerical garb of the Anglican church, apparently about thirty, and with rimless, steel-bowed glasses glistening beneath a sallow, olive forehead of abnormal height.

It was the silent first-comer who had burned his books.

For all the rest of my life, in outward form, I was to be that man!

THE VERY OLD FOLK

DEAR MELMOTH:—
I have myself been carried back to Roman times by my
recent perusal of James Rhoades' *Æneid*, a translation never before
read by me, and more faithful to P. Maro than any other versified
version I have ever seen – including that of my late uncle Dr Clark,
which did not attain publication. This Virgilian diversion, together
with the spectral thoughts incident to All Hallow's Eve with its
Witch-Sabbaths on the hills, produced in me last Monday night a
Roman dream of such supernal clearness and vividness, and such
titanic adumbrations of hidden horror, that I verily believe I shall
some day employ it in fiction. Roman dreams were no uncommon
features of my youth – I used to follow the Divine Julius all over
Gallia as a Tribunus Militum o'nights – but I had so long ceased
to experience them, that the present one impressed me with extraordinary force.

It was a flaming sunset or late afternoon in the tiny provincial
town of Pompelo, at the foot of the Pyrenees in Hispania Citerior.
The year must have been in the late republic, for the province was

still ruled by a senatorial proconsul instead of a prætorian legate of Augustus, and the day was the first before the Kalends of November. The hills rose scarlet and gold to the north of the little town, and the westering sun shone ruddily and mystically on the crude new stone and plaster buildings of the dusty forum and the wooden walls of the circus some distance to the east. Groups of citizens – broad-browed Roman colonists and coarse-haired Romanised natives, together with obvious hybrids of the two strains, alike clad in cheap woollen togas – and sprinklings of helmeted legionaries and coarse-mantled, black-bearded tribesmen of the circum-ambient Vascones – all thronged the few paved streets and forum; moved by some vague and ill-defined uneasiness. I myself had just alighted from a litter, which the Illyrian bearers seemed to have brought in some haste from Calagurris, across the Iberus to the southward. It appeared that I was a provincial quæstor named L. Cælius Rufus, and that I had been summoned by the proconsul, P. Scribonius Libo, who had come from Tarraco some days before. The soldiers were the fifth cohort of the XIIth legion, under the military tribune Sex. Asellius; and the legatus of the whole region, Cn. Balbutius, had also come from Calagurris, where the permanent station was.

The cause of the conference was a horror that brooded on the hills. All the townsfolk were frightened, and had begged the presence of a cohort from Calagurris. It was the Terrible Season of the autumn, and the wild people in the mountains were preparing for the frightful ceremonies which only rumour told of in the towns. They were the very old folk who dwelt higher up in the hills and spoke a choppy language which the Vascones could not understand. One seldom saw them; but a few times a year they sent down little yellow, squint-eyed messengers (who looked like Scythians) to trade with the merchants by means of gestures, and every spring and autumn they held the infamous rites on the peaks, their howlings and altar-fires throwing terror into the villages. Always the same – the night before the Kalends of Maius and the night before the Kalends of November. Townsfolk would disappear just before these nights, and would never be heard of again. And there were whispers that the native shepherds and farmers were not ill-disposed toward the very old folk – that more than one thatched hut was vacant before midnight on the two hideous Sabbaths.

This year the horror was very great, for the people knew that the wrath of the very old folk was upon Pompelo. Three months previously five of the little squint-eyed traders had come down from the hills, and in a market brawl three of them had been killed. The remaining two had gone back wordlessly to their mountains – *and this autumn not a single villager had disappeared.* There was menace in this immunity. It was not like the very old folk to spare their victims at the Sabbath. It was too good to be normal, and the villagers were afraid.

For many nights there had been a hollow drumming on the hills, and at last the ædile Tib. Annæus Stilpo (half native in blood) had sent to Balbutius at Calagurris for a cohort to stamp out the Sabbath on the terrible night. Balbutius had carelessly refused, on the ground that the villagers' fears were empty, and that the loathsome rites of hill folk were of no concern to the Roman People unless our own citizens were menaced. I, however, who seemed to be a close friend of Balbutius, had disagreed with him; averring that I had studied deeply in the black forbidden lore, and that I believed the very old folk capable of visiting almost any nameless doom upon the town, which after all was a Roman settlement and contained a great number of our citizens. The complaining ædile's own mother Helvia was a pure Roman, the daughter of M. Helvius Cinna, who had come over with Scipio's army. Accordingly I had sent a slave – a nimble little Greek called Antipater – to the proconsul with letters, and Scribonius had heeded my plea and ordered Balbutius to send his fifth cohort, under Asellius, to Pompelo; entering the hills at dusk on the eve of November's Kalends and stamping out whatever nameless orgies he might find – bringing such prisoners as he might take to Tarraco for the next proprætor's court. Balbutius, however, had protested, so that more correspondence had ensued.

I had written so much to the proconsul that he had become gravely interested, and had resolved to make a personal inquiry into the horror. He had at length proceeded to Pompelo with his lictors and attendants; there hearing enough rumours to be greatly impressed and disturbed, and standing firmly by his order for the Sabbath's extirpation. Desirous of conferring with one who had studied the subject, he ordered me to accompany Asellius' cohort – and Balbutius had also come along to press his adverse advice, for he honestly believed that drastic military action would stir up a dangerous sentiment of unrest amongst the Vascones both tribal and settled. So here we all were in the mystic sunset of the autumn hills – old Scribonius Libo in his toga prætexta, the golden light glancing on his shiny bald head and wrinkled hawk face, Balbutius with his gleaming helmet and breastplate, blue-shaven lips compressed in conscientiously dogged opposition, young Asellius with his polished greaves and superior sneer, and the curious throng of townsfolk, legionaries, tribesmen, peasants, lictors, slaves, and attendants. I myself seemed to wear a common toga, and to have no especially distinguishing characteristic.

And everywhere horror brooded. The town and country folk scarcely dared speak aloud, and the men of Libo's entourage, who had been there nearly a week, seemed to have caught something of the nameless dread. Old Scribonius himself looked very grave, and the sharp voices of us later comers seemed to hold something of curious inappropriateness, as in a place of death or the temple of some mystic God. We entered the prætorium and held grave converse. Balbutius pressed his objections, and was sustained by Asellius, who appeared to hold all the natives in extreme contempt while at the same time deeming it inadvisable to excite them. Both soldiers maintained that we could better afford to antagonise the minority of colonists and civilised natives by inaction, than to antagonise a probable majority of tribesmen and cottagers by stamping out the dread rites. I, on the other hand, renewed my demand for action, and offered to accompany the cohort on any expedition it might undertake. I pointed out that the barbarous Vascones were at best turbulent and uncertain, so that skirmishes with them were inevitable sooner or later whichever course we might take; that they had not in the past proved dangerous adversaries to our legions, and that it would ill become the representatives of the Roman People to suffer barbarians to interfere with a course which the justice and prestige of the Republic demanded. That, on the other hand, the successful administration of a province depended primarily upon the safety and good-will of the civilised element in whose hands the local machinery of commerce and prosperity reposed, and in whose veins a large mixture of our own Italian blood coursed. These, though in numbers they might form a minority, were the stable element whose constancy might be relied on, and whose co-operation would most firmly bind the province to the Imperium of the Senate and the Roman People. It was at once a duty and an advantage to afford them the protection due to Roman citizens; even (and here I shot a sarcastic look at Balbutius and Asellius) at the expense of a little trouble and activity, and of a slight interruption of the draught-playing and cock-fighting at the camp in Calagurris.

That the danger to the town and inhabitants of Pompelo was a real one, I could not from my studies doubt. I had read many scrolls out of Syria and Ægyptus, and the cryptic towns of Etruria, and had talked at length with the bloodthirsty priest of Diana Aricina in his temple in the woods bordering Lacus Nemorensis. There were shocking dooms that might be called out of the hills on the Sabbaths; dooms which ought not to exist within the territories of the Roman People; and to permit orgies of the kind known to prevail at Sabbaths would be but little in consonance with the customs of those whose forefathers, A. Postumius being consul, had executed so many Roman citizens for the practice of the Bacchanalia – a matter kept ever in memory by the Senatus Consultum de Bacchanalibus, graven upon bronze and set open to every eye.

Checked in time, before the progress of the rites might evoke anything with which the iron of a Roman pilum might not be able to deal, the Sabbath would not be too much for the powers of a single cohort. Only participants need be apprehended, and the sparing of a great number of mere spectators would considerably lessen the resentment which any of the sympathising country folk might feel. In short, both principle and policy demanded stern action; and I could not doubt but that Publius Scribonius, bearing in mind the dignity and obligations of the Roman People, would adhere to his plan of despatching the cohort, me accompanying, despite such objections as Balbutius and Asellius – speaking indeed more like provincials than Romans – might see fit to offer and multiply.

The slanting sun was now very low, and the whole hushed town seemed draped in an unreal and malign glamour. Then P. Scribonius the proconsul signified his approval of my words, and stationed me with the cohort in the provisional capacity of a centurio primipilus; Balbutius and Asellius assenting, the former with better grace than the latter.

As twilight fell on the wild autumnal slopes, a measured, hideous beating of strange drums floated down from afar in terrible rhythm. Some few of the legionarii showed timidity, but sharp commands brought them into line, and the whole cohort was soon drawn up on the open plain east of the circus. Libo himself, as well as Balbutius, insisted on accompanying the cohort; but great difficulty was suffered in getting a native guide to point out the paths up the mountain. Finally a young man named Vercellius, the son of pure Roman parents, agreed to take us at least past the foothills. We began to march in the new dusk, with the thin silver sickle of a young moon trembling over the woods on our left.

That which disquieted us most *was the fact that the Sabbath was to be held at all.* Reports of the coming cohort must have reached the hills, and even the lack of a final decision could not make the rumour less alarming – yet there were the sinister drums as of yore, as if the celebrants had some peculiar reason to be indifferent whether or not the forces of the Roman People marched against them.

The sound grew louder as we entered a rising gap in the hills, steep wooded banks enclosing us narrowly on either side, and displaying curiously fantastic tree-trunks in the light of our bobbing torches. All were afoot save Libo, Balbutius, Asellius, two or three of the centuriones, and myself, and at length the way became so steep and narrow that those who had horses were forced to leave them; a squad of ten men being left to guard them, though robber bands were not likely to be abroad on such a night of terror. Once in a while it seemed as though we detected a skulking form in the woods nearby, and after a half-hour's climb the steepness and narrowness of the way made the advance of so great a body of men – over 300, all told – exceedingly cumbrous and difficult.

Then with utter and horrifying suddenness we heard a frightful sound from below. It was from the tethered horses – they had *screamed*, not neighed, but *screamed* ... and there was no light down there, nor the sound of any human thing, to show why they had done so. At the same moment bonfires blazed out on all the peaks ahead, so that terror seemed to lurk equally well before and behind us. Looking for the youth Vercellius, our guide, we found only a crumpled heap weltering in a pool of blood. In his hand was a short sword snatched from the belt of D. Vibulanus, a subcenturio, and on his face was such a look of terror that the stoutest veterans turned pale at the sight. He had killed himself when the horses screamed ... he, who had been born and lived all his life in that region, and knew what men whispered about the hills.

All the torches now began to dim, and the cries of frightened legionaries mingled with the unceasing screams of the tethered horses. The air grew perceptibly colder, more suddenly so than is usual at November's brink, and seemed stirred by terrible undulations which I could not help connecting with the beating of huge wings. The whole cohort now remained at a standstill, and as the torches faded I watched what I thought were fantastic shadows outlined in the sky by the spectral luminosity of the Via Lactea as it flowed through Perseus, Cassiopeia, Cepheus, and Cygnus.

Then suddenly all the stars were blotted from the sky – even bright Deneb and Vega ahead, and the lone Altair and Fomalhaut behind us. And as the torches died out altogether, there remained above the stricken and shrieking cohort only the noxious and horrible altar-flames on the towering peaks; hellish and red, and now silhouetting the mad, leaping, and colossal forms of such nameless beasts as had never a Phrygian priest or Campanian grandam whispered of in the wildest of furtive tales.

And above the nighted screaming of men and horses that dæmonic drumming rose to louder pitch, whilst an ice-cold wind of shocking sentience and deliberateness swept down from those forbidden heights and coiled about each man separately, till all the cohort was struggling and screaming in the dark, as if acting out the fate of Laocoön and his sons. Only old Scribonius Libo seemed resigned. He uttered words amidst the screaming, and they echo still in my ears. '*Malitia vetus – malitia vetus est ... venit ... tandem venit ...*'

And then I waked. It was the most vivid dream in years, drawing upon wells of the subconscious long untouched and forgotten. Of the fate of that cohort no record exists, but the town at least was saved – for encyclopædias tell of the survival of Pompelo to this day, under the modern Spanish name of Pompelona ...

Yrs for Gothick Supremacy—
C · IVLIVS · VERVS · MAXIMINVS.

THE THING IN THE MOONLIGHT

MORGAN IS NOT A LITERARY MAN; in fact he cannot speak English with any degree of coherency. That is what makes me wonder about the words he wrote, though others have laughed.

He was alone the evening it happened. Suddenly an unconquerable urge to write came over him, and taking pen in hand he wrote the following:

My name is Howard Phillips. I live at 66 College Street, in Providence, Rhode Island. On November 24, 1927 – for I know not even what the year may be now—, I fell asleep and dreamed, since when I have been unable to awaken.

My dream began in a dank, reed-choked marsh that lay under a grey autumn sky, with a rugged cliff of lichen-crusted stone rising to the north. Impelled by some obscure quest, I ascended a rift or cleft in this beetling precipice, noting as I did so the black mouths of many fearsome burrows extending from both walls into the depths of the stony plateau.

At several points the passage was roofed over by the choking of the upper parts of the narrow fissure; these places being exceeding

410

dark, and forbidding the perception of such burrows as may have existed there. In one such dark space I felt conscious of a singular accession of fright, as if some subtle and bodiless emanation from the abyss were engulfing my spirit; but the blackness was too great for me to perceive the source of my alarm.

At length I emerged upon a table-land of moss-grown rock and scanty soil, lit by a faint moonlight which had replaced the expiring orb of day. Casting my eyes about, I beheld no living object; but was sensible of a very peculiar stirring far below me, amongst the whispering rushes of the pestilential swamp I had lately quitted.

After walking for some distance, I encountered the rusty tracks of a street railway, and the worm-eaten poles which still held the limp and sagging trolley wire. Following this line, I soon came upon a yellow, vestibuled car numbered 1852 – of a plain, double-trucked type common from 1900 to 1910. It was untenanted, but evidently, ready to start; the trolley being on the wire and the air-brake now and then throbbing beneath the floor. I boarded it and looked vainly about for the light switch – noting as I did so the absence of the controller handle, which thus implied the brief absence of the motorman. Then I sat down in one of the cross seats of the vehicle.

Presently I heard a swishing in the sparse grass toward the left, and saw the dark forms of two men looming up in the moonlight. They had the regulation caps of a railway company, and I could not doubt but that they were conductor and the motorman. Then one of them sniffed with singular sharpness, and raised his face to howl to the moon. The other dropped on all fours to run toward the car.

I leaped up at once and raced madly out of that car and across endless leagues of plateau till exhaustion forced me to stop – doing this not because the conductor had dropped on all fours, but because the face of the motorman was a mere white cone tapering to one blood-red tentacle ...

I was aware that I only dreamed, but the very awareness was not pleasant. Since that fearful night, I have prayed only for awakening – it has not come! Instead I have found myself an inhabitant of this terrible dream-world! That first night gave way to dawn, and I wandered aimlessly over the lonely swamp-lands. When night came, I still wandered, hoping for awakening. But suddenly I parted the weeds and saw before me the ancient railway car – and to one side a cone-faced thing lifted its head and in the streaming moonlight howled strangely! It has been the same each day. Night takes me always to that place of horror. I have tried not moving, with the coming of nightfall, but I must walk in my slumber, for always I awaken with the thing of dread howling before me in the pale moonlight, and I turn and flee madly.

God! When will I awaken?

That is what Morgan wrote. I would go to 66 College Street in Providence, but I fear for what I might find there.

THE TRANSITION OF JUAN ROMERO

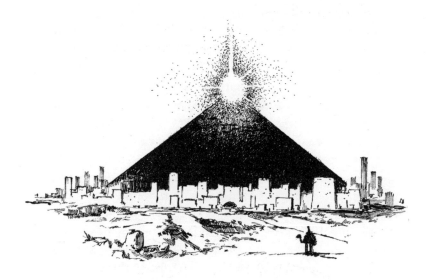

O F THE EVENTS WHICH TOOK PLACE at the Norton Mine
on October eighteenth and nineteenth, 1894, I have no desire
to speak. A sense of duty to science is all that impels me to recall,
in the last years of my life, scenes and happenings fraught with a
terror doubly acute because I cannot wholly define it. But I believe
that before I die I should tell what I know of the – shall I say
transition – of Juan Romero.

My name and origin need not be related to posterity; in fact,
I fancy it is better that they should not be, for when a man suddenly
migrates to the States or the Colonies, he leaves his past behind
him. Besides, what I once was is not in the least relevant to my
narrative; save perhaps the fact that during my service in India
I was more at home amongst white-bearded native teachers than
amongst my brother-officers. I had delved not a little into odd
Eastern lore when overtaken by the calamities which brought about
my new life in America's vast West – a life wherein I found it well
to accept a name – my present one – which is very common and
carries no meaning.

In the summer and autumn of 1894 I dwelt in the drear expanses of the Cactus Mountains, employed as a common labourer at the celebrated Norton Mine, whose discovery by an aged prospector some years before had turned the surrounding region from a nearly unpeopled waste to a seething cauldron of sordid life. A cavern of gold, lying deep beneath a mountain lake, had enriched its venerable finder beyond his wildest dreams, and now formed the seat of extensive tunnelling operations on the part of the corporation to which it had finally been sold. Additional grottoes had been found, and the yield of yellow metal was exceedingly great; so that a mighty and heterogeneous army of miners toiled day and night in the numerous passages and rock hollows. The Superintendent, a Mr Arthur, often discussed the singularity of the local geological formations; speculating on the probable extent of the chain of caves, and estimating the future of the titanic mining enterprises. He considered the auriferous cavities the result of the action of water, and believed the last of them would soon be opened.

It was not long after my arrival and employment that Juan Romero came to the Norton Mine. One of the large herd of unkempt Mexicans attracted thither from the neighbouring country, he at first attracted attention only because of his features; which though plainly of the Red Indian type, were yet remarkable for their light colour and refined conformation, being vastly unlike those of the average 'greaser' or Piute of the locality. It is curious that although he differed so widely from the mass of Hispanicised and tribal Indians, Romero gave not the least impression of Caucasian blood. It was not the Castilian conquistador or the American pioneer, but the ancient and noble Aztec, whom imagination called to view when the silent peon would rise in the early morning and gaze in fascination at the sun as it crept above the eastern hills, meanwhile stretching out his arms to the orb as if in the performance of some rite whose nature he did not himself comprehend. But save for his face, Romero was not in any way suggestive of nobility. Ignorant and dirty, he was at home amongst the other brown-skinned Mexicans; having come (so I was afterward told) from the very lowest sort of surroundings. He had been found as a child in a crude mountain hut, the only survivor of an epidemic which had stalked lethally by. Near the hut, close to a rather unusual rock fissure, had lain two skeletons, newly picked by vultures, and presumably forming the sole remains of his parents. No one recalled their identity, and they were soon forgotten by the many. Indeed, the crumbling of the adobe hut and the closing of the rock-fissure by a subsequent avalanche had helped to efface even the scene from recollection. Reared by a Mexican cattle-thief who had given him his name, Juan differed little from his fellows.

The attachment which Romero manifested toward me was undoubtedly commenced through the quaint and ancient Hindoo ring which I wore when not engaged in active labour. Of its nature, and manner of coming into my possession, I cannot speak. It was my last link with a chapter of my life forever closed, and I valued it highly. Soon I observed that the odd-looking Mexican was likewise interested; eyeing it with an expression that banished all suspicion of mere covetousness. Its hoary hieroglyphs seemed to stir some faint recollection in his untutored but active mind, though he could not possibly have beheld their like before. Within a few weeks after his advent, Romero was like a faithful servant to me; this notwithstanding the fact that I was myself but an ordinary miner. Our conversation was necessarily limited. He knew but a few words of English, while I found my Oxonian Spanish was something quite different from the patois of the peon of New Spain.

The event which I am about to relate was unheralded by long premonitions. Though the man Romero had interested me, and though my ring had affected him peculiarly, I think that neither of us had any expectation of what was to follow when the great blast was set off. Geological considerations had dictated an extension of the mine directly downward from the deepest part of the sub-terranean area; and the belief of the Superintendent that only solid rock would be encountered, had led to the placing of a prodigious charge of dynamite. With this work Romero and I were not con-nected, wherefore our first knowledge of extraordinary conditions came from others. The charge, heavier perhaps than had been estimated, had seemed to shake the entire mountain. Windows in shanties on the slope outside were shattered by the shock, whilst miners throughout the nearer passages were knocked from their feet. Jewel Lake, which lay above the scene of action, heaved as in a tempest. Upon investigation it was seen that a new abyss yawned indefinitely below the seat of the blast; an abyss so monstrous that no handy line might fathom it, nor any lamp illuminate it. Baffled, the excavators sought a conference with the Superintendent, who ordered great lengths of rope to be taken to the pit, and spliced and lowered without cessation till a bottom might be discovered.

Shortly afterward the pale-faced workmen apprised the Superintendent of their failure. Firmly though respectfully, they signified their refusal to revisit the chasm or indeed to work further in the mine until it might be sealed. Something beyond their experience was evidently confronting them, for so far as they could ascertain, the void below was infinite. The Superintendent did not reproach them. Instead, he pondered deeply, and made plans for the following day. The night shift did not go on that evening.

At two in the morning a lone coyote on the mountain began to howl dismally. From somewhere within the works a dog barked an answer; either to the coyote – or to something else. A storm was gathering around the peaks of the range, and weirdly shaped clouds scudded horribly across the blurred patch of celestial light which marked a gibbous moon's¹ attempts to shine through many layers of cirrostratus vapours. It was Romero's voice, coming from the bunk above, that awakened me, a voice excited and tense with some vague expectation I could not understand:

'*¡Madre de Dios! – El sonido – ese sonido – ¡orga Vd! – ¿lo oye Vd? – Señor,* THAT SOUND!'

I listened, wondering what sound he meant. The coyote, the dog, the storm, all were audible; the last named now gaining ascendancy as the wind shrieked more and more frantically. Flashes of lightning were visible through the bunk-house window. I questioned the nervous Mexican, repeating the sounds I had heard:

'*¿El coyote? – ¿el perro? – ¿el viento?*'

But Romero did not reply. Then he commenced whispering as in awe:

'*El ritmo, señor – el ritmo de la tierra –* THAT THROB DOWN IN THE GROUND!'

And now I also heard; heard and shivered and without knowing why. Deep, deep, below me was a sound – a rhythm, just as the peon had said – which, though exceedingly faint, yet dominated even the dog, the coyote, and the increasing tempest. To seek to describe it was useless – for it was such that no description is possible. Perhaps it was like the pulsing of the engines far down in a great liner, as sensed from the deck, yet it was not so mechanical; not so devoid of the element of life and consciousness. Of all its qualities, *remoteness* in the earth most impressed me. To my mind rushed fragments of a passage in Joseph Glanvil which Poe has quoted with tremendous effect[2]:

'... the vastness, profundity, and unsearchableness of His works, *which have a depth in them greater than the well of Democritus.*'

Suddenly Romero leaped from his bunk, pausing before me to gaze at the strange ring on my hand, which glistened queerly in every flash of lightning, and then staring intently in the direction of the mine shaft. I also rose, and both of us stood motionless for a time, straining our ears as the uncanny rhythm seemed more and more to take on a vital quality. Then without apparent volition we began to move toward the door, whose rattling in the gale held a comforting suggestion of earthly reality. The chanting in the depths – for such the sound now seemed to be – grew in volume and distinctness; and we felt irresistibly urged out into the storm and thence to the gaping blackness of the shaft.

We encountered no living creature, for the men of the night shift had been released from duty, and were doubtless at the Dry Gulch settlement pouring sinister rumours into the ear of some drowsy bartender. From the watchman's cabin, however, gleamed a small square of yellow light like a guardian eye. I dimly wondered how the rhythmic sound had affected the watchman; but Romero was moving more swiftly now, and I followed without pausing.

As we descended the shaft, the sound beneath grew definitely composite. It struck me as horribly like a sort of Oriental ceremony, with beating of drums and chanting of many voices. I have, as you are aware, been much in India. Romero and I moved without material hesitancy through drifts and down ladders; ever toward the thing that allured us, yet ever with a pitifully helpless fear and reluctance. At one time I fancied I had gone mad – this was when, on wondering how our way was lighted in the absence of lamp or candle, I realised that the ancient ring on my finger was glowing with eerie radiance, diffusing a pallid lustre through the damp, heavy air around.

It was without warning that Romero, after clambering down one of the many wide ladders, broke into a run and left me alone. Some new and wild note in the drumming and chanting, perceptible but slightly to me, had acted on him in a startling fashion; and with a wild outcry he forged ahead unguided in the cavern's gloom. I heard his repeated shrieks before me, as he stumbled awkwardly along the level places and scrambled madly down the rickety ladders. And frightened as I was, I yet retained enough of my perception to note that his speech, when articulate, was not of any sort known to me. Harsh but impressive polysyllables had replaced the customary mixture of bad Spanish and worse English, and of these, only the oft repeated cry '*Huitzilopotchli*' seemed in the least familiar. Later I definitely placed that word in the works of a great historian[3] – and shuddered when the association came to me.

The climax of that awful night was composite but fairly brief, beginning just as I reached the final cavern of the journey. Out of the darkness immediately ahead burst a final shriek from the Mexican, which was joined by such a chorus of uncouth sound as I could never hear again and survive. In that moment it seemed as if all the hidden terrors and monstrosities of earth had become articulate in an effort to overwhelm the human race. Simultaneously the light from my ring was extinguished, and I saw a new light glimmering from lower space but a few yards ahead of me. I had arrived at the abyss, which was now redly aglow, and which had evidently swallowed up the unfortunate Romero. Advancing, I peered over the edge of that chasm which no line could fathom, and which was now a pandemonium of flickering flame and hideous uproar. At first I beheld nothing but a seething blur of luminosity; but then shapes, all infinitely distant, began to detach themselves from the confusion, and I saw – was it Juan Romero? – *but God! I dare not tell you what I saw!* ... Some power from heaven, coming to my aid, obliterated both sights and sounds in such a crash as may be heard when two universes collide in space. Chaos supervened, and I knew the peace of oblivion.

I hardly know how to continue, since conditions so singular are involved; but I will do my best, not even trying to differentiate betwixt the real and the apparent. When I awakened, I was safe in my bunk and the red glow of dawn was visible at the window. Some distance away the lifeless body of Juan Romero lay upon a table, surrounded by a group of men, including the camp doctor. The men were discussing the strange death of the Mexican as he lay asleep; a death seemingly connected in some way with the terrible bolt of lightning which had struck and shaken the mountain. No direct cause was evident, and an autopsy failed to show any reason why Romero should not be living. Snatches of conversation indicated beyond a doubt that neither Romero nor I had left the bunk-house during the night; that neither of us had been awake during the frightful storm which had passed over the Cactus range. That storm, said men who had ventured down the mine-shaft, had caused extensive caving-in, and had completely closed the deep abyss which had created so much apprehension the day before. When I asked the watchman what sounds he had heard prior to the mighty thunder-bolt; he mentioned a coyote, a dog, and the snarling mountain wind – nothing more. Nor do I doubt his word.

Upon the resumption of work, Superintendent Arthur called upon some especially dependable men to make a few investigations around the spot where the gulf had appeared. Though hardly eager, they obeyed, and a deep boring was made. Results were very curious. The roof of the void, as seen when it was open, was not by any means thick; yet now the drills of the investigators met what appeared to be a limitless extent of solid rock. Finding nothing else, not even gold, the Superintendent abandoned his attempts; but a perplexed look occasionally steals over his countenance as he sits thinking at his desk.

One other thing is curious. Shortly after waking on that morning after the storm, I noticed the unaccountable absence of my Hindoo ring from my finger. I had prized it greatly, yet nevertheless felt a sensation of relief at its disappearance. If one of my fellow-miners appropriated it, he must have been quite clever in disposing of his booty, for despite advertisements and a police search, the ring was never seen again. Somehow I doubt if it was stolen by mortal hands, for many strange things were taught me in India.

My opinion of my whole experience varies from time to time. In broad daylight, and at most seasons I am apt to think the greater part of it a mere dream; but sometimes in the autumn, about two in the morning when the winds and animals howl dismally, there comes from inconceivable depths below a damnable suggestion of rhythmical throbbing ... and I feel that the transition of Juan Romero was a terrible one indeed.

NOTES

[1] AUTHOR'S NOTE: Here is a lesson in scientific accuracy for fiction writers. I have just looked up the moon's phases for October, 1894, to find when a gibbous moon was visible at two a.m., and have changed the dates to fit!

[2] Motto of *A Descent Into the Maelstrom*

[3] Prescott, *Conquest of Mexico*

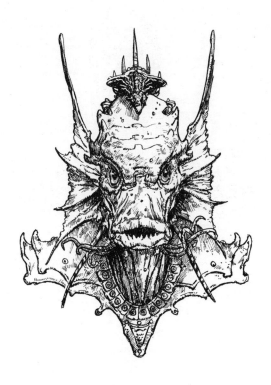

For The Science-Fantasy Correspondent

SUPERNATURAL HORROR IN LITERATURE
By H. P. Lovecraft

(Summary of preceding parts published in The Fantasy Fan)

I. Introduction.

The emotion of fear, and the *imaginative* revolt of the human ego against
the limitations of time, space, and natural law, are so deeply embedded
in our personalities that they have always existed and must always exist
as motivating elements in art and literature. Fantasy must be reckoned with
as a permanent though necessarily restricted element in aesthetics. And
because pain is stronger than pleasure, because religions have absorbed the
brighter side of our myth-making tendencies, and because the unknown always
contains an element of terror despite its fascination, it is the darker
side of fantasy which must necessarily remain the most convincing. The
universality of a leaning toward dark fantasy is shown by the fact that
most authors of all kinds have occasionally produced specimens of spectral
literature. Mere physical gruesomeness or conventional ghosts cannot make
true weird art. A certain atmosphere of breathless and unexplainable dread
of outer, unknown forces must be present; and there must be a hint,
expressed with a seriousness and portentousness becoming its subject, of
that most terrible conception of the human brain---a malign and particular
suspension or defeat of those fixed laws of nature which are our only
safeguard against the assaults of chaos and the daemons of unplumbed space.
The one test of the really weird is simply this---whether or not there be
excited in the reader a profound sense of dread, and of contact with
unknown spheres and powers; a subtle attitude of awed listening, as if for
the beating of black wings or the scratching of outside shapes and entities
on the known universe's utmost rim.

II. The Dawn of the Horror Tale.

Elements of cosmic terror appear in the earliest specimens of human
literature, largely connected with the darker phases of ancient religions.
They are more common, perhaps, in the Oriental and Nordic traditions than
in the classic Graeco-Roman tradition. In the Middle Ages they became
greatly intensified because of the prevailing superstition, and because of
the presence of a persistent "Witch-Cult" of evil and degenerate persons
which kept alive certain very primitive rites from pre-Aryan religions and
held secret and hideously orgiastic meetings or "Sabbats" in lonely places
on traditional dates like May-Eve and Hallowe'en. Another contributing
source was the existence of perverse diabolic groups who parodied and
inverted the rites of Christianity in repulsive ceremonies like the "Black
Mass". Magic and witchcraft were commonly credited, and interest was lent
them by the ceaseless quest of alchemists for the secret of gold-making and
the formula for an elixir of eternal life. At this period touches of weird
horror were scattered all through oral and written literature. They occurred
in the Teutonic myths, in the Celtic legends of the Arthurian cycle, in
poets like Dante, and in every kind of popular balladry. And this condition
continued through the Renaissance, colouring Elizabethan drama and coming
down to meet the rapid development of a special horror-literature in the
eighteenth century.

The weird or horror story as a definite type begins in the eighteenth
century. Its rise was promoted by the translation of the Arabian Nights
into European languages, and by that general reaction from classicism toward
mediaeval wonder and grotesqueness which formed part of the so-called
"romantic movement". Specialised horror-literature first appeared in German
balladry, but very soon took up its chief abode in the domain of the novel.

SUPERNATURAL HORROR
IN LITERATURE

1. Introduction

THE OLDEST AND STRONGEST emotion of mankind is fear, and the oldest and strongest kind of fear is fear of the unknown. These facts few psychologists will dispute, and their admitted truth must establish for all time the genuineness and dignity of the weirdly horrible tale as a literary form. Against it are discharged all the shafts of a materialistic sophistication which clings to frequently felt emotions and external events, and of a naively insipid idealism which deprecates the aesthetic motive and calls for a didactic literature to uplift the reader toward a suitable degree of smirking optimism. But in spite of all this opposition the weird tale has survived, developed, and attained remarkable heights of perfection; founded as it is on a profound and elementary principle whose appeal, if not always universal, must necessarily be poignant and permanent to minds of the requisite sensitiveness.

The appeal of the spectrally macabre is generally narrow because it demands from the reader a certain degree of imagination and a capacity for detachment from every-day life. Relatively few are free enough from the spell of the daily routine to respond to rappings from outside, and tales of ordinary feelings and events, or of common sentimental distortions of such feelings and events, will always take first place in the taste of the majority; rightly, perhaps, since of course these ordinary matters make up the greater part of human experience. But the sensitive are always with us, and sometimes a curious streak of fancy invades an obscure corner of the very hardest head; so that no amount of rationalisation, reform, or Freudian analysis can quite annul the thrill of the chimney-corner whisper or the lonely wood. There is here involved a psychological pattern or tradition as real and as deeply grounded in mental experience as any other pattern or tradition of mankind; coeval with the religious feeling and closely related to many aspects of it, and too much a part of our inmost biological heritage to lose keen potency over a very important, though not numerically great, minority of our species.

Man's first instincts and emotions formed his response to the environment in which he found himself. Definite feelings based on pleasure and pain grew up around the phenomena whose causes and effects he understood, whilst around those which he did not understand – and the universe teemed with them in the early days – were naturally woven such personifications, marvellous interpretations, and sensations of awe and fear as would be hit upon by a race having few and simple ideas and limited experience. The unknown, being likewise the unpredictable, became for our primitive forefathers a terrible and omnipotent source of boons and calamities visited upon mankind for cryptic and wholly extra-terrestrial reasons, and thus clearly belonging to spheres of existence whereof we know nothing and wherein we have no part. The phenomenon of dreaming likewise helped to build up the notion of an unreal or spiritual world; and in general, all the conditions of savage dawn-life so strongly conduced toward a feeling of the supernatural, that we need not wonder at the thoroughness with which man's very hereditary essence has become saturated with religion and superstition. That saturation must, as a matter of plain scientific fact, be regarded as virtually permanent so far as the subconscious mind and inner instincts are concerned; for though the area of the unknown has been steadily contracting for thousands of years, an infinite reservoir of mystery still engulfs most of the outer cosmos, whilst a vast residuum of powerful inherited associations clings around all the objects and processes that were once mysterious, however well they may now be explained. And more than this, there is an actual physiological fixation of the old instincts in our nervous tissue, which would make them obscurely operative even were the conscious mind to be purged of all sources of wonder.

Because we remember pain and the menace of death more vividly than pleasure, and because our feelings toward the beneficent aspects of the unknown have from the first been captured and formalised by conventional religious rituals, it has fallen to the lot of the darker and more maleficent side of cosmic mystery to figure chiefly in our popular supernatural folklore. This tendency, too, is naturally enhanced by the fact that uncertainty and danger are always closely allied; thus making any kind of an unknown world a world of peril and evil possibilities. When to this sense of fear and evil the inevitable fascination of wonder and curiosity is superadded, there is born a composite body of keen emotion and imaginative provocation whose vitality must of necessity endure as long as the human race itself. Children will always be afraid of the dark, and men with minds sensitive to hereditary impulse will always tremble at the thought of the hidden and fathomless worlds of strange life which may pulsate in the gulfs beyond the stars, or press hideously upon our own globe in unholy dimensions which only the dead and the moonstruck can glimpse.

With this foundation, no one need wonder at the existence of a literature of cosmic fear. It has always existed, and always will exist; and no better evidence of its tenacious vigour can be cited than the impulse which now and then drives writers of totally opposite leanings to try their hands at it in isolated tales, as if to discharge from their minds certain phantasmal shapes which would otherwise haunt them. Thus Dickens wrote several eerie narratives; Browning, the hideous poem 'Childe Roland'; Henry James, *The Turn of the Screw;* Dr Holmes, the subtle novel *Elsie Venner;* F. Marion Crawford, 'The Upper Berth' and a number of other examples; Mrs Charlotte Perkins Gilman, social worker, 'The Yellow Wall Paper'; whilst the humourist W. W. Jacobs produced that able melodramatic bit called 'The Monkey's Paw'.

This type of fear-literature must not be confounded with a

type externally similar but psychologically widely different; the literature of mere physical fear and the mundanely gruesome. Such writing, to be sure, has its place, as has the conventional or even whimsical or humorous ghost story where formalism or the author's knowing wink removes the true sense of the morbidly unnatural; but these things are not the literature of cosmic fear in its purest sense. The true weird tale has something more than secret murder, bloody bones, or a sheeted form clanking chains according to rule. A certain atmosphere of breathless and unexplainable dread of outer, unknown forces must be present; and there must be a hint, expressed with a seriousness and portentousness becoming its subject, of that most terrible conception of the human brain – a malign and particular suspension or defeat of those fixed laws of Nature which are our only safeguard against the assaults of chaos and the daemons of unplumbed space.

Naturally we cannot expect all weird tales to conform absolutely to any theoretical model. Creative minds are uneven, and the best of fabrics have their dull spots. Moreover, much of the choicest weird work is unconscious; appearing in memorable fragments scattered through material whose massed effect may be of a very different cast. Atmosphere is the all-important thing, for the final criterion of authenticity is not the dovetailing of a plot but the creation of a given sensation. We may say, as a general thing, that a weird story whose intent is to teach or produce a social effect, or one in which the horrors are finally explained away by natural means, is not a genuine tale of cosmic fear; but it remains a fact that such narratives often possess, in isolated sections, atmospheric touches which fulfil every condition of true supernatural horror-literature. Therefore we must judge a weird tale not by the author's intent, or by the mere mechanics of the plot; but by the emotional level which it attains at its least mundane point. If the proper sensations are excited, such a 'high spot' must be admitted on its own merits as weird literature, no matter how prosaically it is later dragged down. The one test of the really weird is simply this – whether or not there be excited in the reader a profound sense of dread, and of contact with unknown spheres and powers; a subtle attitude of awed listening, as if for the beating of black wings or the scratching of outside shapes and entities on the known universe's utmost rim. And of course, the more completely and unifiedly a story conveys this atmosphere, the better it is as a work of art in the given medium.

2. The Dawn of the Horror-Tale

As may naturally be expected of a form so closely connected with primal emotion, the horror-tale is as old as human thought and speech themselves.

Cosmic terror appears as an ingredient of the earliest folklore of all races, and is crystallised in the most archaic ballads, chronicles, and sacred writings. It was, indeed, a prominent feature of the elaborate ceremonial magic, with its rituals for the evocation of daemons and spectres, which flourished from prehistoric times, and which reached its highest development in Egypt and the Semitic nations. Fragments like the Book of Enoch and the Claviculae of Solomon well illustrate the power of the weird over the ancient Eastern mind, and upon such things were based enduring systems and traditions whose echoes extend obscurely even to the present time. Touches of this transcendental fear are seen in classic literature, and there is evidence of its still greater emphasis in a ballad literature which paralleled the classic stream but vanished for lack of a written medium. The Middle Ages, steeped in fanciful darkness, gave it an enormous impulse toward expression; and East and West alike were busy preserving and amplifying the dark heritage, both of random folklore and of academically formulated magic and cabbalism, which had descended to them. Witch, werewolf, vampire, and ghoul brooded ominously on the lips of bard and grandam, and needed but little encouragement to take the final step across the boundary that divides the chanted tale or song from the formal literary composition. In the Orient, the weird tale tended to assume a gorgeous colouring and sprightliness which almost transmuted it into sheer phantasy. In the West, where the mystical Teuton had come down from his black Boreal forests and the Celt remembered strange sacrifices in Druidic groves, it assumed a terrible intensity and convincing seriousness of atmosphere which doubled the force of its half-told, half-hinted horrors.

Much of the power of Western horror-lore was undoubtedly due to the hidden but often suspected presence of a hideous cult of nocturnal worshippers whose strange customs – descended from pre-Aryan and pre-agricultural times when a squat race of Mongoloids roved over Europe with their flocks and herds – were rooted in the most revolting fertility-rites of immemorial antiquity. This secret religion, stealthily handed down amongst peasants for thousands of years despite the outward reign of the Druidic, Graeco-Roman, and Christian faiths in the regions involved, was marked by wild 'Witches' Sabbaths' in lonely woods and atop distant hills on Walpurgis-Night and Hallowe'en, the traditional breeding-seasons of the goats and sheep and cattle; and became the source of vast riches of sorcery-legend, besides provoking extensive witchcraft-prosecutions of which the Salem affair forms the chief American example. Akin to it in essence, and perhaps connected with it in fact, was the frightful secret system of inverted theology or Satan-worship which produced such horrors as the famous 'Black Mass'; whilst operating toward the same end we may note the activities of those whose aims were somewhat more scientific or philosophical – the astrologers, cabbalists, and alchemists of the Albertus Magnus or Raymond Lully type, with whom such rude ages invariably abound. The prevalence and depth of the mediaeval horror-spirit in Europe, intensified by the dark despair which waves of pestilence brought, may be fairly gauged by the grotesque carvings slyly introduced into much of the finest later Gothic ecclesiastical work of the time; the daemoniac gargoyles of Notre Dame and Mont St Michel being among the most famous specimens. And throughout the period, it must be remembered, there existed amongst educated and uneducated alike a most unquestioning faith in every form of the supernatural; from the gentlest of Christian doctrines to the most monstrous morbidities of witchcraft and black magic. It was from no empty background that the Renaissance magicians and alchemists – Nostradamus, Trithemius, Dr John Dee, Robert Fludd, and the like – were born.

In this fertile soil were nourished types and characters of sombre myth and legend which persist in weird literature to this day, more or less disguised or altered by modern technique. Many of them were taken from the earliest oral sources, and form part of mankind's permanent heritage. The shade which appears and demands the burial of its bones, the daemon lover who comes to bear away his still living bride, the death-fiend or psychopomp riding the night-wind, the man-wolf, the sealed chamber, the deathless sorcerer – all these may be found in that curious body of mediaeval lore which the late Mr Baring-Gould so effectively assembled in book form. Wherever the mystic Northern blood was strongest, the atmosphere of the popular tales became most intense; for in the Latin races there is a touch of basic rationality which denies to even their strangest superstitions many of the overtones of glamour so characteristic of our own forest-born and ice-fostered whisperings.

Just as all fiction first found extensive embodiment in poetry, so is it in poetry that we first encounter the permanent entry of the weird into standard literature. Most of the ancient instances, curiously enough, are in prose; as the werewolf incident in Petronius, the gruesome passages in Apuleius, the brief but celebrated letter of Pliny the Younger to Sura, and the odd compilation *On Wonderful Events* by the Emperor Hadrian's Greek freedman, Phlegon. It is in Phlegon that we first find that hideous tale of the corpse-bride, 'Philinnion and Machates', later related by Proclus and in modern times forming the inspiration of Goethe's 'Bride of Corinth' and Washington Irving's 'German Student'. But by the time the old Northern myths take literary form, and in that later time when the weird appears as a steady element in the literature of the day, we find it mostly in metrical dress; as indeed we find the greater part of the strictly imaginative writing of the Middle Ages and Renaissance. The Scandinavian Eddas and Sagas thunder with cosmic horror, and shake with the stark fear of Ymir and his shapeless spawn; whilst our own Anglo-Saxon *Beowulf* and the later Continental Nibelung tales are full of eldritch weirdness. Dante is a pioneer in the classic capture of macabre atmosphere, and in Spenser's stately stanzas will be seen more than a few touches of fantastic terror in landscape, incident, and character. Prose literature gives us Malory's *Morte d'Arthur*, in which are presented many ghastly situations taken from early ballad sources – the theft of the sword and silk from the corpse in Chapel Perilous by Sir Launcelot, the ghost of Sir Gawaine, and the tomb-fiend seen by Sir Galahad – whilst other and cruder specimens were doubtless set forth in the cheap and sensational 'chapbooks' vulgarly hawked about and devoured by the ignorant. In Elizabethan drama, with its *Dr Faustus*, the witches in *Macbeth*, the ghost in *Hamlet*, and the horrible gruesomeness of Webster, we may easily discern the strong hold of the daemoniac on the public mind; a hold intensified by the very real fear of living witchcraft, whose terrors, first wildest on the Continent, begin to echo loudly in English ears as the witch-hunting crusades of James the First gain headway. To the lurking mystical prose of the ages is added a long line of treatises on witchcraft and daemonology which aid in exciting the imagination of the reading world.

Through the seventeenth and into the eighteenth century we behold a growing mass of fugitive legendry and balladry of dark-some cast; still, however, held down beneath the surface of polite and accepted literature. Chapbooks of horror and weirdness multi-plied, and we glimpse the eager interest of the people through fragments like Defoe's 'Apparition of Mrs Veal', a homely tale of a dead woman's spectral visit to a distant friend, written to advertise covertly a badly selling theological disquisition on death. The upper orders of society were now losing faith in the supernatural, and indulging in a period of classic rationalism. Then, beginning with the translations of Eastern tales in Queen Anne's reign and taking definite form toward the middle of the century, comes the revival of romantic feeling – the era of new joy in Nature, and in the radiance of past times, strange scenes, bold deeds, and incredible marvels. We feel it first in the poets, whose utterances take on new qualities of wonder, strangeness, and shuddering. And finally, after the timid appearance of a few weird scenes in the novels of the day – such as Smollett's *Adventures of Ferdinand, Count Fathom* – the released instinct precipitates itself in the birth of a new school of writing; the 'Gothic' school of horrible and fantastic prose fiction, long and short, whose literary posterity is destined to become so numerous, and in many cases so resplendent in artistic merit. It is, when one reflects upon it, genuinely remarkable that weird nar-ration as a fixed and academically recognised literary form should have been so late of final birth. The impulse and atmosphere are as old as man, but the typical weird tale of standard literature is a child of the eighteenth century.

3. The Early Gothic Novel

The shadow-haunted landscapes of 'Ossian', the chaotic visions of William Blake, the grotesque witch-dances in Burns's 'Tam O'Shanter', the sinister daemonism of Coleridge's *Christabel* and *Ancient Mariner*, the ghostly charm of James Hogg's 'Kilmeny', and the more restrained approaches to cosmic horror in *Lamia* and many of Keats's other poems, are typical British illustrations of the advent of the weird to formal literature. Our Teutonic cousins of the Continent were equally receptive to the rising flood, and Bürger's 'Wild Huntsman' and the even more famous daemon-bridegroom ballad of 'Lenore' – both imitated in English by Scott, whose respect for the supernatural was always great – are only a taste of the eerie wealth which German song had commenced to provide. Thomas Moore adapted from such sources the legend of the ghoulish statue-bride (later used by Prosper Mérimée in 'The Venus of Ille', and traceable back to great antiquity) which echoes so shiveringly in his ballad of 'The Ring'; whilst Goethe's deathless masterpiece *Faust*, crossing from mere balladry into the classic, cosmic tragedy of the ages, may be held as the ultimate height to which this German poetic impulse arose.

But it remained for a very sprightly and worldly Englishman – none other than Horace Walpole himself – to give the growing impulse definite shape and become the actual founder of the literary horror-story as a permanent form. Fond of mediaeval romance and mystery as a dilettante's diversion, and with a quaintly imitated Gothic castle as his abode at Strawberry Hill, Walpole in 1764 published *The Castle of Otranto;* a tale of the supernatural which, though thoroughly unconvincing and mediocre in itself, was destined to exert an almost unparalleled influence on the literature of the weird. First venturing it only as a translation by one 'William Marshal, Gent.' from the Italian of a mythical 'Onuphrio Muralto', the author later acknowledged his connection with the book and took pleasure in its wide and instantaneous popularity – a popularity which extended to many editions, early dramatisation, and wholesale imitation both in England and in Germany.

The story – tedious, artificial, and melodramatic – is further impaired by a brisk and prosaic style whose urbane sprightliness nowhere permits the creation of a truly weird atmosphere. It tells of Manfred, an unscrupulous and usurping prince determined to found a line, who after the mysterious sudden death of his only son Conrad on the latter's bridal morn, attempts to put away his wife Hippolita and wed the lady destined for the unfortunate youth – the lad, by the way, having been crushed by the preternatural fall of a gigantic helmet in the castle courtyard. Isabella, the widowed bride, flees from this design; and encounters in subterranean crypts beneath the castle a noble young preserver, Theodore, who seems to be a peasant yet strangely resembles the old lord Alfonso who ruled the domain before Manfred's time. Shortly thereafter supernatural phenomena assail the castle in divers ways; fragments of gigantic armour being discovered here and there, a portrait walking out of its frame, a thunderclap destroying the edifice, and a colossal armoured spectre of Alfonso rising out of the ruins to ascend through parting clouds to the bosom of St Nicholas. Theodore, having wooed Manfred's daughter Matilda and lost her through death – for she is slain by her father by mistake – is discovered to be the son of Alfonso and rightful heir to the estate. He concludes the tale by wedding Isabella and preparing to live happily ever after, whilst Manfred – whose usurpation was the cause of his son's supernatural death and his own supernatural harassings – retires to a monastery for penitence; his saddened wife seeking asylum in a neighbouring convent.

Such is the tale; flat, stilted, and altogether devoid of the true cosmic horror which makes weird literature. Yet such was the thirst of the age for those touches of strangeness and spectral antiquity which it reflects, that it was seriously received by the soundest readers and raised in spite of its intrinsic ineptness to a pedestal of lofty importance in literary history. What it did above all else was to create a novel type of scene, puppet-characters, and incidents; which, handled to better advantage by writers more naturally adapted to weird creation, stimulated the growth of an imitative Gothic school which in turn inspired the real weavers of cosmic terror – the line of actual artists beginning with Poe. This novel dramatic paraphernalia consisted first of all of the Gothic castle, with its awesome antiquity, vast distances and ramblings, deserted or ruined wings, damp corridors, unwholesome hidden catacombs, and galaxy of ghosts and appalling legends, as a nucleus of suspense and daemoniac fright. In addition, it included the tyrannical and malevolent nobleman as villain; the saintly, long-persecuted, and generally insipid heroine who undergoes the major terrors and serves as a point of view and focus for the reader's sympathies; the valorous and immaculate hero, always of high birth but often in humble disguise; the convention of high-sounding foreign names, mostly Italian, for the characters; and the infinite array of stage properties which includes strange lights, damp trap-doors, extinguished lamps, mouldy hidden manuscripts, creaking hinges, shaking arras, and the like. All this paraphernalia reappears with amusing sameness, yet sometimes with tremendous effect, throughout the history of the Gothic novel; and is by no means extinct even today, though subtler technique now forces it to assume a less naive and obvious form. An harmonious milieu for a new school had been found, and the writing world was not slow to grasp the opportunity.

German romance at once responded to the Walpole influence, and soon became a byword for the weird and ghastly. In England one of the first imitators was the celebrated Mrs Barbauld, then Miss Aikin, who in 1773 published an unfinished fragment called 'Sir Bertrand', in which the strings of genuine terror were truly touched with no clumsy hand. A nobleman on a dark and lonely moor, attracted by a tolling bell and distant light, enters a strange and ancient turreted castle whose doors open and close and whose bluish will-o'-the-wisps lead up mysterious staircases toward dead hands and animated black statues. A coffin with a dead lady, whom Sir Bertrand kisses, is finally reached; and upon the kiss the scene dissolves to give place to a splendid apartment where the lady, restored to life, holds a banquet in honour of her rescuer. Walpole admired this tale, though he accorded less respect to an even more prominent offspring of his *Otranto* – *The Old English Baron*, by Clara Reeve, published in 1777. Truly enough, this tale lacks the real vibration to the note of outer darkness and mystery which distinguishes Mrs Barbauld's fragment; and though less crude than Walpole's novel, and more artistically economical of horror in its possession of only one spectral figure, it is nevertheless too definitely insipid for greatness. Here again we have the virtuous heir to the castle disguised as a peasant and restored to his heritage through the ghost of his father; and here again we have a case of wide popularity leading to many editions, dramatisation, and ultimate translation into French. Miss Reeve wrote another weird novel, unfortunately unpublished and lost.

The Gothic novel was now settled as a literary form, and instances multiply bewilderingly as the eighteenth century draws toward its close. *The Recess*, written in 1785 by Mrs Sophia Lee, has the historic element, revolving round the twin daughters of Mary, Queen of Scots; and though devoid of the supernatural, employs the Walpole scenery and mechanism with great dexterity. Five years later, and all existing lamps are paled by the rising of a fresh luminary of wholly superior order – Mrs Ann Radcliffe (1764–1823), whose famous novels made terror and suspense a fashion, and who set new and higher standards in the domain of macabre and fear-inspiring atmosphere despite a provoking custom of destroying her own phantoms at the last through laboured mechanical explanations. To the familiar Gothic trappings of her predecessors Mrs Radcliffe added a genuine sense of the unearthly in scene and incident which closely approached genius; every touch of setting and action contributing artistically to the impression of illimitable frightfulness which she wished to convey. A few sinister details like a track of blood on castle stairs, a groan from a distant vault, or a weird song in a nocturnal forest can with her conjure up the most powerful images of imminent horror; surpassing by far the extravagant and toilsome elaborations of others. Nor are these images in themselves any the less potent because they are explained away before the end of the novel. Mrs Radcliffe's visual imagination was very strong, and appears as much in her delightful landscape touches – always in broad, glamorously pictorial outline, and never in close detail – as in her weird phantasies. Her prime weaknesses, aside from the habit of prosaic disillusionment, are a tendency toward erroneous geography and history and a fatal predilection for bestrewing her novels with insipid little poems, attributed to one or another of the characters.

Mrs Radcliffe wrote six novels; *The Castles of Athlin and Dunbayne* (1789), *A Sicilian Romance* (1790), *The Romance of the Forest* (1791), *The Mysteries of Udolpho* (1794), *The Italian* (1797), and *Gaston de Blondeville*, composed in 1802 but first published posthumously in 1826. Of these *Udolpho* is by far the most famous, and may be taken as a type of the early Gothic tale at its best. It is the chronicle of Emily, a young Frenchwoman transplanted to an ancient and portentous castle in the Apennines through the death of her parents and the marriage of her aunt to the lord of the castle – the scheming nobleman Montoni. Mysterious sounds, opened doors, frightful legends, and a nameless horror in a niche behind a black veil all operate in quick succession to unnerve the heroine and her faithful attendant Annette; but finally, after the death of her aunt, she escapes with the aid of a fellow-prisoner whom she has discovered. On the way home she stops at a chateau filled with fresh horrors – the abandoned wing where the departed chatelaine dwelt, and the bed of death with the black pall – but is finally restored to security and happiness with her lover Valancourt, after the clearing-up of a secret which seemed for a time to involve her birth in mystery. Clearly, this is only the familiar material re-worked; but it is so well re-worked that *Udolpho* will always be a classic. Mrs Radcliffe's characters are puppets, but they are less markedly so than those of her forerunners. And in atmospheric creation she stands pre-eminent among those of her time.

Of Mrs Radcliffe's countless imitators, the American novelist Charles Brockden Brown stands the closest in spirit and method. Like her, he injured his creations by natural explanations; but also like her, he had an uncanny atmospheric power which gives his horrors a frightful vitality as long as they remain unexplained. He differed from her in contemptuously discarding the external Gothic paraphernalia and properties and choosing modern American scenes for his mysteries; but this repudiation did not extend to the Gothic spirit and type of incident. Brown's novels involve some memorably frightful scenes, and excel even Mrs Radcliffe's in describing the operations of the perturbed mind. *Edgar Huntly* starts with a sleep-walker digging a grave, but is later impaired by touches of Godwinian didacticism. *Ormond* involves a member of a sinister secret brotherhood. That and *Arthur Mervyn* both describe the plague of yellow fever, which the author had witnessed in Philadelphia and New York. But Brown's most famous book is *Wieland; or, The Transformation* (1798), in which a Pennsylvania German, engulfed by a wave of religious fanaticism, hears voices and slays his wife and children as a sacrifice. His sister Clara, who tells the story, narrowly escapes. The scene, laid at the woodland estate of Mittingen on the Schuylkill's remote reaches, is drawn with extreme vividness; and the terrors of Clara, beset by spectral tones, gathering fears, and the sound of strange footsteps in the lonely house, are all shaped with truly artistic force. In the end a lame ventriloquial explanation is offered, but the atmosphere is genuine while it lasts. Carwin, the malign ventriloquist, is a typical villain of the Manfred or Montoni type.

4. The Apex of Gothic Romance

Horror in literature attains a new malignity in the work of Matthew Gregory Lewis (1775–1818), whose novel *The Monk* (1796) achieved marvellous popularity and earned him the nickname of 'Monk' Lewis. This young author, educated in Germany and saturated with a body of wild Teuton lore unknown to Mrs Radcliffe, turned to terror in forms more violent than his gentle predecessor had ever dared to think of; and produced as a result a masterpiece of active nightmare whose general Gothic cast is spiced with added stores of ghoulishness. The story is one of a Spanish monk, Ambrosio, who from a state of overproud virtue is tempted to the very nadir of evil by a fiend in the guise of the maiden Matilda; and who is finally, when awaiting death at the Inquisition's hands, induced to purchase escape at the price of his soul from the Devil, because he deems both body and soul already lost. Forthwith the mocking Fiend snatches him to a lonely place, tells him he has sold his soul in vain since both pardon and a chance for salvation were approaching at the moment of his hideous bargain, and completes the sardonic betrayal by rebuking him for his unnatural crimes, and casting his body down a precipice whilst his soul is borne off for ever to perdition. The novel contains some appalling descriptions such as the incantation in the vaults beneath the convent cemetery, the burning of the convent, and the final end of the wretched abbot. In the sub-plot where the Marquis de las Cisternas meets the spectre of his erring ancestress, The Bleeding Nun, there are many enormously potent strokes; notably the visit of the animated corpse to the Marquis's bedside, and the cabbalistic ritual whereby the Wandering Jew helps him to fathom and banish his dead tormentor. Nevertheless *The Monk* drags sadly when read as a whole. It is too long and too diffuse, and much of its potency is marred by flippancy and by an awkwardly excessive reaction against those canons of decorum which Lewis at first despised as prudish. One great thing may be said of the author; that he never ruined his ghostly visions with a natural explanation. He succeeded in breaking up the Radcliffian tradition and expanding the field of the Gothic novel. Lewis wrote much more than *The Monk*. His drama, *The Castle Spectre*, was produced in 1798, and he later found time to pen other fictions in ballad form – *Tales of Terror* (1799), *Tales of Wonder* (1801), and a succession of translations from the German.

Gothic romances, both English and German, now appeared in multitudinous and mediocre profusion. Most of them were merely ridiculous in the light of mature taste, and Miss Austen's famous satire *Northanger Abbey* was by no means an unmerited rebuke to a school which had sunk far toward absurdity. This particular school was petering out, but before its final subordination there arose its last and greatest figure in the person of Charles Robert Maturin (1782–1824), an obscure and eccentric Irish clergyman. Out of an ample body of miscellaneous writing which includes one confused Radcliffian imitation called *Fatal Revenge; or, The Family of Montorio* (1807), Maturin at length evolved the vivid horror-masterpiece of *Melmoth the Wanderer* (1820), in which the Gothic tale climbed to altitudes of sheer spiritual fright which it had never known before.

Melmoth is the tale of an Irish gentleman who, in the seventeenth century, obtained a preternaturally extended life from the Devil at the price of his soul. If he can persuade another to take the bargain off his hands, and assume his existing state, he can be saved; but this he can never manage to effect, no matter how assiduously he haunts those whom despair has made reckless and frantic. The framework of the story is very clumsy; involving tedious length, digressive episodes, narratives within narratives, and laboured dovetailing and coincidences; but at various points in the endless rambling there is felt a pulse of power undiscoverable in any previous work of this kind – a kinship to the essential truth of human nature, an understanding of the profoundest sources of actual cosmic fear, and a white heat of sympathetic passion on the writer's part which makes the book a true document of aesthetic self-expression rather than a mere clever compound of artifice. No unbiased reader can doubt that with *Melmoth* an enormous stride in the evolution of the horror-tale is represented. Fear is taken out of the realm of the conventional and exalted into a hideous cloud over mankind's very destiny. Maturin's shudders, the work of one capable of shuddering himself, are of the sort that convince. Mrs Radcliffe and Lewis are fair game for the parodist, but it would be difficult to find a false note in the feverishly intensified action and high atmospheric tension of the Irishman whose less sophisticated emotions and strain of Celtic mysticism gave him the finest possible natural equipment for his task. Without a doubt Maturin is a man of authentic genius, and he was so recognised by Balzac, who grouped Melmoth with Molière's Don Juan, Goethe's Faust, and Byron's Manfred as the supreme allegorical figures of modern European literature, and wrote a whimsical piece called 'Melmoth Reconciled', in which the Wanderer succeeds in passing his infernal bargain on to a Parisian bank defaulter, who in turn hands it along a chain of victims until a revelling gambler dies with it in his possession, and by his damnation ends the curse. Scott, Rossetti, Thackeray, and Baudelaire are the other titans who gave Maturin their unqualified admiration, and there is much significance in the fact that Oscar Wilde, after his disgrace and exile, chose for his last days in Paris the assumed name of 'Sebastian Melmoth'.

Melmoth contains scenes which even now have not lost their power to evoke dread. It begins with a deathbed – an old miser is dying of sheer fright because of something he has seen, coupled with a manuscript he has read and a family portrait which hangs in an obscure closet of his centuried home in County Wicklow. He sends to Trinity College, Dublin, for his nephew John; and the latter upon arriving notes many uncanny things. The eyes of the portrait in the closet glow horribly, and twice a figure strangely resembling the portrait appears momentarily at the door. Dread hangs over that house of the Melmoths, one of whose ancestors, 'J. Melmoth, 1646', the portrait represents. The dying miser declares that this man – at a date slightly before 1800 – is alive. Finally the miser dies, and the nephew is told in the will to destroy both the portrait and a manuscript to be found in a certain drawer. Reading the manuscript, which was written late in the seventeenth century by an Englishman named Stanton, young John learns of a terrible incident in Spain in 1677, when the writer met a horrible fellow-countryman and was told of how he had stared to death a priest who tried to denounce him as one filled with fearsome evil. Later, after meeting the man again in London, Stanton is cast into a madhouse and visited by the stranger, whose approach is heralded by spectral music and whose eyes have a more than mortal glare. Melmoth the Wanderer – for such is the malign visitor – offers the captive freedom if he will take over his bargain with the Devil; but like all others whom Melmoth has approached, Stanton is proof against temptation. Melmoth's description of the horrors of a life in a madhouse, used to tempt Stanton, is one of the most potent passages of the book. Stanton is at length liberated, and spends the rest of his life tracking down Melmoth, whose family and ancestral abode he discovers. With the family he leaves the manuscript, which by young John's time is sadly ruinous and fragmentary. John destroys both portrait and manuscript, but in sleep is visited by his horrible ancestor, who leaves a black and blue mark on his wrist.

Young John soon afterward receives as a visitor a shipwrecked Spaniard, Alonzo de Monçada, who has escaped from compulsory monasticism and from the perils of the Inquisition. He has suffered horribly – and the descriptions of his experiences under torment and in the vaults through which he once essays escape are classic – but had the strength to resist Melmoth the Wanderer when approached at his darkest hour in prison. At the house of a Jew who sheltered him after his escape he discovers a wealth of manuscript relating other exploits of Melmoth including his wooing of an Indian island maiden, Immalee, who later comes to her birthright in Spain and is known as Donna Isidora; and of his horrible marriage to her by the corpse of a dead anchorite at midnight in the ruined chapel of a shunned and abhorred monastery. Monçada's narrative to young John takes up the bulk of Maturin's four-volume book; this disproportion being considered one of the chief technical faults of the composition.

At last the colloquies of John and Monçada are interrupted by the entrance of Melmoth the Wanderer himself, his piercing eyes now fading, and decrepitude swiftly overtaking him. The term of his bargain has approached its end, and he has come home after a century and a half to meet his fate. Warning all others from the room, no matter what sounds they may hear in the night, he awaits the end alone. Young John and Monçada hear frightful ululations, but do not intrude till silence comes toward morning. They then find the room empty. Clayey footprints lead out a rear door to a cliff overlooking the sea, and near the edge of the precipice is a track indicating the forcible dragging of some heavy body. The Wanderer's scarf is found on a crag some distance below the brink, but nothing further is ever seen or heard of him.

Such is the story, and none can fail to notice the difference between this modulated, suggestive, and artistically moulded horror and – to use the words of Professor George Saintsbury – 'the artful but rather jejune rationalism of Mrs Radcliffe, and the too often puerile extravagance, the bad taste, and the sometimes slipshod style of Lewis.' Maturin's style in itself deserves particular praise, for its forcible directness and vitality lift it altogether above the pompous artificialities of which his predecessors are guilty. Professor Edith Birkhead, in her history of the Gothic novel, justly observes that with all his faults Maturin was the greatest as well as the last of the Goths. *Melmoth* was widely read and eventually dramatised, but its late date in the evolution of the Gothic tale deprived it of the tumultuous popularity of *Udolpho* and *The Monk*.

5. The Aftermath of Gothic Fiction

Meanwhile other hands had not been idle, so that above the dreary plethora of trash like Marquis von Grosse's *Horrid Mysteries* (1796), Mrs Roche's *Children of the Abbey* (1796), Miss Dacre's *Zofloya; or, The Moor* (1806), and the poet Shelley's schoolboy effusions *Zastrozzi* (1810) and *St Irvyne* (1811) (both imitations of *Zofloya*) there arose many memorable weird works both in English and German. Classic in merit, and markedly different from its fellows because of its foundation in the Oriental tale rather than the Walpolesque Gothic novel, is the celebrated *History of the Caliph Vathek* by the wealthy dilettante William Beckford, first written in the French language but published in an English translation before the appearance of the original. Eastern tales, introduced to European literature early in the eighteenth century through Galland's French translation of the inexhaustibly opulent *Arabian Nights*, had become a reigning fashion; being used both for allegory and for amusement. The sly humour which only the Eastern mind knows how to mix with weirdness had captivated a sophisticated generation, till Baghdad and Damascus names became as freely strown through popular literature as dashing Italian and Spanish ones were soon to be.

Beckford, well read in Eastern romance, caught the atmosphere with unusual receptivity; and in his fantastic volume reflected very potently the haughty luxury, sly disillusion, bland cruelty, urbane treachery, and shadowy spectral horror of the Saracen spirit. His seasoning of the ridiculous seldom mars the force of his sinister theme, and the tale marches onward with a phantasmagoric pomp in which the laughter is that of skeletons feasting under Arabesque domes. *Vathek* is a tale of the grandson of the Caliph Haroun, who, tormented by that ambition for super-terrestrial power, pleasure, and learning which animates the average Gothic villain or Byronic hero (essentially cognate types), is lured by an evil genius to seek the subterranean throne of the mighty and fabulous pre-Adamite sultans in the fiery halls of Eblis, the Mahometan Devil. The descriptions of Vathek's palaces and diversions, of his scheming sorceress-mother Carathis and her witch-tower with the fifty one-eyed negresses, of his pilgrimage to the haunted ruins of Istakhar (Persepolis) and of the impish bride Nouronihar whom he treach-erously acquired on the way, of Istakhar's primordial towers and terraces in the burning moonlight of the waste, and of the terrible Cyclopean halls of Eblis, where, lured by glittering promises, each victim is compelled to wander in anguish for ever, his right hand upon his blazingly ignited and eternally burning heart, are tri-umphs of weird colouring which raise the book to a permanent place in English letters. No less notable are the three *Episodes of Vathek*, intended for insertion in the tale as narratives of Vathek's fellow-victims in Eblis' infernal halls, which remained unpublished throughout the author's lifetime and were discovered as recently as 1909 by the scholar Lewis Melville whilst collecting material for his *Life and Letters of William Beckford*. Beckford, however, lacks the essential mysticism which marks the acutest form of the weird; so that his tales have a certain knowing Latin hardness and clearness preclusive of sheer panic fright.

But Beckford remained alone in his devotion to the Orient. Other writers, closer to the Gothic tradition and to European life in general, were content to follow more faithfully in the lead of Walpole. Among the countless producers of terror-literature in these times may be mentioned the Utopian economic theorist William Godwin, who followed his famous but non-supernatural *Caleb Williams* (1794) with the intendedly weird *St Leon* (1799), in which the theme of the elixir of life, as developed by the imaginary secret order of 'Rosicrucians', is handled with ingeniousness if not with atmospheric convincingness. This element of Rosicrucianism, fostered by a wave of popular magical interest exemplified in the vogue of the charlatan Cagliostro and the publication of Francis Barrett's *The Magus* (1801), a curious and compendious treatise on occult principles and ceremonies, of which a reprint was made as lately as 1896, figures in Bulwer-Lytton and in many late Gothic novels, especially that remote and enfeebled posterity which straggled far down into the nineteenth century and was represented by George W.M. Reynolds' *Faust and the Demon* and *Wagner, the Wehr-wolf*. *Caleb Williams*, though non-supernatural, has many authentic touches of terror. It is the tale of a servant persecuted by a master whom he has found guilty of murder, and displays an invention and skill which have kept it alive in a fashion to this day. It was drama-tised as *The Iron Chest*, and in that form was almost equally cele-brated. Godwin, however, was too much the conscious teacher and prosaic man of thought to create a genuine weird masterpiece.

His daughter, the wife of Shelley, was much more successful; and her inimitable *Frankenstein; or, The Modern Prometheus* (1818) is one of the horror-classics of all time. Composed in competition with her husband, Lord Byron, and Dr John William Polidori in an effort to prove supremacy in horror-making, Mrs Shelley's *Frankenstein* was the only one of the rival narratives to be brought to an elaborate completion; and criticism has failed to prove that the best parts are due to Shelley rather than to her. The novel, somewhat tinged but scarcely marred by moral didacticism, tells of the artificial human being moulded from charnel fragments by Victor Frankenstein, a young Swiss medical student. Created by its designer 'in the mad pride of intellectuality', the monster possesses full intelligence but owns a hideously loathsome form. It is rejected by mankind, becomes embittered, and at length begins the successive murder of all whom young Frankenstein loves best, friends and family. It demands that Frankenstein create a wife for it; and when the student finally refuses in horror lest the world be populated with such monsters, it departs with a hideous threat 'to be with him on his wedding night'. Upon that night the bride is strangled, and from that time on Frankenstein hunts down the monster, even into the wastes of the Arctic. In the end, whilst seeking shelter on the ship of the man who tells the story, Frankenstein himself is killed by the shocking object of his search and creation of his presumptuous pride. Some of the scenes in *Frankenstein* are unforgettable, as when the newly animated monster enters its creator's room, parts the curtains of his bed, and gazes at him in the yellow moonlight with watery eyes – 'if eyes they may be called'. Mrs Shelley wrote other novels, including the fairly notable *Last Man*, but never duplicated the success of her first effort. It has the true touch of cosmic fear, no matter how much the movement may lag in places. Dr Polidori developed his competing idea as a long short story, 'The Vampyre'; in which we behold a suave villain of the true Gothic or Byronic type, and encounter some excellent passages of stark fright, including a terrible nocturnal experience in a shunned Grecian wood.

In this same period Sir Walter Scott frequently concerned himself with the weird, weaving it into many of his novels and poems, and sometimes producing such independent bits of narration as 'The Tapestried Chamber' or 'Wandering Willie's Tale' in *Redgauntlet*, in the latter of which the force of the spectral and the diabolic is enhanced by a grotesque homeliness of speech and atmosphere. In 1830 Scott published his *Letters on Demonology and Witchcraft*, which still forms one of our best compendia of European witch-lore. Washington Irving is another famous figure not unconnected with the weird; for though most of his ghosts are too whimsical and humorous to form genuinely spectral literature, a distinct inclination in this direction is to be noted in many of his productions. 'The German Student' in *Tales of a Traveller* (1824) is a slyly concise and effective presentation of the old legend of the dead bride, whilst woven into the comic tissue of 'The Money-Diggers' in the same volume is more than one hint of piratical apparitions in the realms which Captain Kidd once roamed. Thomas Moore also joined the ranks of the macabre artists in the poem *Alciphron*, which he later elaborated into the prose novel of *The Epicurean* (1827). Though merely relating the adventures of a young Athenian duped by the artifice of cunning Egyptian priests, Moore manages to infuse much genuine horror into his account of subterranean frights and wonders beneath the primordial temples of Memphis. De Quincey more than once revels in grotesque and arabesque terrors, though with a desultoriness and learned pomp which deny him the rank of specialist.

This era likewise saw the rise of William Harrison Ainsworth, whose romantic novels teem with the eerie and the gruesome. Capt. Marryat, besides writing such short tales as 'The Werewolf', made a memorable contribution in *The Phantom Ship* (1839), founded on the legend of the Flying Dutchman, whose spectral and accursed vessel sails for ever near the Cape of Good Hope. Dickens now rises with occasional weird bits like 'The Signalman', a tale of ghostly warning conforming to a very common pattern and touched with a verisimilitude which allies it as much with the coming psychological school as with the dying Gothic school. At this time a wave of interest in spiritualistic charlatanry, mediumism, Hindoo theosophy, and such matters, much like that of the present day, was flourishing; so that the number of weird tales with a 'psychic' or pseudo-scientific basis became very considerable. For a number of these the prolific and popular Lord Edward Bulwer-Lytton was responsible; and despite the large doses of turgid rhetoric and empty romanticism in his products, his success in the weaving of a certain kind of bizarre charm cannot be denied.

'The House and the Brain', which hints of Rosicrucianism and at a malign and deathless figure perhaps suggested by Louis XV's mysterious courtier St Germain, yet survives as one of the best short haunted-house tales ever written. The novel *Zanoni* (1842) contains similar elements more elaborately handled, and introduces a vast unknown sphere of being pressing on our own world and guarded by a horrible 'Dweller of the Threshold' who haunts those who try to enter and fail. Here we have a benign brotherhood kept alive from age to age till finally reduced to a single member, and as a hero an ancient Chaldaean sorcerer surviving in the pristine bloom of youth to perish on the guillotine of the French Revolution. Though full of the conventional spirit of romance, marred by a ponderous network of symbolic and didactic meanings, and left unconvincing through lack of perfect atmospheric realisation of the situations hinging on the spectral world, *Zanoni* is really an excellent performance as a romantic novel; and can be read with genuine interest today by the not too sophisticated reader. It is amusing to note that in describing an attempted initiation into the ancient brotherhood the author cannot escape using the stock Gothic castle of Walpolian lineage.

In *A Strange Story* (1862) Bulwer-Lytton shews a marked

improvement in the creation of weird images and moods. The novel, despite enormous length, a highly artificial plot bolstered up by opportune coincidences, and an atmosphere of homiletic pseudo-science designed to please the matter-of-fact and pur- poseful Victorian reader, is exceedingly effective as a narrative; evoking instantaneous and unflagging interest, and furnishing many potent – if somewhat melodramatic – tableaux and climaxes. Again we have the mysterious user of life's elixir in the person of the soulless magician Margrave, whose dark exploits stand out with dramatic vividness against the modern background of a quiet English town and of the Australian bush; and again we have shadowy intimations of a vast spectral world of the unknown in the very air about us – this time handled with much greater power and vitality than in *Zanoni*. One of the two great incantation passages, where the hero is driven by a luminous evil spirit to rise at night in his sleep, take a strange Egyptian wand, and evoke nameless pres- ences in the haunted and mausoleum-facing pavilion of a famous Renaissance alchemist, truly stands among the major terror scenes of literature. Just enough is suggested, and just little enough is told. Unknown words are twice dictated to the sleep-walker, and as he repeats them the ground trembles, and all the dogs of the coun- tryside begin to bay at half-seen amorphous shadows that stalk athwart the moonlight. When a third set of unknown words is prompted, the sleep-walker's spirit suddenly rebels at uttering them, as if the soul could recognise ultimate abysmal horrors con- cealed from the mind; and at last an apparition of an absent sweet- heart and good angel breaks the malign spell. This fragment well illustrates how far Lord Lytton was capable of progressing beyond his usual pomp and stock romance toward that crystalline essence of artistic fear which belongs to the domain of poetry. In describing certain details of incantations, Lytton was greatly indebted to his amusingly serious occult studies, in the course of which he came in touch with that odd French scholar and cabbalist Alphonse-Louis Constant ('Eliphas Lévi'), who claimed to possess the secrets of ancient magic, and to have evoked the spectre of the old Grecian wizard Apollonius of Tyana, who lived in Nero's time.

The romantic, semi-Gothic, quasi-moral tradition here represented was carried far down the nineteenth century by such authors as Joseph Sheridan LeFanu, Thomas Preskett Prest with his famous *Varney, the Vampyre* (1847), Wilkie Collins, the late Sir H. Rider Haggard (whose *She* is really remarkably good), Sir A. Conan Doyle, H.G. Wells, and Robert Louis Stevenson – the latter of whom, despite an atrocious tendency toward jaunty mannerisms, created permanent classics in 'Markheim', 'The Body-Snatcher', and *Dr Jekyll and Mr Hyde*. Indeed, we may say that this school still survives; for to it clearly belong such of our contemporary horror-tales as specialise in events rather than atmospheric details, address the intellect rather than the impressionistic imagination, cultivate a luminous glamour rather than a malign tensity or psychological verisimilitude, and take a definite stand in sympathy with mankind and its welfare. It has its undeniable strength, and because of its 'human element' commands a wider audience than does the sheer artistic nightmare. If not quite so potent as the latter, it is because a diluted product can never achieve the intensity of a concentrated essence.

Quite alone both as a novel and as a piece of terror-literature stands the famous *Wuthering Heights* (1847) by Emily Brontë, with its mad vista of bleak, windswept Yorkshire moors and the violent, distorted lives they foster. Though primarily a tale of life, and of human passions in agony and conflict, its epically cosmic setting affords room for horror of the most spiritual sort. Heathcliff, the modified Byronic villain-hero, is a strange dark waif found in the streets as a small child and speaking only a strange gibberish till adopted by the family he ultimately ruins. That he is in truth a diabolic spirit rather than a human being is more than once suggested, and the unreal is further approached in the experience of the visitor who encounters a plaintive child-ghost at a bough-brushed upper window. Between Heathcliff and Catherine Earnshaw is a tie deeper and more terrible than human love. After her death he twice disturbs her grave, and is haunted by an impalpable presence which can be nothing less than her spirit. The spirit enters his life more and more, and at last he becomes confident of some imminent mystical reunion. He says he feels a strange change approaching, and ceases to take nourishment. At night he either walks abroad or opens the casement by his bed. When he dies the casement is still swinging open to the pouring rain, and a queer smile pervades the stiffened face. They bury him in a grave beside the mound he has haunted for eighteen years, and small shepherd boys say that he yet walks with his Catherine in the churchyard and on the moor when it rains. Their faces, too, are sometimes seen on rainy nights behind that upper casement at Wuthering Heights. Miss Brontë's eerie terror is no mere Gothic echo, but a tense expression of man's shuddering reaction to the unknown. In this respect, *Wuthering Heights* becomes the symbol of a literary transition, and marks the growth of a new and sounder school.

6. Spectral Literature on the Continent

On the Continent literary horror fared well. The celebrated short tales and novels of Ernst Theodor Wilhelm Hoffmann (1776–1822) are a byword for mellowness of background and maturity of form, though they incline to levity and extravagance, and lack the exalted moments of stark, breathless terror which a less sophisticated writer might have achieved. Generally they convey the grotesque rather than the terrible. Most artistic of all the Continental weird tales is the German classic *Undine* (1811), by Friedrich Heinrich Karl, Baron de la Motte Fouqué. In this story of a water-spirit who married a mortal and gained a human soul there is a delicate fineness of craftsmanship which makes it notable in any department of literature, and an easy naturalness which places it close to the genuine folk-myth. It is, in fact, derived from a tale told by the Renaissance physician and alchemist Paracelsus in his *Treatise on Elemental Sprites*.

Undine, daughter of a powerful water-prince, was exchanged by her father as a small child for a fisherman's daughter, in order that she might acquire a soul by wedding a human being. Meeting the noble youth Huldbrand at the cottage of her foster-father by the sea at the edge of a haunted wood, she soon marries him, and accompanies him to his ancestral castle of Ringstetten. Huldbrand, however, eventually wearies of his wife's supernatural affiliations, and especially of the appearances of her uncle, the malicious woodland waterfall-spirit Kühleborn; a weariness increased by his growing affection for Bertalda, who turns out to be the fisherman's child for whom Undine was exchanged. At length, on a voyage down the Danube, he is provoked by some innocent act of his devoted wife to utter the angry words which consign her back to her supernatural element; from which she can, by the laws of her species, return only once – to kill him, whether she will or no, if ever he prove unfaithful to her memory. Later, when Huldbrand is about to be married to Bertalda, Undine returns for her sad duty, and bears his life away in tears. When he is buried among his fathers in the village churchyard a veiled, snow-white female figure appears among the mourners, but after the prayer is seen no more. In her place is seen a little silver spring, which murmurs its way almost completely around the new grave, and empties into a neighbouring lake. The villagers shew it to this day, and say that Undine and her Huldbrand are thus united in death. Many passages and atmospheric touches in this tale reveal Fouqué as an accomplished artist in the field of the macabre; especially the descriptions of the haunted wood with its gigantic snow-white man and various unnamed terrors, which occur early in the narrative.

Not so well known as *Undine*, but remarkable for its convincing realism and freedom from Gothic stock devices, is the *Amber Witch* of Wilhelm Meinhold, another product of the German fantastic genius of the earlier nineteenth century. This tale, which is laid in the time of the Thirty Years' War, purports to be a clergyman's manuscript found in an old church at Coserow, and centres round the writer's daughter, Maria Schweidler, who is wrongly accused of witchcraft. She has found a deposit of amber which she keeps secret for various reasons, and the unexplained wealth obtained from this lends colour to the accusation; an accusation instigated by the malice of the wolf-hunting nobleman Wittich Appelmann, who has vainly pursued her with ignoble designs. The deeds of a real witch, who afterward comes to a horrible supernatural end in prison, are glibly imputed to the hapless Maria; and after a typical witchcraft trial with forced confessions under torture she is about to be burned at the stake when saved just in time by her lover, a noble youth from a neighbouring district. Meinhold's great strength is in his air of casual and realistic verisimilitude, which intensifies our suspense and sense of the unseen by half persuading us that the menacing events must somehow be either the truth or very close to the truth. Indeed, so thorough is this realism that a popular magazine once published the main points of *The Amber Witch* as an actual occurrence of the seventeenth century!

In the present generation German horror-fiction is most notably represented by Hanns Heinz Ewers, who brings to bear on his dark conceptions an effective knowledge of modern psychology. Novels like *The Sorcerer's Apprentice* and *Alraune*, and short stories like 'The Spider', contain distinctive qualities which raise them to a classic level.

But France as well as Germany has been active in the realm of weirdness. Victor Hugo, in such tales as *Hans of Iceland*, and Balzac, in *The Wild Ass's Skin*, *Séraphîta*, and *Louis Lambert*, both employ supernaturalism to a greater or less extent; though generally only as a means to some more human end, and without the sincere and daemonic intensity which characterises the born artist in shadows. It is in Théophile Gautier that we first seem to find an authentic French sense of the unreal world, and here there appears a spectral mastery which, though not continuously used, is recognisable at once as something alike genuine and profound. Short tales like 'Avatar', 'The Foot of the Mummy', and 'Clarimonde' display glimpses of forbidden visits that allure, tantalise, and sometimes horrify; whilst the Egyptian visions evoked in 'One of Cleopatra's Nights' are of the keenest and most expressive potency. Gautier captured the inmost soul of aeon-weighted Egypt, with its cryptic life and Cyclopean architecture, and uttered once and for all the eternal horror of its nether world of catacombs, where to the end of time millions of stiff, spiced corpses will stare up in the blackness with glassy eyes, awaiting some awesome and unrelatable summons. Gustave Flaubert ably continued the tradition of Gautier in orgies of poetic phantasy like *The Temptation of St Anthony*, and but for a strong realistic bias might have been an arch-weaver of tapestried terrors. Later on we see the stream divide, producing strange poets and fantaisistes of the Symbolist and Decadent schools whose dark interests really centre more in abnormalities of human thought and instinct than in the actual supernatural, and subtle story-tellers whose thrills are quite directly derived from the night-black wells of cosmic unreality. Of the former class of 'artists in sin' the illustrious poet Baudelaire, influenced vastly by Poe, is the supreme type; whilst the psychological novelist Joris-Karl Huysmans, a true child of the eighteen-nineties, is at once the summation and finale. The latter and purely narrative class is continued by Prosper Mérimée, whose 'Venus of Ille' presents in terse and convincing prose the same ancient statue-bride theme which Thomas Moore cast in ballad form in 'The Ring'.

The horror-tales of the powerful and cynical Guy de Maupassant, written as his final madness gradually overtook him, present individualities of their own; being rather the morbid out-pourings of a realistic mind in a pathological state than the healthy imaginative products of a vision naturally disposed toward phantasy and sensitive to the normal illusions of the unseen. Nevertheless they are of the keenest interest and poignancy; suggesting with marvellous force the imminence of nameless terrors, and the relent-less dogging of an ill-starred individual by hideous and menacing representatives of the outer blackness. Of these stories 'The Horla' is generally regarded as the masterpiece. Relating the advent to France of an invisible being who lives on water and milk, sways the minds of others, and seems to be the vanguard of a horde of extra-terrestrial organisms arrived on earth to subjugate and overwhelm mankind, this tense narrative is perhaps without a peer in its par-ticular department; notwithstanding its indebtedness to a tale by the American Fitz-James O'Brien for details in describing the actual presence of the unseen monster. Other potently dark creations of de Maupassant are 'Who Knows?', 'The Spectre', 'He?', 'The Diary of a Madman', 'The White Wolf', 'On the River', and the grisly verses entitled 'Horror'.

The collaborators Erckmann-Chatrian enriched French lit-erature with many spectral fancies like *The Man-Wolf*, in which a transmitted curse works toward its end in a traditional Gothic-castle setting. Their power of creating a shuddering midnight atmosphere was tremendous despite a tendency toward natural explanations and scientific wonders; and few short tales contain greater horror than 'The Invisible Eye', where a malignant old hag weaves nocturnal hypnotic spells which induce the successive occupants of a certain inn chamber to hang themselves on a cross-beam. 'The Owl's Ear' and 'The Waters of Death' are full of engulfing darkness and mystery, the latter embodying the familiar overgrown-spider theme so frequently employed by weird fic-tionists. Villiers de l'Isle-Adam likewise followed the macabre school; his 'Torture by Hope', the tale of a stake-condemned pris-oner permitted to escape in order to feel the pangs of recapture, being held by some to constitute the most harrowing short story in literature. This type, however, is less a part of the weird tradition than a class peculiar to itself – the so-called *conte cruel*, in which the wrenching of the emotions is accomplished through dramatic tantalisations, frustrations, and gruesome physical horrors. Almost wholly devoted to this form is the living writer Maurice Level, whose very brief episodes have lent themselves so readily to theatrical adaptation in the 'thrillers' of the Grand Guignol. As a matter of fact, the French genius is more naturally suited to this dark realism than to the suggestion of the unseen; since the latter process requires, for its best and most sympathetic development on a large scale, the inherent mysticism of the Northern mind.

A very flourishing, though till recently quite hidden, branch of weird literature is that of the Jews, kept alive and nourished in obscurity by the sombre heritage of early Eastern magic, apocalyptic literature, and cabbalism. The Semitic mind, like the Celtic and Teutonic, seems to possess marked mystical inclinations; and the wealth of underground horror-lore surviving in ghettoes and synagogues must be much more considerable than is generally imagined. Cabbalism itself, so prominent during the Middle Ages, is a system of philosophy explaining the universe as emanations of the Deity, and involving the existence of strange spiritual realms and beings apart from the visible world, of which dark glimpses may be obtained through certain secret incantations. Its ritual is bound up with mystical interpretations of the Old Testament, and attributes an esoteric significance to each letter of the Hebrew alphabet – a circumstance which has imparted to Hebrew letters a sort of spectral glamour and potency in the popular literature of magic. Jewish folklore has preserved much of the terror and mystery of the past, and when more thoroughly studied is likely to exert considerable influence on weird fiction. The best examples of its literary use so far are the German novel *The Golem*, by Gustav Meyrink, and the drama *The Dybbuk*, by the Jewish writer using the pseudonym 'Ansky'. The former, with its haunting shadowy suggestions of marvels and horrors just beyond reach, is laid in Prague, and describes with singular mastery that city's ancient ghetto with its spectral, peaked gables. The name is derived from a fabulous artificial giant supposed to be made and animated by mediaeval rabbis according to a certain cryptic formula. *The Dybbuk*, translated and produced in America in 1925, and more recently produced as an opera, describes with singular power the possession of a living body by the evil soul of a dead man. Both golems and dybbuks are fixed types, and serve as frequent ingredients of later Jewish tradition.

7. Edgar Allan Poe

In the eighteen-thirties occurred a literary dawn directly affecting not only the history of the weird tale, but that of short fiction as a whole; and indirectly moulding the trends and fortunes of a great European aesthetic school. It is our good fortune as Americans to be able to claim that dawn as our own, for it came in the person of our illustrious and unfortunate fellow-countryman Edgar Allan Poe. Poe's fame has been subject to curious undulations, and it is now a fashion amongst the 'advanced intelligentsia' to minimise his importance both as an artist and as an influence; but it would be hard for any mature and reflective critic to deny the tremendous value of his work and the pervasive potency of his mind as an opener of artistic vistas. True, his type of outlook may have been anticipated; but it was he who first realised its possibilities and gave it supreme form and systematic expression. True also, that subsequent writers may have produced greater single tales than his; but again we must comprehend that it was only he who taught them by example and precept the art which they, having the way cleared for them and given an explicit guide, were perhaps able to carry to greater lengths. Whatever his limitations, Poe did that which no one else ever did or could have done; and to him we owe the modern horror-story in its final and perfected state.

Before Poe the bulk of weird writers had worked largely in the dark; without an understanding of the psychological basis of the horror appeal, and hampered by more or less of conformity to certain empty literary conventions such as the happy ending, virtue rewarded, and in general a hollow moral didacticism, acceptance of popular standards and values, and striving of the author to obtrude his own emotions into the story and take sides with the partisans of the majority's artificial ideas. Poe, on the other hand, perceived the essential impersonality of the real artist; and knew that the function of creative fiction is merely to express and interpret events and sensations as they are, regardless of how they tend or what they prove – good or evil, attractive or repulsive, stimulating or depressing – with the author always acting as a vivid and detached chronicler rather than as a teacher, sympathiser, or vendor of opinion. He saw clearly that all phases of life and thought are equally eligible as subject-matter for the artist, and being inclined by temperament to strangeness and gloom, decided to be the interpreter of those powerful feelings, and frequent happenings which attend pain rather than pleasure, decay rather than growth, terror rather than tranquillity, and which are fundamentally either adverse or indifferent to the tastes and traditional outward sentiments of mankind, and to the health, sanity, and normal expansive welfare of the species.

Poe's spectres thus acquired a convincing malignity possessed by none of their predecessors, and established a new standard of realism in the annals of literary horror. The impersonal and artistic intent, moreover, was aided by a scientific attitude not often found before; whereby Poe studied the human mind rather than the usages of Gothic fiction, and worked with an analytical knowledge of terror's true sources which doubled the force of his narratives and emancipated him from all the absurdities inherent in merely conventional shudder-coining. This example having been set, later authors were naturally forced to conform to it in order to compete at all; so that in this way a definite change began to affect the main stream of macabre writing. Poe, too, set a fashion in consummate craftsmanship; and although today some of his own work seems slightly melodramatic and unsophisticated, we can constantly trace his influence in such things as the maintenance of a single mood and achievement of a single impression in a tale, and the rigorous paring down of incidents to such as have a direct bearing on the plot and will figure prominently in the climax. Truly may it be said that Poe invented the short story in its present form. His elevation of disease, perversity, and decay to the level of artistically expressible themes was likewise infinitely far-reaching in effect; for avidly seized, sponsored, and intensified by his eminent French admirer Charles Pierre Baudelaire, it became the nucleus of the principal aesthetic movements in France, thus making Poe in a sense the father of the Decadents and the Symbolists.

Poet and critic by nature and supreme attainment, logician and philosopher by taste and mannerism, Poe was by no means immune from defects and affectations. His pretence to profound and obscure scholarship, his blundering ventures in stilted and laboured pseudo-humour, and his often vitriolic outbursts of critical preju-dice must all be recognised and forgiven. Beyond and above them, and dwarfing them to insignificance, was a master's vision of the terror that stalks about and within us, and the worm that writhes and slavers in the hideously close abyss. Penetrating to every festering horror in the gaily painted mockery called existence, and in the solemn masquerade called human thought and feelings that vision had power to project itself in blackly magical crystallisations and transmutations; till there bloomed in the sterile America of the 'thirties and 'forties such a moon-nourished garden of gorgeous poison fungi as not even the nether slope of Saturn might boast. Verses and tales alike sustain the burthen of cosmic panic. The raven whose noisome beak pierces the heart, the ghouls that toll iron bells in pestilential steeples, the vault of Ulalume in the black October night, the shocking spires and domes under the sea, the 'wild, weird clime that lieth, sublime, out of Space – out of Time' – all these things and more leer at us amidst maniacal rattlings in the seething nightmare of the poetry. And in the prose there yawn open for us the very jaws of the pit – inconceivable abnormalities slyly hinted into a horrible half-knowledge by words whose innocence we scarcely doubt till the cracked tension of the speaker's hollow voice bids us fear their nameless implications; daemoniac patterns and presences slumbering noxiously till waked for one phobic instant into a shrieking revelation that cackles itself to sudden madness or explodes in memorable and cataclysmic echoes. A Witches' Sabbath of horror flinging off decorous robes is flashed before us – a sight the more monstrous because of the scientific skill with which every particular is marshalled and brought into an easy apparent relation to the known gruesomeness of material life.

Poe's tales, of course, fall into several classes; some of which contain a purer essence of spiritual horror than others. The tales of logic and ratiocination, forerunners of the modern detective story, are not to be included at all in weird literature; whilst certain others, probably influenced considerably by Hoffmann, possess an extravagance which relegates them to the borderline of the grotesque. Still a third group deal with abnormal psychology and monomania in such a way as to express terror but not weirdness. A substantial residuum, however, represent the literature of supernatural horror in its acutest form; and give their author a permanent and unassailable place as deity and fountain-head of all modern diabolic fiction. Who can forget the terrible swollen ship poised on the billow-chasm's edge in 'MS. Found in a Bottle' – the dark intimations of her unhallowed age and monstrous growth, her sinister crew of unseeing greybeards, and her frightful southward rush under full sail through the ice of the Antarctic night, sucked onward by some resistless devil-current toward a vortex of eldritch enlightenment which must end in destruction? Then there is the unutterable 'M. Valdemar', kept together by hypnotism for seven months after his death, and uttering frantic sounds but a moment before the breaking of the spell leaves him 'a nearly liquid mass of loathsome – of detestable putrescence'. In the *Narrative of A. Gordon Pym* the voyagers reach first a strange south polar land of murderous savages where nothing is white and where vast rocky ravines have the form of titanic Egyptian letters spelling terrible primal arcana of earth; and thereafter a still more mysterious realm where everything is white, and where shrouded giants and snowy-plumed birds guard a cryptic cataract of mist which empties from immeasurable celestial heights into a torrid milky sea. 'Metzengerstein' horrifies with its malign hints of a monstrous metempsychosis – the mad nobleman who burns the stable of his hereditary foe; the colossal unknown horse that issues from the blazing building after the owner has perished therein; the vanishing bit of ancient tapestry where was shewn the giant horse of the victim's ancestor in the Crusades; the madman's wild and constant riding on the great horse, and his fear and hatred of the steed; the meaningless prophecies that brood obscurely over the warring houses; and finally, the burning of the madman's palace and the death therein of the owner, borne helpless into the flames and up the vast staircases astride the beast he has ridden so strangely. Afterward the rising smoke of the ruins takes the form of a gigantic horse. 'The Man of the Crowd', telling of one who roams day and night to mingle with streams of people as if afraid to be alone, has quieter effects, but implies nothing less of cosmic fear. Poe's mind was never far from terror and decay, and we see in every tale, poem, and philosophical dialogue a tense eagerness to fathom unplumbed wells of night, to pierce the veil of death, and to reign in fancy as lord of the frightful mysteries of time and space.

Certain of Poe's tales possess an almost absolute perfection of artistic form which makes them veritable beacon-lights in the province of the short story. Poe could, when he wished, give to his prose a richly poetic cast; employing that archaic and Orientalised style with jewelled phrase, quasi-Biblical repetition, and recurrent burthen so successfully used by later writers like Oscar Wilde and Lord Dunsany; and in the cases where he has done this we have an effect of lyrical phantasy almost narcotic in essence – an opium pageant of dream in the language of dream, with every unnatural colour and grotesque image bodied forth in a symphony of corresponding sound. 'The Masque of the Red Death', 'Silence – A Fable', and 'Shadow – A Parable' are assuredly poems in every sense of the word save the metrical one, and owe as much of their power to aural cadence as to visual imagery. But it is in two of the less openly poetic tales, 'Ligeia' and 'The Fall of the House of Usher' – especially the latter – that one finds those very summits of artistry whereby Poe takes his place at the head of fictional miniaturists. Simple and straightforward in plot, both of these tales owe their supreme magic to the cunning development which appears in the selection and collocation of every least incident. 'Ligeia' tells of a first wife of lofty and mysterious origin, who after death returns through a preternatural force of will to take possession of the body of a second wife; imposing even her physical appearance on the temporary reanimated corpse of her victim at the last moment. Despite a suspicion of prolixity and topheaviness, the narrative reaches its terrific climax with relentless power. 'Usher', whose superiority in detail and proportion is very marked, hints shudderingly of obscure life in inorganic things, and displays an abnormally linked trinity of entities at the end of a long and isolated family history – a brother, his twin sister, and their incredibly ancient house all sharing a single soul and meeting one common dissolution at the same moment.

These bizarre conceptions, so awkward in unskilful hands, become under Poe's spell living and convincing terrors to haunt our nights; and all because the author understood so perfectly the very mechanics and physiology of fear and strangeness – the essential details to emphasise, the precise incongruities and conceits to select as preliminaries or concomitants to horror, the exact incidents and allusions to throw out innocently in advance as symbols or prefigurings of each major step toward the hideous denouement to come, the nice adjustments of cumulative force and the unerring accuracy in linkage of parts which make for faultless unity throughout and thunderous effectiveness at the climactic moment, the delicate nuances of scenic and landscape value to select in establishing and sustaining the desired mood and vitalising the desired illusion – principles of this kind, and dozens of obscurer ones too elusive to be described or even fully comprehended by any ordinary commentator. Melodrama and unsophistication there may be – we are told of one fastidious Frenchman who could not bear to read Poe except in Baudelaire's urbane and Gallically modulated translation – but all traces of such things are wholly overshadowed by a potent and inborn sense of the spectral, the morbid, and the horrible which gushed forth from every cell of the artist's creative mentality and stamped his macabre work with the ineffaceable mark of supreme genius. Poe's weird tales are *alive* in a manner that few others can ever hope to be.

Like most fantaisistes, Poe excels in incidents and broad narrative effects rather than in character drawing. His typical protagonist is generally a dark, handsome, proud, melancholy, intellectual, highly sensitive, capricious, introspective, isolated, and sometimes slightly mad gentleman of ancient family and opulent circumstances; usually deeply learned in strange lore, and darkly ambitious of penetrating to forbidden secrets of the universe. Aside from a high-sounding name, this character obviously derives little from the early Gothic novel; for he is clearly neither the wooden hero nor the diabolical villain of Radcliffian or Ludovician romance. Indirectly, however, he does possess a sort of genealogical con-nection; since his gloomy, ambitious, and anti-social qualities savour strongly of the typical Byronic hero, who in turn is definitely an offspring of the Gothic Manfreds, Montonis, and Ambrosios. More particular qualities appear to be derived from the psychology of Poe himself, who certainly possessed much of the depression, sensitiveness, mad aspiration, loneliness, and extravagant freak-ishness which he attributes to his haughty and solitary victims of Fate.

8. The Weird Tradition in America

The public for whom Poe wrote, though grossly unappreciative of his art, was by no means unaccustomed to the horrors with which he dealt. America, besides inheriting the usual dark folklore of Europe, had an additional fund of weird associations to draw upon; so that spectral legends had already been recognised as fruitful subject-matter for literature. Charles Brockden Brown had achieved phenomenal fame with his Radcliffian romances, and Washington Irving's lighter treatment of eerie themes had quickly become classic. This additional fund proceeded, as Paul Elmer More has pointed out, from the keen spiritual and theological interests of the first colonists, plus the strange and forbidding nature of the scene into which they were plunged. The vast and gloomy virgin forests in whose perpetual twilight all terrors might well lurk; the hordes of coppery Indians whose strange, saturnine visages and violent customs hinted strongly at traces of infernal origin; the free rein given under the influence of Puritan theocracy to all manner of notions respecting man's relation to the stern and venge-ful God of the Calvinists, and to the sulphureous Adversary of that God, about whom so much was thundered in the pulpits each Sunday; and the morbid introspection developed by an isolated backwoods life devoid of normal amusements and of the rec-reational mood, harassed by commands for theological self-exam-ination, keyed to unnatural emotional repression, and forming above all a mere grim struggle for survival – all these things con-spired to produce an environment in which the black whisperings of sinister grandams were heard far beyond the chimney corner, and in which tales of witchcraft and unbelievable secret monstrosities lingered long after the dread days of the Salem nightmare.

Poe represents the newer, more disillusioned, and more tech-nically finished of the weird schools that rose out of this propitious milieu. Another school – the tradition of moral values, gentle restraint, and mild, leisurely phantasy tinged more or less with the whimsical – was represented by another famous, misunderstood, and lonely figure in American letters – the shy and sensitive Nathaniel Hawthorne, scion of antique Salem and great-grandson of one of the bloodiest of the old witchcraft judges. In Hawthorne we have none of the violence, the daring, the high colouring, the intense dramatic sense, the cosmic malignity, and the undivided and impersonal artistry of Poe. Here, instead, is a gentle soul cramped by the Puritanism of early New England; shadowed and wistful, and grieved at an unmoral universe which everywhere transcends the conventional patterns thought by our forefathers to represent divine and immutable law. Evil, a very real force to Hawthorne, appears on every hand as a lurking and conquering adversary; and the visible world becomes in his fancy a theatre of infinite tragedy and woe, with unseen half-existent influences hovering over it and through it, battling for supremacy and moulding the destinies of the hapless mortals who form its vain and self-deluded population. The heritage of American weirdness was his to a most intense degree, and he saw a dismal throng of vague spectres behind the common phenomena of life; but he was not disinterested enough to value impressions, sensations, and beauties of narration for their own sake. He must needs weave his phantasy into some quietly melancholy fabric of didactic or allegorical cast, in which his meekly resigned cynicism may display with naive moral appraisal the perfidy of a human race which he cannot cease to cherish and mourn despite his insight into its hypocrisy. Supernatural horror, then, is never a primary object with Hawthorne; though its impulses were so deeply woven into his personality that he cannot help suggesting it with the force of genius when he calls upon the unreal world to illustrate the pensive sermon he wishes to preach.

Hawthorne's intimations of the weird, always gentle, elusive, and restrained, may be traced throughout his work. The mood that produced them found one delightful vent in the Teutonised retelling of classic myths for children contained in *A Wonder Book* and *Tanglewood Tales*, and at other times exercised itself in casting a certain strangeness and intangible witchery or malevolence over events not meant to be actually supernatural; as in the macabre posthumous novel *Dr Grimshawe's Secret*, which invests with a peculiar sort of repulsion a house existing to this day in Salem, and abutting on the ancient Charter Street Burying Ground. In *The Marble Faun*, whose design was sketched out in an Italian villa reputed to be haunted, a tremendous background of genuine phantasy and mystery palpitates just beyond the common reader's sight;

and glimpses of fabulous blood in mortal veins are hinted at during the course of a romance which cannot help being interesting despite the persistent incubus of moral allegory, anti-Popery propaganda, and a Puritan prudery which has caused the late D.H. Lawrence to express a longing to treat the author in a highly undignified manner. *Septimius Felton*, a posthumous novel whose idea was to have been elaborated and incorporated into the unfinished *Dolliver Romance*, touches on the Elixir of Life in a more or less capable fashion; whilst the notes for a never-written tale to be called 'The Ancestral Footstep' shew what Hawthorne would have done with an intensive treatment of an old English superstition – that of an ancient and accursed line whose members left footprints of blood as they walked – which appears incidentally in both *Septimius Felton* and *Dr Grimshawe's Secret*.

Many of Hawthorne's shorter tales exhibit weirdness, either of atmosphere or of incident, to a remarkable degree. 'Edward Randolph's Portrait', in *Legends of the Province House*, has its diabolic moments. 'The Minister's Black Veil' (founded on an actual incident) and 'The Ambitious Guest' imply much more than they state, whilst 'Ethan Brand' – a fragment of a longer work never completed – rises to genuine heights of cosmic fear with its vignette of the wild hill country and the blazing, desolate lime-kilns, and its delineation of the Byronic 'unpardonable sinner', whose troubled life ends with a peal of fearful laughter in the night as he seeks rest amidst the flames of the furnace. Some of Hawthorne's notes tell of weird tales he would have written had he lived longer – an especially vivid plot being that concerning a baffling stranger who appeared now and then in public assemblies, and who was at last followed and found to come and go from a very ancient grave.

But foremost as a finished, artistic unit among all our author's weird material is the famous and exquisitely wrought novel, *The House of the Seven Gables*, in which the relentless working out of an ancestral curse is developed with astonishing power against the sinister background of a very ancient Salem house – one of those peaked Gothic affairs which formed the first regular building-up of our New England coast towns, but which gave way after the seventeenth century to the more familiar gambrel-roofed or classic Georgian types now known as 'Colonial'. Of these old gabled Gothic houses scarcely a dozen are to be seen today in their original condition throughout the United States, but one well known to Hawthorne still stands in Turner Street, Salem, and is pointed out with doubtful authority as the scene and inspiration of the romance. Such an edifice, with its spectral peaks, its clustered chimneys, its overhanging second story, its grotesque corner-brackets, and its diamond-paned lattice windows, is indeed an object well calculated to evoke sombre reflections; typifying as it does the dark Puritan age of concealed horror and witch-whispers which preceded the beauty, rationality, and spaciousness of the eighteenth century. Hawthorne saw many in his youth, and knew the black tales connected with some of them. He heard, too, many rumours of a curse upon his own line as the result of his great-grandfather's severity as a witchcraft judge in 1692.

From this setting came the immortal tale – New England's greatest contribution to weird literature – and we can feel in an instant the authenticity of the atmosphere presented to us. Stealthy horror and disease lurk within the weather-blackened, moss-crusted, and elm-shadowed walls of the archaic dwelling so vividly displayed, and we grasp the brooding malignity of the place when we read that its builder – old Colonel Pyncheon – snatched the land with peculiar ruthlessness from its original settler, Matthew Maule, whom he condemned to the gallows as a wizard in the year of the panic. Maule died cursing old Pyncheon – 'God will give him blood to drink' – and the waters of the old well on the seized land turned bitter. Maule's carpenter son consented to build the great gabled house for his father's triumphant enemy, but the old Colonel died strangely on the day of its dedication. Then followed generations of odd vicissitudes, with queer whispers about the dark powers of the Maules, and peculiar and sometimes terrible ends befalling the Pyncheons.

The overshadowing malevolence of the ancient house – almost as alive as Poe's House of Usher, though in a subtler way – pervades the tale as a recurrent motif pervades an operatic tragedy; and when the main story is reached, we behold the modern Pyncheons in a pitiable state of decay. Poor old Hepzibah, the eccentric reduced gentlewoman; child-like, unfortunate Clifford, just released from undeserved imprisonment; sly and treacherous Judge Pyncheon, who is the old Colonel all over again – all these figures are tremendous symbols, and are well matched by the stunted vegetation and anaemic fowls in the garden. It was almost a pity to supply a fairly happy ending, with a union of sprightly Phoebe, cousin and last scion of the Pyncheons, to the prepossessing young man who turns out to be the last of the Maules. This union, presumably, ends the curse. Hawthorne avoids all violence of diction or movement, and keeps his implications of terror well in the background; but occasional glimpses amply serve to sustain the mood and redeem the work from pure allegorical aridity. Incidents like the bewitching of Alice Pyncheon in the early eighteenth century, and the spectral music of her harpsichord which precedes a death in the family – the latter a variant of an immemorial type of Aryan myth – link the action directly with the supernatural; whilst the dead nocturnal vigil of old Judge Pyncheon in the ancient parlour, with his frightfully ticking watch, is stark horror of the most poignant and genuine sort. The way in which the Judge's death is first adumbrated by the motions and sniffing of a strange cat outside the window, long before the fact is suspected either by the reader or by any of the characters, is a stroke of genius which Poe could not have surpassed. Later the strange cat watches intently outside that same window in the night and on the next day, for – something. It is clearly the psychopomp of primeval myth, fitted and adapted with infinite deftness to its latter-day setting.

But Hawthorne left no well-defined literary posterity. His mood and attitude belonged to the age which closed with him, and it is the spirit of Poe – who so clearly and realistically understood the natural basis of the horror-appeal and the correct mechanics of its achievement – which survived and blossomed. Among the earliest of Poe's disciples may be reckoned the brilliant young Irishman Fitz-James O'Brien (1828–1862), who became naturalised as an American and perished honourably in the Civil War. It is he who gave us 'What Was It?', the first well-shaped short story of a tangible but invisible being, and the prototype of de Maupassant's 'Horla'; he also who created the inimitable 'Diamond Lens', in which a young microscopist falls in love with a maiden of an infinitesimal world which he has discovered in a drop of water. O'Brien's early death undoubtedly deprived us of some masterful tales of strangeness and terror, though his genius was not, properly speaking, of the same titan quality which characterised Poe and Hawthorne.

Closer to real greatness was the eccentric and saturnine journalist

Ambrose Bierce, born in 1842; who likewise entered the Civil War, but survived to write some immortal tales and to disappear in 1913 in as great a cloud of mystery as any he ever evoked from his nightmare fancy. Bierce was a satirist and pamphleteer of note, but the bulk of his artistic reputation must rest upon his grim and savage short stories; a large number of which deal with the Civil War and form the most vivid and realistic expression which that conflict has yet received in fiction. Virtually all of Bierce's tales are tales of horror; and whilst many of them treat only of the physical and psychological horrors within Nature, a substantial proportion admit the malignly supernatural and form a leading element in America's fund of weird literature. Mr Samuel Loveman, a living poet and critic who was personally acquainted with Bierce, thus sums up the genius of the great shadow-maker in the preface to some of his letters:

> 'In Bierce, the evocation of horror becomes for the first time, not so much the prescription or perversion of Poe and Maupassant, but an atmosphere definite and uncannily precise. Words, so simple that one would be prone to ascribe them to the limitations of a literary hack, take on an unholy horror, a new and unguessed transformation. In Poe one finds it a tour de force, in Maupassant a nervous engagement of the flagellated climax. To Bierce, simply and sincerely, diabolism held in its tormented depth, a legitimate and reliant means to the end. Yet a tacit confirmation with Nature is in every instance insisted upon.
>
> 'In "The Death of Halpin Frayser", flowers, verdure, and the boughs and leaves of trees are magnificently placed as an opposing foil to unnatural malignity. Not the accustomed golden world, but a world pervaded with the mystery of blue and the breathless recalcitrance of dreams, is Bierce's. Yet, curiously, inhumanity is not altogether absent.'

The 'inhumanity' mentioned by Mr Loveman finds vent in a rare strain of sardonic comedy and graveyard humour, and a kind of delight in images of cruelty and tantalising disappointment. The former quality is well illustrated by some of the subtitles in the darker narratives; such as 'One does not always eat what is on the table', describing a body laid out for a coroner's inquest, and 'A man though naked may be in rags', referring to a frightfully mangled corpse.

Bierce's work is in general somewhat uneven. Many of the stories are obviously mechanical, and marred by a jaunty and commonplacely artificial style derived from journalistic models; but the grim malevolence stalking through all of them is unmistakable, and several stand out as permanent mountain-peaks of American weird writing. 'The Death of Halpin Frayser', called by Frederic Taber Cooper the most fiendishly ghastly tale in the literature of the Anglo-Saxon race, tells of a body skulking by night without a soul in a weird and horribly ensanguined wood, and of a man beset by ancestral memories who met death at the claws of that which had been his fervently loved mother. 'The Damned Thing', frequently copied in popular anthologies, chronicles the hideous devastations of an invisible entity that waddles and flounders on the hills and in the wheatfields by night and day. 'The Suitable Surroundings' evokes with singular subtlety yet apparent simplicity a piercing sense of the terror which may reside in the written word. In the story the weird author Colston says to his friend Marsh, 'You are brave enough to read me in a street-car, but – in a deserted house – alone – in the forest – at night! Bah! I have a manuscript in my pocket that would kill you!' Marsh reads the manuscript in 'the suitable surroundings' – and it does kill him. 'The Middle Toe of the Right Foot' is clumsily developed, but has a powerful climax. A man named Manton has horribly killed his two children and his wife, the latter of whom lacked the middle toe of the right foot. Ten years later he returns much altered to the neighbourhood; and, being secretly recognised, is provoked into a bowie-knife duel in the dark, to be held in the now abandoned house where his crime was committed. When the moment of the duel arrives a trick is played upon him; and he is left without an antagonist, shut in a night-black ground floor room of the reputedly haunted edifice, with the thick dust of a decade on every hand. No knife is drawn against him, for only a thorough scare is intended; but on the next day he is found crouched in a corner with distorted face, dead of sheer fright at something he has seen. The only clue visible to the discoverers is one having terrible implications: 'In the dust of years that lay thick upon the floor – leading from the door by which they had entered, straight across the room to within a yard of Manton's crouching corpse – were three parallel lines of footprints – light but definite impressions of bare feet, the outer ones those of small children, the inner a woman's. From the point at which they ended they did not return; they pointed all one way.' And, of course, the woman's prints shewed a lack of the middle toe of the right foot. 'The Spook House', told with a severely homely air of journalistic verisimilitude, conveys terrible hints of shocking mystery. In 1858 an entire family of seven persons disappears suddenly and unaccountably from a plantation house in eastern Kentucky, leaving all its possessions untouched – furniture, clothing, food supplies, horses, cattle, and slaves. About a year later two men of high standing are forced by a storm to take shelter in the deserted dwelling, and in so doing stumble into a strange subterranean room lit by an unaccountable greenish light and having an iron door which cannot be opened from within. In this room lie the decayed corpses of all the missing family; and as one of the discoverers rushes forward to embrace a body he seems to recognise, the other is so overpowered by a strange foetor that he accidentally shuts his companion in the vault and loses consciousness. Recovering his senses six weeks later, the survivor is unable to find the hidden room; and the house is burned during the Civil War. The imprisoned discoverer is never seen or heard of again.

Bierce seldom realises the atmospheric possibilities of his themes as vividly as Poe; and much of his work contains a certain touch of naiveté, prosaic angularity, or early-American provincialism which contrasts somewhat with the efforts of later horror-masters. Nevertheless the genuineness and artistry of his dark intimations are always unmistakable, so that his greatness is in no danger of eclipse. As arranged in his definitively collected works, Bierce's weird tales occur mainly in two volumes, *Can Such Things Be?* and *In the Midst of Life.* The former, indeed, is almost wholly given over to the supernatural.

Much of the best in American horror-literature has come from pens not mainly devoted to that medium. Oliver Wendell Holmes's historic *Elsie Venner* suggests with admirable restraint an unnatural ophidian element in a young woman pre-natally influenced, and sustains the atmosphere with finely discriminating landscape touches. In *The Turn of the Screw* Henry James triumphs over his inevitable pomposity and prolixity sufficiently well to create a truly potent air of sinister menace; depicting the hideous influence of two dead and evil servants, Peter Quint and the governess Miss Jessel, over a small boy and girl who had been under their care. James is perhaps too diffuse, too unctuously urbane, and too much addicted to subtleties of speech to realise fully all the wild and devastating horror in his situations; but for all that there is a rare and mounting tide of fright, culminating in the death of the little boy, which gives the novelette a permanent place in its special class.

F. Marion Crawford produced several weird tales of varying quality, now collected in a volume entitled *Wandering Ghosts*. 'For the Blood Is the Life' touches powerfully on a case of moon-cursed vampirism near an ancient tower on the rocks of the lonely South Italian sea-coast. 'The Dead Smile' treats of family horrors in an old house and an ancestral vault in Ireland, and introduces the banshee with considerable force. 'The Upper Berth', however, is Crawford's weird masterpiece; and is one of the most tremendous horror-stories in all literature. In this tale of a suicide-haunted stateroom such things as the spectral salt-water dampness, the strangely open porthole, and the nightmare struggle with the name-less object are handled with incomparable dexterity.

Very genuine, though not without the typical mannered extrava-gance of the eighteen-nineties, is the strain of horror in the early work of Robert W. Chambers, since renowned for products of a very different quality. *The King in Yellow*, a series of vaguely con-nected short stories having as a background a monstrous and sup-pressed book whose perusal brings fright, madness, and spectral tragedy, really achieves notable heights of cosmic fear in spite of uneven interest and a somewhat trivial and affected cultivation of the Gallic studio atmosphere made popular by Du Maurier's *Trilby*. The most powerful of its tales, perhaps, is 'The Yellow Sign', in which is introduced a silent and terrible churchyard watchman with a face like a puffy grave-worm's. A boy, describing a tussle he has had with this creature, shivers and sickens as he relates a certain detail. 'Well, sir, it's Gawd's truth that when I 'it 'im 'e grabbed me wrists, sir, and when I twisted 'is soft, mushy fist one of 'is fingers come off in me 'and.' An artist, who after seeing him has shared with another a strange dream of a nocturnal hearse, is shocked by the voice with which the watchman accosts him. The fellow emits a muttering sound that fills the head like thick oily smoke from a fat-rendering vat or an odour of noisome decay. What he mumbles is merely this: 'Have you found the Yellow Sign?'

A weirdly hieroglyphed onyx talisman, picked up in the street by the sharer of his dream, is shortly given the artist; and after stumbling queerly upon the hellish and forbidden book of horrors the two learn, among other hideous things which no sane mortal should know, that this talisman is indeed the nameless Yellow Sign handed down from the accursed cult of Hastur – from primordial Carcosa, whereof the volume treats, and some nightmare memory of which seems to lurk latent and ominous at the back of all men's minds. Soon they hear the rumbling of the black-plumed hearse driven by the flabby and corpse-faced watchman. He enters the night-shrouded house in quest of the Yellow Sign, all bolts and bars rotting at his touch. And when the people rush in, drawn by a scream that no human throat could utter, they find three forms on the floor – two dead and one dying. One of the dead shapes is far gone in decay. It is the churchyard watchman, and the doctor exclaims, 'That man must have been dead for months.' It is worth observing that the author derives most of the names and allusions connected with his eldritch land of primal memory from the tales of Ambrose Bierce. Other early works of Mr Chambers displaying the outré and macabre element are *The Maker of Moons* and *In Search of the Unknown*. One cannot help regretting that he did not further develop a vein in which he could so easily have become a recognised master.

Horror material of authentic force may be found in the work of the New England realist Mary E. Wilkins; whose volume of short tales, *The Wind in the Rose-Bush*, contains a number of noteworthy achievements. In 'The Shadows on the Wall' we are shewn with consummate skill the response of a staid New England household to uncanny tragedy; and the sourceless shadow of the poisoned brother well prepares us for the climactic moment when the shadow of the secret murderer, who has killed himself in a neighbouring city, suddenly appears beside it. Charlotte Perkins Gilman, in 'The Yellow Wall Paper', rises to a classic level in subtly delineating the madness which crawls over a woman dwelling in the hideously papered room where a madwoman was once confined.

In 'The Dead Valley' the eminent architect and mediaevalist Ralph Adams Cram achieves a memorably potent degree of vague regional horror through subtleties of atmosphere and description.

Still further carrying on our spectral tradition is the gifted and versatile humourist Irvin S. Cobb, whose work both early and recent contains some finely weird specimens. 'Fishhead', an early achievement, is banefully effective in its portrayal of unnatural affinities between a hybrid idiot and the strange fish of an isolated lake, which at the last avenge their biped kinsman's murder. Later work of Mr Cobb introduces an element of possible science, as in the tale of hereditary memory where a modern man with a negroid strain utters words in African jungle speech when run down by a train under visual and aural circumstances recalling the maiming of his black ancestor by a rhinoceros a century before.

Extremely high in artistic stature is the novel *The Dark Chamber* (1927), by the late Leonard Cline. This is the tale of a man who – with the characteristic ambition of the Gothic or Byronic hero-villain – seeks to defy Nature and recapture every moment of his past life through the abnormal stimulation of memory. To this end he employs endless notes, records, mnemonic objects, and pictures – and finally odours, music, and exotic drugs. At last his ambition goes beyond his personal life and reaches toward the black abysses of *hereditary* memory – even back to pre-human days amidst the steaming swamps of the Carboniferous age, and to still more unimaginable deeps of primal time and entity. He calls for madder music and takes stronger drugs, and finally his great dog grows oddly afraid of him. A noxious animal stench encompasses him, and he grows vacant-faced and sub-human. In the end he takes to the woods, howling at night beneath windows. He is finally found in a thicket, mangled to death. Beside him is the mangled corpse of his dog. They have killed each other. The atmosphere of this novel is malevolently potent, much attention being paid to the central figure's sinister home and household.

A less subtle and well-balanced but nevertheless highly effective creation is Herbert S. Gorman's novel, *The Place Called Dagon*, which relates the dark history of a western Massachusetts backwater where the descendants of refugees from the Salem witchcraft still keep alive the morbid and degenerate horrors of the Black Sabbat.

Sinister House, by Leland Hall, has touches of magnificent atmosphere but is marred by a somewhat mediocre romanticism.

Very notable in their way are some of the weird conceptions of the novelist and short-story writer Edward Lucas White, most of whose themes arise from actual dreams. 'The Song of the Sirens' has a very pervasive strangeness, while such things as 'Lukundoo' and 'The Snout' rouse darker apprehensions. Mr White imparts a very peculiar quality to his tales – an oblique sort of glamour which has its own distinctive type of convincingness.

Of younger Americans, none strikes the note of cosmic terror so well as the California poet, artist, and fictionist Clark Ashton Smith, whose bizarre writings, drawings, paintings, and stories are the delight of a sensitive few. Mr Smith has for his background a universe of remote and paralysing fright – jungles of poisonous and iridescent blossoms on the moons of Saturn, evil and grotesque temples in Atlantis, Lemuria, and forgotten elder worlds, and dank morasses of spotted death-fungi in spectral countries beyond earth's rim. His longest and most ambitious poem, *The Hashish-Eater*, is in pentameter blank verse; and opens up chaotic and incredible vistas of kaleidoscopic nightmare in the spaces between the stars. In sheer daemonic strangeness and fertility of conception, Mr Smith is perhaps unexcelled by any other writer dead or living. Who else has seen such gorgeous, luxuriant, and feverishly distorted visions of infinite spheres and multiple dimensions and lived to tell the tale? His short stories deal powerfully with other galaxies, worlds, and dimensions, as well as with strange regions and aeons on the earth. He tells of primal Hyperborea and its black amorphous god Tsathoggua; of the lost continent Zothique, and of the fabulous, vampire-curst land of Averoigne in mediaeval France. Some of Mr Smith's best work can be found in the brochure entitled *The Double Shadow and Other Fantasies* (1933).

9. The Weird Tradition in the British Isles

Recent British literature, besides including the three or four greatest fantaisistes of the present age, has been gratifyingly fertile in the element of the weird. Rudyard Kipling has often approached it; and has, despite the omnipresent mannerisms, handled it with indubitable mastery in such tales as 'The Phantom 'Rickshaw', '"The Finest Story in the World"', 'The Recrudescence of Imray', and 'The Mark of the Beast'. This latter is of particular poignancy;

the pictures of the naked leper-priest who mewed like an otter, of the spots which appeared on the chest of the man that priest cursed, of the growing carnivorousness of the victim and of the fear which horses began to display toward him, and of the eventually half-accomplished transformation of that victim into a leopard, being things which no reader is ever likely to forget. The final defeat of the malignant sorcery does not impair the force of the tale or the validity of its mystery.

Lafcadio Hearn, strange, wandering, and exotic, departs still farther from the realm of the real; and with the supreme artistry of a sensitive poet weaves phantasies impossible to an author of the solid roast-beef type. His *Fantastics*, written in America, contains some of the most impressive ghoulishness in all literature; whilst his *Kwaidan*, written in Japan, crystallises with matchless skill and delicacy the eerie lore and whispered legends of that richly colour-ful nation. Still more of Hearn's weird wizardry of language is shewn in some of his translations from the French, especially from Gautier and Flaubert. His version of the latter's *Temptation of St Anthony* is a classic of fevered and riotous imagery clad in the magic of singing words.

Oscar Wilde may likewise be given a place amongst weird writers, both for certain of his exquisite fairy tales, and for his vivid *Picture of Dorian Gray*, in which a marvellous portrait for years assumes the duty of ageing and coarsening instead of its original, who meanwhile plunges into every excess of vice and crime without the outward loss of youth, beauty, and freshness. There is a sudden and potent climax when Dorian Gray, at last become a murderer, seeks to destroy the painting whose changes testify to his moral degeneracy. He stabs it with a knife, and a hideous cry and crash are heard; but when the servants enter they find it in all its pristine loveliness. 'Lying on the floor was a dead man, in evening dress, with a knife in his heart. He was withered, wrinkled, and loathsome of visage. It was not till they had examined the rings that they recognised who it was.'

Matthew Phipps Shiel, author of many weird, grotesque, and adventurous novels and tales, occasionally attains a high level of horrific magic. 'Xélucha' is a noxiously hideous fragment, but is excelled by Mr Shiel's undoubted masterpiece, 'The House of Sounds', floridly written in the 'yellow 'nineties', and re-cast with more artistic restraint in the early twentieth century. This story, in final form, deserves a place among the foremost things of its kind. It tells of a creeping horror and menace trickling down the centuries on a sub-arctic island off the coast of Norway; where, amidst the sweep of daemon winds and the ceaseless din of hellish waves and cataracts, a vengeful dead man built a brazen tower of terror. It is vaguely like, yet infinitely unlike, Poe's 'Fall of the House of Usher'. In the novel *The Purple Cloud* Mr Shiel describes with tremendous power a curse which came out of the arctic to destroy mankind, and which for a time appears to have left but a single inhabitant on our planet. The sensations of this lone survivor as he realises his position, and roams through the corpse-littered and treasure-strown cities of the world as their absolute master, are delivered with a skill and artistry falling little short of actual majesty. Unfortunately the second half of the book, with its conventionally romantic element, involves a distinct 'letdown'.

Better known than Shiel is the ingenious Bram Stoker, who created many starkly horrific conceptions in a series of novels whose poor technique sadly impairs their net effect. *The Lair of the White Worm*, dealing with a gigantic primitive entity that lurks in a vault beneath an ancient castle, utterly ruins a magnificent idea by a development almost infantile. *The Jewel of Seven Stars*, touching on a strange Egyptian resurrection, is less crudely written. But best of all is the famous *Dracula*, which has become almost the standard modern exploitation of the frightful vampire myth. Count Dracula, a vampire, dwells in a horrible castle in the Carpathians; but finally migrates to England with the design of populating the country with fellow vampires. How an Englishman fares within Dracula's stronghold of terrors, and how the dead fiend's plot for domination is at last defeated, are elements which unite to form a tale now justly assigned a permanent place in English letters. *Dracula* evoked many similar novels of supernatural horror, among which the best are perhaps *The Beetle*, by Richard Marsh, *Brood of the Witch-Queen*, by 'Sax Rohmer' (Arthur Sarsfield Ward), and *The Door of the Unreal*, by Gerald Biss. The latter handles quite dexterously the standard werewolf superstition. Much subtler and more artistic, and told with singular skill through the juxtaposed narratives of the several characters, is the novel *Cold Harbour*, by Francis Brett Young, in which an ancient house of strange malignancy is powerfully delineated. The mocking and well-nigh omnipotent fiend Humphrey Furnival holds echoes of the Manfred-Montoni type of early Gothic 'villain', but is redeemed from triteness by many clever individualities. Only the slight diffuseness of explanation at the close, and the somewhat too free use of divination as a plot factor, keep this tale from approaching absolute perfection.

In the novel *Witch Wood* John Buchan depicts with tremendous force a survival of the evil Sabbat in a lonely district of Scotland. The description of the black forest with the evil stone, and of the terrible cosmic adumbrations when the horror is finally extirpated, will repay one for wading through the very gradual action and plethora of Scottish dialect. Some of Mr Buchan's short stories are also extremely vivid in their spectral intimations; 'The Green Wildebeest', a tale of African witchcraft, 'The Wind in the Portico', with its awakening of dead Britanno-Roman horrors, and 'Skule Skerry', with its touches of sub-arctic fright, being especially remarkable.

Clemence Housman, in the brief novelette 'The Were-wolf', attains a high degree of gruesome tension and achieves to some extent the atmosphere of authentic folklore. In *The Elixir of Life* Arthur Ransome attains some darkly excellent effects despite a general naiveté of plot, while H.B. Drake's *The Shadowy Thing* summons up strange and terrible vistas. George Macdonald's *Lilith* has a compelling bizarrerie all its own; the first and simpler of the two versions being perhaps the more effective.

Deserving of distinguished notice as a forceful craftsman to whom an unseen mystic world is ever a close and vital reality is the poet Walter de la Mare, whose haunting verse and exquisite prose alike bear consistent traces of a strange vision reaching deeply into veiled spheres of beauty and terrible and forbidden dimensions of being. In the novel *The Return* we see the soul of a dead man reach out of its grave of two centuries and fasten itself upon the flesh of the living, so that even the face of the victim becomes that which had long ago returned to dust. Of the shorter tales, of which several volumes exist, many are unforgettable for their command of fear's and sorcery's darkest ramifications; notably 'Seaton's Aunt', in which there lowers a noxious background of malignant vampirism; 'The Tree', which tells of a frightful vegetable growth in the yard of a starving artist; 'Out of the Deep', wherein we are given leave to imagine what thing answered the summons of a dying wastrel in a dark lonely house when he pulled a long-feared bell-cord in the attic chamber of his dread-haunted boyhood; 'A Recluse', which hints at what sent a chance guest flying from a house in the night; 'Mr Kempe', which shews us a mad clerical hermit in quest of the human soul, dwelling in a frightful sea-cliff region beside an archaic abandoned chapel; and 'All-Hallows', a glimpse of daemoniac forces besieging a lonely mediaeval church and miraculously restoring the rotting masonry. De la Mare does not make fear the sole or even the dominant element of most of his tales, being apparently more interested in the subtleties of character involved. Occasionally he sinks to sheer whimsical phantasy of the Barrie order. Still, he is among the very few to whom unreality is a vivid, living presence; and as such he is able to put into his occasional fear-studies a keen potency which only a rare master can achieve. His poem 'The Listeners' restores the Gothic shudder to modern verse.

The weird short story has fared well of late, an important contributor being the versatile E.F. Benson, whose 'The Man Who Went Too Far' breathes whisperingly of a house at the edge of a dark wood, and of Pan's hoof-mark on the breast of a dead man. Mr Benson's volume, *Visible and Invisible*, contains several stories of singular power; notably 'Negotium Perambulans', whose unfolding reveals an abnormal monster from an ancient ecclesiastical panel which performs an act of miraculous vengeance in a lonely village on the Cornish coast, and 'The Horror-Horn', through which lopes a terrible half-human survival dwelling on unvisited Alpine peaks. 'The Face', in another collection, is lethally potent in its relentless aura of doom. H.R. Wakefield, in his collections *They Return at Evening* and *Others Who Return*, manages now and then to achieve great heights of horror despite a vitiating air of sophistication. The most notable stories are 'The Red Lodge' with its slimy aqueous evil, '"He Cometh and He Passeth By"', '"And He Shall Sing ... "', 'The Cairn', '"Look Up There!"', 'Blind Man's Buff', and that bit of lurking millennial horror, 'The Seventeenth Hole at Duncaster'. Mention has been made of the weird work of H.G. Wells and A. Conan Doyle. The former, in 'The Ghost of Fear', reaches a very high level; while all the items in *Thirty Strange Stories* have strong fantastic implications. Doyle now and then struck a powerfully spectral note, as in 'The Captain of the "Pole-Star"', a tale of arctic ghostliness, and 'Lot No. 249', wherein the reanimated mummy theme is used with more than ordinary skill. Hugh Walpole, of the same family as the founder of Gothic fiction, has sometimes approached the bizarre with much success; his short story 'Mrs Lunt' carrying a very poignant shudder. John Metcalfe, in the collection published as *The Smoking Leg*, attains now and then a rare pitch of potency; the tale entitled 'The Bad Lands' containing graduations of horror that strongly savour of genius. More whimsical and inclined toward the amiable and innocuous phantasy of Sir J.M. Barrie are the short tales of E.M. Forster, grouped under the title of *The Celestial Omnibus*. Of these only one, dealing with a glimpse of Pan and his aura of fright, may be said to hold the true element of cosmic horror. Mrs H.D. Everett, though adhering to very old and conventional models, occasionally reaches singular heights of spiritual terror in her collection of short stories. L.P. Hartley is notable for his incisive and extremely ghastly tale, 'A Visitor from Down Under'. May Sinclair's *Uncanny Stories* contain more of traditional occultism than of that creative treatment of fear which marks mastery in this field, and are inclined to lay more stress on human emotions and psychological delving than upon the stark phenomena of a cosmos utterly unreal. It may be well to remark here that occult believers are probably less effective than materialists in delineating the spectral and the fantastic, since to them the phantom world is so commonplace a reality that they tend to refer to it with less awe, remoteness, and impressiveness than do those who see in it an absolute and stupendous violation of the natural order.

Of rather uneven stylistic quality, but vast occasional power in its suggestion of lurking worlds and beings behind the ordinary surface of life, is the work of William Hope Hodgson, known today far less than it deserves to be. Despite a tendency toward conventionally sentimental conceptions of the universe, and of man's relation to it and to his fellows, Mr Hodgson is perhaps second only to Algernon Blackwood in his serious treatment of unreality. Few can equal him in adumbrating the nearness of nameless forces and monstrous besieging entities through casual hints and insignificant details, or in conveying feelings of the spectral and the abnormal in connection with regions or buildings.

In *The Boats of the 'Glen Carrig'* (1907) we are shewn a variety of malign marvels and accursed unknown lands as encountered by the survivors of a sunken ship. The brooding menace in the earlier parts of the book is impossible to surpass, though a letdown in the direction of ordinary romance and adventure occurs toward the end. An inaccurate and pseudo-romantic attempt to reproduce eighteenth-century prose detracts from the general effect, but the really profound nautical erudition everywhere displayed is a compensating factor.

The House on the Borderland (1908) – perhaps the greatest of all Mr Hodgson's works – tells of a lonely and evilly regarded house in Ireland which forms a focus for hideous other-world forces and sustains a siege by blasphemous hybrid anomalies from a hidden abyss below. The wanderings of the narrator's spirit through limitless light-years of cosmic space and kalpas of eternity, and its witnessing of the solar system's final destruction, constitute something almost unique in standard literature. And everywhere there is manifest the author's power to suggest vague, ambushed horrors in natural scenery. But for a few touches of commonplace sentimentality this book would be a classic of the first water.

The Ghost Pirates (1909), regarded by Mr Hodgson as rounding out a trilogy with the two previously mentioned works, is a powerful account of a doomed and haunted ship on its last voyage, and of the terrible sea-devils (of quasi-human aspect, and perhaps the spirits of bygone buccaneers) that besiege it and finally drag it down to an unknown fate. With its command of maritime knowledge, and its clever selection of hints and incidents suggestive of latent horrors in Nature, this book at times reaches enviable peaks of power.

The Night Land (1912) is a long-extended (583 pp.) tale of the earth's infinitely remote future – billions of billions of years ahead, after the death of the sun. It is told in a rather clumsy fashion, as the dreams of a man in the seventeenth century, whose mind merges with its own future incarnation; and is seriously marred by painful verboseness, repetitiousness, artificial and nauseously sticky romantic sentimentality, and an attempt at archaic language even more grotesque and absurd than that in '*Glen Carrig*'.

Allowing for all its faults, it is yet one of the most potent pieces of macabre imagination ever written. The picture of a night-black, dead planet, with the remains of the human race concentrated in a stupendously vast metal pyramid and besieged by monstrous, hybrid, and altogether unknown forces of the darkness, is something that no reader can ever forget. Shapes and entities of an altogether non-human and inconceivable sort – the prowlers of the black, man-forsaken, and unexplored world outside the pyramid – are *suggested* and *partly* described with ineffable potency; while the night-bound landscape with its chasms and slopes and dying volcanism takes on an almost sentient terror beneath the author's touch.

Midway in the book the central figure ventures outside the pyramid on a quest through death-haunted realms untrod by man for millions of years – and in his slow, minutely described, day-by-day progress over unthinkable leagues of immemorial blackness there is a sense of cosmic alienage, breathless mystery, and terrified expectancy unrivalled in the whole range of literature. The last quarter of the book drags woefully, but fails to spoil the tremendous power of the whole.

Mr Hodgson's later volume, *Carnacki, the Ghost-Finder,* consists of several longish short stories published many years before in magazines. In quality it falls conspicuously below the level of the other books. We here find a more or less conventional stock figure of the 'infallible detective' type – the progeny of M. Dupin and Sherlock Holmes, and the close kin of Algernon Blackwood's John Silence – moving through scenes and events badly marred by an atmosphere of professional 'occultism'. A few of the episodes, however, are of undeniable power; and afford glimpses of the peculiar genius characteristic of the author.

Naturally it is impossible in a brief sketch to trace out all the classic modern uses of the terror element. The ingredient must of necessity enter into all work both prose and verse treating broadly of life; and we are therefore not surprised to find a share in such writers as the poet Browning, whose 'Childe Roland to the Dark Tower Came' is instinct with hideous menace, or the novelist Joseph Conrad, who often wrote of the dark secrets within the sea, and of the daemoniac driving power of Fate as influencing the lives of lonely and maniacally resolute men. Its trail is one of infinite ramifications; but we must here confine ourselves to its appearance in a relatively unmixed state, where it determines and dominates the work of art containing it.

Somewhat separate from the main British stream is that current

476

of weirdness in Irish literature which came to the fore in the Celtic Renaissance of the later nineteenth and early twentieth centuries. Ghost and fairy lore have always been of great prominence in Ireland, and for over an hundred years have been recorded by a line of such faithful transcribers and translators as William Carleton, T. Crofton Croker, Lady Wilde – mother of Oscar Wilde – Douglas Hyde, and W.B. Yeats. Brought to notice by the modern movement, this body of myth has been carefully collected and studied; and its salient features reproduced in the work of later figures like Yeats, J.M. Synge, 'A.E.', Lady Gregory, Padraic Colum, James Stephens, and their colleagues.

Whilst on the whole more whimsically fantastic than terrible, such folklore and its consciously artistic counterparts contain much that falls truly within the domain of cosmic horror. Tales of burials in sunken churches beneath haunted lakes, accounts of death-heralding banshees and sinister changelings, ballads of spectres and 'the unholy creatures of the raths' – all these have their poignant and definite shivers, and mark a strong and distinctive element in weird literature. Despite homely grotesqueness and absolute naiveté, there is genuine nightmare in the class of narrative represented by the yarn of Teig O'Kane, who in punishment for his wild life was ridden all night by a hideous corpse that demanded burial and drove him from churchyard to churchyard as the dead rose up loathsomely in each one and refused to accommodate the newcomer with a berth. Yeats, undoubtedly the greatest figure of the Irish revival if not the greatest of all living poets, has accomplished notable things both in original work and in the codification of old legends.

10. The Modern Masters

The best horror-tales of today, profiting by the long evolution of the type, possess a naturalness, convincingness, artistic smoothness, and skilful intensity of appeal quite beyond comparison with anything in the Gothic work of a century or more ago. Technique, craftsmanship, experience, and psychological knowledge have advanced tremendously with the passing years, so that much of the older work seems naive and artificial; redeemed, when redeemed at all, only by a genius which conquers heavy limitations. The tone of jaunty and inflated romance, full of false motivation and investing every conceivable event with a counterfeit significance and carelessly inclusive glamour, is now confined to lighter and more whimsical phases of supernatural writing. Serious weird stories are either made realistically intense by close consistency and perfect fidelity to Nature except in the one supernatural direction which the author allows himself, or else cast altogether in the realm of phantasy, with atmosphere cunningly adapted to the visualisation of a delicately exotic world of unreality beyond space and time, in which almost anything may happen if it but happen in true accord with certain types of imagination and illusion normal to the sensitive human brain. This, at least, is the dominant tendency; though of course many great contemporary writers slip occasionally into some of the flashy postures of immature romanticism, or into bits of the equally empty and absurd jargon of pseudo-scientific 'occultism', now at one of its periodic high tides.

Of living creators of cosmic fear raised to its most artistic pitch, few if any can hope to equal the versatile Arthur Machen; author of some dozen tales long and short, in which the elements of hidden horror and brooding fright attain an almost incomparable substance and realistic acuteness. Mr Machen, a general man of letters and master of an exquisitely lyrical and expressive prose style, has perhaps put more conscious effort into his picaresque *Chronicle of Clemendy*, his refreshing essays, his vivid autobiographical volumes, his fresh and spirited translations, and above all his memorable epic of the sensitive aesthetic mind, *The Hill of Dreams*, in which the youthful hero responds to the magic of that ancient Welsh environment which is the author's own, and lives a dream-life in the Roman city of Isca Silurum, now shrunk to the relic-strown village of Caerleon-on-Usk. But the fact remains that his powerful horror-material of the 'nineties and earlier nineteen-hundreds stands alone in its class, and marks a distinct epoch in the history of this literary form.

Mr Machen, with an impressionable Celtic heritage linked to keen youthful memories of the wild domed hills, archaic forests, and cryptical Roman ruins of the Gwent countryside, has developed an imaginative life of rare beauty, intensity, and historic background. He has absorbed the mediaeval mystery of dark woods and ancient

478

customs, and is a champion of the Middle Ages in all things – including the Catholic faith. He has yielded, likewise, to the spell of the Britanno-Roman life which once surged over his native region; and finds strange magic in the fortified camps, tessellated pavements, fragments of statues, and kindred things which tell of the day when classicism reigned and Latin was the language of the country. A young American poet, Frank Belknap Long, Jun., has well summarised this dreamer's rich endowments and wizardry of expression in the sonnet 'On Reading Arthur Machen':

> *'There is a glory in the autumn wood;*
> *The ancient lanes of England wind and climb*
> *Past wizard oaks and gorse and tangled thyme*
> *To where a fort of mighty empire stood:*
> *There is a glamour in the autumn sky;*
> *The reddened clouds are writhing in the glow*
> *Of some great fire, and there are glints below*
> *Of tawny yellow where the embers die.*
>
> *I wait, for he will show me, clear and cold,*
> *High-rais'd in splendour, sharp against the North,*
> *The Roman eagles, and thro' mists of gold*
> *The marching legions as they issue forth:*
> *I wait, for I would share with him again*
> *The ancient wisdom, and the ancient pain.'*

Of Mr Machen's horror-tales the most famous is perhaps 'The Great God Pan' (1894), which tells of a singular and terrible experiment and its consequences. A young woman, through surgery of the brain-cells, is made to see the vast and monstrous deity of Nature, and becomes an idiot in consequence, dying less than a year later. Years afterward a strange, ominous, and foreign-looking child named Helen Vaughan is placed to board with a family in rural Wales, and haunts the woods in unaccountable fashion. A little boy is thrown out of his mind at sight of someone or something he spies with her, and a young girl comes to a terrible end in similar fashion. All this mystery is strangely interwoven with the Roman rural deities of the place, as sculptured in antique fragments. After another lapse of years, a woman of strangely exotic beauty appears in society, drives her husband to horror and death, causes an artist to paint unthinkable paintings of Witches' Sabbaths, creates an epidemic of suicide among the men of her acquaintance, and is finally discovered to be a frequenter of the lowest dens of vice in London, where even the most callous degenerates are shocked at her enormities. Through the clever comparing of notes on the part of those who have had word of her at various stages of her career, this woman is discovered to be the girl Helen Vaughan; who is the child – by no mortal father – of the young woman on whom the brain experiment was made. She is a daughter of hideous Pan himself, and at the last is put to death amidst horrible trans-mutations of form involving changes of sex and a descent to the most primal manifestations of the life-principle.

But the charm of the tale is in the telling. No one could begin to describe the cumulative suspense and ultimate horror with which every paragraph abounds without following fully the precise order in which Mr Machen unfolds his gradual hints and revelations. Melodrama is undeniably present, and coincidence is stretched to a length which appears absurd upon analysis; but in the malign witchery of the tale as a whole these trifles are forgotten, and the sensitive reader reaches the end with only an appreciative shudder and a tendency to repeat the words of one of the characters: 'It is too incredible, too monstrous; such things can never be in this quiet world … Why, man, if such a case were possible, our earth would be a nightmare.'

Less famous and less complex in plot than 'The Great God Pan', but definitely finer in atmosphere and general artistic value, is the curious and dimly disquieting chronicle called 'The White People', whose central portion purports to be the diary or notes of a little girl whose nurse has introduced her to some of the forbidden magic and soul-blasting traditions of the noxious witch-cult – the cult whose whispered lore was handed down long lines of peasantry throughout Western Europe, and whose members sometimes stole forth at night, one by one, to meet in black woods and lonely places for the revolting orgies of the Witches' Sabbath. Mr Machen's narrative, a triumph of skilful selectiveness and restraint, accu-mulates enormous power as it flows on in a stream of innocent childish prattle; introducing allusions to strange 'nymphs', 'Dôls', 'voolas', 'White, Green, and Scarlet Ceremonies', 'Aklo letters',

'Chian language', 'Mao games', and the like. The rites learned by the nurse from her witch grandmother are taught to the child by the time she is three years old, and her artless accounts of the dangerous secret revelations possess a lurking terror generously mixed with pathos. Evil charms well known to anthropologists are described with juvenile naiveté, and finally there comes a winter afternoon journey into the old Welsh hills, performed under an imaginative spell which lends to the wild scenery an added weirdness, strangeness, and suggestion of grotesque sentience. The details of this journey are given with marvellous vividness, and form to the keen critic a masterpiece of fantastic writing, with almost unlimited power in the intimation of potent hideousness and cosmic aberration. At length the child – whose age is then thirteen – comes upon a cryptic and banefully beautiful thing in the midst of a dark and inaccessible wood. She flees in awe, but is permanently altered and repeatedly revisits the wood. In the end horror overtakes her in a manner deftly prefigured by an anecdote in the prologue, but she poisons herself in time. Like the mother of Helen Vaughan in 'The Great God Pan', she has seen that frightful deity. She is discovered dead in the dark wood beside the cryptic thing she found; and that thing – a whitely luminous statue of Roman workmanship about which dire mediaeval rumours had clustered – is affrightedly hammered into dust by the searchers.

In the episodic novel of *The Three Impostors*, a work whose merit as a whole is somewhat marred by an imitation of the jaunty Stevenson manner, occur certain tales which perhaps represent the high-water mark of Machen's skill as a terror-weaver. Here we find in its most artistic form a favourite weird conception of the author's; the notion that beneath the mounds and rocks of the wild Welsh hills dwell subterraneously that squat primitive race whose vestiges gave rise to our common folk legends of fairies, elves, and the 'Little People', and whose acts are even now responsible for certain unexplained disappearances, and occasional substitutions of strange dark 'changelings' for normal infants. This theme receives its finest treatment in the episode entitled 'The Novel of the Black Seal'; where a professor, having discovered a singular identity between certain characters scrawled on Welsh limestone rocks and those existing in a prehistoric black seal from Babylon, sets out on a course of discovery which leads him to unknown and terrible things. A queer passage in the ancient geographer Solinus, a series of mysterious disappearances in the lonely reaches of Wales, a strange idiot son born to a rural mother after a fright in which her inmost faculties were shaken; all these things suggest to the professor a hideous connection and a condition revolting to any friend and respecter of the human race. He hires the idiot boy, who jabbers strangely at times in a repulsive hissing voice, and is subject to odd epileptic seizures. Once, after such a seizure in the professor's study by night, disquieting odours and evidences of unnatural presences are found; and soon after that the professor leaves a bulky document and goes into the weird hills with feverish expectancy and strange terror in his heart. He never returns, but beside a fantastic stone in the wild country are found his watch, money, and ring, done up with catgut in a parchment bearing the same terrible characters as those on the black Babylonish seal and the rock in the Welsh mountains.

The bulky document explains enough to bring up the most hideous vistas. Professor Gregg, from the massed evidence presented by the Welsh disappearances, the rock inscription, the accounts of ancient geographers, and the black seal, has decided that a frightful race of dark primal beings of immemorial antiquity and wide former diffusion still dwells beneath the hills of unfrequented Wales. Further research has unriddled the message of the black seal, and proved that the idiot boy, a son of some father more terrible than mankind, is the heir of monstrous memories and possibilities. That strange night in the study the professor invoked 'the awful transmutation of the hills' by the aid of the black seal, and aroused in the hybrid idiot the horrors of his shocking paternity. He 'saw his body swell and become distended as a bladder, while the face blackened ...' And then the supreme effects of the invocation appeared, and Professor Gregg knew the stark frenzy of cosmic panic in its darkest form. He knew the abysmal gulfs of abnormality that he had opened, and went forth into the wild hills prepared and resigned. He would meet the unthinkable 'Little People' – and his document ends with a rational observation: 'If I unhappily do not return from my journey, there is no need to conjure up here a picture of the awfulness of my fate.'

Also in *The Three Impostors* is the 'Novel of the White Powder', which approaches the absolute culmination of loathsome fright. Francis Leicester, a young law student nervously worn out by

seclusion and overwork, has a prescription filled by an old apoth-
ecary none too careful about the state of his drugs. The substance,
it later turns out, is an unusual salt which time and varying temperature have accidentally changed to something very strange and
terrible; nothing less, in short, than the mediaeval *Vinum Sabbati*,
whose consumption at the horrible orgies of the Witches' Sabbath
gave rise to shocking transformations and – if injudiciously used – to
unutterable consequences. Innocently enough, the youth regularly
imbibes the powder in a glass of water after meals; and at first seems
substantially benefited. Gradually, however, his improved spirits
take the form of dissipation; he is absent from home a great deal,
and appears to have undergone a repellent psychological change.
One day an odd livid spot appears on his right hand, and he
afterward returns to his seclusion; finally keeping himself shut
within his room and admitting none of the household. The doctor
calls for an interview, and departs in a palsy of horror, saying that
he can do no more in that house. Two weeks later the patient's
sister, walking outside, sees a monstrous thing at the sickroom
window; and servants report that food left at the locked door is no
longer touched. Summons at the door bring only a sound of
shuffling and a demand in a thick gurgling voice to be let alone. At
last an awful happening is reported by a shuddering housemaid.
The ceiling of the room below Leicester's is stained with a hideous
black fluid, and a pool of viscid abomination has dripped to the bed
beneath. Dr Haberden, now persuaded to return to the house,
breaks down the young man's door and strikes again and again with
an iron bar at the blasphemous semi-living thing he finds there. It
is 'a dark and putrid mass, seething with corruption and hideous
rottenness, neither liquid nor solid, but melting and changing'.
Burning points like eyes shine out of its midst, and before it is
despatched it tries to lift what might have been an arm. Soon
afterward the physician, unable to endure the memory of what he
has beheld, dies at sea while bound for a new life in America.

Mr Machen returns to the daemoniac 'Little People' in 'The Red
Hand' and 'The Shining Pyramid'; and in *The Terror*, a wartime
story, he treats with very potent mystery the effect of man's modern
repudiation of spirituality on the beasts of the world, which are thus
led to question his supremacy and to unite for his extermination. Of
utmost delicacy, and passing from mere horror into true mysticism,

is *The Great Return*, a story of the Graal, also a product of the war period. Too well known to need description here is the tale of 'The Bowmen'; which, taken for authentic narration, gave rise to the widespread legend of the 'Angels of Mons' – ghosts of the old English archers of Crécy and Agincourt who fought in 1914 beside the hard-pressed ranks of England's glorious 'Old Contemptibles'.

Less intense than Mr Machen in delineating the extremes of stark fear, yet infinitely more closely wedded to the idea of an unreal world constantly pressing upon ours, is the inspired and prolific Algernon Blackwood, amidst whose voluminous and uneven work may be found some of the finest spectral literature of this or any age. Of the quality of Mr Blackwood's genius there can be no dispute; for no one has even approached the skill, seriousness, and minute fidelity with which he records the overtones of strangeness in ordinary things and experiences, or the preternatural insight with which he builds up detail by detail the complete sensations and perceptions leading from reality into supernormal life or vision. Without notable command of the poetic witchery of mere words, he is the one absolute and unquestioned master of weird atmosphere; and can evoke what amounts almost to a story from a simple fragment of humourless psychological description. Above all others he understands how fully some sensitive minds dwell forever on the borderland of dream, and how relatively slight is the distinction betwixt those images formed from actual objects and those excited by the play of the imagination.

Mr Blackwood's lesser work is marred by several defects such as ethical didacticism, occasional insipid whimsicality, the flatness of benignant supernaturalism, and a too free use of the trade jargon of modern 'occultism'. A fault of his more serious efforts is that diffuseness and long-windedness which results from an excessively elaborate attempt, under the handicap of a somewhat bald and journalistic style devoid of intrinsic magic, colour, and vitality, to visualise precise sensations and nuances of uncanny suggestion. But in spite of all this, the major products of Mr Blackwood attain a genuinely classic level, and evoke as does nothing else in literature an awed and convinced sense of the immanence of strange spiritual spheres or entities.

The well-nigh endless array of Mr Blackwood's fiction includes both novels and shorter tales, the latter sometimes independent and sometimes arrayed in series. Foremost of all must be reckoned 'The Willows', in which the nameless presences on a desolate Danube island are horribly felt and recognised by a pair of idle voyagers. Here art and restraint in narrative reach their very highest development, and an impression of lasting poignancy is produced without a single strained passage or a single false note. Another amazingly potent though less artistically finished tale is 'The Wendigo', where we are confronted by horrible evidences of a vast forest daemon about which North Woods lumbermen whisper at evening. The manner in which certain footprints tell certain unbelievable things is really a marked triumph in craftsmanship. In 'An Episode in a Lodging House' we behold frightful presences summoned out of black space by a sorcerer, and 'The Listener' tells of the awful psychic residuum creeping about an old house where a leper died. In the volume titled *Incredible Adventures* occur some of the finest tales which the author has yet produced, leading the fancy to wild rites on nocturnal hills, to secret and terrible aspects lurking behind stolid scenes, and to unimaginable vaults of mystery below the sands and pyramids of Egypt; all with a serious finesse and delicacy that convince where a cruder or lighter treatment would merely amuse. Some of these accounts are hardly stories at all, but rather studies in elusive impressions and half-remembered snatches of dream. Plot is everywhere negligible, and atmosphere reigns untrammelled.

John Silence – Physician Extraordinary is a book of five related tales, through which a single character runs his triumphant course. Marred only by traces of the popular and conventional detective-story atmosphere – for Dr Silence is one of those benevolent geniuses who employ their remarkable powers to aid worthy fellow-men in difficulty – these narratives contain some of the author's best work, and produce an illusion at once emphatic and lasting. The opening tale, 'A Psychical Invasion', relates what befell a sensitive author in a house once the scene of dark deeds, and how a legion of fiends was exorcised. 'Ancient Sorceries', perhaps the finest tale in the book, gives an almost hypnotically vivid account of an old French town where once the unholy Sabbath was kept by all the people in the form of cats. In 'The Nemesis of Fire' a hideous elemental is evoked by new-spilt blood, whilst 'Secret Worship' tells of a German school where Satanism held sway, and where long afterward an evil aura remained. 'The Camp of the Dog' is a werewolf tale, but is weakened by moralisation and professional 'occultism'.

Too subtle, perhaps, for definite classification as horror-tales, yet possibly more truly artistic in an absolute sense, are such delicate phantasies as *Jimbo* or *The Centaur.* Mr Blackwood achieves in these novels a close and palpitant approach to the inmost substance of dream, and works enormous havoc with the conventional barriers between reality and imagination.

Unexcelled in the sorcery of crystalline singing prose, and supreme in the creation of a gorgeous and languorous world of iridescently exotic vision, is Edward John Moreton Drax Plunkett, Eighteenth Baron Dunsany, whose tales and short plays form an almost unique element in our literature. Inventor of a new mythology and weaver of surprising folklore, Lord Dunsany stands dedicated to a strange world of fantastic beauty, and pledged to eternal warfare against the coarseness and ugliness of diurnal reality. His point of view is the most truly cosmic of any held in the literature of any period. As sensitive as Poe to dramatic values and the significance of isolated words and details, and far better equipped rhetorically through a simple lyric style based on the prose of the King James Bible, this author draws with tremendous effectiveness on nearly every body of myth and legend within the circle of European culture; producing a composite or eclectic cycle of phantasy in which Eastern colour, Hellenic form, Teutonic sombreness, and Celtic wistfulness are so superbly blended that each sustains and supplements the rest without sacrifice of perfect congruity and homogeneity. In most cases Dunsany's lands are fabulous – 'beyond the East', or 'at the edge of the world'. His system of original personal and place names, with roots drawn from classical, Oriental, and other sources, is a marvel of versatile inventiveness and poetic discrimination; as one may see from such specimens as 'Argimēnēs', 'Bethmoora', 'Poltarnees', 'Camorak', 'Illuriel', or 'Sardathrion'.

Beauty rather than terror is the keynote of Dunsany's work. He loves the vivid green of jade and of copper domes, and the delicate flush of sunset on the ivory minarets of impossible dream-cities. Humour and irony, too, are often present to impart a gentle cynicism and modify what might otherwise possess a naive intensity. Nevertheless, as is inevitable in a master of triumphant unreality, there are occasional touches of cosmic fright which come well within the authentic tradition. Dunsany loves to hint slyly and adroitly of monstrous things and incredible dooms, as one hints in a fairy tale. In *The Book of Wonder* we read of Hlo-hlo, the gigantic spider-idol which does not always stay at home; of what the Sphinx feared in the forest; of Slith, the thief who jumps over the edge of the world after seeing a certain light lit and knowing *who* lit it; of the anthropophagous Gibbelins, who inhabit an evil tower and guard a treasure; of the Gnoles, who live in the forest and from whom it is not well to steal; of the City of Never, and the eyes that watch in the Under Pits; and of kindred things of darkness. *A Dreamer's Tales* tells of the mystery that sent forth all men from Bethmoora in the desert; of the vast gate of Perdóndaris, that was carved from a *single piece* of ivory; and of the voyage of poor old Bill, whose captain cursed the crew and paid calls on nasty-looking isles new-risen from the sea, with low thatched cottages having evil, obscure windows.

Many of Dunsany's short plays are replete with spectral fear. In *The Gods of the Mountain* seven beggars impersonate the seven green idols on a distant hill, and enjoy ease and honour in a city of worshippers until they hear that *the real idols are missing from their wonted seats.* A very ungainly sight in the dusk is reported to them – 'rock should not walk in the evening' – and at last, as they sit awaiting the arrival of a troop of dancers, they note that the approaching footsteps are heavier than those of good dancers ought to be. Then things ensue, and in the end the presumptuous blasphemers are turned to green jade statues by the very walking statues whose sanctity they outraged. But mere plot is the very least merit of this marvellously effective play. The incidents and developments are those of a supreme master, so that the whole forms one of the most important contributions of the present age not only to drama, but to literature in general. *A Night at an Inn* tells of four thieves who have stolen the emerald eye of Klesh, a monstrous Hindoo god. They lure to their room and succeed in slaying the three priestly avengers who are on their track, but in the night Klesh comes gropingly for his eye; and having gained it and departed, calls each of the despoilers out into the darkness for an unnamed punishment. In *The Laughter of the Gods* there is a doomed city at the jungle's edge, and a ghostly lutanist heard only by those about to die (cf. Alice's spectral harpsichord in Hawthorne's *House of the Seven Gables*); whilst *The Queen's Enemies* retells the anecdote of Herodotus in which a vengeful princess invites her foes to a subterranean banquet and lets in the Nile to drown them.

But no amount of mere description can convey more than a fraction of Lord Dunsany's pervasive charm. His prismatic cities and unheard-of rites are touched with a sureness which only mastery can engender, and we thrill with a sense of actual participation in his secret mysteries. To the truly imaginative he is a talisman and a key unlocking rich storehouses of dream and fragmentary memory; so that we may think of him not only as a poet, but as one who makes each reader a poet as well.

At the opposite pole of genius from Lord Dunsany, and gifted with an almost diabolic power of calling horror by gentle steps from the midst of prosaic daily life, is the scholarly Montague Rhodes James, Provost of Eton College, antiquary of note, and recognised authority on mediaeval manuscripts and cathedral history. Dr James, long fond of telling spectral tales at Christmastide, has become by slow degrees a literary weird fictionist of the very first rank; and has developed a distinctive style and method likely to serve as models for an enduring line of disciples.

The art of Dr James is by no means haphazard, and in the preface to one of his collections he has formulated three very sound rules for macabre composition. A ghost story, he believes, should have a familiar setting in the modern period, in order to approach closely the reader's sphere of experience. Its spectral phenomena, moreover, should be malevolent rather than beneficent; since *fear* is the emotion primarily to be excited. And finally, the technical patois of 'occultism' or pseudo-science ought carefully to be avoided; lest the charm of casual verisimilitude be smothered in unconvincing pedantry.

Dr James, practising what he preaches, approaches his themes in a light and often conversational way. Creating the illusion of everyday events, he introduces his abnormal phenomena cautiously and gradually; relieved at every turn by touches of homely and prosaic detail, and sometimes spiced with a snatch or two of antiquarian scholarship. Conscious of the close relation between present weirdness and accumulated tradition, he generally provides remote historical antecedents for his incidents; thus being able to utilise very aptly his exhaustive knowledge of the past, and his ready and convincing command of archaic diction and colouring. A favourite scene for a James tale is some centuried cathedral, which the author can describe with all the familiar minuteness of a specialist in that field.

Sly humorous vignettes and bits of life-like genre portraiture and characterisation are often to be found in Dr James's narratives, and serve in his skilled hands to augment the general effect rather than to spoil it, as the same qualities would tend to do with a lesser craftsman. In inventing a new type of ghost, he has departed considerably from the conventional Gothic tradition; for where the older stock ghosts were pale and stately, and apprehended chiefly through the sense of sight, the average James ghost is lean, dwarfish, and hairy – a sluggish, hellish night-abomination midway betwixt beast and man – and usually *touched* before it is *seen*. Sometimes the spectre is of still more eccentric composition; a roll of flannel with spidery eyes, or an invisible entity which moulds itself in bedding and shews *a face of crumpled linen*. Dr James has, it is clear, an intelligent and scientific knowledge of human nerves and feelings; and knows just how to apportion statement, imagery, and subtle suggestions in order to secure the best results with his readers. He is an artist in incident and arrangement rather than in atmosphere, and reaches the emotions more often through the intellect than directly. This method, of course, with its occasional absences of sharp climax, has its drawbacks as well as its advantages; and many will miss the thorough atmospheric tension which writers like Machen are careful to build up with words and scenes. But only a few of the tales are open to the charge of tameness. Generally the laconic unfolding of abnormal events in adroit order is amply sufficient to produce the desired effect of cumulative horror.

The short stories of Dr James are contained in four small collections, entitled respectively *Ghost-Stories of an Antiquary*, *More Ghost Stories of an Antiquary*, *A Thin Ghost and Others*, and *A Warning to the Curious*. There is also a delightful juvenile phantasy, *The Five Jars*, which has its spectral adumbrations. Amidst this wealth of material it is hard to select a favourite or especially typical tale, though each reader will no doubt have such preferences as his temperament may determine.

'Count Magnus' is assuredly one of the best, forming as it does a veritable Golconda of suspense and suggestion. Mr Wraxall is an English traveller of the middle nineteenth century, sojourning in Sweden to secure material for a book. Becoming interested in the ancient family of De la Gardie, near the village of Råbäck, he studies its records; and finds particular fascination in the builder of the existing manor-house, one Count Magnus, of whom strange and terrible things are whispered. The Count, who flourished early in the seventeenth century, was a stern landlord, and famous for his severity toward poachers and delinquent tenants. His cruel punishments were bywords, and there were dark rumours of influences which even survived his interment in the great mausoleum he built near the church – as in the case of the two peasants who hunted on his preserves one night a century after his death. There were hideous screams in the woods, and near the tomb of Count Magnus an unnatural laugh and the clang of a great door. Next morning the priest found the two men; one a maniac, and the other dead, with the flesh of his face sucked from the bones.

Mr Wraxall hears all these tales, and stumbles on more guarded references to a *Black Pilgrimage* once taken by the Count; a pilgrimage to Chorazin in Palestine, one of the cities denounced by Our Lord in the Scriptures, and in which old priests say that Antichrist is to be born. No one dares to hint just what that Black Pilgrimage was, or what strange being or thing the Count brought back as a companion. Meanwhile Mr Wraxall is increasingly anxious to explore the mausoleum of Count Magnus, and finally secures permission to do so, in the company of a deacon. He finds several monuments and three copper sarcophagi, one of which is the Count's. Round the edge of this latter are several bands of engraved scenes, including a singular and hideous delineation of a pursuit – the pursuit of a frantic man through a forest by a squat muffled figure with a devil-fish's tentacle, directed by a tall cloaked man on a neighbouring hillock. The sarcophagus has three massive steel padlocks, one of which is lying open on the floor, reminding the traveller of a metallic clash he heard the day before when passing the mausoleum and wishing idly that he might see Count Magnus.

His fascination augmented, and the key being accessible, Mr Wraxall pays the mausoleum a second and solitary visit and finds another padlock unfastened. The next day, his last in Råbäck, he again goes alone to bid the long-dead Count farewell. Once more queerly impelled to utter a whimsical wish for a meeting with the buried nobleman, he now sees to his disquiet that only one of the padlocks remains on the great sarcophagus. Even as he looks, that last lock drops noisily to the floor, and there comes a sound as of creaking hinges. Then the monstrous lid appears very slowly to rise, and Mr Wraxall flees in panic fear without refastening the door of the mausoleum.

During his return to England the traveller feels a curious uneasiness about his fellow-passengers on the canal-boat which he employs for the earlier stages. Cloaked figures make him nervous, and he has a sense of being watched and followed. Of twenty-eight persons whom he counts, only twenty-six appear at meals; and the missing two are always a tall cloaked man and a shorter muffled figure. Completing his water travel at Harwich, Mr Wraxall takes frankly to flight in a closed carriage, but sees two cloaked figures at a crossroad. Finally he lodges at a small house in a village and spends the time making frantic notes. On the second morning he is found dead, and during the inquest seven jurors faint at sight of the body. The house where he stayed is never again inhabited, and upon its demolition half a century later his manuscript is discovered in a forgotten cupboard.

In 'The Treasure of Abbot Thomas' a British antiquary unriddles a cipher on some Renaissance painted windows, and thereby discovers a centuried hoard of gold in a niche half way down a well in the courtyard of a German abbey. But the crafty depositor had set a guardian over that treasure, and something in the black well twines its arms around the searcher's neck in such a manner that the quest is abandoned, and a clergyman sent for. Each night after that the discoverer feels a stealthy presence and detects a horrible odour of mould outside the door of his hotel room, till finally the clergyman makes a daylight replacement of the stone at the mouth of the treasure-vault in the well – out of which something had come in the dark to avenge the disturbing of old Abbot Thomas's gold. As he completes his work the cleric observes a curious toad-like carving on the ancient well-head, with the Latin motto '*Depositum custodi* – keep that which is committed to thee'.

Other notable James tales are 'The Stalls of Barchester Cathedral', in which a grotesque carving comes curiously to life to avenge the secret and subtle murder of an old Dean by his ambitious successor; '"Oh, Whistle, and I'll Come to You, My Lad"', which tells of the horror summoned by a strange metal whistle found in a mediaeval church ruin; and 'An Episode of Cathedral History', where the dismantling of a pulpit uncovers an archaic tomb whose lurking daemon spreads panic and pestilence. Dr James, for all his light touch, evokes fright and hideousness in their most shocking forms; and will certainly stand as one of the few really creative masters in his darksome province.

For those who relish speculation regarding the future, the tale of supernatural horror provides an interesting field. Combated by a mounting wave of plodding realism, cynical flippancy, and sophisticated disillusionment, it is yet encouraged by a parallel tide of growing mysticism, as developed both through the fatigued reaction of 'occultists' and religious fundamentalists against materialistic discovery and through the stimulation of wonder and fancy by such enlarged vistas and broken barriers as modern science has given us with its intra-atomic chemistry, advancing astrophysics, doctrines of relativity, and probings into biology and human thought. At the present moment the favouring forces would appear to have somewhat of an advantage; since there is unquestionably more cordiality shewn toward weird writings than when, thirty years ago, the best of Arthur Machen's work fell on the stony ground of the smart and cocksure 'nineties. Ambrose Bierce, almost unknown in his own time, has now reached something like general recognition.

Startling mutations, however, are not to be looked for in either direction. In any case an approximate balance of tendencies will continue to exist; and while we may justly expect a further subtilisation of technique, we have no reason to think that the general position of the spectral in literature will be altered. It is a narrow though essential branch of human expression, and will chiefly appeal as always to a limited audience with keen special sensibilities. Whatever universal masterpiece of tomorrow may be wrought from phantasm or terror will owe its acceptance rather to a supreme workmanship than to a sympathetic theme. Yet who shall declare the dark theme a positive handicap? Radiant with beauty, the Cup of the Ptolemies was carven of onyx.

AFTERWORD:
LOVECRAFT IN BRITAIN

Stephen Jones

Introduction

I N THE SUMMER of 2007, while I was compiling *Necronomicon: The Weird Tales of H.P. Lovecraft* for Gollancz, I was fortunate enough to be given the unique opportunity to look through the publisher's original Lovecraft files, some of the contents of which dated back more than fifty years.

These files comprised around seventy-five scrappy letters and memos (mostly old Xeroxed or carbon copies, still held together with rusty pins instead of paperclips) stuffed haphazardly into two battered brown folders. However, despite the fact that over the years many items had obviously been lost, never properly filed or discarded as the company moved offices, a detailed look at these papers revealed a previously unrecorded insight into the publication of H.P. Lovecraft's fiction in the United Kingdom.

By far the most useful and interesting items were copies of a number of letters between August Derleth and Victor Gollancz employees, some of the original contracts, and various correspondence relating to the licensing of sub-rights to Lovecraft's work to other imprints.

Over the following pages I have attempted to catalogue for the first time a detailed history of the publication of H.P. Lovecraft's fiction in Britain, much of it based on the material contained in these files.

1. A Dark Debut

Howard Phillips Lovecraft is probably the most important and influential author of supernatural fiction in the twentieth century. Today he is acknowledged as a mainstream American writer second only to Edgar Allan Poe. Born in Providence, Rhode Island in 1890, Lovecraft was a life-long antiquarian and voluminous letter-writer whose early work was initially published in the amateur press.

The majority of his tales are set in the fear-haunted towns of an imaginary area of Massachusetts, or in the cosmic vistas that exist beyond space and time. Many of his best stories blend elements of horror and science fiction, and have come to be collectively known as the 'Cthulhu Mythos'.

Most of Lovecraft's tales of horror and the macabre did not see print professionally until the early 1920s, and the bulk of his fiction appeared in pulp magazines like *Weird Tales*, along with a handful of hardcover anthologies. Despite this, his relatively small body of work has influenced countless imitators, and formed the basis of a worldwide industry of books, games and movies based on his concepts and imagination.

Two years after Lovecraft's untimely death in 1937, an

omnibus volume of his best work was published by fledgling imprint Arkham House. Named after Lovecraft's fictional New England town, Arkham House was set up by young authors August Derleth and Donald Wandrei solely to preserve between hardcovers the collected writings of their literary mentor.

August William Derleth sold his first story when he was only fifteen, and began corresponding with Lovecraft *two years later*, in August 1926. Utilising some of the mortgage money Derleth had borrowed from a local bank to build a house, Arkham House published *The Outsider and Others* in 1939. Despite selling the hefty volume for just $5.00 (or $3.50, the pre-publication price), there were only 150 advance subscriptions received, and it eventually took four years to sell out the first – and only – printing and recoup that original investment.

In the meantime, to enable the small press to continue, Derleth was forced to publish collections by himself and other contemporary horror and fantasy authors, to help alleviate the imprint's cash-flow problems.

Victor Gollancz was born in London in 1893, the son of a wholesale jeweller. After serving with the British Army during the First World War, he formed his own eponymous publishing company in 1927. A life-long socialist and humanitarian, he was knighted in 1965 and died two years later at the age of seventy-four.

In May 1950, while staying at The Beverly Hotel at 125 East 50th Street, New York, Victor Gollancz wrote to August Derleth in Sauk City, Wisconsin, to enquire about the possibility of obtaining the British and Commonwealth rights to some of Lovecraft's stories.

In a letter dated May 24 of that year, Derleth replied: 'I am delighted to have your good letter of 22nd May regarding possible publication of the works of the late H.P. Lovecraft in England. We have had several offers for such publication, but have so far turned them all down. Yours, however, seems to us the most decent offer that we have had, and I am confident that we can agree on publication along the lines of the terms you have proposed. Moreover, I personally would prefer to see an imprint like that of Gollancz (many of whose books were on my shelves before I became a publisher) on a British edition of Lovecraft's best work.'

Gollancz's enquiry apparently came as a result of The World Publishing Company's edition of *Best Supernatural Stories of H.P. Lovecraft*, issued in hardcover in 1945. The first 'popular-priced edition' of the author's work, it had been edited by Derleth, who also provided an introduction, and went through three printings in just over a year.

Derleth was quick to assure Gollancz that there would be no problem: 'It is true that I control rights in the Lovecraft stories. The World edition, which is now out of print, but which will go back into print late this year, is in no way bound. But I do believe that you could have a better selection of the stories, of which there are enough to make two collections ultimately, and this I would strongly urge you to consider. Assuming that you have the World collection in your possession, I am supplementing it under separate cover by an incomplete copy of *The Outsider and Others*, from which an essay and three short stories have been deleted. These three short stories will be found in a paperback collection which I am including with the incomplete omnibus edition.'

It is most likely that the paperback collection that Derleth sent to Gollancz was either *The Weird Shadow Over Innsmouth and Other Stories of the Supernatural* (1944) or *The Dunwich Horror* (1945), both published by Bartholomew House, or *The Lurking Fear and Other Pieces* issued in 1947 by the Avon Book Company.

Derleth also helpfully included a list of those titles that he considered Lovecraft's best work:

short novels: AT THE MOUNTAINS OF MADNESS
                 THE CASE OF CHARLES DEXTER WARD

short stories: THE DUNWICH HORROR
                 THE RATS IN THE WALLS

THE COLOUR OUT OF SPACE
THE WHISPERER IN DARKNESS
THE SHADOW OVER INNSMOUTH
THE SHADOW OUT OF TIME
THE CALL OF CTHULHU
THE THING ON THE DOORSTEP
THE DREAMS IN THE WITCH-HOUSE
THE HAUNTER OF THE DARK
PICKMAN'S MODEL
THE SHUNNED HOUSE
THE MUSIC OF ERICH ZANN
THE OUTSIDER
THE CATS OF ULTHAR
COOL AIR
THE HORROR AT RED HOOK
THE NAMELESS CITY
THE TOMB
IN THE VAULT
HE
THE STRANGE HIGH HOUSE IN THE MIST
THE STATEMENT OF RANDOLPH CARTER
THE SILVER KEY
THROUGH THE GATES OF THE SILVER KEY
THE TEMPLE
THE FESTIVAL
ARTHUR JERMYN
THE UNNAMABLE
THE MOON-BOG
THE PICTURE IN THE HOUSE
THE TERRIBLE OLD MAN
HYPNOS
DAGON
POLARIS
CELEPHAÏS
THE HOUND

Derleth did not leave many major stories off his list! He also explained to Gollancz that, with the books he was sending him, he would have copies of all the important work of Lovecraft with the exception of the posthumously published novella 'The Case of Charles Dexter Ward'.

'This exists in ms.,' Derleth continued, 'though it was published in our now out of print collection, *Beyond the Wall of Sleep*, and it can be sent to you if you wish to see it. With proper production, it might be made into a separate book.'

Derleth was also at pains to point out that 'at least two and possibly three volumes as production costs dictate' could be compiled from the list of story titles that he had supplied.

Victor Gollancz had also enquired in his letter about previous British publication of Lovecraft's stories. In fact, the author had enjoyed some previous critical (if not particularly commercial) success in that area. While his work was still being featured in amateur publications and pulp magazines in his native America, in Britain, Christine Campbell Thomson, editor of the *Not at Night* series of popular hardcover horror anthologies, had included 'The Horror at Red Hook' in *You'll Need a Night Light* (1927), 'Pickman's Model' in *By Daylight Only* (1928) and 'The Rats in the Walls' in *Switch on the Light* (1928). Additionally, Gollancz was aware that 'The Music of Erich Zann' had been included in the 'Great Short Stories' series in the October 24, 1932 edition of London's *The Evening Standard* newspaper, illustrated by Philip Mendoza (Montague Phillip Mendoza, 1898–1973).

Around 1936, Brooklyn fan (and later literary agent and legendary comic book editor) Julius Schwartz had attempted to sell a collection of Lovecraft's work to a British book publisher, but his efforts had come to nothing.

'No volume of Lovecraft's

The MUSIC of ERICH ZANN

By H. P. Lovecraft

GREAT SHORT STORIES—No. 91

I HAVE examined maps of the city with the greatest care, yet have never again found the Rue d'Auseil. These maps have not been modern maps alone, for I know that names change. I have, on the contrary, delved deeply into all the antiquities of the place, and have personally explored every region, of whatever name, which could possibly answer to the street I knew as the Rue d'Auseil. But despite all I have done, it remains a humiliating fact that I cannot find the house, the street, or even the locality, where, during the last months of my impoverished life as a student of metaphysics at the university, I heard the music of Erich Zann.

That my memory is broken I do not wonder, for my health, physical and mental, was gravely disturbed throughout the period of my residence in the Rue d'Auseil, and I recall that I took none of my few acquaintances there. But that I cannot find the place again is both singular and perplexing, for it was within a half-hour's walk of the university and was distinguished by peculiarities which could hardly be forgotten by anyone who had been there. I have never met a person who has seen the Rue d'Auseil.

The Rue d'Auseil lay across a dark river bordered by precipitous brick bleak-windowed warehouses and spanned by a ponderous bridge of dark stone.

It was always shadowy along that river, as if the smoke of neighbouring factories shut out the sun perpetually. The river was also odorous with evil stenches which I have never smelled elsewhere, and which may some day help me to find it, since I should recognise them at once. Beyond the bridge were narrow cobbled streets with rails, and then came the ascent, at first gradual but incredibly steep as the Rue d'Auseil was reached.

I have never seen another street so narrow and steep as the Rue d'Auseil. It was almost a cliff, closed to all vehicles, consisting in several places of flights of steps, and ending at the top in a lofty ivied wall. Its paving was irregular, sometimes stone slabs, sometimes cobblestones, and sometimes bare earth with struggling greenish-grey vegetation. The houses were tall, peaked-roofed, incredibly old, and crazily leaning backward, forward, and sidewise. Occasionally an opposite pair, both leaning forward, almost met across the street like an arch, and certainly they kept most of the light from the ground below. There were a few overhead bridges from house to house across the street.

The inhabitants of that street impressed me peculiarly. At first I thought it was because they were all silent and reticent; but later decided it was because they were all very old. I do not know how I came to live on such a street, but I was not myself when I moved there. I had been living in many poor places, always evicted for want of money, until at last I came upon that tottering house in the Rue d'Auseil kept by the paralytic Blandot. It was the third house from the top of the street, and by far the tallest of them all.

My room was on the fifth storey; the only inhabited room there, since the house was almost empty. On the night I arrived I heard strange music from the peaked garret overhead, and the next day asked old Blandot about it. He told me it was an old German viol-player, a strange, dumb man who signed his name as Erich Zann, and who played evenings in a cheap theatre orchestra; adding that Zann's desire to play in the night, after his return from the theatre, was the reason he had chosen this lofty and isolated garret room, whose single gable window was the only point on the street from which one could look over the terminating wall at the declivity and panorama beyond.

Thereafter I heard Zann every night, and although he kept me awake, I was haunted by the weirdness of his music. Knowing little of the art myself, I was yet certain that none of his harmonies had any relation to music I had heard before; and concluded that he was a composer of highly original genius. The longer I listened the more I was fascinated, until after a month or so I resolved to make the old man's acquaintance.

One night, as he was returning from his work, I intercepted Zann in the hallway, and told him I would like to know him and be with him when he played. He was a small, lean, bent person, with shabby clothes, blue eyes, grotesque, satyr-like face, and nearly bald head; and at my first words seemed both angered and frightened. My obvious friendliness, however, finally mellowed him; and he grudgingly motioned to me to follow him up the dark, creaking and rickety attic stairs. His room, one of only two in the steeply pitched garret, was on the west side, toward the high wall that formed the upper end of the street. Its size was very great, and seemed the greater because of its extraordinary bareness and neglect. Of furniture there was only a narrow iron bedstead, a dingy wash-stand, a small table, a large bookcase, an iron music-rack, and three old-fashioned chairs. Sheets of music were piled in disorder about the floor. The walls were of bare boards, and had probably never known plaster; whilst the abundance of dust and cobwebs made the place seem more deserted than inhabited. Evidently Erich Zann's world of beauty lay in some far cosmos of the imagination.

Motioning me to sit down, the dumb man closed the door, turned the large wooden bolt, and lighted a candle to augment the one he had brought with him. He now removed his viol from its moth-eaten covering, and, taking it, seated himself in the least uncomfortable of the chairs. He did not employ the music-rack, but, offering no choice and playing from memory, enchanted me for over an hour with strains I had never heard before; strains which must have been of his own devising. To describe their exact nature is impossible for one unversed in music. They were a kind of fugue, with recurrent passages of the most captivating quality, but to me were notable for the absence of any of those weird notes I had overheard from my room below on other occasions.

Those haunting notes I had remembered and had often hummed and whistled inaccurately to myself, so when the player at length laid down his bow I asked him if he would render some of them. As I began my request the wrinkled satyr-like face lost the bored placidity it had possessed during the playing, and seemed to show the same curious mixture of anger and fright which I had noticed when first I accosted him. For a moment I was inclined to use persuasion, regarding rather lightly the whims of senility; and even tried to awaken my host's weirder mood by whistling a few of the strains to which I had listened the night before.

But I did not pursue this course for more than a moment, for when the dumb musician recognised the whistled air his face grew suddenly distorted with an expression wholly beyond analysis, and his long, cold, bony right hand reached out to stop my mouth and silence the crude imitation. As he did this he further demonstrated his eccentricity by casting a startled glance toward the lone curtained window, as if fearful of some intruder—a glance doubly absurd, since the garret stood high above all the inaccessible roofs, this window being the only point on the street, as the concierge had told me, from which one could see over the wall at the summit.

The old man's glance brought Blandot's remark to my mind, and with a certain capriciousness I felt a wish to look out over the wide and dizzying panorama of moonlit roofs and city lights beyond the hilltop, which of all the dwellers in the Rue d'Auseil only this calloused musician could see. I moved toward the window and would have drawn aside the nondescript curtains, when with a frightened rage even greater than before, the dumb beggar was upon me again; this time motioning with his head toward the door as he nervously strove to drag me thither with both hands. Now thoroughly disgusted with my host, I ordered him to release me, and told him I would go at once. His clutch relaxed, and as he saw my disgust and offence his own anger seemed to subside. He tightened his relaxing grip, but this time in a friendly manner, forcing me into a chair; then, with an appearance of wistfulness, crossing to the littered table, where he wrote many words with a pencil, in the laboured French of a foreigner.

The note which he finally handed me was an appeal for tolerance and forgiveness. Zann said that he was old, lonely, and afflicted with strange fears and nervous disorders connected with his music and with other things. He had enjoyed my listening to his music, and wished I would come again and not mind his eccentricities. But he could not play to another his weird harmonies, and could not bear hearing them from another; nor could he bear having anything in his room touched by another. He had not known until our hallway conversation that I could overhear his playing in my room, and now asked me if I would arrange with Blandot to take a lower room where I could not hear him in the night. He would, he wrote, defray the difference in rent.

As I sat deciphering the execrable French I felt more lenient toward the old man. He was a victim of physical and nervous suffering, as was I; and my metaphysical studies had taught me kindness. In the silence there came a slight sound from the window—the shutter must have rattled in the night wind, and for some reason I started almost as violently as did Erich Zann. So when I had finished reading I shook my host by the hand and departed as a friend.

The next day Blandot gave me a more expensive room on the third floor, between the apartments of an aged moneylender and the room of a respectable upholsterer. There was no one on the fourth floor.

It was not long before I found that Zann's eagerness for my company was not so great as it had seemed whilst he was persuading me to move down from the fifth storey. He did not ask me to call on him, and when I did call he appeared uneasy and played listlessly. This was always at night—in the day he slept, and would admit no one. My liking for him did not grow, though the attic room and the weird music seemed to hold an odd fascination for me. I had a curious desire to look out of that window, over the wall and down the unseen slope at the glittering roofs and spires, which must be outspread there. Once I went up to the garret during the theatre hours, when Zann was away, but the door was locked.

What I did succeed in doing was to overhear the nocturnal playing of the dumb old man. At first I would tip-toe up to my old fifth floor, then I grew bold enough to climb the last creaking staircase to the peaked garret. There in the narrow hall, outside the bolted door with the covered keyhole, I often heard sounds which filled me with an indefinable dread—the dread of vague wonder and brooding mystery. It was not that the sounds were hideous, for they were not; but that they held vibrations suggesting nothing on this globe of earth, and that at certain intervals they assumed a symphonic quality which I could hardly conceive as produced by one player. Certainly, Erich Zann was a genius of wild power. As the weeks passed, the playing grew wilder, whilst the old musician acquired an increasing haggardness and furtiveness pitiful to behold. He now refused to admit me at any time, and shunned me whenever we met on the stairs.

Then one night as I listened at the door I heard the shrieking viol swell into a chaotic babel of sound, a pandemonium which would have led me to doubt my own shaking sanity had there not come from behind that barred portal a piteous proof that the horror was real—the awful, inarticulate cry which only a dumb man can utter, and which rises only in moments of the most terrible fear or anguish. I knocked repeatedly at the door, but received no response. Afterwards I waited in the black hallway, shivering with cold and fear, till I heard the feeble effort of the viol to rise from the floor by the aid of a chair. Believing him conscious after a fainting fit, I renewed my rapping, at the same time calling out my name reassuringly. I heard Zann stumble to the window and close both shutter and sash, then stumble to the door, which he falteringly unfastened to admit me. This time his delight at having me present was real; for his distorted face gleamed with relief whilst he clutched at my coat as a child clutches at its mother's skirts.

Shaking pathetically, the old man forced me into a chair whilst he sank into another, beside which his viol and bow lay carelessly on the floor. He sat for some time inactive, nodding oddly, but having a paradoxical suggestion of intense and frightened listening. Subsequently he seemed to be satisfied, and crossing to a chair by the table wrote a brief note, handed it to me, and returned to the table, where he began to write rapidly and incessantly. The note implored me in the name of mercy, and for the sake of my own curiosity, to wait where I was while he prepared a full account in German of all the marvels and terrors which beset him. I waited, and the dumb man's pencil flew.

It was perhaps an hour later, while I still waited and while the old musician's feverishly written sheets still continued to pile up, that I saw Zann start as from the hint of a horrible shock. Unmistakably he was looking at the curtained window and listening shudderingly. Then I half fancied I heard a sound myself; though it was not a horrible sound, but rather an exquisitely low and infinitely distant musical note, suggesting a player in one of the neighbouring houses, or in some abode beyond the lofty wall over which I had never been able to look. Upon Zann the effect was terrible, for, dropping his pencil, suddenly he rose, seized his viol, and commenced to rend the night with the wildest playing I had ever heard from his bow, save when listening at the barred door.

It would be useless to describe the playing of Erich Zann on that dreadful night. It was more horrible than anything I had ever overheard, because I could now see the expression of his face, and could realise that this time the motive was stark fear. He was trying to make a noise; to ward something off or drown something out—what, I could not imagine, awesome though I felt it must be. The playing grew fantastic, delirious, and hysterical, yet kept to the last the qualities of supreme genius which I knew the strange old man possessed. I recognised the air—it was a wild Hungarian dance popular in the theatres, and I reflected for a moment that this was the first time I had ever heard Zann play the work of another composer.

Louder and louder, wilder and wilder, mounted the shrieking and whining of that desperate viol. The player was dripping with an uncanny perspiration and twisted like a monkey, always looking frantically at the curtained window. In his frenzied strains I could almost see shadowy satyrs and Bacchanals dancing and whirling insanely through seething abysses of clouds and smoke and lightning. And then I thought I heard a shriller, steadier note that was not from the viol; a calm, deliberate, purposeful, mocking note from far away in the West.

At this juncture the shutter began to rattle in a howling night-wind which had sprung up outside as if in answer to the mad playing within. Zann's screaming viol now outdid itself, emitting sounds I had never thought a viol could emit. The shutter rattled more loudly, unfastened, and commenced slamming against the window. Then the glass broke shiveringly under the persistent impacts, and the chill wind rushed in, making the candles sputter and rustling the sheets of paper on the table where Zann had begun to write out his horrible secret. I looked at Zann, and saw that he was past conscious observation. His blue eyes were bulging, glassy and sightless, and the frantic playing had become a blind, mechanical, unrecognisable orgy that no pen could even suggest.

A sudden gust, stronger than the others, caught the manuscript and bore it toward the window. I followed the flying sheets in desperation, but they were gone before I reached the demolished panes. Then I remembered my old wish to gaze from this window, the only window in the Rue d'Auseil from which one might see the slope beyond the wall, and the city outspread beneath. It was very dark, but the city's lights always burned, and I expected to see them there amidst the rain and wind. Yet when I looked from that highest of all gable windows, looked while the candles sputtered and the insane viol howled with the night-wind, I saw no city spread below, and no friendly lights gleamed from remembered streets, but only the blackness of space illimitable; unimagined space alive with motion and music, and having no semblance of anything on earth. And as I stood there looking in terror, the wind blew out both the candles in that ancient peaked garret, leaving me in savage and impenetrable darkness with

(Continued on Next Page)

'Chaos & Pandemonium Before Me'

stories has to my knowledge ever been published in Great Britain,' Derleth reassured Gollancz. 'The World people have the right only to sales in Canada, in addition to the United States. Certain of the Lovecraft stories were published in the *Not at Night* collections published by Selwyn & Blount a decade or so ago; more recently, only "The Dunwich Horror" and "The Rats in the Walls" have appeared in the Fraser-Wise anthology, *Great Tales of Terror and the Supernatural*, published, I believe, by Hammond, Hammond & Company Ltd in 1947. Anthology publication in Great Britain in no way impairs British book collection rights. The only other tale to have been so anthologized, as far as I know, apart from the "Erich Zann" story you mention, has been "The Outsider", which appeared in James Nelson's *The Murder Sampler*, published over there by an associate of Doubleday, the American publisher.'

Concluding his letter on a more business-like note, Derleth proposed to Gollancz that if, after due consideration, he still wanted to go ahead and publish a collection of Lovecraft's work, then he should make an estimate of the word-count and indicate which stories he would like to include in the book.

Derleth also suggested a few additions and modifications to the original offer that Gollancz had proposed. These included a new Foreword to the British edition to be written by Derleth, the advance payment to be split fifty pounds on signature of the contract and fifty pounds on publication, and, perhaps most interesting of all, that 'Arkham House should have the exclusive right to sell the Gollancz edition of this or any further Lovecraft collection in the United States and Canada.'

He signed off by adding that he was sending Gollancz a copy of the Arkham House stocklist under separate cover.

Victor Gollancz replied on May 29, before he left New York, basically agreeing with Derleth's story suggestions but, being concerned about the length of the book, asking Derleth to suggest a possible contents listing that omitted the two short novels.

In the meantime, Derleth had already dispatched a copy of the manuscript of 'The Case of Charles Dexter Ward' to Gollancz's London office in Henrietta Street, Covent Garden, before replying on June 3 to the same address.

His letter contained two proposed contents of varying lengths.

'The wordage adds up to a little over 120,000,' he explained of the first list of eighteen titles, which also included alternatives and details of any previous appearances in the UK, 'but you intend to publish a shorter book in any case; so that this list of "best" stories must necessarily be modified to your needs. These stories are perhaps Lovecraft's best from a literary point-of-view as well as from the perspective of effective fiction.

'This would seem to afford you ample latitude in making a selection of stories. Such short titles as "Dagon", "Polaris", "Beyond the Wall of Sleep", and "The Temple" could be included to pad out the contents page without actually taking up very much space. "The Unnamable" and "The Festival" fit into this category, too, though none is Lovecraft's best work.'

Derleth then went on to present a cut-down version of the contents, with the explanation: 'If I were to launch Lovecraft in England, I would not particularly consider previous anthologization. I would publish, considering space limitations of say 90,000 words, the following stories:

THE OUTSIDER
THE RATS IN THE WALLS
PICKMAN'S MODEL
THE CALL OF CTHULHU
THE DUNWICH HORROR
THE WHISPERER IN DARKNESS
THE COLOUR OUT OF SPACE
THE HAUNTER OF THE DARK
THE THING ON THE DOORSTEP
THE MUSIC OF ERICH ZANN'

Once again, he also suggested a few substitutions, should they be needed, concluding: 'But this selection is your problem, and I shall introduce the stories in accordance with your decision in this matter. It might be well, when you let me know your choice, to indicate a word limit for the foreword.'

Having finally returned from his business trip to New York, Victor Gollancz replied to Derleth again. 'I have now read all the stories and agree completely with your selection,' he wrote on June

23, adding that he had decided that the book should consist of the ten stories initially recommended by Derleth.

'I shall be obliged if you would let me have your Foreword (which should definitely introduce Lovecraft to the British public) as soon as possible,' confirmed Gollancz. 'Please make the length approximately that of your Introduction to the World Publishing Company volume.'

After promising to send off the contract in the next few days, Gollancz concluded his letter with two postscripts. In the first, he told Derleth that he was calling the collection *The Haunter of the Dark & Other Tales of Horror*. In the second note, he asked Derleth to 'Keep me in touch with any "discoveries" in the supernatural field which may come your way.'

Four days later Derleth mailed back his draft of the Introduction. 'It is approximately the same length as that for the World Publishing Company volume,' he confirmed. 'To expedite matters, I wish you would feel perfectly free to make such alterations in the introduction as you would wish to make without consulting me.'

But while Derleth's letter was making its way across the Atlantic, another problem had arisen, one that had the potential to terminate the whole project before it ever got off the ground.

Despite Derleth's flattering claim in his first letter to Victor Gollancz that he had already 'had several offers for such publication', and his assertion that he controlled the rights to the Lovecraft stories, he had failed to mention that for the past year the London literary agency of Pearn, Pollinger & Higham, Ltd had been attempting to sell *Best Supernatural Stories of H.P. Lovecraft* into the British market. When they discovered that Gollancz had already done a deal directly with Arkham House, they were not very pleased.

Co-director Laurence Pollinger wrote to Victor Gollancz on June 29 from his offices around the corner in The Strand to find out what was going on. Gollancz replied the following day:

'*My dear Laurence,*
Many thanks for your letter of 29th June.
As I told Gerald just now, there is a mistake here. When I was first put on to Lovecraft, and was told that Derleth controlled

the rights, I wrote to the latter to find out the position. He told me that
he did control the rights in all Lovecraft's stories: that he had had
requests for volume rights from England: that he had always refused
them: but that he would like to work with me. Negotiations then
followed and we discussed terms. We found no difficulty in arriving
at an agreement, which was clinched. This gives me the sole right to
publish certain of the Lovecraft stories in volume form here, with an
option to publish all the rest of his work in later volumes. My first
volume will consist of a selection made by Derleth which includes most
of the stories in the volume published by the World people, to which
you refer – and Derleth is himself at the moment writing a special
introduction for me to this first collection.
    Yours ever,'

That same day Gollancz wrote to Derleth, to no doubt express
his displeasure at being put in such a difficult position.

Derleth hurriedly responded on July 3: 'I hasten to assure you
that Mr Oscar J. Friend of Otis Kline Associates was instructed
some weeks ago to ask Pearn, Pollinger and Higham to withdraw
The [sic] *Best Supernatural Stories of H.P. Lovecraft*, which they have
been vainly trying to sell for approximately five years. I have thus
no direct connexien [sic] with Mr Pollinger at all, and it is the firm
headed by Mr Friend which has been offering the Lovecraft works
through Pearn, Pollinger and Higham.'

Not only had Derleth let slip in his haste that his claim of 'several
offers' for Lovecraft's work may have been stretching the truth a
bit, but Laurence Pollinger confirmed it in a letter to Gollancz the
following day, although his account did not exactly conform to
Derleth's version of events: 'I find we received copy of this book
from the American agent, Otis Kline on 4th August, 1949, and since
that time it has been submitted to ten publishers without success.
In view of what you write me I am withdrawing it from the publisher
who is now considering it.'

Pollinger also revealed that he had heard that same morning
from the Kline agency, which had been founded by adventure
novelist Otis Adelbert Kline. Kline, like Lovecraft, had also been a
contributor to *Weird Tales* in the 1930s, before concentrating on his
career as a literary agent (most famously for Robert E. Howard).

'I am just in receipt of a letter from Arkham House telling me that they have made their own arrangements for publication of Howard P. Lovecraft material in England and asking me to withdraw all Lovecraft titles from further offer,' instructed Otis Kline Associates. 'I am writing Arkham in some reproof of such action, but will you please withdraw all Lovecraft material.'

Laurence Pollinger was more sanguine about the outcome. 'As you will appreciate Arkham House is the American publisher of this book,' he wrote to Gollancz. 'I take it that you have no objections to my writing to Kline telling him that you have contracted with Derleth for the publication of these stories here. Doubtless upon receipt of this he will then check with Arkham House as to whether they or Derleth should have signed the agreement with you.'

With this final hurdle delaying H.P. Lovecraft's debut British collection now removed, a contract dated July 5, 1950, was signed between Victor Gollancz Ltd and Arkham House Publishers.

The Haunter of the Dark & Other Tales of Horror finally appeared in hardcover from Victor Gollancz in 1951 and quickly went out of print. It was reissued in 1966 and 1969, and a second impression was published in 1971 and reprinted in 1977. The distinctive yellow dust-jacket posed the rhetorical question, 'Who is Lovecraft?', before proceeding to answer itself in some detail.

Although in a different order, all ten stories in the volume had also appeared in the World Publishing edition of *Best Supernatural Stories of H.P. Lovecraft*, which additionally included 'In the Vault', 'The Picture in the House', 'Cool Air' and 'The Terrible Old Man'.

'Remarkable ... It is not too much to say that they are masterpieces in the genre of the super-naturally horrible,' raved the *Birmingham Post*, while the *Yorkshire Post* declared: 'Connoisseurs of the "uncanny" must not miss a most remarkable collection of stories by the American H.P. Lovecraft. His is a narrow but powerful imagination, which has created and peopled a world of its own.'

Derleth's succinct three-page foreword, 'An Introduction to H.P. Lovecraft', achieved its intended aim of introducing the late American horror author to a whole new readership. 'This first selection of Lovecraft's stories to be published outside America is representative of his best work,' concluded Derleth. 'Here are such memorable early stories as "The Outsider", "The Rats in the Walls", and "The Colour Out of Space", which is strangely suggestive of events in our own atomic age, though it was first published in 1927;

here, too, are the best of the Cthulhu Mythology short stories – "The Dunwich Horror", "The Thing on the Doorstep", and others. That these are the best short stories H.P. Lovecraft wrote cannot be gainsaid; but they are not *all* the best. These stories demonstrate conclusively that H.P. Lovecraft has a secure place, however minor, in the same niche as Poe, Hawthorne, and Bierce.'

Despite his reticence about his mentor's position in the pantheon of horror writers, Derleth was no doubt already preparing his British audience for more of Lovecraft's work. As it turned out, they did not have long to wait.

2. Terrors and Tribulations

In his letter of June 27, 1950, Derleth had responded at some length to Victor Gollancz's request to be kept in touch with any discoveries Derleth might make in the supernatural fiction field.

'As for "discoveries" in the supernatural field,' he wrote, 'I should be inclined to think that, apart from Lovecraft, the only Arkham authors in whose work you might conceivably be interested are Clark Ashton Smith, of whose work we have published three volumes, and the late Rev. Henry S. Whitehead, whose two collections under our imprint represent almost his entire prose fiction in the field. Should you be interested in seeing any of these volumes, you have only to let me know and I shall see to it that copies of the books are sent to you.'

Despite a pencilled notation on the original letter that indicates that this information was passed on to someone else in Gollancz, doubtless in the editorial department, nothing came of Derleth's recommendations and it was not until the 1970s that both Smith's and Whitehead's books from Arkham House were reprinted in the UK, not by Gollancz, but by Neville Spearman Ltd.

In fact, it seems out of character for Derleth to have been so reserved at putting forward more authors' names for possible consideration in the British market, as Neville Spearman also went on to publish other well-known Arkham House titles by the likes of Robert E. Howard, Robert Bloch, Carl Jacobi, David H. Keller, Fritz Leiber and even Derleth himself.

Meanwhile, following on from the success of the publication of *The Haunter of the Dark & Other Tales of Horror* in 1951, Gollancz decided to issue Lovecraft's 48,000-word novella *The Case of Charles Dexter Ward* as a stand-alone volume later that same year.

It was written over three months in early 1927 but never published during the author's lifetime. Derleth had retyped Lovecraft's original hand-written manuscript, as he recalled in the May 1941 issue of *Weird Tales*.

'The story was written in longhand on the reverse side of letters he had received, some 130 or 140 sheets of all sizes and colors. He didn't believe in margins or "white space". Every sheet was crowded from top to bottom, from left edge to right, with his small, cramped handwriting.

'That was his original draft; you can imagine what happened when he got through revising, words and sentences crossed out or written in, whole paragraphs added, inserts put on the back of the sheet where they got tangled up with the letters from his correspondents, and the inserts rewritten with additional paragraphs to be put in the insert which was to be put in its proper place in the story.

'Lovecraft's handwriting was not easy to read under the best of circumstances; he had his own peculiarities of spelling, often used Latin and Greek phrases, and often used coined words of his own. These made the problem of deciphering his complex puzzle-pages even more difficult. All in all, working after my classes at the U., it took me four months to get through the labyrinth.'

For the novella's first publication, Arkham House had borrowed the typescript prepared years earlier by Derleth from Lovecraft's literary executor, Robert H. Barlow, and then had it professionally re-typed over a period of two months.

Once again, the press reviews of the Gollancz edition were glowing: The *Manchester Evening Mail* called it a 'superb spine chiller', while the *News Chronicle* advised its readers, 'If you have the least touch of weakness for witchcraft do not miss *The Case of Charles Dexter Ward*'.

Even the usually demure *The Lady*, England's oldest magazine for women, enthused: 'If you like the grim and uncanny fantasy story, then *The Case of Charles Dexter Ward* should not be missed … H.P. Lovecraft, a master of the art, whose *Haunter of the Dark* is well remembered by connoisseurs of terror fiction – and rightly.'

However, despite glowing reviews of the book which, like its predecessor, went rapidly out of print, it would be another fifteen years before Victor Gollancz would publish a further volume of Lovecraft's fiction.

There is nothing in the files to indicate why there was this long hiatus in the publishing schedule.

Responding to a batch of clippings sent by Gollancz's Lester Anderson concerning Count Haraszthy (the founder of Sauk City, Wisconsin), a thank-you letter from August Derleth dated July 22, 1963, not only mentions his latest regional novel, *The Shadow in the Glass* (which he disparagingly dismisses as 'a v. dull, tedious novel'), but also the forthcoming 'Stephen Grendon' Arkham House collection, *Mr George and Other Odd Persons*, candidly revealing that the author is really himself. An Arkham House catalogue was also apparently included with the correspondence.

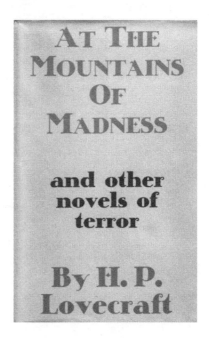

In September 1966, Victor Gollancz reissued *The Haunter of the Dark* while simultaneously publishing *At the Mountains of Madness and Other Tales of Terror* at a price of thirty shillings (£1.50 today)

𝔐𝔢𝔪𝔬𝔯𝔞𝔫𝔡𝔲𝔪 𝔬𝔣 𝔄𝔤𝔯𝔢𝔢𝔪𝔢𝔫𝔱 made this 3rd

day of   January 1967

between   Arkham House,
              c/o Scott Meredith Literary Agency,
              44, Great Russell Street,
              LONDON, W.C. 1

RJB

(who and whose executors administrators and assigns are where the context
permits hereinafter included in the term "the Author") of the one part and   "the Proprietor
VICTOR GOLLANCZ LIMITED of 14, Henrietta Street, Covent Garden,
London, W.C.2 (who and whose successors and assigns are where the context
permits hereinafter included in the term "the Publishers") of the other part
WHEREBY IT IS MUTUALLY AGREED as follows respecting a work by
the Author provisionally entitled:—

DAGON

by H. P. Lovecraft

1. The Publishers shall during the legal term of copyright have the
exclusive right of publishing and producing the said work, or any abridge-
ment or substantial part of the said work, in volume form in the British
Commonwealth and elsewhere subject to the conditions following: English
language in the British Commonwealth as constituted at
1st January 1947, (except Canada) together with all
territories at that date under mandate and in Eire, Burma,
India, Pakistan, Iraq, Transjordan and the British Trusteeships
and the Republic of South Africa, the rest of the world
except the United States of America, its Dependencies,
the Philippine Islands and Canada to be an open market
subject to the conditions following:

2. The Publishers shall, within twelve months of the delivery of the
manuscript ready for press unless otherwise mutually agreed and unless prevented by circumstances over which they have no control, at their own risk
and expense produce and publish the said work and the Author will before the Proprietor
——————————————————deliver to the said Publishers in a state fit
for the printer all the typescript indexes tables of contents illustrations
maps and such other matter as may be required for the said work.

Proprietor
3. The Author warrants to the Publishers that the said work is in no
way a violation of any existing copyright and that it contains nothing
libellous or objectionable and that all the statements purporting to be facts
are truthful and accurate and will indemnify the Publishers against any loss
injury or damage including any legal costs or expenses occasioned to or
incurred by the Publishers in consequence of any breach of this warranty.
But should the said work contain anything which in the opinion of the
Publishers or their legal advisers is libellous or objectionable, the Publishers
shall be at liberty to remove the same.

4. Accounts of the sales of the said work shall be made up to the 25th
March and the 29th September in each year and shall be rendered and paid
Proprietor   to the Author within four months of such making up of account the Publishers
paying the Author as follows:—
Proprietor

15. Should the Publishers sub-lease the said work to a reprint book club or to a cheap edition publisher then provided that the Publishers do not manufacture the book or arrange to participate with the sub-lessee in any way the net sum received from the sub-lease shall be divided equally between the ~~Author~~ Proprietor and the Publishers.

16. Should the Publishers sub-lease the said work with the consent of the ~~Author~~ Proprietor for condensation in volume form then provided that the Publishers do not participate with the sub-lessee in any way the net sum received from the sub-lease shall be divided equally between the ~~Author~~ Proprietor and the Publishers.

~~17. Dramatic and cinematograph rights shall belong to the Author,~~ but if at the Author's request the Publishers shall "handle" any or all of these rights ~~for the Author they shall~~ retain a commission of 10% (ten per ~~cent.) of the net proceeds.~~

18. In the event of a sale of a quantity of copies of not less than 2,000 (two thousand) to the Book Society at a discount of 50% (fifty per cent.) or more of the published price, a royalty shall be arranged.

19. Accounts of monies received by the Publishers in respect of clauses 10 to 18 inclusive shall be made up and the ~~Author's~~ Proprietor share shall be paid to the ~~Author~~ Proprietor on the same dates as those specified in clause 4.

~~20. The Author shall give to the Publishers the first option of publish-ing the next which he may write after the work the subject of this agreement upon terms to be arranged, such terms to be fair and reasonable and to include the same rights and territories as those covered by this agreement. The Publishers shall give their decision as to whether they are prepared to exercise their option on the said work/works within six weeks of the delivery to them of the com-plete copy in each case. In the event of the Publishers declining the first of such works, any further option shall be cancelled.~~

21. The Publishers shall pay all monies due to the Proprietor under this agreement to his Agent, Scott Meredith Inc., of 44, Great Russell Street, London, W.C. 2 whose receipt shall be a good and valid discharge therefor and who shall deal with the Publishers on the Proprietor's behalf on all matters arising in any way out of this agreement.

WITNESS to the signature of

Roderic Meng   *[signature]*

                                  ~~AUTHOR~~
                                  Proprietor

Signed on behalf of
VICTOR GOLLANCZ LTD.

WITNESS to the signature of   by

[signature]   *[signature]*
                                  Director

C.P.—22045/NF

per copy. The contents were identical to the 1964 Arkham House edition, which even included 'The Case of Charles Dexter Ward', published as a stand-alone volume by Gollancz fifteen years earlier.

'These tales of horror are in the true Gothic tradition,' enthused Francis Iles in the *Guardian* newspaper, 'and written in a deliberately Gothic style, full of hinted terrors and unholy stenches. This is something out of the ordinary, a real collector's piece for connoisseurs of the unusual; and at 448 closely printed pages for 30s, it can also be reckoned a "best buy".'

For their edition of *At the Mountains of Madness*, Gollancz dealt directly with Arkham House's New York representatives, the Scott Meredith Literary Agency. The contract, dated February 11, 1966, confirms that Gollancz paid an advance of £200.00 for this volume. With home sales of 1,681 copies and colonial sales – known as export sales these days – of 373 copies, the first printing easily earned out.

For their next Lovecraft volume, Gollancz went through Scott Meredith's London office. In a contract dated January 3, 1967, they paid a smaller advance of £150.00 for the usual British Commonwealth rights (excluding Canada).

Dagon and Other Macabre Tales was released on June 22 that same year, again at thirty shillings for the hardcover edition. Once more, the contents followed the Arkham House edition, published in 1965.

Although sales were slightly down on the previous Lovecraft collection – 1,500 sold in home and 294 in the colonial markets – the book quickly made back what Gollancz had paid for it.

'And now, to all intents and purposes, we are completing publication of the works of H.P. Lovecraft,' trumpeted the dust-jacket flap, which also managed to mis-spell Edgar Allan Poe's middle name as 'Allen'. 'Practically all the stories as yet un-published in England are here ... rounded out with Lovecraft's impressive long essay, "Supernatural Horror in Literature" – an important and much sought-after item.'

However, an astute British reader, P.J. Jeffery of Leigh-on-Sea, Essex, noticed that in Lovecraft's ground-breaking essay, lines 5 and 7 on page 365 were identical and wrote to the publisher. Having photographed the original Arkham volume for the British edition, Gollancz's science fiction editor and managing director John Bush contacted Derleth in a letter dated April 17, 1968, and asked how the paragraph should read, so that it could be corrected in any subsequent printing.

Derleth replied three days later:

'Dear Mr Bush,
 Many thanks for calling attention to a deleted line on page 365 of Dagon & C. The correct line is as follows (I have copied here the entire section from the top of that page through the flawed lines)—

... interest exemplified in the vogue of the charlatan Cagliostro and the publication of Francis Barrett's The Magus (1801), a curious and compendious treatise on occult principles and ceremonies, of which a reprint was made as lately as 1896, figures in Bulwer-Lytton and in many late Gothic novels, especially that remote and enfeebled posterity which straggled far down into the nineteenth century and was represented by George W.M. Reynold's Faust and the Demon and Wagner the Wehr-Wolf. Caleb Williams, though non-supernatural, has many authentic ...'

Never one to miss an opportunity, Derleth signed off by adding that he was taking the liberty of sending under separate cover two of his own books 'for your reading – time permitting'.

John Bush wrote back to the eagle-eyed Mr Jeffery on April 26 to tell him how the missing line should read.

Due to some confusion, or perhaps editorial oversight, Victor Gollancz had publicly announced that with the publication of Dagon and Other Macabre Tales, 'practically all' of H.P. Lovecraft's work was now in print in the United Kingdom. Not unsurprisingly, several dutiful readers begged to differ.

John Bush wrote to Derleth on August 14, 1967:

'*Dear Mr Derleth,*

I enclose a photostat of a letter we have just received from a Lovecraft fan. It appears that we may have been wrong in our assumption that the volumes, <u>Dagon,</u> <u>The Haunter of the Dark and Other Tales of Horror</u> *and* <u>At the Mountains of Madness and Other Novels</u> *represented all Lovecraft's complete works. It would seem that you may have published a further volume which includes the novels and stories mentioned in Mr Valentine's letter: if so, we should be very interested in publishing this.*

Would you let me have your observations on the matter; and to make things easier for you I enclose the contents pages of our editions of the three volumes.

    Yours sincerely,'

It appears that Bush had already been thinking about a fourth Lovecraft collection for some time. On a postcard dated June 11, 1967, Derleth had written: 'I am sending you a copy of the Museum Press *Lurker at the Threshold* rather than an Arkham House, for their typeface is larger and easier to read. It should help to make up an omnibus fully the size of *Dagon* or *At the Mountains of Madness.*'

In fact, the question of exactly which Lovecraft stories Victor Gollancz had published had already come up in March that year when a P.C. Stoyle of Taunton, Somerset, had written to Livia Gollancz, who had by now taken over the company from her late father, and asked about the publication in Britain of the 'Cthulhu Mythos' stories (a term that Livia Gollancz was apparently unfamiliar with).

Derleth replied to John Bush's enquiry on August 18: 'Yes, it is true that Gollancz have *not* published all the Lovecraft stories, and there is a volume that could indeed be made of those that remain.'

He then went on to relate the history of how the British publisher had acquired the rights to Lovecraft's fiction: 'When the late Sir Victor Gollancz visited some years ago this country (ca, 1950), he was much taken with two of our books. These were *Best Supernatural Stories of Lovecraft* and my own '*In Re: Sherlock Holmes*'/*The Adventures of Solar Pons.* I had prepared the former for World Publishing Company from our *Outsider and Others,* a now very rare book commanding $200 and up per copy in any condition. He wanted to take both on, but preferred to publish rather a selection of the stories

ARKHAM HOUSE: PUBLISHERS
SAUK CITY, WISCONSIN

18 August 1967

Mr. John Bush
Victor Gollancz, Ltd.
14 Henrietta Street
London W. 2.

Dear Mr. Bush,

Thank you for your letter of 14th August. Yes, it is true that Gollancz have not published all the Lovecraft stories, and there is a volume that could indeed be made of those that remain. There are the stories listed in Mr. Valentine's letter, with the exception of THE SHUNNED HOUSE, which is in AT THE MOUNTAINS OF MADNESS. This situation came about in this way --

When the late Sir Victor Gollancz visited some years ago in this country (ca. 1950), he was much taken with two of our books. These were BEST SUPERNATURAL STORIES OF LOVECRAFT and my own "IN RE: SHERLOCK HOLMES" / THE ADVENTURES OF SOLAR PONS. I had prepared the former for World Publishing Company from our OUTSIDER AND OTHERS a now very rare book commanding $200 and up per copy in any condition. He wanted to take both on, but preferred to publish rather a selection of the stories from the BEST, with a new introduction by me. This became your volume, THE HAUNTER OF THE DARK.

The stories omitted from the book, together with two which were added later, became (that is, in addition to the stories in HAUNTER), our book THE DUNWICH HORROR & OTHERS. I am now sending you a copy of this, together with a paperback of THE SUR-VIVOR & OTHERS, and two separate volumes entitled, THE SHUTTERED ROOM &C, and THE DARK BROTHERHOOD & C. In these volumes you will find these stories --

by H. P. Lovecraft
  THE SHADOW OUT OF TIME
  THE SHADOW OVER INNSMOUTH
  COOL AIR
  THE PICTURE IN THE HOUSE
  IN THE VAULT
  THE TERRIBLE OLD MAN   all in THE DUNWICH HORROR &C

  by H. P. Lovecraft & August Derleth
  THE SURVIVOR
  WENTWORTH'S DAY
  THE PEABODY HERITAGE
  THE GABLE WINDOW
  THE ANCESTOR
  THE SHADOW OUT OF SPACE
  THE LAMP OF ALHAZRED   all in THE SURVIVOR &C
  THE SHUTTERED ROOM
  THE FISHERMAN OF FALCON POINT   both in THE SHUTTERED ROOM &C
  THE DARK BROTHERHOOD   in the book of that title

These 16 stories could be put into one volume if you are so inclined, perhaps under title of THE SHADOW OUT OF TIME -- or some similar title which need not be reflected in the book: SHADOWS OUT OF TIME AND SPACE, etc. THE LURKER AT THE THRESHOLD is not available over there, for Museum Press issued it in 1948 and have refused to reissue. THE SHUTTERED ROOM, incidentally, became the story used for the film of that title in England (an American production); you may be entertained by a note about it in our house organ, tearsheets also enclosed.

I am taking the liberty of enclosing also a broadside on Solar Pons. Sir Victor's interest in my pastiches did not decline, but it was not sufficient to overcome the blunting his desire to publish in England received from the firm's legal counsel, which feared that the ever-litigous Adrian Conan Doyle would commence an action claiming an invasion of proprietary rights or some such thing. I understand that he has been severely rebuked by the courts, and has considerably mellowed in recent years; it may be that Messrs. Gollancz might be again interested in doing these collections over there. If so, I'll be happy to send the 5 collections over for your inspection.

suggest no reply.

Sincerely,

August Derleth

ad/rm

from the *Best*, with a new introduction by me. This became your volume, *The Haunter of the Dark*.'

It seems that, once again, Derleth could not resist an opportunity to promote his own work. He then continued, 'The stories omitted from the book, together with two which were added later, became (that is, in addition to the stories in *Haunter*), our book *The Dunwich Horror & Others*. I am now sending you a copy of this, together with a paperback of *The Survivor & Others*, and two separate volumes entitled, *The Shuttered Room & C*, and *The Dark Brotherhood & C*.'

After listing all the stories in these volumes (including his own 'posthumous collaborations' with Lovecraft), Derleth suggested: 'These 16 stories could be put into one volume if you're so inclined, perhaps under the title *The Shadow Out of Time* – or some similar title which need not be reflected in the book: *Shadows Out of Time and Space*, etc.'

In a closing paragraph, Derleth made one more attempt to sell his own work by including some information on his Solar Pons detective books. 'Sir Victor's interest in my pastiches did not decline,' he explained, 'but it was not sufficient to overcome the blunting his desire to publish in England received from the firm's legal counsel, which feared that the ever-litigous [sic] Adrian Conan Doyle would commence an action claiming an invasion of proprietary rights or some such thing. I understand that he has been severely rebuked by the courts, and has considerably mellowed in recent years; it may be that Messrs. Gollancz might be again interested in doing these collections over there.'

Scribbled in red ink next to this postscript, in John Bush's handwriting, are the words 'Suggest no reply'.

Derleth also used the same correspondence to mention again his 'collaboration' with Lovecraft: '*The Lurker at the Threshold* is not available over there, incidentally,' he helpfully pointed out, 'for Museum Press issued it in 1948 and have refused to reissue.'

This piece of information seems to have stimulated Bush's interest. A pair of scribbled sheets, containing a list of possible contents for a fourth Lovecraft collection from Gollancz, includes *The Lurker at the Threshold* with the notation 'one of his most famous stories'. Below this note is written: 'Some by Lovecraft & some by L & Derleth'.

On October 18, 1967, Bush wrote to E.D. Nisbet, a director of the

Museum Press Ltd in London: 'Confirming my conversation with you, we are anxious to include the story *The Lurker at the Threshold* by H.P. Lovecraft in the fourth volume of the complete stories of H.P. Lovecraft which we are publishing next spring. August Derleth, the proprietor of Arkham House and Lovecraft's literary executor, writes to say that this story would not be available for us, "Museum Press issued it in 1948 and have refused to reissue".'

Perhaps aware of the previous problems that had arisen over the rights to Lovecraft's work between Derleth and Gollancz, Bush added: 'Derleth has obviously got his facts mixed up a bit but, as there may be some agent or other party involved, I should be most grateful if you could throw any light on the matter.

'I appreciate that you are perfectly willing for us to include this story in our volume, but it is well to get the facts straightened out.

'With many thanks for your co-operation.'

E.D. Nisbet replied two days later:

'Dear Mr Bush,
　　THE LURKER AT THE THRESHOLD
　　　By H.P. Lovecraft
　　I have made an extensive search through our archives, which are deposited in a very dusty vault, but unfortunately I have not succeeded in finding either the agreement or the correspondence relating to the above book. It looks as if they have gone astray during one or other of the moves and reorganizations to which the firm was subjected in the past. I am therefore unable to give you any definite information about this book, since it went out of print long before the time of anyone now connected with the firm.

　　I am afraid it looks as if you will have to rely upon obtaining permission from the author's literary executor, whom you may of

course inform that Museum Press have relinquished all claim to any
rights in the book.
    Yours sincerely,
    for MUSEUM PRESS LIMITED'

This was, of course, exactly the news that John Bush wanted to
hear. He wrote to Derleth on, appropriately, Hallowe'en 1967 to
inform him that the previous publisher had been unable to find
any definite information, adding: 'In view of this letter from the
Museum Press, I am assuming that we may include *The Lurker at
the Threshold* in our new volume.'

Two days later, Bush wrote to Derleth again, noting that
Gollancz did not possess a copy of the book (no mention is made
to what happened to the Museum Press copy Derleth had mailed
to the publisher back in June) and requesting it 'in some shape or
form and we can then get the whole volume cast off and find out
what sort of proposition it is going to be so that we can make you
an offer.'

Derleth was obviously elated by all that was happening and
replied on November 4, 1967: 'By all means include *The Lurker at
the Threshold* in your new Lovecraft book; I am delighted to learn
that Museum Press have relinquished claims on the book. This
time though, since the sale was not made by them, I would prefer
that you bypass Scott Meredith and send your contract, similar to
those made with our agents, directly to me for signature, and
payments likewise.'

The contracts for a fourth Lovecraft collection were drawn up
and sent to Derleth on November 8. The advance offered by
Gollancz had once again returned to £200.00, payable half on
signature and half on publication, against a rising royalty. Derleth
returned a signed copy of the contract on November 24, and terms
were eventually agreed on December 13.

But there was still one final glitch to overcome before the collection could go ahead. At 6:00 p.m. on November 22, a frantic
Gollancz cable-phoned Derleth:

LURKER UNARRIVED. PLEASE AIRMAIL ARKHAM
HOUSE EDITION IMMEDIATELY.

MUSEUM PRESS LTD

PUBLISHERS

Directors:
Chairman: E. H. CODE HOLLAND
B. G. BREWER   D. K. C. DICKENS
E. D. NISBET

39 PARKER STREET
LONDON, W.C.2
HOLBORN 9791
(01-405 9791)

EDN/JB   20th October, 1967

John Bush, Esq.,
Victor Gollancz Ltd.,
14 Henrietta Street,
Covent Garden,
London, W.C.2.

Dear Mr. Bush,

THE LURKER AT THE THRESHOLD
by H.P. Lovecraft

I have made an extensive search through our archives, which are
deposited in a very dusty vault, but unfortunately I have not succeeded
in finding either the agreement or the correspondence relating to the
above book. It looks as if they have gone astray during one or other
of the moves and reorganizations to which the firm was subjected in the
past. I am therefore unable to give you any definite information about
this book, since it went out of print long before the time of anyone
now connected with the firm.

I am afraid it looks as if you will have to rely upon obtaining
permission from the author's literary executor, whom you may of course
inform that Museum Press have relinquished all claim to any rights
in the book.

Yours sincerely,
for MUSEUM PRESS LIMITED

Derleth wrote back to John Bush two days later: 'I was sorry to learn by cable yesterday that the copy of *The Lurker at the Threshold* I had dispatched almost a month ago had not yet reached you. I sent off another copy by first-class airmail, and this ought to come to hand at about the same time as this letter.'

Not only did this replacement copy of *Lurker* arrive at the Gollancz offices on November 27, but the other edition Derleth had dispatched in October was also finally delivered on December 5.

'I'm glad to know that at least one copy of *The Lurker at the Threshold* turned up!' Derleth wrote in a letter dated December 2, 1967. 'Arkham House books are such collector's items over here that books are frequently stolen from the mails – evidently by postal service personnel who recognize the label on the parcel.'

At the same time, over and above his usual author's allowance, Derleth ordered an extra 200 copies of the forthcoming Gollancz collection, because, as he had explained in his letter of November 24: 'Since it reprints material now out of print with us, we will probably want to order a larger number of copies when publication

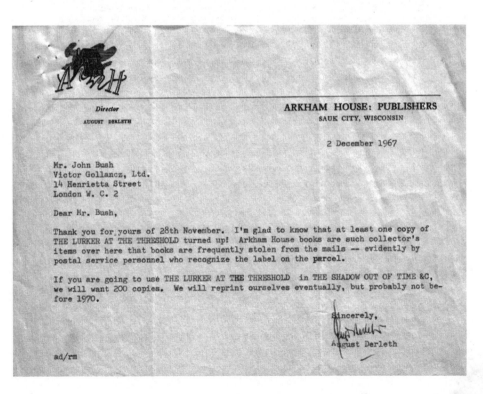

Director
AUGUST DERLETH

ARKHAM HOUSE: PUBLISHERS
SAUK CITY, WISCONSIN

2 December 1967

Mr. John Bush
Victor Gollancz, Ltd.
14 Henrietta Street
London W. C. 2

Dear Mr. Bush,

Thank you for, yours of 28th November. I'm glad to know that at least one copy of THE LURKER AT THE THRESHOLD turned up! Arkham House books are such collector's items over here that books are frequently stolen from the mails — evidently by postal service personnel who recognize the label on the parcel.

If you are going to use THE LURKER AT THE THRESHOLD in THE SHADOW OUT OF TIME &C, we will want 200 copies. We will reprint ourselves eventually, but probably not before 1970.

Sincerely,

August Derleth

ad/rm

looms.' According to a notation, these copies – pre-
sumably for re-sale through
Arkham House – were apparently invoiced at half the cover
price.

With publication set for
May 1968, Gollancz for some
reason sent a proof copy to
their solicitors, Rubinstein,
Nash & Co in London's Gray's
Inn. In a note dated April 2,
the legal firm's consultant, H.F.
Rubinstein, made the pithy
observation: 'This consists of
stories previously published –
presumably without libel trouble resulting.'

**THE
SHADOW
OUT OF
TIME**

**and other
tales of
horror**

**By H. P.
Lovecraft**

including those stories & novellae
that were completed after his death
by August Derleth

The book was issued under Derleth's suggested title of *The
Shadow Out of Time and Other Tales of Horror* at a price of thirty
shillings. The front dust-wrapper flap candidly admitted: 'When
we published H.P. Lovecraft's *Dagon* we made the claim that we had
completed publication of his works. In this we were wrong. We
received several letters from members of the public giving us names
of stories that were not included in any of our three collections. On
investigation, we found that there was a novel, *The Lurker at the
Threshold*, and also two novellae [sic] and five stories outstanding,
together with nine stories completed and edited by his friend,
publisher and Literary Executor, August Derleth. It is these latter
sixteen items that make up the present volume.'

Apparently, the Gollancz copywriter had got confused (or wasn't
very good at mathematics). The five stories and two 'novellae' by
Lovecraft said to be in the book were actually *six* stories: 'In the
Vault', 'The Picture in the House', 'Cool Air', 'The Terrible Old
Man', 'The Shadow Out of Time' and 'The Shadow Over Innsmouth'. The rest of the volume was rounded out with *ten* of
Derleth's so-called 'posthumous collaborations', as the dust-jacket
blurb helpfully explained: 'Among the papers left by Lovecraft, and
found after his death, were various outlines for works which he did
not live to write ... the scattered notes were put together by August

Derleth whose finished stories evolved from Lovecraft's suggested plots.'

No doubt many Lovecraft purists would take exception to that last statement. The second half of the book consisted of 'Stories by H.P. Lovecraft and August Derleth': 'The Survivor', 'Wentworth's Day', 'The Peabody Heritage', 'The Gable Window', 'The Ancestor', 'The Shadow Out of Space', 'The Lamp of Alhazred', 'The Fisherman of Falcon Point', 'The Dark Brotherhood' and 'The Shuttered Room'.

After all the problems with obtaining a copy, and John Bush's assertion to Derleth in his December 7 letter that 'we shall certainly be including *The Lurker at the Threshold*' in the book, that collaborative novel was notably missing from the contents of Gollancz's new Lovecraft collection!

Back in his initial letter to Victor Gollancz in May 1950, August Derleth had mentioned that Museum Press had published *The Lurker at the Threshold* in Britain under both Lovecraft's and his byline.

'This is, however, decidedly inferior work,' he added with unusual candour, 'since 9/10ths of it was written by me from Lovecraft's notes. Yet it has done well enough for them that, in the face of my refusal to permit their publication of the Lovecraft stories in collection, they have asked for a volume of my own tales in this genre, and this is at present being prepared in ms. by my secretary. (This, too, I hasten to add, is secondary work.)'

Interestingly, although no such collection of Derleth's stories ever appeared from Museum Press, they did reprint one other Arkham House title – *The Hounds of Tindalos* by Frank Belknap Long – in 1950.

The Lurker at the Threshold, published under both Lovecraft's and Derleth's names by Arkham House in 1945, was a slim novel based upon a fragment, 'The Round Tower', and other unrelated notes and story ideas discovered amongst Lovecraft's papers following his death. Taken together, this material reportedly amounted to only around 1,200 words.

'I constructed and wrote *The Lurker at the Threshold*,' revealed Derleth later on, 'which had nowhere been laid out, planned, or plotted by Lovecraft.'

The book was reputedly reprinted in Argentina in 1946 by Editorial Molino before Museum Press produced their own British edition two years later.

During the contractual problems about who controlled the British rights to the Lovecraft material, Derleth had complained to Victor Gollancz in his letter of July 3, 1950, that Otis Kline Associates had sold *The Lurker at the Threshold* to Museum Press through the Pearn, Pollinger & Higham literary agency 'at a figure which did not inspire me with confidence in either of the firms which undertook to place material'.

After originally considering including the short novel in *The Shadow Out of Time and Other Tales of Horror,* John Bush apparently changed his mind and decided that, as they had done with *The Case of Charles Dexter Ward* in 1951, the tale was strong enough to stand on its own.

As a result, *The Lurker at the Threshold* was issued as a separate hardcover volume in 1968 at twenty-five shillings (£1.25) and reprinted the following year. 'Lovecraft did not himself finish *The Lurker at the Threshold*,' admitted the jacket copy. 'Notes and plans for the book were left at his death, and enough had been done to indicate the direction of the plot.'

Eighteen years after he had made his first approach to Victor Gollancz, August Derleth finally had a book of his own published by the yellow-jacketed imprint (albeit in conjunction with his late friend and mentor).

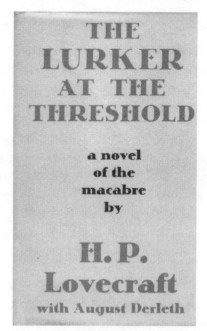

With the publication of *The Haunter of the Dark and Other Tales of Horror, The Case of Charles Dexter Ward, At the Mountains of Madness and Other Novels of Terror, Dagon and Other Macabre Tales, The Shadow Out of Time and Other Tales of Horror* and *The Lurker at the Threshold,*

Gollancz had finally issued all of H.P. Lovecraft's fiction in the United Kingdom. Or had they … ?

The publisher was still receiving letters from devout readers who continued to come up with missing titles from Gollancz's Lovecraft canon.

One such was R. Denton (Mr) from Folkestone, Kent, who wrote to the publisher in February 1970 to point out that he had read another of Lovecraft's 'collaborations' – 'Out of the Eons' by Hazel Heald – in a paperback edition of August Derleth's anthology *The Sleeping and the Dead*. 'Surely, as both your four collections and this anthology have in common August Derleth as editor, there is no excuse for this story's omission from your collections,' complained an obviously disgruntled Mr Denton.

He went on to mention the San Francisco rock band which had adopted Lovecraft's name, and revealed that the album sleeve notes referred to the author's poem cycle 'Fungi from Yuggoth'. 'Poems?!' exclaimed Mr Denton. 'This may, of course, be another one of those commercial "things", or an attempt to identify H.P. Lovecraft (the author) as the original beat/hippy. Nevertheless, I feel you should investigate, and perhaps you will find it necessary to publish yet a fifth collection. I eagerly await your reply.'

Clearly exasperated, John Bush still took the time to respond: 'We rather despair of ever being able to publish *every* story that Lovecraft wrote or had a hand in,' he acknowledged in a letter dated February 9. 'However much we believe – in conjunction with information given us by August Derleth – that we have really got every one, we seem to find that there is something we have missed out.'

Maybe, with this admission, it was time to let some other publisher take up the Lovecraft mantle in Britain …

3: Licence to Chill

Although Victor Gollancz would reprint new hardcover editions of its first four Lovecraft volumes intermittently during the 1960s and '70s, the company had purchased English language volume rights throughout the British Commonwealth (excluding Canada) in its initial dealings with Arkham House.

As a result, they were at liberty to sell paperback rights to the H.P. Lovecraft works in those territories they controlled to another publisher, if they so chose.

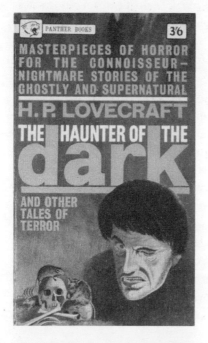

As Gollancz was not producing mass-market softcover books during this period, in July 1962 the publisher signed a five-year contract with Hamilton & Co. (Stafford) Ltd, owners of the Panther Books imprint, to publish *The Haunter of the Dark and Other Stories* (this is the title on the contract) in paperback. Hamilton & Co. paid Gollancz a £200.00 advance against the usual royalty for the sub-rights to this uniquely British Lovecraft collection.

In February the following year, Panther published *The Haunter of the Dark and Other Tales of Terror* at three shillings and sixpence. While the uncredited cover painting adapted an image of the monster from Hammer Films' *The Revenge of Frankenstein* (1958), the contents were the same as the 1951 Gollancz volume. The paperback edition sold well, and it was reprinted in 1965. The license was presumably extended for another five years in 1968, before being renewed for apparently a further eight years in 1973.

Boasting a much classier

cover painting, the short novel *The Case of Charles Dexter Ward* was also issued in a single softcover edition by Panther in May 1963. The publisher was obviously doing well with its Lovecraft reprints – so well, in fact, that they went elsewhere for their next Lovecraft volume.

With all the existing Gollancz material at that time now published in paperback in Britain, Panther apparently decided to put together its own original collection of Lovecraft's work.

The result, published in November 1964 and entitled *The Lurking Fear and Other Stories*, took its title from a 1947 American paperback released by the Avon Book Company (and reissued in the late 1950s and early 1960s in both the US and UK as *Cry Horror!*). However, because the British rights to some stories were already being held by Gollancz, the contents were significantly different.

This new compilation contained 'The Lurking Fear', 'The Shunned House', 'In the Vault', 'Arthur Jermyn', 'Cool Air', 'The Moon-Bog', 'The Nameless City', 'The Unnamable', 'The Picture in the House', 'The Terrible Old Man', 'The Hound', 'The Shadow Over Innsmouth' and 'The Shadow Out of Time'.

Not only did it contain six stories that would appear in the subsequent Gollancz edition of *Dagon and Other Macabre Tales*, and another from *At the Mountains of Madness and Other Tales of Terror*, but the collection also included all six of the remaining Lovecraft stories that John Bush would belatedly gather together in *The Shadow Out of Time and Other Tales of Horror* some four years later!

As a consequence of these differing contents, the *Shadow Out of Time* volume eventually saw print in Britain in an abridged paperback version.

In March 1968, Panther Books bought the sub-rights

for five years to *At the Mountains of Madness and Other
Novels of Terror* for an advance
of £150.00. In May the following year, Panther also
contracted for the *Dagon* collection, splitting it into two
volumes, *Dagon and Other
Macabre Tales* and *The Tomb
and Other Tales*. They paid an
advance of £150.00 for each
book.

Both collections appeared
in paperback that same year.
The six stories that had
already been published in *The
Lurking Fear and Other Stories*
were dropped, and the re-
maining contents slightly
re-ordered to balance out the
two volumes.

Following Gollancz's lead,
Panther issued the short novel
The Lurker at the Threshold as
a single volume in 1970.
Although both H.P. Lovecraft
and August Derleth are
credited as authors, you would
have to look very closely at the
cover to spot the latter's name.

Also released that same
year, for a £300 advance for
the rights in a contract dated
January 2, 1970, Panther's
edition of *The Shuttered Room
and Other Tales of Horror*
contained just the ten
'posthumous collaborations'
between the two authors that

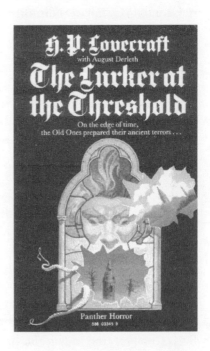

had originally appeared in *The Shadow Out of Time and Other Tales of Horror.*

Across the Atlantic, Ballantine Books had been successfully publishing Lovecraft in paperback in America for a number of years. In the early 1970s, as part of their innovative 'Adult Fantasy' imprint edited by Lin Carter, they decided to repackage some of the author's 'dream' stories and other tales into new editions.

As the 'Adult Fantasy' series was also being imported into Britain through a co-publishing deal with Pan Books, this apparently sent alarm bells ringing in the Gollancz offices.

On July 9, 1971, Giles Gordon wrote to August Derleth in Sauk City: 'There seems to be a little confusion about the rights situation in our market in some of the Lovecraft stories which we have contracted with you for. We have heard that Ballantine are planning to publish early next year two volumes in our territory under the titles *The Dream-Quest of Unknown Kadath* and *The Doom That Came to Sarnath*.'

He went on to point out that twenty of the stories Ballantine proposed to include in their two volumes had previously appeared in the Gollancz editions of *Dagon and Other Macabre Tales* and *At the Mountains of Madness and Other Novels of Terror*. 'Both books which we published in this market holding the exclusive territories from you. Likewise, both books are published in paperback editions here by Panther. They are currently in print in the Panther editions, Panther having sub-contracted for the paperback rights with ourselves.'

After quoting from the pertinent clause in the contract, Gordon concluded his letter: 'No doubt you will agree that the two proposed Ballantine volumes would be in clear violation of the rights you have granted us as both their proposed books reproduce in substantial part our two volumes.

'We very much hope you will be able to give us your assurance as soon as possible that the Ballantine editions will not be sold in the exclusive market which you have granted us.'

What Giles Gordon did not know at the time was that August Derleth had died unexpectedly five days earlier. The man who had almost single-handedly championed the work of his friend H.P. Lovecraft for more than three decades, and who had orchestrated all the dealings between Arkham House and Victor Gollancz, had never fully recovered from gall bladder surgery. He was just 62 years old.

Despite the death of its co-founder, Arkham House continued, initially under the guidance of Forrest D. Hartmann, an attorney in the Wisconsin firm of Hill, Quale & Hartmann who represented the Estate of August Derleth.

In a letter dated November 22, 1971, and copied to Gollancz, Hartmann wrote to Don R. Benson at Ballantine Books: 'I am still staggering under the enormous task presented by the death of August Derleth,' he began. 'However, slowly I am getting control of things and this letter is in regard to one of the problems that should have been taken care of months ago.'

Hartmann included a copy of Giles Gordon's letter and observed, 'If the facts are true as stated, it would seem that the Gollancz people have a very legitimate concern.' He went on to suggest that Ballantine resolve the matter to everyone's satisfaction and that Benson reply directly to the British publisher.

'Though it is unfortunate that this matter has not been called to your attention earlier,' concluded Hartmann, 'it has been very difficult for me to handle some of these matters not being familiar with August Derleth's agreements and contracts. However, now that things are better organized, I can assure you of my fullest cooperation in handling any matters such as these.'

As it turned out, the problem had already been dealt with during the intervening four months. On November 26, Giles Gordon wrote to Forrest Hartmann: 'It was kind of you to write the letter you did to Ballantine Books, but I am delighted to tell you that some months ago they agreed not to proceed any further with attempting to publish the editions of their two volumes of Lovecraft stories in our exclusive territory.'

As a result of these discussions, for British collectors of the Pan/Ballantine 'Adult Fantasy' series, the two volumes by Lovecraft remained available only in the original American editions.

The works of H.P. Lovecraft probably enjoyed their biggest commercial success on both sides of the Atlantic during the fantasy boom of the late 1960s and early '70s, which was initially spurred on by college students discovering J.R.R. Tolkien's *The Lord of the Rings* trilogy.

As a result of this renewed interest, not only did Gollancz reprint some of its Lovecraft hardcovers, but the Panther paperbacks of the author's work went through a number of consecutive printings as well.

But now there was another problem looming. Because there had not been a previous British edition, Panther could go directly to Arkham House to reprint the 1970 collaborative Lovecraft collection *The Horror in the Museum and Other Revisions* (which they split into two volumes in 1975). However, their sub-contracts with Gollancz had been based on five-year licenses. These were starting to run out, and the books were still selling very nicely.

Since 1965 Panther had been owned by Granada Publishing, who eventually phased out the imprint in the early 1980s, and the paperback publisher soon began requesting extensions of their money-making Lovecraft licenses. According to the original contracts, these could be automatically extended for three-year periods, so long as the paperback sales remained at a minimum of 2,500 copies during the final six months of the agreement.

Although Granada renewed their sub-rights deals on the Lovecraft books a number of times during the previous decade, by the early 1980s Gollancz's Rights Department was writing to the publisher informing them that licences had expired for a number of titles and asking if they wanted to renew.

In 1981, apparently in response to an enquiry from another British publisher about licensing the Lovecraft paperback rights, Gollancz confirmed in writing that *At the Mountains of Madness*, *The Case of Charles Dexter Ward*, *The Shuttered Room* (aka *The Shadow Out of Time*) and the first volume of *Dagon* were all available. *The Lurker at the*

Threshold had also been long out of print, although the rights were not officially reverted by Gollancz until March 1989. 'Granada still have two titles under licence but they are not in print and I'm investigating,' the letter continued. 'These are *The Haunter of the Dark* and *The Tomb* (volume 2 of *Dagon*).'

In a letter dated April 2, 1981, Granada confirmed that it was reverting rights to *The Haunter of the Dark*, while the last extension for *The Tomb*, dated March 2, 1978, was for a further five years.

In March 1981, Granada's contracts manager refused a request from Gollancz to revert rights on *The Tomb* because their edition was still in print. After that, there is no indication in the Gollancz files that they ever renewed the rights again.

However, that did not prevent Granada continuing to publish the Lovecraft titles in new editions ...

Surviving correspondence indicates that in 1983 Gollancz had been considering doing their own *Best of H.P. Lovecraft* volume and, in response to an enquiry from Granada, they told the paperback publisher that they would '*probably* retain the rights' in Lovecraft's stories.

However, John Bush (who would step down the following year as Gollancz SF editor and chairman) had somewhat confusingly already confirmed the rever-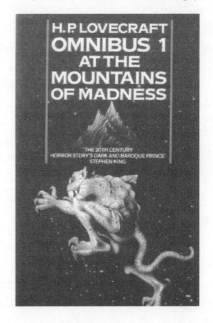sion of Gollancz's rights in *At the Mountains of Madness and Other Tales of Terror* in a note dated June 8, 1982, to A.M. Heath & Co. Ltd, who now represented the Scott Meredith Literary Agency in Britain.

In 1985, Granada Publishing/Panther Books issued three volumes in the *H.P. Lovecraft Omnibus* series, all with distinctive covers by Tim White. The inaugural book, *At the Mountains of Madness and Other Novels of Terror*, should have followed the contents of the earlier paperback editions in the UK but, as a result of an editorial oversight, the first printing of this volume only included August Derleth's introduction, the title story and 'The Case of Charles Dexter Ward'. Subsequent printings reinstated the remaining six stories.

The paperback edition of *The H.P. Lovecraft Omnibus 2: Dagon and Other Macabre Tales* finally returned the collection to a single volume, while *The H.P. Lovecraft Omnibus 3: The Haunter of the Dark and Other Tales* retained the contents of the 1951 Gollancz edition, as well as adding 'The Lurking Fear', 'The Picture in the House', 'The Shadow Over Innsmouth' and 'The Shadow Out of Time'.

On January 1, 1988, the works of H.P. Lovecraft went out of copyright under Britain's Copyright Act of 1911, which conveyed a protection period of fifty years after an author's death. However, when the European Union Directive on Term of Copyright came into force in the UK on January 1, 1996, it retroactively extended copyright protection for a further twenty years to life plus seventy years. As a result, Lovecraft's work went back into copyright until the beginning of 2008.

4. Postscript

During the 1990s, independent imprint Creation Books issued the H.P. Lovecraft collection *Crawling Chaos: Selected Works 1920–1935* with an introduction by Colin Wilson, while Penguin Books imported the three paperback volumes of Lovecraft scholar S.T. Joshi's 'corrected' texts as part of their 'Twentieth Century Classics' series.

More recently, Carlton Books issued *The Best of H.P. Lovecraft* under the Prion imprint, while Wordsworth Editions reprinted Lovecraft's fiction in two 'budget' paperback collections, selected and introduced by M.J. Elliott: *The Whisperer in Darkness: Collected Stories, Volume One* and *The Horror in the Museum: Collected Short Stories, Volume Two* (the latter edition replacing the quickly withdrawn compilation *The Loved Dead & Other Stories*).

Just as Granada Publishing had swallowed up the Panther Books imprint years earlier, so it in turn was absorbed into the mighty HarperCollins empire. As a result, in June 2002 they reissued H.P.

Lovecraft's *At the Mountains of Madness* collection as part of their 'Voyager Classics' series of prestige paperbacks.

Meanwhile, Gollancz (now one of a number of imprints in the Orion Publishing Group) had launched its 'Fantasy Masterworks' series under the guidance of editorial director Jo Fletcher and John Bush's successor, publisher and then managing director Malcolm Edwards.

The series was an avowed attempt to build a library of some of the greatest, most original, and most influential fantasy ever written. As Gollancz had already compiled collections of Robert E. Howard and Clark Ashton Smith's work, it would seem only natural that they would do H.P. Lovecraft next.

In 2002, after checking the copyright situation and confirming that they still retained the rights, Gollancz came up with the idea of publishing all Lovecraft's major fiction in two substantial trade paperback volumes, *The Call of Cthulhu and Other Eldritch Horrors* (containing mostly the author's horror works) and *The Strange High House in the Mist and Other Dream-Quests* (which would feature all the remaining fantastic tales). Each volume would have included around 220,000 words of fiction.

However, the books got bogged down in editorial discussions, and it was not until four years later that the project was eventually revived as an even more exciting concept.

In 2006 Gollancz had combined the two volumes of Howard's 'Conan' stories which had been put together for the 'Fantasy Masterworks' line into a single leather-bound hardcover entitled *The Complete Chronicles of Conan*, and priced to appeal to the mass-market. Along with an expansive historical Afterword, it included numerous interior illustrations by award-winning British artist Les Edwards. The handsome trade edition quickly went through multiple printings.

If it worked for Robert E. Howard, reasoned Gollancz, then why shouldn't it also work for H.P. Lovecraft as well? Consequently, the publisher started putting together the commemorative omnibus *Necronomicon: The Weird Tales of H.P. Lovecraft*.

Produced in an identical format as the Conan volume for publication in early 2008, the book contained around half-a-million words and most of Lovecraft's major weird fiction (but excluded some minor juvenilia and the majority of the author's 'revisions').

Gollancz decided to utilise the 'classic' texts created by Arkham House and *Weird Tales*, but made a number of corrections and revisions based on the vast amounts of research that has been done by Lovecraft scholars over the past two decades.

The hefty volume contained another extensive Afterword, and Les Edwards once again filled the book with his remarkable illustrations.

'Somehow Lovecraft has become permanent,' explained the artist. 'He endures. Even the word "Lovecraftian" has slipped into the language, although there might be strange ambiguities as to what it actually means. For some it refers to the literary style, for others it's to do with bulging gelatinous masses, the chanting of barbarous names and huge, ancient and tentacled beings. It's why the best of Lovecraft's stories are worth returning to.

'How these feelings translate into visual terms is another question. Obviously, the natural tendency for an artist is to concentrate on the visual, but there is limited capital in detailing every drooling fang and ensanguined talon. Certainly there must be tentacles and bat-winged night-gaunts, but, maybe – just maybe – there might also be some of the dread which will stay long after the lights are out.'

As an added bonus, famed American cartoonist Gahan Wilson allowed Gollancz to use his detailed map of 'Arkham circa 1930' (originally produced for August Derleth's magazine *The Arkham Collector* back in 1970).

'In one of the many scrapbook biographical anthologies on Howard Lovecraft produced and published by Arkham House there is a reproduction of a crude map of the witch-haunted village scrawled by HPL's very own hand,' he recalled, 'and I remember my young self latching onto it obsessively and trying to fill in the blank spaces by hunting though memoirs and stories on the place by his friends and fellow authors, with only limited success.'

Some years later, after August Derleth commissioned Wilson to create the cover illustration for the 1970 Arkham House anthology *The Horror in the Museum and Other Revisions* ('Which I did, and for which Derleth broke all payment speed records by sending his check for the artwork via return mail!'), the artist thought to ask Derleth if he could help with the map of Arkham.

'He responded at once and positive by saying he'd love to see such a map printed in *The Arkham Collector* and giving me what he could recall of the missing bits and some valuable addresses,' explains Wilson. 'I drew up a revised map using Derleth's contributions and a few notions of my own (all labelled) and sent copies to people like Frank Long and Bob Bloch and others who had known HPL and surely had asked him Arkhamish questions.

'They all answered (bless their hearts) with generous contributions and brand new suggestions based on what they had been told by the "old Gentleman" (how he would have loved living to be as old as I am now!), giving all sorts of helpful information not only on Arkham itself, but where it sat in relation to Innsmouth and Dunwich and other such matters.

'I sent out another fleet of letters to all concerned to straighten out contradictions and, based on what they told me, drew yet another map, sent it out for their approval and, having got it, did the final map which Derleth printed on the centre double-page in the very next issue of the *Collector*.'

Thirty-eight years later that incredibly detailed map formed the distinctive end-papers of *Necronomicon: The Weird Tales of H.P. Lovecraft*.

Since its initial publication in 2008, Gollancz's 'Commemorative Edition' of Lovecraft's stories has gone through multiple printings (even outstripping the remarkable success of the imprint's 'Conan' collection). Now, with the publication of *Eldritch Tales: A Miscellany of the Macabre by H.P. Lovecraft*, Gollancz finally has – for the first time ever – all of the author's major stories (along with a number of obscure 'revisions', his most important weird poetry and some notable non-fiction) in print in Britain at the same time.

It has been a long and often complicated journey since Victor Gollancz wrote that letter to August Derleth from his New York hotel room in May 1950. Despite the occasional misunderstanding or minor upset, Lovecraft's fiction has enjoyed a healthy publishing history in the United Kingdom, even to the extent that some compilations have been unique to this country.

Now Lovecraft's body of work has finally returned to Gollancz, its spiritual home in the UK, in a prestige format that once again re-establishes the author as one of the most original and influential horror writers of his or any other generation. Nearly seventy-five years after his premature death and exactly sixty years after his books first appeared on these shores, the cosmic wheel has finally turned full circle.

H.P. Lovecraft is definitely back in Britain.

Stephen Jones
London, England

OTHER COLLABORATIONS AND REVISIONS

The following is a list of H.P. Lovecraft's primary collaborations and revisions not included in the present volume.

'Ashes' (with Clifford M. Eddy, Jr.), originally published in *Weird Tales*, March 1924.

'The Ghost-Eater' (with Clifford M. Eddy, Jr.), originally published in *Weird Tales*, April 1924.

'The Loved Dead' (with Clifford M. Eddy, Jr.), originally published in *Weird Tales*, May-July 1924.

'Deaf, Dumb, and Blind' (with Clifford M. Eddy, Jr.), originally published in *Weird Tales*, April 1925.

'The Curse of Yig' (with Zealia B. Bishop), originally published in *Weird Tales*, November 1929.

'The Man of Stone' (with Hazel Heald), originally published in *Wonder Stories*, October 1932.

'The Horror in the Museum' (with Hazel Heald), originally published in *Weird Tales*, July 1933.

'Winged Death' (with Hazel Heald), originally published in *Weird Tales*, March 1934.

'Out of the Aeons' (with Hazel Heald), originally published in *Weird Tales*, April 1935.

'"Till A' the Seas"' (with Robert H. Barlow), originally published in *The Californian* Vol.3, No.1, Summer 1935.

'The Night Ocean' (with Robert H. Barlow), originally published in *The Californian* Vol.4, No.3, Winter 1936.

'The Disinterment' (with Duane W. Rimel), originally published in *Weird Tales*, January 1937.

'The Horror in the Burying-Ground' (with Hazel Heald), originally published in *Weird Tales*, May 1937.

'The Diary of Alonzo Typer' (with William Lumley), originally published in *Weird Tales*, February 1938.

'Collapsing Cosmoses' (with Robert H. Barlow), originally published in *Leaves* No.2, 1938.

'Medusa's Coil' (with Zealia B. Bishop), originally published in *Weird Tales*, January 1939.

'Within the Walls of Eryx' (with Kenneth Sterling), originally published in *Weird Tales* (as 'In the Walls of Eryx'), October 1939.

'The Tree on the Hill' (with Duane W Rimel), originally published in *Polaris*, September 1940.

'The Mound' (with Zealia B. Bishop), originally published in *Weird Tales*, November 1940.

'The Battle That Ended the Century (MS. Found in a Time Machine)' (with Robert H. Barlow), originally published in *The Acolyte* Vol.2, No.4, Fall 1944.

'Four O'Clock' (with Sonia H. Greene), originally published in *Something About Cats* (Arkham House, 1949).

'Satan's Servants' (with Robert Bloch), originally published in *Something About Cats* (Arkham House, 1949).

'The Survivor' (with August Derleth), originally published in *Weird Tales*, July 1954.

HOWARD PHILLIPS LOVE-CRAFT was born in Providence, Rhode Island, in 1890. A life-long antiquarian who had an interest in astronomy, his early work was initially published in the amateur press. His tales of horror and the macabre did not see print professionally until the early 1920s, and even then the bulk of his work appeared in such pulp magazines as *Weird Tales*, along with a handful of hardcover anthologies. A voluminous letter-writer, the only book of his fiction due to be published during his lifetime was the privately printed *Shadows Over Innsmouth* (1938). Following his untimely death in 1937, Lovecraft's work was initially kept in print by Arkham House publishers and today his fiction – notably the influential Cthulhu Mythos – is known all over the world and forms the basis for countless books, movies, comics, collectibles and role-playing games.

STEPHEN JONES is one of Britain's most acclaimed anthologists of horror and dark fantasy. He has more than 100 books to his credit and has won numerous awards. You can visit his web site at www.stephenjoneseditor.com

LES EDWARDS is an award-winning artist who has established himself as a stalwart of the British fantasy, horror and science fiction illustration scene in a career spanning more than thirty-five years. You can visit his website at www.lesedwards.com